JACK HIGGINS

WRATH OF THE LION

HARPER

This novel is entirely a work of fiction.
The names, characters and incidents portrayed in it are the work of the author's imagination. Any resemblance to actual persons, living or dead, events or localities is entirely coincidental.

Harper
An Imprint of HarperCollins*Publishers*
77–85 Fulham Palace Road,
Hammersmith, London W6 8JB

www.harpercollins.co.uk

This paperback edition 2008
1

First published in Great Britain by
John Lang 1964

A catalogue record for this book is available from the British Library

ISBN: 978-0-00-783208-8

Typeset in Sabon by Palimpsest Book Production Limited,
Grangemouth, Stirlingshire

Printed and bound in Great Britain by
Clays Ltd, St Ives plc

Jack Higgins

Jack Higgins lived in Belfast till the age of twelve. Leaving school at fifteen, he spent three years with the Royal Horse Guards, serving on the East German border during the Cold War. His subsequent employment included occupations as diverse as circus roustabout, truck driver, clerk and, after taking an honours degree in sociology and social psychology, teacher and university lecturer.

The Eagle Has Landed turned him into an international bestselling author, and his novels have since sold over 250 million copies and have been translated into fifty-five languages. Many of them have also been made into successful films. His recent bestselling novels include *Bad Company, A Fine Night for Dying, Dark Justice, Toll for the Brave, Without Mercy* and *Storm Warning*.

In 1995 Jack Higgins was awarded an honorary doctorate by Leeds Metropolitan University. He is a fellow of the Royal Society of Arts and an expert scuba diver and marksman. He lives on Jersey.

Visit www.AuthorTracker.co.uk for exclusive updates on Jack Higgins.

Also by Jack Higgins

The Valhalla Exchange
To Catch a King
Dillinger
The Run to Morning
The Eagle Has Landed
A Prayer for the Dying
The Last Place God Made
Storm Warning
Day of Judgment
Solo
Luciano's Luck
Touch the Devil
Exocet
Confessional
Night of the Fox
A Season in Hell
Memoirs of a Dance-Hall Romeo
Cold Harbour
The Eagle Has Flown
Eye of the Storm
Thunder Point
On Dangerous Ground
Sheba
Angel of Death
Drink with the Devil
Year of the Tiger
The President's Daughter
Flight of Eagles
The White House Connection
Pay the Devil
Day of Reckoning
Edge of Danger
The Keys of Hell
Midnight Runner
A Fine Night for Dying
Dark Justice
Bad Company
Toll for the Brave
Without Mercy
East of Desolation
The Savage Day

PUBLISHER'S NOTE

WRATH OF THE LION was first published in the UK by John Lang in 1964 and later by Signet in 1996, but has been out of print for some years.

In 2008, it seemed to the author and his publishers that it was a pity to leave such a good story languishing on his shelves. So we are delighted to be able to bring back WRATH OF THE LION for the pleasure of the vast majority of us who never had a chance to read the earlier editions.

For Joe Cooper – good friend

FOREWORD

This was the first book I wrote that expressed my enduring love for the Channel Islands. St Pierre is a fictional island – at the time of writing it was not fashionable to use real locations – but is heavily based on Alderney. The themes introduced here – boats at sea in bad weather, action at night and diving – have appeared in many of my books since then, and reflect my own abiding passion for scuba-diving.

The wrath of the lion is the wisdom of God.
William Blake

1

Storm Warning

The graticules misted over, momentarily obscured by a curtain of green water, but as the tip of the periscope broke through to the surface the small untidy freighter jumped into focus with astonishing clarity. Lieutenant Fenelon gripped the handles of the eyepiece and his breath escaped in a long sigh.

Beside him, Jacaud said, 'The *Kontoro*?'

Fenelon nodded. 'Not more than five hundred yards away.'

Jacaud dropped his cigarette and ground it into the deck with his heel. 'Let me see.'

Fenelon stood back, conscious of the hollowness at the base of his stomach. He was twenty-six years of age and had never seen action, never known what war was like except through the eyes of other men. But this – this was a new sensation. He felt strangely dizzy and passed a hand across his eyes as he waited.

Jacaud grunted and turned. He was a big, dangerous-looking man badly in need of a shave, a jagged scar bisecting his right cheek.

'Nice of them to be on time.'

Fenelon took another look. The *Kontoro* moved slowly to the right across the little black lines etched on the glass of the periscope and his throat went dry. He was already beginning to taste a little of that special excitement that takes possession of the hunter when his quarry is in plain sight.

'One torpedo,' he said softly. 'That's all it would take.'

Jacaud was watching him, a strange, sardonic smile on his face. 'What would be the point? No one would ever know.'

'I suppose not.' Fenelon called the control room from his voice-pipe. 'Steer one-oh-five and prepare to surface.'

He whipped the periscope down, the hiss

it made as it slid into its well mingling with the clamour of the alarm klaxon. As he turned, brushing sweat from his eyes, Jacaud took a Lüger from his pocket. He removed the clip, checked it with the rapidity of the expert and slammed it back into the butt with a click that somehow carried with it a harsh finality.

He lit another cigarette. When he looked up he was no longer smiling.

In the wheelhouse of the *Kontoro* Janvier, the first officer, yawned as he bent over the chart. He made a quick calculation and threw down his pencil. By dead reckoning they were forty miles west of Ushant and the weather forecast wasn't good. Winds of gale force reported imminent in sea areas Rockall, Shannon, Sole and Finisterre.

For the moment there was only an unnatural calm, the sea lifting in a great oily swell. Janvier was tired, his eyes gritty from lack of sleep. A native of Provence, he had never managed to get used to the cold of these northern seas and he shivered with distaste as he gazed out into the grey dawn.

Behind him the door to the companionway clicked open and the steward entered holding a steaming cup of coffee in each hand. He gave one to Janvier and the other to the helmsman, taking his place at the wheel for a few moments while the man drank.

Janvier opened the door and walked out on to the bridge. He stood at the rail drinking his coffee and breathing deeply of the cold morning air, feeling considerably more cheerful. Once across Biscay there was the long run south to look forward to – Maderia, then the Cape and sun all the way. He finished his coffee, emptied the dregs over the side and started to turn.

A hundred yards to starboard there was a sudden surge in the oily water. It boiled in a white froth and a submarine broke through to the surface, strange and alien like some primeval creature in the dawn of time.

Janvier stood at the rail, trapped by surprise. As he watched, the conning-tower hatch opened and a young officer in peaked cap appeared, followed by a sailor who immediately hoisted a small ensign. A sudden gust of wind lifted it stiffly, the red, white and blue of the tricolour standing out vividly against the grey clouds.

The steward emerged from the wheelhouse and stood at the rail. 'What do you make of her, sir?'

Janvier shrugged. 'God knows. Better get the captain.'

A third sailor appeared in the conning tower, a signalling lamp in his hands. The submarine moved in closer, narrowing the gap, and the lamp started to wink rapidly.

A reserve naval officer, Janvier had no difficulty in reading the signal for himself. When he had deciphered it he stood at the rail frowning for a moment, then went into the wheelhouse and unhooked the signal-lamp.

As he moved back to the rail, the light flickered again from the conning tower, repeating her request. As Janvier replied with the 'Message received' signal, the captain came up the ladder from the well-deck, the quartermaster close behind.

Henri Duclos was nearly fifty, and after thirty years at sea, five of them as a corvette captain with the Free French Navy, he found it difficult to be surprised by anything.

'What's all this?' he demanded.

'They've made the same signal twice,' Janvier told him.

'"Heave to. I wish to come aboard."'

'What have you replied?'

'Message received.'

Duclos went into the wheelhouse and came back with a pair of binoculars. He examined the submarine for a moment and grunted. 'She's French all right. I can see the uniforms. Small for a sub, though.' He handed the binoculars to the quartermaster. 'What do you make of her?'

The old man took his time and then nodded. '*L'Alouette*. I saw her in Oran last year when the fleet was exercising. An ex-U-boat. Experimental job the Germans were working on at the end of the war. One of those the navy took over.'

'So now we know who she is,' Duclos said. 'The point is what in the hell does she want with us?' He turned to Janvier. 'Ask her to be more explicit.'

There was a pause while the lamps flickered again and Janvier turned blankly. 'She says: "Imperative I board you. Matter of national importance. Please observe radio silence."'

The lamp on the conning tower of the submarine was still. 'What shall I reply, sir?' Janvier said.

Duclos raised the binoculars to his eyes for a moment then took them down. 'What can you reply? If it's important enough for them to send a blasted sub after us, then it's important. Signal: "Come aboard."' He grimaced at the quartermaster. 'I was looking forward to all that sun. My rheumatism's been killing me lately. Let's hope we don't have to go into Brest.'

The quartermaster shrugged. 'Stranger things are happening in the Republic these days.'

'Which republic?' Duclos demanded sardonically. 'Stand to all hands and get a ladder over the side.'

The quartermaster moved away and Janvier lowered the lamp. 'They thank us for our co-operation.'

'Do they, now?' Duclos observed. 'Let's hope they aren't wasting our time. Stop all engines.'

Janvier moved into the wheelhouse and Duclos took out his pipe and filled it from a worn leather pouch, watching the submarine as he did so. The forward hatch was opened and a large yellow dinghy hauled out and inflated. As the freighter started to slow, the two vessels drifted together until finally the gap had narrowed to no more than twenty or thirty yards.

The submarine commander climbed down the ladder from the conning tower and paused at the bottom, watching the half-dozen sailors working on the dinghy. He was slim and rather boyish in his reefer jacket and rubber boots, and the peaked cap was tilted rakishly to one side. He glanced up at Duclos, smiled and waved, then walked along the hull and stepped down into the dinghy.

He was followed by half a dozen sailors,

most of whom carried sub-machine-guns slung across their backs. Four of them paddled the boat across the narrow strip of water towards the ladder that had been dropped over the side of the *Kontoro*. Two sailors, still standing by the forward hatch of the submarine, carefully paid out a connecting line.

'Carrying a lot of hardware, aren't they?' Janvier said.

Duclos nodded. 'I don't like the look of this at all. It could be messy enough to rub off on all of us. Perhaps they're after someone in the crew. An O.A.S. man trying to get out of the country or something like that.'

The sailors came over the side quickly. Three of them unslung their sub-machine-guns and stayed in the well-deck and the young officer mounted the ladder to the upper deck, briskly followed by the other three.

He held out his hand and smiled. 'Captain Duclos? My name is Fenelon. Sorry about all this, but I'm only obeying orders, you understand.'

The man who came up the ladder next had a scarred and brutal face and cropped hair.

Like Fenelon, he wore a naval reefer jacket and rubber boots, but no cap. He leaned casually against the rail and lit a cigarette. The other two sailors spaced themselves behind Fenelon, machine-guns ready.

Duclos began to feel distinctly uneasy. 'Look, what's going on? What's this all about?'

'All in good time,' Fenelon said. 'You complied with my request to maintain radio silence?'

'Of course.'

'Good.' Fenelon turned and nodded briefly to one of the sailors, who crossed the deck to the wireless room which stood at the rear of the wheelhouse, opened the door and went inside.

A cry of alarm was followed by a burst of fire. A moment later the radio operator staggered through the door, blood on his face. He dropped to his knees and Janvier moved quickly to pick him up.

'The radio,' the man moaned. 'He put a burst through it.'

There was a sudden, ugly murmur from the crew in the well-deck that was answered by a volley of firing, bullets hissing through the steel rigging lines. Duclos glanced over the rail and saw that a heavy machine-gun had been mounted on a swivel on the rim of the conning tower. Even allowing for the difference in height between the two vessels, it was still capable of reducing most of the deck area of the *Kontoro* to a bloody shambles.

He turned slowly, his face pale. 'Who are you?'

Fenelon smiled. 'Exactly what we seem, Captain. The commanding officer and crew of the submarine *L'Alouette*. Under special orders, but serving France, I assure you.'

'What do you want?' Duclos said.

'One of your passengers, Pierre Bouvier. I understand he is travelling with you as far as Madeira?'

Duclos's rage, hardly contained, flooded out in a roar of anger. 'By God, I'll see you in hell first! I'm still captain of this ship.'

Still leaning comfortably against the rail, Jacaud pulled the Lüger from his pocket and shot him neatly through the left leg. Duclos screamed as the heavy slug splintered his knee-cap and rolled over on the deck, face twisted in agony.

'To encourage the rest of you,' Jacaud said calmly. 'Now get Bouvier up here.'

As Janvier turned, a quiet voice said: 'No need, monsieur. He is here.'

The man who stepped out of the saloon companionway was well past middle age. Tall and thin with stooping shoulders, he had the angular bony face of the ascetic and thinning grey hair. He wore a raincoat over pyjamas and a small grey-haired woman clutched his arm fearfully. Behind them, two other passengers, clothes hastily pulled on, hesitated in the doorway.

'You are Pierre Bouvier?' Fenelon demanded.

'That is correct.'

Jacaud nodded to one of the sailors. 'Bring him over here.'

The woman's voice lifted at once, but Bouvier quietened her and allowed himself to be led forward. The sailor placed him with his back to the rail and went and stood beside Jacaud.

'What do you want with me?' Bouvier said.

'A month ago at Fort-Neuf you were public prosecutor at a trial,' Fenelon said. 'A trial at which six good friends of ours received the death sentence.'

'So, the O.A.S. is in this?' Bouvier shrugged. 'I did my duty as I saw it. No man can do more.'

'You will, I am sure, allow us the same privilege, monsieur.' Fenelon produced a document from his pocket, unfolded it and read rapidly. '"Pierre Bouvier, I must inform you that you have been tried in your absence and found guilty of the crime of treason against the Republic by a military tribunal of the Council of National Resistance."'

He paused and Bouvier cut in gently, 'And the sentence of the court is death?'

'Naturally,' Fenelon said. 'Have you anything to say?'

Bouvier shrugged and an expression of contempt crossed his face. 'Say? Say what? There is no charge to answer. I know it and you know it. Frenchmen everywhere will –'

Jacaud plucked the sub-machine-gun from the hands of the sailor standing next to him, aimed quickly and fired a long burst that drove Bouvier back against the rail. He spun round, the material of his raincoat bursting into flame as bullets hammered across his back, and fell to the deck.

His wife cried his name once, took a single step forward and fainted, one of the passengers catching her as she fell backwards.

From the well-deck there was a strange, muted sigh from the crew and then there was only silence. Jacaud tossed the machine-gun to the sailor he had taken it from and went down the ladder without a backward glance. Fenelon looked as if he might be sick at any moment. He nodded to his men and hurriedly followed the big man, missing a step halfway down and almost falling to the deck.

They went over the side one by one and from the conning tower of the submarine the heavy machine-gun covered them menacingly. When they were all in the dinghy the sailors standing by the forward hatch hauled on the line quickly.

They left the dinghy to drift and everyone scrambled down through the hatch except

Fenelon, who walked along the hull and climbed the ladder to the conning tower. He stood looking up at the freighter for a moment as the two vessels drifted apart, and on the *Kontoro* there was a strange, uncanny silence.

The two sailors dismounted the machine-gun and disappeared. Fenelon remained only a moment or two longer before following. The conning-tower hatch clanged shut, the sound echoing flatly across the water.

On the *Kontoro* it was as if a spell had been broken and everyone surged forward to the rail. Janvier had never felt quite so helpless in his life before and for some unaccountable reason was strangely close to tears.

In the distance the wind was already beginning to lift the waves into whitecaps and he remembered the gale warning. *L'Alouette* sank beneath the waves like a grey ghost, the tricolour waved bravely, then that too disappeared and there was only the sea.

2

To Sup with the Devil

A thin sea fog rolled in from Southampton Water as the taxi turned the corner and pulled into the kerb. Anne Grant peered out through the window at the dim bulk of the building rearing into the night.

The original structure had been Georgian, so much was obvious, but the years had left their mark. A line of uneven steps lifted to the door, the paint cracked and peeling in the diffused yellow light of a street-lamp. Above it a small glass sign said *Regent Hotel*.

She tapped on the partition and the driver opened it. 'Are you sure this is the place?'

'Regent Hotel, Farthing Lane. That's what you said and that's where I've brought you,' the man replied. 'It's only a doss-house, lady. The sort of place sailors come to for a kip on their first night ashore. What did you expect – the Ritz?'

She opened the door and got out, hesitating for a moment as she gazed up at the damp, crumbling façade of the hotel. Except for the lapping of water against the wharf pilings on the other side of the street, it was completely quiet. When a café door was opened somewhere in the middle distance the music and laughter might have been coming from another planet. She gave the driver ten shillings, told him to wait and went up the steps.

The corridor was dimly lit, a flight of stairs rising into the shadows at the far end. She wrinkled her nose in distaste at the stale smell compounded of cooking odours and urine and moved forward.

There was a door to the left, the legend *Bar* etched in acid on its frosted-glass panel. When she opened it she found herself in a long, narrow room, the far end shrouded in darkness. An old marble-topped bar fronted one wall, a cracked mirror behind it, and a man leaned beside the beer pumps reading a newspaper.

In one corner a drunk sprawled across a table face-down, his breath whistling uneasily through the stillness. Two men sat beside a small coal fire talking softly as they played cards. They turned to look at her and she closed the door and walked past them.

The barman was old and balding, with the sagging, disillusioned face of a man who had got past being surprised at anything. He folded his paper neatly and pushed it under the bar.

'What can I do for you?'

'I'm looking for a Mr Van Sondergard,' she said. 'I understand he's staying here.'

Beyond the barman the two men by the fire were watching her in the mirror. One of them was small and squat with an untidy black beard. His companion was at least six feet tall with a hard, raw-boned face and hands that never stopped moving, shuffling the cards ceaselessly. He grinned and she returned his gaze calmly for a moment and looked away.

'Sondergard?' the barman said.

'She'll be meaning the Norwegian,' the tall man said in a soft Irish voice.

'Oh, that fella?' The barman nodded. 'Left yesterday.'

He ran a cloth over the surface of the bar and Anne Grant said blankly: 'But that isn't possible. I only hired him last week through the seamen's pool. I've a new motor-cruiser waiting at Lulworth now. He's supposed to run her over to the Channel Islands tomorrow.'

'You'll have a job catching him,' the Irishman cut in. 'He shipped out as quartermaster on the *Ben Alpin* this morning. Suez and all points east.' He got to his feet and crossed the room slowly. 'Anything I can do?'

Before she could reply a voice cut in harshly: 'How about some service this end for a change?'

She turned in surprise, realising for the first time that a man stood in the shadows at the far end of the bar. The collar of his reefer jacket was turned up and a peaked cap shaded a face that was strangely white, the eyes like dark holes.

The barman moved towards him and the Irishman leaned against the bar and grinned at Anne. 'How about a drink?'

She shook her head gently, turned and walked to the door. She went out into the corridor and paused at the top of the steps. The taxi had gone and the fog was much thicker now, rolling in across the harbour, swirling round the street-lamps like some living thing.

She went down the steps and started along the pavement. When she reached the first lamp she paused and looked back. The Irishman and his friend were standing in the doorway. As she turned to move on, they came down the steps and moved after her.

Neil Mallory lit another cigarette, raised his whisky up to the light, then set it down. 'This glass is dirty.'

The barman walked forward, a truculent frown on his face. 'And what do you expect me to do about it?'

'Get me another one,' Mallory said calmly.

It was some indefinable quality in the voice, a look in the dark eyes, that made the barman swallow his angry retort and force a smile. He filled a fresh glass and pushed it across.

'We aim to please.'

'That's what I thought,' Mallory said, his eyes following the Irishman and his friend as they went through the door after the woman. He took the whisky down in one easy swallow and went after them.

He stood at the top of the steps listening, but the fog smothered everything, even sound. A ship moved across the water, its fog-horn muted, alien and strange, touching something deep inside him. He shivered involuntarily. It was at that moment that Anne Grant cried out.

He went down the steps and stood listening, head slightly forward. The cry sounded again from the left, curiously flat and muffled by the fog, and he started to run.

He turned the corner on to a wharf at the far end of the street, running silently on rubber-soled feet, and took them by surprise. The two men were holding the struggling woman on the ground in the yellow light of a street-lamp.

As the Irishman turned in alarm, Mallory lifted a foot into his face. The man staggered back with a cry, rolled over the edge of the wharf and fell ten feet into the soft sludge of the mudbank.

The bearded man pulled a knife from his pocket and Mallory backed away. The man grinned and rushed him. As the knife came up, Mallory grabbed for the wrist, twisting the arm up and out to one side, taut as a steel bar. The man screamed like a woman and dropped the knife. Mallory struck him a savage blow across the side of the neck with his forearm and he crumpled to the ground.

Anne Grant leaned against the wall, her face pale in the sickly yellow light, blood streaking one cheek from a deep scratch. She laughed shakily and brushed a tendril of dark hair from her forehead.

'You don't do things by halves, do you?'

'What's the point?' he said.

Her Jersey suit was soiled and bedraggled,

the blouse ripped to the waist. When she moved forward, she limped heavily on her right foot. She stopped to pick up her handbag and the bearded man groaned and rolled on his back.

She looked down at him for a moment, then turned to Mallory. 'Are you going to call the police?'

'Do you want me to?'

'Not particularly.' She started to shake slightly. 'Suddenly it seems colder.'

He slipped off his reefer jacket and hung it around her shoulders. 'What you need is a drink. We'll go back to the hotel. You can use my room while I get you a taxi.'

She nodded down at the bearded man. 'Will he be all right?'

'His kind always are.'

He took her arm. They walked to the corner and turned into the street. It started to rain, a thin drizzle that beaded the iron railings like silver. There was a dull, aching pain in her ankle and the old houses floated in the fog, unreal and insubstantial, part of the dark dream from which she had yet to awaken, and the pavement seemed to move beneath her feet.

His arm was instantly around her, strong and reassuring, and she turned and smiled into the strange, pale face, the dark eyes. 'I'll be all right. A little dizzy, that's all.'

The hotel sign swam out of the fog to meet them and they went through the entrance and mounted the rickety stairs. His room was at the end of the corridor and he opened the door, switched on the light and motioned her inside.

'Make yourself at home. I'll be back in a couple of minutes.'

The room had that strange, rather dead, atmosphere typical of cheap hotels the world over. There was a strip of worn carpet on the floor, an iron bed, a cheap wardrobe and locker. The one touch of luxury was the wash-basin in the corner by the window and she hobbled across to it.

Surprisingly, there was plenty of hot water and she washed her face and hands, then examined herself in the mirror that was screwed to the wall above the basin. The scratch on her cheek was only superficial, but her suit was ruined. Otherwise she seemed to have sustained no real damage. She was sitting on the edge of the bed examining her ankle when he returned.

He placed a half-bottle of brandy and two glasses on top of the bedside locker and dropped to one knee beside her. 'Any damage?'

She shook her head. 'A nasty graze, that's all.'

He pulled a battered fibre suitcase from under the bed and took out a heavy fisherman's sweater which he dropped into her lap. 'You'd better put that on. You're wet through.'

When she had pulled it over her head and rolled up the long sleeves, he rested her right foot on his knee and bandaged the damaged ankle expertly with a folded handkerchief. She watched quietly.

He was of medium height, with broad shoulders, and wore the sort of clothes common to sailors. A cheap blue-flannel shirt and heavy working trousers in some dark material, held up by a broad leather belt with a brass buckle.

But this was no ordinary man. He had a strange, hard enigmatic face, the face of a man few would care to trifle with. The skin was clear and bloodless; black, crisp hair in a point to the forehead. The eyes were the strangest feature, so dark that all light died in them.

On the wharf he had been terrible in his anger, competent and deadly, and when he looked up suddenly his dark eyes stared through her like glass. For the first time that night genuine fear moved inside her and then his whole face creased into a smile of quite devastating charm, so great, that he seemed to undergo a complete personality change.

'You look about ten years old in that sweater.'

She smiled warmly and held out her hand. 'My name is Anne Grant and I'm very grateful to you.'

'Mallory,' he said. 'Neil Mallory.'

He touched her hand briefly, opened the brandy, poured a generous measure into one of the glasses and passed it to her. 'I got the barman to phone for a taxi. It might be some time before it gets here.'

'I'd like to know why the driver who brought me didn't wait,' she said. 'I asked him to.'

'They're not too keen on hanging around the dock area at night. It's a rough place and taxi-drivers are obvious targets.' He grinned. 'That goes double for good-looking young women, by the way.'

She smiled ruefully. 'Don't rub it in. I'd no idea what I was letting myself in for, but I was getting desperate. I'd been waiting in Lulworth for someone for most of the day. When it became obvious that he wasn't going to show up I decided to come looking for him.'

'Van Sondergard?' Mallory said. 'I heard you ask the barman about him.'

'Did you know him?'

'He had a room along the corridor from here. I had a drink with him once when he came in the bar. Nothing more than that. Where did you meet him?'

'I didn't,' she said. 'The whole thing was arranged through the seamen's pool. I told them I need someone to take a motor-cruiser across to the Channel Islands for me and captain her for a month or so until my sister-in-law and I were capable of looking after her ourselves. I also told them we'd prefer someone who'd done a little skin-diving. They put me in touch with Sondergard.' She sighed. 'He seemed rather keen on the idea. I'd love to know what changed his mind.'

'It was very simple really. He was sitting in the bar half drunk, feeling rather sorry for himself, when one of his old captains walked in, due out on the morning tide for Suez and short of a quartermaster. Three drinks was all it took for Sondergard to pack his duffel and go off with him. Sailors have a habit of doing things like that.'

He swallowed his brandy, took out an old leather cigarette case and offered her one. 'Are you a sailor, Mr Mallory,' she asked as he struck a match and held it forward in cupped hands.

He shrugged. 'Amongst other things. Why?'

'I wasn't sure. If I'd been asked I'd have said you were a soldier.'

'What makes you say that?'

'I think you could say I know the breed. My father was one and so was my husband. He was killed in Korea.'

There didn't seem anything to say and Mallory lit a cigarette and walked to the window. He peered outside, then turned.

'The motor-cruiser you mentioned, what kind is it?'

'A thirty-footer by Akerboon. Twin screw, steel hull.'

'Only the best?' He looked suitably impressed. 'How's she powered?'

'Penta petrol engine. She'll do about twenty-two knots at full stretch.'

'Depth-sounder, automatic steering, every latest refinement?' He grinned. 'I'd say she must have cost you all of seven thousand pounds.'

'Not me,' she said. 'My father-in-law. All I did was obey orders. He told me exactly what he wanted.'

'Sounds like a man who's used to getting his own way.'

She smiled. 'A habit he finds hard to break. He's a major-general.'

'Grant?' Mallory frowned. 'Are you talking about Iron Grant? The Western Desert man?'

She nodded. 'That's right. He's been living in the Channel Islands since he left the army. I keep house for him.'

'What does the old boy do with himself these days?'

'He's almost blind now,' she said, 'but he's still amazingly active and he's made quite a reputation for himself as a war historian. He uses a tape-recorder and his daughter Fiona and I type up his notes for him.'

'You said you wanted Sondergard to have had some experience as a skin-diver? Why was that?'

'It wasn't essential, but he could have been useful. In the fifteenth century a small fishing village and fortress on Ile de Roc were inundated. The ruins are now about eight fathoms down a few hundred yards off-shore. We're making a survey. Fiona and I have been doing most of the diving so far.'

'Sounds interesting,' he said. 'You shouldn't find any difficulty in getting another man from the pool to take on a job like that.'

As he looked out of the window and down into the yellow fog she said quietly, 'I was wondering whether you might be interested?'

He turned slowly, a slight frown on his face. 'You don't know anything about me.'

'What is there to know? You told me yourself you were a sailor.'

'From necessity,' he said. 'Not choice.'

'You couldn't handle *Foxhunter*, you mean?'

'Is that her name? Oh, yes, I've handled boats like that before. I've even done a little skin-diving.'

'Eighty pounds a month and all found,' she said. 'Does that tempt you?'

He grinned reluctantly. 'It does indeed, Mrs Grant.'

She held out her hand in a strangely boyish gesture. 'I'm glad.'

He held it for a moment, looking into her eyes gravely. Her smile faded, and again she was conscious of that vague irrational fear. Something must have shown on her face. Mallory's hand tightened on hers and he smiled gently. In that single moment her fear disappeared and an inexplicable tenderness flooded through her. A horn sounded outside in the street and he helped her to her feet.

'Time to go. Where are you staying?'

'An hotel in the town centre.'

'You should cause quite a sensation going through the foyer,' he told her as he took her arm and helped her across to the door.

The fog was clearing a little as he handed her into the taxi. She wound down the window and leaned out to him. 'I've several things to attend to tomorrow, so I can't get down to Lulworth again until the evening. I'll see you down there.'

He nodded. 'You could do with a morning in bed.'

She smiled wanly in the pale light, but before she could reply the taxi moved away. Mallory stood looking into the fog, listening to the sound of the engine die into the distance, then turned and went up the steps.

When he entered the bar the barman was still reading his newspaper. 'Where are they?' Mallory asked.

The man lifted the flap and jerked his thumb at the rear door. 'In there.'

When Mallory opened the door he found the Irishman sitting at a wooden table beside a coal fire, a basin of hot water in front of him. His clothes were plastered with mud and he was wiping blood from a gash that ran from his ear to the point of his chin. The man with the black beard lay on an old horse-hair sofa, clutching his right arm and moaning softly.

The Irishman lurched to his feet, his eyes wild. 'You bastard. What were you trying to do, kill us?'

'I told you to frighten the girl a little, that's all, but you tried to be clever. Anything you got, you asked for.' Mallory took several banknotes from his wallet and tossed them on to the table. 'That should settle the account.'

'Ten quid!' the Irishman cried. 'Ten lousy quid!' What about Freddy? You've broken his arm.'

'No skin off my nose,' Mallory said calmly. 'Tell him to try the Health Service.'

He walked out and the Irishman slumped into his chair again, head swimming. The barman came in and stood looking at him. 'How do you feel?'

'Bloody awful. Who is that bastard?'

'Mallory?' The barman shrugged. 'I know one thing. He's the coldest fish I've ever met and I've known a few.' He looked down at the bearded man and shook his head. 'Freddy doesn't look too good. Maybe I should phone for an ambulance?'

'You can do what the hell you like,' the Irishman said violently.

The barman moved to the door, shaking his head. 'You know what they say. When you sup with the devil you need a long spoon. I reckon you and Freddy got a little too close.'

He sighed heavily and disappeared into the bar.

3

London Confidential

The room was half in shadow, the only light the shaded lamp on the desk. The man who sat sideways in the swivel chair, gazing out through the broad window at the glittering lights of London, was small, the parchment face strangely ageless. It was the face of an extraordinary human being, a man who had known pain and who had succeeded in moving beyond it.

The green intercom on his desk buzzed once and he swung round in the chair and flicked a switch. 'Yes?'

'Mr Ashford is here, Sir Charles.'

'Send him in.'

The door opened soundlessly and Ashford

advanced across the thick carpet, a tall, greying man in his forties with the worried face of the professional civil servant who had spent too much of his life close to the seats of power.

He sat down in the chair opposite, opened his briefcase and produced a file which he placed carefully on the desk. Sir Charles pushed a silver cigarette box across to him.

'What's the verdict?'

'Oh, the P.M. agrees with you entirely. The whole thing must be investigated. But we don't want the newspapers getting on to it. You'll have to be damn' careful.'

'We usually are,' Sir Charles said frostily.

'There's just one thing the P.M. isn't too happy about.' Ashford opened the file on the desk. This fellow Mallory. Is he really the best man for the job?'

'More than that,' Sir Charles said. 'He's the best man I've got and he's worked with the *Deuxième Bureau* before with some success. In fact, they've asked for him twice. His mother was French, of course. They like that.'

'It's this shocking affair in Perak in 1954 that the P.M. isn't happy about. Dammit all, the man was lucky to escape prison.'

Sir Charles pulled the file across the desk and turned it round. 'This is the record of a quite exceptional officer.' He put on a pair of rimless spectacles and started to read aloud, selecting items at random. ' "Special Air Service during the war . . . dropped into France three times . . . betrayed to the Gestapo . . . survived six months at Sachsenhausen . . . paratroop captain in Palestine . . . major in Korea . . . two years in a Chinese prison camp in Manchuria . . . released 1953 . . . posted to Malaya, January 1954, on special service." ' He closed the file and looked up. 'A lieutenant-colonel at thirty. Probably the youngest in the army at that time.'

'And kicked-out at thirty-one,' Ashford countered.

Sir Charles shrugged. 'He was told to clear the last Communist guerrilla out of Perak and he did it. A little ruthlessly perhaps, but he did it. His superiors then heaved a sigh of relief and threw him to the wolves.'

'And you were waiting to catch him, I suppose?'

Sir Charles shook his head. 'I let him drift for a year. Bombay, Alexandria, Algiers. I knew where he was. When I was satisfied that the iron was finally in his soul I pulled him in. He's worked for me ever since.'

Ashford sighed and got to his feet. 'Have it your own way, but if anything goes wrong . . .'

Sir Charles smiled softly. 'I know, I end up like Neil Mallory. Out on my ear.'

Ashford flushed, turned and crossed the room quickly. The door closed behind him and Sir Charles sat there thinking about it all. After a while he flicked a switch on the intercom.

'Send in Mallory.'

He lit a cigarette and stood by the window, gazing out over the city, still the greatest in the world, whatever anyone tried to say. When he opened the window he could smell the river and the sound from a ship's hooter drifted faintly on the quiet air as it moved down from the Pool.

He was tired and there was a slight ache somewhere behind his right eye. Something he should really see his doctor about. On the other hand, perhaps it was better not to know? He wondered whether Mallory would survive long enough to ever take his place behind the desk in this quiet room. It would have been a comforting thought, but he knew it was rather unlikely.

The door clicked open behind him and closed again. When he turned Mallory was standing beside the desk. An easy-fitting suit of dark worsted outlined his broad shoulders and in the diffused white light his aquiline face gave an impression of strength and breeding, not out of place anywhere.

Sir Charles moved back to his chair and sat down. 'How are you, Neil?'

'Pretty fit, sir. I've just had six weeks on the island.'

'I know. How's your shoulder?'

'No more trouble. They've done a good job.'

Sir Charles nodded. 'You'll have to be a little more careful next time, won't you?' He opened a file, took out a typewritten document and pushed it across. 'Have a look at that.'

He occupied himself with some other papers and Mallory skimmed through the three closely typed sheets of foolscap. When he had finished he handed them back, face expressionless.

'Where's the *Kontoro* now?'

'The destroyer which found her took her straight into Brest. For the time being the French are holding the lid down tight. Complete security and so on. They can't keep it quiet for more than three or four days. These things always leak out sooner or later.'

'What are they trying to do about it?'

'The usual round-up of anyone who's even remotely suspected of being connected with the O.A.S. or C.N.R. On top of that, the *Deuxième Bureau* and the *Brigade Criminelle*, backed by every available military security agent, have been given one order. Find that submarine.'

'I shouldn't have thought that would be too difficult.'

'I'm not so sure,' Sir Charles said. 'For one

thing this is no ordinary submarine. She's quite small. A thing the Germans were working on at the end of the war.'

'What's her radius?'

'Not much over a thousand.'

'Which means she could be based in Spain or even Portugal?'

'The French are working along those lines right now, but they've got to be careful. On top of that, they're combing the entire Biscay coast, every creek, every island.' He sighed heavily. 'I've a horrible feeling that they're completely wasting their time.'

'I wondered when you were coming to that,' Mallory said.

Sir Charles grinned impishly like a schoolboy, opened a drawer and took out a map which he unfolded across the desk. It was a large-scale Admiralty chart of the Channel Islands and the Golfe de St Malo.

'Ever hear of Philippe de Beaumont?'

'The paratroop colonel? The one who helped bring de Gaulle back to power?'

'That's right. He was one of the leaders of the military coup of May 1958 and a member of the original Committee of Public Safety. Philippe, Comte de Beaumont. Last survivor of one of the greatest of the French military families.'

'And he's living in the Channel Islands?'

'He was the great advocate of a French Algeria. When de Gaulle came down on the side of independence he resigned his commission and left France.' Sir Charles drew a circle on the chart about thirty miles south-west of Guernsey. 'There's an island called Ile de Roc owned by old Hamish Grant.'

'You mean Iron Grant, the Western Desert general?'

'That's right. Been living there for five years with his daughter Fiona, writing up the war. His daughter-in-law Mrs Anne Grant seems to run things. Her husband was killed in Korea. About a mile west of Ile de Roc there's a smaller island called St Pierre.'

'And de Beaumont's living there?'

'He bought it from Grant two years ago. There's a sort of castle up on top of the rock, one of those mock-Gothic jobs some crank built during the nineteenth century.'

'And you think he's up to no good?'

'Let's put it this way. The French have checked on him for two years now and can't find even the hint of a connection with either the O.A.S. or C.N.R., although he's known to be sympathetic to their aims. Frankly, even their Foreign Office think he's simply a *grand seigneur* who won't come home because he's annoyed with the General.'

'And you don't agree?'

'I might have done until yesterday evening.'

'What happened to change your mind?'

'I've had a man keeping an eye on de Beaumont for a year now, just as a precaution. There's a small hotel on Ile de Roc. He was working there as barman. He went missing Tuesday. Yesterday evening he drifted in on the evening tide. The police went over from Guernsey and picked up the body. Needless to say there isn't even a hint of foul play.'

'You think he may have seen something?'

Sir Charles shrugged. 'I don't see why not. *L'Alouette* left Brest on a routine training patrol two days ago. She could have called at St Pierre and our man could have seen her. It's pretty obvious that he came across something, and the *Deuxième* agree with me. They're sending a man across to work with you on this thing.'

'I wondered when we were coming to that,' Mallory said.

Sir Charles pushed a file across. 'Raoul Guyon, aged twenty-nine. He was a captain in a colonial parachute regiment. Went straight to Indo-China from St Cyr in 1952.'

Mallory looked down at the photograph. It showed a young man, slim-hipped and wiry, the sleeves of his camouflaged jacket rolled up to expose sunburnt arms. The calm, sun-blackened face, dark eyes, were shaded by a peaked cap that somehow gave him a strangely sinister, forbidding appearance.

'Why did he leave the army?'

'God knows,' Sir Charles said. 'I should imagine six years in Algeria was enough for any man. He asked to be placed on unpaid leave and Legrande of the *Deuxième* offered him a job.'

'When do I meet him?'

'You don't, for the moment. Apparently, he's quite a talented painter. He's using that as a cover. Should book in at the hotel on Ile de Roc sometime tomorrow.'

'What about me?'

'A little more complicated, I'm afraid. If de Beaumont *is* up to no good, then he'll be expecting company. We need to make your background convincing enough to fool him for at least a day or two, and I might as well tell you now that's all the time we can allow.'

'What do I do?' Mallory asked.

Sir Charles opened another file and passed a photo across. The girl who stared out at Mallory was somewhere in her twenties, dark hair close-cropped like a young boy's, almond-shaped eyes slanting across high cheekbones. She was not beautiful in any conventional sense and yet in a crowd she would have stood out.

'Anne Grant?' he said instinctively.

Sir Charles nodded. 'She came over this morning to finalise the purchase of a thirty-foot motor-cruiser called *Foxhunter*. It's moored at Lulworth now. Apparently, she hired a seaman through the pool to skipper the thing for a couple of months till she and her sister-in-law get used to it for themselves. A big boat for a couple of girls.'

Mallory nodded. 'I ran one in and out of Tangiers for a while back in '59. Remember?'

'Think you could handle one again?'

Mallory grinned. 'I don't see why not.'

Sir Charles nodded in satisfaction. 'First you'll have to get rid of this seaman. After that all you have to do is make sure you get his job.'

'That shouldn't prove too difficult.' Mallory hesitated and went on: 'Couldn't we work something out with General Grant? Let him know what we're after? He'd be certain to co-operate.'

Sir Charles shook his head. 'Before you knew where you were he'd be running the whole damned show. In any case, I'm never happy about bringing amateurs into these things if it can be avoided. They give the game away too easily. Use him by all means, but only in an extreme situation where there's no other way.' He got to his feet abruptly. 'I want results on this one, Neil, and I want them fast. Cut any corners you have to. I'll back you all the way.'

One corner of Mallory's mouth twitched ironically. 'I seem to remember someone saying that to me once before.'

Sir Charles's face was grave and dispassionate, the eyes calm, and Mallory knew beyond a shadow of a doubt that if necessary the old man would not have the slightest compunction in throwing him to the wolves.

'I'm sorry, Neil,' he said.

'At least I know where I stand with you.' Mallory shrugged. 'That's something.'

Sir Charles took an old gold watch from his pocket and checked it quickly. 'You'll have to get moving. I've arranged for you to be fully briefed by G3 at eight o'clock. They'll give you everything. Money, seaman's papers and a special transmitter. Report your arrival. After that, radio silence till you have some news. I've arranged for three M.T.B.s to proceed to Jersey, ostensibly for shallow-water exercises. The moment we get anything positive from you they'll move in so fast de Beaumont won't know what's hit him.

Mallory walked to the door. As he opened it, the old man said: 'Good luck, Neil. With the right kind this could turn out to be a pretty straightforward one.

'Aren't they all?' Mallory said dryly, and the door closed gently behind him.

4

G3

Professor Yoshiyama was little more than five feet in height and wore a judo jacket and trousers many times washed, a black belt around his waist. The face was the man's most outstanding feature, the skin the colour of parchment and almost transparent. There was nothing weak there. Only strength and intelligence and a kind of gentleness. It could have been that of a saint or scholar. It was, in fact, the face of a great master who had practised his art for more than fifty years.

His voice was dry and rather pedantic, the vowels clipped slightly, but the dozen men sitting cross-legged on the floor were giving him all their attention. High in the balcony of the gymnasium, Mallory leaned on the rail and watched.

'The literal meaning of the two Japanese characters which make up the word *karate* is empty hands,' Yoshiyama said. 'This refers to the fact that *karate* developed as a system of self-defence relying solely on unarmed techniques. The system was first developed centuries ago on the island of Okinawa during a time when the inhabitants were forbidden to carry arms on pain of death.'

There was a strangely old-fashioned flavour to everything he said, as if he were repeating a lesson painfully learned. He turned to a large wall chart which carried an outline of a human figure with all vital points, and their respective striking areas, clearly marked.

'The system consists of techniques of blocking or deflecting an attack and of counter-attacking by punching, striking or kicking.' He turned, his face bland, expressionless. 'But there is more to *karate* that well-practised tricks and physical force.' He tapped his head. 'There is also the mental application. You will be taught how to focus all your strength and energy on a single target at any given time. Let me show you what I mean.'

He nodded briefly and his two assistants picked up three lengths of planking. They were perhaps two feet long, each plank an inch thick. The two men took up their positions in front of Yoshiyama, holding the three planks between them and slightly above waist-level. In a single incredibly fluid motion the old man's left foot stamped forward and his right fist moved up from the waist, knuckles extended. There was a report like a gunshot and the planks split from end to end.

A quick murmur rose from the class and Yoshiyama turned, quite unperturbed. 'It is also possible to snap a brick in half with the edge of the hand.' He permitted himself one brief smile. 'But this requires practice. Major Adams, please.'

A small, wiry, middle-aged man with greying hair and a black patch over his right eye stood up at the back of the class and came forward. Like Yoshiyama, he wore a black belt, but where his left arm should have been a metal limb dangled.

'You will observe that Major Adams is rather a small man,' Yoshiyama said. 'He is also no longer in the prime of life. If we add to this the fact that he has only one arm one would not under normal circumstances give him much hope of surviving any kind of physical assault. As it happens, however, his circumstances are far from normal.'

He nodded to one of his assistants and moved out of the way. The assistant, a young, powerfully built Japanese with dark hair, ran to the far side of the gymnasium. He selected a knife from a table which contained an assortment of weapons, turned and ran forward, a blood-curdling cry surging from his throat.

He swerved to one side, came to a dead stop, then moved in quickly, the knife slashing at the Major's face. Adams moved with incredible speed, warding off the attacking arm with an extended knife-hand block. At the same moment he fell diagonally forward to one side and delivered a round-house kick to the groin. In what was virtually the same motion he kicked at his opponent's knee-joint with the same foot. The Japanese somersaulted, ending flat on his back, and the foot thudded across his windpipe.

For a moment they lay there and then both men scrambled to their feet grinning widely. 'In other circumstances, and had the blows been delivered with full force, my assistant would now be dead,' Yoshiyama said simply.

Adams picked up a towel, started to wipe sweat from his face and caught sight of Mallory in the gallery. He nodded briefly, said something to Yoshiyama and moved across to the door. Mallory met him in the corridor outside.

'What are you trying to do, go out in a blaze of glory?'

Adams grinned. 'Every so often I get so sick of the sight of that damned desk that I could blow my top. Yoshiyama provides a most efficient safety-valve.' He ran a hand over his right hip and winced slightly. 'That last fall hurt like hell. I must be getting old.'

As they mounted the stairs at the end of the corridor, Mallory thought about Adams. One of the best agents the department had ever had; all the guts in the world and a mind like a steel trap until the night he'd got too close for someone's comfort and they'd tied a Mills bomb to the handle of his hotel bedroom in Cairo.

And now he was a desk man, running G3, the intelligence section that was the pulse-beat of the whole organisation. Some people would have said he was lucky, but not Adams.

He opened a door and walked through a small, neat office. A middle-aged, desiccated-looking spinster with neat grey hair and rimless spectacles sat behind the typewriter. She glanced up, an expression of disapproval on her face, and Adams grinned.

'Don't say it, Milly. Just tell them I'm ready.'

He led the way into his own office. Like Sir Charles's, it commanded a fine view of the river, the desk standing by the window. He opened a cupboard, took out a heavy bathrobe and pulled it on.

'Sorry about the delay. I thought Sir Charles would keep you for an hour at least.'

'More like fifteen minutes,' Mallory said. 'He always goes straight to the heart of things with the sticky ones.'

'I wouldn't call it that,' Adams said. 'Interesting more than anything else. Whole thing could be just a storm in a teacup. Let's go into the projection room.'

He opened the far door and they descended a few steps into a small hall. There were several rows of comfortable seats and a large screen. The place was quite deserted. They sat down and Mallory offered Adams a cigarette.

'Any gaps in this one?'

Adams exhaled with a sigh of pleasure and shook his head. 'I don't think so. Nothing important, anyway. Has the old man told you much?'

'He's outlined the job, told me who the principals are. No more than that.'

'Let's get started, then.' Adams turned and glanced up at the projection box where a dim light showed. 'Ready when you are.'

A section of film started to run a few moments later. It showed a submarine entering port slowly, her crew lining the deck.

'To start with, that's what all the fuss is about,' Adams said. '*L'Alouette*. Taken at Oran a couple of years ago.'

'She looks rather small. There can't be more than a dozen men on deck.'

'Originally a German U-boat. Type XXIII. Just over a hundred feet long. Does about twelve kilometres submerged. Crew of sixteen.'

'What about armament?'

'Two twenty-one-inch torpedoes in the bow and she doesn't carry spares.'

'Doesn't leave much room for mistakes.'

Adams nodded. 'They never really amounted to anything. This one was built at Deutsches Werft in 1945 and sunk with all hands in the Baltic. She was raised in '46, refitted and handed over to the French.'

The film ended and a slide appeared. It showed a young French naval officer, eyes serious beneath the uniform cap, the rather boyish face schooled to gravity.

'Henri Fenelon, full lieutenant. He's her commander. Age twenty-six, unmarried. Born in Nantes. Father still lives there. Runs a small wine-exporting business.'

Mallory studied the face for a moment or two. 'Looks weak to me. Ever been in action?'

Adams shook his head. 'Why do you ask?'

Mallory shrugged. 'He looks as if he could crack easily. What's his political background?'

'That's the surprising thing. We can't find any evidence of an O.A.S. connection at all.'

'Probably did it for adventure,' Mallory said. 'He only needed half a dozen men in the crew to agree with him. They could have coerced the rest.'

'Sounds feasible,' Adams said. 'Let's move on.'

Various slides followed. There was an Admiralty chart of Ile de Roc, with the harbour, the hotel and General Grant's house all clearly marked. St Pierre was little more than a rock lifting a hundred or so feet out of the sea and crowned by the Victorian Gothic Castle.

Mallory shook his head. 'God knows how they ever managed to build the damned thing out there.'

'Eighteen-sixty-one,' Adams said. 'A self-made industrialist called Bryant. Bit of a megalomaniac. Saw himself as king of the castle and so on. Cost him better than a hundred thousand to build the place and that was real money in those days.'

'I can't see a jetty. Is it on the other side?'

'There's a cave at the base of the cliffs. If you look carefully you can see the entrance. The jetty's inside.'

The castle faded and another picture took its place. It was that of a distinguished-looking man with silvering hair, eyes calm in a sensitive, aquiline face.

'De Beaumont?' Mallory said.

Adams nodded. 'Philippe, Comte de Beaumont. One of the oldest of the great French families. He's even a rather distant blood relation of you-know-who, which makes the whole thing even more complicated.'

'I know quite a lot about his military history,' Mallory said. 'After all, he's something of a hero to paratroopers the world over. He came over here during the war and joined de Gaulle, didn't he?'

'That's right. Received just about every decoration possible. Afterwards he went to Indo-China as a colonel of colonial paratroops.

The Viets picked him up at the surrender of Dien-Bien-Phu in 1954. After his release he returned to France and was posted to Algeria. He was always at loggerheads with the top brass. Once had an argument with the old man himself at an official reception over what constitutes war in the modern sense.'

'That should have been enough to get him put out to grass on its own.'

Adams shrugged. 'They needed him, I suppose. After all, he *was* the most outstanding paratroop colonel in Algeria at that time. Handled all the dirtier jobs the top brass didn't want to soil its fingers with.'

'So he helped bring de Gaulle back to power?'

'That's right. A prime mover in the *Algérie Française* movement. The General, of course, kicked him right in the teeth by granting independence to Algeria after all.'

'And de Beaumont cleared out?'

'After Challe's rather abortive little coup last year. Whether or not he was actually mixed up in that little lot we can't be certain. The point is that he left France and bought this place on St Pierre from Hamish Grant. Caused quite a stir in the French papers at the time.'

'And he's kept his nose clean since then?'

'As a whistle.' Adams grinned. 'Even the French can't turn anything up on him. He runs a boat, by the way. Forty-foot twin-screw motor-yacht named *Fleur de Lys*. The very latest thing for deep-sea cruising with depth-sounder, automatic pilot and 100 h.p. DAF diesels. A bit of a recluse, but he's been seen in St Helier occasionally. What do you think?'

'I'd say he has the kind of inbred arrogance that can only come from a thousand years of always being right, or at least thinking you were,' Mallory said. 'Men like him can never sit still. They usually have to be plotting at one thing or another. Comes from that natural assumption that anything conflicting with their own views must be wrong.'

'Interesting,' Adams said. 'He has more the look of a seventeenth-century puritan to me. One of the thin-lipped intolerant variety. A damned good colonel in the New Model Army.'

'Jesus and no quarter?' Mallory shook his head. 'He's no bigot. Simply a rather arrogant aristocrat with a limited field of vision and an absolute conviction of the rightness of his own actions. When he decides on a plan of attack he follows it through to the bitter end. That's what made him such an outstanding officer. For men like him the rot sets in only if they step outside themselves and see just how much the whole damned thing is costing.'

'An interesting analysis, considering you've only seen his photo.'

'I know about him as a soldier,' Mallory said. 'At Dien-Bien-Phu they offered to fly him out. He was too valuable to lose. He refused. In his last message he said they'd been wrong from headquarters staff down to himself. That the whole Dien-Bien-Phu strategy had been a terrible mistake. He said that if his men had to stay and pay the price the least he could do was stay and pay it with them.'

'Which probably accounted for his popularity with the troops,' Adams said.

'Men like him are never loved by anyone,' Mallory said. 'Even themselves.'

De Beaumont's picture was replaced by another. The face which stared down at them was strong and brutal, the eyes cold, hair close-cropped.

'Paul Jacaud,' Adams said. 'Aged forty. Parents unknown. He was raised by the madame of a waterfront brothel in Marseilles. Three years in the Resistance, joined the paratroops after the war. He was sergeant-major in de Beaumont's regiment. Medaille Militaire plus a court-martial for murder that failed for lack of evidence.'

'And still with his old boss?'

'That's right. You can make what you like out of that. Let's have a look at the angels now.'

A picture of Harnish Grant flashed on the screen, a famous one taken in the Ardennes in the winter of '44. Montgomery stood beside him, grinning as they examined a map. He was every inch Iron Grant, great shoulders bulging under a sheepskin coat.

'Quite a man,' Mallory said.

'And he hasn't changed much. Of course, his sight isn't too good, but he's still going strong. Written a couple of pretty good campaign histories of the last war.'

'What about the family?'

'He's a widower. Son was killed in Korea. At the moment his household consists of his daughter Fiona, daughter-in-law Anne and an ex-Gurkha *naik* called Jagbir who was with him during the war. This is the daughter.'

Fiona Grant had long blonde hair and a heart-shaped face that was utterly appealing. 'Rather a handful, that one,' Adams said. 'She was raised in the south of France, which didn't help. They tried Roedean, but that was a complete fiasco. She was finally settled in a Paris finishing school, which apparently suited her. She's at home at the moment.'

'I like her,' Mallory said. 'She's got a good mouth.'

'Then see what you think of this one. Anne Grant, the old man's daughter-in-law.'

It was the same photograph that Sir Charles had shown him and Mallory stared up at it, his throat for some unaccountable reason going dry. It was as if they had met before and yet he knew that to be impossible. The almond-shaped eyes seemed to come to life, holding his gaze, and he shook his head slightly.

'She's over here now to finalise the purchase of a new boat.'

'Sir Charles told me that much. What about this man Sondergard she's hired through the pool?'

'We'll ship him out somewhere. There's no difficulty there. I've already got a little scheme in mind to bring you and Anne Grant together.'

They next saw the picture of a Frenchwoman called Juliette Vincente who was working at the hotel on Ile de Roc, Nothing was known against her and she seemed quite harmless, as did Owen Morgan, her employer. When the Welshman's face faded away, Mallory straightened in his seat, thinking they had finished. To his surprise another face appeared.

He turned to Adams in surprise. 'But this is Raoul Guyon, the man I'm going to work with. I've already seen his picture. What's the idea?'

Adams shrugged. 'I'm not sure, but I'm

not really happy about the way the French are handling this business. I've got a hunch that old spider Legrande and the *Deuxième* aren't telling us all they could. Under the circumstances it might prove useful to know everything there is to know about Raoul Guyon. He's rather unusual.'

Mallory looked again at the photo Sir Charles had shown him. The slim, wiry figure in the camouflage uniform, the sun-blackened face, the calm, expressionless eyes.

'Tell me about him.'

'Raoul Guyon, aged twenty-nine. Went straight to Indo-China from St Cyr in 1952. He's the only known survivor of his particular cadet class for that year, which is enough to set any man apart for a start.'

'He wasn't at Dien-Bien-Phu?'

Adams shook his head. 'No, but he was at plenty of other hot spots. He was up to his ears in it in Algeria. There was some talk of a girl. Moorish, I think. She was murdered by the F.L.N. and it had a big effect on him. He was badly wounded a day or two later.'

There followed a picture of Guyon half

raised on a stretcher, his chest heavily bandaged, blood soaking through. The face was sunken, beyond pain, the eyes stared into an abyss of loneliness.

'There's a lad who's been through the fire,' Mallory said.

'And then some. Commander of the Legion of Honour, Croix de la Valeur Militaire and half a dozen mentions in despatches. On top of that, he paints like an angel.'

'A man to be reckoned with.'

'And don't you forget it.'

For the next twenty minutes they continued to sit there, discussing questions of time and place, some important technical data and various other items, all of which were relevant to the success of the operation. When they finally returned to the office Adams sat behind his desk and nodded at a large and well-filled in-tray.

'Look at that lot,' he said with an expression of disgust. 'God in heaven, but I'd trade places with you, Neil.'

Mallory grinned. 'I wonder? Is there anything else?'

Adams shook his head. 'Call in at the technical branch. They've got a rather neat line in transmitters for you. They'll give you a call-sign, suitable code and so on. Come back in half an hour. I'll have some identity papers and things ready, plus a rough outline of my little scheme to bring you and Mrs Grant together.'

'Now *that* I look forward to,' Mallory said.

And the strange thing was that he really did. As he went along the corridor and descended the stairs to the technical branch the memory of her haunted him. Those strange eyes searching, looking for something.

He sighed heavily. Taking it all in all, it looked as if this whole affair could become really complicated.

5

Passage by Night

'*Foxhunter!* Ahoy! Ahoy! *Foxhunter!*'

The boat lay at anchor fifty yards out from the beach, her cream and yellow hull a vivid splash of colour against the white cliffs of the cove. A small wind moved in from the sea, lifting the water across the shingle, and darkness was falling fast.

Anne Grant shivered slightly as a light drizzle drifted across her face. She was tired and hungry and her ankle had started to ache again. She opened her mouth to hail the boat a second time and Neil Mallory appeared on deck. He dropped over the stern into the dinghy and rowed towards her.

He was wearing knee-length rubber boots

and when the prow of the fibre-glass dinghy ground on the wet shingle he stepped into the shallows and swung it round so that the stern was beached.

He held out his hand for the girl's suitcase and smiled. 'How do you feel?'

'All the better for being here,' she said. 'It's been a long day. I had a lot of running around to do.'

She was wearing a tweed suit with a narrow skirt and a sheepskin coat. He helped her into the stern seat, pushed off and rowed for the boat.

Anne took in the flared, raking bow and long, sloping deckhouse of *Foxhunter* with a conscious pleasure. As she breathed deeply of the good sea air she smiled at Mallory.

'What do you think of her?'

'*Foxhunter*?' He nodded. 'She's a thoroughbred all right, but that's still an awful lot of boat for two women to handle as a regular thing. How old is your sister-in-law?'

'Fiona is eighteen, whatever that proves. I think you underrate us.'

'What about the engines?' he said. 'They'll need looking after.'

'We've no worries there. Owen Morgan, who runs the hotel on the island, is a retired ship's engineer. He'll give us any help we need and there's always Jagbir.'

'Who's he?' Mallory said quickly, remembering that he wasn't supposed to know.

'The General's orderly. He was a *naik* in a Gurkha regiment. They've been together since the early days of the war. He hasn't had what you would call a formal education, but he's still the best cook I've ever come across, and he has an astonishing aptitude for anything mechanical.'

'Sounds like a good man to have around the house,' Mallory said.

They bumped against the side of *Foxhunter* and he handed her up the short ladder and followed with her suitcase. 'What time would you like to leave?'

She took the case from him. 'As soon as you like. Have you eaten?'

'Not since noon.'

'I'll change and make some supper. We can leave afterwards.'

'When she had gone Mallory pulled the dinghy round to the stern and hoisted it over the rail. By now darkness was falling fast and he turned on the red and green navigation lights and went below.

He found her working at the stove in the galley, wearing old denims and a polo-necked sweater that somehow made her look more feminine than ever. She looked over her shoulder and smiled.

'Bacon and eggs all right?'

'Suits me,' he said.

When it was ready they sat opposite each other at the saloon table and ate in companionable silence. As she poured coffee a sudden flurry of rain drummed against the roof.

She looked up at him, eyebrows raised. 'That doesn't sound too good. What's the forecast?'

'Three-to-four wind – rain squalls. Nothing to get worked up about. Are you worried?'

'Not in the slightest.' She smiled slightly. 'I always like to know what I'm getting into, that's all.'

'Don't we all, Mrs Grant?' He got to his feet. 'I think we ought to get started.'

When he went on deck the wind had increased, scattering the drizzle in silver cobwebs through the navigation lights. He went into the wheelhouse, pulled on his reefer jacket and spent a couple of minutes looking at the chart.

The door swung open, a flurry of wind lifting the chart like a sail, and Anne Grant appeared at his elbow. She was wearing her sheepskin coat and a scarf was tied around her head, peasant-fashion.

'All set?' he said.

She nodded, her eyes gleaming with excitement in the light from the chart table. He pressed the starter. The engines coughed once asthmatically, then roared into life. He took *Foxhunter* round in a long, sweeping curve and out through the entrance of the cove into the Channel.

The masthead light swung rhythmically from side to side as the swell started to roll beneath them and spray scattered against the window. A couple of points to starboard the red and green navigation lights of a steamer were clearly visible a mile out to sea. Mallory reduced speed to ten knots and they ploughed forward into the darkness, the sound of the engines a muted throbbing on the night air.

He grinned at her. 'Nothing much wrong there. With any kind of luck we should have a clear run.'

'When do you want me to take over?'

He shrugged. 'No rush. Get some sleep. I'll call you when I feel tired.'

The door banged behind her and a small trapped wind whistled round the wheelhouse and died in a corner. He pulled the hinged seat down from the wall, lit a cigarette and settled back comfortably, watching the foam curl along the prow.

This was the sort of thing he looked forward to on a voyage. To be alone with the sea and the night. The world outside retreated steadily as *Foxhunter* moved into the darkness and he started to work his way methodically through his briefing from beginning to end, considering each point carefully before moving on to another.

It was in recalling that de Beaumont had been in Indo-China that he remembered that Raoul Guyon had been there also. Mallory frowned and lit another cigarette. There might be a connection, although Adams hadn't said anything about such a possibility. On the other hand, Guyon hadn't been a Viet prisoner, which made a difference. One hell of a difference.

He checked the course, altering it a point to starboard, and settled back again in the seat, turning the collar of his reefer jacket up around his face. Gradually his mind wandered away on old forgotten paths and he thought of people he had known, incidents which had happened, good and bad, with a sort of measured sadness. His life seemed to be like a dark sea rolling towards the edge of the world, hurrying him to nowhere.

He checked his watch, and found, with a sense of surprise that it was after midnight. The door opened softly, coinciding with a spatter of rain on the window, and Anne Grant came in carrying a tray.

'You promised to call me,' she said

reproachfully. 'I couldn't believe my eyes when I wakened and saw the time. You've been up here a good four hours.'

'I feel fine,' he said. 'Could go on all night.'

She placed the tray on the chart table and filled two mugs from a covered pot. 'I've made tea. You didn't seem to care for the coffee at supper.'

'Is there anything you don't notice?' he demanded.

She handed him a mug and smiled in the dim light. 'The soldier's drink.'

'What are you after?' he said. 'The gory details?'

She pulled down the other seat and handed him a sandwich. 'Only what you want to tell me.'

He considered the point and knew that, as always, a partial truth was better than a direct lie. 'I was kicked out in 1954.'

'Go on,' she said.

'My pay didn't stretch far enough.' He shrugged. 'You know how it is. I was in charge of a messing account and borrowed some cash to tide me over. Unfortunately the auditors arrived early that month. They usually do in cases like mine.'

'I don't believe you,' she said deliberately.

'Suit yourself.' He got to his feet and stretched. 'She's on automatic pilot, so you'll be all right for a while. I'll be up at quarter to four to change course.'

She sat there looking at him without speaking, her eyes very large in the half-light, and he turned, opened the door and left her there.

He went down to the cabin and flopped on his bunk, staring up at the bulkhead through the darkness. There had been women before, there always were, but only to satisfy a need, never to get close to. That had been the way for a long time and he had been content. Now this strange, quiet girl with her cropped hair had come into his life and quietly refused to be pushed aside. His last conscious thought was of her face glowing in the darkness, and she was smiling at him.

* * *

He was not aware of having slept, only of being awake and looking at his watch and realising with a sense of shock that it was half-three. He pulled on his jacket and went on deck.

There was quite a sea running and cold rain stung his face as he walked along the heaving deck and opened the glasspanelled door of the wheelhouse. Anne Grant was standing at the wheel, her face disembodied in the compass light.

'How are things going?' he asked.

'I'm enjoying myself. There's been a sea running for about half an hour now.'

He glanced out of the window. 'Likely to get worse before it gets better. I'll take over.'

She made way for him, her soft body pressing against his as they squeezed past each other. 'I don't think I could sleep now even if I wanted to.'

He grinned. 'Make some more tea, then, and come back. Things might get interesting.'

He increased speed a little, racing the heavy weather that threatened from the east, and after a while she returned with the tea. The wheel kicked like a living thing in his hands and he strained his eyes into the grey waste of the morning.

The sea grew rougher, waves rocking *Foxhunter* from side to side, and again Mallory increased speed until the prow seemed to lift clean out of the water each time a wave rolled beneath them.

Half an hour later they raised Alderney and he became aware of that great tidal surge that drives in through the Channel Islands, raising the level of the water in the Golfe de St Malo by as much as thirty feet.

He altered course for Guernsey and asked Anne to get the forecast on the radio in the saloon. She took her time over it and when she came back she carried more tea and sandwiches on a tray.

'It's pretty hopeful,' she said. 'Wind moderating, rain squalls dying away.'

'Anything else?'

'Some fog patches in the islands, but nothing to worry about.'

Gradually the wind died, the sea calmed and they ran into a clear September morning with a slight mist rising from the water. Mallory opened a window and inhaled the freshness. When he turned she was smiling at him.

'You can handle a boat, Mr Mallory. I'll say that for you.'

'Don't forget to mention the fact in my reference.'

She smiled, picked up the tray and went out again. He leaned over the chart and checked the course. *Foxhunter* rounded Les Hanois lighthouse on the western tip of Guernsey an hour and a half later and sea-gulls and cormorants cried harshly in the sky, sweeping in across the deck from the great cliffs.

Already visibility was becoming worse, fog drifting in patches across the open sea as Guernsey dropped behind the horizon. He set the automatic pilot, leaned over the chart and Anne Grant came in.

'How are we doing?'

'With any kind of luck we should reach Ile de Roc in an hour to an hour and a half. Depends on the fog. If we run into any really bad patches things could get tricky.'

'There's a large-scale Admiralty chart of the island and its approaches in the top drawer,' she said. 'I bought it specially.'

He took it out and they leaned over it together. Ile de Roc was perhaps two miles long and three across, the only anchorage a bay at the southern end. The entire area was encircled by a network of sunken reefs with only two deep-water channels giving anything like a safe passage through.

'I'll take her if you like,' Anne said. 'I know these waters like the back of my hand and you need to.'

'The damned place looks like a death-trap.' Mallory shook his head. 'I wouldn't like to be drifting in on those shores on a dirty night.'

'A lot of good ships have done just that. You see St Pierre a mile to the north? In the old days whenever a gale was blowing in from the Atlantic ships were often swept between the two islands to founder on the great sunken reef which links them. At low tide the water-level drops as much as thirty-feet and you can see some of those old wrecks.'

'Dangerous waters to go swimming in.'

She nodded. 'Especially at the wrong time. As a matter of fact, the barman from Owen Morgan's hotel was drowned only the other day. His body drifted in the evening before I left.'

'Not so good.' Mallory moved on quickly. 'I see there's a castle marked on St Pierre.'

'A Gothic mausoleum. It's out on a twenty-year lease to a French count, Philippe de Beaumont.'

'The place is going to be busier than I thought.'

She shook her head. 'We don't see much of him. He stays pretty close to home and we don't get many visitors on the island. The hotel only has six bedrooms. They're booked right through the summer, of course, but Owen usually ends the season at the beginning of September. He likes to enjoy the last of the good weather himself.'

'He won't need much staff, then?'

'Only during the season and then he uses Guernsey girls. He's had a French cook living in full-time for nearly a year now. She should have left at the end of the season, but stayed on.'

'Sounds a rather obvious set-up.'

She shrugged. 'It's their own affair and she's a nice girl. I hope he marries her.'

The fog lifted a little and on either hand the sea broke in a white foam over great reefs. Mallory smiled grimly. 'I think this is where you start doing your stuff.'

She took over the wheel and altered course half a point. A moment later, through a sudden break in the fog, the towering cliffs of the island loomed into view and then the grey curtain dropped into place again.

Mallory reduced speed and Anne Grant took the cruiser forward into the fog. She seemed completely unperturbed and he shrugged fatalistically, pulled down the other seat and took out a cigarette.

At that moment the whole boat rocked violently and Mallory and the girl were thrown across to the other side of the wheelhouse. *Foxhunter* yawed alarmingly and Mallory shoved the girl away and scrambled across to the spinning wheel.

As he pulled the boat back on course, Anne Grant moved beside him and they peered out into the fog. Perhaps a hundred feet to starboard he caught a glimpse of something solid moving through the water and a sizable wave rolled back to rock *Foxhunter* again.

'And what in the hell was that?' he said.

'Probably a basking shark. They're common enough in these waters, but it must have been a big one to leave a wake like that.'

Mallory stared out into the fog, a frown on his face, remembering the force of that wave. Could a shark, however big it was, have set up such a disturbance? He was still thinking about it when they emerged from the last patch of fog and Ile de Roc reared out of the sea a quarter of a mile away.

To the west was St Pierre, much smaller, a little blurred because visibility at that distance still wasn't good. Between the two islands the sea frothed and roared over the great underwater bridge.

'We're in the clear now,' Anne Grant said, and he gave *Foxhunter* everything she had as they roared through the water towards the great round cove which opened to meet them.

The water was a deep translucent blue, reminding him strangely of the Mediterranean. A stone jetty jutted fifty feet out from the shore and above it was the hotel, a two-storeyed, white-painted building sheltering in a hollow from the winter gales.

A fifteen-foot launch was moored on the far side of the cove. A young, dark-haired man in sunglasses was sitting in the stern looking over the side. As he turned towards them a swimmer surfaced and Mallory caught a flash of blonde hair.

When they were a hundred feet from the jetty he cut the engines and *Foxhunter* settled back into the water, drifting in on her own momentum. Anne Grant was already getting the fenders over the side and Mallory ran out to help her. The moment they touched he jumped for the jetty with a line and ran it twice around an iron bollard. *Foxhunter* jerked once, bumped against the jetty and was still.

As he moved to fasten the other line, an engine roared into life, the sound echoing harshly from the cliffs, and the launch came towards the jetty. The swimmer was already almost there. Anne Grant moved to the port rail and Mallory joined her.

'Fiona,' she said simply.

As the girl arrived Mallory leaned down and hauled her up and over the rail. She crouched on deck for a moment, laughing and shaking herself like a young puppy.

'But it's marvellous, Anne. Simply marvellous.'

She didn't even look eighteen, long blonde hair trailing damply to her shoulders. She wore a pair of bathing pants and the upper half of a rubber diving suit in bright yellow that fitted her slim figure like a second skin.

She examined Mallory with interest and her eyes widened in approval. 'And where did you find *him*?'

Anne laughed and kissed her affectionately. 'Now, don't start, Fiona. This is Neil Mallory. He's going to run the boat for us for a month or two till we get the hang of things.'

Fiona Grant pushed a tendril of wet hair out of her eyes and held out her hand. 'I don't know about Anne, but speaking for myself I'll try not to learn too fast.'

The launch was no more than twenty or thirty feet away now and its occupant cut the engine and it drifted in towards *Foxhunter*.

'Who's this, for goodness' sake?' Anne demanded.

Fiona slipped a wet arm in hers. 'A simply marvellous man, Anne. He's French. Staying here for a week or two to paint and do a little skin-diving.'

'But I thought Owen closed the hotel last week?'

'He did, but luckily I was on the jetty when he came in. I persuaded Owen to change his mind.'

The launch bumped against the side and Mallory caught the thrown line. As he looped it round the rail, the Frenchman vaulted on to the deck. He wore a slim-fitting jersey that left his sunburnt arms bare, and the dark glasses gave him the same slightly sinister and anonymous look the peaked military cap had done in the photo in his file.

Fiona took his arm and turned to face them. 'Anne, I'd like you to meet Raoul Guyon,' she said.

6

Iron Grant

The ancient, grey-stone house was firmly rooted into a hollow in the hill, great beech trees flanking it on either side. At some time a large glass conservatory had been added, running along the whole length of the building, and a series of shallow steps dropped down to a stone terrace.

From the terrace the cliffs fell a good two hundred feet into a small funnel-shaped inlet that would have made a wonderfully sheltered mooring had it not been for the jagged line of rocks stretching across the entrance.

Anne Grant leaned on the wall, a cool drink in her hand, and looked out to sea. It had turned into a beautiful day, surprisingly warm for September, with a scattering of white clouds trailing to the horizon. She felt completely relaxed and at peace, happy to be home again. A foot crunched on gravel. When she turned, her father-in-law stood at the top of the steps.

Major-General Hamish Grant, D.S.O., M.C. and bar, had been well named Iron Grant. Six feet four inches in height, with a great breadth of shoulders, his hair was a snow-white mane swept back behind his ears. He wore an old pair of khaki service trousers and a corduroy jacket.

He probed at the top step with his walking stick. 'You there, Anne?'

'Here I am, Hamish.'

She went up the steps and took his arm and his great, craggy face broke into a warm smile. 'Fiona seemed tremendously excited about the new boat, but she was hardly in the house for a moment before she was changed and off out again.'

In a corner of the terrace stood a table containing a tray of drinks and shaded by a large striped umbrella. She led him across and he eased his great bulk into a wicker chair.

'She's gone down to the hotel to meet Raoul Guyon, this young French painter who's staying there. She promised to show him some of the island before lunch.'

'What about this fellow Mallory?'

'He should be here at any moment. I asked him to pick up the diving equipment. There was no real hurry, but I thought you might like to meet him.'

'I certainly would if only to thank him for the way he handled this Southampton affair.' He frowned. 'Mallory. Neil Mallory. There's something familiar about that name. Irish, of course.'

'He certainly doesn't have an accent.'

'And you say he was cashiered for cooking the mess books? That certainly doesn't fit in with the sort of man who'd take on a couple of thugs in a back alley.'

'That's what I thought. He's a strange man, Hamish. At times there's something almost frightening about him. He's so curiously remote and detached from things. I think you'll like him.'

'I'd love to know why they slung him out,' the General said. 'Mind you, the War Office, God bless 'em, do some pretty daft things these days.'

'I'd rather you didn't raise the subject,' she said. 'Promise?'

He frowned for a moment and then shrugged. 'I don't see why not. After all, a man's past is his own affair. Can he sail the boat, that's the main thing?'

She nodded. 'Perfectly.'

'Then what have we got to grumble about?' He squeezed her hand. 'Get me a brandy and soda like a good girl and tell me some more about *Foxhunter*.'

She didn't get the chance. As she was pouring his drink, Jagbir appeared at the top of the steps, Mallory a yard or two behind him.

The Gurkha was short and squat, no more than five feet tall, and wore a neat, sand-coloured linen jacket. He had the ageless, yellow-brown face of the Asiatic and limped heavily on his left foot, relic of a bad wound received at Cassino.

He spoke good English with the easy familiarity of the old servant. 'Mr Mallory's here, General.'

The General sipped a little of his brandy and put the glass down again. 'What's on the stove?'

'Curried chicken. When would you like to have it?'

'Any time you like. Serve it out here.'

Mallory stood at the top of the steps waiting, cap in hand, and Anne smiled up at him. 'Would you care to have lunch with us, Mr Mallory?'

He shook his head. 'It's good of you to offer, but I've already arranged to eat at the hotel.'

She dismissed Jagbir with a quick nod, trying to hide her disappointment, and Mallory came down the steps.

'This is Mr Mallory, General,' she said formally.

Hamish Grant turned towards Mallory, his head slightly to one side. 'Come a bit closer, man. I don't see very well.'

Mallory moved to the table and looked down into the cloudy, opalescent eyes. The General reached out and touched him gently on the chest. 'My daughter-in-law tells me you're a good sailor?'

'I hope so,' Mallory said.

'What was your last ship?'

'An oil-tanker. S.S. *Pilar*. Tampico to Southampton.'

The General turned to Anne. 'Did you check his papers?' she shook her head and he looked up at Mallory again. 'Let's see them.'

Mallory took a wallet from his hip pocket, extracted a folded document and union card and tossed them on the table.

'See when he last paid off and check the union card. There should be a photo.'

She checked the documents quickly and nodded. 'Paid off S.S. *Pilar*, Southampton, 1st September.' She smiled as she handed them back. 'It isn't a very good photo.'

Mallory didn't reply and the General continued: 'The terms Mrs Grant agreed with you, you're quite satisfied with them?'

'Perfectly.'

'There'll be a bonus of one hundred pounds for you on top. Some token of my gratitude for the way you handled this Southampton business.'

'That won't be necessary, sir,' Mallory said coolly.

Blood surged into the General's face in an instant. 'By God, sir, if I say it is necessary it is necessary. You'll take orders like everyone else.'

Mallory adjusted his cap and turned to Anne. 'You mentioned some diving equipment you wanted me to take down to the boat?'

She took a hurried glance at the General's purple face and said quickly: 'You'll find a station wagon in the courtyard at the rear. Jagbir's already loaded it. I'll be down later this afternoon.'

'I'll expect you.' Mallory turned to the General. 'Anything else, sir?'

'No, damn your eyes!' the General exploded.

A smile tugged at the corner of Mallory's mouth. His hand started upwards in an instinctive salute. He caught himself just in time, glanced once at Anne, turned, and ran lightly up the steps.

The General started to laugh. 'Pour me another brandy.'

Anne uncorked the bottle and reached for his glass. 'Am I right in assuming all that was quite deliberate?'

'Of course,' Hamish Grant said, 'and I'll add to your mystery, my dear. There goes a man who once was used to command, and high command at that. I didn't spend forty years in the army for nothing.'

High on the cliffs on the western side of the island Raoul Guyon and Fiona Grant topped a steep hill and paused. Before them the island seemed to tumble over the cliffs and the great jagged spine which joined them to St Pierre was visible under the water.

'There,' she said, making a sweeping gesture with one hand. 'Did I lie to you?'

'You were right,' he said. 'Absolutely magnificent.'

'I'll expect to see you up here with your easel first thing in the morning.'

'You'll be disappointed. I always work from preliminary sketches, never from life.'

She had moved a few feet away, stooping to pick up a flower, and now she turned quickly. 'Fraud.'

He took a small sketch-pad and pencil from the pocket of his corduroy jacket and dropped to the ground. 'Stay where you are, but look out to sea.'

She obeyed him at once. 'All right, but this had better be good.'

'Don't chatter,' he said. 'It distracts me.'

The sun glinted on her straw-coloured hair and her image blurred so that in that one brief moment of time she might have been a painting by Renoir. She looked incredibly young and innocent and yet the wind from the sea moulded the thin cotton dress to her firm young figure with a disturbing sensuousness.

Guyon grunted and pocketed his pencil. 'All right.'

She dropped beside him and snatched the

pad from his hand. In the same moment her smile died and colour stained her cheeks. Inescapably caught in a few brief strokes of the pencil for all eternity, she stood gazing out to sea, and by some strange genius all that was good in her, all the innocence and longing of youth, were there also.

She looked up at him in wonderment. 'It's beautiful.'

'But you are,' he said calmly. 'Has no one ever told you this before?'

'I learned rather early in life that it's dangerous to let them.' She smiled ruefully. 'Until my mother died four years ago we lived in a villa near St Tropez. You know it?'

'Extremely well.'

'In St Tropez, in season, anything female is in demand and fourteen-year-old girls seem to have a strong appeal for some men.'

'So I've heard,' he said gravely.

'Yes, life had its difficulties, but then the General bought this little island and I went to school for a couple of years. I didn't like that at all.'

'What did you do, run away?'

She pushed her long hair back from her face and laughed. 'Persuaded the General to send me to a finishing school in Paris. Now *that* was really something.'

Guyon grinned and lit a cigarette. Tell me, why do you always call him General?'

She shrugged. 'Everyone does – except for Anne, of course. She's special. When she married my brother Angus she was only my age. He was killed in Korea.'

She paused, a few wild flowers held to her face as she stared pensively into the past, and Guyon lay back, gazing up at the sky, sadness sweeping through him as he remembered another time, another girl.

Algiers, 1958. After five months chasing *fellaghas* in the cork forests of the Grande Kabylie he had found himself in that city of fear, leading his men through the narrow streets of the Kasbah and Bab el Oued, locked in the life-or-death struggle that was the Battle of Algiers.

And then Nerida had come into his life, a young Moorish girl fleeing from a mob after a bomb outrage on the Boulevard du Telemly.

He closed his eyes and saw again her dark hair tumbling across a pillow, moonlight streaming through a latticed window. The long nights when they had tried to forget tomorrow.

But the morning had come, the cold grey morning when she had been found on the beach, stripped and defiled, head shaven, body mutilated. The proper ending for a woman who had betrayed her people for a *Frangaoui*. The sniper's bullet of the following day which had sent him back to France on a stretcher had almost carried a welcome oblivion.

Nerida. The scent of her was strong in his nostrils and he reached out and pulled her down, crushing his lips against hers. Her body was soft and yielding and when she swung on to her back her mouth answered sweet as honey. He opened his eyes and Fiona Grant smiled lazily up at him.

'Now what brought that on?'

He leaned on one elbow for a moment and rubbed a hand across his eyes. 'Put it down to the sea air. I'm sorry.'

'I'm not.'

'Then you should be.' He pulled her to her feet. 'Didn't you tell me you were expected for lunch?'

She held on to his hand. 'Come back with me. I'd like you to meet the General.'

'Some other time. I've arranged to eat at the hotel.'

She turned from him like a hurt child. He restrained a strong impulse to take her in his arms, reminded himself strongly that he had work to do – important work – and walked away. When he reached the top of the rise he hesitated and turned reluctantly.

She was standing where he had left her, head drooping, something touchingly despondent about her. The strong sunlight, streaming through the thin cotton of her dress, outlined her firm young thighs perfectly.

'Damn her!' he said softly to himself. 'She might as well have nothing on.'

He sighed heavily and went back down the slope.

* * *

Mallory lay on his bunk in *Foxhunter* watching the blue smoke from his cigarette twist and swirl in the current from the air-conditioner. He'd had an excellent meal at the hotel in company with Owen Morgan, but there had been no sign of the Frenchman.

His mind went back again to his meeting with Hamish Grant at the house on the cliffs. There had been method behind the old man's bullying, of that he was certain. He had been a soldier himself for too long to subscribe to the opinion that all generals were rather stupid, dull-witted blimps who spent their time either needlessly sending men to their deaths or over-indulging at the table.

Behind the worn, leather-coloured face, the half-blind eyes, was a will of iron and a first-rate brain. Iron Grant, who had force-marched his division through the hell that was the Qattara Depression rather than surrender to Rommel, who had led the way down the ramp of the first landing craft to hit Sword Beach on D-Day, was an adversary to be reckoned with by any standards.

And then there was his daughter-in-law.

Mallory closed his eyes, trying to picture her face. There was a calmness about her, a sureness that he found disturbing. Even on the wharf at Southampton she had not seemed afraid. It was as if life had done its worst, could do no more. As if nothing could ever really hurt her again. It came to him quite suddenly that she must have loved her husband very much and he was aware of a vague, irrational jealousy.

He heard no sound and yet it was as if a wind had passed over his face and every muscle came alive and singing, ready for instant action. The lower step of the companionway creaked and he reached for the butt of the revolver under his pillow.

'No need, my friend,' Raoul Guyon said quietly.

As Mallory opened his eyes, the young Frenchman dropped on to the opposite bunk and produced a packet of cigarettes.

'We missed you at lunch,' Mallory said. 'What happened?'

Guyon shrugged. 'Something came up. You know how it is?'

'I certainly do. There's grass on your jacket.'

'A fine day for lying on one's back and contemplating heaven,' Guyon said brazenly.

'Not when there's a job to be done.' Mallory opened a cupboard under the bunk, took out a bottle of whisky and two glasses and set them on the table. 'Business and pleasure don't mix.'

'On occasion, I'm happy to say that they do. Am I not supposed to be a fun-loving young artist on vacation?' Guyon poured himself a generous measure of whisky and raised his glass. '*Santé*.'

Slim-hipped, lean and sinewy, Raoul Guyon possessed that strange quality to be found in the airborne troops of every country, a kind of arrogant self-sufficiency bred of the hazards of the calling. While unaware of this in himself, he recognised it at once in the Englishman, but there was more than that. Much more. Mallory was the same strange mixture of soldier and monk, of man-of-action and mystic, that he had seen in the great paratroop colonels in Algiers. Men like

Philippe de Beaumont. Strange, wild, half-mad fanatics, marred by their experiences in the Viet prison camps, for the time controlling the destiny of a great nation.

But Mallory also had passed through the fire of a Communist prison camp and, like Philippe de Beaumont, he had tried to put into practise those lessons hard learned from his Chinese taskmasters and with the same disastrous result.

Mallory lit a cigarette and leaned back against the bulkhead. 'How good is your skin-diving?'

Guyon shrugged. 'I know what I'm doing. A little out of practice, that's all.'

'Anne Grant wants me to take her out over the reef this afternoon. She's brought a couple of aquamobiles back from the mainland. Wants to try them out. I thought if you asked Fiona nicely you might get yourself invited.'

'As a matter of fact, I already have. All part of my business-cum-pleasure activities.'

'You don't waste much time.' Mallory grinned. 'We'll see how things look. We can make a full-scale reconnaissance later tonight.'

'You really think there maybe something in this business?'

Mallory shrugged. 'I wouldn't like to say. As I was bringing the boat in this morning something damned big passed us underwater. Anne Grant said it was a shark. Apparently they're pretty common round here.'

'Do you think it's worth reporting?'

Mallory shook his head. 'My boss is interested in facts, not possibilities. I've signalled my arrival and nothing more.' He opened the cupboard again, took out what was apparently a small transistor radio and held it up. 'Amazing what they can do with electronics these days. There are three motor torpedo boats based on St Helier now, supposed to be on shallow-water exercises. If I give them the word they'll be in here like a shot.'

'What's the signal?'

'Their codeword is Leviathan. When we need them we simply signal Code Four. That's all that's needed.'

Mallory put the set in a drawer in the table and Guyon helped himself to more whisky. 'I was in touch with my own people before I left Guernsey this morning. They've drawn a complete blank where *L'Alouette* is concerned. It's creating something of a situation.'

'What in the hell are the O.A.S. trying to prove?' Mallory said. 'This sort of thing isn't going to get them anywhere in the long run.'

'Desperate men seek desperate remedies. Eight times since 1960 either the O.A.S. or the C.N.R. have conspired to kill de Gaulle. They came closest last month when they ambushed his car on the way to Villacoublay Airport. They picked the leader of that little affair up only last week.'

'So this latest business is to prove to people they're still a force to be reckoned with?'

'More than that. That they have a long arm which can reach out to punish those who oppose them. This isn't the first member of the judiciary to be assassinated. At this rate there will soon be no one willing to be connected with the trials of O.A.S. members, especially when to take part carries an automatic death sentence.'

'What about Bouvier?'

'He was public prosecutor at a military

tribunal which only last month tried six members of the O.A.S. Two were sentenced to death. His execution was stage-managed to have the maximum dramatic effect and the government can't hope to keep it secret beyond the end of the week.'

'Which doesn't give us long to handle things here.' Mallory frowned. 'Have you ever met de Beaumont personally?'

'Only as one of the crowd. He was a member of the original Committee of Public Safety which brought de Gaulle back to power. When it became obvious that the General wouldn't play along with his dream of an integrated Algeria he fell to plotting, or so we think.'

'Was anything ever proved against him?'

Guyon shook his head. 'It was thought that he was the power behind the scenes in General Challe's abortive coup in 1961, but there was no evidence. Before any could be collected he asked to be placed on unpaid leave and left France. He's extremely wealthy, by the way. One of his uncles married into industry after the first war.'

'What does Legrande think about him?'

Guyon laughed. 'Legrande has little respect for the aristocracy. He would see the guillotine set up in the old situation and smile at the prospect. He has no proof that de Beaumont it directly connected with the O.A.S., but he is unhappy about him. He would be quite content to see him dead. He has a naturally tidy mind.'

'And what's your own opinion?'

'Of de Beaumont?' Guyon hesitated. 'He's a dangerous man and no fool. For a year he was in charge of all military intelligence in Algeria, but he was always at loggerheads with the brasshats. He saw war as the Communists see war – as something to be won – and he believed that the end justified the means. Something the *boi-dois* had beaten into him in the Viet camps.' Guyon half smiled. 'This much at least I would expect you to have in common with him. Legrande told me that you, too, were behind the Communist wire for a time.'

'You make him sound interesting,' Mallory said. 'I'd like to meet him. I've a feeling that would tell me all I need to know.'

'Very possibly.' Guyon emptied his glass. 'Is there anything else you wish me to do?'

'This Frenchwoman who's living at the hotel with Morgan, Juliette Vincente? In my briefing they said she was harmless. What do you think?'

'Our preliminary report certainly didn't indicate anything unusual. Her mother and father have a small farm in Normandy. One brother, killed doing his military service in Algeria in 1958. She worked at an hotel in St Malo for six months before coming here.'

Mallory nodded. 'Sounds all right, but run the usual check on your room, just to make sure it hasn't been searched.'

Guyon put on his sunglasses and got to his feet. 'I'll get changed. See you in about half an hour and we'll have a look at that reef.' He paused in the doorway and stretched. 'It really is a beautiful day. I'm quite looking forward to it.'

After he had gone Mallory sat on the edge of the bunk going over things in his mind, trying to work out what might happen, but he knew that he was wasting his time.

If there was one lesson he had learned above all others it was that in this game nothing was certain. Chance ruled every move. He opened one of the lockers, took out the diving gear and started to check it.

7

On the Reef

Mallory vaulted over the rail into the translucent blue water, paused for a moment to adjust the flow of air from his aqualung and swam down in a long sweeping curve that brought him under the hull of *Foxhunter* to where Fiona Grant swayed beside the anchor chain like some exotic flower in her yellow diving suit. A moment later her sister-in-law appeared beside them in a cloud of silver bubbles.

Fiona jack-knifed at once and followed the anchor chain down into the blue mist, her long hair streaming out behind, and Mallory and Anne went after her.

They were perhaps a hundred yards out

from the shore on the southern side of the island and the water was saturated with sunlight, so that even when they reached bottom at forty feet visibility was good.

The sea-bed was covered by a great spreading forest of seaweed six or seven feet deep which moved rhythmically with every ebb and flow of current, changing colour like some living thing. Fiona swam into it, fish scattering to avoid her. Mallory paused, hovering over the undulating mass, and Anne tapped him on the shoulder and moved away.

They plunged over a great black spine of rock and a wall complete with arched Norman window loomed out of the shadows a few feet to the right. Anne swam effortlessly through it and Mallory followed.

It was obvious that only the strong tidal currents on this side of the island had prevented the building from being completely silted over centuries before. It had no roof and the walls had crumbled until they stood no higher than four feet above the sand. Beyond, the sea-bed sloped gently into another forest of seaweed, broken walls and jumbled blocks of worked masonry strewn on every side.

Fiona Grant appeared from the gloom and swam towards them. She poised a couple of feet away, put a hand into the nylon bag which was looped to her left wrist and produced a piece of red pottery which she waved triumphantly. Anne raised her thumb and they all turned, swam back across the rocks and struck upwards to *Foxhunter*'s curved hull.

They surfaced by the small ladder suspended over the side, and Anne went up first. Mallory followed her, pulled off his mask and turned to give Fiona a hand. She squatted on the deck, taking the pieces of pottery from her bag one by one and laying them out carefully.

Raoul Guyon had set up an easel next to the wheelhouse and was sketching Hamish Grant, who sat in the bows. The Frenchman put down his pencil and moved across to join them.

The General turned his head sharply. 'What's going on?'

'Fiona's found some pottery,' Anne said.

Guyon turned to Mallory, a strange, alien-looking figure in his webbed feet and black rubber suit. 'What's it like down there?'

'Interesting,' Mallory said. 'You should try it.'

'Perhaps later. I'd like to get my sketches of the General finished and the light is just right.'

Fiona unstrapped her aqualung, squatted down on the deck again and started to sort through the pieces of pottery, completely absorbed by her task.

Anne turned to Mallory. 'That's the last we'll see of her today.'

'Do you want to go down again?'

She shook her head. 'I'd like to try out the aquamobiles. You take one and I'll have the other. We'll go round the point to the St Pierre reef. I'll show you the Middle Passage and there's at least one interesting wreck.'

Guyon helped Mallory bring the two aquamobiles up from the saloon. They were bullet-shaped underwater scooters driven by battery-operated propellers, designed to operate at depths of up to one hundred and fifty feet. They carried their own spotlights for use when visibility was bad.

Anne and Mallory went over the side and Guyon passed down the heavy scooters. Anne moved away at once, running on the surface, and Mallory went after her.

The sea was calm, the sun bright on the face of the water, but as they approached the great finger of rock jutting out into the sea at the western end of the island Mallory became aware of cross-currents tugging at his body. Anne raised an arm in a quick signal and disappeared.

The sensation of speed underwater was extraordinary. To Mallory it seemed as if he were hurtling through space as he chased the yellow-clad figure in front of him and yet his effective speed was not much more than three knots.

The red nose of the scooter whipped through the blue-green water, pulling him across a jumbled mass of black rocks. For a moment currents seemed to pull his body in several directions at once and then he was round the point and into calmer water.

They surfaced by a weed-covered shoulder of rock and Anne sat on its slope half out of the water and pulled up her mask. On either side, and stretching across to St Pierre, was white water, surf breaking everywhere over the jagged rocks which made up the central reef mass.

'At low tide most of the reef is twenty feet above water,' she said. 'Stretching all the way to St Pierre like a giant's causeway.'

'Could it be crossed on foot?'

She looked dubious. 'I wouldn't like to try. It's only clear for an hour. Something to do with another flood which moves in this way from the Atlantic.'

A mile away the great, jagged rock of St Pierre lifted out of the sea. The castle was perched on the ultimate edge of the cliffs, its strange, pointed Gothic towers in sharp relief against the blue sky. The sea creamed over rocks two hundred feet below.

'What do you think of it?' she said.

'It must have cost a fortune to build even

on the golden tide of Victorian prosperity.' He shaded his eyes and frowned. 'I can't see a jetty.'

'It's under the island. If you look carefully beyond the last line of rocks you'll see the entrance in the cliffs. At high water there's only ten- or twelve-foot clearance.'

'Is the water very deep in there?' he said casually.

She nodded. 'Even at low water there's a good ten fathoms. There's a fault in the sea-bed which splits the reef along the centre. It runs right under St Pierre.'

'Would that be your famous Middle Passage?'

'That's right, and it's well worth seeing.'

She clamped her rubber mouthpiece between her teeth, pulled down the mask and eased herself back into the water. Visibility was still good and Mallory could see the great boulders of the reef four or five fathoms beneath, and then quite suddenly Anne tilted her scooter over a shelf of granite and went down into space.

They moved through a misty tunnel of

rock, sunlight slanting through fissures and cracks in the roof in wavering bands of light. In places the passage was reminiscent of a cathedral nave, the rock arched up on either side to support the roof, and then the dimness brightened and they moved into a section which was open to the sea.

Anne was twenty or thirty feet in front and she paused, waiting for him. When he approached she jack-knifed. Mallory went after her, the scarlet nose of his scooter cleaving the water, fish crowding to either side. At ten fathoms he moved into a mysterious green dusk with visibility considerably reduced.

Beneath him she had paused, hovering over a ledge. When he joined her he saw, to his astonishment, a three-ton Bedford truck wedged on its side in a large fissure. The canvas tilt had long since disappeared, but when he moved in close he saw painted on the side the white star which all Allied vehicles had carried on D-Day and after.

They moved away again and a moment later the outline of a ship's stern loomed out of the gloom. Every rail, every line, was festooned with strange submarine growths and he followed the curving side to where a ragged torpedo hole gaped darkly at him. Beneath, tilted into a crevasse, was a Churchill tank, beyond it, the shapes of trucks, a solitary field-gun's barrel slanting towards the surface.

Mallory followed Anne across the deck to the wheelhouse. The open door swung gently in the current, the deck around it smashed and broken as if by some internal explosion. The wheel was still intact and also the compass in its mounting, encrusted with scales. When Mallory moved inside he had a strange sensation that someone should be there, that something was missing. A bad end for a good ship, he thought, and moved out again. She tapped him on the shoulder, and together they rose towards the luminosity that was the surface.

They hauled themselves on to the flat top of a large rock, dry in the sun, and Anne pulled up her mask and breathed deeply several times.

'What's the story?' Mallory said.

She shrugged. 'One of the D-Day armada that never made it. She was torpedoed near Guernsey. When her engines stopped the tide carried her straight in across the reef. Apparently, the crew got away earlier in the lifeboats.'

'Where did you get the story?'

'From Owen Morgan. There are plenty of wrecks in these waters and Owen knows them all – and their histories. Something of a hobby with him.'

'Interesting,' Mallory said. 'I'd like to take another look. Feel up to it?'

'I don't think so. I'll wait for you here. Don't stay too long. When the tide starts turning there's quite an undercurrent through the passage.'

He was aware of it almost at once like an invisible hand pushing him to one side as he went down over the edge of the reef. The pressure of the water clawed at his mask as the scooter pulled him down and he swerved as a steel mast pierced the gloom.

He hovered over the tilting deck, considering

his next move. The sight of the black, gaping entrance to a companionway decided him. He moved inside, switching on the spot which was mounted on top of the scooter.

He moved along the angled corridor and opened the first door he came to. It fell inwards slowly, the room beyond it dark and he was aware of a strange, irrational fear. He pushed forward boldly, and the light, spreading through the water, showed him a table bolted to the floor, a bunk against one wall and bottles and assorted debris floating against the ceiling.

He swam out and moved further along the corridor to where it disintegrated into a twisted mass of metal, electric wires draped from the roof and, most poignant sight of all, the broken remnants of a human skeleton crushed beneath a girder.

He moved back along the corridor quickly and, the moment he emerged from the companionway, struck up towards the reef. At twenty feet he paused to decompress for several minutes, aware of the current tugging at his body. He surfaced a few yards from the rock and found Anne Grant waist-deep on the edge of the reef, adjusting her equipment.

'We'll have to get moving,' she shouted, as he approached and pushed up his mask. 'It must be later than I thought. I can feel the tide moving already.'

'Is that bad?' he said.

She nodded. 'Even the aquamobiles aren't going to do us much good with a five-knot current flowing the other way.'

She moved off at once and he went after her. Behind them the entire length of the reef was surging into breakers and he could feel the relentless pressure of the current. He started to flutter-kick with all his strength, and gradually the point grew nearer. Anne turned, gave him a quick wave and they went down.

He could see the weeds on the sea-bed beneath him leaning over on one side, pointing back towards the reef, and the pressure was now a solid wall that he was trying to break through. He kicked again, was dimly aware of the black rocks passing beneath him and then they were round into calm water and his aquamobile seemed to leap forward with a surge of power.

He surfaced and saw Anne at once, over to the right and some distance in front of him. He raised a hand, urging her on, and followed. When he rounded the final point of rock she was perhaps fifty yards in front of him and moving strongly towards *Foxhunter*.

A speedboat was moored beside the ladder, the sunlight gleaming on its scarlet trim, and someone sat in a canvas chair next to General Grant, a tall, distinguished-looking man in dark glasses and linen jacket who stood up and moved to the rail, shading his eyes as Anne approached.

She reached the ladder and he moved to give her a hand. When she climbed up on deck Mallory was still twenty or thirty yards away and he reduced speed.

As he came in under the counter of the speedboat the man who was sitting at the wheel turned to look down at him. He was a large, dangerous-looking individual with a hard face, a jagged scar bisecting the right cheek. Mallory recognised him at once from the photograph he had been shown at his briefing.

He pushed up his mask. 'Hello there.'

Jacaud looked down at him calmly, nodded, then turned away. Mallory pulled himself to the bottom of the ladder where Raoul Guyon was already waiting, a hand outstretched for the aquamobile.

Mallory went over the rail, squatted on deck and took off his aqualung. Anne Grant was standing a yard or two away, an attractive figure in her yellow diving suit as she talked to the man in the linen jacket.

There was little doubt who he was. The handsome aristocratic face, the easy poise, spoke of a man who was supremely aware of the fact that God had created the de Beaumonts first.

'Such a nice surprise,' she was saying.

'Pure luck that I passed, I assure you. I was trying out my new speedboat.' De Beaumont raised her hand to his mouth. 'My dear Anne, you grow more delightful each time I see you.'

She coloured charmingly and the General

cut in: 'And now that we've got you you won't get away so easily. You must come to dinner tonight. It's been far too long.'

'Please do,' Anne said.

He shrugged, still holding her hand. 'How can I refuse?'

Raoul Guyon was standing with Fiona beside the deckhouse and Anne turned towards him. 'Have you met Monsieur Guyon?'

'I have indeed,' de Beaumont said. 'I've been looking at these delightful sketches he's done of the General. If he can spare the time perhaps you could persuade him to come across to St Pierre one day and sketch me?'

'A pleasure,' Guyon said.

Anne turned towards Mallory. 'And this is Mr Neil Mallory. He's running the boat for us for a month or two till Fiona and I get used to things.'

De Beaumont stood for a moment, looking towards Mallory, and then he slowly removed his sun-glasses. His eyes were a strange, metallic blue and very cold, no warmth in them at all, and yet something moved there, something that instantly put Mallory on the alert.

'Mr Mallory.' De Beaumont held out his hand.

Mallory took it and the grip tightened. The Frenchman looked into his eyes for a long moment, then turned back to Anne.

'And now I must go. At what time this evening?'

'Seven,' she said. 'We'll look forward to seeing you.'

He went down the ladder into the speedboat and nodded to Jacaud. The engine roared into life and the boat turned away in a surge of power.

De Beaumont raised his hand in farewell, took a gold cigarette case from an inner pocket, selected a cigarette and lit it.

'Shall I tell Marcel to be ready to run you across tonight?' Jacaud said.

De Beaumont nodded. 'And Pierre, but I shall also require you, Jacaud.'

'Something interesting?'

'I have just seen a ghost,' de Beaumont said calmly. 'A ghost from the past, and ghosts are always interesting.'

He settled back in the seat and Jacaud

spun the wheel in his hands and took the speedboat round the point, his face quite expressionless.

Mallory stood at the wheel of *Foxhunter* thinking about de Beaumont. There had been something there, of that he was sure, but what could it possibly be? They had certainly never met.

The door clicked open behind him and Raoul Guyon came in and leaned against the chart table, lighting a cigarette.

'What did you think of him?'

Mallory shrugged. 'Very charming, very elegant. Seems soft until you look in his eyes. Are you dining with them tonight?'

Guyon shook his head. 'I've been invited for drinks afterwards. What was it like on the reef? Anything interesting?'

Mallory told him everything that had happened. When he had finished Guyon nodded. 'From the sound of it, this cavern under the island would seem like an adequate hiding place for *L'Alouette*.'

'That's what we'll have to find out.'

'And how do we do that?'

'We'll use the aquamobiles. Try the Middle Passage approach I told you about.'

'Straight into the cavern. Do you think they'll let us?'

'That's what we'll have to find out. We'll go in sometime tonight. The forecast's good and there's a moon. If the weather holds it shouldn't be too difficult. We'll go round the point in the dinghy. That should give us a good start.'

Guyon sighed. 'Legrande told me this one would be interesting. Little did he know. I'll see you later.'

The door closed behind him and Mallory increased speed. The strange thing was that as *Foxhunter* ran back towards the jetty he wasn't thinking of the danger that lay ahead, of the long swim through the dark night. He was thinking of two metallic blue eyes and wondering what it was that he had seen in them.

8

The Man from Tangiers

Through the french windows the lawn shimmered palely and the great beeches were silhouetted against the evening sky. Beyond was the timeless sad sough of the sea.

Inside, the room was warm and comfortable, the light softly diffused and a log hissed and spluttered on the hearth-stone. There was a grand piano in one corner, two old comfortable couches drawn to the fire and a print or two on the walls.

It was a room that was lived in, a quiet, comfortable place, and the five people gathered loosely about the fire talked quietly to each other, Fiona Grant's occasional laugh breaking to the surface like a bubble of air in a quiet pool.

De Beaumont and his host wore dinner jackets and the Frenchman looked elegant, completely at his ease as he talked to Anne Grant and the General.

Fiona was wearing a simple green dress in some heavy silk material and sat on the arm of an old tapestry chair. Guyon stood beside her smoking a cigarette, one hand on the high mantelpiece. He was not in evening dress, but a well-cut suit of dark blue fitted his wiry figure to perfection, giving him a touch of distinction.

He leaned close to Fiona, muttered something in her ear, and she chuckled and stood up. 'Raoul and I are going for a little walk. Anyone feel like joining us?'

'And what would you do if we said yes?' her father demanded.

'Brain you!' She kissed him affectionately and moved to the door. 'I'll get a coat, Raoul. It could turn chilly.'

Raoul smiled at de Beaumont. 'Will I see you again before you leave, Colonel?'

De Beaumont shook his head. 'Unlikely, I'm afraid. I keep early hours these days. Strict instructions from my doctor.'

Guyon held out his hand. 'For the present, then.'

'And don't forget about that portrait,' de Beaumont reminded him. 'I meant what I said.'

The young Frenchman nodded to the others and walked across to the door quickly as Fiona called from the hall.

'Seems a nice enough young chap,' the General observed.

'Fiona obviously thinks so,' Anne said. 'And he's certainly talented. He was in the army in Algeria for several years before he took up painting.'

'He's remarkably talented,' de Beaumont said. 'He'll make a name for himself with little difficulty.'

The General turned his head as Jagbir came in and handed round drinks from a tray. 'Any sign of Mr Mallory yet?'

'No, General.'

The General opened a silver box at his

elbow and took out a long black cheroot. 'I wonder what's happened to him?'

'Probably something to do with the boat,' Anne said. 'And he is walking, remember.'

De Beaumont fitted a cigarette into a silver holder and said carefully, 'Have you known him long?'

Hamish Grant shook his head. 'Anne picked him up in Southampton. As a matter of fact, he got her out of a rather nasty scrape.'

'And this is the basis upon which you hired him?'

'His papers were all in order. He'd only just signed off a tanker from Tampico a day or so before. Why do you ask?'

De Beaumont stood up, paced restlessly across to the french windows and turned. 'This is really most difficult for me. I don't want you to think that I am interfering, yet on the other hand I feel that I should speak.'

'You know something about him?' the General said. 'Something to his discredit?'

De Beaumont came back to his chair and sat down. 'You're aware, of course, that during the latter part of my army career I was commanding officer of a parachute regiment in Algeria. During the first few months of 1959 I was seconded to the general staff in Algiers and placed in charge of military security.'

'How does this concern Mallory?'

'We kept a special file on people who were thought to be working for the F.L.N. or the various other nationalist organisations. Neil Mallory was in that file. He was captain of a sea-going motor-yacht berthed in Tangiers. He was a smuggler, engaged in the extremely profitable business of running contraband tobacco into Spain and Italy. He was also thought to be running guns for the F.L.N.'

Hamish Grant emptied his glass, placed it carefully down on the table at his elbow and shrugged. 'In other words he was a tough, rather unscrupulous young man who'd make a pound wherever there was one to be made. You've told me nothing I hadn't already worked out for myself.' He pushed his glass across to Anne. 'Pour me another, my dear.'

'It was the years before Tangiers I found most interesting when I read this file,' de Beaumont said. 'That's why I recalled him so easily. Remember a book you loaned me about a year ago? A War Office manual entitled *A New Concept of Revolutionary Warfare*? You told me it had been written by a brilliant young officer in 1953 during the months following his release from a Chinese prison camp in Korea. I believe it caused quite a stir at the time.'

The General stiffened, one hand tightening on the handle of his walking-stick. 'God in heaven,' he said, 'Mallory! Lieutenant-Colonel Neil Mallory.'

'What was it they called him after that unpleasantness in Malaya?' de Beaumont said gently. 'The Butcher of Perak?'

The glass into which Anne Grant was at that moment pouring whisky splintered sharply against the floor. She stood gazing fixedly at de Beaumont, a puzzled expression on her face, then crossed quickly to her father-in-law.

'What does he mean?'

Hamish Grant patted her hand. 'You're sure it's the same man?'

De Beaumont shrugged. 'The circumstances can hardly be coincidental. Admittedly, until today I had only seen his photograph, but it's a distinctive face. Not the sort one forgets easily.'

'But what is it, Hamish?' Anne demanded.

De Beaumont was clearly embarrassed. 'Perhaps it would be better if I went. Forgive me for having cast a shadow on what otherwise has been a truly delightful evening, but as a friend I felt that I had no choice but to tell you what I knew of this man.'

'You were quite right.' Hamish Grant got to his feet. 'I'm very grateful to you. We'll see you again soon, I hope?'

'But of course.'

The General sat down again and de Beaumont and Anne moved into the hall. 'I'll get Jagbir to run you down to the jetty in the station wagon,' she said.

De Beaumont shook his head. 'No need. A fine evening. The walk will do me good.'

When he raised her hand to his lips it was limp and unresponsive. He picked up his coat, opened the door and smiled. 'Good night, Anne.'

'Good night, Colonel de Beaumont,' she said formally, and the door closed.

He stood on the top step, a slight smile on his face. She was annoyed because he had brought to light something discreditable in Mallory's past and that annoyance could only be the automatic reaction of a woman already deeply involved, which was interesting.

He moved down the steps towards the main gate and Jacaud stepped out of the bushes. 'What happened?'

De Beaumont shrugged. 'Patience, my dear Jacaud. I have set things in motion. Now we must await developments.'

A foot crunched on gravel and Jacaud pulled him quickly into the shadows. A moment later Mallory walked by and went towards the house.

'What do we do now?' Jacaud whispered. 'Return to St Pierre?'

De Beaumont shook his head. 'The night is young and interesting things have yet to happen. I think we will go down to the hotel and sample some of our good friend Owen's contraband brandy. We can await developments there.'

He chuckled gently and led the way out through the gates to the narrow dirt road, white in the gloaming.

'Who was he, Hamish?' Anne said calmly. 'I want to know.'

'Neil Mallory?' Hamish shrugged. 'An outstanding paratroop officer. First-rate war record, decorated several times. Afterwards, Palestine, Malaya, a different kind of war. He went to Korea in '51 was wounded and captured somewhere on the Imjin. Prisoner for two years.'

'And then what?'

'From what one can make out he was the sort of man people were rather afraid of, especially his superiors. A little like Lawrence or Orde Wingate, God rest his soul. The sort of desperate eccentric who doesn't really fit in where peacetime soldiering's concerned.'

'De Beaumont said he was a colonel? He must have been very young.'

'Probably the youngest in the army at the time. He wrote this book *A New Concept of Revolutionary Warfare* for the War Office in 1953. It aroused a lot of talk at the time. Most people seemed to think he'd turned Communist. Kept quoting from Mao Tse-tung's book on guerrilla warfare as if the damned thing were a bible.'

'What happened?'

'He'd been promoted lieutenant-colonel after the Korean business. They had to find him something to do so they sent him to Malaya. Things weren't too good at that time. In some areas the Communist guerrillas virtually controlled everything. They gave Mallory command of some local troops. It wasn't really a regiment. Not much more than a hundred men. Recruiting was bad at the time. Little stocky Malayan peasants straight out of the rice fields. I know the type.'

'Did they make good soldiers?'

'In three months they were probably the most formidable jungle troops in Malaya. Within six they'd proved themselves so efficient in the field they'd earned a nickname: "Mallory's Tigers".'

'What happened in Perak?'

'The climax of the drama, or the tragedy, if you like, because that's what it was. At that time Perak was rotten with Communist guerrillas, especially on the border with Thailand. The powers-that-be told Mallory to go in and clean them out once and for all.'

'And did he?'

'I think you could say that, but when he'd finished he'd earned himself a new name.'

'The Butcher of Perak?'

'That's right. A man who'd ordered the shooting of many prisoners, who had interrogated and tortured captives in custody. A man who was proved to have acted with a single-minded and quite cold-blooded ferocity.'

'And he was cashiered?'

The General shook his head. 'I should imagine that would have involved others. No, they simply retired him. Gave the usual sort of story to the newspapers. Took the line that he'd never really recovered from his experiences in Chinese hands and so on. Nobody could argue with that and the whole thing simply faded away.'

She sat staring into the fire for several moments, then shook her head. 'The man you describe must have been a monster, and Neil Mallory isn't that, I'm sure.'

He stretched out a hand and covered hers. 'You're attracted to him, aren't you?' She made no reply and he sighed. 'God knows it was bound to happen. A long time since Angus went, Anne. A long, long time.'

The door opened and Jagbir appeared, Mallory at his shoulder. 'Mr Mallory is here, General.'

Hamish Grant straightened in his chair, shoulders squared, and said calmly, 'Show Colonel Mallory in, Jagbir.'

Mallory paused just inside the room, his face very white in the soft light, the strange dark eyes showing nothing. 'Who told you?'

'De Beaumont,' the General said. 'When he was head of French Military Intelligence in Algiers in '59 they had a general file on people like you. I understand you were running guns out of Tangiers to the F.L.N. Is that correct?'

For the moment Mallory was aware only of a feeling of profound relief. That de Beaumont should recognise him from the North African days was unfortunate, but at least the front he had used in Tangiers had obviously been accepted and that was the main thing.

'Does it matter?' he said. 'My past, I mean?'

'Good heavens, man, I'm not interested in what you got up to in Tangiers. It's what happened in Perak that I want to know about.'

'And suppose I say that's none of your damned business?'

The old man stayed surprisingly calm, but Anne moved forward and touched Mallory on the sleeve. 'Please, Neil, I must know.'

Her eyes seemed very large as she gazed up at him, and he turned abruptly, crossed to the french window and went down the steps of the terrace outside.

He stood at the wall above the inlet in the desolate light of gloaming, and, below, the lights of a ship out to sea seemed very far away.

He was tired, drained of all emotion, aware out of some strange inner knowledge that whatever a man did came to nothing in the final analysis.

A step sounded on gravel behind him. When he turned, Hamish Grant and his daughter-in-law were standing at the bottom of the steps. They moved to the table, the old man lowered himself into one of the chairs and Anne Grant approached Mallory.

For a long time she stood peering at him, her face in shadow, and then she swayed forward, burying her face against his chest, and his arms went round her instinctively.

The old man was silhouetted sharply against the pale night sky and the sea, hands crossed on top of his stick, rooted into the ground like some ancient statue.

'Right, Colonel Mallory,' he said in a voice that would brook no denial, 'I'm ready when you are.'

9

The Butcher of Perak

Lieutenant Gregson paced nervously up and down, smoking a cigarette, trying to look as unconcerned as the halfdozen Malay soldiers who squatted in the long grass talking quietly. At the edge of the clearing the body of a man was suspended by his ankles above the smouldering embers of a fire, the flesh peeling from his skull.

The smell was nauseating, so bad that Gregson could almost taste it. He shuddered visibly and wondered what was keeping the Colonel. He was only twenty-two, slim with good shoulders, but the face beneath the red beret was fine-drawn, the eyes set too deeply in their sockets.

He heard the sound of the Land Rover coming along the track and snapped his fingers quickly. There was no need. The soldiers had risen as one man with the easy, relaxed discipline of veterans and stood waiting. A moment later Sergeant Tewak pushed his way into the clearing, followed by the Colonel.

Mallory wore a paratrooper's beret and a camouflaged uniform open at the neck, no badges of rank in evidence. He stood staring at the body, dark eyes brooding in that strange white face, and restlessly tapped a bamboo swagger stick against his right knee.

When he spoke his voice was calm. 'When did you find him?'

'About an hour ago. I thought you might want to see him exactly as they left him.'

Mallory nodded. 'Leave Sergeant Tewak in charge here. He can bring the body into Maluban in your Land Rover. You can come back with me.'

He turned abruptly into the jungle and Gregson gave the necessary orders to Tewak and followed. When he reached the Land

Rover Mallory was already sitting behind the wheel and Gregson climbed into the passenger seat.

The Colonel drove away rapidly and Gregson lit a cigarette and said carefully, 'I hope you're not blaming yourself in any way, sir?'

Mallory shook his head. 'He was a good soldier, he knew the risks he was taking. If they'd accepted him we'd have learned a hell of a lot. Probably enough to have put them out of business in the whole of Perak. But they didn't.'

Remembering the pathetic, tortured body, the stench of burning flesh, Gregson shuddered. 'They didn't give him much of a chance, did they, sir?'

'They seldom do,' Mallory observed dryly. 'There are one or two chairborne flunkeys in Singapore who could have learned something this afternoon. Unfortunately they never seem to come this far in.' He took a cigarette from his breast pocket, one hand on the wheel, and lit it. 'There was a signal from H.Q. while you were away. They're sending me a plane Friday. There's to be an enquiry.'

Gregson turned quickly. 'The Kelantang affair?'

Mallory nodded. 'Apparently the papers got hold of it back home.' He slowed to negotiate a steep hill. 'I don't think I'll be coming back.'

'But that's ridiculous,' Gregson said angrily. 'There isn't a guerrilla left in Kelantang. The Tigers have had more success in six months than any other unit since the emergency began.'

'They don't like my methods,' Mallory said. 'It's as simple as that.'

'Neither did I, at first, but I know now that it's the only way. If you don't fight fire with fire you might as well pack up and go home.'

'And they won't let us do either,' Mallory said. 'Britain never likes to let go of anything. That's my Irish father speaking and he had the best of reasons for knowing.'

The Land Rover went over a small rise as it emerged from the jungle, and beneath them, beside the river, was Maluban. There were perhaps forty or fifty thatched houses on stilts, the saw-mill and rubber warehouse on the far side of the jetty.

It was very still, the jungle brooding in that quiet period before night fell, and as Mallory took the Land Rover down into the village a whistle sounded shrilly and the workers started to emerge from the mill.

He braked to a halt outside his command post, a weathered, clapboard bungalow raised on concrete stilts, saluted the sentry and ran up the steps briskly. Inside, a corporal sat at a radio transmitter in one corner. He started to rise and Mallory pushed him down.

'Anything?' he asked in Malayan.

'Not since you left, sir.'

Mallory moved to the large map of the area which was pinned to one wall. He ran a finger along the course of the river. 'Jack must be about there now. A good forty miles.'

Gregson nodded and indicated a small village to the southwest. 'Harry should be at Trebu by nightfall. Between them they'll have swept most of the western side of the river.'

'Without turning up a damned thing.

What's our effective strength here at the moment?'

'Including Sergeant Tewak and the six men bringing in the body, a dozen. Eight men in the sick-bay and all genuine.'

'You don't need to tell me.' Mallory picked up his swagger stick. 'Mr Li's giving a dinner party tonight. I'll probably be there till midnight. Call me if anything turns up.'

'Something special?'

Mallory nodded. 'He's got a journalist staying with him for a few days. A woman called Mary Hume.'

'Isn't she the one who used to be an M.P.?'

'That's right. One of these professional liberals who spend their time visiting the trouble spots and kicking the poor old army up the backside in print.'

'Never mind,' Gregson said. 'Old Li's food is always interesting.'

'Some consolation.' Mallory moved to the door, turned and, for almost the first time since Gregson had known him, smiled. 'Friday – that's just three days. Not much time to clean up Perak, eh?'

When he had gone Gregson went back to the map. There was a hell of a lot of country and he knew in his bones that the patrols they had out along the river were wasting their time. There were perhaps sixty Chinese guerrillas in Perak, certainly no more. And yet they were enough to terrorise an entire state, to fill the people themselves with such fear that all hopes of co-operation were impossible.

And on Friday the Colonel was to fly to Kuala Lumpur to face an enquiry that could well lead to his court-martial and disgrace. Gregson cursed softly. If only Mallory could have flown out with the news that he and his Tigers had done it again. Had destroyed the last effective guerrilla band in the north. That would have given them something to think about at H.Q.

He went into the bedroom at the rear, poured himself a drink and stood on the verandah looking across the small strip of rough grass that was the garden. A loose board creaked and he turned and saw Suwon, Mr Li's secretary, coming up the steps.

She was perhaps twenty and her skin had that creamy look peculiar to Eurasian women, her lips an extra fullness that gave her a faintly sensual air. Her scarlet dress was of heavy red silk, slashed on either side above the knee, and moulded her ripe figure.

He grinned crookedly and raised his glass. 'Surprise, surprise. I thought you'd be at the party.'

'I will be later,' she said. 'But I wanted to see you.'

'Now that's most flattering.'

He moved close and she held a hand against his chest. 'Please, Jack, this is serious. The wife of Sabal, the ferryman, has just been to see me. She's scared out of her wits.'

'What's the trouble?'

'They've been hiding a wounded terrorist at their house for three days now, under the usual threats. He was shot in that patrol clash on the other side of the river last week. His friends took him to Sabal's house because of its isolation. You know where it is?'

Gregson's stomach was hollow with excitement and when he put down his glass his hand was shaking. 'About half a mile upriver. So they've decided to hand him over?'

She shrugged. 'If the man doesn't have medical treatment soon he'll die. Sabal is a Buddhist. He couldn't let that happen.'

'You've told no one else?'

She shook her head. 'I've no desire to become a target. You know how easily these things leak out. That's why I came the back way.'

He buckled on his belt and revolver. 'No one will know who tipped me off, I promise you that.'

'It's Sabal and his family I'm really worried about.'

'No need to be. I'll only take a couple of men with me. Make it look like a routine call.' He kissed her lightly on the mouth. 'You'd better get going. They'll be looking for you at dinner. And not a word about this to anyone. I'd like to surprise the Colonel.'

He went out through the other room and she heard his voice raised as he called to the duty corporal. A few moments later the Land Rover drove away. She stood there, a shadow slanting across her eyes like a mask. It was as if she were waiting for something. Only when the sound of the engine had finally died into the distance did she turn and walk away.

A moth fluttered despairingly beside the oil lamp and shrivelled in the heat. What was left of it fluttered to the table. Mr Li brushed it away and reached for the decanter. It was obvious that he had European blood in him. His eyes lifted slightly at the corners, but they were shrewd and kindly, the lips beneath the straight nose well formed and full of humour.

'More brandy, Mrs Hume?'

She was in her early forties, her greying hair cut short in the current fashion, still attractive in her simple print dress, a kashmir shawl around her shoulders against the cool of the evening.

She pushed her glass across and Mr Li continued, 'You have no idea of the pleasure it gives me to entertain a British Member of Parliament in my own home.'

'I'm afraid you're a little out of date,

Mr Li,' she answered lightly as Suwon came in with the coffee. 'I'm no longer interested in politics. Simply a working journalist on an assignment.'

'To discover for yourself the state of things in the border country?' Mr Li smiled. 'How fortunate that Colonel Mallory agreed to accept my hospitality during his stay. I am sure there can be no greater authority on the troubled times through which we are passing.'

'I've already seen something of Colonel Mallory's methods,' Mary Hume said coldly, and turned to Mallory. who sat at one end of the long table in a beautifully tailored drill uniform, the medal ribbons and S.A.S. wings above his left pocket a splash of colour in the lamplight. 'I drove through a village called Pedak about ten miles south of here on the way in. Every house burned to the ground on your orders. Women and children homeless and the rains due.'

Suwon leaned over Mallory's shoulder to pour coffee into his cup and he was aware of her fragrance. 'One of my patrols was ambushed in Pedak two days ago. Four men killed and two wounded. The villagers could have warned them. They didn't.'

'Because they were afraid,' she said angrily. 'Surely that's obvious. The Communist guerrillas must have forced them to keep silent with threats.'

'Quite right,' Mallory replied calmly. 'That's why I burned their houses. Next time they'll think twice.'

'But you're giving them an impossible choice,' she said. 'To betray their own countrymen.'

'Something people like you never seem to get straight. The men who were ambushed and killed, my soldiers, were Malays. The guerrillas who killed them are Chinese.'

'Not all of them.'

'Some are Malayan Chinese, I wouldn't argue on that point, but the majority are Chinese Communists, trained and armed by the Army of the People's Republic and infiltrated into Malaya from Thailand.'

'What Colonel Mallory says is quite true, Mrs Hume,' Mr Li put in. 'These terrorists are bad people. They have made things very difficult for us in this area.'

'For business, you mean,' she said acidly.

'But of course.' Mr Li was not at all put out. 'Many of the great rubber estates have virtually gone out of business and things will soon be as bad in the timber trade. At the mill my workers are already on half-time. These are the people who really suffer, you know. Two weeks ago the Catholic mission at Kota Banu was attacked. The priest-in-charge was away at the time, but two nuns and thirteen young girls were killed.'

'You're wasting your time, Li,' Mallory said. 'That isn't the sort of story Mrs Hume wants to hear. That rag of hers usually prints items like that in the bottom left-hand corner of page seven.'

He picked up his brandy and walked out on the open verandah, aware of Li's voice raised in apology behind him. In the gathering darkness beyond the river the jungle started to come alive, tree-frogs setting the air vibrating, while howler monkeys challenged each other, swinging through the trees, and through it all the steady, pulsating beat of the crickets.

At his shoulder Mary Hume said in a dry, matter-of-fact voice: 'They're saying in Singapore that you executed your prisoners during the Kelantang operation. Is it true?'

'I was hard on the heels of another gang. I needed every man I had.' Mallory shrugged. 'Prisoners would have delayed me.'

'And now there's to be an enquiry. They'll kick you out, you know.'

He shrugged. 'Isn't that what you want?'

She frowned. 'You don't like me, do you, Colonel Mallory?'

'Not particularly.'

'May I ask why? I'm only doing my job.'

'As I remember, that was the excuse you offered in Korea when you and one or two choice specimens like you accepted an invitation from the Chinese to see what things were really like over on that side.'

'I see now,' she said, and her voice died away in a long sigh.

'You wrote some excellent articles on how good the prison camps were,' Mallory said. 'How well we were all treated. I read them after I was released. Of course, they never showed you over my camp, Mrs Hume, which is hardly surprising. Around about the time you were starting your conducted tour I was doing six months in a rather small bamboo cage. As a matter of fact, about twenty of us were. A salutary experience, particularly as winter was just beginning.'

'I reported the facts as I saw them,' she said calmly.

'People like you always do.' He swallowed about half of his brandy and went on: 'One thing really does interest me. Why has it always got to be your own country? Why is it never the other side? I mean, what exactly *is* eating away at your guts?'

She was obviously only controlling her anger by a supreme effort of will, and when she replied her voice vibrated slightly. 'Where a moral principle is involved I refuse to be hampered by a spurious nationalism.'

'Is that a fact?' Mallory said. 'Well, I've got news for you, Mrs Hume. I'd rather have that lot out there in the jungle than you and your kind any day. At least they fight for what they believe in. I can respect them for that.'

'Even when they butcher nuns and young girls?' she taunted.

'We managed things like that on a much more impressive scale during the war. After all, for a purist like yourself there can't be much difference between the terrorist's grenade and the bombs released at the touch of a button from forty thousand feet.' She was suddenly very still and he said softly: 'But then I was forgetting. Wasn't your husband a bomber pilot during the war? I'm sure his opinion would be most interesting.'

'My husband is dead, Colonel Mallory. He was killed in the war.'

'I know, Mrs Hume,' Mallory said softly.

She turned abruptly and went back inside and Mallory took out a cigarette, striking a match against the verandah rail.

There was a rustle in the bushes below and Sergeant Tewak said quietly: 'Colonel, there is bad news at the command post. It would be well for you to come.'

Mallory glanced over his shoulder quickly. Mr Li and Mary Hume sat at the table, talking earnestly, heads together, and Suwon busied herself preparing drinks at the sideboard. He vaulted over the rail and followed Tewak through the bushes.

The little Malay hurried along without speaking, leading the way out through the rear gate and down the hill to the village. The streets were quiet, but outside the command post Mallory found what seemed to be the whole detachment standing in twos and threes, each man armed and in marching order.

As Tewak led the way round to the store hut at the side of the bungalow Mallory was aware of the emptiness that snatched at the pit of his stomach. The Malay opened the door, switched on the light and led the way in.

The body was covered by a groundsheet and lay on a trestle table in the centre of the room. Mallory knew it was Gregson at once because of the American Paratrooper's boots which he had bought at a second-hand shop in Singapore three months previously. Tewak pulled back the groundsheet and waited, his face like stone.

The teeth were clenched, lips drawn back in the death-agony. His hands had been tied behind him, the eyes gouged out, quite obviously while he was still alive. The rest of him was like a piece of raw meat.

Mallory took a deep breath and turned away. 'When did it happen?'

'About half an hour ago. He was tipped off that a wounded terrorist was hiding at the house of Sabal the ferryman. I arrived back about an hour after he'd left. He only took two men. When he didn't return I thought I'd better investigate.'

'Are they all dead?'

'Also Sabal and his wife and their four children.'

Mallory nodded slowly, a slight frown on his face. He looked down at the body on the table, once more covered with the groundsheet.

'Go to Mr Li's bungalow. There's an Englishwoman there, a Mrs Hume. Tell her I want to see her. If she refuses to come use force.'

The door closed softly and Mallory took

out a cigarette and lit it, thinking about Gregson, about the senseless, needless cruelty of his going. It had been intended as a threat, so much was obvious, and had been directed at him personally. Whoever controlled the sixty or so terrorists in Perak had simply used Gregson as a calling card.

A few minutes later the door opened and Mary Hume was pushed inside. Behind her Mallory was conscious of Li's troubled face in the doorway.

She was trembling with anger, her face very white as she moved forward. Mallory cut in quickly before she could speak.

'So sorry to trouble you, Mrs Hume, but one of my young officers was very anxious to meet you.'

As the frown deepened across her forehead, he pulled the groundsheet away quickly. She stood staring at the table, an expression of wonderment frozen into place, and then her head started to move from side to side, the lips trembling. Mr Li took her gently in his arms and held her close.

'This was not a good thing to do, Colonel.'

'You go to hell,' Mallory said, 'and you can take her with you,' and he turned and covered Gregson carefully. In the distance thunder rumbled and then lightning flared. In the split second of its illumination Mallory saw each item of furniture in his bedroom clearly. He tossed his swagger stick and beret on the bed and opened the shutters. As he stepped on to the verandah the rain came with a sudden, great rush, filling the air with its voice.

He breathed deeply, taking the air into his lungs, and a quiet voice said, 'The night air is not good when the rains start, Colonel.'

Suwon stood a few feet away by the rail and as lightning flared again her face seemed to jump out of the darkness, the embroidered dragon on the scarlet dress coming alive like some strange night creature.

'I was hoping you'd come,' he said.

She moved very close until their bodies touched and her scent was warm in his nostrils, the sharply pointed breasts hard against him. She placed one hand behind his neck, her mouth slack with desire, and he said softly, 'Why did you tell Gregson that a wounded terrorist was hiding out at Sabal's house?'

As his hands slid round to the small of her back her body tensed, taut as a bow-string. She gave a terrified gasp, turned and stumbled down the steps to the lawn. As she started across, lightning exploded again and in that brief moment of illumination Sergeant Tewak and half a dozen men moved forward in a semicircle. As Tewak reached her the sky seemed to split wide open with a crash of thunder that made the earth tremble, drowning her cry of terror as she was turned roughly and pushed towards the steps.

In his room Mallory lit the lamp, pulled out a chair and sat down. Suwon's dress was saturated, clinging to her like a second skin, and her face was very white as Tewak brought her forward.

'Earlier this evening you visited the command post by way of the garden. You told Lieutenant Gregson there was a wounded terrorist at Sabal's house.' She started to shake her head weakly in denial and Mallory went on: 'Don't waste time in stupid lies. The duty corporal overheard the entire conversation.'

Tears started to roll down her face and he said: 'Gregson is dead, but I don't blame you for that. Only the person who gave you your orders. Who was it? You needn't be afraid. I'll see you're protected.'

She shook her head desperately and tried to pull free from Tewak's iron grip. She was wasting her time. The Malay raised his eyebrows. Mallory nodded and Tewak smashed his clenched fist into her mouth, sending her staggering across the room on to the bed.

When Mallory pulled her forward her lips were crushed and bleeding and a couple of teeth were missing.

'Two weeks ago your friends burned down a Catholic mission and butchered thirteen little girls,' he said calmly. 'Last July they derailed a train and killed or injured nearly a hundred peasants. As far as I'm concerned you're expendable. Now either you tell me what I want to know or I'll let Tewak really go to work on you, and one thing I can promise – you'll never want to look in a mirror again.'

Tewak started to take off his belt and she shook her head weakly, the breath bubbling out through her broken mouth.

'Mr Li,' she moaned. 'It was Mr Li.'

Li examined himself in the bathroom mirror, a pair of tweezers in one hand. Very carefully he plucked a couple of gold hairs from his upper lip, then opened a large, goldcapped bottle of perfumed astringent and poured some into his palms. He carefully massaged his face, wincing slightly at the stinging coldness, turned and moved into his bedroom.

Mallory was standing by the open window that led to the verandah. He wore his red beret and the swagger stick in his right hand beat restlessly against his thigh. It was the eyes which told Li his fate, those strange, unfathomable eyes like holes in the white face, staring through and beyond him.

There was nothing to say, nothing at all. He stood there, a slight, careful smile on his face, hands thrust into the pockets of his silk-dressing-gown, and Mallory made a slight gesture with his hand that brought Tewak and his men into the room.

Mr Li moved to a small coffee table, selected a cigarette from a jade box and lit it. 'Who told you?'

Mallory shook his head. 'Suwon was a mistake. Girls like her value their looks too much. They haven't got anything else to trade with.'

The bookcase against the far wall came down with a splintering crash and three of the soldiers rammed the butt ends of their rifles against the wooden panelling. A moment later a large segment fell out, revealing a cupboard, perhaps three feet square, containing a wireless transmitter and several files.

Mallory examined the find, nodded and turned quickly. 'So far, so good. Now let's get down to business. According to our intelligence reports you have between sixty and seventy guerrillas operating in Perak. I'd like to know where they are.'

'You're wasting your time, my dear Mallory,'

Li said. 'And that's something you can't really spare, isn't it? When is it they're coming for you – Friday? Thirty-six hours, that's all.'

He started to laugh and Tewak raised a hand. Mallory shook his head. 'No sense in wasting time on the preliminaries. Bring him into the living-room, there's a fire there.'

Li was aware of a coldness clutching at his inside. The stories he had heard about this man Mallory, of his Tigers and the way they operated. No one really believed it because the English didn't fight in this way. Didn't use such methods, which was their greatest weakness. Brainwashing and psychological pressures he had been prepared for, but this . . . !

They hustled him into the other room and across to the wide stone fireplace in which he had ordered the servants to light a log fire against the dampness of the rains. Mallory nodded and Li's dressing-gown and pyjama jacket were ripped away, baring him to the waist. His hands were jerked roughly behind his back and lashed with a length of rope.

There was a disturbance outside the door and Mallory heard Mary Hume's voice raised shrilly. He crossed the room and moved past his men into the corridor. The dark circles under her eyes accentuated the paleness of her face and she had obviously been crying.

'What's going on in there?' she said. 'I demand to know.'

'I'm questioning Mr Li,' Mallory told her. 'We've just discovered that he's not quite what he seems to be.'

'I don't believe you,' she said.

'Well, that's just too bad. At a later date I'll be happy to show you the transmitting set he had hidden in his room, but right now I'm busy.' He turned to the corporal on his left. 'Escort Mrs Hume to her room and see that she doesn't leave it.'

He went back into the living-room, slamming the door on her sudden, indignant outburst, and crossed to the fire. He sat down in the chair opposite Li, took out a cigarette and lit it.

'Have you ever been tortured?' Li made no reply and Mallory continued: 'In 1943 I was working under cover in France. I was only twenty. The Gestapo got hold of me. The first two days I didn't do too bad, but by the end of the week I was telling them everything they wanted to know. Of course, by that time London had changed everything round, so it didn't really matter.'

'How very interesting,' Li said.

'I thought you might say that.' Mallory picked up a poker and inserted it into the fire. 'I'm afraid I can't wait for a week, you understand that, but I don't think I'll have to. I've had the extra advantage of two years in a Communist prison camp. They taught me a lot, those friends of yours.'

Li gazed at the poker in fascinated horror and his throat went dry. He moistened his lips and croaked: 'You wouldn't dare. The marks would be on my body for all to see. Mrs Hume would be a witness to all that had taken place.'

They told me to clean out Perak,' Mallory said, 'and I've only got till Friday morning to do it. That means cutting a few corners. You understand, I'm sure.'

He took the poker from the fire. It was white hot and he turned and said gently, 'Tell me where your men are, that's all I want to know.'

'You're wasting your time,' Li said. 'You might as well shoot me and get it over with.'

'I don't think so.' Mallory considered him carefully and shook his head. 'I'd say you might last two hours, but I doubt it.'

It was perhaps three hours later when Li regained consciousness on his bed in the cool darkness of his room. His hands had been roughly bandaged and pain coursed through his entire body, sending his senses reeling.

And he had talked. That was the shameful thing. He had poured out everything to the terrible Englishman with the white face and the dark eyes that pierced straight through to the soul.

He pushed himself upright and slowly hobbled across the floor, grinding his teeth together to keep from crying out. He paused at the window and peered outside. The verandah was deserted. There was no one in sight. He pushed the window open and crossed to the steps. He stood there for a moment, inhaling the freshness of the rain, a faint excitement stirring inside him, driving the pain from his mind. He would win. He would beat Mallory in the end and that was the important thing.

He stumbled down the steps and started across the lawn. He was perhaps half-way across when he heard the click of a bolt as a weapon was cocked. He turned, mouth opening to cry out, conscious that even now Mallory had won.

The line of fire erupting from the bushes spun him around twice and drove him down against the earth. For a moment only there was the scent of wet grass in his nostrils, then nothing.

In his office at the command post Mallory heard the rattle of the sub-machine-gun clearly. He paused for a moment, head raised, then returned to the map in front of him.

A few minutes later the door opened and Tewak entered, shaking rain from his groundsheet.

Mallory sat back. 'What happened?'

'The sentry got him as he was crossing the garden. Mrs Hume's outside. Apparently she ran out of the house when she heard the shooting. She saw his condition.'

'Bring her in,' Mallory said.

She was wearing an old Burberry that was far too big for her, the shoulders soaked by the rain. Tewak led her forward and she slumped into a chair and sat looking at Mallory, her face old and careworn.

'I saw Mr Li,' she said dully. 'I saw what you'd done to him.'

'Mr Li was directly responsible for the murder by torture of Lieutenant Gregson and his men,' Mallory said. 'He was responsible for the deaths of thirteen schoolgirls two weeks ago and very many more innocent people during the past two years.'

'You tortured him,' she said. 'Tortured him in cold blood, then shot him down.'

'If he'd gone to Singapore he'd have been

tried and very probably sentenced to ten years at the most as a political offender,' Mallory said. 'His friends would have got him out before then, believe me.'

'You fool,' she whispered. 'You've lost everything. Everything. Don't you see that?'

Mallory leaned forward. 'There are sixty-three Communist guerrillas in Perak, Mrs Hume. That's something I got out of Li. About thirty of them are camped at this moment on an abandoned rubber estate near Trebu. I've got a large patrol in that area now. They'll be in position to attack at 2 a.m. The rest are going to pass downriver hidden in two fishing boats within the next hour. Apparently, they'd intended to destroy the railway bridge at Pegu at dawn. I'm afraid they'll be disappointed.'

She frowned slightly, as if finding difficulty in taking in what he had said. 'But you've only got a handful of men. You can't possibly hope to defeat such a large group.'

'Solicitude for my welfare at this stage, Mrs Hume? You're slipping.' He got to his feet and buckled on his revolver. 'Don't worry, we have our ways.' He crossed to the door, opened it and turned. 'Stay here, and this time I mean it.'

Mary Hume opened her mouth to protest, but no sound came, and suddenly she was afraid. Afraid of this terrible young man. There was nothing she could do, nothing to prevent the tragedy that was taking place. Out of some strange, inner knowledge she knew that Neil Mallory, in the process of destroying the evil that he hated, was also destroying himself. The most surprising thing of all was that she cared.

Mallory moved across to the jetty and paused beside the two men who squatted behind the heavy machine-gun. Another was positioned on top of a small hill fifty yards away and between them they covered the river with an arc of fire.

At the end of the jetty Tewak waited with the rest of the men. Two of them crouched behind the narrow wall, the heavy tanks of their flame-throwers bulging obscenely.

The rain rushed into the river with a heavy, sibilant whispering, and Mallory was aware of a strange, aching sadness. It was as if he had done all this before in another time, another place. As if life were a circle turning endlessly. Everything that had happened during the previous few hours lacked definition, like a dream only half remembered.

And then Tewak grunted. There was the slapping of water against a keel, a sensation of an even darker mass moving through the darkness, and Mallory tapped Tewak lightly on the shoulder.

The little sergeant picked up a portable spot and switched it on. The white beam lanced through the night, picking out two large fishing boats as they slipped downstream, side by side, sails furled, a man in each stern working a sweep.

There was a cry of alarm and the first boat half lifted out of the water as it collided with the ferry hawser which Tewak and his men had suspended across the river an hour earlier.

The boat spun round, crashing into its fellow, and there was another cry, followed by a burst of small-arms fire directed towards the jetty.

Mallory called out and the men with the flame-throwers stood up. Liquid fire arched through the night, splashing across the two boats. Immediately their superstructure and sails started to burn and men poured on to their decks from below.

The two heavy machine-guns opened up, raking the decks, chopping down the guerrillas as soon as they appeared. Tewak dropped the spot, picked up his sub-machine-gun and joined in with the rest of the men.

It was over within a few minutes. A handful jumped from the blazing inferno and struck out desperately for safety, but the flame-throwers searched them out, the fire licking hungrily across the surface of the water, catching them one by one.

By this time the river and the village were brilliantly illuminated and Mallory stood there watching, taking no part in what was happening. He glanced at his watch. It was just after 2 a.m. and he wondered how Harrison was getting on.

He turned and found Mary Hume standing a few yards away. When he walked towards her he saw that she was crying.

'You butcher,' she said. 'You butcher. I'll see you hang for this night's work.'

'I'm sure you will, Mrs Hume,' he said calmly and went past her along the jetty.

Twenty-four hours left now till that plane arrived, that was all, but it was enough. If he moved fast along the river bank to meet up with Harrison and his men coming south they'd be certain to sweep up any survivors of the clash at the rubber estate. Another twenty-four hours and after that . . .

As he went up the bank towards the command post the first fishing boat sank beneath the surface with a hiss of steam.

10

An Affair of Honour

A match flared outlining Hamish Grant's craggy features as he lit a cheroot. 'And the enquiry?'

It was quite dark now, and, below, waves creamed over the rocks in the entrance of the tiny inlet. It was a warm, soft night, stars strung away to the horizon, and when a cloud moved from the face of the moon the terrace was bathed in a hard, white light.

Mallory turned from looking out to sea and shrugged. 'A foregone conclusion. They used terms like: "Previous gallant service." Hinted that I hadn't really recovered from the ordeal of two years in a Chinese prison camp.'

'And spared you the ultimate disgrace.'

'They didn't actually cashier me, if that's what you mean. You could say I was eased into retirement as quietly as possible. For the good of the service, of course.'

'Naturally,' the old man said. 'A bad business. That sort of thing rubs off on everyone concerned.'

'What I did to Li he would have done to me,' Mallory said. 'The purpose of terrorism is to terrorise. Lenin said that. It's on page one of every Communist handbook on revolutionary warfare. You can only fight that kind of fire with fire. Otherwise you might as well lie down and let the waves wash over you. That's what I brought out of that Chinese prison camp, General.'

'An interesting point of view.'

'The only one in the circumstances. I did what had to be done. When I'd finished there was no more terror by night in Perak. No more Kota Banus. No more butchering of little girls. God knows, that should count for something.'

There was silence. In the moonlight Anne

Grant's face seemed very pale, the eyes dark and secret, telling him nothing. When a cloud crossed the moon she became a motionless silhouette, her face turned towards him, but still she didn't speak.

Mallory sighed and tossed his cigarette over the wall in a glowing curve. 'Under the circumstances, perhaps you'll excuse me, General? This has turned out to be one of those evenings when I could do with a drink.'

He turned and went up the steps, the sound of his going fading quickly into the darkness. After a while Hamish Grant said quietly: 'It's not often one meets a man like that. Someone who's willing to carry the guilt for the rest of us. It takes a rather special brand of courage.'

She turned towards him, her face a pale blur, and then, as if coming to a decision, stood up. 'Do you mind?'

He reached for her hand and held it tightly. 'Leave me the car, will you? I might join you later.'

* * *

And that was that, Mallory told himself. *That was very much that.* No question of what she had thought of him. Her silence, that stillness, had been answer enough. And the strange thing was that it mattered, that for the first time in years the protective shell he had grown had cracked and now he was defenceless.

His chin was on his breast, hands in pockets, as he turned on to the springy turf beside the road, white in the moonlight that ran down to the harbour.

A small wind seemed to crawl across his face and he drew in his breath sharply. He heard no sound and yet he knew that she walked beside him. He spoke calmly, but with a faint Irish intonation, inherited from his father, always apparent in moments of great stress.

'And what would you be wanting, Anne Grant?'

'A drink, Neil Mallory,' she said, matching his mood, 'and perhaps another. Would that be asking too much?'

He paused and turned to face her, hands

still thrust into his pockets. In the moonlight she looked very beautiful, more beautiful than he had ever thought a woman could be, and there were tears in her eyes. He slipped an arm about her shoulders and together they went down the hill towards the lights of the hotel.

In the long grass on the hill above the cliffs Raoul Guyon lay on his back and stared into an infinity of stars, his hands clasped behind his head. Beside him Fiona Grant sat cross-legged, combing her hair.

She turned and smiled, her face clear in the moonlight. 'Well, are you going to make an honest woman of me?'

'As always, you have a gift for the difficult question,' he said.

'A plain yes or no would do. I'm reasonably civilised.'

'A word no woman is entitled to use,' he said solemnly, and lit a cigarette. 'Life is seldom as simple as yes or no, Fiona.'

'I don't agree,' she said. 'It's people who

make it complicated. My father likes you, if that's got anything to do with it, and I can't see what they'd have to complain about at your end. After all, I could pass for French.'

'I'm quite sure my mother would adore you. On the other hand, we Bretons are very old-fashioned in certain matters. She would never allow me to marry a girl who couldn't bring a sizable dowry with her.'

'Would eleven thousand pounds do?' Fiona said. 'My favourite uncle died last March.'

'I'm sure *Maman* would be most impressed,' Guyon told her.

She squirmed against him, laying her head on his chest. 'In any case, why should we worry about money? I know most artists have to struggle, but how many of them paint like you?'

'A good point.'

And she was right. Already he had sold many paintings, working between assignments on the family farm near Loudeac that his mother still managed so competently. Mornings on the banks of the Oust with leaves drifting from the beech trees into the river and the smell of wet earth. Country that he had grown up in and loved. He was aware, with a strange wonderment, that he wanted to take this girl there, to see again with her the old grey farmhouse rooted into its hollow amongst the trees, walk with her over the familiar country that he loved so much.

'Of course, there could always be someone else,' she said.

Her voice was light and yet there was a poignancy there. It was as if she was aware of how near to hurt she might be, and he pulled her close instinctively.

'There was a girl once, Fiona, in Algiers a long time ago. She gave me peace when I needed it more than anything else on earth. She paid for that gift with her life. A high price. I've been trying to escape from her ever since.'

There was a short silence, and then she said gently: 'Have you ever considered that it might be Algeria that you're running from? That somehow this girl has come to symbolise everything that ever happened there?'

In that single instant he knew that what she had said was true. That by some strange perception she had struck right to the very heart of things.

'I know I'm young, Raoul,' she continued, 'and on the whole I've only seen the lighter side, but I know this: the war in Algeria wasn't the first to send men home with blood on their hands and it won't be the last. But that's life. There wouldn't be any sweet without sour. People get by.'

'At a guess I'd say you must be about a thousand years old.'

He kissed her passionately and she linked her arms behind his neck and pressed her body against him. After a while she rolled away and lay on her back, breathless, eyes sparkling.

'And now do you think I might get to see that farm in Brittany?'

He pulled her to her feet and held her at arm's length. 'Did I ever have a choice?'

She reached up to kiss him and then turned and ran away down the hill. Guyon gave her a start of perhaps twenty yards and then went after her, laughter bubbling up spontaneously inside him for the first time in years.

The bar at the hotel was a long, pleasant room with white-washed walls, its windows facing out to sea. Two large oil lamps were suspended from one of the oak beams that supported the low roof.

Jacaud and two other men sat at a table in a corner and played cards. Owen Morgan leaned on the bar beside them, watching the play, a small, greying man with hot Welsh eyes and a face hardened by a lifetime of the sea.

Beside an open window Mallory and Anne faced each other across a small table, smoking cigarettes. Far out to sea the lights of a ship moved slowly across the horizon like something from another world and Anne sighed.

'A big one. I wonder where she's going?'

'Tangiers, the Azores. Take your choice.'

'An invitation?'

'Of the most improper kind,' he said, and smiled.

'You should do that more often,' she said. 'It suits you.'

Before he could reply a shadow fell across the table. Juliette Vincente was standing there, a half-bottle of champagne and two glasses on her tray. She was perhaps thirty-five, a plain, rather simple-looking woman in a blue woollen dress, thickening slightly at the waist, but her skin was fresh and clean, the cheeks touched with crimson.

'From Monsieur le Comte, madame,' she said simply, and placed the bottle and glasses on the table.

At the far end of the bar two or three broad steps lifted to another room where de Beaumont sat beside a pleasant fire. Anne nodded and he raised his glass.

'Small return for a delightful meal.'

'Shall I ask him over?' Mallory said.

She shook her head. 'Not unless you want to.'

A moment or two later the station wagon braked to a halt outside and Raoul Guyon and Fiona got out, turning to help the General.

The old man led the way up the steps confidently and entered the bar.

'Over here, Hamish!' Anne called, and he turned and came towards them.

Mallory got to his feet and brought a chair forward and Fiona slipped into the window-seat beside Anne. Guyon picked up the bottle and nodded approvingly.

'Heidsieck, 1952. How typical for the English to reserve the best for themselves. I must really do something to upset the balance.'

He moved across to the bar and Hamish Grant produced a brown leather cheroot case and proffered it to Mallory. 'Try one of these. Filthy things, but nothing quite like 'em. Picked up the habit in India.'

Mallory took one and offered the old man a light as Guyon returned. 'Our good friend Owen is raiding his cellar. He can't guarantee that everything will have necessarily come in through the proper channels, but no matter. He tells me that the revenue man only comes once a year and always warns him in advance.'

'Understandable,' the General said. 'They were in the navy together.'

Owen Morgan appeared a few moments later and came across with a wide grin. 'No need for ice,' he said to Guyon as he offered a bottle for inspection. 'It's cold enough where that's been.'

'Excellent,' Guyon said. 'I'll open it while you fetch some glasses.'

His gaiety was quite infectious and within a few moments he had them all laughing with a description of an outrageous and quite untruthful incident from his past. The conversation which followed moved along spontaneously.

Once or twice Mallory noticed the three men in the corner looking towards them, obviously irritated after some particularly loud burst of laughter from Fiona or Guyon. One of them hammered on the table and called loudly to Owen Morgan for more cognac.

Mallory leaned across to Anne. 'The one on the left with the haircut. He was at the wheel of de Beaumont's boat this afternoon. Who is he?'

'They call him Jacaud,' she said. 'That's all I can tell you. He seems to go everywhere with de Beaumont. I think the others are afraid of him.'

'Hardly surprising,' Guyon put in. There's about fifteen stone of bone and muscle there, mostly muscle from the look of him.'

Jacaud got to his feet, crossed the bar and mounted the steps to the other room. He leaned on de Beaumont's table and they held a short conversation. Mallory watched them over the rim of his glass. Once, de Beaumont turned and looked towards them. He gazed coolly at Mallory for a moment, then turned back to Jacaud.

The big Frenchman rejoined his friends and Owen Morgan turned on the radio, the sound of music filling the room. Guyon pulled Fiona to her feet and grinned.

'Come on, let's liven the place up a little.'

They made an attractive couple as they circled the room. The beautiful young girl on the threshold of womanhood, and Guyon, his lean, sun-blackened face animated and full of life.

Anne Grant watched them wistfully and coloured when she saw that Mallory was looking at her. 'Fiona always makes me feel old,' she said.

'But not too old.' Mallory turned to the General. 'You'll excuse us, sir?'

The General touched the champagne bottle lightly and raised his glass. 'Enjoy yourselves while you can. I'll make do with this.'

They moved into the centre of the floor. She slipped one arm about his neck and danced with her head on his shoulder, her body pressed so closely against him that he could feel the line from breast to thigh.

For a moment, he forgot about everything except the fact that he was dancing with a warm, exciting girl whose perfume filled his nostrils and caused a pleasant ache of longing in the pit of his stomach.

It had been a long time since he had slept with a woman, but that wasn't the whole explanation. That Anne Grant attracted him was undeniable, but there was something more there, something deeper that for the moment was beyond his comprehension.

The music stopped, a pause between records, and they went back to their table.

The others followed a few moments later, and as Fiona seated herself there was a burst of loud laughter from Jacaud and his two friends in the corner, followed by a remark in French, coarse and to the point and quite unprintable.

Guyon swung round, his face hardening. The three men returned his gaze boldly. He took one quick step towards them and Mallory caught him by the sleeve and pulled him down into his chair.

'Let it go.'

Guyon was shaking with suppressed anger. 'You heard what he said?'

Fiona leaned forward and put a hand on his arm. 'Don't let it upset you, Raoul. They've had a little too much to drink, that's all.'

A shadow fell across the table and Mallory looked up into the face of the man he had heard Owen Morgan refer to as Marcel a little earlier. He was of medium height and wore denim pants and a blue seaman's jersey. He was very drunk and clutched at the edge of the table to steady himself.

'I think you'd be better off sitting down,' Mallory told him in French.

Marcel ignored him, leaned across the table, knocking over a glass, and grabbed Anne by one arm. 'You dance with me now?' he mouthed in broken English.

Mallory grabbed for the man's right arm just above the elbow, his thumb hooking into the pressure point. As he swung round, mouth opening in a cry of agony, Guyon kicked him under the right knee-cap. Marcel staggered backwards, lost his balance and sprawled across the other table. Jacaud pushed him to one side, got to his feet and moved forward.

He stood there, swaying slightly as if drunk, and yet the slate-grey eyes were as cold as ice, eternally watchful.

'Two to one, messieurs,' he said in excellent English. 'You made the odds.'

Owen Morgan came round the bar on the run, face very white, eyes blazing. The big Frenchman sent him staggering backwards with a single, contemptuous shove of his hand and laughed harshly.

'He asked for it, Jacaud,' de Beaumont called sharply. 'Let it end there.'

Jacaud ignored him and de Beaumont made no move to come down into the bar, gave no indication of being able or willing to control the situation. He stayed by the fire, a watchful expression on his face.

In that moment Mallory realised that the whole thing had been arranged. That for some reason of his own de Beaumont had deliberately engineered the situation.

Guyon started to rise and Mallory pulled him down again. 'My affair.'

Jacaud stood there swaying a little, still keeping up the pretence of being drunk, his great hands hooked slightly, every muscle tensed and ready. He lurched forward and stood over them.

'Of course, my friend might be willing to settle for a drink.' He nodded at the table. 'A bottle of champagne would do.'

'Anything to oblige,' Mallory said calmly.

He reached for the bottle and, as he turned, reversed his grip and smashed it across the side of the Frenchman's skull. As Anne cried out, Jacaud staggered and fell to one knee. Mallory picked up a chair, moved in fast and smashed it down across the great shoulders. Jacaud grunted, started to heel over and Mallory smashed the broken chair down again and again, until it splintered. He tossed it to one side and waited.

Slowly, painfully, Jacaud reached for the edge of the bar and pulled himself up. He hung there for a moment, then turned to Mallory, wiping blood from his face casually.

And then, incredibly, he charged, head down like a wounded bull, the great hands reaching out to destroy. Mallory judged his moment exactly, swerved to one side, allowing the Frenchman to plunge past, and slashed him across the kidneys with a *karate* blow delivered with the edge of his hand.

Jacaud screamed and fell to the floor. For a little while he stayed there on his hands and knees, and when he got to his feet he was slobbering like an animal. He lurched forward and Mallory kicked his feet from under him. Jacaud crashed to the floor, rolled over and lay still.

In the silence which followed, de Beaumont came down the steps slowly. He dropped to one knee beside Jacaud, examined him and looked up. 'You are a hard man, Colonel Mallory.'

'When I have to be,' Mallory said. 'You could have done something to stop this. Why didn't you?'

He turned without waiting for a reply and went back to the table. 'I think that might do for one night. Shall we go?'

Hamish Grant's face was pale, the nostrils flaring slightly as he got to his feet. 'You know, I really think it's about time I bought you a drink, Neil. I've got some rather special whiskey back at the house. So Irish that you can taste the peat. I'd like to have your opinion on it.'

Anne's face was very white and she was trembling. Mallory squeezed her hand reassuringly and they all walked towards the door. De Beaumont moved to block the way.

'One moment, General. Perhaps I might be allowed to tender my apologies for this distressing affair. At the best of times Jacaud has a short temper. When he's been drinking . . .'

'No need for that, de Beaumont,' Hamish Grant said coldly. 'I think the matter has been handled quite adequately.'

De Beaumont stood there, his smile frozen into place, and then he turned away sharply and they moved outside.

Fiona got behind the wheel, Guyon beside her, and the General and Anne climbed into the back. Mallory slammed the door and leaned in at the open window.

'If you don't mind, General, I'd like to take you up on that drink another time. I've had enough excitement for one night.'

As Anne's head turned sharply towards him he turned quickly, giving them no time to argue, and went down the slope towards the jetty. A few moments later the engine coughed into life behind him and the station wagon moved away.

He turned right at the jetty, following a steeply shelving path which brought him down to a strip of sand, white in the moonlight, waves curling in across the shingle with a gentle sucking sound.

He sat on a boulder and lit a cigarette with

fingers that trembled slightly. He inhaled deeply, drawing the smoke into his lungs and released it with a long sigh.

Behind him Anne Grant said, 'You don't do things by halves, do you?'

'What's the point?' he said simply.

'We seem to have held this conversation before.'

When she whispered his name they came together naturally and easily. Her hands pulled his head down as her mouth sought his and her sweetness drove every other thought from his mind. He picked her up in his arms and laid her down gently in the soft sand.

11

In a Lonely Place

The wind was freshening, lifting the waves into whitecaps, and as the dinghy rounded the point water slopped over the gunwale. Guyon carefully eased his weight into the centre and started to bale. He wore a heavy sweater and reefer jacket against the cold. A pair of night-glasses hung around his neck and one of the aquamobiles lay in the prow behind him.

Mallory sat in the stern wearing a black rubber diving suit, the heavy aqualung already strapped into place on his back. As a cross-current started to turn the dinghy in towards the cliffs he opened the throttle on the outboard motor to compensate and glanced at the luminous dial of his watch.

It was 11.45 and there was very little cloud, the sky brilliant with stars, and the moonlight danced across the waves, leaving a trail of silver behind it. The dinghy lifted high on a large swell and swung in towards the great finger of rock which marked the western tip of the island. Mallory opened the throttle again. For a moment the dinghy seemed to stand still and then it forged ahead.

They rounded the point, fighting the cross-currents, Guyon cursing steadily as water slopped over the sides, and then they were sweeping into calmer water. Beyond, St Pierre and the Gothic towers of the castle were dark against the sky.

Mallory throttled down again and the dinghy coasted on, the sound of her motor a murmur on the wind. The great reef running between the two islands was deceptively innocent in the moonlight. Waves rolling in from the sea splashed lazily across the rocks, now and then a curtain of white spray lifting into the night like silver lace.

He took the dinghy into the calm waters of the Middle Passage until they reached the first point where the roof closed in and water boiled across great jagged black teeth. He cut the motor and the dinghy slowed and ground gently against a sloping, weed-covered shoulder of rock. Guyon hooked the painter into a crevasse and looked towards St Pierre through the night-glasses.

'About a quarter of a mile. A long swim.'

'Not with the aquamobile,' Mallory said.

Guyon got it over the side, the dinghy heeling dangerously. 'Rather you than me. The water's like ice. How long will you be?'

Mallory shrugged. 'No more than half an hour. I've no intention of hanging around at the other end.'

He fitted the rubber mouthpiece between his teeth and adjusted his air supply, touched the knife briefly at his belt and clambered awkwardly over the side on to the reef. He waded into the water, swam to the other side of the dinghy and reached for the aquamobile. Guyon smiled once and Mallory nodded and sank beneath the surface.

Moonlight filtered down through the water, probing into the depths. When he passed beneath the surface of the reef and came into the Middle Passage he entered a darker, more sinister, world.

He switched on the powerful spot mounted on top of the scooter and the shaft of light pierced through the darkness in front of him, splaying against the rocks that arched above his head.

He tilted the nose of the aquamobile and went down gently, levelling out at twenty feet. Although his top speed was no more than three knots, he seemed to rush at a terrifying speed into the wall of grey mist that was the edge of his visibility. The great, arched nave of the reef stretched into infinity before him, the water breaking against his mask.

And then he was through and moving into a strange, unreal landscape of jumbled rocks and pale forests of sea-weed waving languidly in the diffused moonlight. He surfaced and looked up at the cliffs of St Pierre, the pointed towers of the castle dark against the sky.

The moonlight splashed across the face of the cliffs, picking out the dark mouth of the cave. It was now high water and there was no more than a ten- or twelve-foot clearance. Mallory turned the nose of the aquamobile down and levelled out at forty feet. He switched off the spot and moved into a grey phosphorescent mist.

The great fault in the sea-bed dropped beneath him. At least ten fathoms, Anne had said, slicing into the heart of the island. The mist seemed to swing to one side like a curtain, revealing the entrance to the cave, a good sixty feet across as it widened on its way down.

He drifted in, grey-green walls moving past on either side. The water lightened, the grey merging into aquamarine as artificial light seeped down from the surface. He moved in close to the wall and went forward cautiously.

He stopped abruptly, switching off the aquamobile. From this point on the rough wall of the cave merged into the jetty, great square blocks of masonry like the foundations of some ancient fort descending into the depths. He started up cautiously and immediately the grey-black underbelly of the submarine appeared from the mist.

He had found what he was looking for and to stay any longer was to invite trouble. He turned and flutter-kicked towards the entrance. The light dimmed and he was aware of the current tugging at him.

He swam out into that strange, grey, phosphorescent world and paused to switch on the aquamobile. In that same moment it was torn from his grasp with a metallic clang and a shock-wave, spreading through the water, burst around him.

He turned and saw the frogman suspended in the water about twenty feet away, a weird sea-creature, full of menace, the moonlight glinting on his visor as he reloaded his speargun.

Mallory drove forward, pulling the heavy knife from its sheath. When he was perhaps ten feet away the gun exploded again in a shower of silver bubbles. He swung desperately to one side. The spear hurtled past and he moved in fast, his knife cleaving through rubber and flesh.

The man's body bucked agonisingly, blood rising in a dark cloud as Mallory pulled out the knife and snatched at the air-pipe. As it came free in his hand, air burst out at pressure, bubbles swirling past him on the way to the surface.

He could see the man's face quite clearly now, eyes bulging, teeth clamped together in agony. Quite suddenly he went over backwards in a graceful curve, like a leaf spiralling earthwards in autumn, the weight of his aqualung taking him down.

Mallory struck up towards the surface, chasing his aquamobile, which was rising slowly. He grabbed the handles and switched on, already aware of further shock-waves rippling through the water, bouncing from his body.

The aquamobile surged forward, helped by the turning tide. The sea-bed started to shelve again, and, below, he was aware of the pale forest of seaweed, the ribbons of black rock that were the beginnings of the reef.

Once again he was aware of a shock-wave curling around his body and he glanced to his right. Perhaps fifty yards away and coming up fast through moon-drenched water was a large underwater scooter, at least twice as long as his aquamobile, a frogman trailing behind.

Mallory kicked desperately, urging the aquamobile forward. And then the rocks swarmed up out of the gloom on either side and he rushed into the darkness of the Middle Passage. He switched on his spot, planing down to avoid the over-hanging roof. He was aware of a muffled throbbing in his ear and glanced back. A wide band of diffused light spreading through the mist told him that his pursuer wasn't far behind.

He passed through a section where moonlight streamed in through cracks and fissures in the roof and knew that he was about halfway along the passage, somewhere above the wreck of the freighter. As he came into the clear section he plunged down and at ten fathoms a tapering steel mast loomed out of the gloom. Mallory held on with one hand and waited.

The darkness moved in on him with a terrible, suffocating pressure and the mast seemed to move a little as if the old freighter had rolled. He remembered the dark companionway, dead men's bones crushed under a steel girder, and shivered, suddenly aware of the cold.

He could sense the turbulence in the water, waves rippling down. When he looked up there was the weird, incandescent glow of the spot-lamp on the other scooter as it passed overhead. He waited for a moment or two, then went up slowly.

At twenty feet he levelled out, switched on the motor, but not the spot, and went after the other scooter. Only in patches was visibility really bad and at this depth the moonlight streamed in through fissures in the rock like regularly spaced lamps along a dark road.

When he emerged at last from the great central nave into clear water he switched off the aquamobile and surfaced.

Raoul Guyon sat in the stern of the dinghy. A yard or two away the frogman stood waist-deep in water on the shelving reef beside his scooter, a loaded spear-gun in his hands. It was almost as if they were holding a conversation.

Mallory released his grip on the aquamobile, went under the surface and swam forward. He erupted in a surge of power, slid his right arm about the man's neck and fell backwards, towing him into deep water, tearing the air-hose from his mouth.

They sank down through the clear water, the spear-gun spiralling off to one side. Mallory wrenched again with his free hand, pulling away the mask, and the man's face turned up, contorted with fear.

Mallory hung on, even when a clutching hand reached backwards, wrenching away his own air-hose. He compressed his lips and tightened his grip. Blood began to seep from the man's nostrils in two clouds and a moment later he swung loosely against Mallory's arm. Mallory unlocked his fingers and the body bounced away, spun round twice and started to sink.

There was a roaring in his ears and his temples pounded. He kicked for the surface and bumped against the side of the dinghy, gasping and choking for breath. Guyon reached over and grasped his outstretched hand and Mallory stumbled up the sloping shelf of rock and crouched on his hands and knees, chest heaving.

Guyon jumped knee-deep into the water beside him and helped him up, pulling away the mask, his face strained and anxious in the moonlight. When he spoke his voice sounded faint and far away and Mallory shook his head several times.

The roaring subsided abruptly and he gasped: 'No time for questions. I ran into a little trouble. We'd better get moving.'

'You found *L'Alouette*?'

'She's there, all right. Moored to the jetty under the island just like we thought. Room for a couple more from the look of the place.'

He unbuckled the heavy aqualung, swung it into the prow and clambered aboard the dinghy. As he started the outboard motor Guyon unhooked the painter and followed him. A second later and the dinghy was moving back towards Ile de Roc, following the twisting channel between the great rocks which already reared up on either side as the tide turned.

'What happens now?' Guyon said.

'We call up Leviathan the moment we get back. Those motor torpedo boats from St Helier will be here before you know it.'

The dinghy rocked in the turbulence as it swept on a fast current between high black walls and turned towards the point. Behind them a full-throated roar shattered the night and Guyon raised the night-glasses and looked back. When he took them down his face looked very white in the moonlight.

'It's that damned speedboat of de Beaumont's. Coming up fast on this side of the reef. Must be doing all of fifteen knots.'

Mallory glanced back, catching a brief glimpse of the thin pencil of light that was the speedboat's spot, and opened the throttle of the dinghy's outboard motor. The strong current was running against them now as they tried to breast the point, and the light craft was twisted round, a wave splashing across her prow.

'Throw the aqualung overboard,' Mallory shouted.

Guyon scrambled to his knees, reached for the straps, heaved and slid the aqualung over. There was an immediate difference, the prow riding over the next wave, and they turned the point and moved into what should have been calmer water.

The turning tide at this point clashed headlong with the usual strong coastal current, and all around them great patches of white water joined with others, sending irregular waves cascading against the cliffs, the undertow sucking them out again.

The dinghy wallowed in the trough between two great swells, her speed cut in half, and, behind, the roar of the speedboat drew inexorably nearer.

'We'll never make it to the harbour,' Guyon called. 'A couple more minutes and they'll see us.'

A great heaving swell was building up to starboard. As it swept in, lifting the dinghy high into the air, Mallory caught a glimpse of Hamish Grant's house tucked into a fold at the top of the cliffs, a light shining in one of the ground-floor rooms. He swung the tiller over and the current drove the dinghy in towards the cliffs at tremendous speed.

The gap in the inlet had been at least twenty yards across, but the real problem was that line of jagged rocks blocking the entrance as surely as if it had been a steel portcullis. The one slim hope was that the waves, sweeping in, would raise the water-level and carry them over.

He shouted to Guyon: 'This is going to be rough. Hang on and get ready to swim.'

The Frenchman looked back once, his lips moving in reply, but the roaring of the sea drowned his words. Mallory held on to the tiller with both hands. Strange, swirling currents twisted them round and the dinghy was carried helplessly in.

The opening of the cove appeared suddenly in the face of the cliff, water boiling through in a great surge. At one side white spray foamed high in the air, while, all around, dirty cream patches formed as rocks showed through.

The dinghy slewed broadside into the entrance, lifted high and smashed down upon a great green slab of rock. The tiller was wrenched from Mallory's hand and the outboard motor was torn away with a section of the stern.

The dinghy slithered forward across the reef and ground to a halt, a jagged edge of rock smashing through the hull. Guyon went head first over the prow with a cry and Mallory went after him.

The Frenchman tried to stand and Mallory plunged through the boiling surf, hands outstretched to meet him. For a moment they clung together and then another wave, cascading in across the reef, bowled them over.

Guyon went under, and Mallory, striking after him, found himself in deep water. He grabbed the Frenchman by the collar of his jacket and struck out, the current pushing them forward. His feet touched sand and he stood up, pulling Guyon after him. Water boiled waist-high again, tugging at their limbs. As it receded they lurched forward, feet slipping in the shingle, and staggered up the narrow strip of beach at the base of the cliffs.

* * *

Someone was playing the piano, an old, pre-war Cole Porter number with something of the night in it, something of warmth and love and hope that seemed to belong to another age than this.

Crouching in the bushes below the terrace, Mallory was caught for a brief moment, unable to go forward or back. Guyon groaned beside him, coughing up water, and Mallory pulled him to his feet and they staggered up the steps.

The french window was ajar, one end of a red velvet curtain billowing out as a gust of wind lifted it. He took a deep breath and opened it wide.

The fire burned brightly on the stone hearth and Hamish Grant's hair gleamed like silver in the lamplight as he leaned in his wing-backed chair, smoking a cheroot. Anne sat opposite, staring into the fire while Fiona played the piano.

It was Fiona who saw them first. She gave a sudden gasp, her hands striking a false chord, and jumped to her feet. Anne stood up slowly and Hamish Grant turned his head and looked directly at the window.

'Sorry about this,' Mallory said as he moved forward, one arm still around Guyon's shoulders.

Guyon retched suddenly and started to cough again. Mallory helped him to a chair by the fire and the Frenchman fell into it with a groan.

Anne stayed surprisingly calm. 'Brandy, Fiona,' she said. 'Quickly. Two glasses.'

Mallory moved forward, water streaming from his rubber suit, and stretched out his hands to the fire, shivering involuntarily as the warmth enveloped him. Hamish Grant reached out to the dark figure, dimly seen, and touched the wet rubber suit.

'A strange time to go swimming.'

'Under the circumstances we didn't have much choice.' Mallory turned to Anne, who gazed up at him searchingly. 'You're on the phone here, aren't you?'

She nodded. 'Linked to Guernsey by cable, but it hasn't been working since yesterday's storm. That often happens. There's the radio telephone on *Foxhunter*, of course. Is it important?'

'You could say that.' Mallory turned to Guyon, who was gulping the brandy Fiona had passed to him. 'I'll have to get down to the harbour straightaway. I can use the transmitter.'

'We'll both go,' Guyon said. 'There could be trouble waiting down there.'

'Any chance of an explanation?' Hamish Grant enquired mildly.

Mallory took the glass of brandy Fiona offered, swallowed half of it down and coughed as the fiery liquor caught at the back of his throat. 'I'd say you were entitled to one under the circumstances. I was sent here by British Intelligence and Captain Guyon by the same branch on the other side of the Channel. We were asked to do a quick check on de Beaumont.'

'I see,' Hamish Grant said. 'I take it he's up to no good?'

'Very much so. His present activities are a direct threat to the interests of his own government and the fact that he's seen fit to operate from British territory presents a serious complication. On top of that, we don't like what he's doing anyway.'

Hamish Grant smiled faintly. 'How strange. Two great nations side by side through the centuries. We have our quarrels, but somehow they're always in the family. The moment the chips are down we move in to help each other so fast it's almost frightening.'

'Can I ask what happened to Van Sondergard?' Anne asked.

'I paid him double what you would have done and shipped him out.'

'And the incident on the wharf? That was arranged, too?'

He nodded. 'It got a little out of hand. That's why I had to get so rough. I'm sorry.'

'I'm not,' she said simply.

He reached out and touched her face and something glowed deep in her eyes. Her hand went up, holding his against her cheek, and she turned her head, touching her lips to his cold palm. For a brief moment it was as if they were alone. As if the others had ceased to exist. It was Hamish Grant who broke the spell.

'I should imagine dry clothes should be the first step and you'll need the car.'

'I'll get it out of the garage,' Fiona said quickly.

She was standing at the side of Guyon's chair. She smiled down at him, then went out through the french windows. Guyon got to his feet and he and Mallory followed Anne out of the room, leaving a trail of sea-water across the carpet.

She found dry socks, some old service slacks and a couple of heavy sweaters from Hamish Grant's wardrobe and left the two men in his room to change. When they went downstairs ten minutes later Jagbir was pouring coffee into cups arranged on a table beside the fire. Hamish Grant still sat in his chair, but there was no sign of the girls.

The little Gurkha offered them coffee, no visible excitement on his face, and the old man said: 'There was a mention of possible trouble when you go down to the harbour. The violent sort, I presume. Are you armed?'

Guyon answered: 'I had a revolver in the pocket of my reefer coat. I lost it coming through the surf.'

'You'll find another in the top right-hand

drawer of the desk behind you,' the old man said. 'Half a box of cartridges somewhere at the back. There should be a Lüger there as well, but that's already loaded.'

Guyon opened the drawer and came back, the revolver in one hand, the Lüger in the other. 'You can have the Lüger,' the old man went on. 'I'll keep the Webley myself, if you don't mind.'

Guyon slipped the Lüger into his pocket and started to load the Webley. Anne and Fiona came in. They were both wearing heavy sheepskin coats and Anne was binding a scarf about her head, peasant-fashion.

She smiled at Mallory. 'Ready when you are.'

He shook his head gently. 'Not on your life. You stay right here.'

A slight crease appeared between her eyes and Fiona started to protest. Hamish Grant cut in sharply, 'They'll have enough to worry about without you two.'

Fiona turned to Anne, but her sister-in-law sighed and shook her head. 'He's right, Fiona. We'd only be in the way.' She smiled up at Mallory. 'So we sit and wait? How long for?'

'With any luck the whole thing should be wrapped up into a neat parcel by breakfast. And, I warn you, I'll have an appetite.'

'I'll hold you to that.'

He touched her hand briefly and led the way out into the hall. The shooting brake was parked at the bottom of the steps, its engine ticking over, and he climbed behind the wheel and waited for Guyon. The young Frenchman was standing at the top of the steps with Fiona, Anne in the doorway behind them. The young girl reached up, kissed him and hurried inside. He came down the steps and got into the passenger seat, his face grim.

Mallory drove away quickly, turning out through the gates along the white road and down the hill towards the harbour. The hotel was in darkness and the cove was exactly as they had left it, *Foxhunter* moored to one side of the jetty, Guyon's hired launch on the other.

Mallory braked to a halt at the end of the jetty, switched off the engine and got out. Moonlight silvered the water and the night sky was like a warm dark velvet cushion scattered with diamonds.

'So far, so good,' he said to Guyon, and led the way along the jetty.

He jumped to *Foxhunter's* deck and went into the wheelhouse. He switched on the light and cursed softly. The radio telephone had been wrenched from its fastening on the far wall and lay in the corner, smashed beyond repair, a fire-axe beside it.

'They beat us to it after all.'

He pushed past Guyon, hurried down the companionway and through the saloon to the aft cabin. He dropped to one knee, opened the locker beneath his bunk and rummaged inside.

'Is this what you are looking for, Colonel Mallory?' Raoul Guyon said softly.

Mallory got to his feet and turned. Guyon stood on the other side of the table, a drawer open, holding the small electronic transmitter that was Mallory's only link with the department.

'Good man,' Mallory said, and took a step forward.

Guyon dropped the set to the floor and ground his heel into it twice, at the same time taking the Lüger from his coat pocket.

Mallory stood staring at him, a slight frown on his face, and a voice said: 'Excellent, Captain Guyon. I was really beginning to despair of you.'

As Mallory turned, de Beaumont stepped out of the shadows of the dark galley, Jacaud at his side, a submachine-gun in his hands.

12

To the Dark Tower

They were close to the island now and Marcel cut the engine to half-speed and took *Foxhunter* in slowly towards the dark arch. The speedboat bobbed behind them on a long towline and as Mallory looked out to sea a shadow moved in from the horizon, blanketing the stars.

Guyon stood by the rail a few feet away talking to de Beaumont in a low voice and Jacaud leaned against the wheelhouse, the sub-machine-gun in his hands. One of his eyes was half-closed, the right side of his face swollen and disfigured by a huge purple bruise, and his eyes stared at Mallory unblinkingly.

They moved into the dark entrance and Mallory shivered, chilled by the damp air, and then they were through. From end to end the cave was about a hundred yards long and perhaps fifty feet across. Beneath the surface, as he had discovered earlier, it was even wider.

The long stone jetty was brightly illuminated by two arclamps and they coasted in to tie up behind a magnificent forty-foot, steel-hulled motor-yacht, the name *Fleur de Lys* painted across her counter.

The submarine was moored on the far side, squat and black in the water, and looked even smaller than Mallory had imagined. A dozen or so men in the uniform of the French Navy worked busily, loading stores on board under the supervision of a slim, rather boyish-looking lieutenant in peaked cap and reefer jacket. As they went up the short ladder to the jetty, he came forward, saluting de Beaumont casually.

'How are things going, Fenelon?' de Beaumont asked. 'Any snags?'

Fenelon shook his head. 'We'll be ready on schedule.'

'Good, I'll give you a final briefing at 9 a.m.' Fenelon went back to his men and de Beaumont turned to Mallory. 'Magnificent, isn't she? And just the thing for our purposes. Small, compact – only needs a crew of sixteen. You're familiar with the type?'

'Only on paper.'

'This one has quite a history. Built at Deutsche Werft in 1945 and sunk with all hands within a month of commissioning. After she was raised she was transferred to the French.'

'And now she's yours,' Mallory said. 'A chequered career.'

A body was against the far wall covered by a tarpaulin, webbed feet turned to one side, blood streaking the pool of sea-water in which it lay.

'We couldn't find the other one. The current must have taken him under the reef.' De Beaumont shook his head. 'A nasty way to die.'

The words seemed to carry an implicit threat, but Mallory refused to be drawn, and de Beaumont smiled faintly and led the way across to where a flight of stone steps lifted a hundred feet into the gloom, curving round one wall of the cave. They mounted the steps and emerged on to a stone landing, and de Beaumont led the way to the far end of a passage, passing several doors. One or two stood open to show narrow service bunks and grey blankets neatly folded. From a side entrance there came the smell of cooking.

He opened another door and they entered a large hall, great curved beams of oak arching into the gloom. There was a wide marble staircase and, above it, a gallery. At one side logs blazed in an immense medieval fireplace.

'Quite a sight, isn't it? The money these Victorian industrialists must have had to throw around, and every stone brought in by boat.'

His tone was casual, mannered. He might have been a rather complacent host showing a friend over his new place. They went up the great staircase and moved along the gallery to the far end. De Beaumont opened a door to disclose a narrow spiral staircase.

At intervals there were slotted windows and Mallory could see far out to sea as they mounted higher and higher.

They reached a stone landing and paused outside a door. De Beaumont went in, leaving it ajar. The room contained a great deal of radio equipment and an operator sat before a transmitting set, headphones clamped to his ears. He stood up when de Beaumont appeared. There was a murmur of conversation and then de Beaumont came back outside.

He continued up the spiral staircase, Mallory, Guyon and Marcel following behind, Jacaud bringing up the rear. At last they emerged on a small landing and de Beaumont opened his final door.

The room was circular in shape and quite large. It was comfortably furnished, Persian carpets covering the floor, logs burning brightly in the wide fireplace. The walls were lined with books except for a section perhaps twenty feet long covered by a velvet curtain. De Beaumont pulled it to one side, revealing a curved glass window.

'One of my little improvements. On a clear

day you can see France.' He indicated a chair by the fire. 'If you please.'

Mallory sat in the chair and Jacaud moved to stand behind him, the sub-machine-gun held ready. Marcel stood by the window, a revolver in his right hand held against his thigh. Guyon remained by the door and Mallory looked across at him. Guyon returned his gaze calmly, giving nothing away, and Mallory turned to de Beaumont, who was now sitting in the opposite chair.

'I will not insult your intelligence by fencing with you, Colonel Mallory,' he said. 'For some time I was a prisoner of the Viets in Indo-China. There is little they failed to teach me at first hand about the extraction of information from the unco-operative. Jacaud was senior warrant officer of my regiment. He shared my experiences. I need hardly add that he would welcome an opportunity to experiment.'

'No need to go on,' Mallory said. 'I get the point.'

'Excellent,' de Beaumont said. 'We can get down to business. As you may now have deduced for yourself, Captain Guyon is something of a double agent. When the *Deuxième* offered him employment they were not aware that he was already a loyal member of the O.A.S. A most convenient arrangement. He confirms the fact that the *Bureau* had no real grounds for suspecting *L'Alouette* to be in hiding here. That his assignment to Ile de Roc to work with you was at the request of British Intelligence. I'd like to know why.'

'We had a man here watching you,' Mallory said. 'Just routine, because of who you are and what you are. He drifted in on the tide the other evening. Accidental drowning was the coroner's verdict.'

'He had a habit of taking long walks on the cliffs after dark with a pair of night-glasses,' de Beaumont said. 'Rather dangerous. Someone should have warned him.'

'You made a mistake there,' Mallory said. 'To my chief it meant only one thing. Our man had seen something important. With the French combing every creek and inlet on their side of the Channel it gave him a rather nasty feeling to think that she might be sitting it out in the Channel Islands.'

'A pity,' de Beaumont said. 'Now I must move out rather sooner than I had intended. On the other hand, neither my immediate nor long-term plans will be affected in the slightest.' He stood up and smiled politely. 'Under happier circumstances I should have enjoyed talking to you. We must have a great deal in common. I'm sure you'll understand that my time is limited.'

'Naturally,' Mallory said ironically and got to his feet.

He had often wondered about this moment, how it would come and when. The strange thing was that he was not afraid. More curious than anything else. Jacaud moved restlessly behind him and Marcel came away from the wall, the gun still held against his leg.

De Beaumont took a revolver from his pocket, crossed to Guyon and handed it to him. 'Will you do the honours, Captain? A soldier's end, I think.'

Guyon's hand tightened on the butt of the

revolver and he looked across at Mallory, his face very white. Quite suddenly he grabbed de Beaumont by the front of his coat, pulling him forward, and rammed the barrel of the revolver against his throat.

There was a moment of stillness and then de Beaumont laughed gently. 'You know, our friends in Paris have been worried about you for some time now, Guyon. I can understand why. You're slipping. I should have thought an officer of your experience would have been able to tell the difference in weight between a revolver loaded with blanks and one loaded with live ammunition.'

He reached up and took the revolver from Guyon's hand and Guyon looked across at Mallory and smiled wryly. 'Sometimes we can be too clever, my friend.'

'Nice to have you back,' Mallory said.

De Beaumont opened the door and nodded to Marcel. 'Take him below and watch him carefully. I'll send Colonel Mallory down later.'

He closed the door behind them, turned to Mallory and smiled. 'And now that we all know exactly where we are we can perhaps relax for half an hour.' He took a bottle and two glasses from a cupboard in the corner and returned to his chair. 'This is really quite an excellent cognac. I think you'll enjoy it.'

Mallory sat in the opposite chair, aware of Jacaud at his back, and waited for what was to come. He accepted a glass of cognac, drank a little and leaned back. 'I can't understand what you hope to gain from all this. Murder and assassination will only lose you what little support you command.'

'A matter of opinion,' de Beaumont said. 'The only politics which seem to matter in this modern world are the politics of violence. Palestine, Cyprus and Algeria were all examples of victory achieved by a deliberate and carefully planned use of violence and assassination. We can do the same.'

'The circumstances are completely different. In the cases you've quoted, nationalistic elements were opposed to a colonial power. In your own, Frenchmen are murdering Frenchmen.'

'They are not worthy of the name, the

swine we have dealt with so far. Loud-mouths, professional liberals and scheming politicians who feathered their own nests while I and men like me rotted in the Viet prison camps.' De Beaumont laughed bitterly. 'I remember our homecoming only too well. Booed all the way into Marseilles by Communist dock workers.'

'Ancient history,' Mallory said. 'Nobody wants to know. In any case, unless they'd been through the same experience themselves they wouldn't know what you're talking about.'

'But you have,' de Beaumont said. 'Deep inside, I think you know what I mean. You learned a hard lesson from the Chinese. You put it down in cold print in that book of yours. What happened when you put it into practice?'

He stared into the fire, a frown on his face. 'It was going to be different in Algeria, we were certain of that. We fought the *fells* in the *jebel* of the Atlas Mountains, in the heat of the Sahara, in the alleys of Algiers, and we were beating them. In the end we had them by the throat.'

He turned to Mallory. 'I was in the army plot of the 13th May, 1958. They gave us no choice. They would have arrested my friends and me, tried us on trumped-up atrocity charges, designed to please the loud-mouths and fellow-travellers back home in Paris. We put de Gaulle in power because we believed in the ideal of a French Algeria, a greater France.'

'And once he was in control he did exactly the opposite to what you had intended,' Mallory said. 'One of the great ironies of post-war history.'

De Beaumont swallowed some more cognac and continued. 'Even more ironic that I, Phillipe de Beaumont, descendant of one of the greatest of French military families, should have helped place in power the man who has destroyed the greatness of his country.'

'That remains to be seen,' Mallory said. 'I'd say that Charles de Gaulle was moved by one thing only – deep patriotism. Whatever he's done he's done because he thought it best for France.'

De Beaumont shrugged. 'So we disagree? It's of little moment. After his visit to St Malo on the 3rd of next month he will no longer present a problem.'

'I don't know what you have in mind, but I wouldn't count on anything. How many times have your people failed now? Eight, isn't it?'

'I flatter myself that my own organisation has been rather more successful. These affairs need the trained mind, Mallory. Everything I handle is a military operation, planned to the last detail in conditions of the strictest security. *L'Alouette* affair, I have handled personally from the beginning. My colleagues in Paris know nothing about it. I work strictly on my own and use them as an information service only.'

Mallory shook his head. 'You can't last much longer. You're working on too big a scale. Already *L'Alouette*'s become more of a liability than anything else.'

'You couldn't be more wrong.' De Beaumont got to his feet, took a couple of charts from the cupboard beside his chair and crossed to a small table. 'Come over here. You'll find this interesting.'

They were Admiralty charts of the area between Guernsey and the French coast and he joined them together quickly. 'Here is Ile de Roc and St Pierre, thirty miles south-west of Guernsey. The nearest French soil is Pointe du Château, only twenty miles away. You know the area?'

Mallory shook his head. 'The closest I've been is Brest.'

'A dangerous coast of small islands and reefs, lonely and wild. You will notice Ile de Monte only a quarter of a mile off the coast, the Gironde Marshes opposite. There is a small cottage on an island perhaps half a mile into the marsh on the main creek. Eight miles from a road and very lonely. Not even a telephone. There are only two people in residence at the moment.'

'And you want them?'

'Only the man. Henri Granville.'

Mallory straightened, a frown on his face. 'You mean Granville the judge, the Procureur Général who retired last month?'

'I congratulate you on your intimate knowledge of French affairs. He arrived there with his wife yesterday. They are quite alone. Of course, no one is supposed to know. He's fond of solitude – solitude and birds. Unfortunately for him, a contact of mine in Paris got news of his movements last night and let me know at once. I'm sending Jacaud across in *L'Alouette* later today. His execution should cause quite a stir.'

'You're crazy,' Mallory said. 'He must be eighty if he's a day. On top of that, he's one of the best-loved men in France. God in heaven, everybody loves Granville! Politics doesn't enter into it.'

'On three occasions now he has presided at tribunals which have condemned old comrades of mine to death,' de Beaumont said. 'Now he must pay the consequences. By striking at Granville we prove once and for all that we are a force to be reckoned with. That no man, however powerful, no matter what his public standing, is safe from our vengeance.'

'Henri Granville never condemned anyone

in his life without good reason. Harm him in any way and you'll bring the mountain in on you.' Mallory shook his head. 'You'll never get away with it.'

De Beaumont smiled faintly, crossed to the fire and poured more cognac into his glass. 'You think not?' He swallowed a little of the cognac and sighed. 'I will postpone your execution till this evening. By that time Jacaud will have returned. It will give me some satisfaction in sending you to your death with the knowledge that Henri Granville has preceded you.'

'Which remains to be seen,' Mallory said.

De Beaumont turned and indicated a tattered battle standard hanging above the fireplace. 'An ancestor of mine carried that himself at Waterloo when his standard-bearer was shot. It was with me at Dien-Bien-Phu. I managed to hang on to it during all those bitter months of captivity. You will notice it bears the motto of the de Beaumonts.'

'"Who dares, wins",' Mallory said.

'I would remember that if I were you.'

'Something you seem to have forgotten,'

Mallory said. 'When that ancestor of yours picked up that standard at Waterloo he didn't carry it forward on his own. There was a regiment of guards backing him up all the way and I seem to remember that at Dien-Bien-Phu you commanded a regiment of colonial paratroops. But, then, that's France I'm speaking about. The real France. Something you wouldn't know anything about.'

For a moment something glowed in de Beaumont's eyes, but he pushed back his anger and forced a smile. 'Take him below, Jacaud. He and Guyon can spend their last hours together trying to solve an impossible problem. The thought will amuse me.'

Jacaud gave Mallory a push towards the door. As he opened it, de Beaumont said calmly: 'And, Jacaud, when I next see Colonel Mallory I expect him to be in his present condition. You understand?'

Jacaud turned sharply, a growl rising in his throat. For a moment he seemed about to defy de Beaumont and then he turned suddenly and pushed Mallory forward.

They went down the spiral staircase, Mallory

leading, all the time aware of the machine-gun at his back. The gallery was in half-darkness, the fire a heap of glowing ashes, as they crossed the hall and went through the door which led to the living-quarters and the cave.

At the end of a long whitewashed corridor they found Marcel sitting on a chair outside a door, reading a newspaper, the revolver stuck in his belt.

He looked up at Jacaud, eyes raised enquiringly. 'When?'

'This evening when I get back from the mainland.' Jacaud turned to Mallory and patted the sub-machine-gun. A red glow seemed to light up behind the cold eyes. 'Personally, Colonel Mallory.'

Mallory moved into the cell. As the door clanged behind him, Guyon swung his legs to the floor and sat looking at him.

He grinned suddenly. 'You wouldn't by any chance have such a thing as a cigarette on you, would you?'

13

Council of War

'I had lost all belief or interest in right or wrong. In the end you believe only in your friends, the comrade who had his throat cut the previous night. That was what six years in Algeria had done for me.'

Raoul Guyon stood by the small barred window gazing into the night. When he turned he looked tired.

'And this is why you joined the O.A.S.?' Mallory said.

Guyon shook his head. 'I was in Algiers in 1958. So much blood that I was sickened by it. There was a young Moorish girl. For a little while we tried to shelter from the storm together. They found her on the beach one morning, stripped, mutilated. I had to identify the body. The following day I was badly wounded and sent back to France to convalesce. When I returned my comrades seemed to have the only solution. To bring back de Gaulle.'

'You took part in the original plot?'

Guyon shrugged. 'I was on the fringe. Just one more junior officer. But to me de Gaulle stood for order out of chaos. Afterwards most of us were posted to other units. I spent five months on patrol with the Camel Corps in the Hoggar.'

'And did you find what you were looking for?'

'Almost,' Guyon said. 'There was a day of heat and thirst when I almost had it, when the rocks shimmered and the mountains danced in a blue haze and I was a part of it. Almost, but not quite.'

'What happened after that?'

'I was posted back to Algeria to one of the worst districts. A place of barbed wire and fear, where violence erupted like a disease and life was no longer even an act of faith.

I was wounded again last year just before General Challe's abortive coup. Not seriously, but enough to give me a legitimate excuse to put in a request to be placed on unpaid leave. The night before I left, Legrande visited me in my hotel room. Offered me work with the *Deuxième Bureau.*'

'And you accepted?'

'In a strange way it offered me some sort of escape. Later, in Paris, I was approached by O.A.S. agents. As an ex-paratroop officer and supporter of the original coup which had placed de Gaulle in power, I must have seemed an obvious choice.'

'And you informed Legrande?'

'As soon as I could get in touch with him. That was the funny thing. I didn't even have to make a choice. It was almost as if it had been made for me. He told me to accept the offer. From his point of view an agent with contacts in that direction would obviously be valuable.'

'And yet we were informed that the *Deuxième* had no real suspicions about de Beaumont. Surely you must have had some sort of lead on him through your Paris connections with the other side?'

'Not really. I was only on the edge of their organisation. De Beaumont's name was mentioned as one sympathetic to their aims. On the other hand, his political opinions are well known in France. There was certainly never any hint that he might be an active worker.'

'And all this time you were completely accepted?'

'I certainly thought so. As a new recruit to the *Deuxième*, it was obvious that my sources would be limited, but I passed on selected information of Legrande's orders. I certainly never managed to get close to any of the really big men, but I was working towards it. On two occasions he even allowed me to warn some of the lesser fry when their arrest was imminent.'

'What about *L'Alouette*?'

'That was the thing which puzzled us from the beginning. The complete absence of information as to her whereabouts, even in O.A.S. circles. Because of that Legrande told me to inform my Paris contacts that I had been assigned to the Channel Islands merely to run a routine check on de Beaumont, just to make sure that he was behaving himself. Legrande felt that at least it would prove once and for all whether a definite link existed.'

'Something he didn't see fit to inform us at our end.'

'I'm sorry about that, but Legrande never lives in the present – only the future. He envisaged a possible situation in which my other activities could prove useful. Under the circumstances it seemed wiser to present myself merely as Raoul Guyon, an accredited agent of the *Bureau* and nothing more.'

'I see the old fox is still a believer in playing his cards as they fall,' Mallory said. 'It shows in his poker game.'

'A remark strangely similar to one he made about you just before I left.'

Mallory grinned. 'One thing at least has come out of all this. De Beaumont definitely does have a link with the O.A.S. in Paris because he was warned that you were coming. The one thing I don't understand is why he didn't think it strange that you hadn't told them about *L'Alouette* affair.'

'The first thing he asked me coming across on the boat. A difficult question to answer.'

'And how did you?'

'Told him the *Bureau* believed the whole business to be the work of an independent group. That this was confirmed for me personally by the obvious ignorance of the affair in O.A.S. circles. That as an ex-paratroop officer who had taken part in the coup of June '58, only to be betrayed by de Gaulle, I would much prefer to work with him.'

'And he accepted that?'

'He seemed to at the time.'

'It all sounds pretty shaky to me.'

'It obviously did to de Beaumont.' Guyon grinned wryly. 'On the other hand, I didn't have time to think up anything better and I did make my own move against you just before they did, remember?'

'That was quick thinking.'

The young Frenchman shrugged. 'When I saw what they had done to the radio telephone it seemed logical to assume they were still on board, that we were under observation. It seemed wise to establish my credentials while I still could and I remembered seeing you put the transmitter in the table drawer earlier in the afternoon.'

'And you'd never met him previously?'

Guyon shook his head. 'As I told you before, only as one of a crowd. Naturally, I knew a great deal about him. He was one of the really great paratroop officers, you know.'

'I've been going over everything he said to me upstairs,' Mallory said. 'None of it really makes sense. In the end he must lose. The murder of a fine old man like Henri Granville on its own will be sufficient to lose him, and those who think like him, a great deal of sympathy, and yet he goes on. I wonder why?'

'He was always a strange, ascetic man. A cross between religious fanatic and soldier. The surrender at Dien-Bien-Phu, the humiliation of the Viet camps and our subsequent withdrawal from Indo-China were a source of lasting shame to him. Like many of his kind, he swore it would never happen again.'

'And in spite of everything he could do it did.'

Guyon nodded. 'De Beaumont is the last of one of our most noble families, his only heir a brother who is a professor of political history at the Sorbonne. A man with pronounced left-wing sympathies. One of his ancestors was one of the few nobles to give wholehearted support to the revolution in 1789, another was a general under Napoleon. For one hundred and fifty years the de Beaumonts have been one of the greatest of French families.'

'Something of a national calamity if he had to be arrested.'

'Exactly. The government was more than happy when he chose to reside in the Channel Islands. At the time it seemed to dispose of him as an immediate problem.'

'Which he has now become,' Mallory said, 'and in more ways than one.'

'You are thinking of his threat to dispose of de Gaulle during his visit to St Malo next month?' Guyon shook his head, lay on the other bed, pillowing his head on his hands. 'I'm not too worried about that. They won't get de Gaulle. He's indestructible, that one. Like one of those rocks out there on the reef after a storm. A little more weathered, but still standing.'

'Which leaves us with the Granville affair,' Mallory said. 'And the hell of it is there doesn't seem to be a damned thing we can do about it.'

He lit a cigarette and lay on his back, gazing at the ceiling, going over the events of the previous couple of hours in his mind. After a while he said softly: 'The first rule in this game is that the job must come before everything else. Most men I've worked with, in your position, would have played along with de Beaumont, would even have executed me if necessary.'

'Perhaps I saw the situation differently,' Guyon said.

'You moved so fast you didn't even notice the difference in weight the blanks made. Why?'

'Something I've been asking myself on and off for the past hour or more. It's not easy to explain. Let's just say that suddenly people have become important to me again and leave it at that.'

He turned his face to the wall and Mallory lay there, smoking his cigarette, thinking how strange it was that a young man, all feeling burned out of him by the flames of two savage wars, should be brought back to life by that oldest and most elemental of human emotions – love.

He was cold and stiff and his limbs ached. He pulled the blanket over his legs and checked his watch. It was almost 5 a.m. and he lay in the darkness listening to the rain and the wind. After a while he drifted into sleep again.

He became aware that someone was prodding him and opened his eyes. Raoul Guyon squatted beside him. Grey light seeped into the room through the barred window and Mallory swung his legs to the floor.

'Still raining?'

Guyon nodded. 'Hasn't let up all night. It's almost eight.'

Mallory walked to the door and peered through the iron grille into the corridor outside. A young sailor sat in a chair reading a book, a heavy service revolver in the holster at his waist.

Mallory crossed to the window. The casement opened easily enough, but the bars set in the ledge on either side were strong and firm. He looked into the grey morning, out along the reef to Ile de Roc. Rain slanted down and visibility was poor, a cold mist drifting close to the surface of the water.

'I wonder what they're doing over there?' Guyon said at his shoulder.

'They must have realised by now that something's gone wrong.' Mallory shrugged. 'If they've any sense at all they'll have brought in Owen Morgan and gone to Guernsey for help in your launch.'

'Surely de Beaumont will have considered that possibility?'

'He probably has. That's what's worrying me.'

There was a rattle of bolts and the door opened. As they both turned, Marcel entered and stood to one side, a revolver in his right hand. The young sailor followed, carrying a tray which he placed on the bed. They withdrew without saying a word, bolting the door again.

The food was simple, bread and cheese and hot coffee, and Mallory suddenly realised how hungry he was. They sat on either side of the tray to eat and finished off by sharing his last cigarette.

Afterwards he lay on the bed waiting for something to happen, while Guyon paced restlessly up and down the cell, the rain hammering against the window. It was almost ten o'clock when the door opened again and de Beaumont entered, Marcel at his back.

He seemed in a good humour and smiled cheerfully. 'Good morning, gentlemen. I trust you spent a good night? Your quarters are adequate?'

'I've seen worse,' Mallory admitted.

'Anything I can get you?'

'The condemned man's last wish?' Mallory shrugged. 'We could do with some cigarettes. That's about all.'

Marcel took a packet of Gauloise from his pocket and threw them on the bed. 'Anything else?' de Beaumont said politely.

Mallory put a cigarette in his mouth and tossed the packet to Guyon. 'I don't think so.'

'Then you will excuse me? You'll be interested to know that Jacaud and his men left for Pointe du Château fifteen minutes ago as scheduled. Under the circumstances I think it's time I paid a visit to our friends on Ile de Roc.'

'I wouldn't count on anyone being there to meet you.'

'Oh, they'll be there, all right. I can assure you of that.'

De Beaumont smiled faintly as if enjoying some private joke, nodded to Marcel and passed outside. The door closed and the bolts were rammed home with a harsh finality. Guyon turned with a gesture of despair and Mallory motioned him to silence. When he went to the door the young sailor was back on his chair reading a magazine.

Mallory crossed to the window and looked

outside. A minute or two later he heard the sound of an engine and *Foxhunter* came into view, running alongside the reef towards Ile de Roc.

'There he goes.'

Guyon moved to the window, peered out and frowned. 'But why has he taken *Foxhunter*?'

'Easier to handle than *Fleur de Lys* on the short run and there's too much sea for the speedboat.'

Guyon, thinking of Fiona, dropped his cigarette and stamped on it viciously. 'I didn't like his last remark. He sounded far too sure of himself. As if he knew for certain that the General and the girls would still be on the island.'

'I imagine he does,' Mallory said. 'It's been a long night. He could have been up to anything, but that isn't important at the moment. He probably only intends to bring them back here for safe custody until he's ready to move out.'

'You may be right.'

'It's Henri Granville I'm thinking about,

sitting in the middle of the Gironde Marshes not knowing that sometime after noon there'll be a knock at the door. I can see the smile on Jacaud's face now.'

'And nothing we can do about it.'

'Plenty, if we could get out of here. There's always the radio room in the tower, or the *Fleur de Lys* would be a better bet. A boat of that size is bound to have a radio telephone.'

Guyon shook his head. 'Those marshes are one of the most isolated places on the entire coast. Even if we managed to contact my people in Paris it would still be too late for Henri Granville. They'd never reach him in time.'

'But we could,' Mallory said. '*L'Alouette* will have to make the entire run submerged. That will take her a good three hours.'

'It's almost an hour since she left,' Guyon pointed out.

'*Fleur de Lys* has twice the speed. We could still beat Jacaud to the punch.'

'Only if we get out of here within the next half-hour,' Guyon said. 'And I stopped believing in miracles a long time ago.'

'We don't need a miracle. Just a little luck,' Mallory pulled him down on the bed. 'Now listen carefully.'

It was cold in the passage and the young sailor shivered and got to his feet. He stamped vigorously to restore his circulation and walked a few paces away from the chair. He was bored. He was also a little afraid. In the beginning the whole affair had seemed like a great adventure, a crusade. Now he was not so sure. He turned to move back to his chair and a muffled cry sounded from inside the cell.

He stood there, a puzzled frown on his face. There was another cry, followed by the crash of a bed going over. He arrived at the grille in time to see Guyon drive his fist into Mallory's face, knocking him against the wall.

'You got me into this, you bastard!' the young Frenchman cried. 'I'll kill you! I'll kill you!'

He flung himself forward and Mallory ducked under another blow, moved in close and tripped him. A moment later and he was kneeling on Guyon's chest, hands twisted into his collar as he throttled him expertly.

The young sailor gave a cry of alarm. He pulled back the bolts and moved into the cell, revolver ready in his right hand. He reached for Mallory's collar and to his amazement Guyon erupted from the floor, grabbed his wrist savagely and twisted the revolver from his grasp. The sailor's mouth opened in a cry of alarm that was cut short as Mallory's fist moved in a short arc against the side of the jaw.

Mallory picked up the revolver, nodded to Guyon and they went outside quickly. All was quiet. Guyon bolted the door and they hurried along the passage.

A strange quiet reigned until they reached the main corridor when they heard voices in the distance and the clatter of pans from the kitchen. They passed along to the far end and Mallory opened the door cautiously and stepped on to the landing at the top of the steps which led down to the cave.

The jetty was deserted and *Fleur de Lys*

and the speedboat were the only craft moored to the wall. They went down the stone steps quickly, paused for a moment at the bottom, then hurried across to *Fleur de Lys*.

When they went into the wheelhouse they saw at once that the radio telephone had been removed from its housing on the wall. Mallory grinned tightly. 'He's a cautious bastard, I'll say that for him.'

'Only to be expected.' Guyon shrugged. 'A good soldier tries to foresee every eventuality.' He looked around and shook his head. 'This looks one hell of a size for two of us.'

'We'll manage,' Mallory said. 'We'll have to. There's plenty of fuel in the tank, which is the main thing. Go get those lines off the jetty and we'll move out.'

Guyon went forward quickly and untied the first line. As he started aft there was a harsh cry. When he glanced up he saw a sailor standing on the landing at the top of the steps. He ran along the deck and cast off the other line. The sailor drew a revolver and fired two wild shots as he came down the steps.

He was too late. The engines were already roaring into life and Mallory took *Fleur de Lys* out through the entrance. Spray splashed against the window, waves breaking over the deck as he turned through the lee-side of the reef and set course for Pointe du Château.

14

Force of Arms

Hamish Grant opened the door and stood listening to the sound of quiet breathing. Fiona was stretched on the sofa and Anne slept in the wing-backed chair, a rug over her legs.

As he started to close the door she opened her eyes and said softly, 'What time is it?'

'Just after eight. Jagbir's made some fresh tea.'

She got to her feet, draped the rug over Fiona and followed him out. 'Any sign of them?'

The old man shook his head. 'Not yet.'

The kitchen looked out over the courtyard, a large and pleasant room, beams supporting a low ceiling. Jagbir was frying eggs at the stove. When he saw Anne he poured a cup of tea and gave it to her and she stood in front of the fire, drinking it slowly.

Beyond, through the wide window, clouds hung threateningly over the fields, rain dripped from the gutters and brown leaves crawled across the cobbles. She went to the window and gazed out into the rain, thinking of Mallory.

Hamish Grant moved beside her and squeezed her hand. 'He did say it would take till breakfast-time. I shouldn't worry too much if I were you.'

'I'm not,' she said. 'One thing I am sure of is his ability to look after himself, but I'd have thought we'd have heard from them by now.'

'We very probably will before much longer.'

She finished her tea and moved to the door. 'I think I'll run down to the harbour and see what's happening.'

'I'll send Jagbir with you.'

She shook her head. 'Let him get on with

breakfast. I shan't be long. No need to wake Fiona till I get back. She could do with the sleep.'

She went along the hall, pulled on her sheepskin coat and let herself out of the front door. Rain fell steadily and she fastened a scarf about her hair as she went down the drive and turned through the gates.

Visibility was poor, a grey, clinging mist drifting in patches across the water, and the central hill of the island looked very green against the leaden sky. She hurried along the road and paused on the brow of the hill to look down into the harbour. Only one boat was moored there, Raoul Guyon's launch, and the shooting brake was parked at the end of the jetty.

She went down the hill quickly, taking a short cut across the wet grass. The shooting brake was beaded with moisture, the engine cold. She stood there for a moment, a frown on her face, then walked along the jetty and stepped on to the deck of Guyon's launch. She went into the small saloon, stood looking about her for a moment, then turned to go.

She paused, wrinkling her nose, aware of the heavy, acrid taint of oil on the fresh morning air. It seeped into a pool from under the door of the engine compartment. She opened it and looked into a twisted mass of smashed pipes and broken valves.

She crouched on one knee, gazing at the engine, her mind frozen. As she started to rise, steps boomed hollowly on the wooden planking of the jetty and Owen Morgan called, 'Hello below!'

Anne went up the companionway and came out on deck as he stepped down from the jetty. He wore an old blue pilot coat and rubber boots. Rain frosted his grey hair. He started to grin, but his smile faded at the sight of her troubled face.

'What's wrong?'

'Take a look at the engine.'

He went down the companionway quickly. When he reappeared his face was grave. 'Why would anyone want to do a thing like that?'

'To make sure we couldn't get off the island,' she said.

He frowned quickly. 'Look, how about

letting me in on all this? Where's *Foxhunter*? I heard her go out early this morning.'

'That must have been Colonel Mallory and Monsieur Guyon,' she said. 'They should have been back by now. I'm very much afraid something may have happened to them.'

'Are they in some kind of trouble?'

'They could be, but there isn't time to explain now, Owen. We must get to Guernsey as soon as possible. What about your launch?'

'I hauled her up the slipway and into the boathouse ready for winter only two days ago,' he said. 'No trouble to bring her down again if it's all that urgent. I can have her ready for sea in half an hour.'

'Do that,' Anne said. 'I'll go back to the house for the others. I'll explain things more fully when I get back.'

She hurried along the jetty, climbed behind the wheel and switched on the engine. It required a lot of choke before it would turn over and Owen was already half-way up the slope towards the boathouse at the side of the hotel when she finally moved away.

The Welshman's skin crawled with excitement. Whatever was wrong, it was certainly serious. So much had been evident from Anne Grant's manner and actions, and to a man whose entire life had been a series of adventures the prospect of action carried all the kick of a good stiff drink. When he was only a few yards away from the boathouse he remembered that the heavy door was padlocked. He turned and moved up the slope quickly to the side door of the hotel.

When he went into the kitchen Juliette was standing at the sink washing the breakfast dishes. 'Where's the key to the boathouse?' he demanded.

She turned, her eyebrows arching in surprise. 'On the nail behind the door where it always is. What's wrong?'

'I've got to get the boat out,' he said. 'The Grants want me to run them over to Guernsey. Can't explain why. I don't even know myself. But it must be something serious.'

He took down the key and went out again. After he had gone Juliette Vincente stood at the sink, gazing blankly at the door. After a moment she dried her hands carefully, hung up the towel and went up the back stairs to her bedroom.

Owen Morgan opened the heavy doors of the boathouse and moved inside. The launch was seated firmly into a deep concrete slot, a steel cable coiled around a winch at her stern, holding her in place.

He jumped down on to the deck, pulled off the top of the engine housing and paused suddenly, his throat going dry. The engine was in exactly the same state as the one in Guyon's boat. Delicate pipes and valves smashed beyond repair, a heavy hammer from his own tool-kit lying in the ruins.

As he got to his feet there was the scrape of a shoe on stone behind him. He turned and looked up at Juliette. She wore his old corduroy jacket against the cold, her hands thrust deep into the pockets.

'What's wrong, Owen?' she asked.

And then in one single, inexplicable flash of intuition he knew that she was responsible and his eyes widened. 'Why, Juliette?' he said. 'Why did you do it?'

'My brother was killed in Algeria, Owen.' Her voice was flat, lifeless. 'He died for France. They repaid him by giving what he'd died for away. I couldn't stand by and allow that to happen.'

Anger flared inside him like flames through dry leaves. 'What sort of bloody nonsense are you telling me, girl? What about my boat?'

He started to clamber up beside her and she backed away, taking a revolver from her pocket. He stood facing her, very still, the skin on his face so white that it was almost transparent, a bewildered expression on his face.

'It's me, Juliette. Owen.' He took a step forward.

'Move past me very slowly, Owen,' she said. 'Your hands behind your back. Don't make me kill you.'

He stood poised, feet apart, and wild laughter erupted from his mouth. 'Kill me, girl? You?'

In a moment he drove forward, one hand

reaching for the gun, the other grabbing for her coat. In that same instant something seemed to move in her eyes and he knew with the most appalling certainty that he had made the last mistake of his life.

The sound of the shot re-echoed deafeningly between the walls of the boathouse and the force of the bullet, smashing through his body, sent him staggering backwards. He swayed on the edge of the ramp, hands clutching at his stomach, the blood erupted from his mouth in a bright stream and he fell back on the deck.

Juliette Vincente moved to the edge of the ramp and looked down at him. He lay very still, his dark eyes fixed on a point a million miles beyond her. She put the revolver back into her pocket, went outside and started to close the heavy doors. When she turned, *Foxhunter* was just coming round the point into the harbour.

In the kitchen Hamish Grant sat at one end of the table, the remains of his breakfast before him, and listened gravely to what Anne had to tell him.

When she had finished he shook his head briefly. 'No use trying to pretend things look good. They don't. But one thing *is* certain. There isn't much we can do on our own.'

'Then Guernsey is our only hope?'

He nodded and got to his feet. 'I think it would be better if we all went. It never pays to take chances and things could get rather unhealthy.'

Fiona came in from the hall carrying his old British warm. 'You'll need this on, Father. It's rather cold.'

It was the first time she had called him anything but General since she was quite small, and his heart went out to her. He reached for her face, dimly seen, and patted her cheek.

'Not to worry, Fiona. We'll get things sorted out.'

She held his hand tightly for a moment, then turned and led the way into the hall. Anne was already sitting behind the wheel of the brake, the engine ticking over. The General and Jagbir got into the rear, Fiona in the front, and Anne drove away quickly.

It was still raining heavily and she turned on the wipers, leaning forward, watching for pot-holes in the dirt road. As the brake climbed to the crest of the hill she changed to a lower gear, ready for the descent to the harbour. They went over the top of the rise, Fiona gave a cry of alarm and Anne braked quickly.

De Beaumont, Marcel and three sailors stood in the road, looking out towards the sea. About a quarter of a mile offshore, and running strongly south-west towards the French coast, was *Fleur de Lys*. Marcel had one arm outstretched as he pointed. He turned to speak to de Beaumont and saw the shooting brake.

As they fanned across the road, Anne slammed her foot hard against the accelerator in a reflex action that took the old brake forward in a surge of power. She saw the mouths open in alarm, voiceless above the roaring of the engine, and then they were scattering to either side. The brake shot through and bounced down on the road, swerving on the bend at the bottom, cutting across the grass towards the jetty.

She braked hard and the vehicle slewed in a long, breathtaking skid that for one awful moment seemed to be taking them over the edge to the beach and the rocks below. They came to a stop, the front bumper lodged against a boulder, and she opened the door and got out.

There was no sign of Owen Morgan or his launch and when she looked up at the boathouse the great doors were still closed. She turned and found the General scrambling out at the rear, helped by Jagbir. As the little Gurka straightened, his coat fell open to show the ivory-and-silver hilt of his *kukri*, the curved blade in its leather sheath thrust into his waistband.

As Fiona came round from the other side there was a faint cry up on the hill. Anne looked up and saw de Beaumont and his men running towards them. One of them paused, raised his rifle and fired a warning shot that whined across the jetty into the water.

Hamish Grant turned quickly. 'What about Owen?'

'No sign of him or the launch,' Anne said. 'But *Foxhunter*'s moored at the end of the jetty.'

Any brief hope that they might be able to take over the launch before de Beaumont and his men arrived disappeared as a sailor came out of the wheelhouse, looked towards them, then hurried back inside.

'We'd better get up to the hotel,' Anne said.

They started up the hill, Fiona leading the way, Hamish Grant using his walking stick to help him. There was another cry from de Beaumont and the sailor who had been guarding *Foxhunter* rushed out on deck with a rifle and loosed off a quick shot which splintered the woodwork of one of the boat-house doors.

Anne could taste blood in her mouth and there was a pain in her chest. She took Hamish Grant's hand and scrambled on, her feet slipping on the wet turf, and then they were on to the terrace and moving into the porch.

Fiona flung open the door and led the way inside. The bar was quite empty, a small fire burning in the grate. The stillness was so complete that Anne could hear her heart pounding.

Hamish Grant leaned against a table, struggling for breath, and she called out: 'Owen! Owen Morgan! Where are you?'

There was no footfall and yet a quiet voice said with startling suddenness from behind her, 'He isn't here.'

Anne turned quickly and looked into the calm face of Juliette Vincente. 'For God's sake, Juliette. Where is he? What's going on?'

'I think that perhaps you have come to the wrong place, madame.' Juliette's hand came out of her pocket, holding the pistol. 'And now we will all wait quietly for the Comte de Beaumont.'

In the same moment Jagbir drove forward, the terrible Gurkha battle-cry bursting from his throat. His hand swung from under his coat, the razor-sharp blade of the *kukri* hissing softly through space.

Juliette Vincente pulled the trigger twice, bullets smashing into the little Gurkha's body, and then he was on top of her. As she fired again at close quarters the heavy blade swung down, half severing her neck. They fell together, Jagbir on top, the *kukri* as firmly clenched in his right hand in death as it had been in life.

As Fiona screamed, the door swung open. Hamish Grant turned, pulling the Webley from his pocket, thrusting it towards the dark formless shadow against the light that was de Beaumont.

Behind him the window shattered and the barrel of a rifle was rammed painfully into his back. 'If the General is wise he will drop it,' Marcel said.

Hamish Grant stood there, trapped in the moment of decision, and already it was too late. De Beaumont moved forward and pulled the Webley gently from his grasp.

'And now, old friend, perhaps you will be sensible?'

15

The *Fleur de Lys*

Fleur de Lys rolled her slim length into the wind, plunging over a wave as water broke across her prow. In the wheelhouse Mallory leaned over the chart table. Behind him the wheel clicked to one side eerily to compensate as the vessel veered to starboard, the automatic pilot in control.

The Admiralty charts he had found in the flat drawers underneath the table were very comprehensive. The one which covered the Pointe du Château coastline and the Gironde Marshes told him everything he needed to know.

The door of the saloon companionway swung open and Guyon appeared. He wore a yellow oilskin jacket and carried a large mug of coffee in each hand.

'How are we doing?'

Mallory checked his watch. 'Almost noon. Not long now. We're doing about fifteen knots.'

'I heard the weather forecast on the radio in the galley just before I came up,' Guyon said. 'It wasn't good. Winds increasing and fog indicated in the coastal area.'

'We're running into it already.'

Mallory drank some of his coffee and Guyon peered through the window. In the distance the fog waited like a damp shroud and heavy grey skies dropped towards the sea. Already the waves were lifting into white-caps in the northwest.

'How far would you say we're behind *L'Alouette* now?' Guyon said.

Mallory shrugged. 'Submerged, she only has half our speed. Allowing for the start she had, it's going to run things a little close.'

He leaned over the chart again. 'She'll have to surface inshore of Ile de Yeu before moving into the main creek flowing out of the marshes.'

'What depth is it there?'

Mallory traced its course with a pencil. 'Four or five fathoms. *Strong tidal currents constantly changing. Not to be relied on.* I know what *that* means. One day there's a sandbank. The next, six fathoms of clear water. These tidal marshes are all the same.'

'But we could get in with *Fleur de Lys*?'

'I think so. Probably not as far as the central island where the cottage is. It's marked on the chart. Half a mile in.'

Guyon straightened and the inimitable wry grin twisted his mouth. 'Things might get interesting, eh?'

'I think you could say that.'

Gradually the mist enfolded them until they were running through a strange, enclosed world and Mallory took over the wheel and reduced speed to ten knots. About thirty minutes later they emerged into a patch of clear water and saw the coastline of Pointe du Château no more than half a mile to port.

As they approached, a string of rocks and

small islands lifted out of the sea, running parallel to the coast, trailing away towards the great hog-back of the Ile de Yeu, looming out of the mist in the distance.

Mallory called to Guyon to take over the wheel and went back to the chart. When he straightened, his eyes glittered strangely.

'I think we can save a little time here, but it means taking a chance. *L'Alouette* will have to use the inshore passage. She has no other choice. This side of Ile de Yeu there's another passage marked between the island and the reef. Three fathoms.'

'We might take the bottom out of her,' Guyon said.

Mallory shrugged. 'It's de Beaumont's boat, not mine.'

Guyon grinned tightly. 'Then I suggest you take the wheel.'

Mallory changed course a point and the young Frenchman went down the saloon companionway. When he returned he carried two lifejackets.

'When I was a child a gypsy woman told my mother I must always beware of water.

Superstitious nonsense, of course, but unfortunately my Breton blood says otherwise. I'd hate to prove her right at this stage.'

Mallory changed to the automatic pilot, slipped his arms through the straps of the lifejacket and took over the wheel again. They were running parallel with the islands now and *Fleur de Lys* rocked in the turbulence, waves slapping solidly against her hull.

Rain hammered against the window, cascading in a sheet which blurred the outlines of all solid objects, adding a strangely dreamlike quality to the whole scene. Ile de Yeu was very close and he could see white water boiling in a frenzy across the jagged spine of the reef.

He swung the wheel hard to port. *Fleur de Lys* shuddered protestingly, a wave slammed against her hull and the deck tilted. Guyon was thrown across the wheelhouse and Mallory fell to one knee. The wheel started to spin, but already his hands were back in position. As he brought her head round she lurched forward towards the narrow band of clear water between the reef and the island.

He gave her everything the engines had to offer and the boat responded magnificently. The passage rushed towards them at a seemingly impossible speed and then they were into it, water crashing across great rocks on either side, white, curling fingers reaching out to enfold them.

All around, boulders were appearing and disappearing, waves foaming over them and Raoul Guyon hung on to the chart table, his face white.

Strange, swirling currents snatched at the rudder and for one agonising moment *Fleur de Lys* slewed to port. Mallory heaved on the wheel. There was a slight, audible shudder that ran through the entire craft as she slid across a sandbank, and then they were into clear water.

Fog rolled from the land in patches and they could smell the foetid odour of the marshes that was carried towards them on the offshore breeze. Mallory reduced speed and they moved in, the engines rumbling protestingly on a low note.

The marshes drifted out of the fog, dark

and sinister, waiting to receive them, and overhead a long wavering skein of geese passed like wind-blown spirits of the dead. Long, narrow sandbanks lifted out of the water and, landward, miles of rough grass marsh, a maze of creeks, waterlogged mud and wavering barriers of reeds.

They turned the end of a long sandbar and the mouth of the creek opened before them. Guyon leaned forward with a cry of alarm. Squatting just inside the entrance like some land-blown whale was *L'Alouette*, her grey-black plates shining with moisture. Fenelon stood in the conning tower with Jacaud and below three sailors were fitting an outboard motor to the stern of a large rubber dinghy.

Mallory took *Fleur de Lys* forward in a surge of power, her bow wave cascading across the hull of the submarine, knocking one of the sailors into the water. There was a startled cry and as they passed there was no more than ten feet between them. Mallory was aware of the shocked dismay on Fenelon's face, of Jacaud frowning in disbelief, and then they were through and safe in the fog.

He reduced speed to five knots and opened the window. Fog was sucked in, sharp and cold, the taste of it bitter as death. He strained his eyes into the gloom, watching the reeds drift by. A few minutes later they slid gently to a halt with a slight jar.

Mallory quickly reversed the engines. For a moment nothing seemed to be happening and then quite suddenly *Fleur de Lys* slid backwards.

'That settles that,' he said. 'We obviously aren't going to get any further.'

He cut the engines, went out on deck and climbed on top of the wheelhouse. The reeds were very thick at this point, but to the left was a small lagoon, circular in shape and perhaps a hundred feet in diameter.

He pointed to it as Guyon scrambled up beside him. 'Our one chance.'

He jumped to the deck, went into the wheelhouse and started the engines. As they rumbled into life he spun the wheel and crashed the boat into the reeds as she gathered speed.

For a moment they seemed an impenetrable barrier and then they slowly parted and *Fleur de Lys* passed through into the lagoon. Mallory cut the engines and she moved slowly to the far end and came to a halt, her prow grounding gently against a sandbank.

'No time to waste,' he said. 'One of us stays with the boat. The other goes for Granville and his wife.'

'That had better be me,' Guyon said. 'We have mutual acquaintances. I think he would trust me.'

Mallory pulled the chart forward. 'You'll do better by going on foot and swimming the intervening channels.' He opened a drawer and produced a pocket compass. 'Keep due west and you can't miss the central island. About a quarter of a mile away.'

'Getting Granville back here might be difficult,' Guyon said. 'He's an old man.'

'But used to these marshes. That's why he comes here, remember. You'll have to make out the best way you can.' Mallory produced the revolver he had taken from the young sailor at the castle and held it out. 'Not much, but better than nothing.'

Guyon pushed it into the pocket of his

oilskin jacket and went out on deck quickly. He jumped from the prow to the sandbank and plunged into the reeds.

Mallory lit a cigarette and stood on deck in the quiet rain. Perhaps five minutes later he heard the sound of an outboard motor passing along the main channel. It moved into the distance, muffled by the fog, and then there was only silence.

As Guyon went through the reeds a curlew whistled hauntingly somewhere to the left and wildfowl called as they lifted from the water, disturbed by his passing. He came out on higher ground, checked the compass and ran forward, alone in a land of shining mudflats, lonely creeks and everywhere the reeds.

He came to the end of solid ground and waded across a narrow creek, his feet sinking into soft mud. He could taste the salt on his lips and it stung his eyes painfully, but he kept on moving, pushing through the reeds into the grey shroud.

Gradually the ground became firmer again

until he was able to run across sand and coarse marsh-grass. A few moments later he stood on the banks of a shallow lake and the house loomed out of the fog on its island fifty yards away.

The evil, scum-covered waters reached out to meet him as he moved forward, and he took out the revolver and held it above his head. It was not likely that the water would affect it, but there was no point in taking chances.

It was surprisingly easy going, the mud giving way to hard sand, and he was soon moving up on to dry land again. As he ran towards the single-storeyed house a narrow wooden jetty loomed out of the fog and he paused abruptly. No boat was moored there, not even a marsh punt. He stood there, a frown on his face, considering the fact, then turned and went towards the house.

He could smell woodsmoke and saw it lifting in a blue tracer from the rough stone chimney. He went up rickety wooden steps to the porch, opened the door and went in.

The room was furnished simply but comfortably, loose rugs scattered across the polished wooden floor. There were several bookcases, all filled, a sofa and two easy chairs in front of the fireplace.

Logs smouldered fitfully on the stone hearth, heavily banked with ashes that they might not burn too quickly. They told Guyon all he needed to know. Henri Granville and his wife were not there. But, then, they should have always counted on that as a possibility.

Ornithology was the old man's great hobby. He had even written a book on the subject. It was quite obvious that at this moment he and his wife were sitting in their boat somewhere among the reeds which covered so many square miles of the marshes, probably even in some bird-hide since dawn taking photos.

He moved outside and went down to the jetty. Faintly, through the mist, came the sound of an outboard motor. Jacaud and his men. For them the solution would be obvious. They would simply wait for Granville to put in an appearance. No need even to go looking for him.

There was only one answer to the problem and Guyon waded into the lake and pushed towards the other side. He moved up on to high ground and ran along the shore towards the sound of the motor.

In spite of the clammy cold of the marshes sweat trickled from Fenelon's armpits. Ever since that first moment of shock when *Fleur de Lys* had passed them in the mouth of the estuary he had felt sick and frightened. And then de Beaumont's message over the radio, the mind numbing as the operator decoded it.

The message was quite plain. Under the circumstances they were to return at once. But that hadn't been good enough for Jacaud. He had insisted on going on into the marsh and Fenelon had wilted under his cold fury.

The reeds lifted like pale ghosts on either hand, the only sound the steady rattle of the outboard motor. He sat in the stern at the tiller, two sailors in the centre with rifles.

Jacaud sat on the edge of the rounded prow, his sub-machine-gun slung around his neck as he gazed into the fog like some great bird of prey.

He turned, his granite, brutal face running with moisture. 'We must be almost there. Cut the motor. We'll start paddling.'

'You're wasting your time, Jacaud,' Guyon called gaily. 'I beat you to it. By now Henri Granville and his wife are well on their way out of here.'

As the dinghy drifted forward, a sandbank reached out from the reeds like a pointing finger. Guyon stood on a small hillock at the far end. His hand swung up and he fired twice. One of the sailors groaned and went over the side, still clutching his rifle.

Jacaud slipped the sub-machine-gun over his head. It came up in a long, stuttering burst of fire, slicing through the reeds. He was too late. Guyon had disappeared like a ghost into the fog. He laughed mockingly somewhere near at hand and then there was silence.

The remaining sailor leaned over the side to pull in his comrade. Jacaud turned and struck up his arm. 'Leave him. We haven't time.'

The sailor recoiled from the killing fury, the devil's face that confronted him. The curious thing was that when Jacaud spoke his voice was quite calm.

'Back to *L'Alouette* and give that motor everything it's got. Mallory's got to return to Ile de Roc. He's no choice. His girlfriend's still there. If we're lucky we can catch them on their way out to sea.'

To Mallory the rattle of gunfire in the distance was like a physical blow and he walked the deck in impotent fury, hoping desperately that whatever had gone wrong Guyon had been able to handle it. Perhaps ten minutes later he heard the sound of the outboard motor returning along the creek. He stood very still, one foot on the rail, listening as it passed downstream.

He clambered on top of the wheelhouse and looked towards the west, straining into the fog. It was a good fifteen minutes before he heard the sound of brent geese calling bitterly as they lifted from the reeds. As the beating of their wings subsided, he was aware of movement towards the left.

He took a chance, cupped his hands and called: 'Raoul! Over here!'

A couple of minutes later Guyon emerged from the fog and stumbled across the sand-bank. Mallory ran to the prow and hauled him on board. Guyon was soaked to the skin and bitterly cold, his face pale and drawn.

'Have they passed yet?'

Mallory nodded. 'What happened?'

Guyon explained briefly, shivering repeat-edly as the wind cut through his damp clothes. 'What do we do now?'

'Get to hell out of here and fast,' Mallory said. 'Unless I'm very much mistaken Jacaud will wait for us at the estuary. If we can get down there fast enough we might stand a chance of getting out to sea before they're ready.'

'And back to Ile de Roc?'

'That's the general idea. You'd better go below. Find yourself some dry clothes and a drink. I'll get things moving up here.'

He went into the wheelhouse and started the engines. When he put them into reverse *Fleur de Lys* parted easily from the soft mud and he swung the wheel hard over, bringing her prow round until she pointed towards the wall of reeds that barred them from the creek.

He took her forward with a burst of speed, repeating his earlier manoeuvre. Once again it proved successful. The reeds parted protestingly and the boat burst into the creek. He turned the wheel to starboard and she swung round, grazing the mud of the opposite bank.

He took her downstream slowly, the engines a murmur in the rain. Guyon came up from the saloon wearing khaki slacks, rubber boots and a heavy white sweater with a turtle collar. In one hand he carried a bottle of brandy, in the other a tin mug.

'How do you feel?' Mallory said.

Guyon grinned and held up the brandy. 'How would you expect? It's Courvoisier. Like some?'

'I certainly would.'

Mallory took the brandy down in two

quick gulps. As a warm glow started to seep through his entire body he took out the packet of Gauloise that Marcel had given them and threw them to Guyon.

'Better have one while the going's good. Things might get pretty warm within the next ten minutes.'

He took one himself and opened the window of the wheelhouse. Rain kicked into his face and there was a slight wind blowing in from the sea across the marshes, lifting the fog into weird shapes.

Visibility was down to thirty or forty yards, but the reeds were beginning to drop back and the channel widened perceptibly. The water lifted in long swelling ripples and waves kicked against the bottom of the boat. They were almost there now and as a curving sandbank appeared a few yards to port he cut the engines and the current carried them in. There was a slight shudder and they stopped.

'What's the idea?' Guyon asked.

'I'd like to know what the opposition are up to. You stay here. I shan't be long.'

Mallory jumped to the sandbank, landing

knee-deep in water, waded out and followed its length into the fog until he could no longer see *Fleur de Lys*. A few minutes later he stood at the end, water splashing in across the sand, and looked out towards Ile de Yeu. There was no sign of *L'Alouette* and he turned and ran back the way he had come, splashing through the shallows as the tide began to lift over the sandbank.

Fleur de Lys was already swinging out into the deepening channel and he took Guyon's proffered hand and scrambled over the rail.

'Not a sign of them. As far as I'm concerned I'm going to give her everything she's got and head out to sea. They'll have to come up with something pretty good to stop us.'

He went into the wheelhouse, started the engines and reversed into the channel. Visibility was becoming rather better as the fog lifted and *Fleur de Lys* roared down the centre of the channel, her bow wave surging across the water on either side.

The mouth of the estuary appeared, clear and open to the sea, and Mallory swung the wheel to port to negotiate the great sandbank fifty yards beyond the entrance. As they turned the point, the current pushing against them, they found *L'Alouette* waiting.

Jacaud was in the conning tower, a heavy machine-gun mounted on a swivel pin. The moment they came into view he started to fire. Bullets swept across the deck and Mallory ducked as glass shattered in the wheelhouse.

Guyon crouched in the doorway, resting the revolver across one raised arm, trying for a steady shot, but it was impossible. As bullets hammered into their hull, Mallory spun the wheel and the young Frenchman lost his balance.

It was the fog which saved them, a long, solid bank rolling in across the reef before the wind, and it swallowed them in an instant. Guyon picked himself up and stood listening to the impotent chatter of the machine-gun as Jacaud continued to fire. After a while there was silence.

He turned to face Mallory, his breath easing out in a long sigh. 'I'd say that called for another drink.'

As they emerged from the fog-bank, Mallory took them out to sea, giving the engines full power. He turned with a grin. 'Nothing wrong there, thank God.'

Guyon went into the saloon and returned with the Courvoisier. 'He's made one hell of a mess down there. Holes all over the place. I don't think de Beaumont will be pleased.'

Mallory swallowed some of his brandy and lit a cigarette. 'We'll find out about that soon enough.'

Guyon went into the saloon and Mallory inhaled deeply on his cigarette with a conscious pleasure. Everything was going to be all right, he was certain of that. Sometimes one got these feelings. The wind had freshened even more and spray spattered against the shattered windows of the wheelhouse. He pulled down the helmsman's seat and sat.

Some time later Guyon came in with sandwiches and hot coffee and Mallory switched to the automatic pilot. 'Want me to take over?' Guyon asked.

Mallory shook his head. 'In these conditions

it should only take us two hours at the most to get there.'

It was perhaps half an hour later that he became aware that they were slowing perceptibly. His attempts to adjust the controls met with no success and he switched to automatic pilot and went below.

Guyon was lying on one of the saloon divans, his head on his hands, eyes closed. As Mallory entered, he opened them and sat up.'

'What's wrong?'

'God knows,' Mallory said, 'but we're losing speed badly and she isn't answering to the wheel like she should.'

The *Fleur de Lys* heeled to starboard and there was a great rushing of water beneath their feet. He dropped to one knee, pulled back the carpet and peered inside. When he looked up his face was grave.

'There must be two dozen bullet holes along the waterline. We're leaking like a sieve. No wonder the damned thing's slowed down.'

They went on deck quickly and into the wheelhouse. The electric pump was housed in a cupboard in one corner and the condition of the doors, splintered by bullets, told him what he would find.

He surveyed the smashed and twisted metal briefly, then turned, his face grim. 'You'll find a hand-pump aft of the main engine housing. Do the best you can with that. Stick it as long as you can and I'll spell you.'

'I see,' Raoul Guyon said. 'Things look bad, eh?'

'Only if *L'Alouette* catches us in this condition,' Mallory said grimly.

Guyon moved out along the deck without a word and a moment later Mallory became aware of the harsh, rhythmic clangour of the hand-pump. He looked out of the window at the brownish-white stream of water gushing across the deck, took over the wheel and waited for *Fleur de Lys* to lighten.

16

Sea Fury

When Fenelon first caught sight of *Fleur de Lys* his mind froze, refusing to accept for the moment what he knew to be an impossibility. The graticules misted over, temporarily obscured by a wave, and he raised the periscope a little more.

Fleur de Lys jumped into view, her familiar lines quite unmistakable. He said quickly to the rating at his side: 'Fetch Monsieur Jacaud here. Tell him to hurry.'

Jacaud arrived a few moments later. 'What's going on?'

'Take a look.'

The big man gripped the handles of the periscope tightly and lowered his head. When he turned to look at Fenelon a muscle twitched in his right cheek.

'I wonder what went wrong?'

Fenelon shrugged. 'Perhaps you damaged her engines with the machine-gun, or even holed her. Does it matter? Shall I surface? We should be able to board her with very little trouble.'

Jacaud shook his head and something glowed in the cold eyes. 'I've got a better idea. Remember the *Kontoro*? You said that one torpedo was all it would take. Let's see what you can do.'

Fenelon felt the blood surge to his temples and his heart pounded wildly. 'My God, it's perfect! They won't even know what hit them.'

'I don't mind that,' Jacaud said, 'as long as there's nothing left afterwards.'

L'Alouette carried two twenty-one-inch torpedoes, both mounted in the bow. Fenelon took a deep breath, pulled himself together and started to issue firm, crisp orders.

'Enemy's bearing, one-two-five. Course, one-three-one. Speed, six knots. Range, one thousand five hundred.'

These facts, fed into a complicated electrical device, provided the angle of deflection, enabling the torpedoes to be aimed the right distance ahead of the target so that both should arrive in the same place at the same time.

A moment later the petty officer called, 'Deflection, one-three degrees right, sir.'

Fenelon raised the periscope handles, his face pressed to the rubber eyepiece. 'Stand by both tubes.'

'Both tubes ready, sir.'

Fenelon could feel the sweat trickling down his face and his heart seemed to leap inside him. So often he had heard of this moment, had it described to him by men who knew. But for him this was the first.

'Stand by to fire.'

Fleur de Lys seemed to leap into focus, every line of her clear and clean. His hands tightened on the handles. 'Fire one.'

The submarine lurched as the missile shot away and the hydrophone operator reported, 'Torpedo running.'

'Fire two.'

Again the submarine shuddered.

'Torpedo running.'

Fenelon turned to Jacaud. 'Care to watch?'

The big man pushed him roughly to one side and bent to the handles.

On board *Fleur de Lys*, Guyon still sweated at the pump and the boat ran on, the automatic pilot in control while Mallory stood on top of the wheelhouse and swept the sea with a pair of glasses.

That *L'Alouette* would catch up with them now was certain. They were making no more than six knots and barely holding back the water. Submerged, the submarine had three or four knots on them. They were well out of the main shipping lane, he knew that. Their only hope was the chance of an odd fishing boat putting in an appearance, hardly likely considering the weather.

He swung the glasses again in a wide arc and stiffened as something lifted out of the water to starboard. It was a periscope, the telltale bow wave giving it away, and then he saw the great, surging streak of foam boiling under the surface of the water as it ran towards them.

'Torpedo!' he cried, and jumped to the deck, losing his balance and rolling over. He picked himself up, scrambled into the wheel-house and grabbed for the wheel. He spun it round desperately, and slowly she started to turn. Guyon appeared beside him, adding his weight, shoving the wheel over, and then a great swell, rolling in from the west, gave them the final push.

Mallory left Guyon at the wheel and rushed to the rail. He was just in time to see the wash of the torpedo passing to starboard. A few seconds later it was followed by the second.

In the submarine Jacaud gave a growl of rage, turned and grabbed Fenelon by the jacket. 'You missed, damn you! You missed!'

'But that's impossible.'

Fenelon bent to the periscope and Jacaud pulled him away. 'From now on I'm giving the orders. Take her in close and surface.

I'm going to finish Mr Bloody Mallory off personally.'

On the *Fleur de Lys* Mallory was back at the wheel and Guyon worked the pump furiously. But it was no good. The boat rolled heavily, waves breaking across her prow, the weight of the water inside holding her down.

L'Alouette had fired both her tubes and no additional torpedoes were carried by Type XXIII submarines, Mallory knew that. He looked out of the window, watching the fog roll in again in patches. There was no other vessel in sight, and his heart sank. Under the circumstances Jacaud's next move seemed obvious.

Somehow there was still a shock of surprise as the sea boiled in a great cauldron no more than fifty yards away and *L'Alouette* broke through to the surface. Even as the water still spilled from her plates Jacaud appeared in the conning tower. A rating came up beside him and they started to mount the heavy machine-gun on its firing-pin.

Guyon stood in the doorway, the revolver ready in his right hand. 'Now what?'

'I think that's obvious,' Mallory said flatly. 'If I'm going to go I'm taking him with me. It's been nice knowing you.'

'And you, *mon colonel*.' Raoul Guyon drew himself together as if on parade. 'An honour, sir.'

He moved along the deck to the prow and Mallory swung the wheel and brought *Fleur de Lys* into the wind. A moment later and she was bearing down on *L'Alouette*.

Jacaud started to fire, bullets hammering into the prow, and Mallory braced himself, hands firm on the wheel. Guyon lay flat on the deck, one arm around a stanchion, waiting for the moment of impact. There were two rounds left in the revolver and he was praying that at the last he might have the chance of putting them both into Jacaud.

In the conning tower of *L'Alouette* Jacaud still fired the machine-gun, raising it slightly, aiming for Mallory in the wheelhouse. Fenelon appeared beside him, his face white and terrified, mouth open in a soundless scream.

Mallory was aware of all these things, of the bullets hammering into the wheelhouse as he ducked out of sight and then *Fleur de Lys* was lifted high on a swell. She seemed to poise there for a moment, then slid down the other side into *L'Alouette*, her prow grinding against the side of the conning tower where it joined the hull.

There was a terrible crash, a groan of tortured metal as the bow crunched into the plates, cutting through the ballast tanks, crushing the pressure hull. *L'Alouette* heeled, the conning tower leaning over, spilling the machine-gun into the water, and Jacaud and Fenelon hung on desperately.

Guyon was on his feet, leaning over the rail. As he took aim and fired *Fleur de Lys* lurched to one side and he went head first into the sea.

Fleur de Lys kept on moving, her steel hull sliding over the submarine, pushing it down into the water. Suddenly she was across, her prow plunging into a wave. Mallory got to his feet, grabbed the wheel and struggled to bring her round.

Incredibly, she answered, and lifted sluggishly over the swell, her engines still beating. He turned and looked out through the shattered windows at the submarine.

She had righted herself now, but the sea was breaking over her hull in sinister fashion. The forward hatch opened and several sailors emerged. Jacaud came down the outside ladder to join them.

They were pointing at something in the sea and Mallory saw Raoul Guyon, a swell lifting him up and carrying him in towards the submarine. As he was washed across the grey hull they pounced on him.

There was nothing Mallory could do and he kept on going, passing into the fog. When he glanced back five minutes later *L'Alouette* was lost to view.

Gradually the engines lost power and progress became slower. The fog was very patchy, blown by a strengthening wind, and in the distance he could see Ile de Roc low on the horizon. The engines stopped altogether, five minutes later, with a hiss of steam.

He went down into the flooded saloon,

found the bottle of Courvoisier and went back on deck. The fog had cleared even more now, but the wind was cold and the waves were lifting again.

He unshipped the dinghy and waited until the green waters started to slop across the deck, then he slid it over the stern and climbed in. He rowed away, paused and watched *Fleur de Lys* slide under the surface.

The water boiled for a little while, then calmed into a great white patch of froth, a coil of rope, a box and one or two loose spars floating in the centre. It was always a saddening sight, the loss of a good ship. He inflated his lifejacket, raised the bottle of Courvoisier to his lips and started to row.

L'Alouette drifted low in the water, her powerful diesels still working, pushing her towards the island. Progress was agonisingly slow and in the conning tower Jacaud waited, a cigarette in his mouth, watching the island grow nearer in the gathering dusk.

Below, things were bad and getting worse

every minute. The crew worked knee-deep in water and it took the petty officer all his time to keep them under control.

Fenelon lay on the bunk in his tiny cabin, lips moving soundlessly as he stared up at the bulkhead. He shivered as if he had the ague and when someone attempted to speak to him he gazed at the man with vacant eyes.

Guyon lay huddled in a corner of the conning-tower bridge, blood oozing from a nasty gash in his forehead, knocked insensible by Jacaud the moment they had hauled him from the sea.

Jacaud stirred him with his boot, wondering exactly how he was going to kill him. It would have been easy to leave him in the sea or even to put a bullet through his head the moment they hauled him aboard, but that would have been too simple. Guyon deserved something special. He was a traitor and had been all along the line.

The throb of the diesels faltered and stopped and in the silence which followed there was a startled cry from inside the submarine. The forward hatch opened and the crew poured out. They brought with them several inflatable dinghies, including the one with the outboard motor which Jacaud had used in the marshes.

Jacaud picked Guyon up, slung him over one shoulder with easy strength and went down the ladder. He walked along the hull and paused a couple of yards away from the frightened sailors. They were no more than a quarter of a mile from the great reef which linked Ile de Roc and St Pierre, the tide carrying them in. Jacaud did not intend to wait and see what happened to *L'Alouette* when she was pounded across those terrible rocks.

He nodded to the petty officer. 'I'm taking the one with the outboard motor. You're coming with me.'

There was a chorus of startled cries from the men and one of them rushed forward. 'Why you? Why not us?'

Jacaud took a Lüger from his pocket and shot the man twice in the chest, the bullets knocking him into the water, There was a sudden silence and they all crowded back.

A few moments later the largest dinghy was moving away, the petty officer in the stern operating the outboard motor. Jacaud sat in the prow facing him and Guyon sprawled in the bottom.

The power of the current was already swinging the doomed submarine in towards the reef and there was a confused shouting on deck. One by one, the men crowded into the remaining dinghies and the current immediately swept them away.

Below in *L'Alouette* Fenelon lay in his cabin, forgotten by everyone. It was only when the water reached his bunk that he came to his senses. He sat up, stared down at it for a moment, then suddenly seemed to come to life.

He moved outside and started forward. At that moment the lights went out. He screamed as darkness enfolded him and started to feel his way along desperately.

As he reached the control room, light streaming in through the open conning tower, water started to cascade down the ladder and the whole world seemed to turn upside down.

He was aware of the crash, the rending of the metal plates and then a green cascade mercifully engulfed him. The sea swung *L'Alouette* in across the reef. For a brief moment she poised on the edge, then plunged down into the darkness of the Middle Passage.

17

The Run to the Island

The oars dipped and rose and Mallory pulled with all his strength, but his arms were tired and already there was a blister in one palm from a splinter in the rough handles.

It was more than an hour since *Fleur de Lys* had gone down and he had rowed steadily for most of that time, making little progress. The fog still hung low over the water in long, wraith-like patches. On one occasion he seemed to hear a faint cry. When he looked back there was a brief flash of yellow on top of a wave as one of the submarine's rubber dinghies was swept out to sea.

After a while he stopped and rested on the oars. Ile de Roc was still half a mile away and it was quite obvious that the run of the tide was sweeping him on a parallel course with the island that would eventually take him out to sea.

Even if he fetched up in the steamer lane that ran up-Channel from Ushant it would be dark in another hour. He was under no illusions about his ability to survive a night in the Channel in such a frail craft.

There were two good doubles left in the bottle of Courvoisier. He took them down slowly and tossed the empty bottle into the sea. As a thin rain drifted down on the wind he reached for the oars and started to row again.

The freshening wind dispelled the last traces of fog and an ugly chop formed on the water. He pulled steadily, staring into the gathering twilight, his mind a blank, everything he had of brain and muscle concentrated on his impossible task.

When he paused twenty minutes later and looked over his shoulder he saw to his astonishment that he was now quite close to the island. There was a slapping sound against the keel of the dinghy and it swung round, swirling past a long finger of rock, moving in fast, caught by some inshore current.

He bent to the oars with renewed vigour, forgetting the pain in his right hand, the blood that dripped steadily down. The current helped, carrying him closer inshore every minute. The waves were higher now as they pounded in over the rocks and water started to slop across the dinghy's stern.

He heaved on the oars, trying to keep her head round, but it was too much for him. He let them go, knelt in the bottom and waited, holding on with both hands.

The cliffs were very close now, the surf white as it crashed in across the narrow beach, breaking over ledges of rock. Behind Mallory a great, heaving swell rolled in, gathering momentum, sweeping him in before it. A sudden rending crash jarred his spine. Water foamed around, spray lifting high into the air. The dinghy ground forward across jagged rocks, her boards splintering, and came to a halt, the prow wedged into a crevasse.

Mallory hung on, and as the sea receded with a great sucking noise he scrambled out of the dinghy and stumbled across the final line of rocks. A moment later he was safe on the strip of beach at the base of the cliffs.

He sat down, holding his head in his hands, and the world spun away. The taste of the sea was in his throat and he retched, bringing up a quantity of salt-water.

After a while he got to his feet and turned to examine the cliffs behind. They were no more than seventy or eighty feet high and sloped gently backwards, cracked and fissured by great gullies.

It was an easy enough climb and he scrambled over the edge a few minutes later and turned to look out to sea. The fog had disappeared completely now, but darkness was falling fast and the moon was already rising above the horizon.

He hurried through the wet grass, following the slope in a gentle curve that brought him over the edge of the hill ten minutes later on the far side of the harbour from the Grants' house.

The cove looked strangely deserted, no smoke rising from the chimney of the hotel. He was aware of Guyon's launch, of the shooting brake tilted against a rock, the long skidmarks trailing back up the grassy slope to the road. He went down the slope on the run.

He walked round to the front of the hotel, calling loudly without receiving any reply. When he opened the door and stepped into the bar he was already prepared for something out of the ordinary, some evidence of a struggle at least.

Jagbir and Juliette Vincente still crouched together by the bar, a pool of dried blood spreading into the rush matting.

It was very quiet, too quiet, and for a moment Mallory seemed to hear the sea roaring in his ears and there was an element of unreality to it all. It was as if none of this were really happening, and he turned and stumbled outside.

He wasted five minutes in going down to

the jetty in the forlorn hope that Guyon's launch might be seaworthy. It was almost completely dark when he breasted the hill and trotted towards the Grants' house.

He went in through the kitchen and quiet enveloped him, that strange, secret stillness a house wraps about itself when no one is there, and an overwhelming loneliness surged through him.

He spoke aloud, his voice hoarse and broken: 'Anne?'

But only the house listened to him and the quiet ones. He stumbled into the sitting-room, opened the cabinet and poured himself a brandy. He stood there, sipping it quietly, remembering her here by the fireside in the soft lamplight a thousand years ago.

The darkness seemed to move in on him with a strange whispering, and he closed his eyes tightly, fighting the panic, the despair which rose inside him. The moment passed. He put down the glass and went out through the french windows.

The moon was clear and very bright, stars strung away to the horizon. When he topped the hill on the western side of the island St Pierre and the castle were etched out of black cardboard, breathtakingly beautiful like something from a child's fairy-tale.

Beneath him the tide was already on the turn, white water breaking across the great reef, rocks thrusting their heads into the moonlight. Minute by minute the water would continue to drop until for one brief hour a jagged causeway linked the two islands. One hour only and then the tide would come roaring in. But there was no point in thinking about that. Such had been his haste since landing from the dinghy that he had not even had time to rid himself of his lifejacket. He touched it mechanically, moved along the cliffs till he came to a sloping ravine that slanted to the beach below, and started down.

Marcel unbolted the heavy door and de Beaumont moved inside. There was no window, but the room was brightly illuminated by a naked bulb which hung from the centre of the low ceiling. Guyon and Hamish Grant sat on a couple of old packing cases, talking in low tones.

They came to their feet, the old man leaning on his walking stick. Guyon was very pale, dark circles under his eyes, and the gash on his forehead was red and angry.

'It seems I must congratulate you, Captain Guyon,' de Beaumont said calmly.

Guyon shook his head. 'No need. You were doomed from the beginning. A pity you didn't realise that a few lives ago.'

'I wouldn't be too sure. The game isn't over yet.'

'It will be the moment Colonel Mallory makes land.'

'And what if he doesn't? From what I hear, *Fleur de Lys* was in a sinking condition when last seen.'

'You're forgetting Granville and his wife. They must have contacted the authorities now. The sands are running out, de Beaumont. You were wrong from the start, always have been. We don't need you and your bully-boys to tell us how to govern France.'

Marcel took a step forward and de Beaumont pushed him back. 'Let him go on.'

'A country's greatness lies in the hearts of her people, not in the size of her possessions, and France is people. In one way or another, blood and suffering is all they've been given since 1939 and they've had enough. But not you, Colonel. You couldn't stop if you wanted to.'

'Anything I have done I have done to the greater glory of France,' de Beaumont said.

'Or the greater glory of Philippe de Beaumont? Which is it? Can you tell the difference? Have you ever been able to?'

De Beaumont's face seemed to sag, and for the first time since Guyon had known him he looked like an old man. He turned and walked out. Marcel hesitated and then followed him. The door closed and the bolts rasped into place.

'Quite a speech,' Hamish Grant said out of the long silence which followed.

'Accomplishing precisely nothing,' Guyon said wearily, and sat down, his head in his hands.

'Worth hearing, though.' The old man patted him gently on the shoulder, resumed his seat and they waited.

De Beaumont stood in front of the great glass window of the tower room and looked out over the sea. Far, far to the west the rim of the ocean was tipped with orange fire, Ile de Roc dark against the sky.

The beauty of it was too much for a man and he opened the casement and inhaled the good salt air and out beyond the island the lights of a ship seemed very far away.

Life was a series of beginnings and endings, that much at least he had learned. He remembered Dien-Bien-Phu, standing on the edge of a foxhole in the rain as the tricolour was hauled down and little yellow peasants from the rice fields had swarmed over the broken ground to take him and what was left of his men.

And then Algeria. Years of bloodshed. Of death in the streets and death in the hills. He had believed implicitly that the end justified the means, but what if that end was never realised? What if one were left only with the blood on the hands? Blood which had been shed to no purpose, which could never be washed off.

He felt curiously sad and drained of all emotion. A small wind moaned around the tower and then there was only the silence. In that single moment the heart turned to ashes inside him. Looking out over the moonlit sea he knew with a bitter certainty that he had been wrong. That in the final analysis all that he had done came to nothing. That everything Raoul Guyon had said was true.

He walked to the fireplace and looked up at the old battle standard for a long moment. He nodded, as if coming to some secret, hidden decision.

He picked up the telephone and pressed an extension button. When the receiver was lifted at the other end he said briefly, 'Send up Jacaud.'

He replaced the phone, moved across to a narrow door, opened it and stepped into the small turret bedroom. Anne Grant sat in a chair by the window. Fiona lay on the bed.

They got to their feet and faced him. He bowed courteously and stood to one side. 'If you would be so kind.'

They hesitated perceptibly, then brushed past him. He closed the door, moved to the fire and turned.

'What have you done with my father?' Fiona demanded.

'There is no need to alarm yourself. He will come to no harm. I give you my word.'

'And Raoul Guyon?'

De Beaumont smiled faintly. 'A great deal has taken place of which you are not aware. Captain Guyon is at this moment with General Grant. Except for a nasty cut on the head he seemed in fair condition when I saw him an hour ago.'

'You haven't mentioned Colonel Mallory,' Anne said carefully.

De Beaumont shrugged. 'All I can say with truth, my dear, is that at this precise moment I haven't the slightest idea where he is.'

There was a knock at the door, it opened

and Jacaud entered. He came forward and waited, the cold eyes in the brutal, animal face giving nothing away.

'Have *Foxhunter* refuelled and made ready for sea,' de Beaumont said.

'I've already seen to it. Are we leaving?'

'I should imagine it would be the sensible thing to do. Even if Mallory hasn't managed a landfall yet Granville must certainly be in touch with the French authorities by now. Admittedly they will then have to contact British Intelligence, but I shouldn't imagine it will be long before we're faced with some sort of official delegation.'

'Where are we going – Portugal?'

'Perhaps you, but not me, Jacaud.' Philippe de Beaumont extracted a cigarette from his case and fitted it carefully into his holder. 'We leave in half an hour for Jersey. When you have landed me in St Helier you are a free man. You and the others may go where you please.'

Jacaud's eyes narrowed. 'Jersey? Why would you want to go there?'

'Because they possess a more than adequate

airport, my dear Jacaud, and an early-morning flight to Paris. I intend to be on it.'

'You must be mad. You couldn't walk ten yards along the Champs Elysées without somebody recognising you.'

'No need,' de Beaumont said calmly. 'You see, I intend to place myself in the hands of the authorities.'

For once Jacaud's iron composure was shattered. 'Give yourself up? You'd face certain execution.'

'That would be for the court to decide.' De Beaumont shook his head. 'I've been wrong, Jacaud. We all have. I thought I wanted what was best for France. I see now that what I really wanted was what was best for me. Further bloodshed and violence would accomplish nothing. The events of the past few days have taught me that.'

'And what about the women and the old man? What do we do with them?'

'We can release them before we leave. They'll be picked up before long.'

'And Guyon?'

'Him we will also leave.'

Rage erupted from Jacaud's mouth in a growl of anger. 'I'll see that one on his back if it's the last thing I do on top of earth. God in heaven, I could have left him to drown.'

'Sergeant-Major Jacaud!' De Beaumont's voice was like cold steel. 'I have given you certain orders. You will see that they are carried out. Understand?'

For a dangerous moment the fire glimmered in Jacaud's eyes, and then, quite suddenly, he subsided. 'I beg the Colonel's pardon.'

'Accepted. Release Captain Guyon and General Grant and bring them up here. We leave in half an hour.'

Jacaud opened the door and went out. De Beaumont sighed, and said almost to himself: 'Twenty-three years of blood and war. Too much for any man.'

It was Anne who answered him, her face very pale. 'Before God, Colonel de Beaumont, I pity you.'

He took her hand and kissed it gently, then crossed to the door to the turret room and opened it. 'Perhaps you would wait in here?'

They walked past him. He closed the door and went to the fireplace. He looked up at the standard for a long moment, then sat down at his writing desk and picked up a pen.

Marcel sat at the table in his tiny room, a bottle of cognac in front of him. He was reading an old magazine, turning the pages slowly, his mind elsewhere. They should have been out of this place the moment Jacaud had returned with the news of the loss of *L'Alouette*, so much was obvious. He wondered what de Beaumont had wanted, and raised his glass to his lips. Behind him the door crashed open and Jacaud entered.

His face was white, the skin drawn tightly over the prominent cheekbones, and there was a strange, smoky look in his eyes that made Marcel's flesh crawl.

'What is it? What happened up there?'

Jacaud grabbed the glass, filled it with cognac and swallowed it down. 'He wants us to take him to Jersey. From there he intends to fly to Paris to hand himself over to the authorities.'

'He must be mad.' Marcel's face turned a sickly yellow colour. 'Are you going to let him?'

'Am I hell. If they get him they get all of us. It would only be a matter of time.'

'What about the prisoners?'

'He's going to release them.'

Marcel jumped up in alarm. 'We've got to get out of here. This whole thing's going sour.'

'We're getting out of here all right, but on our own,' Jacaud said. 'Just you and me. Everyone else can go to the devil. But first I've got to settle with de Beaumont. He knows too much for his own good.'

'And Guyon?'

'I'll have to forgo that pleasure. You take care of him and the old man. I'll see you on the jetty in fifteen minutes.'

He went out and Marcel raised the bottle of cognac to his lips, swallowed deeply and tossed it into a corner.

* * *

It was quiet in the corridor and he moved quickly along to the end and paused outside a stout wooden door. He took a revolver from his pocket and checked it quickly. There were four rounds in the cylinder and he unbolted the door, kicked it open and moved inside.

Raoul Guyon and General Grant rose to meet him. Marcel closed the door behind him and moved forward.

'You first, Captain,' he said, and his hand swung up.

Guyon flung himself to one side and the bullet chipped stone from the wall. In the same moment Hamish Grant slashed at the light with his walking stick, plunging the room into darkness.

Marcel cried out sharply and fired twice. He was aware of a shadow moving over towards the right in the split-second flash and fired twice again. The second time the hammer clicked on an empty chamber. He flung the useless weapon into the darkness with a sob and reached for the door.

There was the scrape of a foot behind him and a great arm slid around his neck. He was aware of the pain, of the relentless brute strength, and struggled wildly. Hamish Grant increased the pressure, his fingers locked together like steel bands, and the Frenchman went limp.

The old man dropped him to the floor and said hoarsely, 'Raoul, where are you?'

There was a movement in the darkness beside him. 'Here, General.'

Hamish Grant put out a hand and touched him on the shoulder. 'Are you hit?'

'Not a chance,' Guyon said. 'But let's get out of here. We must find the girls.'

The old man opened the door cautiously and walked into the passage. Something moved, a dark shadow against the light. He reached out, a snarl rising in his throat, and his wrists were gripped tightly.

A tired, familiar voice said: 'All right, General. It's me.'

[illegible]

aware of the [illegible] of the [illegible] have [illegible] and [illegible] [illegible] [illegible], the [illegible] [illegible] [illegible] [illegible] [illegible], and the [illegible] [illegible].

He [illegible] [illegible] him. [illegible] [illegible] [illegible]. [illegible] [illegible] [illegible]

[illegible] [illegible] [illegible] [illegible] [illegible]

[illegible] [illegible] [illegible] on his shoulder. [illegible]

[illegible] [illegible] [illegible] [illegible] [illegible]

[illegible] [illegible] [illegible] the [illegible] [illegible] and [illegible] [illegible] [illegible] [illegible] [illegible] [illegible] [illegible] [illegible] [illegible] [illegible] [illegible] were [illegible].

[illegible] [illegible] [illegible] [illegible] [illegible] [illegible]

18

Last Round

Mallory struggled across a great slippery mass of rounded stones and paused on top of a natural escarpment. He had never felt greater loneliness in his entire life. On each side stretched the sea, and before him, clear in the moonlight, the sinister, twisted maze of jagged rocks and great boulders that made up the reef.

At high water the escarpment upon which he was now standing would be a good five fathoms deep, and he moved on, slipping and stumbling across a morass of slimy seaweed, sinking up to his knees in places.

It had taken him three-quarters of an hour to get half-way along the reef. With each passing moment it became more and more apparent that unless he could increase his rate of progress the tide would sweep back in to pound him across these cruel rocks.

He came out on to a strip of wet sand shining in the moonlight, and started to run. For perhaps a hundred yards the sand held true and then petered out into gravel and broken stone.

He entered a forest of dark pointing fingers which lifted into the moonlight like some strange prehistoric monument and wasted ten minutes finding his way through. As he struggled out along a shelving bank of seaweed he paused and looked down at moonlight shining on the waters of the Middle Passage.

It stretched before him, a dark tunnel with at least twenty feet of headroom at low water. The wind blowing in from the sea, scattering spray in his face, decided him. At his present rate of progress he was certain to be caught. There was only one remaining chance of beating the tide and he slid over the edge.

Strangely enough, when he entered the water he wasn't aware of the cold and his lifejacket worked perfectly. He turned on to his back and started to swim, using both arms in a powerful back stroke.

The passage was shadowy in the moonlight and very still and the sound of the sea outside seemed to come from another place. He remembered what lay beneath him, fathoms deep in the darkness, and pushed the thought away, concentrating all his strength on the task in hand.

It was perhaps fifteen minutes later that he became aware of a different note outside and spray foamed through the crannies above his head, splashing across his face. The water-level started to rise at once and with every passing minute the roof came nearer.

He turned on his face and swam forward, thrashing wildly with his feet. A few moments later he came out into a jagged basin. As a swell lifted him up he grabbed for a ledge and hauled himself out of the water.

The tide was already moving in, licking hungrily at the rocks, and far out to sea a flash of sheet lightning illuminated the sky. He came to the end of the main body of the reef and before him a long, thin spine of rock and gravel stretched three hundred yards to St Pierre.

He started to run, aware of the roaring of the sea, hungry for him as she swept in to drown the land, erupting with phosphorescence, blue-green lights dancing on the water, dissolving as rapidly as they appeared.

To the right, lightning flared again and a dark band of shadow moved across the sky, snuffing out the stars. He came to a long strip of shingle and started to run.

Half-way across, the sea splashed in knee-deep. He struggled forward, aware of its strength as it tugged at him. It was already at his waist when he reached the sprawling mass of boulders heaped at the base of the island. As his feet missed bottom, he thrashed forward, grabbed for a ledge and hauled himself out.

Still the sea rose, and he moved on, aware only of the menace behind. He skirted the base of the cliffs and finally reached a point of jagged rock no more than twenty feet from the entrance to the cave.

He jumped into the water and started to swim desperately, but there was no need. The tide swept him into the entrance on the crest of a great swell. A moment later he bumped against the wall of the jetty at *Foxhunter*'s stern. He swam round to a flight of stone steps and climbed out of the water.

He was tired, more tired than he had ever been in his life, and the roaring of the sea seemed to have got inside his head. He pulled off his lifejacket, padded across the jetty and went up the steps, keeping to the wall. When he reached the landing all was quiet. He opened the door cautiously and moved forward.

There were three doors on this section of the corridor, all leading to rooms used as quarters by *L'Alouette*'s crew. He searched them quickly, hoping for a weapon, but found nothing.

As he emerged from the last he heard the muffled reports of several gunshots fired close at hand. He stood listening intently. Another shot sounded. He went along the passage, every sense alert, and paused at the end.

Behind him a door opened. He whirled round, hands coming up, and Hamish Grant stepped into the light.

The great hall was a place of shadows. No fire burned in the hearth and a single light at the far end gave the only illumination. Mallory moved out of the doorway and stood listening, but there was no sound, and he moved forward followed by Guyon and Hamish Grant.

There was a small lamp bracketed to the wall of the gallery and for some reason it seemed to grow dimmer as he went upstairs. He paused, swaying a little, and Guyon's anxious voice seemed to come from a great distance.

'Are you all right?'

Mallory opened his eyes, nodded and moved on, putting one foot in front of the other mechanically. It was only when they reached the door to the tower and he pushed it open that he realised how exhausted he was. There was no strength left in him at all.

Guyon and the old man crowded into the narrow hall and Mallory bolted the door. 'Whatever happens now, no one else gets in,' he said, and the words seemed to be spoken by someone else.

He took a deep breath, summoning together every final resource of body and mind, and led the way up the stairs. The walls spiralled round, the night sky gleaming through the slotted windows, and somewhere thunder rumbled menacingly.

When they emerged on the first landing the door to the radio room stood open and there was no one there. Mallory moved across to the set and switched it on. There was a faint crackling of static. He picked up the microphone and high in the tower three shots were fired in rapid succession. A moment later Fiona Grant screamed.

Jacaud paused on the landing, took the Lüger from the pocket of his reefer coat and removed the clip. It was by no means full, he could tell that by the weight, but there was no time to reload. He slammed it back into the butt, replaced the Lüger in pocket and opened the door.

De Beaumont was sitting at his desk writing, his hair silver in the soft light. He blotted the sheet of paper carefully, put down his pen and looked up.

A frown appeared on his face. 'What's happened, Jacaud? Where are General Grant and Guyon?'

'Marcel is taking care of them now,' Jacaud said calmly.

'Taking care of them? I don't understand.'

'Don't you, my brave colonel?' Jacaud laughed harshly. 'Did you really think I'd stand to one side and allow you to fly off to Paris to play *le grand seigneur*, a de Beaumont to the end?'

'How dare you!' de Beaumont said hoarsely.

'For you it's always been a game,' Jacaud said. 'A great and wonderful game with bugles blowing and standards flying in the breeze like some medieval set-piece. That's the way you've lived and that's the way you want to die, but not this time, Colonel. They'll squeeze you so hard you'll tell them everything that's ever happened to you since you were three years old. Unfortunately for you, that includes me.'

De Beaumont grabbed a glass paperweight, hurled it with all his force and reached for the handle of the drawer containing his revolver. Jacaud jumped to one side, the paperweight smashing against the wall, and fired.

The bullet caught de Beaumont in the left shoulder, spinning him round, and Jacaud fired again twice, the impact driving de Beaumont forward. He clutched at the mantelpiece, the linen material of his jacket bursting into flames, and reached up towards the old battle standard. He started to fall, his fingers catching at the fringe, and it fluttered down to cover him like a scarlet shroud.

The door of the turret room opened and Anne and Fiona Grant appeared. The young girl screamed once, her hands going up to her face. Jacaud ignored them. He walked slowly across the room and stood looking down at de Beaumont, a dazed expression in his eyes.

Behind him the door swung open with a crash. As he turned, Raoul Guyon hurled himself forward. Jacaud's first bullet chipped the wall beside the door, his second caught Guyon just above the left breast, stopping him in his tracks. Guyon groaned and fell to one knee. Jacaud raised the Lüger, took careful aim and fired again.

As the hammer fell on an empty chamber, Anne Grant flung herself forward, grabbing at his arm. He hit her back-handed, slamming her against the wall, and reached into his pocket for some spare rounds.

Mallory seemed to fill the doorway, the eyes dark shadows in a face that was lined with fatigue. He started forward, swaying slightly from side to side, eyes never leaving Jacaud, no expression on his face, a dead man walking.

Jacaud dropped the Lüger, seized the heavy brass poker from the fireplace and weighed it in his hand, a savage smile on his face.

'Come on!' he said. 'Come on, you bastard!'

Mallory stood there, hands hanging loosely at his sides, fatigue washing over his face, and Jacaud sprang forward, the brass poker swinging down, gleaming in the lamplight.

To Mallory that blow was like a branch swaying in the wind. As the poker came down he grabbed for the wrist, twisting the arm up and out to one side, taut as a steel bar, using the same terrible grip he had used on the jetty at Southampton so long ago.

Jacaud screamed, dropping the poker, and the muscles of his shoulder started to tear. Mallory reached for the wrist with his other hand and twisted it round and up.

Again there was a tearing sound as muscle gave and Jacaud screamed again. Still keeping that terrible hold in position, Mallory ran him head first across the room towards the great window. It dissolved in a snowstorm of flying glass and Jacaud dived into darkness, his last cry swept away on the wind like some departing spirit.

Raoul Guyon was propped against Fiona's knee, his face hollow with pain, and Hamish Grant stood in the doorway. When Mallory turned, blood on his face from the flying glass, they were all looking towards him strangely.

He started to fall and strong arms caught him, easing him down to the floor, and he looked up at Anne Grant, that dark, dear face so full of love for him.

'Raoul?' he said. 'How's Raoul? Is it serious?'

'He's going to be fine.'

There was something else, something important. He frowned desperately and then remembered. 'The radio room – downstairs. We must call Jersey. There are three motor torpedo boats just waiting for the right signal.'

'It's all right,' she said. 'Everything's all right. We'll take care of it.'

She pillowed his head against her breast, her arms about him. He turned into their softness, the sound of the sea in his ears, and slept.

Jack Higgins

Jack Higgins lived in Belfast till the age of twelve. Leaving school at fifteen, he spent three years with the Royal Horse Guards, serving on the East German border during the Cold War. His subsequent employment included occupations as diverse as circus roustabout, truck driver, clerk and, after taking an honours degree in sociology and social psychology, teacher and university lecturer.

The Eagle Has Landed turned him into an international bestselling author, and his novels have since sold over 250 million copies and have been translated into fifty-five languages. Many of them have also been made into successful films. His recent bestselling novels include *Bad Company*, *A Fine Night for Dying*, *Dark Justice*, *Toll for the Brave*, *Without Mercy* and *Storm Warning*.

In 1995 Jack Higgins was awarded an honorary doctorate by Leeds Metropolitan University. He is a fellow of the Royal Society of Arts and an expert scuba diver and marksman. He lives on Jersey.

Visit www.AuthorTracker.co.uk for exclusive updates on Jack Higgins.

Also by Jack Higgins

The Valhalla Exchange
To Catch a King
Dillinger
The Run to Morning
The Eagle Has Landed
A Prayer for the Dying
The Last Place God Made
Storm Warning
Day of Judgment
Solo
Luciano's Luck
Touch the Devil
Exocet
Confessional
Night of the Fox
A Season in Hell
Memoirs of a Dance-Hall Romeo
Cold Harbour
The Eagle Has Flown
Eye of the Storm
Thunder Point
On Dangerous Ground
Sheba
Angel of Death
Drink with the Devil
Year of the Tiger
The President's Daughter
Flight of Eagles
The White House Connection
Pay the Devil
Day of Reckoning
Edge of Danger
The Keys of Hell
Midnight Runner
A Fine Night for Dying
Bad Company
Dark Justice
Toll for the Brave
Without Mercy
East of Desolation

JACK HIGGINS

THE IRON TIGER

HARPER

This novel is entirely a work of fiction.
The names, characters and incidents portrayed in it are the work of the author's imagination. Any resemblance to actual persons, living or dead, events or localities is entirely coincidental.

Harper
An imprint of HarperCollins*Publishers*
77–85 Fulham Palace Road,
Hammersmith, London W6 8JB

www.harpercollins.co.uk

This paperback edition 2008
1

First published in Great Britain by
John Long 1966

A catalogue record for this book is
available from the British Library

ISBN 978-0-00-783207-1

Set in Sabon by Palimpsest Book Production Limited,
Grangemouth, Stirlingshire

Printed and bound in Great Britain by
Clays Ltd, St Ives plc

PUBLISHER'S NOTE

THE IRON TIGER was first published in the UK by John Long in 1966, then later by Signet books, but has been out of print for some years.

In 2008, it seemed to the author and his publishers that it was a pity to leave such a good story languishing on his shelves. So we are delighted to be able to bring back THE IRON TIGER for the pleasure of the vast majority of us who never had a chance to read the earlier editions.

For Brenda Godfrey who likes a good story

Foreword

India has always fascinated me, although I had not visited the country when I wrote *The Iron Tiger*. I have since, of course, and was delighted to find that, thanks to careful research, I had got it right. The period during which I wrote the book, the early sixties, was one in which the Chinese occupying power treated the Tibetan people with great brutality and many thousands of those unfortunates died. The Chinese invasion of India hardly made them popular in that country and, because of this, *The Iron Tiger* was a great success with Indian people. However, a strange thing happened. It made me, as the author, highly popular for a while as for some reason people believed that I had simply fictionalised a true story about myself and that the events of the book had actually taken place.

Jack Higgins
July 1996

1

The Place of Silence

Beyond the mountains, the sky was sapphire and blue, a golden glow spreading across the ice caps as the sun slowly lifted. Below, the valleys lay dark and quiet, the only sound the tiny, insignificant drone of the Beaver's engine as it followed the maze through to Tibet.

Jack Drummond was tired and a slight dull ache behind his right eye nagged constantly. Too many late nights, too much whisky and he was getting old. Too old to be dicing in the worst flying area in the world at sixteen thousand feet in a non-pressurised cabin.

He turned to Cheung and grinned. 'There's coffee in a black flask under your seat. I could do with some.'

His companion was Chinese, but it was obvious that he had European blood. The eyes were startlingly blue in the bronzed, healthy face and his mouth lifted slightly in a quirk of ironic good humour.

He wore a heavy sheepskin coat and an astrakhan cap and shivered as he opened the vacuum flask and poured coffee into a plastic cup.

'Is it always as cold as this?'

Drummond nodded. 'The wind comes all the way from Mongolia. There have been times when it's stripped pieces off the fuselage.'

Cheung peered down into the jagged valley below. 'What would happen if the engine stopped?'

Drummond laughed harshly. 'You're joking, of course.'

Cheung sighed. 'It becomes clearer minute-by-minute that you have been earning your money during the past six months.'

'And perhaps a little more?'

The Chinese smiled amiably. 'My dear Jack, in Formosa, we subsist almost entirely on the goodwill of our American friends. If it wasn't for their generosity, we couldn't even afford such minor gestures as this Tibetan venture.'

Drummond shrugged. 'It doesn't worry me. A couple more trips and I'm through. I've done this run too often. I'm on borrowed time.'

Cheung frowned. 'But Jack, there is no one else. What will we do?'

'There's always someone else,' Drummond said. 'You'll find him in one bar or another in Calcutta. Plenty of ex-R.A.F. types who can't settle down or the other kind who've lost their licences to fly commercially. They'll go anywhere if the money's right.'

They moved on through a landscape so barren that it might have been the moon, great snow-covered peaks towering on either side. Drummond handling the plane with the skill of genius. Once they dropped sickeningly in an air pocket, and on another occasion flew along a canyon so narrow that the wingtips seemed to brush the rock face. Finally, they lifted across a snow-covered ridge and plunged into space.

Beneath them an enormous valley dropped ten thousand feet, black with depth, purple and gold, great shimmering banks of cloud strung across it in broken strands. Perhaps seven or eight miles away on the other side was the last frozen barrier between Balpur and Tibet.

The sound of the engine suddenly seemed strangely muted and Cheung sighed through the uncanny quiet. 'The most beautiful sight I've ever seen.'

'The Place of Silence, that's what they call it,' Drummond told him. 'Used to take two days to get across on foot when caravans were still coming through.'

The Beaver seemed to glide on through the enormous blue vault, drifting through the shadows, and then they burst out into golden sunlight and the final barrier rose before them.

Drummond eased back the stick and the Beaver lifted, the sound of the engine deepening into a full-throated roar and a deep valley appeared between the peaks.

'Sangong Pass,' he called above the roar of the engine.

They swept into the pass, a brilliant red and gold leaf, bright against the dark walls, and the frozen earth rose to meet them. Drummond gave the Beaver full power and pulled the stick right into the pit of his stomach.

Cheung held his breath, waiting for the crash as they rushed to meet the skyline, wheels no more than ten feet above the boulder-strewn ground and then they were over the hump and flashing across a great, cold glacier.

Rolling steppes, golden in the morning sun, stretched to the horizon and Drummond grinned. 'Now you know why I charge two thousand a trip.'

Cheung wiped sweat from his forehead with the back of a gloved hand and managed a weak smile. 'I'm beginning to get the point. How much further?'

'Ten or twelve miles, that's all. Better get ready.'

The Chinese reached behind his seat for a sub-machine gun, cocked it and held it across his knees. As the Beaver descended, he could see a narrow river, brawling across a mass of tumbled boulders, widening into a shallow lake. A hundred yards to the left, sheltered against a rock escarpment, was a ruined monastery, a scattering of houses at its feet.

Drummond pointed to a wide sand flat at the far end of the lake. 'That's where we land if we get the signal.'

'And if not?'

'We get the hell out of here.'

He circled, coming in low across the lake, and Cheung pointed excitedly. 'There are people down there, standing in the shallows.'

'Women doing the washing,' Drummond said and swung in across the village, turning away from the escarpment and the fire-blackened ruins of the monastery.

'What happened there?' Cheung demanded.

'It was a headquarters for local resistance back in 1950 when the Chinese Reds first invaded Tibet. There was a siege for a couple of days, but it didn't last long. They brought up a couple of field guns and blew the necessary holes through the walls.'

'Then what?'

Drummond shrugged. 'They saved everything worth having, then burnt the place to the ground and executed a couple of hundred monks.'

'To encourage the others?'

Drummond nodded and took the Beaver round to the other side of the lake in a graceful curve. 'Not that it's done them much good. In areas like this, they only control the towns.'

He took the Beaver down towards the village again and Cheung touched his arm quickly. 'Is that the signal?'

Three flares, spaced out in a crude triangle, started to burn furiously, plumes of white smoke lifting into the cold air and Drummond nodded.

He throttled back, turned the Beaver into the wind, dropped it neatly down on the firm, sandy shore of the lake and taxied along to the far end.

The women washing clothing in the shallows a few yards away, moved up on the shore, their long woollen *shubas* tucked into their belts and stood in a tight little group, watching the plane.

Cheung reached for the door handle and Drummond shook his head. 'Not yet. We've got to be sure.'

At that moment, a horseman galloped over the crest of the slope above them and plunged down towards the plane. Drummond switched off the engine and grinned in the sudden silence.

'There's our man.'

As he opened the door and jumped to the ground, the rider reined in his small Tibetan horse, dismounted and strode towards them. He was tall and muscular with a deeply-tanned face and high Mongolian cheekbones. He wore a long, wide-sleeved robe and sheepskin *shuba* which left his chest bare, and knee-length boots of untanned hide. His hair was coiled into plaits and he wore a sheepskin hat.

'His English isn't much good,' Drummond said to Cheung as the Tibetan approached. 'We'll use Chinese and for God's sake treat him with respect. He's a nobleman. They can be touchy about things like that.'

The Tibetan grinned and held out his hand,

and behind him another dozen men rode down to the shore. 'It is good to see you again, my friend. You have more guns for us?'

Drummond nodded as he shook hands. 'Your men can unload them as soon as they like. I don't want to hang around here for any longer than I have to.'

The Tibetan shouted an order and he and Drummond and Cheung moved out of the way. 'Moro, this is Mr Cheung,' Drummond said. 'He's the Balpur representative of the Chinese National Government, the people who've been supplying the guns and ammunition I've been flying in to you during the past six months.'

Moro took Cheung's hand warmly. 'Before the Lord Buddha brought the way of peace to this land, the Tibetans were warriors. Your guns have helped us prove to the Communists that we can be warriors again. You will take tea with me before you leave?'

Cheung turned to Drummond. 'Have we time?'

'I don't see why not.' Drummond offered

the Tibetan a cigarette. 'Any Reds in the area recently?'

'One patrol,' Moro said. 'Fifteen men. They turned up a week ago.'

'What happened?'

The Tibetan grinned. 'You'll see when we reach the village.'

They went over the escarpment and walked towards the houses, the Tibetan with the bridle of his horse looped over one arm.

'Mr Cheung has to make a special report to his government in Formosa about the state of things here,' Drummond said. 'He thought he'd like to see for himself.'

'How strong are the Reds in this area?' Cheung asked.

'Their nearest real strength is at a town called Juhma about a hundred miles from here,' Moro said. 'Half a regiment of infantry. No more than four hundred men. At larger villages like Hurok which is thirty miles east across the plain, they keep a cavalry troop. Between the villages they are as nothing.'

'There have been no large scale troop

movements, no road building in this area of the border at all?'

'Not here, but further east towards the Aksai Chin and the Ladakh where they fought the Indians in 1962, they have built many roads.' The Tibetan looked surprised. 'Why would they need roads here?'

'They have claimed Balpur,' Cheung said simply.

Moro laughed, showing strong white teeth. 'They have claimed the whole world, is this not so?'

'They came to the outskirts of the village, a small, mean place, single-storey houses of mud and wattle strung along either side of the single street.

Several children ran forward excitedly and followed them, keeping a respectful distance from Moro who occasionally flicked out with the plaited leather whip that hung from his left wrist as someone moved too close.

They came to a house near the centre of the village that seemed larger than the others and he opened the heavy wooden door and led the way in.

There were no windows and in the half-darkness Drummond was aware of the mud walls, the sheepskins on the floor. On a stone hearth in the centre, a fire of yak dung burned brightly and an old Tibetan woman was crumbling brick tea into a cauldron of boiling water. She added butter and a pinch of salt and the men squatted on a sheepskin beside the fire.

They waited in silence for the tea as ritual demanded. The old woman filled three metal cups and gave them one each. Moro took a sip, nodded in approval and they drank.

It was, as always, curiously refreshing and Drummond held out his cup for more. 'How are things going generally?'

Moro shrugged. 'They will not be beaten here, we cannot hope to accomplish so much, but we can keep them occupied, make life difficult.'

'What about arms?' Cheung said. 'You need more?'

'Always more. We can't fight them with broadsword and musket.'

'You were going to tell us about the patrol,' Drummond reminded him.

Moro nodded and got to his feet. 'I was forgetting. If you have finished your tea, I will show you now.'

They moved into the street, blinking in the bright, clear morning sunlight and the Tibetan led the way through the crumbling houses, the small tail of children keeping pace with them.

The great wooden gates in the outer wall of the monastery swung crazily from their hinges, half-burnt away and blackened by fire.

They crossed the courtyard beyond, still followed by the children, and mounted the broad steps to the ruin of what had once been one of the most famous seats of learning in Western Tibet.

The doors had disappeared, splintered into matchwood by high explosive shells, and inside bright sunlight streamed down through holes in the roof.

'There was a library here,' Drummond told Cheung. 'It held more than fifteen thousand books and manuscripts, most of them over a thousand years old. The Chinese burned the lot quite deliberately.'

Beyond, in the shadows, something stirred and a kite rose lazily into the air, great ragged black wings brushing the roof beams and Drummond was aware of Cheung's breath hissing between his teeth sharply.

Disturbed by the bird's passage, something was swinging to and fro, half-in, half-out of the bright shafts of sunlight cutting down through the darkness.

Drummond moved a little closer. It was a Chinese soldier, swinging by a rope from one of the charred beams, tongue protruding obscenely from the black, swollen face. Where the eyes had been, were only empty, ragged sockets and one ear had been torn off.

As his eyes became accustomed to the half-light, he saw the others, each hanging from a beam, staring blindly into eternity.

'We were away when they arrived,' Moro said simply. 'When we returned, the fools were so busy ravishing the women, they had not even thought to post a guard.'

One of the children ran forward with a harsh laugh and grabbed the nearest corpse by the legs, swinging it from side to side furiously and the other children followed suit, running through the shadows, dodging the swinging bodies, helpless with laughter.

Drummond turned and moved into the sunlight again, his mouth dry. 'I think we should be making a move.'

Mr Cheung didn't speak. His face was strangely pale and there was shock and pain in his eyes as they returned to the village. Moro whistled for his horse, caught the bridle and led the way back to the lake.

'What did you bring this time?' he asked Drummond.

'Automatic rifles, sub-machine guns and ten thousand rounds of ammunition.'

The Tibetan nodded. 'Good, but we could do with some explosive next time.'

Drummond glanced at Cheung enquiringly. 'Can you manage that?'

The Chinese nodded. 'I think so. Would a fortnight today be too soon?'

'Not for me,' Drummond said. 'Two more trips and I'm finished. The sooner I get them done, the better I'll like it.'

'A fortnight, then,' Moro said and they

went over the escarpment and down to the shore beside the lake.

His men had unloaded the plane and already several packhorses were on their way to the village. Drummond gave him a final cigarette, climbed in and strapped himself into his seat. As the engine roared into life, Mr Cheung turned and held out his hand.

'We are united in the same struggle,' he said and climbed into the plane.

As he closed the door and fastened his seat belt, the Beaver turned into the wind and started to taxi along the shore, sand whipped up by the propeller rattled against the windows. A moment later, the bluff at the far end of the lake was rushing to meet them and they were rising into the air.

Drummond circled once and Moro, already back in the saddle, waved, turned his horse and galloped back towards the village.

Drummond checked his instruments and started to gain altitude. 'Well, what did you think?'

'Words fail me.'

'I thought they would.'

Cheung lit a cigarette and sighed heavily. 'To you, it is nothing. Jack. Dangerous, unpleasant, yes, but something you are mixed up in for one reason only – money.'

'And to you it's a holy war,' Drummond said. 'I know, only don't start trying to get me to join the crusade. I had a bellyful of that kind of thing in Korea. Enough to last a lifetime.'

'All right,' Cheung said wearily. 'What about these explosives Moro wants on the next trip? If I have them delivered to the rail-head at Juma by next weekend can you pick them up?'

'I'm flying down tomorrow with Major Hamid,' Drummond said. 'He's taking a week's leave. He thought he might enjoy it more if I went along. Why don't you join us?'

Cheung shook his head. 'I'd like to, but I've been getting behind with the paperwork and I'm supposed to be dining with the old Khan on Saturday night.'

'Suit yourself,' Drummond said.

Another two thousand. That brought the

total standing to his credit in the Bank of Geneva to £23,000. Two more trips plus the money Ferguson owed him and he'd have a straight £30,000. After that, he was finished. Time he had a rest. He leaned back in the seat, humming to himself and concentrated on his instruments as he took the Beaver slanting across the glacier and into the pass.

Moro galloped alongside the packhorses, whistling, slashing their bony rumps with the heavy leather riding whip. He urged his mount forward and entered the village first, clattering over the loose stones and dismounted outside his house.

The children had disappeared and the street was quite deserted as he stood there listening to the sound of the Beaver in the distance, drawing happily on the English cigarette Drummond had given him.

Doors opened in the houses along the street and one by one soldiers emerged in peaked caps and drab quilted jackets. As Moro turned, the door to his house opened and a young officer emerged. He wore a beautifully tailored riding coat with fur collar and the red star of the Army of the People's Republic gleamed brightly in his cap.

'I did well?' Moro said.

The young officer took the English cigarette from the Tibetan's lips and inhaled deeply. A sunny smile appeared on his face.

'Excellent. Really quite excellent.'

Moro nodded, the eager smile still firmly in place and together they stood there, listening to the sound of the Beaver fade into the pass.

2

House of Pleasure

Drummond emerged from the hot room, dropped his towel on the tiled floor and dived into the plunge bath, swimming down to touch the brightly coloured mosaic face of Kali, the Great Mother, staring blindly into eternity through the green water as she had done for a thousand years.

He surfaced and one of the house girls moved out of the steam and squatted at the side of the ancient bath, holding a tray containing a slender coffee pot and tiny cups. Drummond swam towards her and she handed him down a cup as he floated there in the water.

She was like all the rest of them, startlingly

beautiful, with delicate features and great kohl-rimmed eyes. Her green silken sari was saturated with steam, outlining to perfection the firm body, the curving breasts.

As Drummond sipped his coffee, he heard a harsh laugh somewhere near at hand and Hamid's great voice boomed between the walls. He was singing the first stanza of *Zukhmee-Dil*, a ballad immensely popular on the North-West Frontier, at one time the favourite march of the Khyber Rifles.

Wullud sureen shuftauloo-maunind duryah,
Ufsose! mun n'shinnah.

Drummond handed his cup back to the girl and threw the song back at the Pathan, translating into English.

There's a boy across the river with a
bottom like a peach, but, alas, I cannot
swim.

Hamid bellowed with laughter as he moved out of the steam, a towel about his waist. He was a Pathan of the Hazara tribe, dark-skinned, bearded. A handsome buccaneer of a man of six feet three with broad muscular shoulders.

He smiled hugely. 'Feeling better, Jack, headache gone?'

'Ready for anything,' Drummond replied.

'Me, too.' The Pathan ran his fingers through the long hair of the girl who still squatted at the side of the bath. 'A good song, that, but where love's concerned, I'm the old-fashioned kind.'

He pulled the girl to her feet and the damp sari parted exposing her left breast. 'Now there's a thing.' He swung her up into his arms and grinned down at Drummond. 'See you later.'

Drummond swam lazily across to the other side of the bath and back again. He repeated the process twice and then hauled himself out over the stone edge, smoothed by time. He picked up his towel, wrapped it around his waist and padded across the warm tiles.

The next room was long and narrow with a vaulted roof and lined with cubicles, some with curtains drawn. From one he heard Hamid's deep chuckle followed by the lighter laughter of the girl and smiled to himself.

He went into the end cubicle, pulled the bell cord in the corner, climbed on to the stone massage slab and waited. After a while, the curtain was drawn and Ram Singh, the proprietor, entered followed by several bearers carrying buckets of hot and cold water.

The Hindu smiled. 'All is in order, Mr Drummond?'

'You've made a new man of me,' Drummond said. 'We could do with you in Sadar.'

The Hindu rolled his eyes to heaven in simulated horror. 'The end of the world, Mr Drummond. The end of the world. I will send Raika.'

He withdrew and Drummond lay there staring up at the ceiling. *The end of the world*. Well, that wasn't far off as a description of Sadar. A capital city with a population of three thousand, which gave some idea of the size of Balpur itself. A barren, ugly land, harsh and cruel as its inhabitants. The last place God made. Well, not for much longer, Praise be to Allah.

The curtain rustled and when he turned his head, Raika had entered. She was strikingly beautiful and wore a ruby in one nostril and great silver ear-rings with little bells on the end that tinkled when she moved her head.

Her sari was of blue silk threaded with gold and outlined every curve of her graceful body. Drummond nodded, and without speaking she started to work.

First came the hot rinse, water so scalding that he had to stifle the cry of pain that rose in his throat. She worked on his limbs to start with, first with the brushes and then with practised hands, loosening taut muscles, relaxing him so completely that he seemed to be floating, suspended in mid-air.

And as always, he was amazed at the matter-of-factness of it all, the lack of overt sensuality. But then this was India where life and death, love and the flesh, were all a part of one great mystery.

She sluiced him down again with another

bucket of hot water that was followed immediately by one so cold it drew the breath from his body. He gasped and there was a glint of laughter in her eyes, barely contained, so that at once she became real, a creature of flesh and blood.

She leaned over him, the damp sari gaping to the waist and Drummond cupped a hand over one sharply pointed breast. She went very still and stayed there in that position, leaning across him, her hand still reaching for the brush.

Drummond stared up at her, the nipple hardening against his palm and something stirred in her eyes. Her head came down slowly, the mouth slightly parted, and as he slid his free hand up around her neck, there was a discreet cough at the entrance.

Raika stood back at once completely unconcerned, and Drummond sat up. Ram Singh peered through the curtain, an anxious frown on his face.

'So sorry, Mr Drummond, but there is a person to see you.'

Drummond frowned. 'A person?'

'A Miss Janet Tate.' Ram Singh laughed nervously. 'An American lady.'

'In this place?'

Hamid appeared at the Hindu's shoulder, a cigarette in his mouth. 'A day for surprises, Jack. Any idea who she is?'

'There's one way of finding out.'

Drummond tightened the towel around his waist, left the cubicle and went into the next room. It was beautifully furnished with heavy carpets, low divans and round brass coffee tables at which several clients were relaxing after the rigours of the bath.

He crossed the room followed by Hamid and the Hindu, knelt on a divan and peered through the latticed partition of wrought iron into Ram Singh's office.

Janet Tate stood at the desk, examining a figurine of a dancer. She put it down, turned and looked around her with interest, moving very slowly across the floor, incredibly lovely in the yellow dress, the long, shoulder-length black hair framing her calm face.

Hamid sighed softly. 'A houri from Paradise itself, sent to delight us.'

Drummond straightened, a frown on his face. 'Get me a robe, will you?'

The Hindu was back in a moment and helped him into it. 'Aren't you going to dress first?' Hamid said.

Drummond grinned. 'My curiosity won't allow me to wait that long.'

When he opened the door and stepped into the office, Janet Tate was examining a tapestry hanging on one wall. She turned quickly and stood quite still.

The man who faced her was about forty, the crisp black hair already greying a little at the temples. He was perhaps six feet in height, well built with good, capable hands. She noticed them particularly as he fastened the belt of his robe.

But it was the face that interested her, the slight ironic quirk to the mouth of someone who laughed at himself and other people too much; the strong, well-defined bones of the Gael. Not handsome, the ugly, puckered scar running from the right eye to the corner of the mouth had taken care of that, but the eyes were like smoke slanting across a hillside on a winter's day and she was aware of a strange, inexplicable hollowness inside her.

'Mr Drummond? I'm Janet Tate.'

She didn't hold out her hand. It was as if she was afraid to touch him, afraid of some elemental contact which, at this first moment, she might be unable to control.

And then he smiled, a smile of such devastating charm that the heart turned over inside her. He shook his head slowly. 'You shouldn't have come here, Miss Tate. It's no place for a woman.'

'That's what the man at the hotel told me,' she said. 'But they have girls here. I saw two as I came in.'

And then she realised and her eyes widened. Drummond helped himself to a cigarette from a sandalwood box on the desk. 'What can I do for you?'

'I'm trying to get to Sadar. I believe you might be able to help.'

He frowned his surprise. 'Why on earth do you want to go to Sadar?'

'I'm a nurse,' she said. 'I've been sent here by the Society of Friends to escort the Khan of Balpur's young son to our Chicago hospital. He's to undergo serious eye surgery there.'

And then Drummond remembered. Father Kerrigan had told him about it before leaving. But the old priest had said they were expecting a doctor.

'So you're a Quaker.'

'That's right,' she said calmly.

'First visit to India.'

She nodded. 'I've just finished a two-year tour of service in Vietnam. I was on my way home on leave anyway, so the Society asked me to make a detour.'

'Some detour.'

'You can take me?'

Drummond nodded. 'No difficulty there. I fly a Beaver, there's plenty of room. Just one other passenger – Major Hamid, Indian Army adviser in Balpur, not that they have much of an army for him to advise. We'll take off about four-thirty, make an over-night stop at Juma and fly on through the mountains to Sadar in the morning. Much safer that way.' He crushed his cigarette into the

Benares ashtray. 'If you'll hang on, I'll go and dress.'

He started for the door and she said quickly, 'I was forgetting, I have a message for you from a Mr Ferguson.'

When he turned, it was the face of a different man, cold, hard, wiped clean of all expression, the eyes like slate.

'Ferguson? Where did you meet Ferguson?'

'On the train from Calcutta. He was very kind to me. He wants you to call on him at the usual place before you leave.' She smiled brightly. 'It all sounds very mysterious.'

An invisible hand seemed to pass across his face and he smiled again. 'A great one for a joke, old Ferguson. I shan't be long.'

He left her there and hurried through the other room to the changing cubicles where he dressed quickly in a cream nylon shirt, knitted tie and single-breasted blue suit of tropical worsted.

When he returned to the office, Hamid was sitting on the edge of the desk, Janet in the chair beside him looking up, a smile on her face.

Drummond was aware of a strange, irrational jealousy as he moved forward. 'I see Ali's managed to make his own introductions, as usual.'

'If I must be formally introduced, then I must.' Hamid grinned down at Janet. 'Jack was at one time a Commander in the Navy. He's never got over it. They're very correct, you know.'

He jumped to his feet and stood there waiting for Drummond to speak, a handsome, challenging figure in his military turban and expertly tailored khaki drill uniform, the medal ribbons a bright splash of colour above his left breast pocket.

Drummond sighed. 'Trapped, as usual. Miss Janet Tate, may I present Major Ali Mohammed Hamid, D.S.O., a British decoration, you'll notice. Winchester, one of our better public schools, and Sandhurst. Rather more class than West Point, don't you think?'

Hamid took her left hand and raised it to his lips gallantly. 'See how the British have left their brand on us, clear to the bone, Miss Tate?'

'Don't look at me,' Drummond said. 'I'm a Scot.'

'The same thing,' Hamid said airily. 'Everyone knows it's the Scots who rule Britain.'

He gave his arm to Janet and they moved out into the bright, hot sunshine. Across the square, there was a low wall and beyond it, the river, usually two miles wide at this point, but as always when winter approached, narrowing to half a mile or less, winding its way through endless sandbanks.

'Is this still the Ganges?' Janet asked.

'Ganges, Light amid the Darkness, Friend of the Helpless. It has a thousand names,' Hamid said as they strolled towards the low wall. 'To bathe in her waters is to be purified of all sin, or so the Hindus believe.'

Janet leaned on the wall and looked down the cobbled bank into the in-shore channel at the brown, silt-laden water. 'It looks pretty unhealthy to me.'

Drummond lit a cigarette and leaned beside her. 'Strangely enough, it does seem to have health-giving properties. During religious festivals pilgrims drink it, often at places where the drains disgorge the filth of the town, but they never seem to suffer. Bottled, it keeps for a year. They say that in the old days when taken on board clipper ships in Calcutta, it outlasted all other waters.'

Down below at the river edge some kind of ceremony was taking place and she glanced up at Hamid. 'Can we go down?'

'But of course. Anything you wish.'

'Not me,' Drummond said. 'If I'm going to see Ferguson before we leave, I'd better be moving.' He glanced at his watch. 'It's almost two o'clock now. I'll see you back at the hotel at four.'

He moved away across the square quickly and Janet watched him go, a slight frown on her face. 'I believe Mr Ferguson said he was in the tea business.'

'That's right,' Hamid said. 'Jack has an air freight contract with him. Ferguson usually comes up to see him once a month. He has a houseboat lower down the river from here.'

'You said Mr Drummond was once a naval commander?'

'Fleet Air Arm.'

'He was a regular officer, then? He would have been too young to have been a full commander during the war.'

'Quite right.' The Pathan still smiled, but there was a slight, cutting edge to his voice, a look in the eye that warned her to go no further. 'Shall we go down?'

They stood on the edge of a small crowd and watched the ceremony that was taking place. Several people stood knee-deep in the water, the men amongst them stripped to the waist and daubed with mud. One of them poured ashes from a muslin bag into a larger paper boat. Another put a match to it and pushed the frail craft away from the bank, out into the channel where the current caught it. Suddenly, the whole boat burst into flames, and a moment later sank beneath the surface.

'What were they doing?' Janet asked.

'The ashes were those of a baby,' Hamid said. 'A man-child because the ceremony is expensive and not worth going through for a girl.'

'And they do this all the time?'

He nodded. 'It is every Hindu's greatest dream to have his ashes scattered on the waters of Ganges. Near here there is a *shamsan*, a burning place for the dead. Would you like to see it?'

'Do you think I can stand it?'

He smiled down at her. 'Two years in Vietnam, you said. If you can take that, you can take anything.'

'I'm not so sure.' She shook her head. 'India's different, like no other place on earth. Ferguson told me that and he was right.'

As they moved along the shore, she could smell woodsmoke, and up ahead there was a bullock cart, three or four people standing beside it.

As they approached, she gave a sudden gasp and moved closer to Hamid. A naked man was lying on a bed of thorns, eyes closed, his tongue protruding, an iron spike pushed through it. His hair and beard were matted and filthy, his body daubed with cowdung and ashes.

'A *saddhu*, a holy man,' Hamid said, throwing a coin into an earthenware jar that stood at the man's head. 'He begs from the mourners and prays for the souls of the dead.'

There was nothing to distinguish the place from any other stretch of the shore, no temples, no monuments. Only the ashes of old fires, the piles of calcined bones and here and there a skull, glaring blindly up at the sky.

The people by the fire laughed and joked with each other and as the flames roared through the criss-crossed logs of the funeral pyre in a sudden gust of wind, she caught the sweetly-sick, distinctive stench of burning flesh and her throat went dry, panic threatening to choke her.

She turned, stumbling against Hamid, and beyond him in the water something turned over in the shallows, a rotting body, arms trailing, a grey headed gull swooping down, beak poised to strike.

There was immediate concern on his face, and unconsciously he used her first name. 'Janet, what is it?'

'The smell,' she said. 'Burning flesh. I was in a village called Nonking north of Saigon last year. The Viet Cong made one of their night raids and set fire to the hospital.' She stared back into the past, horror on her face. 'The patients, we could only get half of them out. There are nights when I can still hear the screams.'

She was aware of his hand under her arm and they were climbing rapidly up the bank, across a narrow stone causeway. Suddenly, they moved into a different world, a place of colour and light, scarlet hibiscus and graceful palms.

They walked through trees along a narrow path and emerged on to a stone, loopholed terrace high above the river, a couple of ancient iron cannon still at their stations as they had been for three hundred ycars.

Hamid pushed her gently forward. 'And behold, said the genie . . .'

She gave an excited gasp and leaned across the wall. Between the sandbanks, hundreds of flamingoes paced through the shallows, setting the very air alight with the glory of their plumage. Hamid picked up a stone and tossed it down, and immediately the sky was filled with the heavy, pulsating beat of their wings as they lifted in a shimmering cloud.

He looked down at her gravely. 'Back there, death, Janet. Here, life in all its magnificence. They are both sides of the same coin. This you must learn.'

She nodded slowly and slipped her hand into his arm. Together, they walked back quietly through the trees without speaking.

Beyond the old quarter of the town, Drummond moved into an area of stately walled villas and beautiful gardens, the homes of rich merchants and government officials. A narrow path, fringed with eucalyptus trees, brought him to the river bank again.

A red houseboat was moored at the end of an old stone wharf about forty yards away and Ferguson's Sikh bearer squatted on the cabin roof. When he saw Drummond, he scrambled to the deck and disappeared below.

Drummond crossed the narrow gangway and stepped on to the deck which had been scrubbed to a dazzling whiteness. Several cane chairs and a table were grouped under an awning at the stern and as he sat down, the Sikh appeared with a tray containing a bottle of gin, ice-water and glasses. He placed the tray on the table and withdrew without speaking.

Drummond helped himself to a drink and walked to the stern rail, staring out across the river and thinking about Janet Tate, as a boat slipped by, sail bellying in the breeze.

There was a clink of a bottle against glass and when he turned, Ferguson was sitting at the table, pouring himself a drink.

'You're looking fit, Jack. Nothing like a steam bath to pull a man round after a hard night.'

'Hullo, Fergy, you old rogue,' Drummond said. 'I got your message. It was delivered in person at Ram Singh's House of Pleasure by a rather delectable little Quaker girl in a yellow dress.'

'God in heaven,' Ferguson said, astonishment on his face. 'She didn't, did she?'

'I'm afraid so.' Drummond sat down and took a cheroot from an old leather case. 'Her first visit to India, apparently. She's a lot to learn.'

'I found her travelling from Calcutta second class,' Ferguson said. 'Can you imagine that? What's all this about the Khan's son needing eye surgery?'

'The boy fell from his horse a month ago and took a nasty knock. The sight started to fail in the right eye, so the old man had me fly a specialist up from Calcutta. He's got a detached retina and his balance has been affected.'

'Tricky surgery to put that right.'

'It seems the big expert's on the staff of some Quaker foundation hospital in Chicago. Father Kerrigan got in touch with them and they agreed to take the case. Said they'd send a doctor to escort the boy.'

'Instead, you get Janet Tate.'

'Who was already in Vietnam and due home on leave, so they saved on the fare.' Drummond grinned. 'Never look a gift horse in the mouth, Fergy.'

Ferguson frowned slightly. 'She's a nice girl, Jack. A hell of a nice girl. I wouldn't like to see her get hurt.'

'So?' Drummond said coolly.

Ferguson sighed. 'All right, let it go. What have you got for me this time?'

Drummond took several spools of film from his pocket and pushed them across. 'That's the lot. You've got the whole Balpur-Tibet border region now.'

'You've finished?'

Drummond nodded. 'Trip before last. A good job, too. Cheung decided to fly in with me on the last trip, so I couldn't have set the camera up if I'd wanted to.'

Ferguson smiled and shook his head. 'Our Nationalist friends are still at it, are they? I wonder what Washington would say if they knew?'

'I couldn't care less,' Drummond said. 'A couple more trips and I'm through. I've told Cheung that already.'

Ferguson applied a match to the bowl of his old briar pipe and coughed as the smoke caught at the back of his throat. 'How did you find things last trip? Any signs of Chinese activity?'

'Swinging on the end of a rope,' Drummond said. 'Moro and his band dealt with a cavalry patrol in their own inimitable fashion, that's all.'

'Nothing else? You're sure about that?'

Drummond nodded. 'Moro says that all the activity's still in the Aksai Chin, Ladakh region. No sign of any large scale interest in the Balpur border area at all.'

'That's strange, you know. They've claimed it officially and the brutal truth is they're on pretty firm ground this time, historically speaking.'

'They can have it, for all I care,' Drummond said. 'Another month, and I'm out.'

Ferguson poked a match into the end of his pipe to clear the air hole and said casually, 'What were you thinking of doing?'

'Nothing you'd be interested in. I'm finished, Fergy. I've had enough. How long have I given you now; four years, five? I've played this sort of game on every border from Sarawak to Kashmir. I can't go on forever. Nobody can.'

'You've done a good job, Jack. I'm not denying that,' Ferguson said. 'But you've been well paid.'

'What about last year when the Indonesians shot me down in Borneo?' Drummond reminded him. 'They chased me through that jungle for three weeks before I managed to scramble across the border.' He ran a finger down the ugly scar that stretched from his right eye to the corner of his mouth. 'I spent a month in hospital and what happened? You paid me the same as always. No more, no less.'

Ferguson sighed, took an envelope from his pocket and pushed it across. 'Three thousand, deposited as usual with your Geneva bankers. You know how to get in touch with me if you change your mind.'

'That'll be the day.' Drummond opened the envelope, examined the deposit slip, then put it in his wallet. 'It's been fun, Fergy.'

He moved along the deck to the gangplank and stepped on to the wharf. 'One more thing, Jack,' Ferguson called. 'Don't forget who the Beaver belongs to when you've finished up there. Government property, you know.'

'And just how would you like to set about proving that?' Drummond said and started to laugh as he walked away along the wharf.

3

The Nightwalkers

Janet stepped out of the shower, dried herself quickly and went into the bedroom, the towel wrapped around her slim body. The window to the terrace was open and she stood in the shadows and looked out.

A bank of cloud rolled away from the moon and Juma was bathed in a hard white light, flat-roofed houses straggling down to the river below. The night sky was incredibly beautiful with stars strung away to the horizon where the mountains lifted uneasily to meet them.

It was peaceful and quiet, a dog barking hollowly somewhere in the night. In the streets below, she could see torches flaring and then a drum started to beat monotonously, joined a moment later by some stringed instrument, and the sound of laughter drifted up on the warm air.

There was a discreet tap on the door and she called quickly, 'Who is it?'

'Ali – can I speak to you for a moment?'

She pulled on her dressing gown, fastened the cord and opened the door. Hamid came in, resplendent in his best uniform.

'How are you feeling?'

'Fine. I slept for an hour, then had a shower.'

'Good.' He hesitated and then went on apologetically. 'I'm sorry about this, Janet, but I'm afraid I'd already arranged something for this evening.' He glanced at his watch. 'As it is, I'm pressed for time.'

'A lady?'

'I hope not,' he said solemnly.

She chuckled. 'You're quite incorrigible. Better not keep her waiting.'

'Jack went out to the airstrip to check on some cargo we're taking with us tomorrow. Motor spares, I think. He shouldn't be more than half an hour.'

She listened to the sound of his footsteps fade along the narrow passage and then closed the door. She stood with her back to it, a slight frown on her face and then walked slowly across to the window.

The drumming was louder now, an insistent throbbing that filled the night and someone was singing in a high, reedy voice, hardly moving from one note to another, monotonous and yet strangely exciting.

She hurried across to the bed, opened her second suitcase and took out a sleeveless black dress in heavy silk that she had purchased in a moment of weakness in Saigon. She held it against herself for a moment in the mirror, and then smiled and started to dress. When she was ready, she pulled on a white linen duster coat against the night air, wound a silk scarf around her head and went downstairs.

The Hindu night clerk dozed at his desk, but came awake at once when she touched him lightly on the shoulder. 'I want to go to the airstrip. Can you get me a *tonga*?'

'Certainly, memsahib. Come this way.'

He took her out through the entrance and

down the steps to the street. A light, two-wheeled *tonga* was parked at the kerb, a magnificent affair, a beautiful, high-stepping horse between the shafts, his brass harness gleaming in the lamplight.

The driver squatted on the pavement, chatting to an old beggar, but he sprang to his feet at once and ran forward. The Hindu desk clerk handed Janet in, gave the man his destination and then moved away.

The sky was scattered with the fire of a million stars, the moon so large that it seemed unreal like a paste-board cut-out. The wind blew in through the darkness carrying the last heat of the day across the river and she breathed deeply, wondering what the night might bring, her body shaking with a strange, nervous excitement.

The airstrip was half a mile outside Juma on a flat plain beside the river. It was not an official stopping place for any of the big airlines and had been constructed by the R.A.F. as an emergency strip during the war.

There was one prefabricated concrete hangar still painted in the camouflage of wartime, and the plane squatted inside, the scarlet and gold of its fuselage gleaming in the light of a hurricane lamp suspended from a beam.

Drummond leaned against a trestle table beside a wall-eyed Bengali merchant named Samil, Cheung's agent in Juma, and watched two porters load the narrow boxes into the plane.

'What's in this one?' he asked, kicking a wooden crate that carried the neatly stencilled legend *Machine Parts, F. Cheung, Esq., Sadar, Sikkim.*

Samil produced a bunch of keys, unfastened the padlock which secured the lid of the crate and opened it. He removed a mass of cotton waste and revealed a layer of rifles, each one still coated in grease from the factory.

Drummond took one out. It was a Garrand automatic, a beautiful weapon. He examined it closely and frowned. 'What about this?' He indicated the legend, *United States Army* on the butt plate. 'A bit stupid, isn't it? I don't think our American friends would be amused.'

'That's what they sent me this time,' Samil shrugged. 'Surplus stock always comes cheaper, you should know that.'

'Somehow, I don't think Cheung is going to like it.' He raised the Garrand, took an imaginary sight out of the door and stiffened suddenly as Janet Tate moved out of the shadows.

'What in the hell are you doing here?' he demanded.

'I'm sorry,' she said, her face serious. 'Hamid's gone off for the night. Before he left he called and told me you were out here. I thought you might like to take me to dinner or something.'

'Exactly what I intended to do.'

The two porters had stopped working and glanced at Samil uncertainly. Drummond was still holding the Garrand in both hands, close to his chest and Janet said gravely, 'Hamid said he thought you were loading motor spares.'

He put the rifle back with the others, wiped his hands clean on a lump of cotton waste and nodded to Samil. 'You finish up here. Nothing to worry about. I'll handle it.'

He turned, straightening his tie. 'How did you get here?'

'I came in a *tonga* from the hotel. I told the driver to wait.'

'Shall we go, then?'

He took her arm, aware of the stiff restraint, the tilt of her chin and knew that in some way he had disappointed her. In the *tonga* she sat silently in her corner, as far away from him as possible and Drummond chuckled.

'I'm sorry to spoil the image of the big bad gunrunner for you, but Ali knows damn well what I fly up to Sikkim in boxes labelled Machine Parts.'

She turned quickly in the darkness and he was aware of her perfume, delicate on the cool air.

'So does everyone else including the Khan himself.' He groped for her hand in the darkness and held it tight. 'Look, I'll tell you about it because it's coming to an end anyway and because I don't want my dinner spoiled. I've been looking forward to it.'

'Go on,' she said.

'There's a Chinese gentleman called Cheung up at Sadar. He's been there for six or seven months now. He's supposed to be a general merchant, but he happens to be an agent of the Chinese Nationalist Government on Formosa. He supplies the guns and I run them over the border into Tibet.'

'To help Tibetan guerrilla fighters against the Communist government?'

'Exactly.'

She reached over and touched his arm, the breath going out of her in a gentle sigh. 'Oh, Jack. I'm so glad.'

'Well that's a hell of a thing for a clean living Quaker girl to say,' he said. 'And don't go putting me on any pedestal. I do it for hard cash, not out of any political idealism.'

'You don't think the Tibetans stand any chance of winning then?'

He laughed harshly. 'Not in a thousand years. Their battle will be won or lost in other places. Vietnam, Malaysia, Sarawak, perhaps on the floor of the United Nations. But to hell with that. Where would you like to eat?'

'Somewhere full of colour, not just a tourist trap. I want to see the real India.'

'Good for you. We'll make a woman of you yet.'

They were moving into the centre of Juma now and he tapped the driver on the shoulder and told him to stop. 'We'll walk from here. You want to see the real India, I'll show it to you.'

He paid the driver, took her arm and they moved along the street. As they neared the centre, it became busier and busier. Vendors of cooked food squatted inside their wooden stalls beside charcoal fires, busy with their pans, the scent of spices and cooked meats pungent on the cooling air.

And then they turned into the old quarter where lamps hung from the houses and the bazaar was even more crowded than during the daylight hours as people walked abroad to savour the cool night air.

The pavements were jammed with wooden stalls, overflowing with masses of paper flowers, shoddy plastic sandals imported from Hong Kong, aluminium pots and pans looking somehow incongruous and out of place.

Craftsmen sat cross-legged in their booths behind the stalls of the brass merchants, still plying their ancient craft next to the silversmiths and the garment-makers where they embroidered dancing girls' clothes.

There were Bohara carpets, rugs from Isfahan and, at the far end, prostitutes waiting in their booths, unveiled and heavily painted, and even here the curtain of night, the flickering lamps shining on cheap bangles and jewellery, cloaked the filth and disease, the squalor of the daylight hours.

They moved on, Drummond pushing to one side the numerous beggars who whined for alms, and finally turned into a narrow, quiet street leading to the river. Faintly on the night air, Janet could hear music. It grew louder and then they came to a narrow arched door.

'You wanted India? Well, this is it,' Drummond said.

They went along a narrow passage and came out on to a small landing at the head of a flight of steps overlooking a large, square room. It was crowded with Indians, mainly men, most of them wearing traditional dress. They were all eating hugely and talking loudly at the same time.

In the centre on a raised platform, a young, womanish *tabla* player, eyes rimmed with kohl, beat his drums with an insolent skill, looking around at the crowd as he did so, a bored and haughty expression on his face. His companion, an older man in baggy white trousers, three-quarter length black frock coat buttoned to the neck, looked strangely formal and played the *zita*, his fingers moving across the strings with incredible dexterity.

A small, neat Hindu in scarlet turban, his eyes flickering towards Janet with frank admiration, approached with a ready smile. 'A table, Mr Drummond? You wish to dine?'

'A booth, I think,' Drummond told him.

They threaded their way between the

tables, all eyes turning towards Janet and gasps of admiration, even clapping, followed them to their booth.

They sat facing each other across a small brass table, a bead curtain partially obscuring them from the other diners and Drummond ordered.

It was a simple meal, but superbly cooked. Curried chicken so strong that Janet gasped for breath, swallowing great draughts of cold water, thoughtfully provided by the proprietor, to cool her burning mouth. Afterwards, they had green mangoes soaked in syrup, followed by Yemeni *mocha*, the finest coffee in the world, in tiny, exquisite cups.

'Satisfied?' he asked her as he lit a cheroot.

She nodded, her eyes shining. 'Marvellous, I wouldn't have missed it for anything.'

'There's a floor show of sorts,' he said. 'Do you want to see it? Not exactly the Copacabana, I warn you.'

There was an unmistakable challenge in his voice and she responded immediately. 'I've never refused a dare since I was old enough to walk.'

'Suit yourself.'

There was a sudden roll on the drum, the lights dimmed a little and there was silence. There was an atmosphere of expectancy that she could sense at once and then a gentle, universal sigh echoed through the room.

A woman stepped through a curtain at the rear and poised for a moment, a dark silhouette against the light. 'Saida! Saida!' the name echoed faintly through the crowd.

'One of the few great *nautch* dancers left,' Drummond whispered to Janet. 'She's fifty if she's a day, but you'd never guess it.'

The right arm extended slowly and a tiny, tinkling cymbal sounded. Immediately the musicians responded on the *tabla* and *zita* and Saida started to sway sensuously, moving into the centre of the room.

Her face was heavily painted, a symbolic mask that never changed expression, but the body beneath the swirling, silken veils was that of a young and vibrant girl.

Gradually, the music increased in tempo and she moved in time, swaying from side to side, discarding her veils one by one until she stood before them, naked except for a small, beaded girdle low across her loins.

She stood quite still as the music stopped and the audience waited. The *tabla* player's fingers broke into a fast monotonous tattoo and she started to sway, hands above her head, clapping rhythmically, and the audience swayed with her, clapping in time, crying aloud with delight.

Round and round the perimeter of the floor she moved, faster and faster, sweat glistening on her body, until, with a sudden fierce gesture, she ripped the girdle from her loins and flung herself forward on her knees, sliding to a halt in front of a large, richly dressed merchant who squatted on cushions before a low table with two companions.

There was another abrupt silence and then the drum sounded again, slower this time, the beat becoming more insistent each moment as she writhed sinuously, thrusting her pointed breasts at him, twisting effortlessly from knees to buttocks, sliding away from his grasping hands, sharp cries rising from the crowd.

And then he had her, fingers hooking into her buttocks. As the crowd roared its approval, the drum stopped. She twisted from his grasp, her oiled body slipping between his hands, ran across the floor and melted through the curtain.

The musicians started to play again on a more muted key and the audience returned to their food, discussing the performance with much laughter and joking. When Drummond turned to look at Janet, her face was strangely pale.

'I warned you,' he said. 'You wanted to see the real India and this is a country where sex is as much a part of daily life as eating and drinking, an appetite to be satisfied, that's all.'

'Do you believe that?'

'Depends what a man's looking for, doesn't it? Had enough?'

She nodded and he called for the bill and paid it. The room was by this time heavy with smoke and there was the sound of drunken laughter everywhere. As they threaded their way between the tables, eyes turned on Janet, there were winks and leers and sly nudges.

Someone stood up at the edge of the floor and made an obscene gesture. There was a roar of spontaneous laughter and as she turned her head, flushing angrily, she was aware of a hand on her right leg, sliding up beneath the skirt.

She cried out in rage and mortification and swung round. There were four men seated at a low table, three of them typical of a breed to be found the world over in spite of their turbans and loose robes, young, vicious animals, spoiling for trouble. The man who had grabbed at her was older with wild, drunken eyes in a bearded face. He wore a black outer robe threaded with gold and his hands were a blaze of jewels.

As his chin tilted, the mouth wide with laughter, her hand caught him full across the face. His head rocked to one side, there was a general gasp and the room was silent.

His head turned slowly and there was rage and madness in the eyes. As he grabbed at her coat, Drummond spun her to one side.

The bearded man was only half-way to his feet when Drummond's right foot swung into his crutch. The man screamed, doubling over, and Drummond raised a knee into the descending face, smashing the nose, sending him crashing back across the coffee table.

And the thing Janet couldn't understand was the silence. No one moved to stop them when Drummond turned, straightening his jacket, took her arm, and pushed her through the crowd to the stairs.

Outside in the street, he urged her on, turning and twisting through several alleys until, finally, they emerged on an old stone embankment above the river.

'Why the rush?' she said. 'Did you think they might follow us?'

'That's the general idea.' He lit a cheroot, the match flaring in his cupped hands to reveal the strong, sardonic face. 'The young squirt-about-town I treated so roughly back there happens to be the son of the town governor.'

'Will there be trouble?'

'Not the official kind, if that's what you

mean. He's got away with too much in the past for anyone to start crying over his ruined looks at this stage. He might put someone on to me privately, but I can handle that.'

'Did you really need to be so rough?'

'It never pays to do things by halves, not here. This isn't tourist India, you know. The only thing I'm sorry about is taking you there in the first place. I should have had more sense.'

'I'm not,' she said. 'You weren't responsible for what happened. To tell you the truth, I rather enjoyed myself.'

'Including the *nautch* dance?'

She laughed. 'I'll reserve my opinion on that part of the programme. It was very educational, mind you.'

'Something of an understatement. You know, you're quite a girl, and for someone who believes in turning the other cheek, you throw a good punch. You certainly rocked him back there.'

'A quick temper was always my besetting sin,' she said. 'My old grannie used to warn me about that when I was a little girl back home in Maine. Quakers are really quite nice when you get to know them. Flesh and blood, too.'

He grinned and took her arm. 'All right, I surrender. Let's walk.'

They went on to the beach below the embankment and strolled through the moonlight without talking for a while. Now and then, sandbanks collapsed into the water with a thunderous roar and cranes threshed through the shallows, disturbed by the noise.

Huge pale flowers swam out of the night, and beyond the trees the sky was violet and purple, more beautiful than anything she had ever seen before. They passed a solitary fisherman cooking a supper of fish over a small fire of dried cowdung and Drummond gave him a greeting in Urdu.

'What do you do in Balpur beside fly in guns for Mr Cheung?' she said after a while.

'Survey work for the Indian government, freight general cargo or passengers. Anything that comes to hand.'

'I shouldn't have thought there was much of a living in that.'

'There isn't but Cheung pays well for the Tibetan trips. And I'll be leaving soon, anyway. I've had enough of the place.'

'What's it like?'

'Balpur?' he shrugged. 'Barren, treacherous mountains. A capital of three thousand people that's more like an overgrown village. An army, if you can call it that, of seventy-five. When winter comes, it's absolute hell and that's in another month. The roads are the worst in the world at the best of times, but during the winter, they're completely snowed up.'

'What about the Khan?'

'An old mountain hawk, proud as Lucifer. Quite a warrior in his day. To his people, something very special. Not only king, but priest, and that makes for quite a distinction. You'll like Kerim, his son. A great pity about his accident. I hope your people in Chicago can fix him up all right.'

'He's eight, isn't he?'

'Nine in three months.'

'My instructions told me to get in touch with a Father Kerrigan when I arrive. Apparently he's in charge of all the arrangements.'

'You'll like him,' Drummond said. 'He's about sixty. A marvellous old Irishman who just won't give in. He's been twelve years in Sikkim and hasn't made a single convert and the people adore him. It's fantastic.'

'If he hasn't got a congregation, what does he do with himself?'

'As it happens, he's a qualified doctor. Runs a small mission hospital about a mile outside of Sadar, completely on his own. There's one other European up there, a man called Brackenhurst. A geologist for some British firm or other. They've also made him British Consul, but don't let that impress you. It doesn't mean a thing.'

'You don't like him, I take it?'

'Not much.'

He stopped to light another cheroot and she said casually, 'Why did you leave the Navy, Jack?'

He paused, the match flaring in his fingers, his eyes dark shadows. 'You really want to know?'

She didn't answer and he shrugged, flicking the match into the night. 'They kicked me out, or advised me to leave, which comes to the same thing for a career officer.'

She could sense the pain in his voice and put a hand on his arm instinctively. 'What happened?'

'I was a Fleet Air Arm pilot during the Korean War. One bright morning in July, 1952, I took my squadron to the wrong target. When we left, it was a smoking ruin. We did a good job. We managed to kill twenty-three American marines and ten Royal Marine Commandos who had been serving with them.'

There was bewilderment in her voice. 'But how could such a thing happen?'

'The briefing officer gave me the wrong information.'

'So it wasn't your fault?'

'Depends how you look at it. If I'd checked my orders more carefully, I'd have spotted the mistake. I was too tired, that was the trouble. Overtired. Too many missions, not enough sleep. I should have grounded myself weeks before, but I didn't.'

'So they couldn't court-martial you?'

'A quiet chat with someone with gold rings

all the way up to his elbow, that's all it took. I got the message.'

'I'm sorry, Jack. Sorrier than I can say.'

Her voice was warm and full of sympathy. They had reached a flight of stone steps leading up from the shore and he paused and looked at her.

Her mouth opened to cry a warning and he ducked, turning to meet the rush of feet from the darkness.

A fist grazed his cheek, he lost his balance and rolled over and over, hands protecting his genitals as feet swung in viciously.

He sprang up and backed to the wall. There were three of them, dark, shadowy figures in tattered robes, scum from the market place hired for a few rupees. Above them on the steps below the lamp, stood the man from the cafe, supported by two of his friends, blood on his face.

A knife gleamed dully and Janet ran in past the three men to join Drummond against the wall. 'Kill him!' the bearded man cried. 'Kill the swine!'

Drummond was tired. It had been a long

evening. His hand disappeared inside his coat reaching to the leather holster on his left hip and reappeared holding a Smith & Wesson .38 Magnum revolver with a three-inch barrel.

He fired into the air and there was a sudden stillness. 'Go on, get out of it!' he shouted angrily and fired a shot towards the man on the steps that ricocheted into the night.

The men from the market place were already running away along the shore, cursing volubly, and the governor's son and his two friends staggered into the darkness.

Drummond slipped the revolver back into its holster and looked down at her calmly. 'You know, I really think it's time we went back to thc hotcl, don't you?'

She started to tremble uncontrollably and he reached out, pulling her into his arms. 'It's all right. Everything's all right now.'

He stroked her hair gently with one hand and his lips brushed her forehead. In the heavy stillness of the night, she could almost hear her heart beating. When he tilted her chin and kissed her gently on the mouth, it was like nothing she had ever known before.

He slipped her arm in his without speaking, and together they went up the steps to the embankment.

4

The Last Place God Made

The air was bumpy as they flew out of the pass for a forty-knot wind was blowing across the mountains. They climbed through a heat haze that was already blurring the horizon and levelled out at 9,000 feet to cross the mountains between India and Balpur.

Janet Tate was in the front passenger seat beside Drummond and Hamid sat behind her. She was wearing a white blouse, collar turned down over the neck of a cashmere sweater, cream whipcord slacks and a sheepskin coat that Drummond had provided.

Hamid poured coffee into a plastic cup and handed it to her. 'We're moving into Balpur now,' he said. 'The mountains to the east are in Bhutan with Assam far beyond in the haze. The Chinese broke through in strength there in 1962.'

'Were you there?'

He shook his head. 'No, I was on the Ladakh front in the north-west.'

'It was supposed to be pretty bad up there, wasn't it?'

'A vision from hell,' he said grimly. 'Can you imagine what it's like trying to live at 20,000 feet, never mind fight? The mules died of asthma, the men of pulmonary oedema. You've heard of it, I suppose.'

She nodded. 'The lungs fill with water, don't they?'

'An ironic way for a man to die in battle – by drowning. We could never get them down to the base hospitals in time for treatment, that was the trouble.'

'Hadn't you any air support, helicopters?'

He laughed harshly. 'Until October, 1962, we hadn't needed them. The way of peace was the way for India.' He shook his head. 'No, we didn't have the necessary planes. Even if we had, there weren't the pilots.

Certainly not the kind who could fly in that sort of country. That's where I met Jack, you know.'

She turned to Drummond in surprise. 'You were flying for the Indian Army?'

'Five hundred quid a week,' he said. 'Good money by any standards.'

'Don't listen to him,' Hamid broke in. 'A game he plays. From Leh, he flew three operational flights a day into the Ladakh mountains to one small airstrip at 18,000 feet, taking in supplies and ammunition, bringing out the sick and wounded. In five weeks, he flew just over a hundred sorties, then collapsed and spent three weeks in hospital suffering from complete exhaustion. His contract called for five flights a week, no more.'

'He should have added that they didn't pay me for the time in hospital,' Drummond told her. 'That's the wily oriental for you.'

He increased speed and banked in a long, sweeping curve that took them out of a shallow pass and into a valley beyond. A broad river flowed sluggishly, snaking between jagged cliffs, a thread of silver in a landscape so savage and sterile that it took the breath away.

'Remember what I told you,' Drummond said. 'The last place God made. And to think the Chinese have laid claim to this bloody lot.'

'But why?' she said.

'The same psychology the Roman Emperors used,' Hamid told her. 'Give the mob circuses to take their minds off the more important problems. In China in 1962, the harvest was bad and thousands starved, so their army invaded India, a country completely unprepared for such an attack, and presented their people with a ready made victory. In Pekin, they were able to tighten their belts and wave banners.'

'Have they really laid claim to Balpur?'

'Along with almost every other border country. Actually, Balpur *was* a part of the Chinese Empire in ancient times. The people are Mongolian. Only the ruling class are Muslims, descendants of the original invaders. But no one seriously imagines that they would invade. For one thing, the old Khan has preferred to stay completely neutral. He's the only ruler of a border state who hasn't signed a mutual defence pact with India.'

'Yet he accepts you as an adviser?'

'To an army of seventy-five men. A political gesture only. In Pekin they laugh about it.'

She almost mentioned Mr Cheung, but remembering what Drummond had told her on the previous evening, kept silent. Even if Hamid did know the truth, that Cheung was in fact a Chinese Nationalist agent, that Drummond was flying in guns to Tibetan guerrilla fighters, he would probably prefer to know nothing officially. Remembering Vietnam, she sighed heavily. The same pattern, violence, blood and suffering turning on each other in a circle that had no ending.

They were flying at no more than a thousand feet above the floor of the valley and suddenly, in a bend of the river, she saw Sadar, flat-roofed houses scattered untidily across a broad plateau, the Khan's palace like a fortress in a walled garden.

The Beaver banked tightly and swept in past the graceful tower of a mosque, and beyond the town on the plain to the south she could see the airstrip, a narrow slot laboriously carved out of the rough terrain, a windsock on a tall pole at one end. Drummond circled once then turned into the wind for a perfect landing between two rows of empty oil drums.

There was a small improvised hanger constructed of rusting corrugated iron, barely large enough to house the Beaver from the look of it. He taxied towards it and switched off the engine.

He unfastened his seat belt, jumped to the ground and turned to give Janet a hand. At the same moment, a Land Rover appeared from among the houses on the edge of the town and came towards them in a cloud of dust.

She shivered and wrapped her sheepskin coat more tightly around her. 'It's colder than I thought it would be.'

'Winter coming,' Drummond said. 'Maybe it'll be early this year.'

An old army jeep, still painted in the grey-green camouflage of wartime, its canvas tilt patched and mended in many places, was parked inside the hangar. He and Hamid had just started to transfer the luggage to it from the plane when the Land Rover arrived.

Mr Cheung jumped out of the passenger seat and came towards them wearing a heavy blue quilted jacket and an astrakhan hat. His driver was a young fair-haired man with a bronzed, reckless face. He wore a sheepskin jacket in untanned hide and knee-length boots. A revolver, slung low on his right hip in a black holster, seemed theatrical and out of place.

He came forward with a ready smile, eyes fixed on Janet, and Hamid said maliciously, 'Why the gun, Tony? Expecting trouble?'

The young man flushed. 'I'm driving up to my base camp at Howeel for a couple of days. They'd cut your throat for the shoes on your feet up there. I've come for that new theodolite I ordered if Drummond's remembered to bring it.'

'It's in the plane,' Drummond said coldly. 'Help yourself.'

'So this is Miss Tate?' Cheung took both of her hands in his. 'We must try to make your stay a pleasant one.'

'You knew I was coming?'

Hamid grinned. 'I had Indian Army Headquarters in Juma send a signal to warn the Khan.'

Cheung nodded. 'Colonel Dil got the message last night by radio.'

'And probably told you before the Khan.'

Brackenhurst jumped down from the Beaver and turned to lift out a wooden case containing his theodolite. 'A hell of a lot of machine parts you seem to bring through these days,' he commented and turned to Janet before Drummond could reply. 'I'm Tony Brackenhurst, Miss Tate. I'm doing geological survey work up here, but I'm also the British Consul. If I can help you in any way, don't hesitate to ask.'

'She happens to be an American, so that's hardly likely,' Drummond said acidly.

Brackenhurst ignored him, holding her

hand for longer than was necessary, an eager smile on his lips, and it was the smile which betrayed him, somehow revealing an essential weakness, a lack of strength.

'Why, that's very kind of you, Mr Brackenhurst.'

'I'll be back in two days,' he said. 'You'll probably still be here from what they tell me of the boy's condition.'

He carried the theodolite across to the Land Rover and Cheung said quickly, 'I'll go back with him. You'll have enough in the jeep with the three of you and the luggage. You'll call on me this afternoon, Jack?'

'After lunch. I'll take Janet out to the mission first. Is the boy still out there?'

Cheung nodded and smiled down at her. 'And you, I will have the pleasure of seeing you again this evening, Miss Tate. The Khan is to give a small dinner party for you. He has honoured me with an invitation.'

'I'll look forward to that, Mr Cheung.'

The Land Rover moved back towards town and Drummond drove the jeep out of the hangar. He and Hamid pushed the Beaver inside and padlocked the door.

'I'll take Janet out to Father Kerrigan now. What about you, Ali?'

Hamid shrugged. 'You can drop me at Colonel Dil's headquarters. I'll probably see you both tonight at the palace unless the old boy's decided to change his usual guest list.'

They got into the jeep and Drummond drove towards the town, following the rutted track that did service as a road. He changed down, scattering a herd of goats, and they entered the outskirts of Sadar.

Janet looked about her with interest, but there was nothing of the gaiety and colour of Juma and Altaf here. The people were small, squat Mongolians with skins the colour of weathered parchment and slanting eyes. The men wore boots of untanned hide, baggy trousers and sheepskin jackets. Only a few sported the turban, the majority preferring conical sheepskin caps with earflaps. The women's attire differed in only one significant detail. Instead of the sheepskin jacket, they wore three-quarter length blanket coats of black and brown, relieved in some cases by a necklace of silver coins.

They were dour and unsmiling, drab as the rocky land that bred them. Even the children in the market place lacked the energy and humour of their Indian counterparts, and there was a strange absence of bustle and vitality as they drove through the bazaar.

'No one seems to smile,' Janet said. 'Have you noticed that?'

'This is a poor country,' Hamid told her. 'Anything they get has to be squeezed out of the very rocks. Life is hard, work from dawn till dusk. It leaves little time for laughter.'

Across the square stood a barrack-like building, the flag of Balpur, a black eagle against a grey and gold background, lifting in the slight breeze above the entrance. Two sentries, almost incongruously smart in neat khaki uniforms and military turbans, presented arms as Drummond braked and Hamid got out.

He reached for his canvas grip and an orderly ran down the steps and relieved him of it. 'I'll see you tonight, then,' he said and his hand lifted in a brief salute.

The palace was a hundred yards further on and looked considerably less forbidding than it had done from the air, wrought iron gates standing open to reveal a gravel drive, tall cypress trees fringing the wall, a profusion of greenery beyond to where a fountain lifted gracefully into the calm air.

'I must say that looks rather more inviting,' Janet remarked.

'Not surprising,' Drummond said. 'The Khan's a Muslim, remember. At least they know how to live.'

'What's the religion of his people generally?'

'A lot pay lip service to Islam and a great many still adhere to Buddhism, but in a bastardised form. And then there's a minority group of Hindus who've kept themselves apart over the centuries. Not more than two or three thousand in the entire country.'

They were by now moving out of the town again and the houses were more scattered, two-storeyed walled villas in the main, obviously the homes of the rich of Sadar, whoever they were.

Drummond slowed, swung the jeep in through an arched entrance and braked to a halt in the courtyard of a small bungalow surrounded by a walled garden.

'This is my place,' he said. 'If you don't mind hanging on, I'll drop my things and be straight out again.'

As he got out, a small, greying woman, swathed in a dark robe, her face seamed and wrinkled, opened the front door and moved out on to the verandah inclining her head in greeting, hands together, Indian style.

'Your housekeeper?' Janet asked.

He nodded and reached for his canvas holdall. 'I won't be a minute.'

'Mind if I come in?' she said. 'I'd love to see inside.'

He hesitated perceptibly and then shrugged. 'If you'd like to, but there really isn't much to see.'

She followed him up the steps. At the top, he murmured something quickly to the old woman who went back in, then stood to one side. 'After you.'

She found herself in a narrow entrance hall with rough cast walls and a floor of polished wood. He opened a door to the right and she moved into the main living room. There was a great stone fireplace, skin rugs on the wood floor and the furniture was of the simplest; a dining table, several easy chairs and a couple of shelves of books.

'I'll be with you in a minute,' Drummond said and he crossed the room and went through another door.

She walked slowly around the room, examining everything and paused at the bookshelves. There was a small figurine of a dancer on the table beneath, carved from some dark wood of incredible hardness. She picked it up and examined it closely. The breasts were of a ripeness that was almost lifelike, hands extended in a ritualistic pose, the unsmiling, grave face fixed for all eternity. There was a slight sound from behind and she swung round and found a woman standing in the doorway to the hall.

Like the old housekeeper she was an Indian, but quite young with a pale, flawless complexion, set off to perfection by her scarlet sari. There was a silver rope necklace around her neck, gold bracelets on the wrists and her dark eyes were rimmed with kohl.

In that same moment, Drummond came in from the bedroom. He said something quietly in Urdu and the girl turned at once and disappeared into the hall.

'Who was that?' Janet said.

'The old girl's daughter, Famia.' He took the figurine gently from her hands. 'You like this?'

'Yes, is it very old?' she replied automatically.

'Greco-Buddhist. Probably second century. You'll find things like this all over Balpur. As I said before, Buddhism used to be very strong up here, real Buddhism, I mean. Monasteries all over the place.'

'Are there any left?'

'One or two.' He glanced at his watch. 'We'd better get moving. It's almost eleven o'clock and Father Kerrigan holds his daily surgery at half-past. We'll try and catch him before it starts.'

They went out to the jeep and he handed her in and drove away as if nothing had happened. But things were not the same and there was a constraint between them that had not been present before.

Janet remembered the girl, her shapely body, the pale beauty of her skin against the scarlet sari, and a burning anger took possession of her that she found impossible to analyse.

The mission was on a hill above the river. It was a long, low, flat-roofed building, walled in by grey stone, as seemed to be the custom with all houses in this stark country, and the tiny belfry of a small chapel reared above it.

Flocks of goats, sheep and a few small horses grazed on the sparse grass at the entrance, and thirty or forty people waited patiently, squatting on the ground or leaning against the wall.

As Drummond slowed the jeep to drive

through, Janet leaned out, her trained eye quickly taking in the evidence of disease. Rickets and ringworm in the children, old people with faces eaten away by yaws, eyes encrusted with dried pus and, here and there, a broken limb held awkwardly in a crude bandage.

'He doesn't handle all this on his own?' she demanded, turning to Drummond as they drove in through the entrance and braked at the bottom of a flight of stone steps.

He switched off the engine and nodded. 'Don't ask me how, but he does. Has an old woman to do the cooking, but that's all. Here she comes now.'

The woman who opened the front door and came out into the porch had the same ageless Mongolian face as the people in the market place, but wore a long cotton skirt and an Indian Army issue khaki sweater with cloth epaulets. The red scarf around her head and gold ear-rings made her look like a gypsy.

Drummond went up the steps with Janet's two cases, put them down and spoke to her in slow, careful English. He came back down the steps and took Janet's arm.

'He's in the chapel.'

They crossed the courtyard to the tiny, grey-stone building, he opened the heavy wooden door and they went inside. The lights were very dim, and down by the altar the candles flickered and the statue of the Holy Mother seemed to float out of the darkness.

Father Terence Kerrigan knelt in prayer, his rugged, stubborn old Irish face momentarily relaxed, almost childlike in its purity, his white hair gleaming like silver. When he crossed himself and got to his feet, she saw that he was a big man, built like a tree with shoulders as wide as Hamid's.

He turned, narrowing his eyes shortsightedly when he saw them there in the shadows and came forward with a ready smile.

'Jack, is it yourself, and this will be Miss Tate?' He took her hands in his, holding them tightly. 'It's good to see you here, my dear. I got word from Colonel Dil that you were coming in today. He had a message last night from Ali Hamid over the radio.'

'I feel like a fraud, Father,' she said. 'I believe you were expecting a doctor.'

'Nonsense, my dear, a qualified nursing sister with two years' experience in Vietnam refugee camps will do for me any day of the week.' He chuckled at her astonishment, 'Major Hamid is always most thorough.'

They crossed the courtyard, mounted the steps and went inside. The entrance hall had been turned into a dispensary, the stone walls whitewashed, drugs, medicines and equipment neatly arranged on white-painted shelves giving an overall impression of cleanliness and efficiency.

'This is where most of the work is done and as I'm the only qualified doctor in Balpur the pace is usually fast and furious.' He glanced at his watch. 'You'll see for yourself in precisely fifteen minutes.'

'What about my patient?' Janet asked.

'Kerim?' the old man sighed. 'Frankly, he's not been too marvellous. He's been staying here, of course, so that I can give him constant supervision. The Khan wanted me to take up residence at the palace, but naturally, I had to refuse. As I pointed out, I do have other patients.'

'And how is Kerim now?'

'Rather better. He's been very feverish, but we seen to be over the worst of that now. In any event, I think we should wait for a few days before contemplating such a long journey.'

'So Janet stays here?' Drummond said.

'If she can put up with a crotchety old fool.' Father Kerrigan smiled. 'Would you like to take a peep at Kerim?'

He led the way through into a narrow whitewashed passage and opened a door on the left. The boy looked very frail as he slept, head turned to one side on the white pillow, a heavy bandage crossing his right eye and they withdrew softly.

The priest opened the opposite door and ushered her into a small room, simply furnished with a narrow bed and wooden locker. The one touch of luxury was a large sheepskin rug on the floor. A french window opened on to a verandah overlooking an overgrown and neglected garden.

'The best I can do, I'm afraid,' he said apologetically.

'A palace compared to what I was used to in Vietnam.'

They returned to the dispensary and found Drummond standing at the door looking outside. The courtyard had filled with people, all squatting together in the dust, waiting patiently for the old priest to begin.

He took out his watch again and pursed his lips. 'Five minutes late. This will never do. I'll have to say goodbye for now, Jack. We'll be seeing you tonight at the palace, I imagine.'

'I expect so.'

Drummond turned to Janet, but she was touching Father Kerrigan on the arm as he moved away. 'Could I help, Father?'

The old man looked down at her searchingly and then a slow smile broke across his face. 'I'd be glad to have you, my dear. I'll find you a robe.'

She nodded briefly to Drummond. 'See you tonight, Jack.'

She turned away, different now, holding

herself straighter, competent, assured. She and the old man stood at the back of the dispensary, talking as she pulled on the white robe he had found for her, a strange intimacy between them.

Drummond turned abruptly, pushed his way through the crowd, climbed into the jeep and drove quickly away.

5

Dinner at the Palace

Through the french windows, the white balustrade of the terrace shimmered palely and the tall cypress trees were silhouetted against the evening sky. From the garden came the timeless, incessant chirping of the crickets.

Inside, the soft lamplight gleamed on delicate crystal decanters and silver and gold tableware, and the great ruby in the centre of the Khan's turban glowed dimly like an ember stirred by a soft wind.

He was seventy years of age, but carried himself well in his London tailored mohair and silk dinner jacket, and the face beneath the turban was still that of a warrior, proud and strong with the touch of arrogance of one born to rule.

He sat at the head of the table, Janet Tate on his left, and he turned to her with a smile, speaking in careful, precise English. 'More brandy, Miss Tate?'

'I don't think so, thank you.'

'A little more coffee, then?'

He snapped a finger and a servant came forward quickly. There were five of them at the table besides the Khan, Janet, supremely beautiful in her simple black silk dress, and Jack Drummond on her left in a white dinner jacket. Father Kerrigan sat on the Khan's right hand next to Mr Cheung, and Hamid and Colonel Sher Dil, commander of the Khan's small army, faced each other, magnificent in dress uniform.

'Father Kerrigan has made you comfortable, Miss Tate?' the Khan asked.

'He couldn't have done more.'

The Khan sighed. 'It would have pleased me to have had you as my guest here at the palace, but he is a stubborn old man.'

'And if that's true, then I know another

not a thousand miles from here,' the priest said, speaking with the familiarity of an old friend and reaching for the brandy decanter. 'Would you imagine it, Janet, he wanted me to forsake every other blessed patient I have, close the mission and move in here?'

The Khan shrugged helplessly. 'What can one do? He even refused the soldiers I sent. At this moment, who guards the Hope of Balpur?' he challenged the old priest.

'Tell me first who in Balpur would harm him,' Father Kerrigan countered.

The Khan sighed. 'You see, Miss Tate, I am not even ruler in my own house.'

'If you must know, old Nerida's sitting at the boy's bedside this very moment,' Father Kerrigan told him. 'She'd cut off her arm rather than move from that spot before I return.'

'You have seen Kerim today?' the Khan said to Janet. 'He is well?'

She nodded. 'But still a little weak. An injury of this kind is a great shock to the whole system, especially for a child.'

'A child who will be a man in another

three years, an important distinction. Under our customs, he must then be presented to the people, ready to take my place if need be. That is why I am anxious that he starts on the journey to America with as little delay as possible.'

'We must wait for another few days,' Father Kerrigan said. 'I'm sure Miss Tate agrees with me.'

The Khan glanced at Janet and she nodded. 'I think Father Kerrigan is right. And we've time to spare. Kerim can be back within a month of the operation, you know.'

He threw his arms wide. 'Then I must bow before the wind. You play chess, Miss Tate?'

'Not very well, I'm afraid.'

'Father Kerrigan considers himself a master. It is my painful and frequent duty to prove otherwise.'

'Indeed, so?' the priest said, pushing back his chair and rising, glass of brandy in hand. 'If your Highness would be good enough to lead the way to the usual place, we can get down to the business of making you eat your words.'

'A pleasure.' The Khan got to his feet and looked enquiringly at the others. 'Gentlemen?'

Hamid glanced at Drummond and Sher Dil. 'Billiards?'

They both nodded and Cheung smiled across at Janet. 'Which leaves Miss Tate and myself. With the Khan's permission, perhaps I could show her some of the treasures of the palace?'

'Please do. It should take me no longer than an hour to encompass the downfall of this turbulent priest.'

'Is that a fact, now?' Father Kerrigan said in mock anger and they went out.

Hamid, Sher Dil and Drummond had their heads together for a moment, something to do with a report over the radio from Indian Army Headquarters about patrol clashes in the Ladakh area. Cheung joined them and Janet moved to the window and looked into the garden.

It was very beautiful. Great, Grecian-style jars were spaced along the terrace, filled with dwarf iris, and the scent of hibiscus was heavy on the night air. Lower down in the shadows, the slender cypress trees stood like straight sentinels, dark against the sky, and the moon was full.

Cheung paused beside her. 'A startling contrast, isn't it? In here all the beauty in the world, a garden by night. Beyond those walls, a harsh, sterile land where even mere existence is a struggle.'

'Has it always been this way?'

He nodded. 'In the old days, the tribesmen raided into India like wolves. Their name was a byword for cruelty. But those days are gone. Now they must live off the land and the land has little to give.'

'Can nothing be done?'

He shrugged. 'Who knows? Brackenhurst may turn up with something in his survey, evidence of mineral deposits worth developing, perhaps. The Khan has his hopes, but I doubt if they will come to much. Brackenhurst would not be the first geologist to waste his time here.'

'And yet Hamid tells me the Chinese Government in Pekin has laid claim to Balpur.'

'And Nepal and Bhutan, even parts of Assam.' He shrugged. 'Words, merely words. But as a matter of interest, there can be little doubt that in other times Balpur *was* part of the Chinese Empire. Come, I will show you.'

They went back inside, moved into the central hall, and he opened another door. The room was in darkness. Janet heard the click of the switch, but was totally unprepared for what followed.

On every side a row of glass showcases, each with its own illumination, sprang into view to float in the darkness. But it was their contents which drew from her an involuntary gasp of admiration. They contained the most superb collection of pottery she had ever seen.

There were alabaster jars, pale, translucent and delicate, glazed urns in red and black, their colours as vivid as on the day they had been fired.

Most were unmistakably Chinese and others showed a distinct Chinese influence. There was also a collection of figurines like the one she had seen at Drummond's bungalow.

'Jack has one of these,' she said. 'He told me it was Greco-Buddhist.'

'That's right. As you're probably aware, Alexander the Great invaded India. Amazing to what extent Greek culture penetrated the entire border area and yet in India, their literature doesn't even mention his name.'

She reached out and touched a delicate and beautiful wine jar which had been painstakingly put together piece-by-piece to judge by the network of fine lines that covered it.

'Where was this discovered?'

'A burial mound south of the city near the river. There are many such sites. You must visit some of them while you are here. There is a most interesting ruin of a Buddhist temple not far from the mission. Breathtaking by moonlight. I can recommend it.'

He smiled charmingly and Janet, hesitating, was saved by Hamid who entered at that moment. 'There you are.'

'I thought you were playing billiards?' she said.

'A variation of our own, a sort of knock-out competition. Jack and Sher Dil were too good for me.'

'Mr Cheung was showing me the Khan's collection. I had no idea the Chinese had so much influence in this area in ancient times.'

'God knows why,' he said. 'The damned place must have been an economic liability even in those days.'

Cheung glanced at his watch. 'It's getting late. I really think I must be going. I leave Miss Tate in your capable hands, Major.'

He went out quickly and she turned to Hamid with a sigh. 'I feel rather sorry for him. We've been standing here talking about the splendours of China past and he isn't even permitted to be a part of China present. It must be a terrible thing to be an exile from one's own country.'

'The tragedy of the twentieth century,' Hamid said. 'Did you like him?'

'It's difficult to say. He puts himself out to be pleasant, but I feel that he's looking at me from behind his eyes if you know what I mean.'

'An excellent description. What about Sher Dil?'

'A wonderful man. He's so beautifully correct, so . . .'

She hesitated and Hamid chuckled. 'So positively British? The Imperial taint still lies heavy upon us. Sher Dil was a Sword of Honour man at Sandhurst in his day. He was also a colonel in the Indian Army as long ago as 1945.'

'What went wrong?'

'For many years we tried to follow the way of peace in India. Nehru was sure that such a neutrality would be respected by all. Many men like Sher Dil, high ranking regular army officers, were not so sure and said so. When the army was reduced, they were the first to go.'

'And so Sher Dil came here?'

'To command an army of seventy-five men for the Khan, most of them recruited in India. The locals don't take kindly to uniforms.' He laughed. 'But a night like this is made for love and laughter and nothing else. I will show you the delights of the garden.'

'Which Mr Cheung has already done.'

'Not with my superb efficiency.'

They left the display room and moved out to the terrace, pausing at the top of a flight of shallow steps for Hamid to light a cigar.

The moon was caught in the dark meshes of the cypress trees, the night air heavy with the scent of flowers and a fountain splashed into a fish pool amongst the trees as they went down the steps, her hand on his arm.

'The Hour of the Dove they call it.' He waved a hand theatrically. 'The time for lovers to unburden their hearts to each other.'

They came to the fountain in the centre of the garden and she sat on the low wall that ringed the pool, dabbling her hand in the water, and somewhere a bird called sweetly through the night.

'This place is like finding the Garden of Eden in the wilderness. How does he do it?'

'An army of gardeners and careful cultivation and the walls keep out the winds, remember.' Hamid breathed in deeply and sighed. 'And the strange thing is that it can all die in a single night. When winter comes here, it strikes suddenly, like a sword biting into warm flesh.'

She gazed down into the moonlit water, watching the fish nibbling gently at her trailing fingers. 'Jack told me about what happened in Korea.'

Hamid raised her chin with one hand and looked into her eyes. 'You like him, don't you?'

'Very much. I've never met anyone quite like him. He's a strange man, violent and bitter, and yet he can be the gentlest person I've ever known.'

'The story of my life.' Hamid sighed. 'What would you like to know?'

'We stopped at his bungalow this afternoon. There was a girl there. Famia, I think he called her.'

'His housekeeper's daughter.'

She seemed to hesitate and then plunged on, 'Is she his mistress?'

'So that's it?' Hamid chuckled gently and took her hands. 'He's a grown man, Janet, not a boy. There would be something strange if he didn't feel the need for a woman occasionally, now wouldn't there?'

Momentarily, her hands tightened on his as anger swept through her like an uncontrollable fire, and Hamid touched her gently on the right cheek.

'Poor Janet. India makes a harsh taskmaster.'

'I think I love him, you see,' she said in a low voice. 'It's as simple as that.'

'It's never as simple as that,' he said solemnly and pulled her to her feet. 'I think we'd better go back while I can still remember that fact.'

'Just one more thing,' she said. 'Is he as embittered over this Korean business as he appears to be sometimes?'

Hamid shook his head. 'Not really. He's too intelligent to blame himself for what was really an accident of war, but he loved the Navy. That was his greatest loss.'

'And what does he believe in now?'

'Nothing. At least this is what he tells himself, and spends his time living dangerously, working for the highest bidder to amass a fortune.' He chuckled gently. 'Only to end by betraying all his hard won principles when he looks upon the face of suffering, as he did in Ladakh during the Chinese invasion.'

'You like him a great deal, don't you?'

'I value real friendship,' he said simply. 'Jack Drummond has shown that to me many times.'

They walked back through the garden in silence. As they mounted the steps to the terrace, Drummond came through the windows.

'There you are. Father Kerrigan thinks he should be going. He doesn't like leaving Kerim for too long. I'll run you back in the jeep.'

'I'll get your coat,' Hamid told her and went inside.

'Did you win your game?' she asked.

'No, did you?'

Janet smiled faintly. 'You couldn't be more wrong.'

She brushed past him and went inside and Drummond stood there in the half-darkness, listening to the rise and fall of the voices, a cold finger of excitement moving inside him, leaving his stomach hollow and empty.

She sat next to him on the way back, Father Kerrigan on the other side, and now and then the wind lifted the edge of her silken headscarf into Drummond's face.

He was aware of her warmth, the softness of the thigh against his, the delicate perfume, and gripped the wheel tightly, inhaling her sweetness, aware of feelings he had not experienced for a very long time.

The old priest kept chuckling to himself. 'I wish you could have been there, the pair of you. And didn't I show him? It'll be many a long day before he comes crowing over Terence Kerrigan again.'

Drummond glanced at Janet and grinned as he turned the jeep into the courtyard of the mission. 'I think he must have won.'

'Ah, get away with you!' The old man snorted as he got out of the jeep and then smiled, his face clear in the moonlight. 'A fine night for a drive.'

Drummond hesitated and Janet said calmly, 'Mr Cheung mentioned the ruins of a Buddhist temple not far from here. He seemed to think they were worth seeing by moonlight.'

'And maybe he had a point there.' Father Kerrigan slapped the side of the jeep with his bare palm. 'Off with you, now, and don't be late.'

Drummond took the jeep out through the entrance and turned across the moonlit plain beside the river. He had taken down the canvas tilt earlier and the wind was sharp and cold, carrying with it the scent of wet earth. A few minutes later, they came over the edge of an escarpment and the ruins of the temple lay before them in the centre of a small plateau, bare and windswept, crumbling with the years.

He braked, switched off the engine and they walked the last few yards. The full moon touched the scene with a pale luminosity and the dark shadows of half-ruined pillars fell across the mosaic floor like iron bars.

The statue of the Buddha was at the far end, chipped and cracked by time and the weather, one arm missing, but the great, serene face was still complete, hooded eyes staring blindly into eternity across the river.

Janet walked towards it slowly and Drummond paused to light a cheroot. When he raised his head, she was standing at the edge of the crumbling terrace, staring pensively into the night.

The moon was directly behind her, outlining her shapely limbs through the thin silk of the dress, and when she turned and looked at him, she looked unreal and ethereal like some dark goddess of the night who might fly away at any moment.

They stood like that, trapped by a moment of time, looking at each other, and then she came forward slowly, reached up and gently touched his face.

Drummond turned his head, brushing her palm with his lips and slipped his arm about her waist. She leaned against him, trembling a little and in the distance, thunder rumbled menacingly.

She glanced up quickly. 'What was that?'

'Storm on the way.' He pointed to where sheet lightning flickered over the mountains. 'We'd better get moving.'

She was conscious of the unnatural stillness.

A blanket of dark moved in from the horizon, blotting out the stars as it came. Drummond took her hand and they ran back towards the jeep.

He pressed the starter and moved away immediately, and in the same moment, great heavy drops started to splash against the windscreen. He pressed his foot flat against the boards, but it was no good. There was a tremendous clap of thunder overhead and the skies opened.

There was no time to put up the canvas tilt and he crouched behind the wheel, eyes narrowed against the stinging, ice-cold rain and Janet huddled at his side.

He drove into the courtyard at the mission, braked to a halt and they scrambled out and ran up the steps to the porch.

The thin silken dress was plastered to her body like a second skin and she shivered uncontrollably, laughing at the same time.

'That was marvellous, simply marvellous.'

'Better get out of those wet things,' he said. 'You'll catch your death.'

'You could use a towel yourself.' She took his hand.

'We'll go round this way. Father Kerrigan's probably gone to bed.'

They followed the verandah to the garden at the rear where the window of her bedroom stood ajar. She went in, turned up the lamp and found a spare towel.

'Do what you can with that while I get changed.'

'Like me to dry your back?' he said.

She gave him a quick push towards the window. 'Go on, get out of here.'

She pulled the curtain, peeled off her wet clothes and towelled herself briskly, still shivering. After a while, the shaking stopped and a warm glow spread through her body. She pulled on her dressing gown, tying the cord at her waist and went back outside.

Drummond wiped the rain from his head and face and hung the towel across the rail. It was bitterly cold by now and he stood there breathing deeply, taking the freshness into his lungs, filled with a strange inward restlessness.

'Feeling better?' she said quietly.

He turned slowly. Janet Tate was standing a few feet away by the rail and as lightning exploded, her face seemed to jump out of the night, the hair like a dark curtain to her shoulders. And she was beautiful, that was the thing which came to him with a sense of real wonder. Not just attractive, but beautiful, and he took two stumbling steps towards her, pulling her close.

The drumming of the rain on the corrugated iron roof increased into a solid roaring that seemed to fill her ears. She was aware of his strength, the arms crushing her to him and as her loose dressing gown parted, his lips found her bare shoulders, her breasts.

She leaned against him, caught in a strong current there was no denying, and was aware of his hands, fumbling at the cord of her dressing gown.

As it opened, she pulled away, struggling frantically. 'No, Jack, no!' He paused, head slightly forward, trying to see her more clearly in the half-darkness, and she pushed him away violently with both hands. 'Not this way, Jack! I'm not one of your kept women!'

For a long moment he stood there, almost invisible in the shadows, staring at her, and then, without a word, he walked rapidly away.

As another brilliant flash of lightning illuminated the empty verandah, Janet turned with a dry sob, went back inside and threw herself on the bed, anger and frustration sweeping through her.

Drummond had left the window of his bedroom open deliberately in spite of the cold. He lay in bed, propped against a pillow smoking a cigarette and thinking about Janet Tate as the rain drummed endlessly on the roof.

If that was the way she wanted it, then to hell with her. As he reached to stub out his cigarette in the ashtray on the locker at his bedside, there was a movement by the window, something stirred and Famia emerged from the shadows.

Her hair was unbound, hanging to her waist and she wore a loose silken robe fastened with a scarlet sash. There was a slight rustling of silk and as she moved into the narrow circle of the lamplight, the robe slipped to the ground.

She stood there for a moment, magnificent in her nakedness, breasts pointed with desire, hands flat against her thighs.

She moved forward quickly and his arms went out to enfold her, crushing her softness against him. He held her close, staring blindly out of the open window at the night as she moaned softly, digging her nails into his shoulder.

And after all, why not? This was one kind of answer and as good as any other.

In the darkness of the terrace, the old woman listened for a moment, then nodded to herself in satisfaction and crept quietly away.

It was close to dawn when he awakened, the sweat cold on his flesh. It was still raining hard outside and he hitched the blanket over his shoulders and turned into her warmth to sleep again.

Outside, the sound that had awakened him came nearer, the roar of an engine thundering through the rain. There was a squeal of brakes, boots running across the courtyard. Drummond got out of bed, reached for his dressing gown and padded to the window. As he moved out on to the verandah, Tony Brackenhurst stumbled on the top step and dropped to one knee, his face wild and strained in the light of the porch lamp.

'For God's sake, man, what is it?' Drummond demanded.

'Chinese troops,' Brackenhurst gasped. 'At Howeel. They over-ran my camp, slaughtered my men.'

'Chinese?' Drummond said. 'A patrol, you mean?'

'Hundreds of the bastards! Hundreds!' Brackenhurst sobbed.

Drummond stood stock-still for a moment and then pulled Brackenhurst to his feet. 'Have you told anyone else about this?'

Brackenhurst shook his head. 'No, I haven't had time.'

'Good, if word gets out too soon we might have a general panic and that plane of mine can take no more then fifteen in this kind of flying country.'

'That's what I thought,' Brackenhurst said.

'I bet you did. Now this is what we do. From here, we go to the mission to warn Father Kerrigan and Janet. We'll leave them my jeep and they can follow us in with Kerim as soon as they're ready.'

'What do we do then?'

'Come back to town in your Land Rover and break the news to the Khan. This might prove to him just how useless it was to rely on the border tribes for information.'

He returned to his bedroom and dressed quickly, pulling on fur-lined boots and his old naval flying jacket. Famia sat up in bed, the blankets clutched to her breast and watched him.

'When will you be back?' she said.

He took the Smith & Wesson .38 from a drawer, checked that it was loaded and slipped a box of spare cartridges into his pocket. 'God knows, but you'll be all right. You don't need me. You never did.'

He went out through the window and a moment later she heard the two engines break into life, one after the other, and the sound of them faded into the rain.

The door creaked open and the old woman crept in. 'Did you hear?' the girl said softly in Urdu.

The woman nodded and pulled the blankets aside. 'Come, girl, there is not much time and you know what must be done.'

Famia dressed quickly in an old pair of Drummond's drill pants and a white naval sweater that dropped over her slim hips. She pulled on slippers, nodded to her mother and moved out on to the verandah. A moment later, she was running through the quiet streets, head down against the rain.

Within five minutes, she came to a bungalow almost identical with Drummond's, ran up the steps to the verandah and knocked on the door furiously.

'Mr Cheung! Mr Cheung!' she called.

6

Action by Night

It was the rain which saved Brackenhurst, the sudden torrential downpour which turned a normally quiet mountain stream into a brawling torrent, in one place filling a dip in the road with a ford of ice-cold water.

He had spent a long, hard day in the mountains on his own, prospecting for ore specimens and now, on his way back to his base camp at Howeel, the sudden rush of water gleaming white and brown in his head-lights caused him to stamp hard on the brake.

He got out, found a branch at the side of the road and poked it carefully into the water. It was at least four feet deep. He might be able to drive through, but on the other hand, if the damned thing bogged down, he'd had it. He climbed back into the Land Rover and reversed to the top of the hill, switched off his headlights and returned on foot.

The water was cold, damned cold, and it swirled around his thighs, numbing him to the bone. He floundered forward with a curse and found dry land again. Thank God the camp was no more than half a mile away.

He trudged along the dirt road, head down against the driving rain, the light from his electric torch reaching into the darkness. Somewhere up ahead he seemed to hear a cry and then another, confused shouting and the dull, flat report of a gunshot muffled by the rain. A second later came the deadly staccato of a machine gun.

He stood at the top of a small rise, a slight frown on his face as he looked down through the pine trees at the flickering light of the campfire. There was a flurry of movement, the noise of vehicles, a shouted command.

He moved off the road and went down through the trees cautiously until he was no more than twenty or thirty yards away from the camp, but above it on the hillside.

The hollow was alive with Chinese troops, little stocky peasants in quilted uniforms and peaked caps, shining Burp guns in their hands, and the heart seemed to freeze inside him.

He could see two of his men, Galur and old Abdul, standing beside the fire, hands raised high in the air. There was the sudden roll of an automatic weapon and Abdul fell back across the fire. Galur turned, burst through the ring of men and ran for the trees, head down. For a moment it seemed that he might make it and then a burst from a submachine gun drove him on to his knees.

The soldiers were calling excitedly to each other as they started to search the tents. More and more of them pressed into the camp and with a sudden roar, a troop carrier came down the road, followed by another and yet another, half-tracks at the rear for mountain warfare, instead of wheels.

Brackenhurst had seen enough. He turned and scrambled back up the hill. From somewhere to his left, there was a cry and a bullet passed through the trees severing a branch.

He put down his head and ran faster, one arm raised before his face to ward off flailing branches. A moment later he floundered across the ford and staggered up the hill to the Land Rover.

The engine was still warm and it burst into life with a surge of power when he pressed the starter. He reversed quickly, the tyres skidded for a moment, searching for a grip on the soft, crumbling edge of the track, and then they found it and he drove away rapidly.

Sitting at the wheel of the Land Rover in the courtyard of the mission and remembering what had happened at Howeel, Brackenhurst shivered involuntarily. He could hear the rise and fall of voices and looked out again at Father Kerrigan, at Drummond standing in the doorway, the old priest holding a lamp in one hand.

After a moment, Father Kerrigan went back inside, closing the door and Drummond ran down the steps and scrambled into the passenger seat.

'Right, let's get moving.'

'What did the old man have to say?' Brackenhurst asked as he drove away.

'What could he say? He's going to pack up as fast as he can and follow on in the jeep with Janet and the boy. No sense in staying to face what's coming. You know what they do to people like him.'

'What do you think the Khan will do?'

'What in the hell can he do except get out? He hasn't got a defence pact with India, which means they're going to sit tight on their side of the border, and if I know them, the Chinese will be smart enough to go just that far and no further.'

'But why?' Brackenhurst demanded. 'What in the hell can they possibly want with a dump like this? There's nothing here that's worth having.'

'You could say the same about the Aksai Chin and the Ladakh, but they moved in there and for the same reason. Prestige, a paper victory. The glorious Army of the People's

Republic takes back what was part of the Chinese Empire a thousand years ago. The fact that Balpur is a few thousand square miles of the most sterile territory on God's earth doesn't matter. It'll take the people's mind off the bad harvest back home.'

As they drove through the deserted streets, the sky was beginning to lighten over the mountains, and beyond the scattered, flat-roofed houses, grey and sombre, the river roared through the valley, swollen by the rain.

Later, at the palace, waiting for the Khan in the room where they had dined in what now seemed another age, another time, Drummond opened the french windows and stood on the terrace in the rain, listening.

The Khan was taking his time, but when he came in, he was wearing a khaki drill uniform, the medals above the left hand pocket, a splash of vivid colour in the grey morning. The major domo to whom Drummond had given the original message followed him with a decanter of brandy and glasses on a silver tray.

The Khan had dropped twenty years and

there was a new vitality in his step. 'It seemed to me that a drink might be in order, gentlemen. If what Ahmed has told me is anywhere near the truth, it may well be some considerable time before we have another.' The major domo filled three glasses, passed them round and left the room. The Khan toasted them silently. 'Now, Mr Brackenhurst, perhaps you would be good enough to tell me in your own words exactly what happened at Howeel.'

When Brackenhurst had finished, the old man turned to Drummond. 'What do you think?'

'I don't understand it,' Drummond said. 'Last time I was up there, there was nothing. Not a damned thing.'

'But that was ten days ago now, am I right?'

'What are you going to do?'

'I'm not sure. First I must confer with Colonel Sher Dil and Major Hamid. I have sent messengers already telling them both to meet me urgently at Army Headquarters.'

'Seventy-five men,' Drummond said. 'They won't go far and you can't rely on the tribesmen. They'll simply take to the hills and stay out of trouble. And I don't think the Indian Army will interfere.'

'A pessimistic view, but a correct one, I fear. How many can your plane take?'

'Not more than fifteen in this kind of country. I've got to get over those mountains, remember, and if we're going we must go quickly. Once the people get hold of the news we'll have a howling mob running for the airstrip. Father Kerrigan's the only other person I've told so far. We called at the mission and left my jeep. He's going to pack up as quickly as he can and follow us in with Kerim and Miss Tate.'

The Khan nodded. 'Good, my son must certainly be saved at all costs.'

'Then by my reckoning that gives us a possible passenger list consisting of yourself, Kerim, Father Kerrigan, Miss Tate, Brackenhurst here and Major Hamid, Colonel Sher Dil, too, of course, if he wants to come.'

'What about Cheung?' Brackenhurst put in.

'I was forgetting him.' Drummond turned to the Khan. 'Your Highness is probably well aware of Mr Cheung's true politics. God alone knows what the Reds would do if they got their hands on him.'

The major domo returned and handed the Khan a polished leather belt and holster containing a heavy British Army service revolver. He belted it around his waist, and smiled grimly.

'Then I think it is time to move, gentlemen. You may drop me at Colonel Sher Dil's headquarters. I suggest you then continue on to the airstrip and prepare the plane for immediate take-off.'

Outside, it was even lighter now, the sky a heavy uniform grey, the rain turning the dirt road into a quagmire as they drove down through the streets to the main square, braking to a halt outside the grim, barrack-like building that was Sher Dil's headquarters.

There was already a bustle of activity, and as the Khan got out the colonel came down the steps to meet him, Major Hamid at his shoulder. The Pathan glanced enquiringly at Drummond who held his thumb down and Brackenhurst drove away quickly.

Beyond the city, one or two tents were pitched, a flock of heavy, mountain sheep crowding in close to where a herdsman's fire already trailed grey smoke into the morning.

They bounced over the rutted track, skidding slightly in the mud, and went over the escarpment and down towards the airstrip.

The corrugated iron hangar looked ugly and forsaken in the grey morning and Brackenhurst braked to a halt a few yards away and nodded towards the airstrip itself, already a sea of mud.

'Not much of a surface to take off on.'

'Anything will do for a Beaver,' Drummond said. 'That's why they're so good for this kind of country.'

He took out his key, unlocked the padlock and pulled the doors wide, revealing the red and gold plane, and a quiet, precise voice said, 'Excellent, my friend, now move away, please.'

Cheung came round the corner of the building, an automatic pistol in one hand. In the other, he held a grenade. 'Going somewhere, Jack?'

'That was the general idea.' Drummond slipped his hands casually into the slanting pockets of his flying jacket, fingers closing around the butt of the Smith & Wesson. 'What is this?'

Famia moved from behind one of the doors and stood at Cheung's shoulder, looking faintly ridiculous in Drummond's sweater, which was by now so sodden and heavy with rain that it almost reached her knees.

'Well, I'll be damned,' he said.

Cheung smiled gently. 'No one is going anywhere, Jack. It was not in the plan.'

In one quick movement, he pulled the ring from the grenade with his teeth and tossed it inside the hangar. In the same moment, Drummond pulled the Smith & Wesson from his pocket and loosed off a wild shot that splintered the door behind Cheung's head, sending him running for cover.

Drummond turned and ran. Brackenhurst was already scrambling behind the wheel of the Land Rover. As the engine roared into life, the grenade exploded, hot air reached out to enfold Drummond, and the entire hangar seemed to sag.

As he jumped in, the Land Rover shot away, wheels churning the mud to liquid. Cheung moved into the open, firing steadily, the gun held in both hands with all the expertise of the marksman.

Brackenhurst took the Land Rover into a gully that slanted up the hillside giving them some kind of cover, and a moment later the Beaver's fuel tank blew up.

'And I hope that's taken the bastard with it!' he shouted.

They roared out of the gully on to a plateau which jutted like a shelf from the side of the mountain and gave a view of the plain below.

Cheung was standing a little distance away from the burning hangar looking up towards them and the girl lay face down in the mud a yard or two away from him.

Drummond was conscious of nothing, no anger, no pain. There was no time to wonder about what had happened or why. Survival was the thing from now on. The only thing that mattered.

Brackenhurst braked on the edge of the plateau seeking the safest way down, and beneath them the town was spread out like a map. Already people were stirring, moving in the streets in spite of the heavy rain.

'Bad news travels fast,' Drummond said.

In the square outside headquarters there was considerable activity. Three trucks moved up and parked outside and the drivers got down and stood in a small knot, obviously discussing what was happening.

Somewhere, Drummond was conscious of the noise, dulled by the rain, and then Brackenhurst screamed and pointed up into the sky to where a couple of planes flew out of the grey morning side by side, turned and broke formation, spiralling down like leaves falling from the branches of a tree.

The leading jet roared down the valley beside the river, banking so close to the mountain that for one frozen moment Drummond was able to distinguish the red stars on the wings.

'God in heaven, Chinese Migs!' Brackenhurst cried.

In the town below there were cries of alarm, people were standing in groups looking up at the sky, and as they scattered to run, the leading Mig swooped and fired its rockets, ploughing a double furrow across the square and scoring a direct hit on the first truck in line outside Sher Dil's headquarters. The truck's petrol tank exploded and debris and flames cascaded outwards to enfold the panic-stricken people who ran past.

The second Mig came in fast, rockets ploughing into the other two trucks and the flimsy mud and wattle houses beyond. As it swooped up into the grey morning, the leader was already banking, turning in to make his second run. He roared down, rockets hammering into the closely packed houses, and scored a direct hit on the ammunition store on the other side of Sher Dil's headquarters. A tremendous explosion sent a column of flame shooting up through the dark pall of smoke that was already enveloping the town as the second Mig followed the other in fast.

'Let's get moving.' Drummond slapped Brackenhurst on the shoulder.

Brackenhurst turned, his face very white, eyes staring. 'Down there? You must be mad.'

Drummond didn't argue. He dragged Brackenhurst across the seat and scrambled into his place behind the wheel. He took the Land Rover down the steep hillside and across the plain, and the smoke enveloped them so that he had to drive blind for several moments, swerving as a half-ruined house loomed out of the gloom. They bounced across a tangled mass of timber and masonry and turned into the main square.

A man ran out of the swirling darkness, his petrol-soaked body flaming like a torch. He vanished in the direction of the river. Someone screamed monotonously above the crackling of the flames and ammunition started to explode.

The Land Rover crunched across a burned and blackened body and Drummond braked hard. The screaming had stopped and the silence was somehow intensified by the crackling of the flames. On this side of the square there was hardly a house standing, and one end of Sher Dil's headquarters was a heap of rubble.

As Drummond jumped to the ground, Hamid staggered out of the entrance and leaned against the wall at the top of the steps, gasping for air, his uniform smouldering in several places.

Drummond ran up the steps and caught him as he started to fall. 'Easy does it. I've got you. What about the Khan?'

There was blood on Hamid's right cheek and he wiped it away mechanically. 'I don't know. Inside somewhere. The place is a bloody shambles.'

As Brackenhurst came up the steps to join them, the Migs came down the valley again. They grabbed Hamid between them and ran. As they staggered in through the door and hit the floor, cannon fire ripped up the surface of the square again, fragments of stone rattling against the shattered windows.

Drummond lay against the wall and waited while the earth trembled. Two soldiers sprawled on their faces in the centre of the room and Brackenhurst crouched in the far corner, eyes wide and staring.

The firing ceased as quickly as it had begun and the Migs faded into the distance, leaving only the smoke and the flames and the ruins behind.

Drummond got up and helped Hamid to his feet and Brackenhurst joined them. When he spoke, his voice shook a little. 'We've got to get out of here, Drummond. We've got to get moving.'

Drummond ignored him and turned to Hamid who was leaning against the wall, shaking his head from side to side like a wounded bull. 'Where was the Khan when the attack began?'

Something clicked in Hamid's eyes and he took a deep breath. 'In the radio room. Through here.'

The door was off its hinges and the room beyond was a shambles. Four or five men, dead or badly wounded, lay sprawled amid the wreckage and Colonel Sher Dil knelt by the window, the Khan in his arms. In one corner, the wireless operator still crouched by his seat, earphones in place.

Sher Dil was covered in dust, his uniform

singed and torn, but he seemed otherwise unharmed. Drummond dropped on one knee beside him and looked down at the Khan. The front of the old warrior's uniform was soaked in blood and when he opened his eyes, death stared out.

He gazed uncomprehendingly at Drummond for a moment and then his eyes seemed to clear. He reached out one bloodstained hand and held on tight, his mouth opening and closing as he tried to speak.

'Kerim,' he croaked. 'You will save Kerim? Your word on it.'

'It's all right,' Drummond said. 'I give you my word. We'll get the boy to safety, I promise you.'

The hand tightened on the front of his flying jacket, there was a hollow rattling in the Khan's throat and blood erupted in a sudden flow between his lips.

Drummond forced the bloodstained fingers apart and Sher Dil laid the Khan gently down on his back. The colonel removed his tattered tunic and covered the face and Drummond stood up and turned to Hamid.

'Any sign of the party from the mission?'

Hamid shook his head as Brackenhurst stepped in through the shattered doorway. 'The Land Rover's still intact, thank God. At least we've got transport. I hope that bastard Cheung rots in hell.'

Hamid turned to Drummond. 'What's he talking about?'

'It seems our good friend Cheung was working for the opposition all along. He got to the plane with a grenade before the Migs came in.'

'But we checked him out with Formosa,' Hamid said. 'He *was* a Nationalist agent, there can be no doubt about that. They communicated with him regularly. We looked the other way for obvious reasons, but we knew all about it.'

'Probably a double agent,' Drummond said and turned to Sher Dil. 'If you heard that, you'll know we're on our own and it's one hell of a step to the border. Have you managed to contact the Indian Army yet?'

'No, but the operator's still trying.'

There was the sound of sporadic gunfire

and they all turned and looked out of the window. A current of warm air had momentarily snatched away the veil of smoke revealing a small sugar loaf hill on the other side of the town. People were running towards the river, refugees from the town, men, women and children, a few herdsmen on horseback, their panic-stricken flocks rushing this way and that, getting in everyone's way.

A second later, the top of the hill was alive with troops in drab quilted uniforms. They started to fire as they swept on and the screams of the mob rose into the air like the smoke as they started to fall.

The tidal wave surged on, the soldiers calling to each other like hounds in full cry, running down the hill towards Sadar and the pall of smoke dropped back into place.

Hamid turned to Sher Dil. 'We've got perhaps five minutes before they get here. You must contact Indian Army Headquarters.'

A section of the roof crashed through into the room, scattering flame and sparks, and as Hamid and Drummond ran forward to stamp it out, Brackenhurst rushed outside. A second later, the engine of the Land Rover roared into life. When Drummond reached the door, it was already disappearing into the smoke.

Hamid cursed savagely and went back inside and Drummond stayed there, listening to the sound of the Land Rover fade into the distance, aware of the wireless operator's excited voice as he finally contacted Indian Army Headquarters.

The smoke swirled around him, touched with crimson, and the sickly-sweet stench of burning flesh was everywhere. In the great heat, things seemed to lack definition and nothing was real any more.

A bullet splintered the wooden framework of the door and several Chinese ran out of the smoke. He ducked inside as Hamid appeared at a shattered window and emptied a Sten gun, driving them back into the smoke.

Sher Dil turned from the radio and dropped the hand mike he had been using. 'From the sound of things we'd better get moving. Every man for himself, and try to get across the river. There's a village called Bandong ten miles due south on the road. We'll meet there.'

The rear door led into a fenced yard. It was strangely quiet and the smoke hung low in the heavy rain, reducing visibility considerably.

The wireless operator climbed up on the fence and swung a leg over. There was a sudden cry and a group of Chinese appeared about forty yards to the left. Several of them fired at once and he screamed and fell backwards into the yard, clutching his face.

Sher Dil scrambled through a gap in the fence and started up the slope and Drummond went after him, weaving desperately from side to side as the Chinese continued to fire. He was aware of Hamid hard on his heels, of Sher Dil disappearing over the rim of the escarpment.

He could taste blood in his mouth as he clawed his way up, slipping on the wet earth, and then the jagged rocks on the skyline loomed above him. He went over the top, head down, sobbing for breath and tripped over an outstretched foot.

He had one brief impression of Sher Dil sliding down the steep slope of shale to the river below, picking himself up at the bottom and plunging into the water, and then they moved out of the swirling smoke to surround him, small and misshapen in their quilted uniforms, each carrying a rifle that seemed too large for him, an old-fashioned sword bayonet on the end.

Hamid was lying on the ground a few yards away and a soldier stood over him, a foot on his neck. Drummond backed against a boulder and the brown peasant faces moved in on him.

7

Edge of the Sword

The town gaol was one of the few major buildings left undamaged by the attack, and from the small cell on the corner of the second floor, Drummond had an interesting view of the city through the barred window.

It was 10 a.m., four hours since the initial attack, but smoke still drifted across the stricken city through the heavy rain and a heavy grey mist moved up from the river and crouched at the end of the streets.

It was unbelievably cold and rain drifted in a fine spray through the bars as Drummond dropped to the ground. 'It's going to be an early winter this year. I feel it in my bones.'

'For us, a matter of academic interest only,' Hamid said from his bunk.

'You think so?'

There was the sullen chatter of a machine gun from down by the river and Hamid smiled bleakly. 'There's your answer. Nothing like cutting down on the opposition. They haven't stopped since this morning.'

'Then why have they let us last this long? Why the special treatment?'

There was no time for a reply. A key grated in the lock, the door opened and a small sergeant stepped in, flanked by two privates armed with sub-machine guns. Hamid got to his feet and the sergeant shook his head.

'Not you, this one.'

They pushed Drummond into the corridor before he had a chance to say anything, and the door clanged into place with a grim finality.

The sergeant turned without a word and started along the corridor and Drummond followed, the two privates bringing up the rear. They mounted a flight of stone steps to the top floor and halted outside a door. The sergeant knocked, listened for a moment and then led the way in.

The room had once been the governor's office. The walls were hung with Bohara rugs, sheepskins covered the floor and logs burned in the large stone fireplace.

A Chinese officer stared down into the fire, one foot on the hearth, and tapped his booted leg with a leather swagger stick impatiently. The heavy greatcoat with the fur collar which swung from his shoulders carried the epaulets of a full colonel.

He turned and examined Drummond calmly. 'You don't look too good, Jack.'

'No thanks to you, you bastard.'

'Nothing personal, Jack. We just happen to be on different sides. Regrettable, but true.'

'What are you, Military Intelligence?'

'That's right.'

'Am I allowed to ask for how long you've been making a monkey out of them back on Formosa?'

'I've never been to Formosa,' Cheung said. 'The Nationalists *did* have an agent called Cheung and they *did* send him on a mission to Nikkim. He got as far as Singapore. I took his place from there.'

'What about the guns I flew into Tibet and Moro and his boys? All that was a fake, too, I suppose?'

'An elaborate pretence which enabled me to communicate constantly with my superiors to help pave the way for the regaining of what has always been legally a part of the Chinese Empire by the Army of the People's Republic.'

'I can do without the speeches,' Drummond said. 'Where did Famia fit in?'

'She and her mother were of no particular importance. I paid them well to keep me informed of your movements.'

'You speak in the past tense.'

'Only where Famia is concerned. She was struck in the head by a piece of sharpnel back at the airstrip.'

Remembering the months of pretence, Drummond dismissed her with no particular regret. 'Do you really think you're going to get away with this?'

'Why not?' Cheung said. 'India will not interfere. She is interested only in maintaining the status quo and the two countries have never had a mutual defence pact. In the United Nations, there will be an emergency session, they will talk far into the night and do precisely nothing. No one wants to rock the boat, Jack. A phrase you taught me.'

'You've got it all nicely worked out, haven't you?'

'Except for one rather important detail. The Khan is dead, which is something of a convenience, but these are a superstitious people, and to them the Khan is priest as well as king. Prince Kerim can be his only successor.'

'And as such, an obstacle to the setting up of a People's Republic.'

'Not at all.' Cheung smiled briefly. 'With our guidance, he could be of great help to his people. He could lead them along the true path.'

'Now I've heard everything,' Drummond said.

'Good, then perhaps you will be sensible enough to help me in this matter. After all, you always did have an eye to the main chance. Where is the boy?'

Drummond stared at him in astonishment. 'You mean you don't know?'

'He is not at the mission. Neither are Father Kerrigan nor the American girl. My men have spent hours checking the crowds and searching the immediate area of the city.'

'And you expect me to help?'

'I know you went straight to the mission from your bungalow after Brackenhurst brought you news of the invasion. Famia told me.'

Drummond decided to take refuge in the truth. 'That's right. We left my jeep and told Father Kerrigan to pack up as quickly as possible and meet us at the airstrip. Your men moved too fast for him, I suppose.'

'But Brackenhurst also is proving difficult to locate. You arranged an alternative plan in case of trouble. I know you, Jack. I know how your mind works.'

'Can I go now?'

'You might find it wiser to co-operate. I could make things easier for you.'

'Do me a favour, for God's sake,' Drummond said. 'That's like a line from a bad play.'

Colonel Cheung stared at him, apparently calm, the leather swagger stick beating against his right boot. 'All right, take him away, Sergeant,' he said abruptly in Chinese. 'Bring the other one.'

Drummond paused in the doorway and shook his head. 'Now you really are wasting your time,' he said.

Chinese headquarters had been set up at the palace and the commanding officer, General Ho Tsen, stood on the terrace and looked out over the garden. He seemed far from happy and paced up and down impatiently.

There was a slight cough from behind and he turned to find Cheung standing in the window. 'You have found him?' he demanded eagerly.

'I'm afraid not, General.'

Ho Tsen slammed a hand hard down on the balustrade. 'This is your direct responsibility, Colonel. I expected to find the boy ready and waiting when I arrived.'

'It seems that the priest and the American

girl left the mission with the boy shortly before our men arrived. We've confirmed this by questioning herdsmen at a camp up-river. I've just had a report that their jeep has been found abandoned ten miles north of here at a village called Quala. There was a vehicle ferry there which has apparently been destroyed so I'm assuming they've crossed by boat. A Land Rover belonging to the man Brackenhurst has been found in the same place.'

'Has the patrol gone after them?'

'Unfortunately there were no other boats. The village was quite deserted. Obviously the entire population had crossed over. Since then the level of the water has risen with the rains.'

'Is there any place where the river may be crossed with vehicles?'

'Certainly not here. The current was always too swift for a ferry.'

Cheung spread out a map on a wrought iron table. 'Twenty miles north of here at Kama. The river is very wide and shallow there. We could cross in half-tracks.' His finger traced a line to the border. 'There is only one road to India and they have no transport, remember. We should catch them easily. They must stay on the road. The priest is an old man and in any case, with the woman and the boy, he couldn't hope to get through the mountains on foot by any other route.'

Ho Tsen nodded. 'I hope so, for your sake. Pekin will not be pleased if you fail. I will also send other patrols south on this side of the river in troop carriers. They should find boats sooner or later. Once across, they can proceed on foot and cut the road ahead of you.'

'An excellent idea.'

Ho Tsen put a cigarette in his mouth and leaned to the match Cheung offered. 'One thing worries me. What if the priest had an alternative plan? Perhaps a vehicle waiting on the other side. It would explain why they did not drive north to Kama and attempt to cross in the jeep. This man Drummond you spoke of? You are certain he knows nothing?'

'He is a difficult man to be sure of and

the Pathan is as stubborn as the breed usually are.'

'You have exhausted the accepted methods?'

'They take time, General, and in any case, Drummond must be preserved for a more searching examination in Pekin.'

'Why is this?'

'He is known to have worked for British Intelligence.'

'I see!'

Cheung hesitated. 'I would like to have one last try before leaving in case they do have information of value. A small subterfuge which often has remarkable results.'

'Which sounds interesting,' General Ho Tsen said. 'I think I shall accompany you, Colonel. Let us hope I'm not wasting my time.'

The wind across the river was like a bayonet in the back and Drummond shivered as it cut into him. He flexed his hands to ease his cramped muscles and winced with pain as the wire that was twisted about his wrists bit into his flesh.

Hamid was next to him and on the other side one of Sher Dil's soldiers in tattered uniform was silently weeping. Every few moments the man coughed and a trickle of blood came from his mouth. After a while, he slumped on his face and lay motionless. The guards standing talking a few yards away took no notice.

Two troop carriers, half-tracks biting into the mud, drove up and parked thirty or forty yards away, each containing a dozen men and a heavy machine gun mounted on a pivot.

Drummond eased back on to his heels and looked along the line of kneeling men. There were at least thirty of them, mostly Sher Dil's soldiers with a few tribesmen who'd been caught carrying weapons. In his mind's eye he saw them keel over one by one as the machine gun curved in an arc and finally reached him and he shuddered.

A jeep drove up and parked behind the troop carriers and Hamid said quickly, 'We've got company, Jack.'

Cheung walked across the broken ground

towards them, General Ho Tsen at his side. They paused a few yards away and the General said calmly, 'These are the men?'

Cheung nodded. 'They both speak Chinese.'

'Excellent.' The General came closer. 'Let us not waste any more time, gentlemen, I find this rain most unpleasant. We wish to know the whereabouts of the Catholic priest and the young Khan. If you are sensible and help us, I will see that you are well treated. If not . . .'

Drummond and Hamid stared up at him without speaking and Cheung sighed with exasperation. 'You're a damned fool, Jack,' he said in English. 'You always were. We've found the jeep at Quala which means they've crossed the river. They won't get far, I promise you.'

He and the General turned and walked back to the troop carriers. Ho Tsen climbed into the shelter of the jeep and Cheung looked up at the sergeant who stood beside the heavy machine gun in the first troop carrier.

'You have your orders. Stop firing when you reach the Indian and the Englishman.

If you harm either of them, I'll have your head.'

He climbed into the jeep beside the General and Ho Tsen smiled and offered him a cigarette. 'You were quite right, Colonel. This should prove most interesting.'

Drummond stared at the sodden earth, numb with cold and waited for what was to come. He wondered about Father Kerrigan and Janet and the boy, somewhere on the other side of the river in the mist, and prayed that the old man would have the sense to keep on the move. But the Indian border was a long way off, all of three hundred miles.

A burst of shrill, girlish laughter came from the Chinese and he stiffened. They strutted towards the line of prisoners, their thin voices bird-like on the wind and Drummond dropped his head and waited.

A boot thudded into his chest and he rolled on his face and fought for breath. The wire was torn from his wrists and a kick in the side drove him to his feet. The Chinese soldier grinned amiably and held out a spade.

Drummond glanced once at Hamid and

they started to dig. The soil was soft and sandy and lifted easily. Beside them the other prisoners worked silently, and as Drummond bent to his task, he knew with a feeling of utter hopelessness that it wouldn't take very long.

The rain increased into a heavy downpour and the Chinese turned and ran to the shelter of their vehicles leaving one man on guard, a sub-machine gun crooked in one arm.

The trench was now a couple of feet down and Drummond wondered how deep they wanted it. Six feet was the statutory requirement for a grave back home, but it was unlikely that the Chinese bothered about such niceties.

He leaned on his spade for a moment and Hamid moved closer. 'I don't suppose we've got much longer,' Drummond said.

Hamid glanced once over his shoulder at the mist rolling up from the river. 'Not if I can help it. Any good at the hundred yard dash, Jack?'

Drummond frowned in bewilderment. 'What in the hell are you talking about?'

'This,' Hamid said crisply and slapped him heavily in the face.

As Drummond staggered back, momentarily dazed, the guard hurried across to see what the disturbance was about. He leaned over the trench, the sub-machine gun pointed threateningly and Hamid swung the edge of the spade against his neck. The man fell into the trench without a sound.

The rain was now a heavy grey curtain that almost shrouded them from the troop carriers and the jeep. Hamid snatched up the guard's sub-machine gun, scrambled out of the trench and ran towards the river. Drummond went after him, slipping and stumbling in the mud.

Behind him he heard a cry and glanced over his shoulder. The other prisoners were strung out in a ragged line, running for dear life. Beyond them, the first Chinese had already reached the trench, firing as they advanced, and one of the troop carrier's heavy machine guns opened up above their heads.

The river was very close now and he increased his pace as he smelled water. A bullet plucked at his heel and he tripped and fell heavily. Hamid was beside him in an instant. He dragged him to his feet and together they stumbled down the slope to the water.

The river was in a sullen, angry mood. It ran smoothly through the heavy rain, but sudden swirls on the surface indicated dangerous currents and the speed with which tree branches drifted by argued against any attempt to reach the other side.

There was a rattle of stones and earth behind and one of Sher Dil's soldiers ran past, his face purple with effort so that a scar which stretched from one eye to the corner of his mouth gleamed whitely. He plunged into the water and began to swim furiously.

In a few moments, the swift current had carried him out of sight into the heavy rain. Others followed, some bleeding from wounds, crying with fear as they stumbled down the slope and flung themselves into the river.

'They won't last five minutes,' Hamid shouted. 'The water must be near freezing.'

A bullet landed at their feet, showering them with dirt. He turned as four Chinese appeared at the top of the slope and swung the sub-machine gun in a wide arc, firing from the hip. Two of them crumpled to the ground.

As their companions dropped behind an outcrop of rock, several more appeared on the skyline and Hamid drove them back with a long burst that emptied the gun.

As one of the troop carriers came into view, Hamid tossed the useless weapon to one side and they ran into the river and splashed through the shallows towards a line of dense, thorny bushes that grew down into the water. Bullets churned around them and then they were waist deep and hidden by the rain.

The water was bitterly cold and Drummond could feel it eating its way into his bones. They could hear the cries of the soldiers coming nearer and began to move further downstream aided by the strong current.

The land curved out for about fifty yards making a natural breakwater, imprisoning a floating mass of smashed trees and branches. They pushed towards it and the current, taking pity on them, swept them into the safety of the floating jungle.

They rested side by side, holding the branches of a tree, gasping for breath. Voices came from the shore and half a dozen soldiers appeared, pushing their way through the bushes along the water's edge.

They were no more than ten yards away from the shore and through the branches Drummond could see the Chinese clearly, the peaked caps pulled down over the eyes, the red star prominent, the shining Burp guns and rubber, knee-length boots.

The breathless minutes passed slowly and the cold gradually numbed their limbs. The soldiers appeared to be having a conference. After a while, they split into pairs and disappeared into the driving rain.

'Now what?' Drummond said.

'Only one thing for it,' Hamid said, his lips blue with the cold. 'We'll have to try to get across on one of these logs. They'll be swarming around like flies on this side of the river. We wouldn't last five minutes.'

He let go of the tree and splashed to the

next one, progressing slowly through the floating mass and Drummond followed. When they reached the edge, they found a large tree that was already swinging out into the river, straining to be free.

Hamid pulled himself into the branches and Drummond said, 'I'll try to guide it from the other end.'

He lifted a foot from the water and pushed against the next tree. There was a snapping of branches and the tree lifted into the current. In a few moments they were drifting rapidly away and the floating mass of trees and the promontory disappeared into the mist.

Drummond soon found that it was impossible to guide the tree. It went with the current and his feeble kicking had no effect. He gave up the struggle and tried to heave himself into a more secure position, but his frozen limbs refused to help him. He trailed helplessly through the water, arms hooking over a projecting branch and gradually all discomfort and pain left him.

* * *

When Cheung scrambled up the steep bank from the river's edge, he found General Ho Tsen still sitting in the front of the jeep, a cigarette in a long jade holder between his teeth.

'Well?' the General demanded.

Cheung seemed tired. 'As yet there is no sign of them, General.'

'A small subterfuge which often leads to remarkable results,' said Ho Tsen. 'Wasn't that what you promised me?'

Cheung wiped rain from his face mechanically. 'What can I say?'

'Nothing,' Ho Tsen told him. 'That would be much better. As it happens, in such weather it is more than likely that Drummond and his friend are already floating face down somewhere out there in the flood. In any case, I shall take charge here, Colonel. Take your men and go north to Kama. Cross the river and bring me back the young Khan.' He paused and neatly ejected the end of his cigarette from the holder. When he looked up again, his eyes were cold. 'Without him, there would be little point in returning at all. You follow me?'

Cheung stood there in the rain, staring at him for a moment, his face quite white. He seemed to pull himself together, saluted, turned and clambered up beside the driver of the first troop carrier. A moment later, the two vehicles moved up the slope, their tracks spurning the wet earth and disappeared into the mist.

8

Forced March

Vaguely through his numbed mind, Drummond became aware that something was digging into him. After a while, he realised that another large tree had drifted into them. They floated together, branches intertwined, their combined weight considerably slowing down the speed at which they were travelling.

Hamid was still secure in his perch amongst the branches and after a while he called, 'I can see the other side. The river must be narrowing.'

Drummond turned his head. Through the torrential rain, the opposite bank was just visible and it seemed to draw nearer every moment. The water became rougher and trees and flotsam of every description raced through the white-capped waves.

Suddenly, the bank was very close and seemed to increase in size as the river churned through a deeper and narrowing channel. There was a sickening, body-shaking jar and the tree grounded.

Drummond heard a cry and saw Hamid flung into the water. He unhooked his cramped limbs and found that he could stand waist deep. He forced his way along, pushed by the current, and caught Hamid by the belt before the river took him. There was a crashing sound behind and, as he turned, the trees were lifted by a sudden swell of the water and swept away again.

The water boiled around them as they braced themselves against the current. Slowly they forced their way to the steeply shelving banks and scrambled to temporary safety. They lay face down, their battered bodies heaving as they retched up river water.

After a while, they got to their feet and clambered up the mud bank away from the river. They stood looking across the river through the mist, listening. Hamid was shaking with cold, his uniform moulded to his body although strangely enough, his turban was still intact.

'Sooner or later they'll get men across by boat,' he said. 'They're bound to find an odd one or two missed by the refugees.'

'But they'll be on foot, just like us,' Drummond reminded him. 'The nearest place they have a hope of crossing with vehicles is Kama and that's twenty miles north from here. The shallows there could well be impassable because of the rain.'

'Well, one thing is certain,' Hamid said with a savage grin. 'There's only one road out to India and there's only one way we're going to get to it.'

They began to walk south through the rain, slowly, because the ground was fast turning into a quagmire. Drummond found it an effort to lift one foot in front of the other, and after a while found himself falling behind the hardy hillman.

They moved into a grey impenetrable mist that shrouded them completely from the outside world. Nothing existed now except the two of them and the rain and Drummond stumbled on through the mud, wondering what he was doing here and where it was all going to end.

It was perhaps half an hour later that he became aware that Hamid was calling to him. He was standing on top of a small hill about fifty yards away. When Drummond joined him, he saw a herdsman's hut in a small hollow below.

There was no sign of life and they moved cautiously down into the hollow. Drummond didn't feel tired any more. He didn't feel anything. He knew he was alive and that was about all.

It was a poor place of mud and wattle construction and a thin tracer of smoke lifted through a hole in the straw roof. Hamid opened the door and led the way in.

The fire on the stone hearth was banked with earth and smoke drifted in a heavy layer against the ceiling. It was filthy and it smelled and Drummond knew the place was very probably lousy with fleas as well, but it was warm and dry, and at the moment that was all that mattered.

He raked the soil from the fire and brought wood from a pile in one corner. Hamid rummaged amongst the sheepskins at the back and came up with a couple of stone jars.

He brought them to the fire with a grin. 'Goat's milk and cheese. Pretty rancid, but good for the constitution.'

'At the moment, I could face anything except going out there in these wet clothes again,' Drummond said.

He built the fire into a great, roaring pyramid and Hamid gave the sheepskins a shake. 'God alone knows what we'll get from this lot.'

But it didn't matter, nothing mattered except that it was warm and the fire was hot on the skin. Drummond crouched there watching the steam rise from his clothes suspended from the ridge pole, a sheepskin around his shoulders, and after a while he slept.

* * *

He awakened slowly and stared through the dim grey light at his clothes hanging from the ridge pole of the but, wondering where he was. After a while he remembered and sat up.

Hamid squatted on the other side of the fire. He was wearing his uniform again and grinned. 'How do you feel?'

'Bloody awful!' Drummond stretched his arms and blood started to flow through cramped limbs. 'How long have we been here?'

'A couple of hours, that's all. Must be about two o'clock. We'd better get moving. Your clothes are pretty dry by now. Better than they were, anyway.'

Drummond started to dress and Hamid peered outside. 'From the looks of it, this rain is never going to stop. I think it'll turn to snow before it does.'

'As if we haven't got enough to worry about.'

Hamid shrugged. 'The weather should help if anything. It makes things just as difficult for the Chinese.'

Drummond moved to the entrance, zipping up the front of his flying jacket and looked out. The rain was lancing into the earth with steady force and a slight mist rising from the cold ground combined with it to reduce visibility to a few yards.

'I think you're right about the snow.'

'Which means we've got to move fast. We can't be more than seven or eight miles from the road. Anyone else who got across the river is bound to move in the same direction. They've no other choice.'

'You're thinking of Father Kerrigan and Janet?'

'Or Sher Dil, but the Chinese will follow the same route once they get across and we must keep ahead of them. If we can only reach the village Sher Dil mentioned, Bandong, and get horses, we might stand a chance.'

He picked up a couple of sheepskins and tossed one to Drummond. 'Better wear that over your shoulders. It'll keep out some of the rain.'

In the same moment, he drew back from

the entrance, a finger to his mouth and dropped to one knee.

They crouched side by side, soundless and waiting. At first there was only the savage drumming of the rain and then Drummond heard it. A slipping, stumbling sound of feet trailing through the wet ground outside.

As the steps approached the hut and paused, Hamid launched himself through the entrance. There was a sudden splashing through the mud outside, the sound of a blow.

Drummond went after him, fists ready, but there was no need. Hamid stood over the huddled figure of a man who crouched in the mud. He grabbed a handful of hair and jerked the head back savagely. A great scar ran from the man's right eye to the corner of his mouth. The tattered remnants of a khaki uniform with corporal's stripes on the right sleeve still clung to his wiry body.

'It's the one who plunged into the river ahead of us,' Drummond said. 'You remember? He's one of Sher Dil's men.'

The man's face split into a wide, impudent grin. 'You know me, Major Hamid. Ahmed

Hussein, Corporal in Number One Section.' His English was almost perfect, but with a slight, sing-song accent. 'Drummond Sahib, I have seen many times.'

Hamid started to laugh. 'I know this one, all right. One of the greatest rogues you'll ever meet in your life. An old Indian Army man, Khyber Rifles, wasn't it?'

'That's right, sahib.' Ahmed got to his feet and indicated the row of medal ribbons above his left breast. 'D.C.M. from King George himself, sahib.'

'Probably bought in the bazaar at Peshawar,' Hamid said. 'But he's an Afridi. They're good fighting men.'

They went outside and Ahmed crouched over the fire, warming his hands. 'What are we going to do with him?' Drummond said. 'We can't afford to wait for him to dry off.'

'No need, sahib.' Ahmed picked up another sheepskin. 'This will do fine. The cold is nothing to me. Hardship is nothing.' He grinned hugely. 'I'm an Afridi.'

'Which also means liar, cheat and rogue,' Hamid said. 'There's goat's cheese in one of the jars. If you're hungry, you'll have to carry it with you and eat on the way.'

'Where do we go, sahib?'

'To the road, where else? The road out of this accursed country. Colonel Sher Dil told us to meet at Bandong if we managed to cross the river. Do you know it?'

'About eight miles south, sahib. I take you there.'

When they climbed out of the hollow, Drummond paused for a moment and looked down at the small hut, the smoke rising into the air. Somehow it represented security and safety and now he was moving into the unknown again. He shivered and hurried after his two companions.

For the first quarter of a mile, Ahmed trailed at the rear scooping handfuls of the soft cheese from the jar, devouring it avidly with groans of delight. Finally, he tossed the jar to one side and ran ahead to take the lead.

Drummond kept a pace or two behind Hamid. The world was a few cubic feet covered on all sides by walls and a ceiling of mist and rain and they were the only inhabitants.

They had been marching for about half an hour when he stumbled into Hamid who grabbed his arm. 'Listen for a moment.'

Ahmed joined them and they stood in a small group, strange figures in their sheepskins, streaming with rain and somehow symbolic like a piece of modern sculpture.

'I thought I heard firing,' Hamid said and at that moment it sounded again, a faint echo to the west.

'Sounded like a machine gun,' Drummond said.

Again, there was a faint, deadly echo of small arms fire and then there was silence.

'Probably back across the river,' Hamid said. 'We're still moving parallel with it, remember, but I think one of us should scout ahead from now on.'

'I will go, sahib,' Ahmed said with a grin and ran into the mist.

They commenced to march again. Drummond's senses were on the alert for danger at first, but gradually he succumbed to his surroundings. There was a safety, an anonymity about the rain and the mist that was vaguely comforting.

He withdrew into himself, an old trick, forgot about fatigue, discomfort, the danger of his present situation. He didn't even feel fear when Ahmed suddenly emerged from the mist and ran towards them.

Hamid grabbed hold of the Afridi and steadied him. 'What is it?'

'There is a village up ahead, sahib.'

'Good, lead the way.'

He walked into the mist and they followed him. Drummond found that he was sweating a little, the ground sloped and then dipped suddenly as they descended into a large hollow.

The houses loomed out of the mist. There were no more than six of them, poor, mean places of mud and wattle like the herdsman's hut scattered alongside the banks of a small stream.

They went forward quickly and Drummond was aware of the acrid smell of woodsmoke on the damp air. Ahmed opened the first door and went in. He reappeared a moment later.

'Empty, sahib, everything gone.'

He ran along the line of huts, opening the crude, wooden doors and finally came back to meet them despondently. 'Picked clean, sahib. Picked clean.'

Hamid looked in through the door of the nearest house at the embers of the fire which still glowed on the hearth. 'I said bad news travels fast, didn't I? They've gone, every last one of them. Horses, livestock, the lot. Taken to the hills I suppose, to wait things out and see what happens.'

Ahmed looked at them enquiringly. 'We move on now? Nothing for us here.'

'That's right, Ahmed,' Drummond said. 'Nothing for us here.'

They moved up out of the hollow and started to march again. The rain-soaked earth made the going very heavy and the ground itself was boulder-strewn and very difficult so that they had to pick their way with care.

Gradually a change became noticeable. The air seemed colder and drifted steadily into their faces and the ground began to slope steeply. They paused to take stock of the situation.

'We must be coming to the edge of the rift valley,' Hamid said. 'And that means the road can't be far away. We should cut across it in another mile or so.'

They started to make their way down the hillside. The ground began to fall away until at times, they were compelled to climb very carefully, feeling for handholds.

Finally, they found themselves on the lower slopes and the going was easier over rough, moss-covered ground. Ahmed moved ahead again and was soon lost to sight, for as they descended through the rain, the mist became thicker until visibility was almost nil.

It was Drummond who heard the motor. He stopped quickly and called to Hamid. They both stood there on the hillside listening and heard the sound of truck engines.

Ahmed came running out of the mist. 'Bandong just below in the valley, sahib,' he said to Hamid. 'Four trucks stopping there. Big ones, sahib, I think they are ours.'

'What do you mean, ours?' Drummond said.

'Army trucks, sahib. Convoy from India making its way to Sadar.'

'He's right,' Drummond said. 'I'd forgotten about that. Don't they make the run once a month?'

'Only one difficulty,' Hamid said. 'If it is the usual convoy to Sadar, then it's going in the wrong direction.'

'Not if they'd heard what's happened.'

They covered the rest of the distance quickly, running and sliding down the slippery slopes until they came to a boulder-filled stream bed. On the other side they scrambled up on to a dirt road, and Ahmed motioned them to silence as a flat-roofed house loomed out of the mist.

'Bandong,' he whispered.

The truck engines had stopped and the whole world seemed to have died with them. A vague unease stirred in Drummond and then he heard the voice, the rough, familiar Irish voice, and ran forward between the houses scattered on either side of the road.

Four trucks were drawn up in a line, old Bedford three-tonners, pointing south towards India. Father Kerrigan stood bareheaded in the rain talking to a tribesman in sheepskin coat and fur hat who held an old .303 Enfield rifle in one hand and the bridle of a rough hill pony in the other.

A stone rattled under Drummond's foot and they swung round. The hillman was Colonel Sher Dil.

'Well, praise be,' Father Kerrigan said softly.

The door of one of the trucks opened and Janet Tate dropped to the ground. She was wearing the same clothes she had worn on the flight in, fur-lined boots, cord pants and the sheepskin jacket Drummond had provided for her, but he didn't really notice these things. Only her eyes and the deep incredulous joy in them as she ran towards him.

9

Council of War

A corporal and three privates walked forward slowly, curiosity written on their faces, and behind them, lagging slightly, his left arm heavily bandaged, came Tony Brackenhurst.

'We didn't expect to see any of you again,' Father Kerrigan said. 'The Chinese arrived so quickly that we only got out of the mission by the skin of our teeth. I drove up-river to Quala and found that the headman had already had the vehicle ferry destroyed to prevent the Chinese crossing the river with transport. Everyone in the village was being ferried over by small boats in relays.'

'Mr Brackenhurst arrived while we were waiting our turn,' Janet continued. 'He was pretty badly burned. He told us what happened at Sadar. He thought he was the only one to get away.'

'So he was for a while,' Hamid replied calmly.

Brackenhurst looked very pale and swayed slightly, groping for the side of the truck to steady himself. Two of the soldiers moved to catch him and Father Kerrigan said, 'I think you ought to lie down again, my boy, you don't look too good. Will you see to him, Janet?'

Brackenhurst stumbled away between the two privates, Janet walking beside them, and the priest turned back to the others.

'I don't think I've ever had a greater surprise in my life than I did ten minutes ago when this tribesman here emerged from the mist and turned out to be Sher Dil.'

'I arrived on foot about four hours ago,' Sher Dil said. 'When I told the villagers what was happening, they decided to move into the mountains while they still could. They wanted me to go with them, but I'd told Drummond and Major Hamid to meet here if they managed to get across the river.' He grinned. 'I was beginning to think you weren't going to make it.'

'We very nearly didn't,' Hamid said. 'They insisted on our staying for a while. You'll be interested to know, by the way, that friend Cheung is an Intelligence Colonel.'

'God bless my soul,' Father Kerrigan said. 'Are you sure about this?'

'We've the best of reasons for knowing, Father,' Drummond said. 'How's Kerim?'

'Taking it all surprisingly well. Of course, he's not had things too bad as yet. After crossing the river we were in an ox cart for nine or ten miles, but then we met the convoy. As soon as Corporal Nadin heard our story, he turned round at once. He didn't have much choice. He couldn't have gone any further.'

'Does he know about his father's death?'

'So it's certain? Brackenhurst seemed to think so, but I kept hoping he might have been mistaken.' Father Kerrigan sighed. 'No, I've told the boy nothing. Later, perhaps, when we're safe across the border.'

'If we can get there, Father. A debatable point at the moment.'

Ahmed splashed towards them through the rain, two tin mugs in each hand. 'Tea, Colonel?'

'So, you survived, you rogue?' Sher Dil said in mock anger. 'Am I never to be rid of you?'

'As Allah wills, Colonel.'

Ahmed grinned impudently. He wore brand new leather combat boots and a quilted khaki parka of the kind specially issued for winter warfare, the fur-lined hood pulled up over his head.

'Where did you get the clothes?' Drummond asked.

'One of the trucks was carrying general equipment for the army, sahib. There is still some left although we unloaded most of it back there on the road to make room for the women and children.'

'Women and children?'

'Refugees we found on the road. We could not leave them for the Chinese.'

'Tell Corporal Nadin to bring me a map,' Sher Dil said.

They squatted on the verandah of the nearest house to drink their tea and Nadin, a thin, sinewy Indian with a brown face and long black moustache, brought the map.

Sher Dil unfolded it. 'Three hundred miles to the Indian border and one road out – this one. The usual way to cross the river with transport was by the ferry at Quala, but according to Father Kerrigan, the villagers have burned it.'

'It might be possible to cross in the shallows at Kama,' Drummond said. 'Especially with half-tracks, and they've got those.'

'Do you think they'll try?' Father Kerrigan said.

Hamid nodded. 'I'm afraid so. They want the young Khan, Cheung made that quite plain. A puppet to sit on the throne of Balpur, a mouthpiece for the People's Republic. As Sher Dil says, there's only one road out. They're certain to follow.'

'Then we must keep moving. We have a good lead.'

'Only for a time.' Sher Dil ran his finger along the course of the river. 'Here, seventy miles south of Sadar is a village called Huma. If the Chinese get their hands on the boats there, they can put men across.'

'But not vehicles.'

'That is true, but see how the river swings to follow the valley. They would be no more than ten to fifteen miles from the road, no distance for active, well-trained troops.'

'So you think they may try to cut the road ahead of us?' Drummond said.

Hamid shrugged. 'I don't know who their commanding officer is, but that's what I'd do if I was in his place.'

'Then the sooner we're on the move, the better.'

Sher Dil looked up at the leaden sky. 'About two hours of daylight left. We can go a long way in that time.'

'You don't think we should push on through the night?'

'On this road?' Hamid laughed harshly. 'It would be suicide in vehicles like these. Much better to camp at a suitable spot and move on at first light. The Chinese won't have anyone across the river yet, there hasn't been enough time. We'll have a good start on them.'

Sher Dil got to his feet and turned to Corporal Nadin. 'What about petrol?'

'There is plenty, Colonel, enough for all the trucks.'

'Why not dump two and push on in the others?' Drummond said. 'Plenty of room for all of us if we unload.'

Sher Dil laughed and made a sweeping gesture that took in all four of the Bedfords. 'Look at them. Twenty years old if they're a day. They've been running since the Burma campaign and it shows.' He turned to Nadin. 'How often do they break down?'

The corporal shrugged. 'All the time, Colonel. First one thing and then another.'

'That settles it. We push on with all four. If one breaks down, we still have three left and so on. One of the damned things is bound to last out to the border. In any case, the ammunition they carry may prove useful.'

The three privates had been standing in a little group a yard or two away listening to this conversation and as Corporal Nadin turned to move away, one of them grabbed his sleeve and muttered something quickly.

Sher Dil frowned and stepped down into the mud. 'What's going on?'

Nadin turned, indecision on his face. 'Two of the men, sir, Piroo and Yussuf. They are local men. Their wives are in Sadar. They would rather stay. They do not wish to return to India.'

Only the rush of the rain and the rattle of water in the stream bed on the other side of the village disturbed the silence after he had finished speaking.

Father Kerrigan looked worried and Hamid was quite composed, ready for anything. When Drummond glanced quickly at Sher Dil, the colonel's face had turned pale with anger and the eyes blazed fire.

'For a soldier who disobeys an order in the face of the enemy, there can be only one punishment.' He unslung the old Lee Enfield rifle and rammed home a round, the bolt making an audible click. 'Is that understood?'

The two men in question looked scared to death. Sher Dil slung the rifle over his shoulder again. 'Right, Corporal Nadin. Prepare to move out.'

Nadin and the three privates hurried away and Father Kerrigan heaved a sigh of relief. 'You almost frightened me.'

'A bad business,' Hamid said. 'Once it starts, you can never tell where it's going to end.'

Sher Dil nodded. 'We've wasted enough time. Get what you need in the way of arms and so on and we'll move out.'

The refugees, a dozen women and five children, huddled together in the shadows at the back of the truck, clutching the pathetic bundles which contained their worldly possessions.

They sat there patiently, watching with no visible emotion as Drummond and Hamid looked through what was left of the general equipment the truck had been carrying. They found quilted parkas similar to the one Ahmed was wearing and Drummond discarded his flying boots, still saturated from their immersion in the river, and helped himself to a pair of heavy mountain warfare combat boots. He pulled on waterproof mittens and jumped to the ground.

Hamid was at the second truck with Sher Dil. The colonel had discovered a case of sub-machine guns and had broken it open.

'These are very good,' he said with a grin. 'A gift from Moscow. One of the happier results of adopting a policy of strict neutrality.'

He prised open a box of ammunition and another of grenades and turned as Corporal Nadin approached. 'Bring the others, I'm going to issue automatic weapons.'

Nadin called and a moment later, Ahmed and the third driver, a tall Bengali named Amal, hurried out of the mist.

'Yussuf and Piroo – where are they?'

The two men glanced at each other uncertainly and Nadin ran along the line of trucks. He was back in a moment. 'They have gone, Colonel.'

Sher Dil grabbed Ahmed by the front of his parka. 'Did you see them go, you rogue?'

Ahmed raised his hands, palms outwards. 'On my father's grave, Colonel. They were here only five minutes ago. I was talking to them.'

'What about?'

'They were very angry with the Colonel. They said that the Chinese would catch us all. That we would never reach India.' He shrugged. 'They didn't want to stay.'

Sher Dill cursed and Hamid shook his head. 'We're better off without them. There's no problem. We've enough drivers between us. I can take a truck myself.'

Sher Dil nodded. 'Very well. I'll go first with Corporal Nadin. You follow in the supplies truck, Major. Father Kerrigan, Miss Tate and the young Khan can travel with you.'

'What about me?' Drummond said.

'You can bring up the rear with Ahmed. Mr Brackenhurst can travel with Amal in the third truck with the refugees. As soon as everyone's in, we'll move out.'

As they broke away, Drummond heard his name and saw Janet leaning over the tail-board of the second truck.

He climbed up beside her quickly. 'Anything wrong?'

'No, what's been happening?'

'A couple of drivers have deserted, but, there's nothing to worry about. How's Kerim?'

'Asleep at the moment. We've made him as comfortable as possible.'

Boxes had been moved away from the far end creating an alcove in which the young Khan lay covered with blankets, his face very pale against the white bandage. Janet leaned down to straighten a blanket and when she stood up again, Drummond took her hands.

'Are you worried?'

She shook her head. 'Nothing's really sunk in yet. I can't quite believe it's happening.'

His hands tightened, pulling her close and he kissed her. 'Not even this?'

She looked up at him, her eyes dark and serious, and then she smiled and touched his face gently. She didn't speak, there was no need and they kissed again.

'I'll see you later,' he said and left her there.

When he vaulted over the tailboard, Father Kerrigan was standing in the rain, a long cheroot jutting from his teeth beneath the shovel hat.

'And would it be all right if I got in now?' he demanded.

Drummond grinned and gave him a push up over the tailboard. 'Where did you get the smokes?'

'See Ahmed. He's been foraging amongst the supplies again.'

Drummond trudged through the mud to the rear truck. When he climbed up into the cab, he found Ahmed sitting behind the wheel wreathed in tobacco smoke.

The Afridi grinned and took a carton from the dash-board. 'Cheroots, sahib, very strong. Specially made for Indian Army.'

'The way I feel, I could smoke any damned thing,' Drummond said.

He lit one, coughing as the smoke caught at the back of his throat, the door was pulled open and Sher Dil appeared.

'The next village is Hasa which is a good ninety miles further on.'

'We haven't a hope of getting that far before darkness in weather like this,' Drummond said.

Sher Dil nodded. 'If we can make forty

miles I'll be satisfied. We'll camp at the side of the road and push on at dawn.'

He slammed the door, and Ahmed pressed the starter. After several moments and a liberal use of the choke, the engine rumbled into life. The truck in front of them lurched forward and he eased off the handbrake and followed.

There was a warm smell of petrol and oil in the cab and rain splashed against the windscreen. Suddenly, Drummond had that same feeling of temporary security and safety he'd known in the herdsman's hut after they'd got across the river. He leaned back in his seat, laid the sub-machine gun across his knees and started to clean the grease from it with a piece of rag.

As the sound of the truck engines faded into the mist and rain, Piroo and Yussuf scrambled up from the stream bed and stood in the rain listening.

As the last echo died away, Piroo nodded

in satisfaction. 'Good, they have gone. Sher Dil was very angry.'

'No matter,' Yussuf replied. 'His day is done.' He looked up at the smoke rising from the headman's house. 'There is still a fire on the hearth. We will stay here for the night. We can move on in the morning.'

They went up the steps to the verandah, opened the heavy door and went inside leaving the street empty again. Rain hammered into the mud, mist enfolded the silent houses and the village waited as night fell.

The truck rocked violently as it ground its way along the muddy, pot-holed road and Drummond leaned forward, straining his eyes into the swirling mist.

The truck in front stopped suddenly and Ahmed stamped his foot on the brake. Drummond opened the door, sub-machine gun ready, and Sher Dil appeared.

'We've bogged down. You'll have to lend a hand.'

Drummond and Ahmed tramped through the mud to the front truck. Its offside wheel was deep in a waterfilled pothole and Nadin and Hamid were already busy with spades.

It took twenty minutes of hard work on the part of everybody to get it moving. When Drummond climbed back into his seat, he was plastered with mud to the knees and his fine new parka looked as if it had been through a hard campaign. Half an hour later, the whole performance had to be repeated.

When he settled himself back in his seat for the second time he was past feeling anything. His feet were numb, his hands raw and bleeding from handling the rocks and stones which had gone to fill the potholes.

Visibility was bad now and he began to feel very tired as he strained his eyes through the gathering gloom. The front truck's horn sounded once and as the convoy slowed, he was aware of scattered pine trees on the left.

Ahmed turned off the road and followed the dimly-seen tail of the truck in front and there was a sudden stillness as all engines were cut.

10

Nightwatch

The camp site Sher Dil had chosen was a rocky flat, thinly scattered with pine trees that gave them some sort of a screen from the road.

When Drummond walked up the line, Hamid, Sher Dil and Father Kerrigan were standing at the rear of the second truck talking in low voices. Janet leaned over the tailboard.

'We've decided we don't need to worry too much about a blackout in this mist,' Sher Dil said. 'We'll set up one of the oil stoves in the back of the supply truck. Miss Tate can cook in there away from the rain. The refugees can do the same. There's plenty of food to go round.'

'A good hot meal should go a long way towards raising everyone's spirits,' Father Kerrigan said.

Drummond nodded. 'What about the boy?'

'He'll be all right. I've kept him under strong sedation so far.'

'What about sleeping arrangements?' Hamid asked.

'In the trucks. We'll need a guard, of course. Two at a time. One here, the other at the roadside. I'll work out a rota after we've eaten.'

Sher Dil moved away and Father Kerrigan smiled up at Janet. 'Hand me my bag, my dear. I'd better have a look at Brackenhurst.'

'I'll go with you,' Hamid said.

They walked away together and Drummond called to Ahmed and helped Janet down. The little Afridi arrived on the run. 'Yes, sahib?'

'Miss Tate's going to cook a meal for us in the back of the supply truck,' Drummond said. 'Get the spirit stove going for her and open a few tins. If you don't do everything she tells you at the double, I'll cut your throat.'

Ahmed grinned at Janet. 'The sahib has a

kind heart, memsahib. He could never do such a terrible thing. You come with me. I will see to everything.'

They moved away and Drummond went after Father Kerrigan and Hamid. He found them in the back of the third truck with the refugees. An engine inspection light had been rigged up to illuminate the interior. Brackenhurst sat on an ammunition box, stripped to the waist, as Father Kerrigan carefully peeled layers of bandage away from his left arm and the women and children watched solemnly.

He looked pale and drawn and every so often glanced furtively at Hamid who watched calmly. The priest removed the final bandage, examined the arm and nodded.

'Nothing like as bad as I thought at first. You'll be fine in a day or two.'

'It hurts like hell,' Brackenhurst said.

'What a shame.' Drummond pulled himself up and looked over the tailboard. 'Don't you think that's a shame, Ali?'

'Undoubtedly,' Hamid replied calmly. 'You must rest, Tony. We wouldn't want anything to happen to you.'

Brackenhurst threw them both a glance of pure hatred and Drummond dropped to the ground and moved back to the supply truck. He could smell cooking, and a sudden, hollow ache told him how long it had been since he'd eaten. When he climbed inside, Janet and Ahmed crouched over the stove and Sher Dil sat on a packing case, the map across his knees.

'You look worried.'

'I'm thinking about tomorrow. We swing very close to the river again. If the Chinese have moved fast along the other side in their troop carriers and get a few patrols across, we could run into trouble. The bridge across the Sokim Ravine, for example – if that was destroyed, we would be on foot.'

'We can worry about that in the morning,' Drummond said. 'I'm only interested in one thing at the moment – food.'

Ahmed passed plates of stewed meat and beans across, and as they started to eat Father Kerrigan climbed up, followed by Hamid.

'Will you see that Mr Brackenhurst gets something to eat,' the priest said to Ahmed and frowned at Drummond. 'Weren't you a little hard on him back there? Any man's nerve can go for a while in a situation like this.'

'He never had any in the first place,' Drummond said flatly.

The old priest frowned, glancing from one to the other, aware that there was something here that he did not understand. Drummond jumped over the tailboard and went round to the cab.

He sat in the warm darkness smoking and Ahmed brought him a mug of strong, scalding tea. A little later Sher Dil opened the door.

'I've worked out a guard rota. I'd like you to take over from Amal up on the road at ten. You'll also be on guard down here for an hour from 4 a.m. I want everyone up at five. We've got a long day ahead of us.'

He vanished into the darkness and Drummond pulled the fur-lined hood of his parka over his head. Ten o'clock. That left time for a couple of hours sleep. He settled into the corner and closed his eyes.

* * *

He was running down a long, dark road and somewhere ahead of him was Janet. She was calling to him and he knew that something terrible was close behind. He ran faster and then the surface of the road changed to mud and his feet began to stick in it, ankle-deep. Clouds of rain blew across his path, blotting her from sight, and only the sound of her voice told him she was still there. It became fainter and fainter and then he felt terribly afraid and the thing behind him, the nameless evil that made him so afraid, grabbed him violently by the shoulder.

He awakened suddenly to the cold night and realised that somebody was shaking him. He groaned and sat up. Ahmed said from the darkness. 'You were having a bad dream, I think, sahib.'

'Is it time?'

'Yes, sahib.'

Drummond breathed deeply a couple of times to steady himself, then pulled on his mittens. He picked up his sub-machine gun, opened the door and jumped down into the mud.

The rain rushed steadily through the darkness and the mist still blanketed the wet ground as he moved through the pine trees to the road.

After a while, he paused and called in a low voice, 'Amal, where are you?'

The Bengali moved out of the night to join him. 'Drummond sahib?'

'Anything doing?'

'Nothing, only the rain and yet more rain. Soon it will be snow. I have known it happen before this early in the year.'

'Let's hope not,' Drummond said and the Bengali faded into the darkness.

He found a fallen tree and sat on it, arms folded, sub-machine gun across his knee, but the cold ate into his bones and from time to time he stood up and walked around a little, stamping his feet to restore the circulation. Finally, with a complete disregard for caution, he lit a cheroot. It tasted terrible, but the glowing end somehow comforted him. When he had finished it, he lit another.

He became aware of the noise very gradually. He straightened up and listened carefully.

He could hear the sound of feet squelching through the mud from the direction of the camp. There was silence for a moment as if the person approaching was momentarily at a loss and then the steps sounded again, this time much more cautiously.

Very carefully, Drummond placed his still burning cheroot in a branch of the fallen tree, then slipped quietly into the darkness.

He worked his way round in a wide circle until he was certain he was behind the intruder and then moved forward. The dim bulk of a man appeared from the gloom, and glowing faintly through the dark beyond him was the cheroot.

It was the stillness of the man that decided Drummond, that and the slight, ominous rattle of a gun sling as he eased from one foot to the other, still peering towards the glowing cheroot. Drummond took a pace forward, tapped him on the shoulder and punched him in the stomach as he turned round.

He lay moaning on the ground and Drummond struck a match. It was Brackenhurst, one of the Russian sub-machine guns lying in the mud beside him. The match hissed and was extinguished by the rain.

After a while, Brackenhurst groaned and sat up. 'What happened?' His voice quavered and he sounded sick.

'You shouldn't go creeping around in the dark like that,' Drummond said. 'People might get the wrong idea.'

'I wanted a word with you, that's all,' Brackenhurst said. 'Away from the others. I wanted to explain about what happened at Sadar. When the roof started to come down, I panicked. Didn't know what was happening. I got to the Land Rover and when no one else followed, I thought you'd all bought it.'

Which was a straight lie, but Drummond let it go. 'That's all right. These things happen.'

Brackenhurst hesitated. 'Have you told anyone else?'

Drummond shook his head. 'Only Hamid and I know and we've more important things to worry about.' He stood there, calm and somehow uncompromising in the darkness. 'You'd better get some sleep. You're going to need it.' He picked up the sub-machine gun and held it out. 'Better take this with you.'

Brackenhurst stumbled away without speaking and Drummond went back to his tree. Half an hour later, Sher Dil relieved him. 'Anything happened?'

Drummond shook his head. 'No, everything quiet up here,' he replied and trudged through the mud back to the camp.

He climbed into the back of the truck and lay down, hitching a blanket over his shoulders. He was cold, numb all over and yet he wasn't miserable. He was long past that point.

He came awake slowly, yawned and turned on one side. Janet crouched over the oil stove, waiting for the kettle to boil, her face half in shadow in the subdued glow.

'What time is it?' he asked softly.

She glanced at her watch. 'Just after three. I couldn't sleep.'

She made tea in two tin mugs and handed him one and they sat in companionable silence in the glow of the stove. After a while, he said gently, 'What is it, Janet? Are you afraid?'

'I think I am,' she said simply. 'Even Vietnam didn't prepare me for anything like this. Do you think we'll get out?'

He was tempted to answer with a false assurance and then looked into that calm, grave face and knew that he couldn't. 'I'm not sure. As Sher Dil says, if the Chinese have moved fast along the other side, they could be ahead of us. They're bound to find boats at Huma or one of the other riverside villages. They could put men across to cut the road with no trouble.'

'This bridge up ahead that Sher Dil mentioned. Do you think there may be trouble there?'

'Trouble is where you find it. There's never any sense in worrying too much in advance.' He smiled. 'What will you do when all this is over?'

'Carry on to Chicago with Kerim, I suppose. That still stands whatever else may be changed. I'm due three months leave anyway.'

'And afterwards?'

'I'm not sure. I go wherever the Society sends me.'

'Isn't it time you thought about settling down?'

'Is that a straight offer?'

He shook his head. 'I could offer you money, Janet, enough and to spare. But take a look at the debit side. I'm forty years old, a beat-up ex-Navy flyer who's seen too much of hot countries and strange cities, had enough of flying to places where no one else will go. I want to rest my head somewhere for a while. That doesn't sound like much of a catch to me.'

'I know one thing,' she said quietly. 'If we don't try, we'll regret it for the rest of our lives.'

He sat staring down at the light of the stove, her hand in his, sighed and got to his feet. 'I'll get a little air. I've got some thinking to do.'

Janet sat there in the darkness, and after a while Hamid climbed over the tailboard. He helped himself to tea and squatted on the other side of the stove from her.

'I should wake Jack. He's supposed to take over from me at four.'

'That's all right. He was here. He's just gone for some air.'

'Trouble?' Hamid said.

She shrugged. 'Four o'clock in the morning talk, that's all. He's just decided he's too old for me.'

Hamid nodded. 'He's tired, that's all.' He hesitated and then decided to carry on. 'Jack isn't aware that I know this, Janet, but for the past five years at least, he's been working for British Intelligence, mainly flying illegal reconnaissance flights across the borders of what might be termed the less friendly powers.'

The breath went out of her in a long sigh. 'You're sure about this?'

'Oh, yes, the information comes to me from friends in Indian Army Intelligence. A long time for a man to live on his nerves.'

'Which explains a great many things.'

'Last year he crashed in the Borneo jungle and was badly wounded. They nearly got him that time and the Indonesians do not care for the British these days. His fate would hardly have been a pleasant one.'

'Is that when he got that terrible scar on his face?'

He nodded and leaned across, his face grave in the diffused light of the stove. 'He's a good man, Janet, but he's had enough. Take him home, wherever that turns out to be.'

There was an obvious change in her, she seemed confident, assured, smiled suddenly and squeezed his hand. 'I will, Ali, I will.' She got to her feet. 'I'd better check on Kerim.'

Hamid poured himself some more tea, feeling strangely sad, and after a while Drummond climbed over the tailboard and joined him.

'Where's Janet?'

'Gone to have a look at Kerim. Who's on duty at the road?'

'Ahmed, I think.' Drummond hesitated and then went on, 'Brackenhurst turned up when I was doing my hour up there last night.'

'What did he want?'

'I'm not sure. I rather got the impression he was toying with the idea of killing me, but basically he just wanted to make sure that we hadn't told the others what really happened at Sadar.'

He explained what had taken place. When he had finished, Hamid nodded slowly, a frown on his face. 'Of course, he could argue that he was carrying the gun merely as precaution in case of trouble. He could never have used it. Far too noisy. The knife is the weapon for darkness, Jack.'

'I'm not sure that he's rational enough to look at things in that way any more,' Drummond said. 'He's badly scared, and he's certainly never possessed the kind of cold-blooded guts it takes to go after a man with a knife.'

'We'll have to watch him from now on, that's all,' Hamid shivered suddenly. 'I don't like it at this time in the morning, Jack. Makes me think of other dawnings, other places and a lot of good men dead.' He laughed in a peculiar fashion. 'I must be getting old.'

'Aren't we all?' Drummond said.

He got to his feet and moved to the tailboard. It was already dawn, a grey light seeping through the mist. The heavy rain lanced into the ground and he stared out at it morosely, wondering what the day would bring.

Wrapped in a sheepskin on the floor in front of the fire in the headman's house at Bandong, Piroo was awakened suddenly by a savage kick in the side. He sat up with a start, aware, as if in a dream, of faces staring down at him, the shining Burp guns, the red stars in the peaked caps.

Somewhere, Yussuf cried aloud, running for the door. A foot tripped him and a rifle butt thudded savagely against the back of his skull, cracking the bone.

Piroo was dragged to his feet, gibbering with fear and then a sharp voice cut across the noise and confusion and there was silence.

Colonel Cheung paused in the doorway, the fur collar of his greatcoat pulled up around his neck, the face beneath the fur hat lined and drawn with fatigue.

There had been considerable delay in

crossing the river at Kama. For one thing, the shallows had been deeper than usual owing to the heavy rain and one of the troop carriers had bogged down. They had wasted several hours in trying to salvage it. It had been almost dark when he had finally decided to push on with the remaining vehicle and a dozen men.

He had kept on the move for most of the night, often at no more than ten miles an hour in the appalling conditions, on several occasions almost losing the vehicle, but there was always the hope that Father Kerrigan and his party might be at Bandong. It was an obvious stopping place. When they had reached the village, he had sent the sergeant and ten men in on foot, giving them five minutes' start before following in the troop carrier.

'What's going on here?' he demanded.

The sergeant, a small, hard-faced Cantonese named Ng, hurried forward. 'The village is empty, Colonel, except for these two. Deserters from the look of them.'

'Deserters?' Cheung's face changed, went

pale with excitement as he pushed his men aside and examined Piroo. 'Who are you?' he demanded in Urdu. 'One of Colonel Sher Dil's men? Did you escape across the river?'

'No, sahib,' Piroo said. 'I was with the supply convoy.'

'The convoy was here?' Cheung said. 'Where is it now?'

'Gone, sahib, to India with Colonel Sher Dil and the young Khan. They are hoping to reach the border.'

'Sher Dil was here?' Cheung said in amazement.

'Oh, yes, sahib,' Piroo babbled. 'Also Major Hamid and Drummond sahib. They all crossed the river from Sadar.'

'When did they leave?'

'Yesterday, two hours before dark. They intended to camp somewhere along the road when night fell. I heard the colonel say so.'

Cheung laughed excitedly, slapping his leather swagger stick across his gloved palm. 'Get the men together at once, Sergeant. We're going on.'

He turned to the door and Sergeant Ng

said quickly, 'What shall I do with this one, sir?'

Cheung looked at Piroo with something close to affection. 'Let him go free, he has served us well.'

He went out and Piroo, to whom the interchange in Chinese had been completely unintelligible, turned eagerly to Sergeant Ng.

A strange man, the colonel, the sergeant told himself. Full of wild fancies, but a good officer for all that. He nodded to one of his men who grabbed Piroo suddenly, clamping a hand over his mouth.

Piroo saw the knife coming up, felt a coldness streaking under the ribs to the heart and plunged into darkness. They left him there by the fire, and a moment later the troop carrier moved away, its tracks scattering mud from the street across the walls of the houses.

11

The Bridge at Sokim

'I can see the bridge,' Sher Dil said, 'and it's still standing.'

'Thank God for that.' Drummond took the binoculars and focussed them quickly. 'There certainly doesn't seem to be anybody about.'

'And no cover for an ambush,' Hamid said. 'We'd better cross now while the going's good.'

They dispersed to the trucks and Drummond ploughed through the mud and heaved himself up beside Ahmed, glad to be back inside. It had rained without pause all morning, turning the road into a rutted quagmire through which they had progressed at little more than fifteen miles per hour.

They went over the hill and the road dropped steeply towards the great ravine which cut its way through the heart of the mountains. Ahmed selected bottom gear and followed Sher Dil cautiously.

The bridge was a narrow spindly thing, fit only for one-way traffic. As the road levelled off to approach it, the other trucks slowed to a halt and Ahmed braked quickly.

'I'll see what's happening,' Drummond said and jumped down.

Sher Dil leaned over the parapet examining the web of rusty steel girders. He turned as Drummond approached.

'It would take the Chinese a long time to construct another. A demolition expert's dream.'

'Thinking of doing it yourself?'

'I don't see why not. It wouldn't take long. We'll cross over first, though.'

As Drummond went back to his own vehicle, Hamid leaned out of the cab of the supply truck. 'What was he up to?'

'He wants to stop and blow up the bridge. What do you think?'

'An excellent idea. It would block the road for months.'

'Don't you think it might advertise our presence?'

'I can't see that it makes much difference. If there's anyone up ahead, they'll still be there whether we blow the bridge or not.'

Drummond climbed up beside Ahmed and the truck lurched forward and started the slow ascent on the other side. When they pulled over the hill, they saw that Sher Dil had stopped a little way up the road. They joined him as Amal and Brackenhurst drove up behind.

Brackenhurst came forward, his face white and strained. 'Why are we stopping?'

'I've decided to destroy the bridge before moving on,' Sher Dil said.

Father Kerrigan climbed down to join them and Janet stayed in the cab, an arm around young Kerim who was now sitting beside her.

'For God's sake,' Brackenhurst said. 'Haven't we lost enough time?'

'If we blow the bridge, the Chinese will lose even more,' Sher Dil said patiently. 'We'll use the contents of my truck, grenades, ammunition and some demolition charges. You can all help. We'll unload the stuff more quickly that way.' He turned to Father Kerrigan. 'You stay with Miss Tate and the Khan. We shan't be long.'

He took the wheel himself on the journey back down the hill. When they reached the bridge, he turned and reversed as far as the centre. Drummond climbed into the back with Hamid and handed the boxes out to the others. They worked fast and each time he passed a box down to Brackenhurst, he noticed that he was sweating.

'That's about it,' Sher Dil said at last as he surveyed the boxes stacked across the bridge. 'When that lot goes up, they'll hear it in Sadar.'

'What now?' Hamid said.

'I'll set the fuses myself. Corporal Nadin and Amal can stay and help me. The rest of you better get back up the hill. You'll have to walk. We'll need the truck to make a quick exit before the big bang.'

Brackenhurst was already hurrying back

across the bridge and Nadin stood rooted to the spot, dismay in his eyes. Sher Dil tossed him a coil of fuse wire which the Indian almost dropped.

'Pull yourself together, Corporal,' the colonel snapped. 'The sooner we get this set up, the sooner we can get out.'

At the top of the hill, Drummond turned and looked down. The bridge and the truck seemed like toys and the whole scene had an unreal, fake look.

Hamid came up the hill carrying Sher Dil's binoculars. He sat on a boulder and adjusted them until the truck and the bridge jumped sharply into focus.

'How are they doing?' Drummond asked.

'He's laying the charges. I must say Nadin doesn't look too happy. Neither does Amal.'

'They're both scared to death. I think that's why Sher Dil made them stay.'

Below on the bridge, they worked rapidly. Nadin running the fuse wire to the far end. He walked back towards the colonel, paused and pointed dramatically. His cry rose thin and clear in the rain.

As a Chinese troop carrier came over the crest of the hill on the other side of the ravine, Hamid focussed the binoculars quickly and the face of the officer standing upright beside the driver jumped out to meet him.

'It's Cheung.'

As the troop carrier started the descent, Drummond said, 'They haven't got time to blow the bridge now. We'd better get moving.'

'In the troop carrier, they would catch us within five minutes,' Hamid said calmly. 'Sher Dil knows that. He will blow the bridge. He will do it for the young Khan.'

Drummond turned to watch the drama being enacted below, saw Sher Dil take a step towards the charges and knew with cold certainty that Hamid was right, that he intended to blow the bridge even if it meant going up with it.

Amal seemed rooted to the ground, but Nadin rushed at him in complete panic, clawing at his shoulder. Sher Dil knocked him down with a blow of his fist and turned again to the charges. Nadin scrambled to his feet, wrenched the truck's spade from its fastenings near the door and struck Sher Dil on the head with all his force.

He turned and jumped into the cab. The truck moved forward and stalled and Amal, seizing his chance, scrambled over the tail-board. Sher Dil managed to reach his knees. He took a grenade from one of his pockets, pulled out the pin and tossed it towards the stacked boxes.

At that moment, the truck lurched forward. It had moved perhaps ten yards when the centre of the bridge erupted in a cloud of smoke. Pieces of stone girder lifted skywards as a series of violent explosions sounded one after the other and then the entire middle section of the bridge fell in, the truck slipped back into the gaping chasm and disappeared.

The troop carrier had slewed to a halt on the other side and now its heavy machine gun opened up, firing blindly through the pall of smoke, bullets ripping up earth and stone on the hilltop beside the trucks.

Brackenhurst was already behind the wheel of Amal's truck, lurching down the road to a chorus of terrified screaming from the women and children in the back.

There was no time to talk. Hamid scrambled up behind Father Kerrigan and drove away quickly and Drummond and Ahmed followed in the supply truck. For a heart-stopping moment, bullets ripped through the canvas hood and then they were over the hill.

Ten minutes later, Hamid sounded his horn, Brackenhurst slowed, turning in to the side of the road and Ahmed and Drummond pulled in ahead of him.

Drummond jumped down to join the Pathan and Brackenhurst stumbled towards them, his eyes wild. 'What do we do now, for Christ's sake?'

Hamid ignored him and held up Sher Dil's map. 'He left this in the cab, that's one good thing.' They leaned over it and he nodded. 'I thought so. There's another village fifteen miles further on and the border, fifty miles beyond that.'

'One thing's certain,' Drummond said. 'Cheung can't hope to catch us now.'

Hamid nodded. 'As long as there's no one

waiting at the next village we should be all right.'

'What about ditching a couple of the trucks?'

Hamid shook his head. 'If anything went wrong with the truck we were travelling in, we really would be in trouble. Another thing – three trucks give us more of a show of strength than one. That could be useful if we run into any small patrols.'

'What about the women?' Brackenhurst demanded. 'Don't you think it's time we left them?'

'For the Chinese to get their hands on? Even for you, that isn't such a sparkling idea. Get back to your truck and take up third position.'

The contempt in Hamid's voice was obvious to them all. Brackenhurst turned as if he had been struck and stumbled away.

'For heaven's sake, Major,' Father Kerrigan said, leaning out of the cab of Hamid's truck. 'The man's at the end of his tether, can't you see that?'

'Which means he's got to be driven, Father. It's the only way, I'm afraid.' Hamid turned to Drummond. 'You and Ahmed take the lead in the supply truck, Jack, and I'll follow. If you do run into trouble, try to block the road with your truck. That'll give the rest of us a chance to turn round. If you run fast enough, you should be in time for a lift.'

'I hope so,' Drummond said.

He went round the front of Hamid's truck and waved to Janet. She waved back and so did the boy, the first real sign of life Drummond had noticed from him.

He climbed up beside Ahmed and they drove away. The mist had lifted even more which wasn't too healthy and the rain sluiced down relentlessly. It was bitterly cold and there was a bad taste in his mouth. He ran a hand over the stubble on his chin and leaned back in the seat watching the road, a sub-machine gun in his lap.

They had been driving for no more than twenty minutes when Hamid sounded his horn a couple of times. Ahmed turned in to the side of the road and Hamid pulled in ahead.

He jumped down and came to meet them. 'Brackenhurst doesn't seem to be following.'

'I wonder what the stupid bastard's up to now?' Drummond said.

'As far as I'm concerned, I'd leave him to stew, but we've the women to think of.'

Drummond nodded. 'You wait here. We'll run back in the supply truck. It's always possible that he's just broken down. I can't understand how the things have kept going this long.'

Ahmed reversed and drove back along the road. Within five minutes they saw the truck parked at the edge, the women and Brackenhurst standing beside it.

He drove past, turned in a tight circle and parked a few yards away. Drummond jumped down and walked back. Brackenhurst was smiling nervously, relief on his face.

'Thank God you came. I knew you would.'

'What happened?' Drummond asked.

'It's the brakes. They're hydraulic on this truck. They've stopped working. There must be a leak.'

'That's all we needed.'

'We'll have to leave the women now,' Brackenhurst said.

'Take a look underneath, Ahmed,' Drummond said and he climbed into the cab of Brackenhurst's truck.

He pumped the brake pedal up and down several times, but there was no answering pressure. At that moment, Ahmed called to him. He jumped down, pushed his way through the women who had crowded silently around and crawled under the truck.

'See, sahib,' Ahmed said grimly. 'The pipe has been deliberately fractured.'

As Drummond started to examine it, the engine of the supply truck burst into life. He scrambled out frantically, but he was too late. As he shoved the women out of the way, Brackenhurst accelerated. For a little while there was the sound of the engine and then that too died away and there was silence.

Ahmed moved to his side. 'I think there must be a special place in hell reserved for Mr Brackenhurst. What do we do now, sahib?'

'Go after him, what else can we do?'

'Without brakes, sahib?'

'It wouldn't be the first time. I'll take the wheel.'

He turned wearily to the women as a small child started to cry. Its mother hushed it and there was silence again as they waited, stolid and patient.

'Get in!' he said. 'Go on, all of you! Get back in!'

God knows what Brackenhurst would do when he reached Hamid and the others, probably keep right on going. And there was no means of knowing what Hamid might do. Best to try and catch up with him as soon as possible. They could unload the ammunition and transfer the women. If he drove carefully and used the gears, he could manage without the foot brake.

He climbed behind the wheel, eased off the handbrake and took the truck slowly forward. After a while, he gained more confidence, moved into top gear and put on speed. Within five minutes he reached the place where he and Hamid had stopped and rolled slowly to a halt. He could see the tyre marks at the side of the road, and an oil splash, but that was all.

Which wasn't good and he took the truck forward again grimly. There was hail mixed in with the rain now, building up against the windscreen and the wipers were having difficulty in handling it. After half an hour, the road started to slope down.

He changed to a low gear and proceeded more cautiously. The valley widened until it stretched away into the rain for about half a mile, lifting into the mountains that could be seen dimly on his left. The road dropped even more abruptly and peering through the misty windscreen, he saw a small bridge.

He crawled the rest of the way down the hill in bottom gear. The bridge consisted of a flat surface of planks crossing what would otherwise have been a deep ford. There was still no sign of either of the other trucks and he drove across and kept on moving.

The road started to lift steeply, hugging the side of the mountain which now towered above his head and he began to sweat a little. The truck churned steadily upwards through the mud, Drummond gripping the wheel tightly, an expression of utter concentration on his face. He rounded a curve and came to the crest of a hill and the road dropped steeply into the valley below. He leaned across quickly and looked out. There was no fence, only the crumbling, rain-soaked edge and two hundred feet of steeply sloping mountainside.

The truck began the descent, skidding occasionally with a sickening lurch. Drummond was trembling, and beside him Ahmed's face was wet with sweat. The truck lurched again as he negotiated a corner and then the wheels skidded on the shaky surface and slid forward for about fifteen yards. He turned into a skid and then out of it, and by a miracle regained control.

The sweat soaked through his shirt, ran from his forehead into his eyes and he took the truck forward again, hail rattling against the windscreen in a flurry of wind.

The road curved around a great outcrop of black rock and he followed it, hugging the side, turning the corner to where an apron of brown and white water flooded the road, rushing down from the mountain above and cascading into space.

As he started across, the front wheels dipped and the surface of the road dissolved beneath him, washed out in a great sliding scoop, and the truck slewed towards the edge.

For a moment, it seemed to halt and Drummond tugged frantically at the hand-brake, but it was not enough. The truck lurched and one of the front wheels dipped over the edge.

'Jump for it!' he cried to Ahmed.

He got the door open and went out head first, landing on his hands and knees, slipping in the thick mud as the truck slid past him and went over the edge.

It hung there for a split second, and Ahmed, whose door had jammed, got it open a second too late. The truck went over with a chorus of screams from the wretches imprisoned inside. There were three terrible, metal-wrenching crashes as it bounced its way down the valley, a brief moment of silence and then a tremendous explosion.

Drummond moved cautiously to the side and looked down at the bright, orange tongue of flames and turned away, his body heaving in a great, uncontrollable spasm that emptied his stomach.

He leaned against the rock for a while and then scrambled across the washed-out portion of the road and walked on into the rain.

For half a mile the road dropped steeply into the valley and he caught a brief glimpse of the river, winding through the mist below. The rain became colder and darkness started to fall.

There was only one way to go, though God knew where it would take him. He wasn't even armed. His sub-machine gun had gone over the edge with the truck.

Something brushed his face. He raised a gloved hand and saw that it was covered with large melting snowflakes. He looked up and all around him, snow fell intermingled with the rain.

From further along the road came the rattle of small arms fire and he paused for a moment, the snow gently covering him. Who was it? Hamid or Brackenhurst? But there was no means of knowing and he started to walk again.

Darkness increased and the snow gradually took the place of the rain until it was falling all about him, covering the muddy road with a white mantle. Again there came the rattle of small arms fire, much nearer this time.

The situation was beginning to look desperate. If he stayed on the road, he was bound to run into trouble sooner or later to judge from the sound of that firing. Without shelter, he would freeze to death on a night like this.

Trees had now begun to cover the valley bottom and he moved into their shelter and stumbled along, parallel with the road, his gloved hands tucked into his armpits against the intense cold.

Somewhere up the road, there was the clatter of a hoof against stone, and a horse snickered softly. Drummond dropped behind a tree and waited.

There was a soft drubbing of hooves muffled by snow and half a dozen horsemen cantered by. They wore the typical rough sheepskin coat of the hillmen, but the red stars in the peaked caps, the Burp guns slung across their backs, told him what they were.

'What do I do now?' he said softly as the hoofbeats faded into the night.

There was a quiet chuckle almost in his ear and Ali Hamid said, 'Exactly what I was wondering.'

12

The Long Night

'When I first heard you coming, I thought it meant trouble. I was about to become most unpleasant.' Hamid smiled, his teeth gleaming in the darkness. 'A good thing those soldiers rode by. The moment you took cover, I knew you were on the right side.'

It was impossible to see his face in the darkness and Drummond reached out to touch him in sheer relief. 'Ali, you old bastard. What happened?'

'You tell me. We were waiting for you to come back with news of Brackenhurst and you went by as if half the Chinese Army was on your tail.'

'That was Brackenhurst, not me,' Drummond

said and explained quickly what had happened, including the loss of the truck.

There was a moment's silence when he finished and Hamid said softly, 'There was heavy firing up ahead, I think he may have paid the price already, Jack.'

'He couldn't,' Drummond said flatly. 'It's too heavy.'

'Perhaps, but since Sadar, I don't think he's really been responsible for his actions.'

'Where's the truck?'

'About fifty yards back in the woods. I decided to leave the road when we heard the firing up ahead. We obviously weren't going to get any further. I came back to make sure that the snow covered our tracks.'

'Judging by the soldiers, the next village is obviously in Chinese hands. What are we going to do?'

'I haven't the slightest idea. We'll discuss it in more comfortable surroundings. At least we should be safe here for the night.'

Drummond stumbled after him through the darkness and the truck loomed out of the night. 'Not exactly the Savoy,' Hamid said, 'but better than a snowdrift on a night like this. Careful, there are boxes all over the place. I dumped half the load.'

The canvas curtain at the back of the truck moved slightly, showing a chink of light and Father Kerrigan said softly, 'Major Hamid?'

'And guest,' Hamid said. 'The wanderer returns.'

Drummond followed him over the tail-board. He dropped the canvas curtain back into place and turned. As Hamid had said, half the vehicle's load had gone and the remaining boxes had been stacked so as to create a small enclosed alcove. An oil stove was set on a box in the centre throwing out life-giving warmth as well as a dim light.

Father Kerrigan murmured something, a hand on his shoulder, but Drummond had eyes only for Janet kneeling on the other side of the cooker next to the young Khan.

'Jack,' she said in a whisper. 'Jack?'

He moved close, dropped on one knee and took her hand. There were no words, none that would say the things he wanted to say and he touched it to his lips briefly.

'What happened?'

He told his story again in a few brief sentences. When he finished, there were tears in her eyes. 'Those women, those poor women and children. And Ahmed.'

'There was nothing I could do,' he said. 'Nothing.'

'I thought we'd never get round that mountain ourselves,' Hamid said.

In the silence that followed, Janet seemed to pull herself together and put the kettle on the stove. Father Kerrigan said slowly, 'Then the shooting we heard earlier? That must have been Brackenhurst?'

Hamid nodded. 'There were Chinese on horseback up on the road, That means they must be in the next village.'

'Are we safe here?'

'For tonight.'

'And in the morning?'

Hamid shrugged. 'I don't honestly know. Even if we could get the truck out of here again, which I doubt, there's nowhere to go. We'd never get through the village and we all know who's coming up behind.' He held out his hands to the stove. 'We've got shelter, food and warmth and that's a lot under the circumstances.'

'Beans,' Janet said. 'Beans and tea.'

'Sufficient unto the day, isn't that what the Bible says?'

She poured tea into two tin mugs and passed them to Hamid and Drummond. 'Those are all we've got. We'll have to share.'

Drummond took off his mittens and wrapped his frozen hands around the mug, conscious of the warmth and from the shadows opposite, Kerim watched him solemnly, swathed in blankets.

He smiled, showing even white teeth and Drummond smiled back at him. 'He's beginning to liven up.'

Father Kerrigan nodded. 'The natural resilience of the young, I suppose.'

Drummond sat there, staring into the fire, remembering many things. The city burning, the old Khan's eyes blazing into his as he exacted that final promise, Cheung's pale, handsome face. Strange how things turned out. They'd been very good friends, really. And what happened now?

He emptied the mug and passed it to Janet. 'Where's the map?'

Hamid produced it from a pocket of his parka. 'Any ideas?'

'Not at the moment. How far are we from the village?'

'Here.' Hamid pointed as Drummond spread the map on the floor. 'Perhaps five miles. It's called Chamdo. The border's about fifty miles on the other side.'

Drummond examined the map carefully and frowned. 'Where does this track go to running over the mountain from the village? There's a place up on top on the plateau. Ladong Gompa.'

'Ladong Gompa?' Father Kerrigan put in. 'But that's a monastery, a Buddhist monastery. There's a shrine in the next valley, very famous in the old days. Pilgrims used to cross over the mountain and stay overnight at the monastery. I believe that's why it was built in the first place. The old Khan told me about it once.'

Hamid examined the map and shook his head. 'That's eight or nine thousand feet up,

Jack, and the snow starting. Father Kerrigan and Janet could never get across.'

'But you could with the boy,' the priest said.

Drummond cut in quickly. 'We all could if we had horses.'

'Horses?' Hamid said with a frown. 'And where are we going to get horses?'

'As you said, the village is only five miles along the road. If we slipped in just before dawn, we shouldn't have too much trouble.'

'All of us?' Hamid said.

Drummond shook his head. 'Just you and I. The others can wait for us here. When we come back with the horses, we can cut up across the shoulder of the mountain and join the track above the village.'

'If we come back with the horses.'

'At least it gives us a chance.' Drummond shrugged. 'Can you think of anything better?'

Hamid shook his head slowly. 'That's the trouble, Jack, I can't. I don't suppose we have much choice.'

'Then I suggest we get some sleep. We're going to need it.'

Janet passed him a blanket and he wrapped himself in it and lay down next to Hamid and the old priest. Surprising how warm the stove had made the interior now. He looked across at Janet sitting against the boxes, head bowed, the young Khan sleeping in the hollow of her arm.

A wonderful girl. The shadows thrown by the stove on to the canvas hood moved in and out, now coming together, now separating. Just like people, he thought. Now they need each other, now they don't. Now they mingle with each other, now they go their own way.

He slept well in spite of the cold that crept into the truck during the night and found himself crushed between the old priest and Hamid. When he awakened he sat up and lit the stove. The bright flame reflected suddenly from Kerim's unbandaged eye and Drummond grinned at the little boy, huddled in the corner next to Janet.

He motioned him to silence and looked outside. It was that time just before dawn when things begin to take on shape again, to have definition. There wasn't anything like as much snow as he had expected. Quite obviously, it had stopped falling hours before.

He felt curiously refreshed and jumped down into the snow, enjoying the fresh air in his nostrils after the close atmosphere of the truck. As he stood there, the trees started to stand out with a sort of hard luminosity and he knew that dawn was not far away.

'Enjoying the morning air?' Janet said quietly from the truck.

He turned and smiled. 'I don't know if you could say that exactly.' He spread his hands in a vaguely French gesture. 'I feel funny this morning. Close to home, wherever that is, and yet I know I'm not.'

She reached down for his hand in the darkness and gripped it tightly. 'We'll get there, Jack, I know we will.'

'Well just go on believing that.' He grinned. 'Better put some tea on the stove and wake Ali. We haven't got much time.'

'No need.' Hamid looked out of the canvas

screen beside her and Janet moved back. 'What's the day like?'

'Could be worse. It can't have snowed for very long.'

'It'll be back, I can promise you that. We'd better get ready.'

Drummond climbed back into the truck and found Father Kerrigan crouched at the stove beside Janet, opening tins of beans.

'How do you feel?' Drummond asked.

Father Kerrigan smiled. 'The old bones are beginning to creak a little, but I'll manage.'

'One thing I didn't check last night. Can you both ride?'

Janet nodded. 'Since I was a child.'

The priest smiled. 'I should imagine you've been used to a rather more sedate mount than the local variety, my dear. Intractable brutes, I know from bitter experience.'

'I'll manage,' she said confidently. 'What about you, Jack?'

'I get by, but only just. Ali's your man. He's a Hazara. They spent about a thousand years galloping down into India and back again, usually with a woman across the saddle.'

Hamid grinned and broke open a case of Garrand automatic rifles and Drummond cleaned one quickly. He found a box of ammunition and slipped several spare clips into his pockets. Hamid primed half a dozen grenades and they took three each.

Janet called softly and they sat in a circle round the oil stove, drinking hot tea and eating beans. 'That's the last of the food,' she said. 'I can fill the big Thermos with hot tea before we leave, but after that, we've had it.'

Drummond finished his tea and handed her the mug. He glanced at Hamid. 'Ready?'

'As ready as I ever will be.'

Drummond shouldered his Garrand and dropped over the tailboard. When he turned to look up, Father Kerrigan and Janet were pale shadows in the darkness. 'We'll be back in a couple of hours,' he said, trying to sound confident and they moved off.

Hamid led the way through the trees, his boots crunching the crusted snow and as Drummond pushed frost-covered branches to one side with a gloved hand, a feeling of exhilaration took possession of him. It was going to be all right. It had to be. They'd come too far, suffered too much.

Hamid raised an arm and they halted. The road lay just in front of them. As they stood in silence looking at it, snow began to fall quietly in large, firm flakes.

A tall, black finger of rock lifted out of the gloom on the other side and he pointed to it. 'That's as good a marker as any. We might as well use the road, it'll be quicker, but keep your eyes open. I've a nasty feeling we've left a little late. It's getting lighter by the minute.'

And he was right. One by one, the trees seemed to step out of the darkness as they marched along the road. The muddy ruts were ice-bound and iron-hard with just enough snow covering them to make walking easy. They moved quickly, Hamid in the lead, Drummond behind him and keeping to the other side.

The snow was quite heavy now and reduced visibility considerably. There was that strange, absolute quiet that snow always brings and it affected Drummond powerfully so that for a while, he walked with his head bowed, oblivious to all possible danger, alone with his thoughts.

They had travelled for no more than half a mile when he was brought back to reality sharply by Hamid's low, urgent call. He was standing at the side of the road and Drummond hurried to join him.

The tail of a truck was sticking out from the trees at an unnatural angle perhaps twenty-five yards into the wood. They stood there for a moment, not speaking, both thinking the same thought and then Hamid led the way forward, following the snow-covered path the vehicle had made for itself.

It was the supply truck. Drummond brushed snow from the side of the vehicle and his glove snagged on rough edges. He regarded the bullet holes dispassionately.

'The thing's like a sieve. He must have run straight into trouble.'

He wrenched open the door, but the cab was empty and then Hamid called from the other side. Brackenhurst lay huddled under a tree, his face turned slightly, fingers frozen into tallons. There were three gaping holes in his chest.

They stood looking down at him and somewhere, a horse snorted softly. There was the jingle of harness and voices, soft on the morning air. Someone laughed and Hamid and Drummond slipped into the shelter of the trees.

At the end of the jagged lane the truck had made into the wood, two horsemen appeared, Chinese dressed in great sheepskin coats and peaked caps, guns slung across their backs. They reined in, looking down towards the truck and one of them laughed again.

Hamid handed his sub-machine gun to Drummond and said softly, 'Give me your rifle. We can't let them go on. They'll spot the other truck.'

Drummond gave him the Garrand and Hamid rested the barrel against the tree trunk in front of him. The horsemen had just started forward again when his first shot tumbled the lead man from the saddle. He screamed, turning on to his face in the snow. As both horses plunged in panic, the second rider fought to turn his mount. He was still trying when two bullets in the back lifted him from the saddle.

As Drummond and Hamid ran forward, one horse cantered away slowly, back towards the village. The other stood patiently beside the body of its rider. Hamid slung his rifle across his back, gathered the reins and vaulted into the crude sheepskin saddle.

'I'll catch the other one, Jack.'

He urged his mount forward and disappeared into the curtain of snow. Drummond checked the action of the sub-machine gun and waited impatiently. Somewhere in the distance, he seemed to hear a faint cry and then Hamid galloped back along the road, the reins of the second horse in his right hand.

'We'd better get moving. More horsemen back along the road. The bastards are out early this morning.'

Drummond slung the sub-machine gun across his back and took the reins. The horse moved away from him, rolling an eye and he pulled it back savagely and scrambled into the crude saddle.

Hamid urged his mount into a gallop and Drummond hung on grimly as his own horse followed. There was excited shouting somewhere to the rear, but no shooting and then the black finger of rock loomed out of the falling snow on their left and Hamid turned into the trees.

Father Kerrigan was standing anxiously beside the truck and Janet leaned over the tailboard as they dismounted. 'What happened?' the old priest said.

'Never mind now,' Drummond told him. 'Get the boy. We've got to get out of here.'

Janet handed Kerim down, slung a small military haversack over her back and followed him. Swathed in the grey army blankets, the boy looked like a little old woman and didn't seem to be in the least afraid, his large, dark eye taking in everything with interest.

Drummond gave Janet a leg up on to his horse and handed her the child. She settled him in front of her and took the reins.

'Across the road and up the hillside,' he said, 'and don't waste any time getting there.'

As Hamid helped Father Kerrigan into the saddle of the other horse, there was movement up on the road, voices called excitedly and then, quite suddenly, the sharp report of a rifle and a bullet thudded into the side of the truck.

Drummond unslung his sub-machine gun and gave Hamid a violent shove. 'Get out of it, Ali! I'll hold them.'

Hamid didn't argue. He vaulted up behind Father Kerrigan and smashed his clenched fist against the horse's hindquarters. It bounded forward into the trees and the other horse followed instinctively.

Drummond fired a quick burst through the brush towards the excited voices and someone cried out sharply. He ran from the shelter of the truck and dropped on one knee behind a tree.

He could hear the sound of his friends' progress somewhere to the left as Hamid took them away on a diagonal course, obviously intending to cross the road lower down.

A mounted soldier burst through the trees towards the truck, another behind him. Drummond loosed off a long burst that sent both men and horses down in a confused heap, turned and ran headlong through the trees, following the trail left in the snow by the others.

There was movement over to his right, dark shadows against the snow and he emptied the sub-machine gun in a great, sweeping arc and ran on.

As he emerged into a small clearing, a Chinese soldier ran out of the trees on his right. Drummond's sub-machine gun was empty. He dropped it and rushed straight at the Chinese at the same headlong pace.

The man was badly shaken. Instead of trying to aim his Burp gun, he raised it defensively. Drummond ducked under the flailing weapon, grabbed for the throat and lifted a knee into the man's crutch. As the Chinese sank into the snow, he tore the weapon from his grasp and ran on.

He was sobbing for air as he stumbled through the trees and scrambled up the little slope to the road. He slipped and fell to one knee. As he stood up and made to cross, he heard voices through the falling snow.

At least a dozen soldiers were running towards him, but these weren't mounted, they were on foot and wore normal quilted uniforms. And then he saw Cheung in his long greatcoat with the fur collar, mouth open in a soundless cry.

Drummond emptied the magazine in one continuous, clumsy burst that ripped up the surface of the road for twenty yards in front of the Chinese, ran across and started to scramble up the hillside.

He heard the roars of the men behind as they followed then a cry of alarm echoed by an explosion. A few seconds later, there was another. He kept on moving and fell on his face.

Hands dragged him to his feet and Hamid said, 'A good thing I had those grenades.'

Drummond leaned against him, feet splayed and fought for breath. 'The lot I ran into just now,' he said. 'Not soldiers from the village. Cheung and his men. They must have followed on foot from the bridge. Isn't the bastard ever going to give up?'

'I shouldn't imagine so,' Hamid slapped him on the shoulder. 'We'd better get moving. He'll need horses if he's going to follow and that means going to the village. It'll take time.' He grinned savagely. 'With any luck, one of my grenades may have finished him off. He could be lying down there in his own blood right now.'

And then the wind tore a hole in the curtain, and for a moment they saw the road below, the bodies sprawled in the snow, the living moving amongst them and one man who stood quite still, staring up at the mountain, the fur collar of his greatcoat framing the pale face.

'No such luck,' Drummond said with a shudder.

As the curtain swept back into place, he turned and followed Hamid upwards into the driving snow.

On the road, the carnage was absolute as Cheung turned to examine the dead and the dying. Only Sergeant Ng and three men were left on their feet, and then one of the soldiers from the village limped out of the wood clutching a bloody arm, his sheepskin wet with snow.

Cheung went to meet him, the sergeant at his side. 'You are from Chamdo, the next village?'

'Yes, Colonel.'

'How did you get there?'

'By boat from Huma. Two patrols crossed straight over, we came down river.'

'And there are horses there?'

'As many as you need, Colonel.'

Cheung took out his map and examined it quickly, the sergeant peering over his shoulder. He traced a finger along the track leading from Chamdo up over the mountain to Ladong Gompa.

'So that's where they're going,' he said softly and turned to the sergeant. 'A Tibetan name.'

'A monastery, from the sound of it, Colonel,' the sergeant said.

Cheung folded the map and turned to the

wounded soldier from Chamdo. 'How far is the village from here?'

'Five miles, Colonel.'

'Then we've no time to waste.' He nodded to the sergeant. 'We'll march there as quickly as possible and get horses.'

'And the wounded, Colonel?'

'Leave them. We'll send someone from the village.'

He pulled up his collar and started to walk along the iron hard road into the falling snow.

13

The Mountain of God

The snow was a living thing through which they stumbled blindly. Death and the valley had slipped far away and they were alone with man's oldest enemy – the elements.

The hillside was rough, strewn with boulders, and the carpet of snow made the going difficult and unsure. At one point, Father Kerrigan's mount plunged to its knees and Hamid grabbed its bridle, pulling it up again by brute strength.

Janet reined in and Drummond moved up beside her. She was covered in snow and her cheeks were flushed as she smiled down at him.

'How are you doing?'

'Fine and so is Kerim.'

The boy was so swathed in blankets that only his single eye showed, but it sparkled suddenly and Drummond knew that he had smiled.

'These horses are used to this kind of country,' Hamid said. 'Let them choose their own way. They know what they're doing.'

'Do you think we'll find the track?' Drummond said.

'I don't see why not. If we keep climbing on a diagonal line to the east, I can't see how we could miss it.'

They started again, Hamid leading followed by Father Kerrigan, Drummond bringing up the rear. The slope steepened as they moved higher and the full blast of the snow, driven by the wind, hit them as they came out on to the bare mountainside.

At one point half-way up a shelving bank, Janet's horse started to slide. Drummond scrambled forward beating it hard across the rump with his clenched fist and it plunged forward.

It was the snow that showed them the

track, the shape of it clear under the white carpet, zig-zagging up the steep slope beneath them and turning into a narrow ravine about a hundred yards to the right.

When they moved into the ravine, they were sheltered from the wind for a while and climbed upwards, the clatter of hooves against the hard ground echoing between the walls. Gradually, the slope steepened, the walls of the ravine fading into the ground and they came out on the bare mountainside again.

As they climbed, the mountain seemed to rise more steeply, and after another hour they went over the rim of an escarpment and looked across a narrow plateau to where the rock face tilted backwards in great, overlapping slabs, most of which were split and fissured into a thousand cracks.

They moved on, heads down against the driving snow, and after another hour Hamid grabbed the bridle of Father Kerrigan's horse and led it into the shelter of some boulders.

'We'll rest for a while,' he said.

Janet handed Kerim down to Drummond and slipped from the saddle. She wiped the snow from her face and smiled wanly. 'It's cold.'

'Too damned cold,' Drummond said.

Father Kerrigan walked forward stiffly, slapping his arms to restore the circulation. 'I'd better have a look at Kerim.'

Drummond crouched down in the shelter of the boulders and Father Kerrigan knelt beside him and gently parted the blankets. 'God bless my soul, but the child's sleeping.'

'Is he all right?' Janet said anxiously. 'He's warm enough, isn't he?'

'Warmer than any of us in that cocoon.' The old man sat down against the rocks. 'Did you bring the contents of my medical bag?'

Janet nodded and slipped her arms through the straps of the military haversack she'd been carrying on her back. She opened it and took out the Thermos flask of tea she had prepared at breakfast.

'What was it you wanted?'

'Never mind, I'll find it for myself.'

The old priest looked grey and haggard and the lines in his face scoured deep into the flesh. He searched through the contents of the haversack and found what he was looking for, a small bottle of red capsules. He slipped a couple into his mouth and Janet passed him tea in the one tin mug that she had brought.

Father Kerrigan took a mouthful down and leaned back with a sigh. Hamid said anxiously, 'Are you all right, Father?'

The old man opened his eyes and grinned. 'Let's just say I'm not as young as I was, but the pills I've taken start acting straight away. I'll make it. The luck of the Irish.'

The mug came round in turn and when it reached Drummond, he swallowed the hot tea gratefully. Hamid produced a couple of cheroots from one of his breast pockets and they lit them and moved away from the others, looking back down the track into the snow.

'The old man doesn't look too good,' Drummond said. 'How long till we reach the monastery?'

'Maybe three hours,' Hamid said. 'It all depends on the state of the track.'

'I've been thinking,' Drummond said. 'What

guarantee have we got that there will be anyone there when we do reach the place? It could have fallen into disuse years ago. There are ruined monasteries all over the mountains, you know that as well as I do.'

'At least we'll find some sort of shelter,' Hamid said. 'And that's something we're going to need just as soon as we can find it. It's no use pretending the old man or Janet and the child, for that matter, can stand much of this sort of thing.'

They moved back to the others and Father Kerrigan got to his feet. Whatever he had taken had certainly had a miraculous effect and he smiled, cheeks slightly flushed.

'I'm ready when you are.'

Hamid helped him into the saddle, Drummond passed the boy up to Janet and they moved on, skirting the base of the great face of rock slabs.

Over the years, the track had been marked by pilgrims placing their stones on conical cairns which marked quarter-mile intervals and these were still clearly visible in the snow.

An hour later, the track turned into a

narrow ravine that slanted up into the rock. It was choked with boulders and loose stones, an indication of years of neglect.

Hamid took the lead, holding Father Kerrigan's horse by the bridle and Drummond did the same for Janet. He was soon tired and his arm ached with the strain of holding in the unwilling horse. He constantly slipped on the snow, sending loose stones rattling through the maze of boulders below.

Once or twice when they paused, he looked up at Janet and was shocked at the weariness in her eyes. Somehow she managed to smile and he smiled back.

Half an hour later they emerged from the ravine on to a ledge perhaps forty feet across that slanted upwards to the left, jutting out from the cliff face.

Hamid turned, still holding on to the bridle of the old man's horse. 'Everyone all right?'

Drummond glanced up at Janet and she nodded. 'Fine. Keep going.'

The ledge lifted steeply, following the curve of the wall and a sea of swirling snow cloaked the valley below. Drummond followed Hamid and Father Kerrigan, holding the horse as close in to the wall as possible.

And then the ledge narrowed until there hardly seemed room for man and animal together. He pushed forward frantically and came out on the edge of a great plateau.

Beyond them, the ultimate peaks of the mountains stabbed into the sky and great sterile valleys ran between, cutting their way through to the other side.

'The main plateau,' Hamid shouted above the wind. 'The monastery can't be very far away. We'll keep on going.'

It was cold at that height, very cold. No more snow fell, but the wind blew harder and harder until it cut through their clothing, whipping their bruised bodies with cold fingers and the child started to cry.

Janet held him close in her arms and Drummond took the reins of the horse, pulling it forward and then they moved over the crest of a small hill and paused.

Below them was a great natural arena into which many valleys spilled, and squarely in the entrance of one of them stood the monastery of Ladong Gompa. Hamid urged Father Kerrigan's mount forward with a savage cry and Drummond went after him.

The monastery walls had been painted red, green and black to signify the nature of the order, but the colours had faded with the years. It was of no great size and had a bleak, deserted look about it. There was no encircling outer wall, a usual feature of larger establishments, and the entrance was at the top of several steps, protected against the weather by a stone porch.

Snow had drifted in an unbroken line across the steps and a chain hung through a hole high in the wall, jingling faintly as it swung in the wind. When Hamid pulled hard on it, a bell rang hollowly somewhere inside and they waited as its brazen sound died.

After a while, they heard a rattle of wooden clogs on stone and a metallic rasping as bolts were withdrawn. The door swung back to reveal a Buddhist monk in faded yellow robes. He showed no particular surprise and came forward at once to give his hand to Father Kerrigan as the old man stumbled up the steps. Drummond held Kerim until Janet had dismounted, then handed him to her and she followed Father Kerrigan.

Another monk, a younger man, came down the steps and Hamid said, 'What about the horses?'

Like the other one, the young man did not speak, but motioned them to follow him and when he tucked his robe into his girdle so that it didn't trail in the snow, Drummond saw that his feet were bare.

There was an enclosed courtyard at the rear. They waited at the gate and after a while it was opened from inside and they moved in. There were the usual stables and a young novice took the horses from them and they followed the other monk into the monastery.

They walked along a narrow, stone-flagged corridor and entered a large, poorly-furnished room at the far end with a fire of logs burning on a large stone hearth.

Janet was sitting by the fire, Kerim nursed in her arms, while Father Kerrigan sat on a bench by a large wooden table, engaged in animated conversation in English with a much older monk in a yellow, conical hat with ear-flaps.

Father Kerrigan got to his feet and the monk rose with him. 'Major Hamid and Mr Drummond.' He made the introductions in English. 'This is the Abbot of Ladong Gompa. I've been giving him a brief account of our misfortunes. Apparently they still get a few pilgrims across during the summer. Lucky for us, eh?'

'I suppose we're pilgrims in a sense,' Drummond said. 'Pilgrims of hope.'

The Abbot smiled. 'I've been explaining to Father Kerrigan that the other members of our order here are under a strict vow of silence. Please accept that they mean no discourtesy.'

His English was slightly stilted and technically excellent, but was delivered in the grave, expressionless tone of a man who did not use his voice often.

'Can we stay here for a while?' Drummond said.

'As long as you wish.'

'Has Father Kerrigan told you that we are being followed by Communist troops?'

The Abbot nodded. 'Sound travels great distances at this height. We could hear your party coming when you were still crossing the main plateau. There will be ample warning. I will have food sent to you and then blankets. I suggest you all try to get some sleep.'

'And that's the most sensible thing I've heard in a long time,' Drummond said.

'I shall pray for your continuing good fortune.'

The Abbot left the room. Hot food was brought to them, steaming in a great copper bowl, and afterwards blankets.

Drummond draped one over his shoulders and Hamid spread the map out on the table. 'Where do we go from here?'

Hamid ran his finger along another valley, following the track over the top and down the other side of the mountain. 'About fifteen miles to the Indian border from here, that's all.'

Drummond looked across to where Father Kerrigan and Janet were already asleep in front of the fire wrapped in their blankets, Kerim between them.

'Do you think they can make it?'

'They'll have to. We don't have any choice.'

He lay down on the floor beside the others, pulling his blanket over his head, and Drummond stayed at the table. It was peaceful, quiet after the storm, the regular breathing of the sleepers rising and falling gently and after a while he rested his head in his arms and slept.

He awakened suddenly, yawned and stretched his arms so that the blanket fell from him. As he bent down to retrieve it he became aware that the Abbot was standing just inside the door watching him.

'How long have I been asleep?'

The Abbot came forward and sat on the bench on the other side of the table. 'About three hours. It is almost night.'

Drummond glanced across at the others sleeping quietly beside the fire. 'They're very tired. They've been through a great deal.'

The Abbot nodded and brooded quietly, face expressionless and calm as the firelight played across it. Drummond felt completely rested and wide awake, but his feet pained him and the toes on his right foot were numb and lifeless.

He fumbled half-heartedly with the laces of his combat boots, but the knots were swollen and tightened by the constant damp of the past two days and he finally gave up trying.

'It would interest me to know what you think of my country,' the Abbot said.

'Frankly, I can't get out fast enough. I've seen enough of places like this, smoke rising from burning cities, refugees on the move.'

'But you came by choice in the first place, did you not?'

'I once read somewhere that life is action and passion,' Drummond said. 'That if a man failed to take part in it, he wasn't really living.'

He absentmindedly banged his right foot against the floor in an endeavour to restore the circulation and the Abbot said, 'A mistake to take that too literally. It was said by a man who, having experienced the horrors of war, devoted himself to the rule of law for the rest of his life.'

The Abbot crossed the floor and opened

a pair of large wooden shutters revealing the night and the mountains. Drummond joined him on a small stone terrace.

It was very cold and he pulled his blanket more closely about him and shivered. During the past few days, his body had been alternately wet and frozen so many times, that he was now at a stage where his resistance was at a very low ebb.

Night was beginning to fall, cold and clear with great scatterings of stars, brilliant and luminous, strung away across the peaks. As he looked, it darkened quickly from east to west and the stars were blotted out before his eyes as though someone moved among them quickly, snuffing them out between finger and thumb.

'It will snow very heavily soon,' the Abbot said.

A small wind lifted the hair on Drummond's head as it skidded round the corner of the building. Gradually, the shadow moved across the night sky until there were no more stars to be seen and the wind howled mournfully as it sped down the valleys towards them.

'It isn't a night I'd like to be out in.'

The Abbot lifted a hand, motioning him to silence. Drummond strained his ears, but heard nothing. He was about to speak when quite suddenly, as the wind lifted, there was a faint jingling sound.

'They are coming,' the Abbot said simply.

'Are you sure?'

The Abbot nodded. 'Crossing the main plateau.'

'Is there anywhere we could hide?'

The Abbot shook his head. 'This is a small place, not like some. As they are looking for you, they will search thoroughly.'

Drummond dropped his blanket, moved to the fireplace and shook the others awake quickly.

Hamid sat up at once. 'What is it? Trouble?'

Drummond nodded. 'We're about to have company. We'll have to get moving again, I'm afraid.'

'I will have your horses made ready,' the Abbot said and he hurried out.

As Father Kerrigan and Janet got to their

feet, Hamid and Drummond moved across to the shutters. Hamid opened one and peered out. He closed it, his face grim. 'It's snowing again. How long are we going to last in the open on a night like this?'

Drummond turned to Father Kerrigan and Janet, standing by the fire. 'If we stay, Cheung will catch us, there's no doubt of that. He'll take this place apart looking for a hiding place.'

'That's all right, Jack,' Father Kerrigan said in a tired voice. 'It isn't your fault.'

The door opened and the Abbot came in with one of the monks, bundles of sheepskins in their arms. 'A sheepskin coat for each of you. Our shepherds find them very useful at this time of the year.'

As they pulled them on, Hamid said urgently, 'Is there anywhere we can go, anywhere at all? We won't last long on a night like this.'

'I think I can help you,' the Abbot said. 'I'll show you as you leave.'

Kerim was still asleep. Janet lifted him gently in her arms and the Abbot led the way along the dark corridor to the courtyard at the rear.

A monk brought the horses forward and helped Father Kerrigan and Janet into the saddle. They all crossed to the gate and the Abbot moved outside with them.

He pointed to the valley beyond. 'This is the best way, the only way. Eight miles and you're through to the other side of the mountain. You'll find a shepherd's hut at the end with wood for a fire, a lantern, everything you need. From there into the valley is easy. Five miles from the mountain and you will come to an Indian border post.'

Powdery snowflakes were already beginning to stick to their sheepskins as the small cavalcade moved away, Hamid leading Janet's horse, Father Kerrigan behind.

'Thanks for everything,' Drummond said.

The wind lifted snow around his legs as he walked away and the Abbot called quietly, 'Do not worry, my friend. You will reach India.'

The snow began to fall steadily till it filled the night and they were alone with it.

* * *

As they advanced towards the end of the narrow valley, the going became heavier and Drummond's feet sank ankle-deep into the snow. He walked with his head bowed against the wind, alone with his thoughts, and when a sharp stab of pain cut into his face, he winced and came to a halt.

To his surprise, he found that he was knee-deep in snow. When he wrenched off a mitten and touched his face, he felt caked snow and ice on his cheeks and his flesh had split in several places. He frowned and pulled on his mitten, and when he looked up saw that he was alone.

The wind was whipping the snow into a frenzy and it spun around his head and sliced at his cheeks, until his face was so numb he could feel no pain.

How long since they had left the monastery? *An hour? Two hours?* There was no knowing, and as a horse whinnied somewhere near at hand he blundered forward.

He peered down at the ground and saw great slurred hoofprints leading away through the snow and stumbled forward, half-bent so that he could follow them.

Time had stopped and his frozen mind had difficulty in thinking what to do next. The wind was howling like a lost thing and he was completely covered with frozen snow until he no longer resembled an ordinary man. He fell several times, and each time lay in the snow for a little longer before getting up.

A terrible iron band settled around his chest and he seemed to be struggling for breath. Again he heard the whinny of a horse and then it appeared from the whirling darkness, rearing up above his head, Father Kerrigan falling over the hindquarters and knocking him to the ground.

As Drummond sat up, the wind carried the sound of the horse's desperate cry and there was a coldness sweeping into his face, a sense of space, of limitless distance. He crawled forward, feeling the ground in front of him and then his hand touched nothing but air.

He crawled backwards, turned and went back to the old man. Father Kerrigan was on his hands and knees like an animal, his body coated with snow, and Drummond heaved him to his feet and they staggered forward.

It was no good. He was on his knees, the old man beside him in the snow, his arms moving feebly. Drummond took a deep breath, something deep inside, some essential courage that refused to be beaten giving him the strength to haul the old man to his feet.

They stood there, swaying together and then the other horse loomed out of the night, Hamid in the saddle.

What happened after that was something Drummond could never really remember afterwards. He was aware of Hamid pulling the old man up across the saddle with a supreme effort, of shouted directions that were snatched away by the wind and then the horse plunged forward, taking him with it, his right hand hooked firmly around the saddle girth.

It was Janet at the door of the hut with the lantern that saved them and the light drew them out of the storm. Hamid slid to the ground, pulling Father Kerrigan after him and staggered towards the door while Drummond hung on to the horse.

It was no use. As a sudden gust of wind slashed in from the valley driving razor-sharp particles of ice before it, the terrified animal reared up, knocking Drummond to the ground and galloped madly into the night.

He was on his hands and knees again, crawling towards the doorway and the wind seemed to have got inside his brain, dragging him down into the whirling darkness.

14

The Last Round

He awakened slowly and lay for several moments staring up through the gloom, trying to decide where he was. Realisation came suddenly and completely and he tried to sit up.

The hut was low roofed and built of blocks of rough stone. He was lying on a pile of mouldy hay with Hamid beside him. In the middle of the floor a fire burned brightly.

All his outer clothing had been removed and he was only wearing his underwear. He had been covered with sheepskin coats and he pulled them aside and examined his swollen, chapped hands. Gingerly, he touched his face and winced as fingertips probed great splits in his flesh.

His right foot felt heavy and numb and when he sat up, he saw that it had been bandaged. He reached to touch it and Hamid opened his eyes and pushed himself up on one elbow.

'How do you feel?'

'Bloody awful. What's wrong with my foot?'

'A touch of frostbite, nothing serious. All your toes are still there, if that's what you're thinking.'

'I can't feel a damned thing.'

'Janet gave you an injection. Something from the old man's medical kit.'

Drummond looked across to the other side of the fire to where Janet, Father Kerrigan and the young Khan slept peacefully. 'How is he?'

'He had a heart attack when I got him inside last night. Luckily he'd brought the right sort of drugs along and Janet was able to give him an injection.'

'He's in pretty bad shape then?'

'Couldn't walk another step and, in case you don't remember, we lost both horses last night.'

He took a cheroot from his pocket, broke it in two and handed Drummond half. 'The last one so make the most of it.' He walked to the door, opened it slightly and peered out. 'Dawn's coming and the snow seems to be lifting.' He returned to the fire and pulled on his boots. 'I'll take a walk and find out exactly where we are.'

The door closed behind him softly and a small, trapped wind raced round the walls seeking an outlet and then died. There was a sudden movement in the shadows on the other side of the fire and Janet sat up.

'Jack, are you all right?'

'Fine,' he said softly. 'Ali's gone to have a look round.'

He started to dress, fumbling over the buttons with his swollen fingers and she threw some more wood on the fire. 'How's your foot?'

'I'm just beginning to feel it again.'

'I'd better give you another injection.'

He was hardly aware of the needle going in. 'How long will that last?'

'Four or five hours.'

He found the laces of his combat boots quite impossible and she tied them for him after fitting the right boot over the bandaged foot gently.

'How's that?'

'Fine.' He took her hand. 'You look just about ready to fall down. How's Father Kerrigan?'

'Not too good, I'm afraid. He needs hospital treatment.'

'And Kerim?'

She chuckled. 'In better shape than the rest of us put together, I think.'

There was a sudden draught as the door opened, then closed and Hamid dropped by the fire, cursing softly and holding his hands to the flames.

'What's it like?' Drummond said.

'Cold enough to freeze you to the ground, but it's stopped snowing.'

'What about getting out of here?'

'We're in the hollow of a small plateau overlooking the lower slopes of the mountain. According to the Abbot, it's five miles down to the big valley and the Indian border.'

'How rough is the going?'

Hamid shrugged. 'Impossible to tell, it's not quite dawn yet, but it shouldn't take us more than a couple of hours even if conditions are bad. It's all downhill.'

Drummond got to his feet and swayed slightly, suddenly light-headed. 'Are you all right?' Janet said anxiously.

He nodded and walked carefully to the door. Outside it was still dark, but towards the east, a pale, grey light was lifting over the peaks. He followed the line of Hamid's footsteps, climbing up out of the hollow and stood on the rim, looking down into the darkness of the valley.

After a while, he turned and went back to the hut. Hamid glanced up at him as he dropped beside the fire.

'Well, what do you think?'

'The old man will never make it.'

'We could carry him.'

Drummond shook his head. 'We'd have enough trouble getting ourselves down there on foot. Even Janet would find it a struggle.'

'Then what do we do?' Hamid said. 'We can't leave him.'

There was a tired chuckle from the other side of the fire and Father Kerrigan said in a faint voice, 'You haven't any choice, have you?'

'I'm damned if I will,' Drummond said. 'If we assume that Cheung and his men stayed overnight at the monastery because of the storm, then we've got to expect that he'll start out again at first light, especially as it's stopped snowing. He's come this far, he won't stop till he reaches the border and has to accept the inevitable.'

'So what do we do?' Hamid said. 'Stay here and try to beat him off?' He picked up the Garrand. 'With one rifle.'

'What's your suggestion?'

'If we got to the border post fast enough, we could get help.'

'And come straight back?'

'That's right. For all we know, they may have air support down there, helicopters even. They're bound to be reinforcing the entire area in view of what's happened.'

Drummond stood there, indecision on his face and Janet said quietly, 'He's right, Jack, it's the only plan that makes any sense. I'll stay here with Father Kerrigan.'

'Now just wait a minute . . .' Drummond began.

She shook her head, her face grave. 'I'm staying, Jack, he needs me, but you must take Kerim with you.'

'But why, for God's sake?' Drummond demanded. 'We'll be coming back for all of you.'

'You may not be in time.'

She stood before him, arms hanging straight at her sides, calm and determined, her eyes very tired, and then she smiled and there was all the love in the world there for him.

'Hurry back, Jack! Hurry back!'

He reached blindly for her and Hamid took him firmly by the arm. 'We're wasting time, Jack.'

Drummond turned and stumbled to the door and Hamid offered her the rifle. 'I'll leave you this.'

She shook her head. 'I couldn't use it, Ali,' she said simply.

Hamid stood there for a moment, a frown

on his face and then he slung the rifle over his back and went round the fire to where Kerim slept beside the old priest, swathed in his blankets.

He picked the boy up gently, cradling him in his arms and Father Kerrigan smiled. 'I'd take it as a personal favour if you'd run all the way, Major.'

Hamid turned and went out, the lump that rose in his throat threatening to choke him. Drummond was waiting outside and the Pathan walked past him without speaking, the boy held close to his chest.

Drummond stumbled after him. On the rim of the hollow he paused to look back at the hut. Janet was standing in the entrance. She gazed towards him for a long moment and then went back inside. The door closed with a strange finality and Drummond turned and went down the slope after Hamid.

Progress was slow at first for on the upper slopes, sheltered by a shoulder of the mountain, the snow had not been swept away and had fallen in a deep blanket that made walking difficult.

Drummond soon realised how weak he was. They had not covered a mile before he was gritting his teeth and placing one foot in front of the other with a dogged persistence. Hamid seemed tireless and ploughed ahead through the snow without faltering, but his face, when they rested in the lee of a large boulder, told another story.

Kerim's single eye over the edge of the blanket was round with wonder and Hamid laughed. 'I wonder how much of this he'll remember in the years to come?'

'God knows,' Drummond said hoarsely. 'Here, give him to me. I'll take him for a while.'

Hamid didn't even try to argue, a bad sign, and they started to walk again. The boy seemed heavy, which was a strange thing, and Drummond held him close and leaned well back as he went down the slope.

Another mile and his legs were trembling and when he tried to take another pace forward, he overbalanced and rolled over and over down the mountainside.

He held on tight to the boy and the world spun and red sparks flashed before his eyes. Faintly, through a great roaring, he heard Hamid calling to him and he came to rest in a great drift of snow.

The boy was crying and Hamid picked him up and brushed snow from his face as Drummond got painfully to his feet. Hamid's eyes seemed to have receded into their sockets, and lines of fatigue were etched deeply into his face. They didn't speak – there was nothing to say. He started to march, the boy against his chest and Drummond followed.

Time no longer had any significance for Drummond. He placed one foot doggedly in front of the other, and after a while they left the slopes and struggled over a flat plain of deep snow. Half-way across, they had to rest, completely exhausted.

Darkness had fled across the mountains and day had dawned, grey and sullen, more snow threatening in the heavy clouds as they finally struggled out of the deep snow and entered a thinly wooded stretch that sloped down to the valley bottom.

Drummond sucked a piece of ice, delighting in the coolness of it as it melted in his mouth and trickled down his throat and hobbled along in a strange, trance-like mood.

It was with a sense of shock that he found himself lying in the snow, the taste of it cold in his mouth and then a foot dug into his side and he heard Hamid's dead, washed-out voice.

'Get up, Jack. I haven't the strength to lift you.'

He turned away and Drummond with a supreme effort got to his feet and went after him. He bowed his head and placed one foot in front of the other. He repeated that simple action until he had lost count of time and suddenly heard a shout in front.

Hamid had stopped on top of a slight rise twenty or thirty yards away and called to him in a strange, cracked voice. Drummond broke into a stumbling run and reached the top of the rise in time to see Hamid staggering down towards the camp in the hollow below. There were field guns deeply entrenched, supply trucks parked at the rear and a sprinkling of snow-covered huts.

Men were flooding forward, men in familiar uniforms and khaki turbans, some riding supply mules. They reached Hamid and Drummond saw him hand the boy carefully to a great, bearded Sikh. He turned, looked back at Drummond, took a single hesitant step and fell on his face in the snow.

Drummond slid to the ground and sat there, tears rolling down his cracked cheeks as the soldiers moved towards him.

It was warm in the hut and he sat before the stove, a blanket round his shoulders and sipped hot tea slowly, holding the mug in both hands. After a while, the door to the other room opened and a young Bengali medical corps sergeant came in.

'How is he?' Drummond asked.

'Fine,' the sergeant said. 'He's fallen asleep now, quite exhausted.'

'And the boy?'

'Having a meal in the officers' mess, such as it is.' The sergeant laughed. 'There's nothing wrong with that one. He seems to have enjoyed himself, if anything, during the past few days. More brandy?'

Drummond nodded and held out his mug. 'How much longer will your commanding officer be?'

'He shouldn't be long now. The main command post is only three miles away, but since the snow, of course, we're having to use mules.'

The door swung open, a cold wind whistling round the room and young Lieutenant Singh entered. 'Major Naru's coming now, Mr Drummond.'

'Thank God for that.'

Drummond got to his feet and hobbled to the window in time to see the major and an escort of two privates ride up on mules. They dismounted and the major came up the steps to the hut, brushing snow from his parka with both hands.

Lieutenant Singh opened the door for him and he came in and moved straight to the fire, a tall, handsome man with a clipped moustache.

'Mr Drummond?' He pulled off his gloves and held out a hand. 'A pleasure to see you here, sir.'

'Believe me, it's a pleasure to be here, Major,' Drummond said. 'Did Lieutenant Singh give you the whole story?'

The major nodded. 'We spoke over the field telephone. Where is Major Hamid?'

'Asleep in the other room. He's done the work of ten men during the past few days.'

'And the young Khan?'

'We're looking after him in the officers' mess, sir,' Lieutenant Singh put in.

'What about my friends, Major?' Drummond said. 'When can we make a start? I wanted to return with men and mules straight away, but the lieutenant said he couldn't move without the good word from you.'

Major Naru sighed. 'I'm afraid it's rather more complicated than that. The Chinese invasion of Balpur is something my government must handle with the greatest care. An emergency session has already started at the United Nations. Under these circumstances, all units on the border have been ordered to avoid any confrontation with Chinese units at whatever the cost. It would be impossible for me to even consider sending a patrol into Balpur territory.'

'But that hut's no more than five miles from here,' Drummond said. 'With mules, we could be there in less than an hour and time is vital. As I explained to Lieutenant Singh, Colonel Cheung could beat us to the punch.'

'All the more reason to avoid a situation which could lead to possible military action.'

'We'll see what Major Hamid has to say about this,' Drummond said angrily and he moved to the door of the inner room.

'Major Hamid is an officer of the Indian Army. He will do what I have to do – obey orders.' Major Naru's voice cracked suddenly. 'Do you think I'm enjoying this, Mr Drummond? If I had my way, I'd move over that border now with every man I've got.' He pulled on his gloves. 'I'm going to get in touch with Headquarters by radio immediately. If they give me the word, I'll lead my men in myself, I promise you.'

'How long will that take?'

'To get a reply?' Major Naru shrugged. 'An hour, perhaps two. It is something they will have to consider carefully.' He moved to the door and Singh opened it for him. 'I am sorry, Mr Drummond.'

The door closed behind them and Drummond went to the window. Major Naru walked across to the command post, Singh at his shoulder. The three mules he and his escort had used were tethered outside. Drummond looked at them for a moment, then made his decision.

The medical sergeant was standing by the stove, his face troubled, and Drummond moved past him and opened the door to the inner room. Hamid lay on his back on one of the bunks, breathing gently, the harsh lines smoothed from his handsome face.

When they had carried him in, someone had brought his rifle and it stood in the corner by the window. Drummond slung it over his back and looked down at Hamid for a moment.

'Good luck, Ali,' he said softly and returned to the other room.

He uncorked the brandy bottle, poured some into his mug and swallowed it quickly and the medical sergeant watched, a frown on his face.

'Why the rifle, Mr Drummond?'

'I'm going for a little ride,' Drummond said. 'It might come in useful.'

He went to the door and opened it, the sergeant hurrying at his shoulder. 'But this is madness.'

Drummond ignored him, went down the steps pulling on his mittens and crossed to the mules. As he unhitched them, the medical sergeant ran past him, mounted the steps to the command post and went inside.

Drummond took his time, lopped the reins of two of the mules to the pommel of the saddle of the third, mounted, and rode away.

He passed between the field guns, men standing up to stare at him, and then Major Naru and Lieutenant Singh emerged from the command post, the medical sergeant at their backs, and hurried after him.

As Drummond passed the last gun emplacement, they caught up with him and Major Naru reached for the bridle of the mule he was riding.

'I can't let you do this, Mr Drummond.'

'Then you'd better start shooting,' Drummond said calmly. 'It's the only way you're going to stop me.'

He jerked the bridle from the major's grasp, dug his heels into the mule's flanks and moved forward. When he reached the crest of the small hill and looked back into the hollow, Major Naru was still standing there in front of the gun, but Lieutenant Singh was running back towards the command post.

The clouds had dropped down towards the jagged peaks, heavy with snow, and as the mules moved out of the valley and started up the mountain, the first few flakes started to fall.

Drummond no longer felt tired, but there was a strange singing inside his head, perhaps the brandy talking, and he was alone in a great white silence, following the double track in the snow that he and Hamid had made on their way down.

He pushed the mules as much as he could, moving up into the white stillness towards the peaks as the snow continued to fall. It was just under an hour after leaving the camp that he came out of a ravine on to the final slope and moved up towards the plateau.

From the rim of the plateau, sheltered by a group of jagged rocks, Sergeant Ng watched his progress from the moment he emerged from the ravine. As Drummond drew closer, he turned and hurried down to Colonel Cheung who stood beside the horses outside the hut in the hollow below.

Cheung looked tired and the skin of his face stretched tightly over his cheekbones, was raw with frostbite. 'One man coming with three mules,' Sergeant Ng said.

'Take the horses inside,' Cheung told him and he moved up out of the hollow to the rim of the plateau.

He watched Drummond for a full minute

and there was no excitement in his heart. He had failed, utterly and completely, and in Pekin he would have to face the consequences of that failure, but at least he would have something of value to take back with him.

He ran down into the hollow and went inside the hut. The horses had crowded to the far end and were quietly feeding on the hay. Father Kerrigan was sitting up on the other side of the fire. Janet standing beside him and Ng waited by the door.

'It's Drummond,' Cheung said. 'I'll stay down here. You wait for him in the rocks on the edge of the hollow. Let him ride past you before you make your move.'

'Do you want him alive?' Ng asked calmly.

'At all costs.'

Ng went out, closing the door behind him and Cheung drew his revolver. He smiled gently across the fire at Janet and Father Kerrigan.

'It would be unwise for either of you to attempt to make the slightest noise, do I make myself clear?'

* * *

Drummond came over the edge of the plateau and reined in. It was a peaceful scene, the hut standing below in the hollow, smoke rising into the gently falling snow. He had unslung the Garrand as a precaution while still in the ravine and now it rested across the saddle in front of him.

He dug his heels into his mule's flanks and started into the hollow. He was perhaps half-way down the slope, when there was a commotion inside the hut, the door was flung open and Janet ran outside.

'Behind you, Jack!' she called. 'Behind you!'

Drummond released the two lead mules and jerked savagely on the bridle of his own mount, pulling it round as Sergent Ng emerged from the rocks at the top of the hollow, sub-machine gun in his hands.

He fired a warning burst into the air and Drummond's mule reared, throwing him over its hindquarters as he reached for the Garrand.

He came to his knees in deep snow, the Garrand still in his hands, the three mules milling around him. Sergeant Ng crouched, trying to get a clear view, and Drummond fired twice in rapid succession, the bullets somersaulting the Chinese back over the rocks.

As the mules broke away, trotting down to the hut, he turned and saw Janet on one knee, Cheung holding her by the hair, the barrel of his revolver rammed against her neck.

Drummond walked forward, the rifle at his hip, and stopped a yard or two away. 'Let her and the old man go, Cheung, take me. I could be of real value, more than you could ever realise.'

'No bargains, Jack, quickly now.'

Cheung's voice was as soft as ever, but quite implacable, and as he thumbed back the hammer of his revolver, Drummond threw the Garrand far away into the snow.

'That's better.'

As Cheung released his hold, Janet came to her feet and ran into Drummond's arms. He held her close for a moment. 'Is Father Kerrigan all right?'

She nodded. 'What about Ali and Kerim?'

'We reached the border safely, but the Indian Army has strict orders about crossing over. I had to come back alone.'

'How very fortunate for me,' Cheung said and he pulled Janet back against him. 'You've caused me a great deal of trouble, Jack. I tried to follow you from Ladong Gompa last night and got caught in the blizzard. We had to turn back. Only Sergeant Ng and I made it. I knew I'd be too late and yet I still came on this morning. That's the kind of man I am.'

'Father Kerrigan and the girl can't be of any use to you. Let them go. I won't give you any trouble.'

'They want you in Pekin, Jack,' Cheung said. 'They know all about the work you've been doing for Ferguson. When you stand before a military tribunal, these two will stand beside you, I'll see to that personally.'

Drummond shook his head. 'You'll be facing your own tribunal, Colonel. You lost the young Khan, remember?'

Something glowed in Cheung's eyes, he

pushed the girl away from him and the revolver came up. Drummond tensed himself to spring, knowing already that he was too late.

Cheung took a deep breath and shook his head. 'Oh, no, Jack, nothing as easy as that, I promise you.'

Somewhere horses plunged and snorted and a hard, familiar voice called, 'Over here, Cheung!'

Hamid was already sliding from the back of a mule up on the rim of the hollow, an automatic rifle in his hands. Cheung turned, crouching, and Hamid fired three times so quickly that they sounded like one, the first shot catching Cheung in the shoulder, spinning him round, the second and third driving him hard against the wall.

Janet turned away quickly, stumbling into Drummond's arms as Cheung struggled for life, clawing for the revolver he had dropped, and then blood erupted from his mouth in a bright flow and he coughed once and lay still.

Lieutenant Singh came over the skyline on a mule, reaching for the bridle of Hamid's mount, following him down into the hollow. Hamid turned Cheung over with his toe and looked down at him.

'The face of the damned.'

'What happened?' Drummond said. 'I thought the Indian Army was supposed to stay on its own side of the border?'

'It still is,' Hamid said. 'Young Singh here, woke me just after you left. He thought I might have other ideas, which I did. Being a young man of spirit, he decided to come with me.'

'And Major Naru?'

'Most unhappy.'

'Do I detect the possibility of a court martial in the near future?'

'A matter of supreme indifference to either of us, but, in any event, unlikely. The newspapers wouldn't like it. Is Father Kerrigan all right?'

'As right as he ever will be,' the old priest said, appearing in the doorway. 'Nothing that a bottle of Jamiesons' and a decent meal wouldn't cure.'

'Then I suggest we take you to where we

can obtain both items as quickly as possible. Poor Naru will be most uncomfortable until we cross the border.'

They brought out the horses and helped Father Kerrigan and Janet into the saddle. The old man looked down at Cheung, crossed himself and muttered a prayer as he moved off between Singh and Hamid, and Janet followed.

Drummond was the last to leave, and after he'd mounted, he sat on his mule for a moment or two looking down at Cheung, feeling strangely sad.

But nothing mattered now except that life began again, and as he rode up towards Janet, waiting for him on the edge of the plateau, he was smiling.

Jack Higgins

Jack Higgins lived in Belfast till the age of twelve. Leaving school at fifteen, he spent three years with the Royal Horse Guards, serving on the East German border during the Cold War. His subsequent employment included occupations as diverse as circus roustabout, truck driver, clerk and, after taking an honours degree in sociology and social psychology, teacher and university lecturer.

The Eagle Has Landed turned him into an international bestselling author, and his novels have since sold over 250 million copies and have been translated into fifty-five languages. Many of them have also been made into successful films. His recent bestselling novels include *Bad Company, A Fine Night for Dying, Dark Justice*, *Toll for the Brave, Without Mercy* and *Storm Warning*.

In 1995 Jack Higgins was awarded an honorary doctorate by Leeds Metropolitan University. He is a fellow of the Royal Society of Arts and an expert scuba diver and marksman. He lives on Jersey.

Visit www.AuthorTracker.co.uk for exclusive updates on Jack Higgins.

Also by Jack Higgins

The Valhalla Exchange
To Catch a King
Dillinger
The Run to Morning
The Eagle Has Landed
A Prayer for the Dying
The Last Place God Made
Storm Warning
Day of Judgment
Solo
Luciano's Luck
Touch the Devil
Exocet
Confessional
Night of the Fox
A Season in Hell
Memoirs of a Dance-Hall Romeo
Cold Harbour
The Eagle Has Flown
Eye of the Storm
Thunder Point
On Dangerous Ground
Sheba
Angel of Death
Drink with the Devil
Year of the Tiger
The President's Daughter
Flight of Eagles
The White House Connection
Pay the Devil
Day of Reckoning
Edge of Danger
The Keys of Hell
Midnight Runner
Bad Company
A Fine Night for Dying
Dark Justice
Toll for the Brave
Without Mercy
East of Desolation

JACK HIGGINS

TOUCH THE DEVIL

HARPER

This novel is entirely a work of fiction.
The names, characters and incidents portrayed in it are the work of the author's imagination. Any resemblance to actual persons, living or dead, events or localities is entirely coincidental.

Harper
An Imprint of HarperCollins*Publishers*
77–85 Fulham Palace Road,
Hammersmith, London W6 8JB

www.harpercollins.co.uk

This paperback edition 2007
1

First published in Great Britain by
William Collins Sons & Co Ltd 1982

A catalogue record for this book is available from the British Library

ISBN: 978-0-00-783206-4

Typeset in Sabon by Palimpsest Book Production Limited, Grangemouth, Stirlingshire

Printed and bound in Great Britain by
Clays Ltd, St Ives plc

PUBLISHER'S NOTE

TOUCH THE DEVIL was first published in the UK by William Collins Sons & Co Ltd in 1982 and in 1983 by Pan Books, but has been out of print for some years.

In 2008, it seemed to the author and his publishers that it was a pity to leave such a good story languishing on his shelves. So we are delighted to be able to bring back TOUCH THE DEVIL for the pleasure of the vast majority of us who never had a chance to read the earlier editions.

For Margaret Hewitt

Between two groups of men that want to make inconsistent kinds of worlds. I see no remedy except force . . . It seems to me that every society rests on the death of men.

Oliver Wendell Holmes

Vietnam 1968

PROLOGUE

The Medevac helicopter drifted across the delta at a thousand feet, her escort a Huey Cobra gunship keeping station to the left. Rain threatened, the clouds over the jungle in the far distance heavy with it, and thunder rumbled on the distant horizon.

Inside the Medevac, Anne-Marie Audin sat in a corner, eyes closed, her back supported by a case of medical supplies. She was a small, olive-skinned girl with black hair razor-cut close to the skull, a concession to the living conditions of the Vietnam war front. She wore a camouflage jump jacket, unzipped at the front, a khaki bush shirt and pants tucked into French paratroopers' boots. The most interesting features were the cameras, two Nikons strung around her neck by leather straps; the pouches of the jump jacket contained, not ammunition, but a variety of lenses and dozens of packets of 35 millimetre film.

The young medic squatting beside the negro Crew Chief gazed at her in frank admiration. The first two buttons of the khaki bush shirt were undone, giving a hint, no more, of the firm breasts rising and falling gently as she slept.

'A long time since I saw anything like that,' he said. 'A real lady.'

'And then some, boy.' The Crew Chief passed him a cigarette. 'There's nowhere that girl hasn't been. She even jumped with the 503rd Paras at Katum last year. You name it, she's done it. *Life* magazine did an article on her six or seven months back. She's from Paris, would you believe that? And from the kind of family that owns a large slice of the Bank of France.'

The boy's eyes widened in amazement. 'Then what in the hell is she doing here?'

The Crew Chief grinned. 'Don't ask me, kid. I don't even know what I'm doing here.'

'Have you a cigarette? I seem to have run out,' Anne-Marie said.

Her eyes were greener than anything he had ever seen, the Crew Chief realised that as he tossed a pack across to her. 'Keep them.'

She shook one out and lit it with an old brass lighter fashioned from a bullet, then closed her eyes again, the cigarette lax in her fingers. The boy had been right, of course. What was she doing here, the girl who had everything? A grandfather who doted on her, one of the richest and most powerful industrialists in France. A father who had survived Indo-China only to die in Algeria, an infantry colonel, five times decorated, Chevalier of the Legion of Honour. An authentic hero and just as dead.

Her mother had never recovered from the shock, had died in a car crash near Nice two years later. The thought often crossed Anne-Marie's mind that perhaps it had been a deliberate turn of the wheel which had taken the Porsche over the edge of that mountain road that night.

Poor little rich girl. Her mouth twisted in a derisory smile, her eyes still closed. The houses, the villas, the servants, the good English schools, and then the Sorbonne; a year of that stifling academic atmosphere had been enough. Not forgetting the affairs, of course, and the brief flirtation with drugs.

It was the camera which had saved her. From her first Kodak at the age of eight, she had had an instinctive genius for photography, which had developed over the years into what her grandfather described as Anne-Marie's little hobby.

After the Sorbonne, she had made it more than that. Had apprenticed herself to one of the finest fashion photographers in Paris for six months, had then joined *Paris-Match* as a staff photographer. Her reputation had soared astonishingly within one short year, but it was not enough – not nearly enough – and when she asked to be assigned to Vietnam, they had laughed at her.

So, she had resigned, turned freelance and in a final confrontation with her grandfather, had forced from him a promise to use all his formidable political power to obtain for her the necessary credentials from the Department of Defense. It was a new Anne-Marie he had seen that day: a girl filled with a single-minded ruthlessness which had surprised him. And yet had also filled him with reluctant admiration. Six months, he had said. Six months only, and she had promised, knowing beyond any shadow of a doubt that she would break that promise.

Which she did, for when her time was up, it was too late to turn back. She was famous, her material used by every major magazine in Europe and America. *Time, Paris-Match, Life*, had all clamoured for the exclusive services of this mad French girl who had jumped with the paratroopers at Katum. The girl for whom no assignment was too rough or too dangerous.

Whatever it was she was looking for, she discovered what war was about, at least in Vietnam. No set-piece battles. No trumpets in the wind, no distant drum to stir the heart. It was savage street fighting in Saigon during the *Tet* offensive. It was the swamps of the

Mekong Delta, the jungles of the central highlands. The leg ulcers that ate their way through the bone like acid, leaving scars which would never go away.

Which brought her to today. A morning spent waiting in the rain at Pleikic trying to arrange transportation to Din To until she'd managed to thumb a lift in the Medevac. God, but she was tired – more tired than she had ever been in her life. It occurred to her, that perhaps she'd reached the end of something. She frowned slightly. And then the Crew Chief called out sharply.

He was hanging in the open doorway, pointing to where a flame had soared into the sky a few hundred yards to the east. The Medevac swung towards it and started to go down, followed by the Huey Cobra gunship.

Anne-Marie was on her feet and standing beside the Crew Chief, peering out. There was the burnt-out wreck of a helicopter in a corner of a paddy field, several bodies sprawled beside it. The man who waved frantically from the dyke was in American uniform.

The Medevac went on down, her escort circling warily, and Anne-Marie locked a lens into place on one of her Nikons and started to take pictures one after the other, braced against the Crew Chief's shoulder.

He turned his head to smile at her once and then, when they were no more than thirty feet up, she realised, with a strange kind of detachment, that the face she was focusing on below was Vietnamese, not American. A couple of heavy machine guns opened up from the jungle fifty yards away and at that range they couldn't miss.

The Crew Chief didn't stand a chance, standing in the open door. Bullets hammered into him, punching him back against Anne-Marie who was hurled against the medical supplies. She pushed him to one side and got to one knee. The young medic was huddled in the corner, clutching a bloody arm and as another solid burst of machine gun fire raked the cockpit, she heard the pilot cry out.

She lurched forward, grabbing at a strut for support; at the same moment the aircraft lifted violently and she was thrown out through the open door to fall into the mud and water of the paddy field. The Medevac bucked twenty or thirty feet up in the air, veered sharply to the left and exploded in a great ball of fire, burning fuel and debris scattering like shrapnel.

Anne-Marie managed to stand, plastered with mud, and found herself facing the man on the dyke in American uniform who, she could see now, was very definitely Vietnamese. The rifle he pointed at her was a Russian AK47. Further along the dyke, half a dozen Vietcong in straw hats and black pyjamas climbed from the ditch and moved towards her.

The Huey Cobra swept in, its heavy machine guns kicking dirt along the dyke, driving the Vietcong backwards into the ditch. Anne-Marie glanced up and the gunship hovered; then forty or fifty North Vietnamese regular troops in khaki uniforms appeared from the jungle on the far side of the paddy field and started to fire at the gunship with everything they had. The gunship moved towards them, loosing off its rocket pods,

lighter back to her. She shook her head and for some reason she couldn't possibly explain, said, 'No, keep it.'

'As my memento?'

'*Memento mori*,' she said. 'We'll never get out of this place alive.'

'Oh, I don't know. That Cobra's still on station. I'd say the cavalry should arrive within the next twenty minutes, just like Stage Six at MGM. In the nick of time. I'd better let them know they're not wasting it.'

He took a flare pistol from a side pouch and fired a red flare high into the sky.

'Couldn't that be the Vietcong playing games again?'

'Not really.' He fired another red flare, then a green. 'Colours of the day.'

Her leg was just starting to hurt. She said, 'So now they know where we are, the Vietcong, I mean.'

'They already did.'

'And will they come?'

'I should imagine so.'

He wiped the M16 clean with a rag and she raised the Nikon and focused it. As she discovered later, he was twenty-three and just under six feet in height with good shoulders, the dark hair held back by the sweatband giving him the look of some sixteenth century bravo. The skin was stretched tightly over Celtic cheekbones and a stubble of beard covered the hollow cheeks and strongly pointed chin. But it was the eyes which were the most remarkable feature, grey, like water over a stone, calm, expressionless, holding their own secrets.

'What are you?' she said.

'Airborne Rangers. Sergeant Martin Brosnan.'

'What happened here?'

'A bad foul-up is what happened. Those clever little peasants, half our size, who we were supposed to walk all over, caught us very much as they caught you. We were on our way to Din To after being picked up from a routine patrol. Fourteen of us plus the crew. Now there's only me for certain. Maybe a few out there still alive.'

She took several more pictures and he frowned. 'You can't stop, can you, just like the guy said in the article he wrote about you in *Life* last year. It's obsessional. Christ, you were actually going to take a picture of that kid as he was about to shoot you.'

She lowered the Nikon. 'You know who I am?'

He smiled. 'How many women photographers have made the cover of *Time* magazine?'

He lit another cigarette and passed it to her. There was something about the voice which puzzled her.

'Brosnan,' she said. 'I'm not familiar with that name.'

'Irish,' he said. 'Well, County Kerry to be exact. You'll seldom find it anywhere else in Ireland.'

'Frankly, I thought you sounded English.'

He looked at her in mock horror, 'My father would turn in his grave and my mother, God bless her, would forget she was a lady and spit in your eye. Good Irish-American, Boston variety. The Brosnans came over during the famine a long time ago, all Protestants, would you believe? My mother was born in Dublin herself. A good Catholic and could never forgive my father for not raising me the same.'

He was talking to keep her mind off the situation, she knew that and liked him for it. 'And the accent?' she said.

'Oh, that's part acquired by way of the right prep school, Andover in my case, and the right university, of course.'

'Let me guess. Yale?'

'My family have always gone there, but I decided to give Princeton a chance. It was good enough for Scott Fitzgerald and I'd pretensions to being a writer myself. Majored in English last year.'

'So,' she said, 'What's a spoiled preppy brat doing in Vietnam, serving in the ranks in the toughest outfit in the Army?'

'I often ask myself that,' Brosnan said. 'I was going to carry straight on and do my doctorate and then I found Harry, our gardener, crying in the conservatory one day. When I asked him what was wrong, he apologised and said he'd just heard his son, Joe, had been killed in Nam.' Brosnan wasn't smiling now. 'But the real trouble was that there'd been another son called Elie, killed in the Delta the year before.'

There was a heavy silence, the rain flooded down. 'Then what?'

'My mother had him in and gave him a thousand dollars. I remember it well because the cashmere and silk jacket I was wearing at the time had cost me eight hundred in Savile Row on a London trip the year before. And he was so damn grateful.'

He shook his head and Anne-Marie said softly, 'So, you made the big gesture.'

'He made me feel ashamed, and when I feel, I act. I'm a very existentialist person.'

He smiled again and she said, 'And how have you found it?'

'Nam?' He shrugged. 'Hell without a map.'

'But you've enjoyed it? You have an aptitude for killing, I think.' He had stopped smiling, the grey eyes watchful. She carried on, 'You must excuse me, my friend, but faces you see, are my business.'

'I'm not so sure about liking it,' he said. 'I'm damned good at it, I know that. Out here you have to be if the fellow coming at you has a gun in his hand and you want to get home for Christmas.'

There was silence, a long silence, and then he added, 'I. know one thing, I've had enough. My time's up in January and that can't come soon enough for me. Remember what Eliot said about the passage we didn't take towards the door we never opened into the rose garden? Well, from now on, I'm going to open every door in sight.'

The morphine was really working now. The pain had gone, but also her senses had lost their sharpness. 'Then what?' she said. 'Back to Princeton for that doctorate?'

'No,' he said. 'I've been giving that a lot of thought. I've changed too much for that. I'm going to go to Dublin, Trinity College. Peace, tranquillity. Look up my roots. I speak a fair amount of Irish, something my mother drummed into me as a kid.'

'And before that?' she said. 'No girl waiting back home?'

'No more than eighteen or twenty, but I'd rather be sitting at one of those pavement cafes on the Champs Elysée sipping Pernod and you in one of those Paris frocks.'

'And rain, my friend.' Anne-Marie closed her eyes drowsily. 'An absolute necessity. So that we may smell the damp chestnut trees,' she explained. 'An indispensable part of the Paris experience.'

'If you say so,' he said, and his hands tightened on the M16 as there was a stirring in the reeds close by.

'Oh, but I do, Martin Brosnan.' Her voice was very sleepy now. 'It would give me infinite pleasure to show you.'

'That's a date then,' he said softly and came up on one knee crouching, firing into the reeds.

There was a cry of anguish and then a long burst in reply and something punched Brosnan high in the left side of the chest and he went over backwards across the girl.

She stirred feebly and he came up, firing one-handed at the man who charged through the reeds, that smile on his face again, and as the M16 emptied, he hurled it into the face of the last man, drawing his combat knife, probing for the heart up under the ribs as they went down together.

He lay in the mud for quite some time, holding the Vietcong against him, waiting for him to die and suddenly, two Skyraiders swooped overhead and half a dozen gunships moved in out of the rain, line astern.

Brosnan got up awkwardly and lifted Anne-Marie in his arms, grimacing against the pain. He started to wade through the reeds towards the open paddy field.

'I told you the cavalry would arrive.'

She opened her eyes. 'In the nick of time? And then what?'

He grinned. 'One thing's for sure. After this, it can only get better.'

Paris 1979

1

A cold wind lifted across the Seine and dashed rain against the windows of the all-night cafe by the bridge. It was a small, sad place, half a dozen tables and chairs, no more, usually much frequented by prostitutes. But not on a night like this.

The barman leaned on the zinc-topped counter reading a newspaper. Jack Corder sat at a table by the window, the only customer, a tall, dark-haired man in his early thirties. His jeans, worn leather jacket and cloth cap gave him the look of a night porter at the fish market up the street, which he very definitely was not.

Barry had said eleven-thirty so Corder had

arrived at eleven, just to be on the safe side. Now, it was half-past midnight. Not that he was worried. Where Frank Barry was concerned, you never knew where you were, but then, that was all part of the technique.

Corder lit a cigarette and called, 'Black coffee and another cognac.'

The barman nodded, pushed the newspaper to one side and at that moment the telephone behind the bar started to ring. He answered it at once, then turned enquiringly.

'Your name is Corder?'

'That's right.'

'It would seem there is a taxi waiting for you on the corner.' He replaced the receiver. 'You still wish the coffee and the cognac, Monsieur?'

'The cognac only, I think.'

Corder shivered for no accountable reason and took the cognac down in one quick swallow. 'It's cold even for November.'

The barman shrugged. 'On a night like this, even the *poules* stay home.'

'Sensible girls.'

Corder pushed a note across the table and

went out. The wind dashed rain in his face and he turned up the collar of his jacket, ran to the old Renault taxi waiting on the corner, wrenched open the rear door and got in. It moved away instantly and he sank back against the seat. They turned across the bridge and the lights in their heavy glass globes made him think of Oxford with a strange sense of *déjà vu*.

Twelve years of my life, he thought. What would I have been now? Fellow of Balliol? Possibly even a professor at some rather less interesting university? Instead . . . But that kind of thinking did no good – no good at all.

The driver was an old man, badly in need of a shave, and Corder was aware of the eyes watching him in the driving mirror. Not a word was said as they drove through darkness and rain, moving through a maze of back streets, finally turning into a wharf in the dock area and braking to a halt outside a warehouse. A small light illuminated a sign which read *Renoir & Sons – Importers*. The taxi driver sat there without a word. Corder got out, closing the door behind him, and the Renault drove away.

It was very quiet, only the lapping of the water in the basin where dozens of barges were moored. Rain hammered down, silver in the light of the sign. There was a small judas gate in the main entrance. When Corder tried the handle it opened instantly and he stepped inside.

The warehouse was crammed with bales and packing cases of every description. It was dark, but there was a light at the far end and he moved towards it. A man sat at a trestle table beneath a naked bulb. There was a map spread across the table in front of him, a briefcase beside it, and he was making notes in a small, leather-bound diary.

'Hello, Frank,' Corder said.

Frank Barry looked up. 'Ah, there you are, Jack. Sorry to mess you about.'

The voice was good public school English with just a hint of an Ulster inflection here and there. He leaned back in the chair. His blond hair curled crisply, making him look considerably younger than his forty-eight years, and the black Burberry trenchcoat gave him a curiously elegant appearance. A handsome, lean-faced man with one side of his mouth hooked into a slight perpetual half-smile, as if permanently amused by the world and its inhabitants.

'Something big?' Corder asked.

'You could say that. Did you know the British Foreign Secretary was visiting the President at the moment?'

'Lord Carrington?' Corder frowned. 'No, I didn't know that.'

'Neither does anyone else. All very hush-hush. The new Tory government trying to cement the *entente cordiale* which has been more than bruised of late years. Not that it will do any good. Giscard d'Estaing will always put France top of his list, no matter what the situation. Their final meeting in the morning is taking place at a villa at Rigny.' He stabbed at the map on the table with his finger. 'Here, about forty miles from Paris.'

'So?' Corder said.

'He leaves at noon by car for Vezelay. There's an airforce emergency field there from where the RAF will be waiting to whisk him back to good old England, to all intents and purposes as if he's never been away.'

'So where's all this leading?'

'Here.' Barry tapped the map again. 'St Etienne, fifteen miles from Rigny, which consists of a petrol station and a roadside cafe at present closed. A perfect spot.'

'For what?'

'To hit the bugger as he passes through. One car, four CRS escorts on motorbikes. No problem that I can see.'

Corder was conscious of the cold now eating deep into his bones. 'You're joking. We'd never get away with it. I mean, a thing like this needs preparation, split second timing.'

'All taken care of,' Barry said cheerfully. 'You should know me by now, Jack. I always prefer people who are working for wages. Thorough-going fanatics like yourself – honest Marxists who believe in the cause – you take it all too seriously and that tends to cloud your thinking. You can't beat the professional touch.'

The Ulster accent was more in evidence now, all part of a deliberate exercise in charm.

'Who have you got?' Corder asked.

'Three hoods from Marseilles on the run from the *Union Corse* after the wrong kind of underworld killing. One of them has his girl with him. They'll do anything in return for the right price, four false passports and tickets to the Argentine.'

Corder stared down at the map. 'So how does it happen?'

'Simple. As I said, the cafe is closed. That only leaves the proprietor and his wife in the garage. They'll be taken care of and my men will be in position, dressed as mechanics, from twelve-fifteen, working on a car on the forecourt.'

Corder shook his head. 'From what I can see, the convoy will be passing at a fairly high speed at that point. Remember what happened at Petit-Clamart when Bastien Thiry and his boys tried to ambush General de Gaulle? Even with machine guns at point-blank range they didn't do any good because the old man's car just kept on going. A second is all you get and away.'

'So what we have to do is stop the car,' Barry said.

'Impossible. These days those VIP drivers are trained for just this kind of situation. From what I can see on the map, it's a straight road giving a good view long before he gets there. Block it with a vehicle or anything else and they'll simply turn round and get the hell out of there.' He shook his head. 'He won't stop, Frank, that driver, and there's no way you can make him.'

'Oh, yes, there is,' Barry said. 'Which is where the girl I mentioned comes into the picture. At the appropriate moment, she tries to cross the road from the garage pushing a pram. She stumbles, the pram runs away from her into the road.'

'You're crazy,' Corder said.

'Am I? It worked for the Red Army Faction a couple of years back when they snatched Schleyer, the head of the German Industries Federation in Cologne.' Barry smiled. 'You see, Jack, human nature being what it is, I think that I can positively guarantee that when that driver sees a runaway pram in his path he'll do only one thing. Swerve to avoid it and come to a dead halt.'

Which was true. Had to be. Corder nodded. 'Put that way, I suppose you're right.'

'I always am, old son.' He opened the brief-case and took out a hand transceiver. 'This is for you. There's a side road on a hill covered by an apple orchard which overlooks the chateau at Rigny nicely. I want you there by eleven o'clock in the morning. You'll find a Peugeot estate car in the yard outside, keys in the lock. Use that.'

'Then what?'

'The moment you see Carrington making preparations to leave, you call in on the trans-ceiver, Channel 42. You say: This is Red calling. The package is about to be delivered. I'll say: Green here. The package will be collected. Then you get to hell out of there. I want you at St Etienne before Carrington arrives.'

'Will you be there?'

Barry looked surprised. 'And where else would I be?' He smiled. 'I was a National Service second lieutenant with the Ulster Rifles in Korea in 1950, Jack. You didn't know that, did you? But I'll tell you one thing.

When my lads went over the top, I was always in front.'

'With a swagger stick in one hand?'

'And now you're thinking of the Somme,' Barry laughed gently. 'I killed an awful lot of Maoists out there, Jack, which is ironic, considering my present circumstances.' He clapped him on the shoulder. 'Anyway, you'd best be off. A decent night's sleep and no booze. You'll need a clear head for what you must do tomorrow.' He glanced at his watch and laughed. 'Correction – today.'

Corder weighed the transceiver in his hand, then slipped it into his pocket. 'I'll say good-night then.'

His footsteps echoed in the lofty warehouse as he walked to the entrance, opened the judas and stepped out. It was still raining as he moved into the yard at the side of the building. The Peugeot was parked by the main entrance, the key in the lock as Barry had indicated. Corder drove away, his palms sweating, slipping on the wheel, stomach churning.

Kill Carrington, one of the most decent and humane of politicians. My God, what would the bastard come up with next? But no, that question didn't need an answer, because now Barry was very definitely finished. This was it. What Corder had been waiting for for more than a year.

He found what he was looking for a moment later, a small all-night cafe on the corner of one of the main boulevards into the city. There was a public telephone in a glass booth inside. He ordered coffee, then bought the necessary tokens from the barman and went into the booth, closing the door. His fingers were shaking as he carefully dialled the London code number and then the number following.

The Security Service in Great Britain, more correctly known as Directorate General of the Security Service, DI5, does not officially exist as far as the law is concerned although it does, in fact occupy a large white and red brick building near the Hilton Hotel. It was that establishment which Jack Corder was calling now; more specifically, an office known as Group Four which was manned twenty-four hours a day.

The 'phone was lifted and an anonymous voice said, 'Say who you are.'

'Lysander. I must speak with Brigadier Ferguson at once. Priority One. No denial possible.'

'Your present number?' He dictated it carefully. The voice said, 'If security clearance confirmed, you will be called.'

The 'phone went dead. Corder pushed open the booth door and went to the bar. There was a man in a blue suit asleep on a chair in the corner, mouth gaping. Otherwise the place was empty.

The barman pushed the coffee across. 'You want something to eat? A ham sandwich perhaps?'

'Why not?' Corder said. 'I'm waiting for a call.'

The barman turned to the stove and Corder spooned sugar into his coffee. All calls to DI5 were automatically recorded. At this moment the computer would be matching his voice print on file against the tape of his call.

Ferguson would probably be at home in bed. They would ring him, give him the number. Ten minutes in all.

But he was wrong, for it needed no more than five and as he took his first bite into the sandwich, the 'phone rang. He squeezed into the booth, closed the door and picked up the receiver.

'Lysander here.'

'Ferguson.' The voice was plummy, a little over-done, rather like the ageing actor in a second-rate touring company who wants to make sure they can hear him at the back of the theatre. 'It's been a long time, Jack. Priority One, I understand.'

'Frank Barry, sir, out in the open at last.'

Ferguson's voice sharpened. 'Now that *is* interesting.'

'Lord Carrington, sir. He's visiting President Giscard d'Estaing at the moment?'

There was a slight pause. Ferguson said, 'No one's supposed to know that officially.'

'Frank Barry does.'

'Not good, Jack, not good at all. I think you'd better explain.'

Which Corder did, speaking in low urgent tones. Five minutes later, he emerged from the booth and went to the counter.

'Your sandwich, Monsieur – it has gone cold. You want another?'

'What an excellent idea,' Corder said. 'And I'll have a cognac while I'm waiting.'

He lit a cigarette and sat back on the bar stool, smiling for the first time that night.

In his flat in Cavendish Square, Brigadier Charles Ferguson stood beside the bed, pulling on his dressing gown as he listened to the tape recording he had just taken of his conversation with Corder. He was a large, kindly-looking man and distinctly overweight with rumpled grey hair and a double chin. There was nothing military about him at all and the half-moon spectacles he put on to consult a small pocket book gave him the air of a minor professor. He was, in fact, as ruthless as Cesare Borgia and totally without scruples when it came to his country's interest.

There was a tap at the door and his manservant, an ex-Ghurkha *naik*, peered in, tying the belt of a dressing gown about his waist.

'Sorry, Kim, work to be done.' Ferguson said. 'Lots of tea, bacon and eggs to follow. I won't be going back to bed.'

The little Ghurkha withdrew and Ferguson went into the sitting room, stirred the fire in the Adam fireplace, poured himself a large brandy, sat down by the telephone and dialled a number in Paris.

The French Security Service, the *Service de Documentation Extérieure et de Contre Espionnage*, the SDECE, is divided into five sections and many departments. The most interesting is certainly Section Five, most commonly known as the Action Service, the department which more than any other had been responsible for the smashing of the OAS. It was the number of Service Five which Ferguson dialled now.

He said, 'Ferguson here, DI5. Colonel Guyon, if you please.' He frowned impatiently. 'Well, of course he's at home in bed. So was I. I've only rung you to establish credentials.

Tell him to call me back on this number.' He dictated it quickly. 'Most urgent. Priority One.'

He put down the 'phone and Kim entered with bacon and eggs, bread, butter and marmalade on a silver tray. 'Delicious,' Ferguson said, as the little Ghurkha placed a small table before him. 'Breakfast at two-thirty in the morning. What a capital idea. We should do this more often.'

As he tucked a napkin around his neck the 'phone rang. He picked it up instantly. 'Ah, Pierre,' he said in rapid and excellent French. 'I've got something for you. Very nasty indeed. You won't be pleased, so listen carefully.'

In the warehouse, it was quiet after Jack Corder had left. Barry walked to the entrance and locked the judas gate. He paused to light a cigarette and as he turned, a man emerged from the shadows and perched himself on the edge of the table.

Nikolai Romanov was fifty years of age and for ten of them had been a cultural attaché at the Soviet Embassy in Paris. His dark suit was Savile Row, as was the blue overcoat which fitted him to perfection. He was handsome enough in a slightly decadent way, with a face like Oscar Wilde or Nero himself and a mane of silver hair which made him look more like a distinguished actor than what he was, which was a Colonel in the KGB.

'I'm not too sure about that one, Frank,' he said in excellent English.

'I'm not too sure about anyone,' Barry said, 'including you, old son, but for what it's worth, Jack Corder's a dedicated Marxist.'

'Oh dear,' Romanov said. 'That's what I was afraid of.'

'He tried to join the British Communist Party when he was an undergraduate at Oxford years ago. It was suggested that someone like him could do more good by keeping his mouth shut and joining the Labour Party, which he did. Trade Union Organiser for six years, then he blotted his copybook by losing his cool during a miners' strike three or four years ago and assaulting a policeman in the picket line with a pickaxe handle. Put him in hospital for six weeks.'

'And Corder?'

'Two years in gaol. The Union wouldn't touch him with a barge pole after that. Deep down inside, those lads are as conservative as Margaret Thatcher when it comes to being British. Jack came over here when he got out and involved himself with an anarchist group well to the left of the French Communist Party which is where I picked him up. Anyway, why should you worry, or has the Disinformation Department of the KGB changed its aims?'

'No,' Romanov said. 'Chaos is still our business, Frank, and we need to create as much as possible in the Western world. Chaos, disorder, fear and uncertainty, which is why we employ people like you.'

'You haven't left much out, have you?' Barry said cheerfully.

Romanov looked down at the map. 'Is this going to work?'

'Come on, now, Nikolai,' Barry said. 'You don't really want Carrington shot dead on a French country road, do you? Very counterproductive, just like the IRA shooting the Queen. Too much to lose, so it isn't worth it.'

Romanov looked bewildered. 'What game are you playing now?'

'Oh, you know me,' Barry said, 'the game's the thing,' and added briskly, 'I'll still take the cash, by the way. Chaos, disorder, fear and uncertainty. I'll do my best to see you get your money's-worth.'

Romanov hesitated, then took a large manilla envelope from his pocket and pushed it across. Barry dropped it into the briefcase along with the map.

'Shall we?'

He led the way to the entrance and unlocked the judas gate. A flurry of wind tossed rain into their faces. Romanov shivered and turned up his collar.

'When I was fourteen years old in nineteen forty-three, I joined a partisan group in the Ukraine. I was with them two years. It was simpler then. We were fighting Nazis. We knew where we were. But now?'

'A different world,' Barry said.

'And one in which you, my friend, don't even believe in your own country.'

'Ulster?' Barry laughed harshly. 'I gave up on that mess a long time ago. As someone once said, there's nothing worse than a collection of ignorant people with legitimate grievances. Now let's get to hell out of here.'

The apples in the orchard on the hill above Rigny should have been picked weeks before, were already over-ripe, and the air was heavy with the smell of them, warm in the unexpected noon-day sun.

Jack Corder lay in the long grass, a pair of Zeiss binoculars beside him, and watched the villa below. It was a pleasant house, built in the eighteenth century from the look of it with a broad flight of steps leading up to the portico over the main entrance.

There were four cars in the courtyard, at least a dozen CRS police waiting beside their motor cycles and uniformed gendarmes at the gate. Nothing too ostentatious. The President was known to imitate General de Gaulle in that respect and hated fuss.

For a while, Corder was a boy again lying in long grass by the River Wharfe, the bridge below him, good Yorkshire sheep scattered across the meadow on the other side. Sixteen years old with a girl beside him whose name he couldn't even remember, and life had seemed to have an infinite possibility to it. He felt an aching longing to be back, for everything in between to be just a dream, and then the President of France, Valéry Giscard d'Estaing, stepped out of the house below, followed by the British Foreign Secretary.

The two men stood in the portico flanked by their aides as Corder focused his binoculars.

'Jesus,' he whispered. 'One man with a decent rifle is all it would take to knock out both of them.'

The President shook the Foreign Secretary's hand. No formal embrace. That was not his style. Lord Carrington went down the steps and was ushered into the black Citroen.

Corder's throat was dry. He took the

transceiver from his pocket, pressed the channel button and said urgently. 'This is Red calling. This is Red calling. The package is about to be delivered.'

A second later he heard Barry's reply, cool, detached. 'Green here. The package will be collected.'

Carrington's car was moving towards the entrance followed by four CRS motorcyclists, just as Barry had promised and Corder jumped to his feet, turned and ran through the orchard to where he had left the Peugeot. He had plenty of time to reach the main road before the convoy and the moment he turned on to it, he put his foot down, pushing the Peugeot up to seventy-five.

His palms were sweating again, his throat dry, and he lit a cigarette one-handed. He didn't know what was going to happen at St Etienne, that was the trouble. Probably CRS riot cops descending in droves, shooting everything that moved which could include him. But he had to turn up; had no other choice, for if he didn't, Barry, being Barry, would smell an instant rat, call the thing off and disappear into the blue as he had done so many times before.

He was close to St Etienne now, no more than two or three miles to go, when it happened. As he passed a side turning, a CRS motorcyclist emerged and came after him, a sinister figure in crash helmet and goggles and dark, caped coat. He pulled alongside and waved him down and Corder pulled in to the edge of the road. Was this Ferguson's way of keeping him out of it?

The CRS man pulled in front, got off his heavy BMW machine and pushed it on its stand. He walked towards the Peugeot, a gloved finger hooked into the trigger guard of the MAT49 machine carbine slung across his chest. He stood looking down at Corder, anonymous in the dark goggles, then pushed them up.

'A slight change of plan, old son.' Frank Barry grinned. 'I lead, you follow.'

'You've called it off?' Corder demanded in astonishment.

Barry looked mildly surprised. 'Jesus, no, why should I do a thing like that?'

He got back on the BMW and drove away. Corder followed him, totally lost now, not knowing what to do for the best. For a moment Corder fingered the butt of the Walther PPK he carried, not that there was much joy there. He'd never shot anyone in his life. It was unlikely that he could start now.

About a mile outside St Etienne, Barry turned into a narrow country lane and Corder followed, climbing up between high hedgerows past a small farm. There was a grove of trees on the brow of a green hill and Barry waved him down and turned into them. He pushed the BMW up on its stand and Corder joined him.

'Look, what's going on, Frank?'

'Did I ever tell you about my grandmother on my mother's side, Jack? Whenever she got a terrible headache there'd be a thunder-storm within the hour. Now with me, it's different. I only get a headache when I smell stinking fish and I've got a real blinder at the moment.'

Corder went cold. 'I don't understand.'

'Nice view from up here.' Barry walked through the trees and indicated St Etienne spread neatly below like a child's model. The garage and forecourt were on one side of the road, the cafe and carpark on the other.

He took some binoculars from the pocket of his raincoat and passed them across. 'Have a look. I have a feeling it may be a bit more interesting to sit this one out.'

Corder focused the binoculars on the forecourt of the garage. Two of the men, wearing yellow overalls, worked on the engine of a car. The third waiting in the glass office beside the petrol pumps talking to the girl who stood at the door with the pram, wearing a scarlet headscarf, woollen jumper and neat skirt.

'Any sign of the car?' Barry demanded.

Corder swung the binoculars to examine the road. 'No, but there's a truck coming.'

'Is there, now? That's interesting.'

The truck was of the trailer type, an eight-wheeler with high green canvas sides. As it entered the village, it slowed and turned into the carpark. The driver, a tall man in khaki overalls jumped down from the cab and strolled to the cafe door.

Barry took the binoculars from Corder and

focused them on the truck. 'Bouvier Brothers, Long Distant Transport, Paris and Marseilles.'

'He'll move on when he finds the cafe's closed,' Corder said.

'Pigs might fly, old son,' Frank Barry told him, 'But I doubt it.'

There was a sudden firestorm from inside the truck at that moment, machine gun fire raking the entire forecourt area, shattering the glass of the office, driving the girl back over the pram, cutting down the two gunmen working on the car, riddling its fuel tank, petrol spilling on to the concrete. It was the work of an instant, no more, there was a flicker of flame as petrol ignited and then the tank exploded in a ball of fire, pieces of wreckage flying high in the air. The holocaust was complete and at least twenty CRS riot police in uniform leapt from the rear of the truck and ran across the road.

'Efficient,' Barry said calmly. 'You've got to give the buggers that.'

Corder licked dry lips nervously and his left hand went into the pocket of his leather jacket, groping for the butt of the Walther.

'What could have gone wrong?'

'One of those bastards from Marseilles must have had a big mouth,' Barry said. 'And if word got back to the Union Corse . . .' He shrugged, 'Thieving's one thing, politics is another. They'd inform without a second's hesitation.' He clapped Corder on the shoulder. 'But we'd better get out of this. Just follow my tail, like you did before. Nobody is likely to stop us when they see me escorting you.'

He pushed the BMW off its stand and rode away. Corder followed. The whole thing was like a bad dream and he could still see, vivid as any image on the cinema screen, the body of the girl, bouncing back across the pram in a hail of machine gun fire. And Barry had expected it. Expected it, and yet he had still let those poor sods go through with it.

He followed the BMW closely, through narrow country lanes, twisting and turning. They met no one and then, a good ten miles on the other side of St Etienne, came to a small garage and cafe at the side of the road.

Barry turned in beside the cafe and braked to a halt. As Corder joined him, he was taking a canvas grip from one of the side panniers.

'I know this place,' he said. 'There's a wash room at the back. I'm going to change. We'll leave the BMW here and carry on in the Peugeot.'

He went round to the rear before Corder could reply and the young woman in the glass office beside the petrol pumps emerged and approached him. She was perhaps twenty-five with a flat, pleasant face, and wore a man's tweed jacket that was too large for her.

'Petrol, monsieur?'

'Is there a telephone?' Corder asked.

'In the cafe, monsieur, but it's not open for business. I'm the only one here today.'

'I must use it. It's very urgent.' He pushed a hundred franc note at her. 'Just give me some tokens. You keep the rest.'

She shrugged, went into her office and opened the till. She came back with the tokens. 'I'll show you,' she said.

The cafe wasn't much: a few tables and chairs, a counter with bottles of beer and mineral water and rows of glasses ranged behind, a door which obviously led to the kitchen. The telephone was on the wall, a directory hanging beside it.

The girl said, 'Look, seeing I'm here I'll make some coffee. Okay?'

'Fine,' Corder told her.

She disappeared into the kitchen and he quickly checked in the directory to find the district number to link him with the international line. His fingers were shaking as he dialled the area code for London followed by the DI5 number.

He didn't even have time to pray. The receiver was lifted at the other end and a woman's voice this time, the day operator, said, 'Say who you are.'

'Lysander,' Corder said urgently. 'Clear line please. I must speak to Brigadier Ferguson at once. Total Priority.'

Ferguson's voice cut in instantly, almost as if he'd been listening in. 'Jack, what is it?'

'Total cock-up, sir. Barry smelt a rat, so he and I stayed out of things. The rest of the team were knocked out by CRS police.'

'You've got clean away, presumably.'

'Yes.'

'And does he suspect you?'

'No – he thinks it's down to one of those Marseilles hoods speaking out of turn.'

In the kitchen Frank Barry, listening on the extension, smiled, anonymous in the dark goggles. The girl lay on the floor at his feet, blood oozing from an ugly cut in her temple where he had clubbed her with his pistol. He left the receiver hanging on its cord, took a Carswell Silencer from his pocket, and screwed it on to the barrel of his pistol as he walked into the cafe.

Corder was still talking in a low urgent voice. 'No, I don't know how much more I can take, that's the trouble.'

Barry said softly, 'Jack!'

Corder swung round and Barry shot him twice through the heart, slamming him back. He bounced off the wall and fell to the floor on his face.

The receiver dangled on the end of its cord. Barry picked it up and said, 'That you, Ferguson, old son? Frank Barry here. If you want Corder back, you'd better send a box for him to Cafe Rosco, St Julien.'

'You bastard,' Charles Ferguson said.

'It's been said before.'

Barry replaced the receiver and went out, whistling softly as he unscrewed the silencer. He slipped the pistol back into its holster, pushed the BMW off its stand and rode away.

2

It was raining on the following morning when Ferguson's car dropped him outside Number Ten Downing Street, ten minutes early for his eleven o'clock appointment with the Prime Minister. His driver moved away instantly and Ferguson crossed the pavement to the entrance. In spite of the rain, there was the usual small crowd of sightseers on the other side of the road, mainly tourists, kept in place by a couple of police constables. Another stood in his usual place by the door, not much protection for the best-known address in England, the seat of political power as well as the Prime Minister's private residence, but that didn't mean a thing, as Ferguson well knew. There were others, more inconspicuously attired, situated at certain strategic points in the area, ready to swarm in at the first hint of trouble.

The policeman saluted and the door was opened, even before Ferguson reached it. He passed inside.

The young man who greeted him said, 'Brigadier Ferguson? This way, sir.'

There was the hum of activity from the Press Room on the right as he crossed the entrance hall and entered the corridor leading to the rear of the house and the Cabinet Room.

The main staircase to the first floor was lined with portraits of previous Prime Ministers: Peel, Wellington, Disraeli, Gladstone. Ferguson always felt an acute sense of history as he mounted those stairs, although this was the first time he had done so to meet the present Prime Minister. The first time he had had to explain himself to a woman, and a damn clever woman, if it came to that. Definitely a new experience. But did anything change? How many attempts to assassinate Queen Victoria? And Disraeli and Gladstone had both had their hands full of Fenians, dynamiters and anarchists with their bombs, at one time or another.

On the top corridor the young man knocked on a door, opened it and ushered Ferguson inside. 'Brigadier Ferguson, Prime Minister,' he said and left, closing the door behind him.

The study was more elegant now than Ferguson remembered it, with pale green walls, gold curtains and comfortable furniture in perfect taste. But nothing was more elegant in the entire room than the woman behind the desk. The blue suit with the froth of white lace at the throat perfectly offset the blonde hair. An elegant, handsome woman of the world, and yet the eyes, when she glanced up at Ferguson from the paper she was reading, were hard and intelligent.

'I've had a personal assurance from the French President this morning that this whole wretched business will be hushed up. It never happened. You understand me?'

'Perfectly, ma'am.'

She looked at the paper before her. 'This agent of yours, Corder. If it hadn't been for him . . .' She gestured to a chair. 'Sit down, Brigadier. Tell me about him.'

'We recruited Jack Corder some twelve years ago when he was still an undergraduate at Balliol. The route he chose was to immerse himself totally in left wing politics. We often hear of moles within our intelligence service working for the Russians, ma'am. Jack was the other side of the coin. He endured prison sentences twice for his apparent militancy. Afterwards, I transferred him to the European terrorist scene. Frank Barry was his most important assignment.'

She nodded. 'I've already spoken to the Director General of DI5. He tells me that as long ago as nineteen seventy-two, one of my predecessors authorised the setting up within DI5 of a section known as Group Four which has powers, held directly from the Prime Minister, to co-ordinate the handling of all cases of terrorism, subversion and the like.'

'That is correct, Prime Minister.'

'With you in charge, Brigadier?'

'Yes, ma'am.'

There was a longish pause while she stared down at the paper thoughtfully. Ferguson cleared his throat. 'Naturally, if you would prefer to initiate some change, I will offer my resignation without hesitation.'

'If I want it, I'll ask for it. Brigadier,' she said sharply. 'But you can't expect me to have much faith in the activities of your section when one of the chief ministers of the Crown comes within an inch of assassination. Now tell me about this man, Barry? Why is he so important, and more to the point, how does he remain so elusive?'

'A brilliant madman, ma'am. A genius in his own way. As important to the international terrorist scene as Carlos, but not so familiar to the public.'

'And why is that?'

'A question of his personal psychology. Many terrorists, take some of those involved with the Baader-Meinhoff gang, for example, have a craving for public display. They want people to know not only who they are, but that they can make fools of the police and intelligence departments they confront, any time they wish. Barry doesn't seem to have a need for that kind of publicity, and as it suits our purposes best to give him none, he has remained an unknown quantity as far as the public is concerned.'

'What about his personal background?'

'I'm afraid it couldn't be worse from the point of view of media sensationalism. He is an Ulsterman by birth. Held a commission as a National Service second-lieutenant with the Ulster Rifles. Served in Korea. Excellent record in the field, I might add. He's a Protestant. His uncle is an Irish Peer, Lord Stramore. Much involved in Orange politics for most of his life, but now in ailing health. Barry is his heir.'

'Good God,' the Prime Minister said.

'During the early years of the Irish Troubles, Barry professed to be a Republican. As usual, he did his own thing. Organised a group called the Sons of Erin, which gave us tremendous problems in the Province. Repudiated totally by the Provisional IRA. In nineteen seventy-two, when Group Four was first set up, I managed to penetrate Barry's organisation with an agent of mine, a Major Vaughan. The upshot of that little affair was that Barry was badly wounded.

That he lived at all was only due to the skill of the surgeons of the Military Wing of the Musgrave Park Hospital in Belfast.'

'What happened then?'

'He escaped, ma'am. Not even capable of walking, according to his doctors, but walk he did, right out of the hospital, dressed as a porter. Turned up in Dublin within twenty-four hours. We couldn't touch him there, of course. He was in and out of hospital there and in Switzerland for more than a year.'

'And afterwards?'

'Since then, ma'am, he has in some cases to our certain knowledge, and in others to the best of our belief, been responsible for at least fifteen assassinations and a number of bombing incidents. His touch is distinctive and unmistakable, and political commitment seems to be the least of his considerations. A résumé of his activities during the past few years will explain what I mean. In nineteen seventy-three he assassinated the General in command of Spanish Military Intelligence in the Basque country. Responsibility was claimed by the Basque Nationalist Movement, ETA.'

'Go on.'

'On the other hand, he was also responsible for the murder of General Hans Grosch during a visit to Munich in nineteen seventy-five. A source of considerable embarrassment to the West German Government. Grosch held a post roughly equivalent to my own in the East German Ministry for State Security. So, as you can see, ma'am, on the one hand Barry kills a Fascist, on the other, a Communist.'

'You're saying he has no politics?'

'None at all.' Ferguson took a sheet from his briefcase and passed it across. 'A list of the jobs we think he's been concerned with. As you can see, his victims have been from every part of the political scene.'

The Prime Minister read the list slowly and frowned. 'Are you saying then that he works for whoever will pay him?'

'No, ma'am, I think it's more subtle than that. Everything he does falls into a pattern, in that it causes maximum damage wherever it happens. For instance, he kills a Spanish diplomat visiting Paris in nineteen seventy-seven – a Fascist. The French government have to react appropriately and within twenty-four hours, every left-wing agitator in Paris is in police hands. Not only Communists, but Socialists. The Socialist Party didn't like that, which meant the Unions also didn't like it. Result, unrest amongst the workers, strikes, disruption.'

She paused suddenly lower down his list and glanced up, her face bleak. 'You mention here a possible involvement in the Mountbatten assassination?'

'We've the best of reasons for believing his advice was sought.'

She shook her head. 'It doesn't make sense.'

'It does if one considers his known links with the KGB. I believe that most of the incidents he has been responsible for were commissioned by the KGB, even the assassination of those supposed to be their friends, with the sole purpose of causing the maximum amount of disruption possible in the West.'

'But Barry is no Marxist?'

'Frank Barry, ma'am, isn't anything. Oh, he'll take their money, I'm sure of that, but he'll do what he does for the hell of it.

I suppose the psychiatrists would have fancy terms to describe his mental condition. Psychopath would only be the start. I'm not really interested. I just want to see him dead.'

The Prime Minister passed the list back to him. 'Then get on with it, Brigadier.'

Ferguson took the list from her as she pressed a buzzer on her desk. 'Ma'am?'

'Department Four has the power – total authority from this office so it would seem. Use it, man. I'm not going to tell you how to do your own job, you're too good at it. I've read your record. The only thing I will say is that it seems obvious to me you must put everything on one side and concentrate all your activities on Barry.'

Ferguson got to his feet and slipped the paper back in his briefcase. 'Very well, Prime Minister.'

The door opened behind him and the young secretary appeared. The Prime Minister picked up her pen and returned to work as Ferguson moved to the door and was ushered out.

* * *

Ferguson usually preferred to work from his Cavendish Square flat. He was sitting by the fire drinking tea and toasting crumpets on a long brass fork when Kim opened the door and ushered in Harry Fox.

'Ah, there you are, Harry. Got what I wanted?'

'Yes, sir, every last piece of paper in the file on Frank Barry.'

Fox was thirty, a slim elegant young man who wore a Guards tie, not surprising in someone who until two years previously had been an acting-Captain in the Blues. The neat leather glove which he wore permanently on his left hand concealed the fact that he had lost the original in a bomb explosion during his third tour of duty in Belfast. He had been Ferguson's assistant for just over a year.

'What exactly are we looking for, sir?'

'I'm not sure, Harry. Jack Corder was the third man I've put up against Frank Barry and two out of the three have ended up in a box. We've got to come up with something different, that's all I know for certain.'

'You're right, sir. Takes a thief to catch a thief, I suppose.'

Ferguson paused in the act of spearing another crumpet on his fork. 'What did you say?'

'Jack Grand of Special Branch was telling me the other day they put one of their men into Parkhurst Prison, posing as a convict. He was attacked within two days and badly injured. I suppose the truth is most crooks can spot a copper a mile away. Frank Barry will be the same, if you think about it. He'd smell a rat in almost anyone you tried to infiltrate into his kind of action.'

'You could be right,' Ferguson said. 'Start reading through those files, aloud, if you please.'

They were at it for six hours, only Kim disturbing them from time to time to replenish the tea and coffee. It was dark when Ferguson got up and stretched and waved to the window.

'I'd like to know where the bastard is now.'

Fox said, 'The photos on him are a bit sparse, sir. Nothing since nineteen seventy-two.

The earliest seems to be this one taken from a *Paris-Match* article done by some woman journalist in nineteen seventy-one. Who are the other two with him? Devlin, is it? Liam Devlin and Martin Brosnan.'

Ferguson crossed the room with surprising speed for a man of his bulk and took the news clipping from him. 'My God, Liam Devlin – and Brosnan. I'd forgotten they'd had dealings with Barry, it's so long ago.'

'But who were they, sir?'

'Oh, a couple of anachronisms from the early days of the Irish Troubles. Before the worst of the bombings and the butchery. The kind of men who thought it was still nineteen twenty-one with Michael Collins carrying the flag for Ireland. Gallant guerrillas up against the might of the British Empire, Flying Columns, action by night.'

'I think I saw the movie once, sir,' Fox said.

'There was a man called Sean McEoin, a Flying Column leader who later became a General in the Free State Army. In nineteen twenty-one, he was surrounded by Black and

Tans in a cottage near his own village. There were women and children inside so McEoin ran out in the open with a gun in each hand and shot his way through the police cordon. Devlin and Brosnan are the same kind of idiots.'

'I can't say I came up against anyone like that during my time in Ulster,' Fox said, feelingly.

'No, well it's as well to remember that the IRA, like the British Army or any other institution, consists of a wide range of human beings. Still, you cut along now. I want to give this some think time.'

Fox left. Ferguson poured himself a brandy and went and stood at the window, looking down into the square, thinking, with regret, of Jack Corder and the others he had sent against Barry.

'Somewhere,' he said softly, 'that bastard is still laughing at me.'

Barry, at that precise moment, was doing roughly what Ferguson was: standing at a window with a large cognac in his hand. In his case, the apartment was in Paris and the view was of the Seine. There was a discreet tap at the door and when he opened it on the chain, Romanov was outside.

'Well?' Barry demanded as the Russian entered.

'Considerable Service Five activity, Frank. They know you were behind the whole affair so they're leaving no stone unturned to find you, with full assistance from British Intelligence on this one, I might add. Your Brigadier Ferguson and Colonel Guyon of Service Five are old friends.'

'Well, that makes a change. I didn't think DI5 and the French Intelligence Service were on speaking terms. How can you be sure that Ferguson and Guyon are such good pals, or have you an informer in Guyon's department?'

'Anything is possible,' Romanov told him.

Barry was surprised and showed it. 'You're kidding. I thought British Intelligence had cleaned out all its moles by now. Your man certainly didn't do me any good. What about

Corder? I had to find out about him for myself.'

'To be honest, Frank, at the moment we're only getting peripheral information, but we expect that to improve.'

'I don't get it,' Barry said. 'You'd expect DI5 to check its employees' credentials right back to the womb.'

'Perhaps they do, Frank. But in this case it wouldn't do them any good.'

'One good thing. At least there's no one left who can finger me at the moment, except you, of course, old son.'

Romanov's smile was forced. 'On the whole, I think it would be sensible if you dropped out of sight for a while.'

'And where would you suggest?'

'England.'

Barry laughed. 'Well, it's a novel enough idea. The last place they'd expect. Would you have somewhere specific in mind?'

'The Lake District.'

'They say it's lovely at this time of the year.' Barry poured himself another cognac. 'All right, Nikolai, let's be having it.'

The Russian opened his briefcase and took out a selection of maps. 'It's painfully simple. The balance of power as regards ground forces in Europe is hugely in our favour, mainly because we would be able to put at least four thousand more tanks in the field than the NATO forces.'

'So?'

'The West Germans have come up with a rather brilliant new weapon. Light enough to be carried by any infantry section. When fired, its pod releases twelve rockets simultaneously. Imagine them as missiles in miniature. Heat seeking, of course. Any one of these rockets is capable of knocking out our largest tank.'

'Jesus,' Barry said. 'You'd wonder how they lost the war. What'll they come up with next?'

'We've tried every way possible to get hold of one, but so far, we've failed. We must have one, Frank.'

'So, where do I come into it?'

Romanov started to unfold the maps. 'I've had a report today of a rather interesting development. The Germans intend to demonstrate this weapon to the British and others at the British Army Rocket Proving Ground near Wast Water in the Lake District, next Thursday. There's a team of Germans taking one over on Wednesday. An officer and six men. There's a disused RAF base at Brisingham which is only twenty miles from the Proving Ground. They'll land there to be taken the rest of the way by truck.'

'Interesting.' Barry opened the maps right across the table.

'Frank, pull this off for me and it would be worth half a million.'

Barry didn't seem to hear him. 'I'd need ground support. Someone I could rely on in the general area of things. A thorough-going crook preferably. Could your people in London arrange that?'

'Anything, Frank.'

'And more maps. English Ordnance Survey maps. I want to know that area like the back of my hand.'

'I'll have them round to you in the morning.'

'Tonight,' Barry said. 'I'll also need fake

passports. One British, one French and one American, just to vary things. Details like who I am, I'll leave to your experts.'

'All right,' Romanov said.

'And keep the SDECE off my back. Tell them I've been in Turkey or gone to the Argentine.'

Since the *Sapphire* scandal, the intelligence networks of most Western countries had had a rather poor opinion of the French Intelligence Service, believing it to be penetrated by the KGB, which it was – certainly enough for Romanov to be able to agree to Barry's request.

'And one more thing,' Barry added as Romanov opened the door. 'A banking account in my English identity for fifty thousand pounds' working capital.' He smiled softly. 'And it'll cost you a million, Nikolai. This one will cost you a million.'

Romanov shrugged. 'Frank, just get it for us and you can name your own price, I promise you.'

He went out and Barry locked and chained the door, then returned to the table, sat down at the maps and started to give the whole thing some thought.

Back in London, Harry Fox was just about to step into the shower when his 'phone rang. He cursed, pulled a towel around him and went to answer it.

'Harry, Ferguson here. You know what you said earlier about setting a thief to catch a thief. You've given me a very interesting idea. Go to the office and bring me Martin Brosnan's file. You might as well bring Devlin's while you're at it.'

Fox glanced at his watch. 'You mean in the morning, sir?'

'I mean now, damn you!'

Ferguson slammed down his 'phone and Fox replaced his receiver and checked his watch. It was just after two a.m. He sighed, returned to the bathroom and started to dress.

3

'Martin Aodh Brosnan,' Ferguson said. 'The Aodh is Gaelic for Hugh, if you're interested, after his maternal grandfather, a well-known Dublin Union leader in his day.'

The fire was burning well. It was four o'clock in the morning and Harry Fox felt unaccountably alive, except for the hand, of course, which ached a little as if it were still there. That always happened under stress.

'According to the file he was born in Boston in nineteen forty-five, sir, of Irish-American parentage. His great, great-grandfather emigrated from Kerry during the famine. Made the family fortune out of shipping during the second half of the nineteenth century, since when they've never looked back. Oil, construction, chemical plants – you name it. And very social register.' Fox frowned and looked up. 'A Protestant. That's astonishing.'

'Why?' Ferguson said. 'A lot of prejudice against the Catholics in America in the old days. Probably one of his ancestors changed sides. He's hardly the first Protestant to want a United Ireland. What about Wolfe Tone? He started it all. And the man who came closest to getting it from the British Government of his day, Charles Stewart Parnell, was another.'

'According to this, Brosnan's mother is a Catholic.'

'Unremittingly so. Mass four times a week. Born in Dublin. Met her husband when she was a student at Boston University. He's been dead for some years. She rules the family empire with a rod of iron. I believe the only human being she has never been able to bend to her will is her son.'

'He did all the right things, it seems. Very Ivy League stuff. Top prep school, Andover. Took a degree in English literature at Princeton.'

'Majored,' Ferguson corrected him.

'I beg your pardon, sir?'

'Majored in English, that's what our American friends say.'

Fox shrugged and returned to the file. 'Then in nineteen sixty-six he volunteered for Vietnam. Airborne Rangers and Special Services. And in the ranks, sir, that's the puzzling thing.'

'A very important point, that, Harry.'

Ferguson poured himself more tea. 'Vietnam was never exactly a popular issue in America. If you were at University or College, it was possible to avoid the draft, which was exactly what most young men with Brosnan's background did. He could have continued to avoid service by staying on at University and taking a doctorate. He didn't. What's the word that's so popular these days, Harry, *macho?* Maybe that had something to do with it? Perhaps he felt less of a man because he'd avoided it for so long. In the end, the important thing is that he went.'

'And to some purpose, sir.' Fox whistled. 'Distinguished Service Cross, Silver Star with

Oak Leaves, Vietnamese Cross of Valor.' He frowned. 'And the Legion of Honour. How in the hell did the French get involved?'

Ferguson stood up and walked to the window. 'An interesting one, that. His last flamboyant gesture. He saved the neck of a famous French war photographer, a woman, would you believe it, name of Anne-Marie Audin. Some ambush or other. She pops up in the story again. The photo from the *Paris-Match* article, remember, with Brosnan, Liam Devlin and Frank Barry? The good Mademoiselle Audin took that, amongst others. She wrote the same story for *Life* Magazine and got a Pulitzer Prize for it. A behind-the-scenes look at the Irish struggle. Went down very well in Boston.'

Fox reached for the next file. 'But how in the hell did he move on from that to the IRA?'

'Wildly illogical, but beautifully simple,' Ferguson turned and walked back to the fire. 'I'll shorthand it for you and save you some time. On leaving the army, Brosnan went to Trinity College, Dublin, to work for that doctorate we mentioned. In August, nineteen sixty-nine, he was visiting an old Catholic uncle on his mother's side, a priest-in-charge of a Church on the Falls Road in Belfast. When did you first visit that fair city, Harry?'

'Nineteen seventy-six, sir.'

Ferguson nodded. 'So much has happened, so much water under the bridge, that the first wild years of the Troubles must seem like ancient history to people like you. So many names, faces.' He sighed and sat down. 'During Brosnan's visit, Orange mobs led by "B" Specials, an organisation now happily defunct, went on the rampage. They burnt down Brosnan's uncle's Church. In fact, the old man was so badly beaten he lost an eye.'

'I see,' Fox said soberly.

'No you don't, Harry. I had an agent once called Vaughan – Major Simon Vaughan. Won't work for me now, but that's another story. He really did see, because like Brosnan, he had an Irish mother. Oh, the IRA has its fair share of thugs and mad bombers and too many men like Frank Barry, perhaps, but it also has its Liam Devlins and its Martin

Brosnans. Genuine idealists in the Pearse and Connolly and Michael Collins tradition. Whether you agree with them or not, men who believe passionately that they're engaged in a struggle for which the stake is nothing less than the freedom of their country.'

Fox raised his gloved hand. 'Sorry, sir, but I've seen women and kids run screaming from a bombing too many times to believe that one any more.'

'Exactly,' Ferguson said. 'Men like Devlin and Brosnan want to be able to fight with clean hands and a little honour. Their tragedy is that in this kind of war that just is not possible.'

He got up again and paced the room restlessly. 'You see, I can't blame Brosnan for what happened in Belfast that night in August, 'sixty-nine. A handful of Republicans, no more than six in all led by Liam Devlin, took to the streets. They had three rifles, two revolvers and a rather antiquated Thompson sub-machine gun. Brosnan found himself caught up in the thick of it during the defence of the Church, and when one of them was shot dead at Devlin's side, he picked up the man's rifle instinctively. He was far and away the most experienced fighting man there, remember. From then on he was caught up in the IRA cause, Devlin's right-hand man during the period Devlin was Chief of Staff in Ulster.'

'Then what?'

'During the first couple of years or so, it was fine. Men like Devlin and Brosnan were able to fight the good old-fashioned guerrilla kind of war that would have delighted Michael Collins' heart. No bombs – they left that to men like Frank Barry. Taking on the army was the way Devlin saw it. He believed that was the way to gain world sympathy for the Cause. By the way, how would you feel if you were the General Officer commanding Northern Ireland, and you went into the private office of your headquarters at Lisburn one fine morning and found a rose on your desk?'

'Good God.'

'Yes, Brosnan loved that sort of nonsensical and foolhardy gesture. The rose was a play on his own name of course. Not only did he do it to the G.O.C., he also left one for the then Ulster Prime Minister and for the Secretary of State for Northern Ireland. The implication was clear enough.'

'He could have killed and didn't.'

'That's right. Brosnan's rose.' Ferguson laughed. 'We had to make it classified to keep it out of the papers, not that they'd have believed it. Who would?'

'What happened later?'

'All changed, didn't it? An escalation of the worst kind of bloodshed, the bombers gained the ascendancy in the movement. Devlin became Chief Intelligence Officer in Dublin. Brosnan worked with him as a kind of roving aide.'

Reading on through the file, Fox said, 'It says here he's got Irish Nationality. How's that, sir?'

'Well, the American Government was not exactly delighted with his activities. Then in nineteen seventy-four, Devlin sent him to New York to execute an informer who'd been helped to seek refuge in America by the Ulster

Constabulary after selling information which had led to the arrest of nearly every member of the North Belfast Brigade. Brosnan accomplished his task with his usual ruthless efficiency, got out of New York by the skin of his teeth. When the American State Department tried to extradite him, he claimed Irish Nationality, which he was entitled to do under Irish law because his mother was born there. If you're interested, Harry, I could do the same. My grandmother was born in Cork.'

Fox quickly glanced through the rest of the file. 'And then the French business.'

'That's right. Devlin sent him to France in nineteen seventy-five to negotiate an arms consignment. The middle man concerned turned out to be a police informer. When Brosnan arrived at a fishing village on the Brittany coast to take delivery, a large consignment of riot police was waiting for him. In the ensuing fracas, he wounded two and shot one dead, for which he was sentenced to life imprisonment on Belle Isle.'

'Belle Isle, sir?'

'The French don't have Devil's Island any more, Harry. They just have Belle Isle. In the Mediterranean, of course, which sounds pleasanter, but it isn't.'

Fox closed the files. 'All right, sir, but where is all this getting us?'

'Set a thief to catch a thief, Harry. You said it.'

Fox gazed at him in astonishment. 'But he's in prison, sir. You said so yourself.'

'For the past four years,' Ferguson said. 'But what if we could do something about that?'

The internal 'phone rang and Ferguson went to it and picked it up. He nodded. 'Fine. Tell him we'll be straight down.' He turned to Fox. 'Right, Harry, grab your coat and let's get moving. We haven't got much time.'

He moved to the door and Fox followed him. 'With respect, sir, where to?'

'Bradbury Lines Barracks at Hereford, Harry. Headquarters of Twenty-second Special Air Service, to be precise. I'll explain it on the way,' and he hustled on through the door like a strong wind.

It was cold in the street outside, rain

reflecting on the black asphalt, and as the big black Bentley pulled away, Harry Fox leaned back against the seat and buttoned his old cavalry overcoat one-handed. So many things circling in his mind, so much had happened and Brosnan simply wouldn't go away, this man he had never met and yet felt he knew as intimately as a brother. He closed his eyes and wondered what Brosnan was doing now.

Belle Isle is a rock situated forty miles to the east of Marseilles and some ten miles from the coast. The fortress, an eighteenth century anachronism, seems to grow out of the very cliffs themselves, one of the grimmest sights in the whole of the Mediterranean. There is the fortress, there is the granite quarry, and there are some six hundred prisoners, political offenders or criminals of the most dangerous kind. Most of them are serving life sentences and, the French authorities taking the term seriously, most of them will die there. One thing is certain. No one has ever escaped from Belle Isle.

The reasons are simple. No vessel may approach closer than four miles and the designated clear area around the island is closely monitored by an excellent approach radar system. And Belle Isle has another highly efficient protection system provided by nature itself, a phenomenom known to local fishermen as the Mill Race, a ferocious ten knot current that churns the water into white foam on even a calm day. Hell on earth in a storm.

Martin Brosnan lay on his bed in a cell on the upper landing, reading, head pillowed on his hands. He was stripped to the waist, strong and muscular, his body toughened by hard labour in the granite quarry. There were the ugly puckered scars of two old bullet wounds in his left breast. His dark hair was too long, almost shoulder-length. In such matters the authorities were surprisingly civilised, as the books on the wooden shelf above the bed indicated.

The man on the opposite bed, tossed a pack of Gitanes across. 'Have a smoke, Martin,' he said in French.

He looked about sixty-five with very white

hair and eyes a vivid blue in a wrinkled humorous face. His name was Jacques Savary, a Union Corse godfather and one of the most famous gangsters in Marseilles in his day. He had been a prisoner in Belle Isle since 1965, would remain there until he died, an unusual circumstance in one of his background for usually the Union Corse, the largest organised crime syndicate in France, was able to use its formidable influence with the judiciary to pull strings on behalf of members of Jacques Savary's standing who found themselves in trouble.

But Savary was different. He had chosen to ally himself to the cause of the OAS. It has been said that Charles de Gaulle survived at least thirty attempts on his life, but he had never been closer to death than during the attack masterminded by Jacques Savary in March, 1965. The Union had at least saved him from execution, settling instead for a life sentence on Belle Isle, mistakenly assuming that his release could be arranged at some future date.

Rain lashed the window, the wind howled. Savary said, 'What are you reading?'

'Eliot,' Brosnan told him. '"What we call the beginning is often the end and to make an end is to make a beginning. The end is where we start from."'

'*The Four Quartets*. "Little Gidding",' Savary said.

'Good man,' Brosnan told him. 'See, all the benefits of an expensive education, Jacques, and you're getting it for free.'

'And you also, my friend, have learnt many things. Can you still open the door the way I showed you?'

Brosnan shrugged, swung his legs to the floor, picked up a spoon from his bedside locker and went to the door. The lock was covered by a steel plate and he quickly forced the handle of the spoon between the edge of the plate and the jamb. He worked it across for a few seconds, there was a click and he opened the door a few inches.

'The same locks since eighteen fifty-two or something like that,' Savary said.

'So what, it doesn't get me anywhere, only to the landing,' Brosnan said. 'I never told you this before, but I once worked out a way to get out. A little climbing, a certain amount of wading through the central sewage system and I could be outside. Found that out three years ago.'

Savary sat up, his face pale. 'Then why have you never done anything about it?'

'Because it gets you nothing. You're still on the rock and nowhere to go.'

There was the sound of footsteps ascending the steel steps at the far end of the landing and Brosnan quickly closed the door and worked the spoon around again. There was a slight click and he hurried across to the bed and lay down.

The footsteps halted outside, a key turned in the lock, the door opened. The uniformed guard who looked in was an amiable looking man named Lebel with a heavy Walrus moustache. He wore an oilskin.

'Stir it you two, I need your services.'

'And what have we done to deserve the honour, Pierre?' Savary demanded.

'When I suffer, you suffer; you know I like you,' Lebel said as they moved past him on to the landing. 'The bastards have just given me the burial detail for the next month and you know the regulations. When they take their last swim, it must be at night.'

They paused for Lebel to unlock the door in the great steel mesh curtain at the end of the landing and Brosnan peered through it to the central hall below.

'Who's dead?' Savary demanded.

Lebel looked at the paper in his hand. '67824 Bouvier. Served thirty-two years. Cancer of the bowel.'

It was a sobering enough thought to kill any further conversation as they descended to the hall and went over to the outer door where the judas gate was unlocked for them by another officer. They crossed the courtyard outside and climbed the steps to the mortuary.

It was a simple enough room with whitewashed walls, and lit by a single naked light. There were several well scrubbed wooden benches in a neat row. The corpse waited on one of them, strapped in a canvas body bag. An old convict in overalls that were too large for him, shoulders bent with age, scrubbed carbolic across the floor. He paused, leaning on his broom.

'All ready for you, sir.'

Brosnan knew the form, had performed the task many times before. There was a simple wooden cart against one wall which he trundled across and he and Savary got the body on to it.

'Right,' Lebel said. 'Let's go.'

'What about the chaplain?' Savary demanded as they manoeuvred the cart down the steps.

'Said he didn't want one. An atheist.'

Savary was shocked. 'Hell, everybody should be entitled to a priest when he goes.' He glanced sideways at Brosnan. 'You make sure they do things right for me.'

'You won't die, you old bastard,' Brosnan said. 'You'll live for ever.'

The guard on duty at the gatehouse emerged to open the gates and they moved outside and followed the road, not down toward the harbour, but curving up to the left. It was hard work, pushing uphill. Finally, they came out on to a small plateau on the edge of the cliffs.

There was no moon and the rock dropped sheer, a good forty feet into the water. There was an impression of waves out there, broken water, white foam, and Brosnan could feel salt on his lips like the taste of freedom.

Behind them, Lebel switched on a light above a wooden door and unlocked it. 'All right, let's get the weights on him.'

The room was small with a wooden bench in the centre on which Brosnan and Savary placed the body. One of the walls was hung with a selection of oilskins and orange life jackets. The most interesting feature was the piles of heavy steel chain coiled neatly on the floor, each one in a different weight category according to a painted board on the wall behind it.

'Right.' Lebel consulted his document. 'He weighed seven and a half stone at death. Christ, we can't have that. He'll float like a cork on that current.' He turned to a sheet on the wall. 'Ninety pounds of chain according to this. Get it on him.'

Brosnan took a chain from the correct pile and they proceeded to pass it through the loops specially provided for the purpose on the body bag.

'I've often wondered why you make all this fuss over the weights, Pierre.' Savary remarked. 'The way you change it, according to the body weight?'

Lebel produced a pack of Gauloises and offered them one. 'Simple. The Mill Race isn't one current as most people imagine. It's two. Stay on the surface, you'd end on the rocks at St Denise ten miles up the coast and bodies drifting in as regularly as that would scare old ladies walking the dog. But drop the body down to thirty fathoms, the current takes it out to sea. So, the weight factor is critical. Anyway, let's get this over with.'

Brosnan and Savary carried the body between them to the edge of the cliff. They stood there for a moment and Savary said, 'I tell you he should have a priest. This isn't right.'

Lebel, his essential decency coming to the surface, removed his cap and said, 'All right. Lord, into thy hands we commend the spirit of 67824 Jean Bouvier. He didn't get much out of this life. Maybe you can do more for him in the next.' He replaced his cap. 'Okay, over with him.'

Brosnan and Savary swung a couple of times, then let go. The body turned over once, plunged into white foam below and disappeared. They stood staring down at the water.

Savary whispered, 'The only way I'm ever going to get off this rock. I'm going to die here, Martin.'

There was desolation in his voice, total despair, and Brosnan put a hand on his shoulder. 'Maybe – on the other hand, maybe not.'

Savary turned to stare at him, frowning, and Lebel closed and locked the door and switched off the light. 'Okay, let's go,' and they turned and followed him back down the track, heads bowed against the rain.

At six a.m. Ferguson and Harry Fox were having breakfast in a truck drivers' cafe on the A40 just outside Cheltenham. The bacon and eggs were the best Fox could remember enjoying since the Officers' Mess at Combermere Barracks in Windsor. Ferguson was obviously just as impressed.

'What about Devlin, sir?'

'Remarkable man. Must be sixty-one now. An Ulsterman. County Down, I believe. Father executed during the Anglo-Irish war in nineteen twenty-one for serving in a flying column. Educated by Jesuits, took first class honours in English Literature at Trinity College. Scholar, writer, poet and highly dangerous gunman for the IRA during the thirties. Went to Spain in nineteen thirty-six. Served in the Washington Brigade against Franco. Captured by Italian troops and imprisoned in Spain until nineteen forty when the Abwehr had him freed and brought to Berlin to see if he could be of any use to German Intelligence.'

'And was he, sir?'

'The trouble was, from their point of view, he was a bad risk. Very anti-fascist, you see. The Abwehr's Irish Section did use him once. They'd sent an agent to Ireland, a Captain Goertz. When he got stuck, they parachuted

Devlin in to get him out for them. Unfortunately Goertz was caught and Devlin spent several months on the run before he managed to make it back to Berlin via Portugal. From then on, Ireland was a dead end as far as the Abwehr was concerned and Devlin took a job lecturing at the University of Berlin. Until the autumn of nineteen forty-three.' Ferguson reached for the marmalade. 'This really is very good. I think I'll ask him for a jar.'

'The autumn of nineteen forty-three,' Fox said patiently.

'How much do you know about the German attempt on Churchill's life in November of that year, Harry?'

Fox laughed out loud. 'Come on, sir, an old wives' tale, that one.' And then, continuing to watch Ferguson's face, he stopped laughing. 'Isn't it, sir?'

'Well, let's assume it's just a good story, Harry. The scenario would run something like this. Devlin, bored to tears at University of Berlin, is offered a job by the Abwehr. He's to parachute into Ireland, then make his way to Norfolk to act as middle man between the most successful woman agent the Abwehr had in the entire war and a crack force of German paratroopers, led by a Colonel Kurt Steiner, the object of the exercise being to apprehend Churchill who was staying at a country house outside the village of Studley Constable.'

'Go on, sir.'

'All for nothing, of course. Wasn't even Churchill, just a stand-in while the great man was going to Tehran. They died anyway, Steiner and his men. Well, all except one, and Devlin, with his usual Irish deviousness, got away.'

Harry Fox said in amazement, 'You mean it's all true, sir?'

'A few years yet before those classified files are opened, Harry. You'll have to wait and see.'

'And Devlin worked for the Nazis? I don't get it. I thought you said he was anti-fascist?'

'Rather more complicated than that. I think if someone had suggested on our side that he should attempt to kidnap Adolf Hitler, he'd have thrown himself into the task with even greater enthusiasm. Very frequently in life we're not playing the game, Harry. It's playing us. You'll learn that as you get older.'

'And wiser, sir?'

'That's it, Harry, learn to laugh at yourself. A priceless asset. During the post-war period Devlin was a professor at a mid-Western college in America. He returned to Ulster briefly during the border war of the late fifties. Went back again during the civil rights disturbances of nineteen sixty-nine. One of the original architects of the Provisional IRA. As I said earlier, he never approved of the bombing campaign. In nineteen seventy-five, increasingly disillusioned, he officially retired from the movement. A living legend, whatever that trite phrase means. Since nineteen seventy-six, against considerable opposition from some quarters, he's held a post as additional professor in the English Faculty at his old University, Trinity College.'

Ferguson pushed back his chair and they got up to go. 'And he and Brosnan were friends?' Fox asked.

'I think you could say that. I also think what happened to Brosnan in France was a sort of final straw for Devlin. Still.' He stood in the entrance looking across the dingy carpark and waved to his driver. 'All right, Harry, let's press on to Hereford.'

Barry was working at the maps in his apartment, soon after breakfast, when there was a discreet knock at the door. He opened it to admit Romanov.

'How about the passports?' Barry demanded.

'No problem. Go to the usual place at ten o'clock for the photos. The passports will be ready this afternoon. Is there anything else you need?'

'Yes, documentation for the Jersey route. That's the way I'll go. French tourist on holiday.'

'No problem,' Romanov told him.

Once in Jersey, he would be on British soil and able to take an internal flight to a selection of airports on the British mainland where customs and immigration procedures were considerably less strict than they would have been landing at London Heathrow.

'If I collect the package Wednesday afternoon, you must be prepared to take delivery that night,' Barry said. 'Preferably a trawler, say fifteen miles off the coast.'

'And how will you rendezvous?'

'We'll get whoever your people in London find to work for me, to arrange a boat. A good forty-foot deep-sea launch will do to operate somewhere out of this area.' He tapped the map. 'Somewhere on the coast opposite the Isle of Man. South of Ravenglass.'

'Good.'

'I'll leave for St Malo tonight, cross to Jersey tomorrow, using the French passport. There's a British Airways flight to Manchester from Jersey at midday. I'll meet your London contact man the following day on the pier at Morecambe at noon. That's a seaside resort on the coast below the Lake District. He'll recognise me from the photograph you keep on file at the KGB office at your London Embassy, I'm sure.'

Romanov looked down at the map. 'Frank, if this comes off, it will be the biggest coup of my career. Are you sure? Are you really sure?'

'That you'll be a hero of the Soviet Union decorated by old Leonid Ilyich Brezhnev himself?' Barry clapped him on the shoulder. 'Don't worry, Nikolai, old son. A piece of cake.'

4

The 22nd Regiment, Special Air Service, is what the military refer to as an élite unit. Someone once remarked that they were the nearest thing the British Army has to the SS. A sour tribute to the unit's astonishing success in counter-insurgency operations and urban guerrilla warfare, areas in which the SAS are undoubtedly world experts with thirty years' experience gained in the jungles of Malaya and Borneo, the deserts of Southern Arabia and the Oman, the green country-side of South Armagh, the back streets of Belfast. It accepts only volunteers, soldiers already serving with other units. Its selection procedure is so demanding, both physically and mentally, that only five per cent of those applying are accepted.

The office of the commanding officer of 22nd SAS at Bradbury Lines Barracks in Hereford was neat and functional, if rather spartan. Most surprising was the CO himself, young for a half-colonel with a keen intelligent face, bronzed from much exposure to desert sun. The medal ribbons above his pocket included the Military Cross. He sat there, leaning back in his seat, listening intently.

When Ferguson had finished speaking the colonel nodded 'Very interesting.'

'But can it be done?' Ferguson asked.

The colonel smiled slightly. 'Oh, yes, Brigadier, no trouble at all as far as I can see. The sort of thing my chaps are doing in South Armagh all the time. Tony Villiers is the man for this one, I think.' He flicked his intercom. 'Captain Villiers, quick as you like, and we'll have tea for three while we're waiting.'

The tea was excellent, the conversation mainly army gossip. It was perhaps fifteen minutes before there was a knock at the door and a young man of twenty-six or seven entered. At some time or other his nose had been broken, probably in the boxing ring from the look of him. He wore a black track suit but the most surprising feature about him was his hair which was black and tangled and almost shoulder length.

'Sorry about the delay, sir, I was on the track.'

'That's okay, Tony. I'd like you to meet Brigadier Ferguson and Captain Fox.'

'Gentlemen.' Villiers nodded.

'Brigadier Ferguson is from DI5, Tony. He has a job of the kind to which we are particularly suited. Top priority. Seemed to me it could be your department.'

'Ireland, sir?'

Ferguson said, 'That's right. I want you to kidnap someone for me. My information is that he'll be spending the weekend at his cottage in County Mayo on the coast near Killala Bay. I need him within thirty-six hours, delivered to me Sunday morning in London. Do you think you can manage that?'

'I don't see why not, sir.' Villiers strolled to the map of Ireland on the wall. 'Only sixty or seventy miles from the Ulster Border.'

'Excellent,' Ferguson said.

'Presumably IRA, sir? Anyone important?'

'A university professor called Devlin. You'll be thoroughly briefed.'

Villiers actually reacted. 'Liam Devlin, sir? I thought he'd retired?'

'That's what he thinks too,' Ferguson said. He hesitated, 'Are you certain you can mount this thing right off the cuff, just like that?'

Villiers grinned and ran a hand over his hair. 'That's why I never have a haircut, sir. Special dispensation. I mean, in Crossmaglen you've got to look the part.' His shoulders hunched and his voice changed, the hard, distinctive Ulster accent taking over. 'Personal camouflage is very important, sir. Other people use language labs to learn how to speak French or whatever. In the SAS, we can teach you how to speak with the accent of any Irish county you care to name within a fortnight.'

'Soldiering,' Ferguson said, 'has certainly changed since my day.'

The colonel stood up. 'Right, gentlemen, I think we'll go over to operations now. Get this thing thoroughly sorted out. You lead the way, Tony.'

Villiers flicked Fox's Guard Division tie as they went through the door. 'Which regiment?'

Fox, who knew a guardsman when he saw one, long hair or not, said, 'Blues and Royals. And you?'

'Grenadiers,' Villiers said. 'You lost the hand over there?'

'That's right,' Fox said. 'Picked up the wrong briefcase.'

'That's the way it goes.'

It was a misty morning as they crossed the parade ground. The clock tower loomed above them. Villiers paused. 'If you're interested, the name of every member of the regiment killed since nineteen fifty is recorded up there.'

Fox paused and peered at the names of men who had died in every possible theatre of war. He frowned, 'Good God, there's a chap listed as having died in Ethiopia in nineteen sixty-eight. What on earth was he doing there?'

'Search me,' Villiers said. 'Ours not to reason why and all that sort of good old British rubbish. You might as well ask ten years from now what I was doing in Mayo tomorrow night.'

Later, as the Bentley turned out through the main gates and they started back to London, Fox said, 'You really think they'll pull it off, sir?'

'By the beginning of nineteen seventy-six, Harry, forty-nine British soldiers had been killed in South Armagh and not a single member of the IRA, so the SAS were moved in to operate undercover. In the year following, only two part-time members of the Ulster Defence Regiment were killed in the entire area. That result speaks for itself.'

'All right, sir, but one thing worries me. So Tony Villiers and his boys are good. The two men he's taking with him were very impressive, I admit that. But Devlin's good, too. I know he's a bit long in the tooth, but what if he decides to shoot first himself . . . ?'

'Just what the bastard would do,' Ferguson said. 'But you heard my orders to Villiers. I want him untouched by human hand. No use to me if he's dragging his left leg or something.' He yawned. 'I'm going to get a little shut-eye, Harry. Wake me at Cheltenham and we'll have something to eat at that superb cafe.'

He closed his eyes, folded his hands across his stomach, leaned back in the corner and was instantly asleep.

At that moment, Frank Barry was disembarking from the hydrofoil in St Helier harbour on the island of Jersey having just completed the run from St Malo. According to the forged French passport supplied by the KGB, he was a commercial traveller from Paris named Pierre Dubois. His hair had been soaked in brilliantine and carefully parted at one side and he wore a large pair of black horn-rimmed glasses. His appearance exactly fitted the photo they'd taken. Amazing how different he looked, but then, as he had discovered so often in the past, a little was all that it took.

Fifteen minutes later, a taxi deposited him at the entrance to the airport. He went straight to the British Airways desk and booked a seat on the Manchester flight.

An hour to kill. He stopped at the duty free shop to buy a carton of cigarettes and a bottle of cognac and the girl behind the counter put them in a plastic bag and smiled.

'I hope you enjoyed your visit.'

'Certainly did,' Barry said. 'Wonderful place. Come back any time,' and he walked away to the departure lounge.

The old farmhouse that nestled amongst beech trees on the hillside above Killala Bay enjoyed one of the best views of the entire west coast of Ireland. Devlin never tired of it. From the terrace he'd built in his spare time the year before, he could see out beyond the cliffs all the way to Newfoundland, the sun slipping into the sea like a blood orange, and to his right, Sligo Bay and across to the mountains of Donegal. He turned and went into the house.

Liam Devlin was a small man, no more than five foot five or six, and at sixty-one, his dark, wavy hair showed no visible signs of grey. There was a faded scar on the right side of his forehead, an old bullet wound, his face was pale, the eyes a vivid blue, and a slight ironic smile seemed permanently to lift the corner of his mouth. The look of a man who'd found life a bad joke and had decided that the only thing to do was laugh about it.

He went into the kitchen, rolled up the sleeves of his black woollen shirt and prepared a stew, peeling potatoes and vegetables methodically, whistling to himself. He was still unmarried, circumstances of his life having dictated the situation more than anything else, but now, it suited him. He liked to be alone; to find his own space, although there were women enough still, even a student or two, who would have been happy to spend their weekends in Mayo with him.

He put the stew on the stove, went into the sitting room and replenished the fire. It was dark outside now. He pulled the curtains at the French windows and poured himself an Irish whiskey, Bushmills, his favourite and settled down by the fire. He ran a hand along the shelf at the side of the fire place, selected a copy of *The Midnight Court* in Irish and started to read.

A breath of cold air touched his cheek, the fire stirred. As he glanced up, instantly alert, the door from the hall swung open and Tony Villiers stepped in. He wore a dark reefer jacket and jeans and badly needed a shave. The combination made him look a thoroughly dangerous man. The Browning automatic pistol in his right hand confirmed it. He ran an expert hand over Devlin, seeking a concealed weapon, found none and stepped back satisfied.

'Would you look at that now,' Devlin said softly and stood up, leaning against the mantelpiece of the great stone fireplace, one foot on the hearth. 'And which club are you from, son? Red Hand of Ulster, UVF or what?'

'Easy now, Professor,' Tony Villiers said in impeccable public school English.

'Christ Jesus,' Devlin said amiably. 'Not you bloody lot again.'

His right hand went up inside the hearth and grasped the butt of a Walther pistol which hung on a nail there is case of just such an emergency. His hand swung and he fired in one smooth motion, hitting Villiers in the left shoulder, knocking him back against the wall, the Browning falling to the floor.

Villiers struggled to one knee, blood oozing between his fingers where he clutched his shoulder. 'Good,' he said. 'Really very good.'

'Flattery will get you nowhere, son,' Devlin said. There was a crash behind him as the kitchen door was flung open and Villiers' two companions erupted into the room, machine pistols at the ready.

'Alive,' Tony Villiers cried. 'Don't harm a hair on his bloody head, that's an order.' He smiled savagely. 'I'm expecting rather a lot, Professor, they're only trained to kill. I'd advise you to drop it.'

'SAS, is it?' Devlin said.

'I'm afraid so.'

'Mother Mary, why didn't they send the Devil instead. Now with him, I'm on good terms.' He turned to the other two. 'Do you think one of you could do something about his shoulder? It's the carpet I'm thinking of. Persian. A gift from a friend.'

Tony Villiers shook his head. 'Later, Professor. For now, you will please pack a suitcase with whatever you feel you need for an extended trip.'

'And just exactly where might we be going?'

'Well, if things go according to plan, we should cross into Ulster about three hours from now. Onward transportation, courtesy of the Army Air Corps, tomorrow morning. You should be in London by noon. I'd take a raincoat, if I were you.' Villiers had produced a field service dressing pack from one pocket and was opening it with his teeth. 'The weather over there's been terrible lately.'

Devlin shook his head. 'Where did you go to school, son?'

'Eton.'

'Jesus and I might have known. What would the Empire have been without you?'

'Not very much, I suspect,' Tony Villiers said crisply. 'But time is limited, Professor. Please do as I say without any further delay.'

'And so I will.' Devlin walked to the door followed by one of the troopers. 'But only because I'm fascinated. Can't wait to find out what all this is about. Help yourself to the Bushmills.'

He smiled and moved out into the hall.

Morecambe is a seaside resort on the Lancashire coast, south of the English Lake District, a quiet town which even during the holiday season caters mainly for older people. Not a great deal goes on there. Someone once unkindly said that when people die in Morecambe, they don't bury them, they simply sit them up in the town bus shelters to make the place look busy.

Frank Barry found it pleasant enough. Not many people on the front, which was only to be expected in November, but then he'd always found seaside resorts out of season stimulating places. The cafes and shops closed for the winter, the empty boardwalks: he walked out along the pier, feeling unaccountably cheerful, and stood at the rail, breathing in the good salt air. The dark waters of Morecambe Bay were being whipped into whitecaps by the wind and north, through the mist, he could see the mountains of the Lake District, a blur, on the horizon.

He lit a cigarette and waited. After a while, he heard footsteps booming hollowly on the boardwalk behind him. The man who leaned on the rail on his right wore a dark raincoat and hat. He was perhaps thirty with a young intelligent face and his steel-rimmed glasses were giving him trouble in the rain.

Barry, who had discarded his horn-rimmed spectacles and washed the brilliantine from his hair at the motel where he had stayed the night before, turned and smiled. 'A hell of a problem those things in weather like this.'

The young man nodded, put down the briefcase he was carrying and wiped his glasses with a handkerchief. 'True, Mr Barry. I tried contact lenses a few years ago, but unfortunately had an allergy to them.' His English was excellent with just a trace of an accent.

'You have something for me?'

The young man touched the briefcase with his foot. 'Everything you need.'

'Well, that makes a change,' Barry said. 'I mean, it's not often you get everything in this life.'

'I have also included a contact in London by which you may reach me in the event of an emergency, Mr Barry. Please memorise and destroy.'

Barry picked up the briefcase and grinned. 'Son, I was doing this sort of thing when you were still hanging on your mother's left breast.'

He walked away along the pier, his feet echoing on the boards. The young man stayed where he was. Only when the sound of them had faded did he turn from the rail.

Barry had picked up a hire car at Manchester Airport, a Ford Cortina, and he was driving it through Lancaster, turning on to the A6 and heading north for the Lake District, within twenty minutes of leaving his KGB contact on Morecambe pier. He drove for some ten or twelve miles, then turned into a convenient layby, stopped the engine and opened the briefcase.

There was, as the young man had said, everything he needed. His contact at a place called Marsh End, south of Ravenglass on the Cumbrian coast, very convenient for the Wast Water proving ground. Details of the rendezvous for Thursday night – they'd provided a deep sea trawler for that from the Russian northern fishing fleet. And, of course, the young man's number in London. Even more interesting was the pistol with the silencer screwed on the end, a Czech Ceska 7.5mm. There were also several additional clips of ammunition and fifty thousand pounds in twenty pound notes, neatly packeted.

'Well, would you look at that, now?' Barry said softly, hefting the Ceska in one hand.

He slipped it into his raincoat pocket. He

closed the briefcase, placing it on the passenger seat beside him with the typed list on top and drove away. Occasionally, he glanced at the list, memorising the details it contained line-by-line. A little later, he left the A6 at Levens Bridge and pulled into a roadside cafe. He went into the men's room, locked himself in a stall, lit a cigarette and touched the lighter flame to the list. Only when it was reduced to dark ashes did he drop it into the toilet bowl to flush away. Then he went outside, got back into the car and took the road for Broughton-in-Furness and the Cumbrian coast, whistling softly between his teeth.

Kim opened the door of Ferguson's sitting room and ushered Tony Villiers and Liam Devlin inside. Ferguson was at his desk, Harry Fox standing beside him. Ferguson glanced up, peering at the two men over his half-moon spectacles, then removed them slowly.

Tony Villiers' dark reefer coat hung from his shoulders, loosely buttoned. Underneath, he was swathed in bandages, his left arm in a sling. His face was white and drawn, lines of pain deeply etched there in spite of the injection they'd given him at the Military Wing of Musgrave Park Hospital in Belfast.

'Professor Devlin, sir, as ordered,' he said.

'Now then, you old bastard,' Devlin said amiably. 'You've got a good lad here and you not deserving it.'

Ferguson got to his feet. 'You should be in hospital, Captain, now, and that's an order. See to it Harry. Get my car.'

Villiers swayed and Devlin moved in fast and got an arm around him. 'Easy boy, you've done enough and more.'

Villiers managed to smile. 'Damn it, Professor, but I like you. I really do, and that's a hell of a thing to say considering the situation.'

'You're not so bad yourself,' Devlin told him. 'Only the uniform I'm not too happy about, not the man wearing it.'

Harry Fox had Villiers by the elbow. 'All right, let's go.'

He got the door open and Villiers turned.

'One thing, Professor. You could have killed me and you didn't. Why?'

'The terrible waste that would have been,' Devlin said, and suddenly the blue eyes were bleak. 'And hasn't there been waste enough?' Villiers stared at him, frowning and Devlin laughed. 'Go on, boy, out of it, before I totally corrupt you.'

The door closed behind them and Devlin turned to face Ferguson, unbuckling the belt of his dark trenchcoat. 'So, here we are.'

'Here we are indeed.'

'Would there be any chance of a cup of tea, would you think? It's been a hell of a journey.'

Ferguson smiled and flicked the intercom. 'Tea, Kim. My usual and another pot, extra strong, Irish variety.' He turned back to Devlin. 'Satisfactory?'

'As long as I can stand up a spoon in it.'

He helped himself to a cigarette from a box on Ferguson's desk, lit it and went and sprawled in one of the chairs by the fire. 'They do you well, DI5, I must say.'

The door opened and Kim came in with

the tea on a silver tray followed by Harry Fox. 'I've packed him straight off in the Bentley to the Special Wing at Melbury House, sir. I've rung through and notified Colonel Jackson that he's on his way.'

'Good,' Ferguson said. 'And let's make sure he gets only the best.'

Kim withdrew and Devlin helped himself to the tea. 'And who have we got here?'

'Captain Fox is my personal aide,' Ferguson said.

Devlin's eyes took in the gloved hand. 'And not much time for people like me, I should imagine.'

'Not really,' Fox said.

'That's fine, boy. Just so we know where we stand.'

There was silence. Ferguson got up and peered out of the window into the square. 'You're in a bad hole, Devlin, you realise that, don't you? There are outstanding crimes listed against you which would draw you twenty years at least, if not life. How does the Central Criminal Court at the Old Bailey appeal to you?'

Devlin laughed out loud. 'Go teach your grandmother to suck eggs, Brigadier. I'm not standing in the dock at the Bailey or anywhere else. You know it, I know it and so does the boy here, if he has an ounce of sense. I was taken against my will, from one sovereign state to another, kidnapped by British troops, carried over the border from the Republic of Ireland into Ulster. Now, I know things haven't been going too well between our two wonderful countries, but if you think the British Cabinet is going to want the stink that this would cause, all the way up to the United Nations, you've lost your marbles.'

He was right. He knew it and so did they. It was Harry Fox who put it into words. 'He's got a point, sir. A hell of a point. There's no way we can make this work against his will. If he won't play, we'll have to send him back.'

'Don't be a fool, Harry. I've known that all along,' Ferguson told him.

'So,' Devlin said. 'Let's be having it.'

Ferguson said calmly, 'When did you last see Brosnan?'

Devlin's eyes were wary. 'Martin? Four years ago.'

'That's right, February, nineteen seventy-five, when you sent him to France, since when he's taken up permanent residence in a very unpleasant establishment called Belle Isle off the French Mediterranean coast, which you may have heard of.

'A small corner in hell, so they tell me,' Devlin said.

'Aptly put and he's there for life. An establishment which like Alcatraz, proudly boasts that no one has ever escaped from it.'

'So.'

'What if I could get him out?'

Devlin frowned. 'And how would you do that?'

'Some sort of deal with the French authorities.'

'But why would you? Why should you go to the trouble?'

'Frank Barry.'

There was total amazement on Devlin's face. 'Frank Barry?' he said. 'And what in the name of Christ has he to do with it?'

'Well, if you can keep that Irish tongue of yours still for fifteen minutes, I'll tell you.'

Devlin walked up and down the room, the cigarette hanging from the corner of his mouth, smoke curling. 'All right,' he said. 'A fine mad bastard, Frank Barry is, I'll not deny that, nor my personal dislike of the man. Frank believes in what some people call the purity of violence; a fancy term which when you come down to it means a licence to kill anyone who gets in your way. When that includes innocent women and kids, I want no part in it. But it's your flesh he's the thorn in and nailing him to the cross is your affair. Not Martin Brosnan's and certainly not mine.'

'Frank Barry is at war with the world, Mr Devlin,' Harry Fox said.

Devlin laughed. 'Oh, but you have a way with the words, Captain. Is there just a touch of Irish in your blood somewhere?'

'Be reasonable, Devlin,' Ferguson said. 'Barry's activities never exactly helped your cause, you've got to admit that. He's done as much as anyone to blacken your image in his time and that was before he was mixed up in the Mountbatten affair. One of the worst things that ever happened to the IRA as far as world opinion was concerned.'

'I'm with you there,' Devlin said. 'But you're wrong in one respect. It isn't my cause any longer.'

Fox was thunderstruck. 'You mean that?'

Devlin nodded. 'Oh, I'm still one hundred per cent for a United Ireland, but ten years is enough as far as I'm concerned. Too many dead, Captain. A bloody charnel house and what have we got to show for it? Frankly, I think you'll find Martin Brosnan to be of the same opinion.'

'Put it to him,' Ferguson said. 'Go and see him, that's all I ask.'

'And how could that be arranged?'

Ferguson nodded to Harry Fox, who opened a file and took out a British passport which he pushed across the desk. Devlin picked it up. It was in the name of Charles Gorman and when he opened it, his own picture stared out at him.

'And who would Charles Gorman be?'

'A highly respectable lawyer. Offices in Lincoln's Inn. Visiting Brosnan to discuss legal matters in connection with the family business. Also the possibility of an appeal for clemency.'

Devlin shook his head in amazement. 'Are you trying to tell me I'm expected or something?'

'Certainly. Tuesday morning, day after tomorrow. You catch the prison supply boat from a place called St Denise along the coast from Marseilles.'

Devlin tapped the passport with a finger, frowning. 'To set up a thing like this must have taken some pull in France, even for you.'

'Not really,' Ferguson said. 'The right SDECE contact. Colonel Guyon who heads Service Five now, has a vested interest in running Frank Barry to earth himself, particularly after the attempt to assassinate Lord Carrington on French soil. It's through his influence that your appointment to see Brosnan was arranged so expeditiously.'

'Service Five?' Devlin grimaced. 'They

could have given Himmler and his bunch a run for their money. The way I hear it, they enjoy playing with electricity.'

'Yes, well we don't exactly have much choice, do we?'

'And Guyon can arrange Martin's release, is that what you're saying?'

'Not at all.' Ferguson shook his head. 'That would take some delicate negotiations at a rather higher level. No, for the moment all I want you to do is see Brosnan and find out if he'll agree in principle.'

'To what? Freedom if he agrees to hunt down Frank Barry and act as a kind of public executioner for you?'

'Why not? A simple enough quid pro quo, or do you really think he'd rather spend the rest of his life in a cell on Belle Isle?'

Devlin shook his head. 'I don't know about this. To start with, you're making a mistake to think Frank Barry would welcome him with open arms. They always disliked each other. Martin thought him a butcher from the beginning and told him so. On the other hand, he's a very complex man, our Martin. The killer's hand is the instinctual part of him that surfaced in Vietnam and wouldn't go away, but up here,' he tapped his forehead, 'is a scholar, philosopher and poet of no mean distinction. You could never tell which way he'd jump.'

'You mean he needs to be angry?' Ferguson said. 'I think I can arrange that, too.' He nodded to Fox, who took a photo from the file and passed it across.

The girl on it sat on a sand dune with tall grass around her, hugging her knees, face pushed forward, laughing. She was no more than seventeen, with shoulder-length black hair and a face of extraordinary beauty. Devlin's own face was very pale as he picked the photo up.

'You recognise her?' Ferguson asked.

'Yes,' Devlin said softly. 'Norah Cassidy, Martin's cousin once removed. A nice Belfast girl.'

'And what happened to her?'

'She died a year back, so I believe. In France.' Devlin paused a hand over his face, then froze. 'France?' he whispered. 'And just what are you getting at now, Ferguson?'

'She went to the Sorbonne to study French in nineteen seventy-six,' Ferguson said. 'As you might expect from a girl with her political views, she soon made contact with various extremist political organisations at the University. Then Frank Barry appeared on the scene.'

'Barry?' Devlin said. 'Barry and Norah? I don't believe it.'

'She was his mistress for over a year, but Belfast had left its mark. Like many young women from that city, she'd been on tranquillisers for years. In Barry's company, she progressed to harder drugs. Finally, she was mainlining on heroin. She became more and more dependent on the drug, which suited Barry because it made her more and more dependent on him. The police almost caught him on a farm in Normandy just over a year ago. He escaped by the skin of his teeth, but dumped her.'

'The bastard,' Devlin said.

'What you're going to see now isn't nice, but I think it necessary.' Ferguson nodded to Fox. 'Now, Harry.'

There was a television set in the corner, a video machine underneath it. Fox switched it on and Ferguson said, 'I got this through Guyon from French Intelligence. As I said, not nice, but there it is.'

The video rolled for a moment, then focused. Norah Cassidy's face filled the screen, ravaged, wasted, only a hint of that smiling girl in the photo. She was crying helplessly and the camera pulled back to show her being held by two nurses. One of them pushed up the wide sleeve of the hospital robe and the camera moved in to show the dozens of cracks in her arm from the heroin fixes, running sores, most of them.

The scene changed. She was in bed now, a narrow hospital cot in a white room, straps across the bed to control her as she thrashed wildly. The scene cut sharply to be replaced by another close-up of the face, in total repose, relaxed, at peace, only she wasn't sleeping, she was dead and the camera pulled back to reveal her lying naked on a mortuary slab, her head cradled on a wooden block. The pathologist leaned over her with a scalpel.

Ferguson said, 'That'll do, Harry, no need to prolong the agony.'

Fox hurriedly switched off the video. Devlin turned to the windows, tears in his eyes. He stayed there, shoulders hunched. He said quietly, 'I'm going to be sick. Where's the bathroom?'

'Straight through that door,' Ferguson told him and Fox hurried across and held it open for him.

Devlin went out and Fox removed the video from the machine, crossed to Ferguson's desk and laid it down carefully.

'You know something, sir?' His voice was shaky. 'On the whole, I think I'd really prefer to be back in Belfast.'

'I know, Harry, I know. A dirty, dirty business, you'll find that out the longer you're in it, but someone has to do it.'

The door opened and Devlin came back in. He went to the sideboard, helped himself to a large Scotch and stood there, savouring it.

'Martin loved that girl like a sister, you know that? August sixty-nine, in the Falls

Road, she carried ammunition to us under fire. She was all of twelve years old then.'

Ferguson said, 'You'll go?'

'Oh, yes,' Devlin said in a low voice. 'I think you could say that.'

'Good. You can 'phone whoever you have to at Trinity College from here. Tell them you're taking extended leave or something. Anything you like. You can stay at Harry's flat tonight. Fly on to Marseilles tomorrow. Papers, money, everything you need you'll be provided with. You've got two days, then I want you back here.'

'Fine by me,' Devlin said.

'We think Barry's Russian contact in Paris is a man called Nikolai Romanov. Supposed to be a cultural attaché at the Soviet Embassy. Actually a colonel in the KGB. There's the address of his apartment in St Germain in Paris, his cottage at Neuilly and a photo.'

He passed them across and Devlin examined the photo, frowning. 'Surely French Intelligence know about this man?'

'Of course.'

'Then why don't they do something about him?'

'Officially he's a diplomat so they'd have to catch him at it. And we have reason to believe that the KGB is still well entrenched within French Intelligence. I think he's got friends there. One more thing that may help.' Ferguson held up the old *Paris-Match* photo of Devlin, Brosnan and Frank Barry. 'Remember the girl who took this?'

'Anne-Marie Audin.' Devlin took the photo from him. 'Nineteen seventy-one. Belfast was crawling with journalists in those days. All of them wanting stories. Secret interviews with the gallant lads of the IRA. She scooped them all, that girl.'

'But then she would, wouldn't she?' Ferguson said. 'After all, she'd known him in Vietnam. All she had to do was put the word out in Belfast that she was there. She must have known he'd contact her.'

'Exactly,' Devlin said. 'She stayed with us for a week and a hell of a time of it she had, but what a story.'

'She visited him twice in Dublin,' Ferguson

said. 'They met again in Paris at least once. Rather more than journalistic interest, I'd say.'

'That's her business,' Devlin said flatly.

'Well, she *is* thirty-three and still unmarried. She's also in London this week-end on an assignment for the French edition of *Vogue*. Do you think it's worth seeing her? After all, she's hardly likely to call copper on you.'

'No, she wouldn't do that.' Devlin nodded, remembering those heady days in 1971, hustling through the Armagh countryside by night, crashing an army roadblock, bullets shattering the windows of their car and flinging himself on Anne-Marie, holding her safe against the floor.

'Good,' Ferguson said. 'Arrange it then, Harry.' He pushed the 'phone across. 'Only one more thing to do then. Ring the University and make your excuses.'

Devlin picked up the receiver and held it for a moment 'You know, there's an old Irish saying. Touch the Devil and you can't let go.'

'Interesting,' Ferguson said. 'And what exactly does it mean?'

'Oh, I think you know well enough. You and me, the boy here, Martin in his cell. Frank Barry. None of us can stop, can we? No going back. Bloody undertakers the lot of us, always carrying some poor bugger out in a coffin.' He started to dial. 'The trouble is, you see, that we're not playing the game any more. The game's playing us.'

5

The Grenadier Guard in black busby and scarlet tunic stood at his post outside St James's Palace, rigidly at attention, rifle at the slope and stared into infinity, trying to ignore the young model in the white silk pantaloon suit and gold high-heeled shoes who positioned herself against him.

It was ludicrous really, rain falling, and in spite of that her perfume filled his nostrils, so that he had to breath deeply to steady himself.

There was a lighting man, a second camera-man, wardrobe mistress with two assistants, three other models, just now changing in the large van, and a curious crowd of onlookers, pausing to watch Anne-Marie Audin at work.

She wore knee-high brown boots, a khaki

jumpsuit of the kind that could be purchased at any military surplus shop. Her hair was long, shoulder length, at present held back in a ponytail. The face was very brown and the only make-up she wore was a pale lipstick.

Fox parked the car at the kerb and followed the Irishman down towards the crowd. They moved round to the other side of the van.

'Has she changed much?'

Devlin shook his head. 'Big for the cause of women, but a darling girl, though she'd belt me for saying it.'

'She and Brosnan were lovers then?' Fox said gently.

'Oh yes.' Devlin continued to watch her as she took one photo after another. 'I wasn't going to tell that old bugger that, though. Tell me, Captain, when were you born? End of March, beginning of April, I'd say.'

Fox was astonished. 'How did you know that? It's actually the seventh of April.'

'I was right though. Aries the Ram. That's the doctor's sign. Surprising to find a soldier and you a healer by nature. Now take

Ferguson. He's a Scorpio for sure. According to my favourite book of astrology, published in the eighteenth century, I might add, if his stars are badly aspected, which I'm certain they are, he's a lover of murder and thieving, a promoter of sedition, perjured, obscene, rash and inhumane. Recognise any of his more lovable traits there?' He put a hand up. 'No, don't bother to answer.'

Anne-Marie turned to her assistant. 'All right,' she said in French. 'Now we move into the Park. Buckingham Palace last.'

Her eyes passed over Devlin. She paused and looked back slowly. 'Good-day to you, *a colleen*,' he said cheerfully. 'God save the good work.'

Anne-Marie Audin turned pale under her tan. He took her hands and kissed them gently.

Devlin and Anne-Marie sat on a bench in the rain in St James's Park. Below, the crew were setting up for more pictures by the lake.

The content of Devlin's French was excellent,

rapid and fluent. The accent was terrible. He said, 'You're wearing well, girl.'

'And you, Liam. Still up to your ears in that cause of yours? I would have thought London dangerous territory for you.'

'Ancient history,' Devlin told her. 'No more causes. I'm getting old, my love.'

'That will be the day.' She ruffled his hair without thinking.

He offered her a cigarette from his battered old silver case. She shook her head and he took one himself. 'Fashion photography?' He nodded down towards the crew by the lake. 'Isn't that a bit of a come down for France's favourite war photographer? The girl who won a Pulitzer Prize?'

'And there's the Professor talking,' she said. 'Don't be a snob, Liam. The best fashion magazine in the world and I never give less than my best. I'd have thought you'd have known that. There's always far more to any highly popular art form than the critics are willing to admit. Anyway, it's not the only reason I'm here. Later tonight I'm doing a feature for *Paris-Match* on down-and-outs in London.'

'I might have known.' He grinned crookedly. 'And still big for the cause of women and still not married and all of thirty-five.'

'Thirty-three,' she sparked and punched him in the shoulder.

'But still not married for all that and we both know why.' She glanced at him, face blank, then looked out across the lake. Devlin said softly, 'Have you seen him lately?'

'The last time I tried was three years ago. I received permission through the Judiciary Department and went to Belle Isle. He refused to see me. Sent me a letter later, his last one, in which he said I was to look upon him as dead.'

'And?'

She smiled wanly. 'I got some good pictures, Liam. A terrible place.'

'I can imagine. I'm seeing him Tuesday, myself. It should be an enlivening encounter.'

She turned instantly, eyes dark. 'You are seeing Martin? You? But how can this be?' She frowned, glancing across at Fox sheltering from the rain under a tree. 'Who is that man, Liam? What game are you playing now?'

So he told her, rapidly and concisely, leaving nothing out. When he was finished, she sat there staring at him in astonishment.

'But this is incredible. Insane.'

'It might get him out, or would you rather he spent the rest of his life on that rock?'

'No, of course not. I would do anything – anything to see him free,' she said savagely. 'Not for my own sake, Liam, not for love, but for him.' Her fingers hooked painfully into his arm.

'I know, girl, I know,' he soothed her.

There was a call from the lake below, her assistant waving. She said, 'I'll have to go. Look, I must see you again.'

'I'm leaving for Marseilles in the morning.'

'Tonight at nine o'clock. I'm doing the feature I mentioned to you. Filming the work of one of the Welfare canteens serving the homeless. The south side of Lincoln's Inn Fields. Please be there, Liam.'

Her voice was low, urgent. He took her hand as they got up. 'You always were hard to refuse.'

She kissed him on the cheek and started down the slope to the lake.

It was early evening when Barry reached Marsh End, not that Marsh End itself was anything much. A scattering of cottages beside the road, most of them derelict. The place he was looking for was a mile on the other side. Iron gates stood open, a gravel drive passing through the beech trees and rhododendrons to a grey stone house beyond. The board at the gate carried the legend in gold lettering *Henry Salter – Undertaker. House of Rest and Crematorium.*

Barry drove up the drive and parked the Cortina at the bottom of the steps leading to the entrance. As he got out, a girl emerged from the stable yard to the right and paused, looked at him. She wore rubber boots, an old raincoat and headscarf and carried a bucket in each hand. Her face was calm, touched by an impossible beauty in the evening light.

'Mr Salter about?' Barry asked.

She spoke with the strong and distinctive

Cumbrian accent and yet there was a dead quality to her voice.

'I'll see, sir. No one else here with it being Sunday. Who shall I say?'

'Sinclair's the name,' Barry told her cheerfully. 'Maurice Sinclair. I think you'll find he's expecting me.'

'I'll see then, shall I?' She went up the steps and Barry followed her.

It was very quiet in the embalming room and Henry Salter worked alone, his rubber apron smeared with blood. The body upon which he was working was that of a young woman and he was in the process of removing her viscera. The door opened behind him and the girl entered. She had taken off the headscarf, revealing tangled dark hair, and the old cotton dress she wore was a size too small, the seams splitting in several places.

Salter said, 'I've told you never to disturb me while I'm working, Jenny.'

'There's a gentleman to see you, sir. A Mr Sinclair. He's waiting downstairs.'

Salter paused and glanced at her sharply. 'Ah, yes, Mr Sinclair. He'll be staying the night, Jenny, so make sure the spare bedroom is ready. Then you can get him something to eat.'

'Yes, sir,' she said in that curiously dead voice and looked down at the body. 'She was really beautiful.'

'I know, Jenny, but this is what we all come to in the end. Now be a good girl and run along.'

She went out and Salter picked up the body and lowered it into a stone sink filled with formaldehyde. It slid under the surface and hung suspended an inch or two from the bottom, the hair fanning out. He removed his rubber apron and gloves, went into the small washroom at the other end of the embalming room and started to clean himself up.

Afterwards, he slipped on a dark alpaca jacket and straightened his black tie. The iron grey hair, the gaunt face, the rimless glasses, gave him exactly the appearance that he felt the public had a right to expect from an undertaker. Death was a serious business and nobody believed that more sincerely than Salter himself. Certainly there was little to link the grave and respectable face which confronted him in the mirror with the second-rate thief who had served three prison sentences as a young man before coming to terms with the real facts of life.

As he went along the corridor, he wondered about this man Sinclair. The offer of the work had been something he'd found impossible to refuse. The ten thousand pounds mentioned would come in very handy indeed. Only the previous week he'd had the new incinerator installed in the crematorium, which could consume a human body in fifteen minutes. Not like the older one, which was so inefficient that it was necessary to pound up the skull and pelvic bones later.

Another reason he'd not been able to refuse the work, even if he'd wanted to, was the source of the request; people of consequence in the London underworld whom he'd dealt with on a number of occasions. The coast around Marsh End was a lonely, sombre world of creeks and marshes, ideal for a fast boat by night, in and out, and Salter had acted as middle man for many a drug consignment on its way to London. When you'd done that sort of thing once, the truth was you could never say no again.

He went down the staircase and found Frank Barry standing by the reception desk. 'Mr Sinclair?' he said and held out a hand. 'Henry Salter. Let's go into my private sitting room. Far more comfortable.'

Barry followed him along a narrow corridor and Salter opened a door and led the way into a room that was crowded with Victorian furniture. The walls were dark green damask, the curtain a dull red velvet. Salter stirred the fire with a brass poker.

'A drink, Mr Sinclair?'

'Not yet,' Barry said. 'Business first.'

He took the Ceska from his pocket and placed it on the table. Salter licked his lips nervously. Barry put the briefcase down and opened it. He took out several packets of twenty-pound notes and tossed them across.

'Five thousand there. You get the other half on completion. Satisfactory?'

'Perfectly, Mr Sinclair.' Salter scooped the money up instantly and put it in a drawer.

'Now, my requirements. You have everything?'

'You can see the boat in the morning. It's moored in a creek not far away. I thought you might like to stay the night here.'

'What else do you have to offer?'

'A small farmhouse at the head of the valley, four miles from here. The two men I was asked to recruit arrived this afternoon. They're there now.'

'What are their backgrounds?'

'Liverpool underworld. They have both done time for robbery with violence and the like. Rather rough, I'm afraid.'

'Exactly what I need,' Barry told him. 'Soon enough to see them tomorrow. And the equipment?'

'Two suitcases were delivered this morning very early.'

'Who by?'

'I haven't the slightest idea. A young man

in a dark coat and hat. I've never seen him before.' Barry smiled and Salter said, 'Your people seem remarkably efficient, Mr Sinclair.'

'And why wouldn't they be? Let's have a look at those suitcases.'

Salter opened a cupboard at the side of the fireplace. The cases were well made in real leather, their catches held in place by tumbler locks, the combination of which Barry had memorised from the list in his briefcase.

He quickly lined up the right sequence of numbers and opened the first case. It contained two sterling sub-machine guns, two British Army issue Smith and Wesson revolvers, a Browning automatic and several gas canisters. Salter's eyes opened wide. Barry closed the case, locked it and opened the other disclosing Army camouflage uniforms, several dark blue berets and webbing belts.

'Can I ask what all this is about, Mr Sinclair?' Salter said nervously. 'It all looks pretty heavy to me.'

'That's what you're getting paid for,' Barry told him. He locked the second case 'Now let's have that drink.'

At that moment, there was a knock at the door, it opened and Jenny came in with a tray. 'I told you not to disturb me,' Salter said angrily.

'I thought you might like some tea, Mr Salter, you and the gentleman.'

She glanced at Barry and in the light of the room and without the headscar he saw now that she was at best plain with high cheekbones, olive skin and overfull lips.

'All right, girl, run along and get a meal ready for Mr Sinclair.'

She went out and Frank Barry ignored the tea, went to the sideboard and helped himself to a Scotch. 'Is she all there?'

Salter poured himself a cup of tea. 'Oh, yes, just a little slow, that's all. She used to live at the farm I mentioned up the valley, with her father, a fine old drunk. Ran his car into a wall one night and killed himself. She would have been destitute if I hadn't taken her in and bought the place.'

'A philanthropist,' Barry said. 'I could tell right away.'

'But she never seems to come to life,' Salter

said. 'Her flesh has – has a deadness to it. She never responds.' It was as if he was talking to himself for a moment and then he looked up. 'You understand me?'

'Oh, yes,' Barry said in disgust. 'I think so.'

Salter swallowed the rest of his tea hurriedly. 'Well, if you'll excuse me, I've got a job to finish. A burial tomorrow afternoon so it won't wait. Jenny will look after you.'

He went out. Barry drank the rest of his Scotch. The room was very quiet except for the grandfather clock in the corner. There was an indefinable musty smell to everything, like an old room opened for the first time in many years. It went well with the overstuffed furniture and the nature of the establishment.

When he opened the door, he could smell cooking and followed it along the passage to the old stone-flagged kitchen. The girl stood at the stove stirring something in a pan with a wooden spoon and she glanced over her shoulder.

'It's almost ready,' she said in that dead voice, put down the spoon and smoothed her hands over her thighs. 'I'm just going out to the shed for more wood for the stove.'

She took a large red spotlight from under the sink and moved to the door. Barry was there before her and opened it. 'I'll come with you. You could probably do with some help.'

She looked up at him, uncertain, then handed him the lamp. 'All right, it's across the yard.'

It was treacherous underfoot and Barry picked his way carefully, cursing when he stepped into a puddle. When the girl opened the door of the barn, he saw several vehicles parked inside: a black hearse, a large black limousine, a van and a Land-Rover.

The woodpile was to one side under a gallery stuffed with hay. She said, 'Over here, Mr Sinclair,' and for a moment, in the lamp-light, she looked as beautiful as she had done at their first meeting.

She leaned over the woodpile, one knee forward so that the old cotton dress tight-ened across her thighs. Barry reached out, cupping a hand around her thigh. She glanced back over her shoulder and it was there, whatever Salter had thought, in her eyes.

Barry handed her the torch and smiled. 'You take that, I'll carry the wood.'

She stood waiting for him, her face above the spotlight in shadow. He piled half a dozen logs in the crook of one arm and led the way out.

Like any other great city in the world, London has its share of derelicts, down-and-outs who can no longer help themselves. Who sleep rough because they have to.

When Devlin and Harry Fox arrived at Lincoln's Inn Fields just before nine o'clock, a Salvation Army mobile canteen was in position, the French camera crew already setting up their equipment. Fox parked the car and he and Devlin started across to where Anne-Marie, wrapped in a bulky Afghan sheepskin jacket, stood talking to a cheerful-looking woman who wore the uniform of a Salvation Army major. She turned away, caught sight of Devlin and Fox approaching and went to meet them.

'Time you two met,' Devlin said. 'Harry Fox.'

'A pleasure, Miss Audin,' Fox said gallantly.

'And what would you be doing here then?' Devlin demanded. 'Aren't those film cameras?'

'Video,' she said. 'A documentary I'm doing for French television on the underside of London life.' She pointed to the figures shambling out from underneath the plane trees. 'Men without hope,' she said. 'Sometimes women. Unemployed, alcoholic, socially inadequate or just out of prison. When the hostels are full, those who can't get in sleep rough. The soup and sandwiches they get here are probably the only meal they've had today.'

They watched for a while as the canteen workers served as derelict a crowd of human beings as Harry Fox had ever seen in his life before.

'This is terrible,' he said. 'I never realised.'

'Some of them sleep over the grilles in the pavement of the hotel round the corner, warmed by the steam from the boiler room,' she said. 'The rest wrap themselves in old newspapers and crowd together in the pavilion in the garden over there. At least its dry.'

'All right,' Devlin said. 'What are you trying to prove? That you care? I know that. What did you want to see me about?'

'I want to come with you,' she said, 'in the morning. To Marseilles. You could ask Martin to see me. He might listen to you.'

'What about this?' Devlin looked around him.

'Oh, I'll get all the footage I need of this business tonight. I'd intended to return to Paris Tuesday, anyway.'

Devlin turned to Fox and nodded. 'She could be very useful.'

Fox said, 'All right, Miss Audin. We'll see you at Heathrow in the morning. No later than ten o'clock, if you don't mind. I'll see to your ticket for you. We'll meet at the entrance to the International Lounge.'

'Good,' she said, and reached up and kissed Devlin gravely on each cheek. 'Thank you, Liam. And now, I must work, I think.'

She walked towards the cameras. At the

head of the queue at the canteen someone was being violently sick.

'Jesus Mary,' Devlin said. 'The one thing in this life that I can't stand. Let's get out of it,' and they hurried back to the car.

Salter led the way up a flight of narrow wooden stairs covered in cheap linoleum. The landing was long and narrow and he opened a door at the end and switched on the light. Barry moved in after him, humping the two suitcases, and put them down. There was a double bed with a brass frame, a wardrobe and a dressing table in Victorian mahogany and a marble washstand.

'You'll be nicely out of the way here,' Salter said. 'The back stairs are very handy. I'm at the front of the house myself. Just you and Jenny back here.' He smiled weakly. 'I'll see you in the morning. Look at the boat first thing, then I'll take you up to the farm to meet the others.'

He backed out, closing the door. Barry took off his jacket and draped it over a chair. He stood frowning at himself in the cracked mirror above the washstand. There was something wrong. It spoke aloud in the girl's silence, in Salter's sly eyes.

'An unreliable sod if ever I've seen one,' Barry said softly and he went to the door and turned the key.

He undressed, got into bed with only the lamp switched on and sat propped against the pillows, smoking, and considered the job in hand. It was really very simple. Stop the truck, put the Germans and their escort out of action, drive down to Marsh End with the rocket pod, load it on to the boat Salter had arranged, and put to sea for the rendezvous with the Russian trawler later that night. Absurdly simple. So much so that something was bound to go wrong.

He lit another cigarette and at the same moment watched the door knob turn slowly. He reached for the Ceska, was across the room in an instant and turning the key. He wrenched open the door to see Jenny moving back along the passage. She was barefoot and wore a white cotton nightdress, a shawl about her shoulders.

She turned and stared at him dumbly. Her eyes took in the gun in his hand and yet she showed no reaction – no reaction at all. He stood to one side and she moved past him into the room and went and lay on the bed without a word, staring up at the ceiling, hands folded across the shawl. Barry locked the door, put the Ceska where he could reach it and got on the bed beside her.

He was surprised at the strength of his own desire. When he kissed her, he was shaking like a boy and yet there was no response, not even when his hands roamed freely over her body, pushing the shift up above her thighs.

She lay there quite passively, allowing him to do anything he would with her, but still not responding in the slightest degree, staring up at the ceiling, eyes wide. By then, he was past caring, needing her in a way he hadn't needed a woman in years.

Afterwards, he rolled to one side, exhausted and reached for a cigarette. She lay there for a moment longer, then stood up without a word, unlocked the door and went out.

Barry lay there, smoking, looking up at the ceiling. It was crazy. Didn't make sense. A long time since he'd needed anyone like that. A hell of a long time. He closed his eyes and thought of Norah Cassidy.

6

The tide was drifting in, gurgling in crab holes, covering the mud flats with an expanse of shining water that moved amongst sea asters. Somewhere a curlew cried, lonely in a sombre world.

Barry and the girl crossed a narrow stone causeway and followed a path through rough marsh grass and reeds that were head high. Beyond, the reeds stretched in an unbroken line towards the distant sea on either side of the estuary, swaying, the wind passing through them with an uneasy whispering sound.

Barry said soberly, 'You'd swear there were eyes watching you from every thicket.'

'Spirits of the dead,' she said. 'My father used to tell me the Romans were here two thousand years ago. Ravenglass up the coast was a port even then.' She stood there for a moment, a strange, archaic figure in the head-scarf and old raincoat, and shivered visibly. 'I don't like this place. It frightens me. No one comes here, no local people, unless they can help it.'

She intoned the words in that dead voice of hers like the chorus from some Greek play. Barry said, 'Fine. That's exactly how I want it.'

She moved on along the causeway and he followed. A few moments later they emerged beside a narrow creek. There was a decaying wooden jetty stretching out into the water on rotting pilings. To Barry's surprise there were two boats moored there, not one.

The first had real class with a sharp raking prow and trim lines, painted white with a black line along the watermark and obviously lovingly cared for. The name *Kathleen* was neatly printed across the bow in gold.

'Mr Salter's own boat,' she said. 'He brought the other down from a boatyard outside Ravenglass yesterday.'

It was a different proposition altogether, a forty foot motor cruiser painted black, the name *Jason – Fowey* so faded that Barry had difficulty reading it. He climbed over the rail and went into the wheelhouse and the girl followed.

'It doesn't look much, but it's a good boat at sea.'

'You've been out in her?'

She nodded. 'Mr Salter uses her from time to time.'

'What for?'

She shrugged. 'Fishing, when he's in the mood. He won't go out in the *Kathleen* unless the weather's perfect.'

'Spends his spare time polishing the binnacle and so on?'

She looked at him in surprise. 'How did you know?'

'Oh, it figures.' He lit a cigarette and offered her one. She shook her head and he said, 'The men at the farm, have you seen them yet?'

'I took milk up this morning.'

'Old friends of Mr Salter's?'

'I wouldn't know that. I've never seen them before.'

'But you didn't like them?' They were standing close, shoulders touching and he was filled with that irrational excitement again. She turned almost unwillingly, eyes down and he gently stroked her face with the back of one hand. She leaned close and, outside, footsteps boomed on the jetty.

Barry went on deck as Salter stepped over the rail. 'Ah, there you are, Mr Sinclair,' Salter said. 'Will she do?'

'The other looks a better proposition to me,' Barry told him.

Salter was dismayed and showed it. 'My own boat, Mr Sinclair. A beautiful boat as you can see. You could sail to the Mediterranean in that boat. But the *Jason* here – there's more to her than meets the eye, I can assure you. She may not look much, but if you check the engine room, you'll find a Penta petrol engine. She'll do twenty-two knots. Depth sounder, automatic steering.'

'All right,' Barry said. 'I'll take your word for it.'

Salter looked relieved. 'Good, and now, if you don't mind, I'll take you up to the farm and introduce you to Preston and Varley. As I told you, I have a funeral today and I really am rather pressed for time.'

Hedley Preston came awake and stared up at the ceiling. For a moment, he couldn't think where he was and then he remembered. His mouth tasted bad, his throat dry, and he got up and reached for the whisky bottle on the locker. It was empty and he tossed it into a corner. He pulled on a pair of jeans and a sweater; a lean, sardonic-looking man with tangled dark hair and a face that was just beginning to show the first signs of dissipation.

He lit a cigarette, coughing as the smoke caught at the back of his throat, and peered out of the window at the sodden hillside. 'Jesus,' he said softly. 'The joys of the countryside,' and he opened the door.

Jenny Crowther, her mouth open in fear, stumbled into him. Sam Varley just behind her. Varley was an ox of a man in soiled sweatshirt and corduroy trousers and the eyes were wild in the fleshy face. Preston held the girl in the crook of his arm and fended Varley off.

'Okay, what's the problem?'

'I had a two hundred pack of fags in my room last night. Now they're gone. That bitch must have taken them.'

His breath was sour and not only with the stench of last night's drinking, for there was a sharp, fresh edge to it that indicated he had already been at the bottle.

'You lost the whole pack to me at poker last night,' Preston said patiently. 'Too bloody drunk to remember, that's your trouble.'

'To hell with that,' Varley said. 'You're just trying to protect her.'

The girl pulled herself free from Preston's encircling arm and ran. Varley shoved him to one side and went after her. She got the door open, was already on her way out, when his hand fastened on her shoulder. And then he seemed to stumble, went down hard on the cobbles of the yard.

He tried to get up, his feet were kicked from under him expertly and he was flat on his back, a foot across his throat. He struggled, glaring up into Frank Barry's implaccable face. Barry increased the pressure and Varley started to choke and then the pressure was relieved. Barry took the Ceska from his pocket and touched the muzzle to Varley's forehead.

The girl cried out, a hand to her mouth and Henry Salter said desperately, 'For God's sake, Mr Sinclair.'

Barry said softly, 'Touch her again, I'll put you on sticks.'

And Varley knew fear then, as well as rage, the kind of fear that almost turned his bowels to water. Barry removed his foot and stepped back. As the big man got up, Preston, lounging in the doorway, laughed.

'A touching scene.' He came forward as Barry picked up his briefcase. 'I'm Hedley Preston, Mr Sinclair. This throw-back to a more primitive age is Sam Varley. You must forgive him, but he's only just learned how to walk erect.'

'I'll close that mouth of yours for good one of these days,' Varley said and went into the house.

Preston stood to one side with a slight mocking grin and Barry walked past, followed by the girl and Salter. When they went into the sitting room, Varley was in a chair by the fire, clutching a bottle.

Barry put the briefcase on the table and said to the girl, 'You cut along to the kitchen and make us a nice cup of tea or something.' She hesitated and he nodded reassuringly. 'Go on, it'll be all right.'

She went out. Salter closed the door and leaned against it. Barry nodded to Varley and said to Preston, 'He starts early.'

'Just his little weakness. Like they say in show business, Mr Sinclair, he'll be all right on the night.'

'Is that a fact?' Barry put the Ceska on the table beside the briefcase and unbuttoned his coat.

'So what's the job?' Preston asked.

'Simple enough. We stop a truck, on a country road twenty miles from here on

Wednesday morning. Off-load what it contains and bring it back here.'

'And what does it contain?' Preston asked.

'That's none of your business.' Barry opened the case. 'This is.' He tossed several packets of twenty-pound notes across. 'Five thousand quid each there. You get the other half on completion.'

Varley got up and moved to the table, reaching. Preston slapped his hand away. 'And that's all you're telling us?'

'It's a simple job,' Barry said. 'Very simple. You get told what to do on Wednesday morning. Three hours' work at the most and you'll be on your way. Of course, if you're not interested . . .'

Preston said, 'Oh, but we are.' He quickly pushed the packets together into a neat pile. 'Anything you say, Mr Sinclair. Like the guy out of the brass lamp said, to hear is to obey.'

'See that you do.' Barry snapped the brief-case shut and turned to Salter. 'I'll go back with you now. I want that Land-Rover of yours. Somewhere I have to go this after-noon.'

Preston said. 'You'll be back?'

'Oh, yes,' Barry told him. 'You can count on it.'

He and Salter went out into the passageway as Jenny appeared from the kitchen with a tray. 'You're going?' she said.

'I'll be back this evening.' Barry smiled. 'Don't worry. The ape man won't touch you again. The clever bugger will see to that.'

He winked in a conspiratorial fashion, went out, got into Salter's limousine and they drove away.

Watching through the sitting room window, Varley said viciously, 'When I've finished with that little bastard . . .'

'Don't be stupid, Samuel,' Preston said. 'Unless I'm much mistaken, he could take you apart any time he wanted.' He tapped the packets of money in front of him. 'Ten grand here, Samuel, another ten to come which means whatever is in that truck he mentioned must be very interesting indeed.'

Varley smiled slowly. 'Here, are you meaning what I think you are?'

'I used to learn Latin at school, Samuel.

Festina lente. Hasten slowly. That way you get it all in the end.'

'Including him?'

'I don't see why not.'

Varley laughed delightedly and reached for the bottle. 'I'll drink to that.'

Back at the house, Barry and Salter stood beside the Land-Rover in the barn. Salter said, 'I didn't try to dress them up. You must admit that. I was told hard men were required, men who would do anything. They certainly fit the bill.'

'What's Preston's background?'

'Middle-class respectable. His father was an accountant in Bradford and Preston went to Grammar School there, so he's decently educated. I understand he was training to be an accountant himself and went to prison for some fraud or other. Since then, he's never looked back. Was released from prison six months ago after serving three years of a five year sentence for armed robbery of a supermarket. Varley, of course, is just an animal.'

'A drunken animal,' Barry amended. 'Still, never mind. At least I know what I'm dealing with. I'll see you later.'

He drove the Land-Rover out of the barn and across the yard. Salter turned to the hearse, which had a coffin inside now. He took out a handkerchief and very carefully inspected the whole vehicle, occasionally pausing to give the chrome a quick polish.

The Air France jet touched down exactly on time at Marignane Airport, fifteen miles outside Marseilles. As it was only a quarter full, the passengers passed through Customs and, where needs be, immigration, with no delay. Within forty-five minutes of landing, Devlin and Anne-Marie were driving down towards the coast road in a hired Peugeot.

Devlin said, 'We'll find a hotel in St Denise for tonight, that's where the prison supply boat leaves from.' She nodded, not saying anything, concentrating on her driving and Devlin added, 'You realise you can't come with me tomorrow? I mean, I'll have to see how the land lies.'

'I know that, Liam.' She glanced sideways and smiled. 'Just as I know that he may still not wish to see me. I learned a long time ago to expect nothing from Martin.'

'You really mean that?'

'Once, in Vietnam, when it looked as if we both would very probably die, we spoke of a rendezvous in Paris. A pavement cafe in the rain, the smell of damp chestnut trees.'

'Absolutely essential,' Devlin said.

She smiled without looking at him. 'Dear Liam, why could it not have been you I loved? I was to wear a Paris frock, very chic.'

'Just like the adverts on television. Dreams for the masses.'

'Only ours came true, Liam. He had a rest from Ulster, met me in Paris. We found our pavement cafe, the chestnut trees behaved perfectly. Two weeks and then he went back.' She shrugged. 'You see he had a mistress waiting for him. Darker than me and infinitely more demanding.'

They drove on in silence for there was really nothing left to say.

The bar at the village pub at Brisingham was a large comfortable room with a low beamed ceiling, several high-backed benches and a couple of wooden tables. There was a fire on the open hearth.

Barry was the only customer and he stood at the end of the bar devouring the last of the beef sandwiches the landlady, a large matronly blonde, had provided for him.

'Great,' Barry said, 'couldn't be better.' He reached for his beer. 'Where's all the customers then?'

'Don't get many tourists through in the winter. Mainly evening trade. Locals.'

'But I thought there was an RAF airfield here? This is Brisingham, isn't it?'

'Closed down years ago. They have a dozen men up there at the most. Oh, planes still land, but not very often.' She sighed. 'I remember a time twelve year or so ago, when you couldn't get near the bar on a night for boys in RAF blue.'

'That's life,' Barry said. 'Everything changes. Thanks for the sandwiches.'

Ten minutes later, he slowed the Land-Rover as he came to the perimeter wire of the airfield. He coasted along past the main gate which was padlocked and then picked up speed and drove on. Five miles further on, a signpost indicated Wast Water to the right, a narrow country road climbing up into the mountains.

He found what he was looking for without too much trouble. A small wood, a plateau of grass beside the road. When he stopped the engine, there wasn't a sound except for a curlew calling. He could have been the only man left alive on the face of the earth.

He got out of the Land-Rover and stood there looking around him, smiling. 'Frank, me old son,' he said softly. 'I think this will do very nicely indeed.'

The granite from Belle Isle was famous throughout France, was still so much in demand that the authorities had constructed a new deep water jetty so that larger container ships could be used. The quarry itself was hewn out of the northern cliffs and they were blasting as Lebel approached, the red flag fluttering in the wind.

The explosion, when it came, echoed from the cliffs like thunder as a great shoulder of rock cracked in a thousand pieces and cascaded down. A whistle blew, and convicts and their armed guards emerged from the shelter and went back to work.

Brosnan and Savary toiled together, Savary loading into a skip standing on the crude rail track beside them, Brosnan splitting larger pieces with a sledgehammer and wedge. He was stripped to the waist, his hair held back by a sweatband. The muscles in his back rippled as the hammer came down and his prison number was clear to see, tattooed on his right forearm.

As Lebel approached, Savary paused, leaning on the skip, wiping his face with a rag. 'Hey, Pierre, I'm getting old. What about a job in the kitchen or even the library. I'm not fussy.'

'Nonsense,' Lebel said. 'Look what magnificent shape you're in for a man of your age. All thanks to regular exercise and hard work.' He turned to Brosnan and took a paper and pen from his pocket. 'You've got a visitor due on the morning boat, my friend. Are you willing to receive him?'

Brosnan paused, leaning on the sledgehammer. 'Who is it?'

Lebel looked at the paper. 'Monsieur Charles Gorman. Solicitor, Lincoln's Inn Fields, London.' He looked puzzled. 'Solicitor?'

'What the English call their lawyers, Pierre,' Savary advised him.

'Reason for visit, legal business.' Lebel repeated the question. 'Will you receive him?'

'Why not?' Brosnan said.

Lebel held out the paper and pen. 'Then sign in the appropriate section.' Brosnan complied and handed them back. 'Okay,' Lebel said. 'Back to work,' and he folded the document and stuck it in his pocket. 'I may have a treat for you tonight. Another body. They're expecting some old guy up in the Infirmary to die any minute.'

'So kind of you to think of us.' Savary picked up another rock as Lebel walked away. 'Interesting, Martin. You didn't tell me your lawyer was coming to see you.'

'What's even more interesting is that he isn't my lawyer,' Brosnan said. 'I've never heard of Charles Gorman in my life.'

He brought the hammer down with all his strength and split in half the rock that was his target.

It was dark when Barry turned the Land-Rover into the farmyard and braked to a halt. While he switched off the engine, a woman screamed. As Barry jumped to the ground, the front door was flung open, light flooding into the yard. Jenny Crowther almost made it, and then Varley had her.

Her dress was torn, one shoulder bare, and Varley laughed drunkenly and tried to kiss her. She tried to pull away, disgust and loathing on her face as her hands clawed at him. Barry moved in fast and punched Varley in the kidneys, then grabbed him by the collar and pulled him back.

Varley cried out in pain and went down on one knee. He stayed there for a moment, shaking his head, then looked up at Barry. He got up slowly, shook his head again as if to clear it, then charged, hands reaching out to destroy.

Barry moved to one side, grabbing for the right wrist, twisting it round and up in an armlock and using Varley's own momentum, ran him into the wall. Varley, on his knees for the second time that night, tried to stand and Barry kicked him in the stomach.

Varley lay on his back, groaning and Hedley Preston standing in the doorway, laughed drunkenly. 'I told you he could take you apart any time he wanted, Sam. You should have listened. I'm always right, never wrong.' He raised his glass. 'To you, Mr Sinclair, and all who sail in you.'

Barry said, 'You could have stopped this, you bastard. I told you to keep him in line.' His right hand swung up, the Ceska coughed once and Preston dropped his glass and cried out, clutching his neck.

He leaned against the doorpost, blood oozing between his fingers Barry tapped him gently between the eyes with the muzzle.

'Don't worry, Preston. Just a scratch, that's how good I am with one of these things. Next time, old son, you're dead.'

He turned, took the girl by the arm and pushed her towards the Land-Rover. 'I'll take you down to Salter's place. In fact, I'll stay there again tonight myself.' She was trembling and clutched his arm and once again, he was aware of that strange surging excitement. 'It's all right,' he said as they drove out of the farmyard and he reached across and took her hand. 'It's all right.'

Later that night, standing at the window of his bedroom, smoking and looking down into the yard, he saw her come out of the kitchen with the lamp and cross to the barn. Barry opened the door and went downstairs quickly.

When he went into the barn, she was filling

a basket with wood. 'Here, let me do that,' he said.

'That's all right, I can manage,' she replied in a low voice without turning round.

He lit a cigarette, aware of a sudden unbearable tightness in his chest that threatened to choke him. She had changed out of the torn cotton dress and the black one she now wore, like the other, was too small and stretched tightly across her buttocks and thighs.

She stood up and Barry dropped his cigarette and moved close, his arms sliding about her, pulling her against him. He held her for a moment, his lips against her neck and then pushed her gently forward and down into the hay.

And then she truly did come to life, her hands tightening in his hair, her mouth fastening on his with great bruising kisses that were almost frightening in their intensity.

7

It was Lebel's duty, as the officer on Brosnan's landing, to take him down to the visiting room on Tuesday morning. When he opened the door and ushered Brosnan in, Devlin was standing with his back to them peering out of the window. Brosnan had received no greater shock in his life than he did when the small man turned to face him.

'Ah, Mr Brosnan. My name is Charles Gorman. My firm has been retained by the Brosnan Corporation in Boston, Massachusetts, to discuss certain legal matters affecting your future. There is also the matter of an appeal for clemency on your behalf to the President of France. Your mother feels . . .'

'My mother,' Brosnan said, 'is wasting her

time, Mr Gorman. The only way she'll ever get me off this rock is in a box.'

'Monsieur Gorman, please,' Lebel said. 'You and your client must sit on either side of the table, otherwise you may be alone. As his legal adviser, you are entitled to this. I will lock the door. When you are ready to leave, please ring the bell.'

'Can we smoke?' Devlin asked.

'But of course, monsieur.'

Lebel went out, the key turned in the lock. Brosnan reached across the table and Devlin took his hand and held it for a long moment.

'*Cead mile failte*,' he said in Irish. 'A hundred thousand welcomes.'

Devlin smiled. '*Go raibh maith agat*,' he replied. 'My thanks. Let's stick to the Irish, just to confuse the buggers if they happen to be listening in.' He sat down, lit a cigarette and pushed the pack across. 'Good to see you, Marteen.'

It was the affectionate diminutive of the name which normally would be used with a child. In the old days, Brosnan had not cared to be called Little Martin by a man considerably smaller than himself. And then, of course, he had come to know Devlin rather better.

'You look well, Martin, considering.'

'Never fitter. I work in the quarry most days. You look good yourself. Still at Trinity?'

'They keep me out of kindness. I was invited as visiting professor to Yale this year.'

'God help them.'

'Came to nothing. The State Department refused me a visa.'

Devlin glanced about him, his face sombre. 'Was this what it was all about – truly?'

Brosnan said, 'They closed down Devil's Island, but they still had this in reserve. Tell me, Liam, how you've been? Did you ever find those Plains of Mayo you were always looking for? Remember Blind Raftery's poem?'

Devlin said, 'Once, a thousand years ago. November, nineteen forty-three to be precise, at what you might call the hour of maximum danger.'

'The Churchill affair?'

'A lovely ugly little peasant,' Devlin

quoted, 'Who turned my heart not once, but twice. She was seventeen and I was thirty-five.'

'And too old?'

'Not for that one. But there was a problem. I was the enemy.'

'So, what you're trying to say is that you found your Plains of Mayo twenty-six years ago?'

Devlin smiled with infinite sadness. 'And lost them again in the finding. Now wouldn't that make you laugh all the way to hell and back?'

'Not really. What's all this about?'

'It's simple enough. How would you like to get out of here?'

Brosnan didn't take it seriously for a moment. 'Well, a little divine intervention would be divine, because that's what it would take. Even my mother, formidable lady as she is, discovered a long time ago that neither lighting a candle, saying her prayers or offering large sums of money would do any good.'

'Has she been to see you?'

'Once, four years ago. I saw her then only to make it clear I wouldn't see her again.'

'And Anne-Marie?'

Brosnan paused and went very still. 'What about Anne-Marie?'

'I left her in St Denise this morning. She begs you to see her.'

'No,' Brosnan said in a low voice. 'I will not do it.'

He jumped to his feet and went to the window, reaching for the bars, his cheek to the stone. After a while, he turned.

The rusting barred window had no glass in it and wind whistled through. Devlin shivered. 'God save us, *avic*, but I hate to see you in this place.'

Brosnan came back to the table, helped himself to another cigarette and sat down. 'All right, Liam, what's this all about? What are you after?'

Devlin grinned crookedly. 'Just consider me that divine intervention you were looking for, shut your mouth and listen.'

* * *

When he was finished, Brosnan sat back in his chair, brooding, the grey eyes giving nothing away.

'Well?' Devlin said.

'I don't know,' Brosnan told him. 'I used to be big on slogans like Ireland must be free. It came naturally from a love of literature, a joy in words, but then you discover that the reality is that you must be prepared to walk over corpses to achieve your end.'

'And it isn't worth it?'

'I'm beginning to wonder whether any cause is worth the loss of a single human life.'

'I know, Marteen, your revolutionary ardour has cooled a little. So has mine and I was at it longer than you.'

Brosnan got up, went to the window and held the bars again, looking out. 'Suddenly, I feel old, Liam. Really old, you know what I mean? I can't get worked up about things any more. Not even Frank Barry and the KGB and Ferguson and DI5 and the stupid senseless bloody games they're all involved in.'

'Not even to get out of here?'

'There's no way Ferguson can get me out of this place,' Brosnan said flatly.

'Ferguson thinks he can.'

Brosnan didn't reply and Devlin came to the one issue he had been avoiding, no help for it now. 'Martin, you heard what happened to Norah?'

Brosnan nodded without turning round. 'I heard. She died about eighteen months ago.'

Devlin cleared his throat. 'But the way that she died, that's the thing.'

Brosnan turned, his face blank, the eyes very dark. 'You've something to tell me?'

Devlin said, 'It's difficult to know where to begin, Marteen.'

Brosnan was across the room in three quick strides, had him back across the table, his hands on his throat. 'Tell me!' he said in a low hoarse voice. 'Tell me!'

Afterwards, he sat at the table, his head in his hands for a long time without saying anything, then suddenly stood up, went and rang the bell.

He turned to Devlin. 'I need to think. I'll speak to you again later.' Before Devlin could reply, the key turned in the lock and Lebel appeared. 'Mr Gorman has papers for me to sign. I'd like some time to think about it. Can I go back to my cell for an hour?'

Lebel turned to Devlin. 'You have no objection, monsieur?'

'None at all.'

'Then please wait here. I shall return and take you to the Officers' Canteen. A little refreshment might be in order while you wait.'

Savary had just been returned to the cell for the noon break. He was lying on his bed smoking a cigarette when the door was unlocked and Lebel ushered Brosnan in.

'An hour, then,' the prison officer said and departed.

'How did you get on?' Savary started to say. Brosnan waved him to silence, listening at the door.

'So, a mystery?' the old man said as Brosnan came and sat on the other bed facing him. 'Oh, I get it,' he added shrewdly. 'This Gorman – someone you knew after all?'

'Just shut up and listen,' Brosnan said. 'I haven't got much time.'

When he was finished, Savary sat there, clenching and unclenching his hands in excitement. 'For God's sake, seize this chance with both hands, Martin. Go!'

Brosnan reached across and put a hand on his shoulder to still him. 'No, Jacques, listen to me – just a little while longer. In the first place, I don't believe Ferguson can swing this thing with the French authorities. I'm not some little thief – some cat burglar or confidence man. I killed a policeman and you know how they look at that sort of thing at the Palais de Justice. In the second place, even if Ferguson could arrange it, it would take time – too much time to suit me.'

'So what's your alternative.'

'I'm crashing out,' Brosnan said simply.

'But Martin, this is impossible. No one has ever escaped from this damn rock.'

'I've always known I could get outside the

walls via the sewer. I told you that,' Brosnan explained. 'But that gets you nowhere because you're still on the island. And then, while we were on the burial detail with Lebel the other night, I saw it. We break into the stores, steal a couple of lifejackets each and enter the water from the burial rock.'

Savary gazed at him in awe. 'We? You said we?'

'Sure, both of us, Jacques. Stay on this rock, you'll end up in the sea in a canvas bag sooner or later, so why not take a chance on the sea while you can still fight?'

'But the Mill Race,' Savary said. 'It would be the death of us.'

'Or the saving of us, don't you see?' Brosnan said. 'That current runs up to ten knots, curving towards St Denise. Now, if a boat was waiting in the appropriate area.'

Savary broke in, shaking his head. 'No fishing boat is allowed within a four mile radius of the island. You know that.'

'The current would take us that far in half an hour.'

'But such a boat would never find us. Be

reasonable, Martin. That sea out there and at night.'

'I've thought of that,' Brosnan said. 'All we need is one of those electronic homing beacons. They're standard issue in all airforces now. Pilots have them stitched to their life-jackets, so when they ditch at sea the rescue craft can home in on them.'

'And if they missed us?' Savary whispered.

'Or if your heart gave out or you couldn't stand the cold?'

'All right, all right.' Savary waved a hand. 'You've infected me with your madness. When do we go?'

'I don't see any reason to hang about. We can get everything we need right here except that homing device. They're only the size of a cigarette pack. Devlin will have to get hold of one and smuggle it in to me. I don't see any problem there.'

'And the boat?'

'I was thinking that was where that son of yours could come in.'

'Jean-Paul?'

'If the Union Corse can't organise a fast

run by night in a trawler out of St Denise, they must be slipping.'

'But of course.' Savary was laughing now, excitement boiling over. 'Jesus, Martin, but I feel alive again like I haven't done in years.'

He embraced Brosnan enthusiastically, kissing him on both cheeks. Brosnan turned and hammered on the cell door. 'Come on, Pierre!' he called. 'Let's be having you.'

Anne-Marie, sitting on the balcony of the hotel in St Denise, had seen the prison supply boat enter the harbour so she was not surprised when Devlin appeared on the adjoining balcony twenty minutes later. He clambered over and sank into the wicker chair opposite her.

'You saw him?' she asked eagerly.

'Oh, yes, I saw him.'

'And he was well?'

'Never fitter. In fact, fighting fit.'

Her face clouded. 'What happened?'

'It's simple really. At first, when I outlined the deal, he wasn't particularly interested and in any case, he didn't believe that Ferguson could get him out. And to be frank with you there, I'm inclined to agree with him.'

'So?'

'I told him about Norah.' He shook his head. 'He took it hard. If Frank Barry had been within touching distance, Martin would have broken him in his two hands.'

Anne-Marie got up, went to the drinks cabinet and poured him a whisky. She came back to the table. 'And that changed his point of view?'

'You could say that.' Devlin swallowed a little whisky. 'God, I needed that. Now, he intends to break out within the next two or three days in company with his cell mate, a man called Savary.'

'But how can this be done?' she said.

Devlin told her. When he was finished, he went and poured himself another whisky. 'As hairbrained a scheme as I'd ever heard of.'

To his astonishment, Anne-Marie got up and stood at the rail, looking out to sea to where Belle Isle crouched behind the horizon. 'Oh, I don't know. I can see the logic of it.

It's so beautifully simple. He could be right. It could work.'

'It could just as easily go the other way.' Devlin moved to the rail beside her. 'I was talking to the captain of the supply boat coming over. He tells me that some nights that thing they call the Mill Race out there is like a river in flood.'

'So, what did you tell Martin? That you would help?'

'I didn't have much choice. He said if I didn't have something working by Thursday night, he'd take to the water anyway and take a chance of floating the ten miles to St Denise.'

'Not possible.' She shook her head. 'The cold would have killed them by then. Tell me, this Savary you mentioned? Would that be Jacques Savary, the gangster?'

'That's right. Apparently he has a son, Jean-Paul, who's following enthusiastically in his father's footsteps. I'm supposed to contact him as soon as possible at a night club called *Maison d'Or*.'

'Oh, yes,' she said. 'The most notorious

establishment in Marseilles. It will be interesting to see how you get on there. With your accent, my dear Liam, I think you may well need the services of an interpreter.'

He frowned and put a hand on her arm as she turned away. 'Are you sure about this? If it goes wrong, if your involvement became public, you could end up in prison yourself.'

'Liam, dear Liam.' She kissed him gently. 'Such a clever, devious human being and such a child. Is there any possible way you could keep me out?' and she turned and went into the bedroom.

It was raining again as Frank Barry and Jenny Crowther walked along the track through the reeds at Marsh End. The two boats swung on their lines beside the jetty. It was the *Kathleen*, Salter's own craft, that Barry boarded now, humping the case he carried over the rail.

He went into the gleaming wheelhouse and examined the interior carefully, going down on his hands and knees until he found what he wanted. Under the instrument panel there was a large inspection flap which gave access to the electrics. When he pulled the release catch, it swung down on hinges.

Barry said to Jenny, 'Keep a weather eye out for Salter, there's a good girl, just in case he decides to show up.'

He took from his pocket several items he had purchased that morning at the local general store: a screw driver, screws, a bradawl and a small hacksaw. There were also a number of brackets of the type used to secure tools on some convenient spot on a wall.

He neatly and methodically bored the necessary holes in the flap and screwed the brackets into place. Then he opened the case, took out one of the Sterling submachine guns, loaded it, then slipped it into place, held by the brackets. Then he carefully loaded one of the Smith and Wessons and positioned that underneath the Sterling. He pushed the flap up, the catch clicked into place.

Jenny, standing outside in the rain

watching the shore, had been keeping one eye on him also. 'What's all that for then?' she asked and her voice was totally different, like a new person's.

'What I call an ace-in-the-hole.'

He took out the other Sterling and quickly removed the end of the firing pin with the hacksaw. Not too much, just enough. He fired it up into the air, to make sure, a round up the spout. Then he did the same with the other Smith and Wesson.

He put them back in the case with the gas canisters and turned to Jenny, who was staring at him curiously. 'Now, they won't shoot.'

'That's it, darling.' Barry moved out in the rain and slipped an arm around her waist. 'I'm very ordered, you see, Jenny. I always like to know exactly where I am.'

She held on to him tightly, her face glowing and he kissed her. 'I love the rain. It makes me come alive in a way nothing else does. A fine day, thanks be to God.' He smiled down at her. 'And with the rest of it stretching before us, I suggest you take me into the thriving metropolis you call Ravenglass and show me the sights.'

Twenty minutes later and five miles out of Marsh End on the way into Ravenglass he pulled into the side of the road and braked suddenly.

'What's wrong?' she said.

'That place over there? What is it?'

There was a watch tower, several decaying hangars and an overgrown runway crossed by another The perimeter wire around the place was rusting.

'Tanningley Field,' she said. 'The RAF built it in the war. Someone tried to run an aero club there a few years ago, but it didn't work. It hasn't been used for years.'

'Is that so?' Barry said. 'Now that is really very interesting.'

He started the engine and drove away.

The *Maison d'Or* was in the old quarter of Marseilles and could only be approached on foot along a narrow cobbled street, lined with houses four or five storeys high with small iron balconies and shuttered windows. In spite of the new and stricter laws the police were supposed to invoke, prostitutes sat outside most of the doors in the warm night air, dressed in a myriad different ways to attract the clients, most of them holding cheerful conversations with each other across the narrow alley.

As Devlin passed, Anne-Marie on his arm, they were the target for a number of humorous remarks, mainly vulgar. He was astonished at the cheerful ease with which Anne-Marie handled the situation and at the fluency of her own gutter language when she replied.

He said, 'One thing's for sure, the oldest profession is anything but oppressed. How does that sit with your women's struggle?'

'That women should have a choice, a free choice, is all I ask,' she said. 'What they do with that choice is their own affair.'

The door of the *Maison d'Or* was locked and Anne-Marie rang the bell. A panel slid back instantly and a pair of hard blue eyes inspected them.

'We're looking for a little fun,' she said.

'Aren't we all, sweetheart. Are you members?'

'No, from out of town, but I promised my friend here a good time.' She made an obscene gesture with the fingers of one hand.

The door opened to admit them. The doorman looked as if he'd been a useful middle-weight prize fighter in his day, the eyes swollen with scar tissue. He looked Anne-Marie over approvingly and whistled.

'You look such a nice girl, too.'

The foyer was decorated in scarlet and gold. The two girls behind the cloakroom counter wore elegant black dresses and one of them came forward to take their coats.

'I told you the *Maison d'Or* was special,' Anne-Marie said.

In the ornate mirror, Devlin was aware of a young man who had appeared from a small doorway almost hidden beside the gold draped entrance to the club itself. He was enormously attractive with dark hair that curled slightly and black eyes that moved over everything with a kind of amused contempt. The badly broken nose for some reason fitted perfectly with the elegant Yves St Laurent suit in dark blue flannel. He watched them for a moment, a Gauloise drooping from the corner of his mouth, then came forward.

'Monsieur,' he said to Devlin. 'You will permit me?'

Devlin raised his arms, smiling slowly and the young man ran hands over him expertly.

'What is this?' Anne-Marie demanded indignantly.

'Hush, girl,' Devlin told her. 'No problem. I'm clean.'

'No offence, Monsieur,' the young man said at last, satisfied.

'None taken,' Devlin said cheerfully. 'It takes one to know one. We'd like to see Monsieur Savary.'

'That isn't possible,' the young man said. 'Monsieur Savary isn't here. I could take a message.'

'I don't think so,' Devlin told him. 'This is the kind he'd prefer to receive himself. From his father.'

The doorman said, 'Heh, what in the hell is this?'

The young man waved him down, the slight smile still fixed firmly in place, but the eyes had stopped smiling. 'How interesting, monsieur.'

'Yes, well when Savary comes in, maybe you could mention it to him. We're in no hurry.'

Devlin took Anne-Marie by the elbow and headed for the draped entrance to the club. The young man snapped his fingers and a head waiter materialised from nowhere to lead them to a table.

'Champagne,' Anne-Marie said. 'Irish whiskey for the gentleman.'

'You wouldn't happen to have a bottle of Bushmills available?' Devlin put in.

'But of course, Monsieur,' the head waiter replied. 'We pride ourselves at *Maison d'Or* on our ability to provide all our customers' requirements.'

'And I expect that covers a wide field,' Devlin said and looked around him.

It was typical of such establishments the

world over. A trio playing intimate music, a small dance floor, tables crowded together and a gaming room through an archway. In this case the only surprise was the decor for everything, wall coverings, curtains, carpets and furniture, was in excellent taste.

The head waiter returned with their drinks himself. 'Something to eat, perhaps?'

It was Anne-Marie who answered him. 'Later. For the moment, we wait for Monsieur Savary.'

The head waiter shrugged and walked away. Devlin said, 'Do you get just the slightest impression we're not wanted?'

He toasted her, she sipped her champagne. It was too early for the club to be busy, that curious half-way point in the life of such establishments, a kind of lull before the real action of the night takes place.

The doorman was leaning against the bar, a glass in his hand, watching them closely. He emptied his glass and moved towards them.

'Get ready,' Devlin muttered. 'Unless I miss my guess, this is action stations.'

The doorman said, 'Look, Monsieur Savary isn't coming in tonight so I'd drink up and move on, if I were you. Of course the *poule* can stay.' His hand dropped to Anne-Marie's shoulder, the broad fingers sliding inside the open neck of her shirt.

She didn't even flinch. 'Could I have some more champagne?' she asked Devlin.

'Of course.' He reached for the bottle. 'And by the way,' he said to the doorman. 'You'd oblige me by not doing that. I mean, she doesn't know where you've been, does she?'

Very slowly, the doorman released his grip. 'You little jerk,' he said. 'You know what I'm going to do with you?'

'No,' Devlin said. 'Do tell me.'

He was in the act of pouring Anne-Marie's champagne and in an almost casual gesture, he reversed his grip and smashed the bottle across the side of the doorman's head. The man cried out, going down on one knee, clenching at the table cloth, glasses bouncing to the floor.

There was immediate consternation, diners crying out in alarm. The band stopped playing and several hard-looking specimens in dinner jackets moved in fast. There was a sudden shouted command as the young man with the broken nose appeared, waving his arms.

Everyone backed off, the doorman stood up, shaking his head like a bull, holding a napkin to the blood mingling with the champagne. 'You were right, boss,' he said. 'Not what he seems, this one.'

The young man inspected the damage. 'Not too bad, Claude, you've known worse. Go and get yourself patched up.'

Already half a dozen waiters were tidying things up. The young man turned. 'Very good, Monsieur . . . ?'

'Devlin.'

'I like your style.'

'And I yours,' Devlin said. 'You are Jean-Paul Savary?'

'Guilty.' Savary gave them a mock bow.

'Then why the performance?'

'Because I recognised Mademoiselle Audin here.' He took her hand and kissed it gallantly. 'You have no greater admirer of your work. Anyway, it gave me pause for thought. I don't like to jump straight in, I like to think.' He sat down and snapped his fingers for the head waiter. 'Now, a message from my father, you say? How can this be?'

'He shares a cell at Belle Isle with a friend of mine.'

'Prisoner 38930 Martin Brosnan,' Savary said.

'That's right.' Devlin frowned. 'You even know his number?'

'There is nothing affecting my father and Belle Isle that I do not know, and on the rock, a man's number stays with him till death. They make certain by tattooing it on their right forearm.'

Anne-Marie said, 'He's been there a long time, your father. I'm surprised the Union Corse haven't managed to do something about it.'

'If it had been any other crime than the one he is in for.' He shook his head. 'He tried to knock off de Gaulle. Not only that, he came damn close. They'll never forgive him. He's there till he dies.'

There was a sudden savagery in his voice.

Anne-Marie continued. 'And you've never tried to break him out?'

'Off Belle Isle?' he laughed incredulously. 'No one has ever escaped from that damned rock. No one.'

Devlin said cheerfully, 'Well, Thursday night, Martin Brosnan and your father are going to attempt to break the record, with your help or without it. That's the message I bring from your father.'

Jean-Paul Savary sat there, hands flat on the table, staring at Devlin. He turned slowly to Anne-Marie. 'This is true?'

'Absolutely.'

He took a deep breath and stood up. 'Then I suggest we adjourn to my private suite upstairs and discuss the matter.'

It was very warm in the comfortable sitting room and Anne-Marie opened the windows to the balcony, went outside and looked out over the harbour below. After a while, she turned and went back in

Devlin and Jean-Paul had their jackets off

and leaned over the table which was covered by a large scale chart of the Belle Isle area.

'Could it work?' Devlin said.

'In theory. The homing system Brosnan mentioned is no problem. I have heavy connections with the smuggling business in this area. We often recover stuff dropped over the rail of a passing ship at sea using just such a device. And the boat is no problem. We took over a fish company on the docks last year. Own six trawlers. I can have one round to St Denise tomorrow.'

'In other words, there's no technical reason why it shouldn't work.'

'True, but it's still a hell of a thing to step off the rock in that sea and take a chance which I would put at no better than fifty-fifty.'

'You seem cheerful enough about it.'

'He's been in a stone tomb for fourteen years, Mr Devlin. This is the only chance he'll ever get to beat the game. Who am I to refuse him that? But there are other things to consider. Many important points which do not seem to have occurred to you.'

There was a knock at the door and big Claude, the doorman, looked in. 'Doctor Cresson is here.'

'Good, show him in.'

Anne-Marie said, 'What do we need a doctor for?'

Jean-Paul lit a Gauloise and smiled. 'You'll see, *chèrie*. You'll see.'

André Cresson was a large man with dark, sad eyes and a double chin. His tan gaberdine suit looked as if it hadn't been pressed in months and he chain-smoked incessantly, lighting one cigarette from the stub of another, his black shirt smothered with ash.

He said, 'You say they intend to come out through the sewers?'

'That's right,' Devlin told him.

Cresson made a face. 'Not good. Sewers are a bad scene at the best of times, but in a place like Belle Isle.' He shrugged. 'Probably the original tunnels from the eighteenth century. The effluent of years.'

'What are you saying?' Jean-Paul demanded.

'Well, there are often pockets of CO_2 and methane. The first will suffocate. The second will not only suffocate, but will explode from a spark if conditions are right. But that's just a chance they have to take.'

'The point is, no candles or matches?' Devlin said.

'Exactly. You will be seeing this man Brosnan again before the attempt, Monsieur?'

'That's right. I saw the assistant governor. Made it clear there were further matters of business to iron out before I could finalise them with my client. There was no problem. I see Brosnan Thursday morning.'

'Then I suggest a small pocket torch might be in order. A thing perhaps difficult to come by in prison. You see the main danger would occur if they were to fall in the effluent. Nausea, vomiting and a rapid death within a few hours can occur due to a gutful of human pathogens. There is also the possibility of viral hepatitis.'

There was a profound silence. It was Anne-Marie who said, 'And what can be done about all this, Doctor?'

'Oh, immediate drug therapy the moment they are retrieved.' He smiled sadly. 'If, indeed, they are retrieved. The waters of the Mill Race, my friends, even on a mild night, will reduce body temperature rapidly. This would particularly affect my old friend Jacques, who is not, to be frank, as young as he was.'

Jean-Paul said, 'All right, then you come with us on the trawler to administer whatever drugs are necessary the moment we have them over the side. Naturally, I'll see that you're well taken care of for this service.'

Cresson shook his head. 'No, Jean-Paul, your father and I go back more years than I care to remember. He was always my good friend. This one, I do for him.'

Jean-Paul smiled. 'Then in his name, I gratefully accept.'

Devlin said, 'Let's assume it works like a charm and they make it. What happens next?'

'As I told you,' Anne-Marie said. 'I have a small farm in the hills above Nice. I use it when I want to get away from things. It's very remote and up high. You can see anyone approaching for miles. They can go there during the recovery period.'

'What about your staff?' he asked.

'No problem. I only keep sheep there, a Spanish mountain variety. One shepherd, old Louis, and he's away up in the hills most of the time.'

'Sounds good to me.'

Jean-Paul said, 'I appreciate the offer, but I'll take care of my father.'

'They'll need to lie low for some time,' Devlin pointed out. 'This thing will cause one hell of a stink. We'll have every cop in France looking for them. Interpol on the alert.'

'True,' Jean-Paul said. 'But let's look at it another way. What if the sea claimed them? What if they died from exposure and the Mill Race carried them in to the rocks outside St Denise?'

There was a long silence. Anne-Marie said in a low voice, 'If you're implying what I think you are, there is the obvious problem that the bodies would not be Jacques Savary and Martin Brosnan.'

'And wouldn't stand up to any kind of forensic examination,' Devlin added.

'Battered beyond recognition, wearing prison uniform, stencilled with their own numbers, floating in on stolen prison life jackets?' Jean-Paul shook his head. 'I would think it unlikely that they would take the examination any further than that.' He eased his back, staring down at the chart thoughtfully. 'I made a considerable amount of money from the operation of gambling casinos. We always win because the odds favour the house. I'll make you a prophecy on this one – a gambler's hunch. I think that if the authorities recover those two bodies, they'll dispose of them as quickly as possible, and simply announce that prisoners Brosnan and Savary have died, either from natural causes or perhaps in an accident at the granite quarry.'

'What you're saying is that they would kill the escape story altogether?' Devlin said. 'In other words it never happened.'

'Eminently sensible if you think of it. That way the authorities are not left with egg on their face and Belle Isle's reputation for being escape-proof is left intact.'

Anne-Marie said, 'He could be right. It would make a great deal of sense.'

'Perhaps,' Devlin said. 'Only time will tell on that one. So, what's the next move?'

Jean-Paul turned to Cresson. 'We're in your hands now, André. Scour the city. Mortuaries, undertakers, all the usual places. The trawler leaves for St Denise tomorrow afternoon. When it does, I want two suitable bodies in its cold store.'

André Cresson lit a fresh cigarette from the stub of the one he was smoking and took a pen and a small leather-bound notebook from his pocket. He said to Devlin, 'I know where I am where Jacques is concerned, I was his doctor for years. Perhaps Monsieur, in the interests of accuracy, you'd care to give me a description of your friend Brosnan?'

8

Frank Barry lay in bed smoking, staring up at the ceiling. It was seven o'clock in the morning and November cold, rain drifting against the window. Jenny Crowther slept beside him, breathing gently, her lips slightly parted. She looked, in repose, incredibly innocent, even childlike. He considered her dispassionately, his mind busy on more important things.

He slid from between the blankets, padded across to the chair on which he'd left his clothes and pulled on slacks and an old sweater. He ran fingers through his hair and went to pick up his suitcases

Jenny stirred and sat up. 'You're going?' she said, and there was alarm in her voice.

He put the cases down and moved to the

bed. 'No, you stay where you are. I don't want you up at the farm today, understand?'

She gazed at him searchingly. 'You'll be back?'

'Later,' he said.

She flung her arms around his neck and kissed him passionately. It had no effect on him at all and he was conscious of a strange feeling of regret.

'Be a good girl,' he said, and he picked up his suitcases and went out.

There was a smell of bacon cooking and he found Salter in the kitchen at the stove.

'Ah, Mr Sinclair,' he said. 'Can I offer you a little something?'

'Not really.' Barry poured himself a cup of tea and drank it quickly. 'I always prefer to work on an empty stomach.'

Salter stopped smiling. 'This is the big day then?'

'I'd have thought a devious old sod like you would have learned by now that the less you know the better off you are,' Barry said as he picked up the suitcases and moved to the door. 'I've told Jenny to stay away from the farm today. That applies to you as well.'

The threat was implicit. Salter stood there clutching the frying pan looking thoroughly alarmed. Barry went out and crossed the yard to the barn.

Fifteen minutes later he parked the Land-Rover at the end of the jetty. The rain was fine and soft in the mist and, as usual, there wasn't a soul about. He slipped over the rail of the *Kathleen* and went into the wheel-house. First, he dropped the inspection flap under the instrument panel to check that the Smith and Wesson and the Sterling were still there. Satisfied, he went outside. *Kathleen*'s tender swung at the stern on a line, a yellow inflatable with an outboard motor. He pulled it into the jetty, clambered down and cast off. The outboard, like everything else about Salter's boat, was brand new. It started with no trouble at all and he moved away along the creek towards the sea.

He turned into a side channel, followed it for a while, then tried another, for some twenty minutes beating back and forth, even turning towards the land again before he pushed through a bank of reeds and found what he wanted. It was a pool, roughly circular in shape, perhaps sixty or seventy feet across. It shelved steeply towards the centre and at that point was about fifteen feet deep.

It was as if he was the first person to enter that place. There wasn't a sound, only the rain, and he shivered, remembering stories he'd heard as a child back home in Ireland of fairy pools and the like. Strange, but it was as if it had been waiting for him. As if he had been there before. Nonsense, of course, but in any case, it would suit his purpose admirably. He started the engine of the inflatable again and made his way back to the boats.

Hedley Preston stood in front of the wardrobe mirror and adjusted the blue army beret to a suitably rakish angle. The camouflaged battle dress gave him a sinister appearance and he adjusted the webbing belt at his waist.

'Well, now,' he said softly. 'Who'd have thought it.'

He went downstairs and found Varley, similarly attired, standing at the fire, a glass in his hand. Varley turned to glance over his shoulder and said sourly, 'Look at you. Quite the hero.'

'One thing's certain,' Preston told him cheerfully. 'You won't be if Sinclair finds you with that in your hand.'

'Stuff Sinclair,' Varley said, but at the sound of steps in the passageway he hurriedly put the glass on the mantelpiece behind a photo.

Barry appeared in the doorway, one of the suitcases in his hand. The uniform suited him. He looked a soldier down to the last inch and the Browning in the webbing holster at his waist fitted the picture perfectly.

'So, here we are,' Preston said. 'Now we get to know what it's all about.'

'Just as much as you need to.'

Barry put the brown suitcase on the table, opened it and took out a map of the area, which he unfolded. 'One truck, possibly two, passing this point on the road to Wast Water. Half a dozen soldiers in one for certain. They'll also have an escort. I shan't know how many until later.'

'Soldiers?' Varley said. 'Here, what is this?'

'Don't wet yourself,' Barry said. 'They don't let armed soldiers go racketing round the countryside in Britain so you've nothing to worry about. We block the road with the Land-Rover to stop them.' He took one of the gas grenades from the case. 'Lob one of these in the back of the truck. The gas it contains works instantly. They'll be unconscious for an hour.'

'And what about us?' Preston asked.

'All catered for.' Barry held up a small khaki-coloured gas mask with a green canister dangling from it.

'So, they're all sleeping like babies,' Preston said. 'What do we do?'

'Off-load what we find in the truck into the Land-Rover Thirty minutes back to the coast where I've got a boat waiting. We load up and that's you two finished. You can get the hell out of it.'

'With another five thousand pounds each,' Preston said. 'Let's not forget the most important item.'

Barry took the Sterling sub-machine gun and the Smith and Wesson from the suitcase. 'Both these are loaded for bear in case anything goes wrong, but no shooting, not unless I give the word. Understood?'

'Perfectly, Mr Sinclair.' Preston picked up the Sterling lovingly. 'A thing of beauty is a joy for ever.'

Varley handled the Smith and Wesson gingerly, then slipped it into his webbing holster. 'One thing I'd like to know,' he said belligerently. 'What's in this bloody truck that's so important?'

Barry closed the suitcase and stood looking at them, holding it against his leg. There was a long moment before he said, 'Right, let's get going.'

He walked out. 'Now look here,' Varley began and Preston choked him off instantly.

'Shut it, Sam, understand? Everything comes to he who waits as I've already told you, so for the moment, let's just do as the man says.' He picked up his Sterling and followed Barry out.

The funeral parlour was on one side of a small cobbled square in the old city. When Jean-Paul Savary, Devlin and Anne-Marie approached there was a horse-drawn hearse outside, a splendid baroque creation in black with weeping golden angels at each corner and black plumes stuck up between the horses' ears.

'Ostrich feathers,' Jean-Paul said. 'Actually, it's illegal now, but when people are as conservative as they are around here, it's difficult to break such ancient customs.'

He pulled on a bell rope at the side entrance. It was opened immediately by a tall, thin old man in a rusty black suit. 'This way, Monsieur Savary,' he said.

They followed him along a dark passage. The smell of incense and wax candles filled the air, heavy and oppressive. There were chapels of rest on either side of the passage, most of them with a corpse lying in state in an open coffin so that the relatives and friends might visit.

Devlin said, 'Thank you very much, but I'd rather go some other way.'

'Does it really matter?' Anne-Marie asked. 'When you're dead, you're dead.' They paused in a doorway to look at an old man propped up in a coffin lined with black satin. He wore a blue suit, collar and tie, his hair was neatly combed and his face had been coloured with stage make-up, the lips vermilion. 'What can it possibly matter to him that they've made him into a waxworks freak?'

'As long as it comforts his old mother, you mean?' Devlin shivered. 'No thanks. As a bad Catholic I think I'll stipulate cremation.'

The old man opened a door at the end of the passage and stood to one side. The room they entered was the preparation room where bodies were washed or embalmed if required before actual burial. Dr Cresson, the eternal cigarette in his mouth, was standing by a stone sink talking to a tiny, rat-faced man who wore a shiny blue suit and carried a black bag in one hand.

Cresson turned to greet them. 'Ah, there you are.'

There were two stone mortuary slabs in the centre of the room, a body on each covered by a sheet.

'Everything going according to plan?' Jean-Paul asked.

'I think so. Both these individuals died in automobile crashes.'

'Can we have a look?'

'I wouldn't advise it. Not unless you actually enjoy that kind of thing. They don't look too good.'

'Will they pass?' Devlin asked.

Cresson nodded. 'I think so, after I've done a little more work on them.' He beckoned the rat-faced man over. 'Jean-Paul, this is the tattooist I mentioned, Mr Black. English, but he's been in Marseilles some time now.'

Jean-Paul took the little man's hand. 'I am grateful for your help in this matter. The Union Corse does not forget its friends, believe me.'

'A pleasure, monsieur. May I start now?' Black said.

'But of course.' Jean-Paul turned to Cresson. 'You have the numbers?'

'Yes.'

'Then all that remains is to make sure the right one goes on the right corpse.'

Anne-Marie and Devlin watched fascinated, as the little man opened his bag, produced a battery-operated tattooist's needle and a bottle of dye and went to work.

'An extra, but essential touch,' Jean-Paul said.

As they watched, the little man neatly tattooed Brosnan's number on the forearm of the taller corpse. He rubbed in the dye, then swabbed the flesh and held the forearm up.

'Satisfactory, Monsieur Savary?'

'Beautiful,' Jean-Paul told him. 'You are a true artist, my friend. And now my father, 28917.'

'Very well, Monsieur.'

Jean-Paul turned to Anne-Marie and Devlin. 'The rest, I think, is in the hands of fate.'

* * *

From a vantage point amongst trees at the side of the road two hundred yards north of Brisingham Airfield, Barry watched through binoculars as they unloaded the Luftwaffe transport plane. He could see only two vehicles, a large three-ton truck and a jeep. As he watched, the Bundeswehr soldiers loaded three crates into the back of the truck and then climbed in after them.

Their officer stood talking for a while to a young man in the uniform of a Captain in the British Army. After a while, they got into a jeep which moved off across the tarmac, followed by the truck. Barry waited until both vehicles were turning out of the gate into the road, just to make sure, then he jumped into the Land-Rover and drove away.

The rain had increased into a solid driving downpour since Barry had gone and it was not too pleasant crouched out of sight behind a greystone wall in the trees at the side of the road. Varley had a half bottle of Scotch from which he took frequent swallows.

Preston said, 'You really are a daft bastard, aren't you?'

'Mind your own sodding business,' Varley snarled. 'Nobody tells me what to do. Not you and certainly not Mr God-Almighty Sinclair.' He emptied the bottle and dropped it to the ground. 'I'll fix him when I'm good and ready.' He put a finger to his nose. 'You see if I don't.'

Preston shook his head in disgust. Varley was a liability, not only now but for the future, so much was obvious. On the other hand, who needed him? Preston caressed the barrel of the Sterling and stiffened, suddenly alert at the sound of an engine.

'Here, I think he's coming.'

A moment later the Land-Rover appeared. Barry turned it across the road, got out and moved through the trees to join them.

'Everything all right?' Preston demanded.

'Fine,' Barry told him. 'Two vehicles. A jeep leading that's got three in it, followed by a three-ton truck. The driver and a sergeant in the cab, half a dozen Krauts in the back. That means three grenades. I'll slip the first one into the jeep when I go to talk to them. You and Varley take the truck, one in the cab, another in the back.'

'Fine by me, General.' Varley saluted drunkenly.

Barry bent down, picked up the empty whisky bottle and threw it from him with a curse. He grabbed the big man by the front of his battledress. 'Spoil this for me, you drunken pig, and I'll blow your head off. That's a promise.'

There was no time for more, for suddenly there was the deepening note of an engine as a vehicle started up the hill.

'All right,' Barry said. 'Get your masks on,' and he turned and ran down to the road. He opened the door of the Land-Rover, got his gas mask, slung it around his neck and stood there waiting. The German Major of Artillery was in the rear seat of the jeep while the young English Captain sat up front beside the driver, half turned towards him while they spoke. He didn't see Barry until the driver drew his attention to him and slowed.

The Captain said, 'I wonder what this is

all about?' and wound down the window. 'What's going on?' he demanded as Barry approached.

'Change of plan, old boy, didn't they tell you?' Barry said. 'Well, isn't that bloody typical?'

He pulled the pin and lobbed the gas grenade through the open window, turning away instantly to pull his mask up over his face.

Preston and Varley ran out from the trees, Preston cutting across the road to the rear of the truck, tossing his grenade over the tail-board.

It was Varley who fouled things up. He pulled the pin of his grenade as he ran forward, tripped and went sprawling, the grenade rolling away from him in a curl of white smoke.

The truck door swung open and a big Sergeant of Artillery jumped to the ground. Barry, having no option, drew his Browning and shot him twice as the Sergeant launched himself at Varley. In the same moment Barry picked up the smoking grenade and threw it into the cab where the driver still sat behind the wheel.

It was suddenly very quiet. Preston came round from the back of the truck while Barry pulled Varley to his feet and shook him in anger, his voice muffled inside the gas mask.

He turned and hurried round to the back of the truck, let down the tailboard, clambered over the inert bodies of the German Artillery men and examined the three green containers he found there.

Preston and Varley joined him. It took them exactly four minutes to move the containers across to the Land-Rover. Within five, they were driving away, leaving the two army vehicles silent in the rain at the side of the road.

Jenny Crowther walked along the path beside the estuary in the rain, a forlorn looking figure in the headscarf and old raincoat. Her life until Barry had been nothing, one grey day after another. Now, he circled in her brain constantly so that she could think of nothing else.

She moved along the jetty and stood, hands in pockets, looking at the two boats. After a while, she stepped over the rail of the *Kathleen* and went into the wheelhouse. She sat on the bench, her back against the bulkhead, staring at the instrument panel. Finally, she reached underneath and dropped the inspection flap. The Sterling and the revolver hung there, neat and deadly in their brackets. She touched gingerly, then pushed the flap back up into place and went out again.

She moved along to the *Jason* next and stood looking at it, wondering what it was all about, a slight, puzzled frown on her face. She stepped over the rail and went into the wheelhouse and stood there undecided, not certain what she was doing there at all. Suddenly, in the distance, she heard the sound of an engine.

By the time she got out on deck it was very close. She hesitated, then went down the companionway quickly and closed the door.

* * *

The Land-Rover braked to a halt at the end of the jetty and Barry got out and went round to the rear where Preston and Varley sat with the three containers.

'All right, let's have these on board the *Jason*, quick as you like,' he said. 'Pass me the first one. I can manage it on my own.'

'Anything to oblige,' Preston said as he pushed it across.

It was comparatively light. Barry had no difficulty in negotiating the rail and the companionway. Jenny, hearing him coming, moved to the other end of the saloon and hid in the toilet.

Barry got the door of the saloon open and moved in with the container. He put it down on the floor and Preston and Varley appeared, carrying the second which was larger.

'Good,' Barry said. 'One more and we're done and you two can be out of it.'

Varley gave Preston a sly glance, but they went back up the companionway. Barry went after them. When they reached the Land-Rover he stood watching them manhandle the third container. As they started back along the jetty, he reached under the driving seat, found the briefcase and followed them.

It would be interesting to see when they made their move. The only certainty was that Preston would make a drama out of it. Barry went and stood by the stern rail, put the briefcase on the ground at his feet and unclipped the holding strap of the webbing holster at its belt. He could hear the rumble of their voices in the cabin below, as he took out the Browning, cocked it and replaced it in the holster. He lit a cigarette and waited.

They came back on deck and Preston said, 'You've got the money there, I hope?'

'That's right.'

'Yes, well we'd like to talk to you about that. About what's below in those containers and how much there really is in that brief-case.'

'In other words, clever bastard,' Varley cut in, 'we want it all.'

Barry turned, a slight smile on his face, the cigarette hanging from the corner of his mouth. Preston had him covered with the

Sterling and Varley drew his Smith and Wesson.

'Do I walk away from this?'

'I'm afraid not, Mr Sinclair.' Preston shrugged. 'You lose, all the way round.'

'A crying shame.' Barry tossed his cigarette over the side. 'And to think you could have had your wages and been away.'

His hand dropped to his side, reaching for the Browning and Preston pulled the trigger of the Sterling. There was only the mechanical chatter of the bolt reciprocating. Preston stopped smiling as in that final dreadful moment, he saw it all.

And as Barry fired, Jenny erupted from the companionway. 'No!' she cried, flinging herself at Preston. The bullet caught her full in the back, driving her against him.

Preston held her as a shield, trying to back away and Barry shot him through the head, fragmenting the top of his skull, punching him back against the wheelhouse still clutching the girl.

Varley was firing his Smith and Wesson frantically, one metallic click after another.

With a desperate cry, he flung the useless weapon at Barry and turned to run. Barry shot him twice in the back, shattering his spine, and Varley fell to his knees and hung across the rail.

Birds drifted up from the reeds, circling in panic, the air filled with their cries and the beating of their wings. Barry holstered the Browning, dropped on his knees and cradled Jenny Crowther in his arms. She was quite dead, her eyes wide, staring. He closed them gently.

'Poor stupid little bitch,' he said and kissed her on the forehead. 'There was no need – no need at all. I had it all sewn up.'

He picked her up in his arms, went down the companionway and laid her on one of the bench seats. Then he went back on deck and knelt beside Preston, opening the battledress blouse and searching him quickly. As he had expected, Preston was carrying the five thousand pounds on him, as was Varley. He tumbled them down the companionway one after the other, then retrieved his briefcase, went over the rail and hurried along to the *Kathleen*.

He went into the wheelhouse and looked

about him. Simplest places were always the best, or so he'd found. There was a bench seat against the wall. The padded leather top lifted easily enough. There was an accumulation of rubbish inside, ropes, oilcans, plastic bags. He concealed the briefcase under the plastic bags and went outside.

Next, he swiftly wrapped the containers in a waterproof sheet, untied the *Kathleen*'s tender, hauled it along the side of the jetty and attached it to the *Jason*'s stern. Then he went back on board, cast off, hurried into the wheelhouse and started the engine. Ten minutes later he was nosing through the great bank of reeds to enter the pool he had discovered earlier that day.

He switched off the engines. The *Jason* glided to a halt. He went down the companionway, ignoring the bodies, and worked his way from the prow to the stern, opening the sea-cocks. The *Jason* was already beginning to settle as he went out on deck. He hauled in the inflatable, dropped into it and pulled away to the side of the pool.

The *Jason* was sinking fast now, the water

almost at deck level. He lit a cigarette and waited and then, with a final sudden rush, she dipped beneath the surface and settled on the bottom. Only then did he start the outboard and push his way back through the reeds to the estuary.

Henry Salter was sitting in the kitchen drinking tea. His nerves were bad and his hand shook a little as he added a tot of brandy. Wind rattled the window and rain slapped against the pane. He hated the winter. It worried him, filled him with unease, but not as much as Barry did. He could hear him moving about above him now and, a moment later, descending the stairs.

When Barry came into the room, he was wearing the dark raincoat he had arrived in and carried one of the brown leather cases. He sat in the chair opposite and put the case on the table.

'Well, that's that. I've cleared up at the farm. You wouldn't know anyone's been there.'

'And Preston and Varley?'

'Couldn't wait to get their hands on the cash and away. And speaking of cash,' he opened the case, took out Preston's five thousand pounds and pushed it across. 'As promised.'

Salter was sweating a little, as he reached out to touch. 'I've been listening on the radio, Mr Sinclair. There hasn't been any mention of any untoward incident on the local news.'

'And why should that sort of thing concern a respectable man like you, Mr Salter?'

'Of course,' Salter said. 'Why indeed. You're leaving in the *Jason* now?'

'The *Jason* has already left, old son.' Barry smiled. 'All taken care of. I'm very organised, you see.' He reached into the case, produced Varley's money and tossed it across the table, packet by packet. Salter watched, fascinated. 'A bonus, Mr Salter. You've been more than helpful, you see, and I always say the labourer is worthy of his hire. I expect to be back this way again very soon. Nothing too demanding this time, but it would be nice to think that you were here and ready and waiting to take care of my requirements.'

'Of course, Mr Sinclair. Anything you say,' Salter gabbled.

'Good, I'll be off then.'

Barry picked up his case and moved to the door. Salter said, 'One more thing, Mr Sinclair. What about Jenny?'

Barry turned slowly. 'You've no need to worry about Jenny any longer, Mr Salter, she's my concern from now on.'

'I see.' Salter nodded knowingly. 'I'm hardly surprised. Very fond of you, that girl. A love match, eh?'

Barry managed a smile. 'Well, as they say, that's what makes the world go round.'

He went out. Salter sat there listening. Only when he heard the hire car drive away did he start to count the money with trembling fingers.

9

By the time Barry reached Manchester Airport, his hair was soaked in brilliantine again and neatly parted and he was wearing the thick horn-rimmed spectacles. He made the Jersey plane with only twenty minutes to spare and sank into his seat with a certain amount of relief, for there wasn't another until the following day.

He ordered a large Scotch from the pretty British Airways stewardess in her blue uniform, lit a cigarette and sat looking out of the window, going over it all in his mind, giving particular attention to Romanov.

'Poor Nikolai,' he said softly. 'You certainly are in for one hell of a shock, old son.'

His Scotch came and he sipped it slowly,

with conscious pleasure. Things were going well, very well indeed.

One hour later he was walking out of the main entrance to Jersey airport to hail a taxi to take him down to the harbour and it was here that he ran into his first snag. According to a notice chalked up on a blackboard, there was no further sailing to St Malo that day.

Barry went into the shipping office and spoke to the clerk, who exhibited the usual competent indifference that such people do. 'Technical trouble, I'm afraid, sir. No problem with the morning sailing. They'll have another craft over if there is.'

Barry, bowing to the inevitable, walked back along the quay into town and booked himself a room for the night at the Royal Yacht Hotel.

Sitting on the balcony of the hotel room at St Denise, Anne-Marie searched the horizon for Belle Isle, for it had been a calm day with excellent visibility. She found it at last, a shadow, no more than that, even when she focused the binoculars.

Devlin came out of his room in a bath robe, towelling his hair dry from the shower. 'If you're interested, the trawler docked an hour ago at the fish quay.'

'Is Jean-Paul on board?'

'No, he comes tomorrow afternoon with Cresson. He'll 'phone me here after I've visited the island again, just to make sure everything's all right.'

'You'll be going with them tomorrow night?'

'Yes.'

'Can I come?'

She wasn't pleading, she wasn't that sort of human being. Devlin said, 'What a scoop this all would have been for you. What pictures. Another Pulitzer.'

'Bastard,' she said amiably.

'You've considered the worst implications. The fact that we may miss them altogether . . .'

'Or that they may come aboard dead?' she nodded gravely 'Whichever way it goes, I'd like to be there, Liam.'

'And why not?'

'Thank you.'

'Thanks is it?' he said. 'God save us and what for? Anyway, I must away out of this and take care of a 'phone call I've been avoiding making for twenty-four hours at least.'

'Important?'

'Ferguson,' he said.

Ferguson had been called away at a moment's notice by the Director General. When the 'phone rang at the Cavendish Square flat, Harry Fox was sitting at the desk in the study working on some papers.

'Brigadier Ferguson, please?'

'Not here, I'm afraid. Can I help?'

'Harry, me boy. It's your long-lost Uncle Liam.'

Fox was immediately alert. 'For God's sake, Professor, where have you been? Ferguson's been kicking the furniture to pieces. You were supposed to keep in touch.'

'Jesus, Harry, do you think you could stop calling me Professor? Makes me sound like some old character actor playing Einstein in a bad television play. I've been working like a dog, tell Ferguson.'

'So what's happened? You saw Brosnan?'

'I did indeed and didn't get very far until I mentioned Norah. That set him alight with vengeance.'

'So he's willing to play along?'

'In a manner of speaking. Look, Harry, Ferguson isn't going to like this, but the truth is Martin doesn't rate his chances of getting him out very highly so he's taking care of it himself.'

'He's what?' Fox was shocked and it was clear in his voice. 'That's madness. It can't be done.'

'He thinks differently. You're getting all this down on your little recorder, I trust.'

Fox laughed in spite of himself. 'Of course. Is Miss Audin with you?'

'She is indeed. I'll be off now.'

'Just a minute,' Fox cried. 'Where can we get in touch with you?'

Devlin chuckled. 'Don't ring us, we'll ring you,' he said and replaced his phone.

* * *

It was half an hour later that Ferguson appeared. He looked tired and went to the sideboard and poured himself a brandy. 'What a day.'

'Did the Director General want you for anything special, sir?'

'Had us all in, Harry, all department and section heads. Nasty little fracas up in the Lake District earlier today. A West German Artillery team were on their way to the Wast Water Proving Ground by road to demonstrate this new antitank rocket of theirs. Somebody walked all over them on one of those country back roads. Very professional. Gas grenades in the back of the vehicle, ours apparently. Type the SAS use on those smash-your-way-in jobs.'

'Any shooting, sir?'

'One death – Artillery Sergeant. Apparently the characters involved were in combat uniform, gas masks, the lot. Took the rocket pod, of course, and away.'

'Anything in it for us, sir?'

'I'm not sure. Strictly speaking it's a job for the local police. Special Branch are assisting, naturally, and I've sent Carter up there with them, just in case. In view of the delicacy of the situation, the Director General has managed to get a security clamp-down placed in force. Not a word to the media. The West Germans aren't going to like this one little bit.'

Fox said, 'Devlin telephoned in, sir.'

Ferguson's eyes gleamed. 'Did he, by God? What's he been up to?'

'I think you'd better hear for yourself, sir.' Fox turned on the recorder.

Ferguson sat listening, his face darkening. When the tape was finished, he jumped up and paced angrily across the room.

'Damn you, Devlin!'

'Frankly, sir, I don't really see how Devlin's had much to do with it. It's Brosnan's choice after all.'

'Madness,' Ferguson said. 'If by some miracle he does escape it will cause an absolute sensation in France. The man would become a folk hero. The authorities would be bound to turn the country upside down to find him as an act of self-preservation.'

He stood at the window fuming. Fox said cheerfully, 'You could stop it, sir, very simply.'

'By alerting the governor of Belle Isle? Could you do that, Harry?'

'No, sir, not really.'

'Neither can I and Devlin knows that damn well, otherwise he wouldn't have told us.' He shook his head. 'I don't know. Is the Audin woman still with him?'

'Apparently so, sir. What would you like me to do?'

'Nothing much you can do, Harry.' Ferguson frowned suddenly. 'No, there is. I want you to put together a brief account of this affair so far. The salient facts, who's involved, what we've done. Everything except the business about Norah Cassidy.'

Fox was surprised. 'May I ask why, sir?'

'I'll explain later, Harry. One copy for my personal file and one for the eyes of the Prime Minister only.'

'Shall I send it round to Number Ten, sir?'

'Not yet. I'd like to be prepared. That's all. She might send for me at any time. You never can tell. A mind like a Swiss watch, that lady. Security One, needless to say. Tell Meg Johnson she does this one herself. No one else touches it.'

Meg Johnson was a formidable, grey-haired lady in her late fifties, widowed since 1951 when her husband had been killed in Korea. She had been Senior Secretary of Administration in Ferguson's department since its inception.

The report on the Brosnan affair which Harry Fox had dictated to her fitted neatly on to a single sheet of A4. It was typed exquisitely, the margin size exact. If it was for the Prime Minister's eyes, then it had to be perfection. Nothing less would do.

She took it in to Fox who read it quickly and nodded his approval. 'Excellent, Mrs Johnson. You've excelled yourself. One copy, please, for the Prime Minister, which for the moment will be held with the original in Brigadier Ferguson's Red file.'

She went back along the corridor to her office, reading the report again, strictly in the interests of accuracy. Its contents did not concern her. She never allowed the details of any report to sink in. That, she had found over the years, was the best way.

Satisfied, she opened the door of her office which communicated with the copying room. The woman on duty was Mary Baxter, Senior Secretarial Assistant. They were old friends and had worked together for years.

Mrs Johnson said, 'Hello, Mary, what are you doing here?'

'Young Jean was taken ill at lunchtime. I'm just filling in.'

Meg Johnson passed her the report. 'One copy of that, please.'

Mary Baxter set the machine up quickly. *For the eyes of the Prime Minister only*. She took in that much and then the phone started to ring in Meg Johnson's office. Meg turned and hurried in to answer it.

It was a routine matter, taking only three or four minutes to handle. As she was writing a memo there was a nervous cough and she looked up and found Mary Baxter standing there holding the report.

'One copy, you said?'

'Thanks, Mary. Just put them on the desk,' Meg Johnson replied, still concentrating on her memo.

The other woman did as she was told and went out. Back in the copying room, she closed the door carefully, then took out the two extra copies of the Brosnan report she had made. She folded them neatly and slipped them into the pocket of her tweed skirt. She checked her watch. Almost time to go home. She switched off the light and went out.

Mary Baxter, as Nikolai Romanov had indicated to Barry, was of impeccable background. Her father had spent his entire career as an army doctor, and as her mother had died when she was five, she had spent all her impressionable years at a succession of boarding schools.

A plain, even rather ugly girl, she had few friends, had entered the Civil Service as a Ministry Secretary to start with. Her total reliability had led to promotion, then after a while, a transfer to DI5 once her security clearance had gone through.

She had money left her by her father, a good flat in St John's Wood and very little else. She was forty-two, still plain, her hair drawn back in a tight bun, and the tweed suits and sensible flat shoes she wore did little to enhance her appearance.

And then she had met Peter Yasnov. She'd had an invitation to a cultural evening at the Brazilian Embassy, the sort of thing that came up occasionally. Usually, she didn't go to such affairs, but for some reason, she had done so that time and that's where she'd met Yasnov.

He'd been more than attentive. Had stayed with her all evening. Had not only taken her home, but had arranged to squire her to a concert at the Albert Hall the following week.

His slow insistent seduction had finally taken her to bed where she had discovered the delights of sex for the first time in her life. By the time she also discovered that he was a commercial attaché at the Soviet Embassy, she was hooked, so that she didn't care. Anything he wanted, she gave him, and that included any information of value that she came across in the office. Usually, her access to the interesting stuff was limited, but this was really something special.

She wasn't supposed to see him for another four days, an eternity of waiting, and he had always forbidden her ever to call at his flat. But for this . . .

She had taken two copies to make sure she got a good one. She slipped one into her dressing table drawer, put the other in her handbag and went out.

Peter Yasnov had been commercial attaché at the Soviet Embassy in London for two years. A Captain in the KGB, his previous posting had been at the Paris Embassy where under Nikolai Romanov's tutelage, he had made remarkable progress. A handsome, dark-haired and elegant young man, he was particularly attractive to women; a circumstance which had its uses and explained why his masters had thought it worthwhile to indulge him in the small town house in Ebury Court, not far from the Palace of St James.

He emerged from the shower, humming softly to himself, pulled on a robe and went into the living room to get a cigarette. He was standing at the window, looking down idly into the court when Mary Baxter came round the corner, passed the two telephone engineers with their green tent over the manhole in the pavement, and came towards the house. Yasnov cursed softly and went downstairs.

The main function of the Special Branch of the Metropolitan Police based at Scotland Yard is to act as the executive arm of the Security Services. Surveillance forms a large part of Special Branch work and the two detective-sergeants posing as telephone engineers in their tent in Ebury Court had been watching Peter Yasnov in one way or another for a month now.

Mary Baxter rang the bell and turned, looking back along the court while she waited, enabling the SB man with the camera to take several excellent photos.

'I haven't seen her before, have you?'

'Hardly his style, I would have thought,' his colleague said. 'She's no dolly-bird.'

The door opened and Yasnov appeared in his white bathrobe. Mary Baxter flung her arm round his neck and kissed him and the sergeant's camera clicked again.

'Now that is interesting,' he said, as she passed inside and the door closed. 'He didn't look pleased at all. You'd better follow the lady, George, when she comes out. Find out who she is. There could be something in this one.'

Yasnov was thoroughly angry as he made clear. 'I told you never to visit me here.' He shook her by the shoulders. 'Are you trying to ruin everything?'

'Please, Peter, I didn't mean any harm.'

There were tears in her eyes and he was filled with disgust, but made a brave effort to conceal it. He held her close to him for a moment.

'All right, I'm sorry I lost my temper, but you must understand my position.'

'I know, Peter, I'm so sorry.' She got her handbag open. 'But I felt sure you'd be interested in this. I thought you might want to see it.'

For the eyes of the Prime Minister only. The moment Yasnov saw that, his stomach tightened with excitement and the paper trembled slightly in his hand as he took in the contents. He turned away from her and walked to the fireplace. *The biggest touch he'd ever had by far.* It was inconceivable that this block of wood in the tweed skirt had come up with such a thing.

She approached him hesitatingly. 'Did I do right? Is it what you wanted?'

He turned with a dazzling smile and pulled her close. 'For an exceptionally good girl, an exceptional kiss,' and he crushed his mouth on hers.

She clung to him, trembling. 'Oh, Peter, I'd do anything for you. Anything.'

He cradled her head in his shoulder and checked his watch. Fifteen minutes was all it would take and if it kept her happy. He put an arm round her. 'Come upstairs, my darling,' he whispered, and led her out of the room.

Mary Baxter left half an hour later. She had never felt so alive. It was as if something which had been locked up inside her for years had been released. She felt so full of energy that she walked a considerable part of the way home before taking to the tube, totally unaware of the man following her.

Yasnov left his house an hour later and walked a couple of streets before hailing a cab. He alighted in Kensington High Street and went the rest of the way on foot to the Soviet Embassy in Kensington Palace Gardens. Five minutes later, he was closeted with his immediate superior, Colonel Josef Golchek.

Golchek read the report through twice and nodded. 'Very interesting.' He lit an American cigarette. 'Of course, it isn't going to prevent the start of the Third World War or anything.

Its real importance lies not in the substance of this report, but in the implication that the woman Baxter can actually get her hands on a report intended for the eyes of the British Prime Minister only. The possibilities for the future would seem to me to be fantastic!'

'And this report. What do I do with it?' Yasnov demanded.

'Send it to Nikolai Romanov in Paris. Code Three, for his own eyes. He'll know how best to handle it.'

'Very well.' Yasnov moved to the door.

As he opened it, Golchek said, 'One more thing, Peter.'

'What's that?'

'You'll have to continue to keep her happy.'

'For that,' Peter Yasnov said with feeling, 'I should be made a Hero of the Soviet Union.'

It was nine o'clock that night when Mary Baxter was led by a woman Detective-Sergeant of Special Branch into Charles Ferguson's office. He nodded to the Detective-Sergeant and she went out, closing the door.

'Sit down, Miss Baxter.'

She did as she was told, suddenly tired. She was not afraid. The shock of her arrest had a numbing effect so that she was not really capable of taking anything in. It had never occurred to her, not for one moment, that this kind of thing might happen.

'You know why you're here?' Ferguson said.

'I've no idea. If there has been some mistake in my work.'

He pushed the surveillance photos across the desk. She looked at them blankly, then picked up the one which showed her kissing Yasnov in the doorway. 'You've no right,' she began . . .

'We have every right,' he said gently. 'You work for the British Security Service. All right, in a minor capacity perhaps, but that makes your association with a man like Yasnov very suspect.'

'All right,' she said, 'so he's a commercial attaché at the Soviet Embassy.'

'And also, Miss Baxter, a Captain in the KGB.'

She gazed at him, incredulously. 'I don't believe you.'

'I have a photo of him here in uniform. Excellent likeness, don't you agree?'

There was a knock at the door and Harry Fox entered, face grave. He glanced at Mary Baxter, then put the second copy of the Brosnan report she had made on the desk in front of Ferguson.

'I found this, sir, in one of her dressing table drawers,' he said grimly.

'Dear God Almighty.' Ferguson got up, beckoned to Fox and went out into the corridor. 'Watch her,' he said to the Detective Sergeant, and she went into the office and closed the door.

'Well, sir?' Harry Fox said. 'What do we do?'

'What can we do, Harry, except hope and pray Devlin calls us again. This could give him real problems.'

'What about the Baxter woman?'

'Let's see, shall we?'

They went back into the office and the Detective Sergeant stepped out again. Mary Baxter sat holding the photo of Yasnov in uniform in her lap. She had stopped crying, there was something close to anger on her swollen face now and Ferguson seized on that fact instantly.

'He certainly made a bloody fool out of you, didn't he?'

'He told me he loved me,' she said bitterly. 'All lies. Nothing but lies.' She tore the photo into several pieces. 'I could kill him.'

'Much more sensible to pay him back in his own coin.' Ferguson gave her a cigarette and a light.

'What do you mean?' she asked.

'You could go to prison,' he said. 'For a long time. On the other hand, it does seem rather a pity when there's another way of handling this matter.' He held up the copy of the report. 'This, after all, is past history. Not much we can do about it now.'

'What exactly do you mean?'

'Simple enough. You continue to see Yasnov as if nothing had happened. Feed him the information I give you.'

She shook her head, shocked. 'I don't think I could do that.'

'Why not?' Ferguson demanded. 'He used you for his own purposes, didn't he? I should have thought it truly poetic justice for you to use him for yours.'

She was like a different person now, her face hardening. 'You know, I think I'd rather enjoy that, Brigadier.' She stood up. 'Do you think I could wash my face?'

'Certainly.' Ferguson indicated the door. 'Bathroom through there.'

'My God,' Fox said softly after she'd gone out.

'I know, Harry, I warned you just how dirty a business it was. You can tell that girl from Special Branch to clear off. We shan't be needing her.'

In Paris, the coding machine chattered in the radio room of the intelligence section of the Soviet Embassy. The woman operator watched the message appear line by line on the display screen. When it was finished she removed the tape which had recorded it and summoned the Supervisor.

'A Code Three from London for Colonel Romanov's eyes alone. It also includes as ancillary information three photos over the wire. Here are the serial numbers.'

'He's in Berlin,' the Supervisor said. 'Due back tomorrow afternoon or evening. Hold it till then. You can't do anything with it anyway. It requires his personal key to decode. I'll get those photos from the wire room. You can hold those too.'

She walked away and the operator placed the tape in her data drawer, locked it and returned to work.

It was almost midnight and chilly on the balcony of Anne-Marie's hotel room at St Denise. She went inside and returned, putting on her Afghan sheepskin jacket. She sat down beside Devlin again.

'This time tomorrow night, it could be all over.'

'True.' Devlin's cigarette glowed in the dark.

'How will I find him, Liam?'

'Changed, girl, and considerably. Be prepared for some big differences.'

'I don't mind that. An essential requirement for any human being is to grow or change or learn how to become reconciled to their limitations.'

'Ah, you're talking about the rocky road to maturity,' Devlin shook his head. 'I mean something else. He's not the wild man who saved you in that swamp in Vietnam and he isn't the brave soldier who stood at my side in Ulster in sixty-nine. To be honest with you, if he's learned anything at all it's that he's been used too much for other people's purposes. I don't think he believes in anything any more.'

'I can't accept that.'

Devlin said, 'Girl, dear, don't try to make him into some mythological hero. Whatever else he is, he is not that. I'm turning in now. The supply boat leaves at seven.'

He swung a leg over the balcony rail and went into his room, leaving her there, staring out into the darkness.

10

When Lebel opened the door of the interview room and ushered Brosnan in, Devlin was standing by the window, peering out through the bars.

He turned, smiling. 'Ah, there you are.'

'Mr Gorman.' Brosnan shook hands and sat down and Devlin took the chair opposite.

'If you need me, Monsieur, remember the bell.' Lebel went out, locking the door.

They spoke in Irish. Devlin said, 'Will he search you before taking you back to your cell?'

'Pierre?' Brosnan shook his head. 'All for a quiet life, that one. What have you got for me?'

Devlin opened his briefcase. 'Have a cigarette.' He pushed a pack across and followed it with another. 'One contains the homing device, the other a pocket torch. I wasn't sure if you could lay your hands on one. I was thinking of the sewers.'

'We've got candles and matches.'

'Holy Mother of God,' Devlin said. 'The worst thing you could do. You'd blow yourself to hell. Now listen to me.'

He went over everything thoroughly. When he was finished, Brosnan nodded. 'You've certainly got it all wrapped up, but then you always were the organising type. I like the touch with the two corpses. That should amuse Jacques. Obviously the son takes after the father.'

'What time will you be leaving?'

'We're locked up for the night by eight-thirty. It's dark by then, at the moment anyway, so we might as well make our move straight away. There isn't another landing check until midnight.'

'So they'll discover you've gone then?'

'Not the way Lebel checks the cells. With luck, the first they'll know is at seven o'clock in the morning.'

Devlin nodded 'How long in the sewers?'

'There's some climbing to do first. I'd give it an hour. With luck, we'll be at the funeral rock by nine-thirty. The current should have us outside the four mile limit by ten-fifteen.'

Devlin sat there frowning. 'This is a desperate ploy, you know that?'

Brosnan said, 'Of course I do.'

Devlin got up and rolled a small plastic ball across the table. 'When you peel the skin off, it's luminous inside. A signalling device we used in the war. My own life was saved by one once. I know there are lights on the lifejackets, but . . .'

He shrugged and went to the window and peered through the bars. The Mill Race was clear to see, flecked with white caps in spite of the calm weather.

Brosnan clapped him on the shoulder. 'Don't worry, Liam, Jacques Savary and I know what we're doing. We all come to a box in the end, anyway. The important thing is to go kicking like hell.'

* * *

The hydrofoil from Jersey to St Malo took around an hour to complete the journey. Frank Barry spent the time working his way through all the English national newspapers which he'd purchased before leaving St Helier.

There wasn't a mention, not even a hint, of the Wast Water affair in any of them, which was interesting. On the other hand, it made a great deal of sense. Not exactly the sort of thing that even the West Germans would want to advertise.

He passed through Customs experiencing no difficulty at all using the French passport, and immediately went to a telephone and phoned Romanov at his Paris apartment.

The phone was answered by the Russian's personal secretary from the Embassy, Irana Vronsky. She told him that she'd just been speaking to Romanov in East Berlin and that he wouldn't be back until the flight arrived at midnight

Barry said, 'If he speaks to you again, tell him that I'll be back in touch in the morning.'

He picked up his suitcase and left the booth. The train for Paris departed in twenty minutes. On the other hand, there was no reason to hurry. He had most of the day still before him and a fine soft day it was and to be enjoyed. He walked across the forecourt to the hire car company on the other side and, fifteen minutes later, drove out into the main road in a Peugeot coupe with the top down.

It was dark and the trawler was slipping out through the harbour entrance at St Denise when Devlin followed Jean-Paul Savary down the ladder into the fish hold. The door to the cold store was open and Dr Cresson and big Claude from the club stood inside at the slab on which fish were usually gutted, cutting away the plastic bags which contained the two corpses.

From what Devlin could see in the shadowy light, the faces were disfigured beyond recognition.

'Jesus,' he said.

'The force of the Mill Race pounding in on the granite rocks along the shore outside

St Denise,' Jean-Paul said. 'It is not unreasonable to expect such a result.'

Devlin touched the leg of one of the corpses. It was like marble. 'If there ever was an autopsy, it would indicate entirely the wrong time of death, wouldn't it?'

'Keeping the bodies frozen as we have done takes care of that to a certain degree,' Cresson said. 'It considerably arrests the process of decay. But frankly, my friend, if this is to succeed at all, it will be because the authorities accept these two gentlemen at face value.'

'Or without it,' Devlin said.

He followed Jean-Paul back up on deck and they went into the wheelhouse. The Captain was older than Devlin had expected, with a weatherbeaten face beneath the peaked hat. He wore a black oilskin. The cheroot he was smoking smelt foul and Devlin stayed in the doorway.

'Now then, Marcel,' Jean-Paul said. 'What's the score?'

'Not good, boss,' the old man said. 'A bad blow forecast, winds, seven-to-eight. Not enough to blow anyone's roof off, but for men out there in the waters of the Race . . .' He shrugged.

Jean-Paul turned to Devlin, his face pale in the dim light. 'Don't worry, this old sea rat is the finest skipper on the coast. If anyone can bring this off it's him, with the help of this gadget, of course.' He tapped the gleaming blue box on the chart table. 'The very latest thing. I had it installed yesterday. Microchip and digital read-out, so it really thinks for itself. Once locked on to the wavelength of that homing device, it will give us a course straight to it, whatever the weather.'

'Fine,' Devlin said, 'but if you've got any candles handy, I'd like to light a couple, just in case.'

Jean-Paul returned to the charts and Devlin went out on to the bridge where Anne-Marie stood at the rail, muffled in her Afghan jacket. White caps stretched into the darkness and spray scattered across the deck as the trawler dipped its prow into the waves.

'It's not good, is it?' she said.

'Not from the sound of it.' He grabbed the rail tightly 'You might as well know it all. The Captain thinks it will get worse before it gets better.'

'Enough to put them off?' she said. 'Martin and Savary, I mean?'

'I can only speak for Martin, but in my opinion, nothing could stop him entering the water if he makes it outside those walls, no matter how bad the storm. He's prepared to die if necessary, you see. That's the important thing.'

'My God,' she whispered and then suddenly clutched his arm as the wind carried a strange roaring sound from the far distance. 'Did you hear that, Liam? What is it?'

'Why, from the sound of it, I'd say that must be the Mill Race.'

She didn't say a word. He slipped an arm about her shoulders and, together, they stood there at the rail listening.

Pierre Lebel pulled back the flap on the spyhole of the cell on the upper landing. Brosnan and Savary sat opposite each other with a wooden box between them. Savary had a pack of Tarot cards in one hand and was laying out the wheel of fortune.

'This gives an answer to a specific question,' he said. 'And the outcome of events in the immediate future.'

'Really?' Brosnan said. 'You amaze me. Do I cross your palm with silver?'

'I've told you before, I've got gypsy blood.'

Lebel called. 'You should be in bed you two. Lights out.'

The cell was plunged into darkness. Savary called, 'God bless you, too, Pierre, and thanks for everything. You've been swell.'

'Idiot!' Brosnan whispered.

Lebel checked the next cell, they listened to his footsteps work their way along the landing. The barred gate at the end clanged, he descended the iron stairs and the footsteps faded.

'Switch on the torch,' Savary said. 'I just want to see what I've laid out.' Brosnan produced the small pocket torch Devlin had given him which had a surprisingly powerful beam. Savary turned over the first card. It showed death, a skeleton on horseback riding across a field of corpses. Savary gathered up the cards and put them on the shelf. 'Now that I can very definitely do without. I'm not looking any more. Let's get moving.'

Brosnan turned over his mattress, slid his hand through the seam at one side and pulled out a coil of nylon rope and a sling with snap links at the end, items he had frequently used at the quarry when placing dynamite charges in the cliff face. He also produced a narrow-handled screwdriver and a pair of twelve-inch heavy-gauge wire-cutters which Savary had obtained from a convict who worked in the machine shop. They each arranged their beds with extra clothes, a few books, a pillow to give the appearance of a human form.

'Do you think it will pass?' Savary asked.

'With Lebel? Most nights, he doesn't even look in and I reckon that will be good enough if he does. Now let's get moving. We've got a tight schedule.'

They pulled on their heavy reefer coats, prison issue for working outside in bad weather, and leather and canvas gloves. Brosnan picked up the rope and Savary knelt at the door with a spoon. There was a slight click and he stood up. 'That's it, Martin, let's go.'

They moved outside and closed the door carefully behind them. They stood in the shadows of the wall for a moment, then moved quietly to the end of the landing.

The central hall was illuminated by a single light and music drifted up from the radio in the duty officer's glass office. The roof and the dome were shrouded in darkness. Brosnan climbed on to the rail and scrambled up the steel mesh curtain to the roof of the cell block. He hooked the snap links of his sling into the wire to hold himself secure and took out the wire-cutters.

It took him no more than five minutes to make a hole about three feet across through which he pulled himself. Once on the other side he stepped on to one of the steel support girders. He looked down at Savary, his face pale in the darkness, and beckoned and the Frenchman followed him.

They balanced together on one girder and held on to another. Brosnan hooked a line to the sling around Savary's waist and touched him briefly on the shoulder. There was no need to say anything for they had discussed, in detail, the route and what to expect.

The difficult part came now for the grille he needed to reach was thirty feet up in the darkness and the girder curved out, following the line of the wall. Brosnan slipped his sling around it, fastened the links at his waist and started to climb, bracing himself against the girder, using a well-proven climbing technique.

It was now that his strength and excellent physical condition stood him in good stead. He heaved himself up, inch-by-inch, until he reached his objective, a large ventilation grille.

It was held in place by four screws and he took out his screwdriver, braced himself against the girder and set to work. The screws were brass and came out easily enough. He left the one on the bottom left hand corner partly in position so that the grille swung down, no longer obscuring the entrance, but still held securely.

So far so good. He looked down at Savary,

waved and tugged on the line and the Frenchman secured himself to the girder with his sling and started to climb.

Brosnan kept the tension on the line, giving Savary all the help that he could. It went well enough for a while and then a door clanged far below. Savary, shocked by the unexpected noise, lost his hold and slipped.

Brosnan clenched his teeth and leaned back against the girder, a foot on the wall, and held on, the line cutting into his back and shoulder. Savary hung there, while below, a prison officer crossed the hall and went into the office. There was a rumble of voices, laughter.

Savary swung back against the girder and started to climb again. Finally he reached Brosnan.

They poised there for a few moments and Brosnan whispered, 'Okay, Jacques, you first.'

Savary unhooked himself from the beam, leaned forward, and went headfirst into the shaft. Brosnan coiled the line neatly about his waist and went after him.

Clouds of dry dust filled his nostrils and

he took out the torch and switched it on, the spot travelling ahead of Savary, picking out the dirt-encrusted metal sides of the shaft. The Frenchman started to pull himself along, no room to crawl, and Brosnan followed. Then there was a distinct current of air, a low humming sound far below, and the shaft emerged into a sort of central chamber, the dark mouths of other shafts at intervals around it.

The noise came from a hole about three feet in diameter in the centre of the chamber. Brosnan crouched beside Savary and shone his torch down.

'This is it,' he said. 'I saw the plans for the ventilation system of this place two years ago when I was working with the heating engineer's detail at the hospital. From what I remember, this shaft goes down sixty or seventy feet to the boiler room. How are you doing?'

'Fine,' Savary said. 'Don't worry about me. I haven't felt so good in years.'

Brosnan examined the interior of the shaft with his torch. The circular metal sheets were held in place by steel stays.

'Good foot-holds,' he said. 'If you get tired, just wedge yourself against the sides for a few moments. I'll go first, then if you fall, you can drop on me.'

Savary's teeth gleamed in the darkness. 'Good luck, Martin.'

Brosnan started down, holding the torch in one hand. It was easy enough, far easier than the earlier climb up the girder in the central hall. The hum of the generators increased as he got closer to the bottom of the shaft. There was light down there, shining up through a grille. He braced himself against the sides of the shaft and tried to peer through. All he could see was the boiler room floor. Usually, there was no one on duty at this time of night and if there was, it was likely to be a Trusty anyway. Not that he had much choice.

He flashed his torch up and found Savary poised just above him. 'Hang on,' Brosnan whispered. 'I'm going through.'

He slipped the torch into his pocket, braced himself against the sides, then stamped on the grille with both feet. It buckled, started to give, and at the third attempt, gave way completely and crashed to the floor eight feet below, followed by Brosnan himself.

He got up, shaken but unhurt, and looked about him. The boiler room was in semi-darkness, the only light a small bulb which hung over the dials on the instrument panel on the far wall. Most important of all, there was no one there.

He called up the shaft, 'Okay, Jacques, let's be having you. Just let yourself go.' A moment later he caught the Frenchman as he dropped through.

They moved to the door at once. Brosnan opened it and peered outside. Rain fell heavily, bouncing from the cobbled courtyard.

'The manhole cover is over there,' he said. 'To the right of the hospital entrance. Keep your head down and let's go.'

He kept to the shadows of the wall, working his way round the courtyard, Savary at his heels, until he reached the manhole cover and crouched down. He got the screw-driver out and cleaned the dirt from the iron handles which were set into the cover, but when he heaved, it refused to budge.

'What is it, for God's sake?' For the first time there was panic in Savary's voice.

'Nothing,' Brosnan said. 'Probably hasn't been up in years. I'll fix it, don't worry.'

He worked the screwdriver around the edge of the manhole cover methodically, stifling an insane desire to laugh. There had been a notice on the command board at Khe Sahn. *For those who fight for it, life has a flavour the sheltered never know.* Whoever wrote that had certainly known what he was talking about.

He tried again, exerting all his strength, Savary wrapping his hands around him to assist. The manhole gave suddenly and easily, so that Brosnan lost his balance and they fell together.

The stench was immediate and appalling, accentuated by the freshness of the rain. Savary said, 'Oh, my God, I didn't realise.'

'The only way, Jacques,' Brosnan said. 'Down you go.'

Savary disappeared into darkness and Brosnan followed, descending a short iron ladder, pausing only to slide the manhole cover back into place. When he switched on the torch he found Savary standing in three feet of stinking water and excrement. The Frenchman leaned against the wall and vomited.

He turned, his pale face. 'I can't take much of this, Martin.'

'You don't have to,' Brosnan lied. 'A couple of hundred yards, that's all, I promise you.'

The tunnel was six feet high and very old, the brickwork crumbling, and, as they advanced, the torchlight picked out rats by the dozen, scampering along the ledges on either side. Fifty or sixty yards further on, the tunnel emptied itself into a pool over a concrete apron. It was obviously the main catchment chamber for the entire system, several other tunnels emptying into it.

Brosnan slid down the apron, holding the torch high, and found himself almost chest deep. Savary came after him, lost his balance and went under. Brosnan pulled him up by the collar and the Frenchman surfaced in a dreadful state, his face smeared with filth. He was badly shocked.

Brosnan said, 'Come on, Jacques, keep going. Just keep going.'

He worked his way across the pool and pulled himself up on a concrete ledge, heaving Savary behind him. He followed the ledge and came to an iron ladder, the water from the sewer cascading down beside it for some thirty feet.

They descended the ladder and moved on, negotiating two more before the walkway ended.

'We must be close to the shoreline now,' Brosnan said. 'It can't be much further.'

He eased himself down into the water and Savary followed him. The water rose higher and higher as Brosnan advanced. There was a ground swell now and the stench was not so apparent; then suddenly, a yard or two ahead, the tunnel simply disappeared.

Savary said, 'Now what?'

'The outfall must be under the surface,' Brosnan said. 'I hadn't counted on that.'

'So what do we do?'

'Swim for it.'

'Under water?' The Frenchman shook his head. 'I don't think I can.'

Brosnan gave him the torch. 'Hang on to this and I'll take a look.'

He took a couple of deep breaths, went under and swam forward, sliding against the roof of the tunnel. Ten feet, fifteen, twenty and he was through and surfaced immediately in a channel amongst rocks at the foot of the cliffs.

It was dark, rain falling, a heavy swell running. He floated there for a moment, took a breath and went down into the mouth of the tunnel again. The return journey was more difficult, but he surfaced beside Savary a few moments later and braced himself against the tunnel wall, gasping for breath.

'Bad?' Savary asked.

'Twenty feet, Jacques, that's all and you're out.'

'I can't,' Savary said.

Brosnan was untying the line from about his waist and he snapped it to the link on Savary's sling. 'You want to go back?'

'No, I'd rather die.'

'Good. I'm going to swim out again now. When you're ready, pull twice on the line and hold your breath. I'll haul you through.'

He didn't give Savary time to think about it, simply dived under the water again and swam back along the tunnel. He surfaced and floated for a moment in the pool, then found that his feet could touch bottom and that it was no more than five feet deep. He pulled in the slack on the line until it was tight and waited. The tugs, when they came, were quite distinct. He started to haul in with all his strength, pulling steadily, never stopping until Savary surfaced beside him, gasping for air.

Brosnan held him for a moment, then said, 'Okay, let's get out of here.' Together they waded out of the water and scrambled up the hillside, the walls of Belle Isle towering into the night above them.

Lightning flickered on the far horizon of things as they crouched at the door of the store while Savary worked the lock. Finally, it clicked open. They moved inside, Brosnan closed the door and switched on the light.

'All right?' he said to Savary.

The Frenchman nodded, nervous, excited. The sea had washed the filth from his body and he seemed to have recovered his spirits. 'We beat the bastards, eh, Martin?'

'Not yet,' Brosnan told him. 'Get ready, quick as you like. Two lifejackets, remember, not one. We'll need all the flotation we can get out there.'

Five minutes later, they were ready. Brosnan took the homing device Devlin had given him, activated it, then strapped it to one of his lifejackets.

He said to Savary, 'Let's go,' switched off the light, opened the door and they left.

The rain hammered down and when the sheet lightning crackled, they saw waves lashing into foam stretching as far as the eye could see. They descended the cliffs, following the course of a ravine that finally emptied itself into the water.

The funeral rock towered into the night above their heads and Savary looked up at it. 'Maybe we're just saving Lebel a job.'

Brosnan uncoiled the line and secured it, first to Savary's sling and then to his own, leaving an umbilical cord perhaps six feet long between them.

'Together, or not at all?' Savary said.

'Exactly.'

They shook hands, then made their way to a ledge on the outer reaches of the rocks where the sea roared by. Brosnan turned enquiringly, Savary nodded and they jumped, committing themselves to the waters of the Mill Race.

They were carried along at a terrific rate, for the current was running at nine or ten knots. Strangely enough, it didn't seem particularly cold at first, but that would come later. The clothing helped, of course, and the heavy reefer coats.

There was no real sense of passing time, just the sea and the roaring and the tug of the line at Brosnan's waist as Savary pulled at it. Occasionally lightning flickered again, but all it illuminated was the sea, a waste of broken water in which they were quite alone.

After fifteen or twenty minutes Brosnan

did begin to feel the cold. He wondered how Savary was doing, tugged on the line, and, a moment later, got a response. Belle Isle was so far back in the darkness that there seemed no longer any need to fear detection and he switched on the light on his lifejacket. A moment later Savary did the same, and they continued on, dipping over the waves like two will-o'-the-wisps in the darkness.

On the bridge of the trawler, Anne-Marie and Devlin stood at the rail as the ship plunged into the waves. They both wore oilskin coats and sou'westers and water streamed from them.

As lightning flickered, illuminating the size of the seas breaking, the white carpet of foam, Devlin said desperately, 'This is no good – no good at all.'

And then Jean-Paul leaned out of the wheelhouse, his voice full of excitement. 'We've got them!' he cried exultantly.

Anne-Marie and Devlin hurried into the wheelhouse. Jean-Paul and Claude bent over the blue box on the chart table. Lines moved across the screen, there was a rythmic pinging sound and the red illuminated figures on the digital read-out altered with incredible rapidity and finally stopped.

Jean-Paul made a quick calculation. 'That's it,' he said to old Marcel at the wheel. 'They're about a mile to the south-west. Steer two-four-two.' As they altered course he said to Devlin, 'When the regular beat of that signal becomes continuous and high-pitched, we're there.'

Anne-Marie held Devlin's hand and together they stood there watching the screen.

Brosnan was cold and his face and eyes were sore from the salt water. He was tired, completely at the end of his tether. When Savary's light went out, he tugged on the line, but got no response, and when he tried to haul the Frenchman in to him, realised he simply didn't have the strength.

A few moments later, the light on his own lifejacket went out. So that was it then. Now it had come, it didn't seem to matter. He floated, eyes closed, head back and was lifted high on the crest of a wave. He opened his eyes and saw the lights of a ship to the right of him.

It was enough. As he went down into a trough, he opened his mouth and yelled at the top of his lungs, and yet in the roaring of the sea, he couldn't even hear it himself.

He lifted on another wave, Savary trailing behind him. The ship was closer now, close enough for him to see that it was a trawler, her lines plain in her deck lights. He shouted and waved, all to no purpose, went down again, then suddenly remembered Devlin's parting present at the prison, the signalling ball.

He felt for it in his right hand pocket, got it out, desperately clutching it in numb fingers, and tore at the plastic covering with his teeth. The phosphorescence dazzled him with its beauty, shining in the night like a glow worm, and he cupped it in his right palm and held it aloft.

It was big Claude who caught sight of the

light to port and ran to the wheelhouse instantly. Marcel cut back the engines and brought the trawler round, curving in. Devlin and Anne-Marie ran to the port rail where Jean-Paul and Claude were throwing a boarding net over the side.

'What do you think?' Devlin demanded.

'It's got to be them. Must be,' Jean-Paul said savagely.

He took the spotlight Claude passed him, switched it on and played it across the water.

'Nothing!' Anne-Marie said. 'Not a damn thing!'

And then Brosnan rose high on the crest of a wave, arm raised, Savary trailing behind him.

11

Brosnan coughed as the whiskey caught at the back of his throat. He looked up at Devlin, sitting on the edge of the bunk. 'Bushmills?' he asked hoarsely.

'What else? I brought the bottle specially. And now that you're back in the land of the living, there's someone to see you. I'll see how Savary's getting on.'

He moved out of the way and Anne-Marie sat down. She still wore the oilskin and pushed damp hair back from her forehead in an inimitable gesture.

'Here we are again then,' Brosnan said.

'So it would appear.' She reached across and touched his face briefly. 'You're still cold.'

'Frozen to the bone. I'll have nightmares

about the Mill Race for the rest of my life. How's Jacques?'

'Dr Cresson is working on him in the next cabin.'

'You mean he's still unconscious?'

'I'm afraid so.'

Brosnan sat up, pulling the blanket around him. 'Show me.'

She led the way to the next cabin. Jacques Savary lay on the bunk swathed in blankets, his face white and shrunken, eyes closed. Jean-Paul watched anxiously with Devlin while the doctor worked over his father.

'He's cold,' he said. 'Too cold. At his age . . .' He filled a hypodermic and injected the contents into Savary's right forearm. 'The most powerful stimulant I dare use.' He turned to Jean-Paul. 'The pulse is very weak. He needs hospitalization as soon as possible.'

'Who in the hell says so,' said Jacques Savary in a low voice.

His eyes were open, he smiled weakly, and Jean-Paul seized his hand and dropped to one knee beside the bunk. 'What were you trying to do, scare the hell out of me?'

'Something like that.' Savary's eyes sought Brosnan and found him. 'We showed the bastards, eh?'

'Definitely,' Brosnan said.

Cresson said, 'Everybody out. He needs sleep.'

Savary grabbed Jean-Paul's coat as he got up. 'I'm not going back to that place, not ever. You understand?'

'Sure, papa.'

'So now we're out, the most important thing is dumping those bodies in the right place. Get on with that and never mind about me. Lots of time to sleep later.'

Brosnan went back into the other cabin, followed by Devlin and Anne-Marie. He sat on the bunk. 'What happens now?'

'The Captain is going to land us at St Denise about an hour from now. Jean-Paul has his own plans for his father. We three will move on to Anne-Marie's farm in the hills above Nice.'

'And Barry?'

'Plenty of time for him when you've rested a few days. Now I suggest you lie down again and get a little shut-eye before we land.'

'He's right, Martin,' Anne-Marie said. 'We'll leave you for a while.'

They went out. Brosnan pulled the blanket around him, lay back and closed his eyes, but there was no comfort there, simply a distorted pattern of images, waves breaking in the darkness. His eyes were sore from the salt. But he was free, that was the amazing thing. Free again after four years in one of the grimmest prisons in Europe and the strange thing was, the thought had no effect on him at all.

He slept for a short while in the end, came awake suddenly and realised that the trawler had virtually stopped. He lay there for a moment thinking about it, then got up and dressed in the clothes which had been provided, jeans, a heavy fisherman's sweater and a reefer coat.

When he went out on deck it was still raining, but the sea was calmer as they rode in the lee of the shore. Anne-Marie stood at the rail watching while Devlin and Jean-Paul lowered one of the corpses over the side to Claude in an inflatable. The other lay on the deck on its back. The face was bound with a cloth to mask the mutilation and it had been dressed in Brosnan's prison uniform and reefer coat and the two lifejackets.

'Your other self.' Devlin knelt down and pushed up the sleeve, baring the tattooed prison number.

'You think of everything,' Brosnan said.

'Jean-Paul, not me. I can see why that boy is such a successful crook.'

They picked up the corpse between them and lowered it over the side to Claude and Jean-Paul, who had joined him. Brosnan said, 'Roped together, don't forget that. The authentic touch.'

'I will.' Jean-Paul started the outboard and turned the inflatable towards the shore.

The three of them leaned on the rail and watched it go. 'And how does it feel attending your own funeral?'

'Like Lazarus, risen again,' Brosnan told him. 'Washed clean.'

'What for?' Anne-Marie said. 'A reprise of the old life? Or a fresh start?'

'After I've dealt with Frank Barry, perhaps.'

She shook her head. 'There's the smell of

death on you, Martin, do you know that? You'll never change.'

She turned from the rail and went below. Brosnan said, 'What's wrong with her?'

'Well, if you don't know, son, I can't tell you,' Liam Devlin said.

There was considerable activity on the fish dock at St Denise as more than twenty trawlers unloaded their catch. Jacques Savary sat with Cresson in the back of a black BMW limousine. He looked much more his usual self, wore a cashmere sweater and expensive sports jacket. Jean-Paul leaned in to tuck a travelling rug around his father's knees.

Brosnan, Devlin and Anne-Marie stood watching. As Jean-Paul stepped back, Brosnan leaned in the car and took Savary's hand. 'Maybe we can do it again some time?'

Savary held his hand for a moment and then, in an excess of emotion, pulled Brosnan close and embraced him.

Brosnan turned away and Jean-Paul took his hand, his face serious in the yellow light of the lamp bracketed to the wall of the warehouse above their heads.

'To repay what you have done is an impossibility, but just remember this. We of the Union Corse can accomplish most things.' He took out his wallet, extracted a card and passed it across. 'My private numbers.' He smiled crookedly. 'All four of them. If there is ever anything you need and I do mean anything . . .'

He embraced Brosnan, holding him for a moment, shook hands with Devlin and Anne-Marie, got into the BMW and nodded to Claude who had the wheel. The big limousine moved away along the fish quay.

Brosnan watched it go, suddenly tired, at the end of things in some strange way. He turned to Devlin and Anne-Marie. 'Now what?'

Anne-Marie took his arm. 'Come on, soldier, from the looks of you I'd say you need to sleep for about a week.'

She took the wheel of the Citroen hire car, Devlin sat beside her leaving Brosnan on his own in the rear. 'How long?' he asked us she drove away.

'This time in the morning, three hours if we're lucky. Go to sleep.'

Brosnan closed his eyes, leaning back against the seat. At first there was only the Mill Race, the waters passing over him, his head filled with the stink of it, and then, suddenly, darkness.

It was just after six o'clock, dawn touching the horizon with light, as Pierre Gaudier left his cabin in the sand dunes a mile outside St Denise. A packer on the day shift at the fish quay, he always started the day at first light, scavenging the beach before anyone else got down.

The handcart he pushed in front of him sported old automobile tyres which moved well over the wet sand and he paused every so often to pick up driftwood. When his cart was almost full, he was at the end of the beach where the final kick of the Mill Race hammered in across jagged black rocks. He paused to light a cigarette before turning back and suddenly noticed a flash of orange in the rocks up ahead. He flicked his match away and walked forward.

One of the bodies was draped across a rock, the other floated beside it in a pool, and the waves broke across both of them constantly. Gaudier crossed himself, then waded into the water, caught hold of the body in the pool and tried to pull it back to the beach. It was only then that he became aware of the line that held them together.

He scrambled up to the body on the rocks, fumbled at the line to untie it and immediately saw two things: the legend, *Department of Correction – Belle Isle* stamped on the lifejacket, and the prison number stencilled in white across the back of the reefer coat.

'Holy Mother of God,' Gaudier said, crossing himself again, and tried to turn the corpse over.

He saw the face then, or what was left of it and staggered back in horror, losing his balance and falling into the pool beside the other body. He pushed it away from him with a hoarse cry, scrambled out of the water and ran back along the beach to St Denise.

It was just after nine o'clock and Pierre Lebel sat in the ante-room of the governor's office at Belle Isle, totally crushed. What had happened was so unbelievable that he had been unable to take it in. His discovery of the empty cell on the upper landing at seven o'clock had coincided with the phone call from the Chief of Police in St Denise to the Governor.

How it had happened, how Savary and Brosnan had managed to achieve the impossible, was not relevant now. The only important thing was the consequences. For Lebel, they could only lead in one direction; instant dismissal with twenty-five years of service down the drain and no pension.

The door opened and the Governor beckoned to him. Lebel went in and stood at the desk while the Governor lit a cigar and went to the window and peered out. What he said next was a total surprise.

'To enter such a sea as was running last night. Quite incredible.' He shook his head. 'Magnificent idiots, that's what they were, Lebel. Why would they do such a thing, risk everything?'

Lebel amazed himself by saying, 'To get off the rock, sir.'

The Governor nodded, still looking out to sea. 'Yes, well we'd all like to do that, wouldn't we?'

There was a knock at the door and the Chief Officer appeared. 'The bodies have arrived from St Denise, sir.'

'Good,' said the Governor. 'We'll take a look, shall, we?'

It was cold in the mortuary, bitterly cold, and the two bodies dripped seawater as they lay on the slabs, still wearing the clothes and life-jackets. The Governor pushed back the sleeve of first one corpse and then the other and examined the tattooed numbers. He lifted the sheers to peer at the faces and replaced them hurriedly.

'So, that's what the Mill Race and those rocks at St Denise do to a man.' He turned to the Chief Officer. 'Pity we can't show photos to every convict in the place.'

'Yes, sir.' The Chief Officer hesitated. 'What happens now, sir?'

'I've spoken to the Minister of Justice in Paris. The story will be released to the press. No reason not to. All it proves is what we've known all along. That nobody escapes from Belle Isle.'

'And the bodies, sir?'

'Disposed of in the usual way, exactly according to regulations, and today. I don't want any nonsense with relatives trying to claim them, particularly that son of Savary's. He's as big a crook as his father was.' He turned to Lebel. 'As for you, taking all the circumstances into consideration, I don't think you were really to blame for any of this. On the other hand, I must do something, if only for the record, so I'll fine you a month's salary.'

Lebel, overcome with joy, could hardly speak. 'Thank you, sir,' he stammered.

The Governor went out and the Chief Officer said, 'You're a lucky man, Pierre.'

'You don't have to tell me,' Lebel said fervently.

'Just as I don't have to remind you you've still got the funeral detail, so get on with it.'

He went out. Lebel turned and found old Jean, the mortuary orderly, standing between the two slabs. 'Jacques Savary and Brosnan, eh?' He shook his head. 'Who'd have thought it.'

The orderly leaned down and examined the number on the forearm of the body on his right, then turned to the other. 'Strange,' he said.

'What is?'

'Savary's number. The seven is done the way the English do it.'

Lebel put on his reading glasses, raised the arm and checked the number. The old man was right. The figure seven was plain, no line across the stem in the continental manner.

The old man gazed at him searchingly. 'Maybe the tattooist made a mistake?'

Lebel put his glasses away and said quietly, 'Bag them up, Jean, now. And this one, we do together. Okay?'

The old man smiled and turned and shuffled away to his store.

They took them out through the main gate and pushed the hand cart up the winding road to the funeral rock. Lebel got the necessary weights from the store and they threaded them through the straps, taking one body each, not speaking.

It was a fine day, no rain now, only the sea stretching to a grey horizon where the sun was trying to come through. They pushed the cart to the outer edge of the rock, tipped it and slid both bodies off together. They plunged into the swirling waters below and disappeared instantly.

Old Jean said, 'The only way anyone gets off Belle Isle.'

He turned and walked away, pushing the cart in front of him. Lebel said, 'That's right,' and then he added softly, 'and good luck, you bastards, wherever you are.'

Ferguson was working at his desk at Cavendish Place when the phone rang.

Harry Fox said, 'Bad news, sir, just over the wire from Paris. Not had time to make the papers yet. Brosnan and Savary were drowned last night trying to escape from Belle Isle.'

Ferguson put down his pen. 'Are you sure about this, Harry?'

'No doubt about it, sir. The bodies were found on the beach outside a place called St Denise this morning.'

'So that's that,' Ferguson said.

'Afraid so, sir. Any word from Devlin?'

'Not a thing.'

'I should think he'll probably phone in any time now, sir, in view of what's happened.'

'Very probably. Carry on, Harry. I'll see you later.'

Ferguson replaced the receiver and sat there

brooding for a moment, then got to his feet and went and stood at the window.

'Damn you, Brosnan,' he whispered. 'Why couldn't you have waited?'

Nikolai Romanov's plane had been delayed for fourteen hours in Berlin because of fog and he didn't arrive at Charles de Gaulle Airport until noon. He drove straight to the Soviet Embassy and was taking off his overcoat when Irana Vronsky came in with a cup of coffee.

She was a handsome, full-bodied woman of thirty-two with calm eyes, black hair tied back with a velvet bow. The neat grey skirt, white silk blouse, dark stockings and good shoes only accentuated her undeniable attractiveness.

She had been Romanov's secretary for eight years and he had seduced her within a month of her taking up the appointment. She was totally devoted to him, brushed aside his affairs with other women as being of no consequence. She was the one certainty in his life and was content.

There was nothing that went on in the office that she was not fully conversant with and he had already spoken to her on the telephone the previous night.

'A bad flight, Colonel?' she always addressed him formally in the office.

'I prefer to forget the entire experience. That airport really is appalling, but never mind that now. Has Barry been in touch again?'

'Just over an hour ago. He said he'd ring back.'

'And gave no explanation why he didn't make the rendezvous with the Northern Fleet trawler?'

'None, Colonel.'

'Have you checked the British papers?'

She nodded. 'Not a word of anything remotely similar to what Barry intended. There is an urgent communication from our London Embassy, marked for your eyes only, Code Three. Perhaps that contains the relevant information.'

'Let's go and see.'

Romanov went out. She followed him

down to the Coding Room and went and got the relevant tape and the photos. The operator inserted it into the machine, Romanov keyed it to his personal code. The machine chattered briefly, the decoded information appeared on a print-out sheet which Irana tore off and handed to him.

The message gave Romanov the fullest of briefings on the Brosnan affair and also contained a full profile of Devlin and Anne-Marie Audin, illustrated by the photos he held in his hand.

He handed the lot to Irana. 'What do you make of that?'

She read the report and frowned. 'But there's something about this in the latest edition of the morning paper, Colonel.'

'Are you sure?'

'I'll show you.' They went back along the corridor to her office which was next to his. The Paris morning papers were on her desk. She hunted through them and finally said triumphantly, 'There you are. Stop Press. Prisoners drowned trying to escape from Belle Isle prison. Martin Brosnan and Jacques Savary.'

Romanov took the paper from her, sat on the edge of the desk and read it. 'This man, Savary, was quite a character,' he said, 'I thought his name sounded familiar.'

'And Brosnan must have been a handful too,' she said.

'Yes, it could have developed into a troublesome situation if it had come to anything.'

The phone rang on her desk. She picked it up, spoke briefly, then turned to Romanov. 'Barry.'

Romanov took the phone and didn't waste any time. 'You're in Paris?'

'So it would appear,' Barry said cheerfully.

'My apartment in thirty minutes,' Romanov said, and put down the phone.

Barry stood at the rail of the terrace of the apartment in the Boulevard St Germain and looked out across the river. 'They really do you very well, your people,' he said, as Romanov came through the open window and handed him a Scotch and soda.

'Never mind that sort of nonsense.

Explanations, Frank, that's what I want. What went wrong over there?'

'Not a thing.' Barry helped himself to a cigarette and sat down in a wicker chair. 'Couldn't have gone better.'

Romanov was astonished. 'You mean you actually did the job? But that's not possible. There hasn't been a word in the English newspapers.'

'Security clampdown,' Barry said. 'Which makes sense if you think of it. Anyway, all that's important is that I do have that rocket pod.'

'Then why didn't you make the rendezvous with the Northern Fleet trawler?'

Barry chuckled. 'Nikolai, this may come as a shock in view of our long relationship, but I don't trust your lot and it occurred to me that if I once boarded that trawler with that valuable piece of merchandise, I might well never get off again. You do follow me?'

'Nonsense.' Romanov was genuinely angry. 'Haven't I always treated you fairly? When have I ever let you down?'

'Not you, old son, the sods back at headquarters I'm thinking of,' Barry said. 'This one is big, Nikolai. The biggest thing you've ever handled. You said that yourself. Maybe too big.'

Romanov took a deep breath. 'What do you want?'

'A plane ready and waiting whenever I need it. A Cessna will do. I'll fly her myself, of course.'

'Where to?'

'Back to the Lake District. No problem. I'll find some suitable abandoned strip near where I want to be. I'll leave the plane there.'

'And what about British Air Traffic Control? They like to know who's flying in their air space.'

'Oh, I'll be long gone by the time they discover where I put down.'

Romanov nodded reluctantly. 'All right. There's a small aero club near Croix just outside Paris. We've found it useful in certain instances in the past. I'll see a suitable plane is ready and waiting for you. Now, what other nasty surprises have you in store for me?'

'Number one, the exchange takes place in Ireland, south of the border, of course.' Romanov started to explode and Barry shook his head. 'I won't have it any other way. Anything I've ever done can be construed as political, so I can't be extradited. I'm safe there. An old aunt of mine has an estate ten miles outside Cork on the coast. Very suitable place to do business. I'll let you have details, naturally.'

Romanov put up a hand. 'I wouldn't dream of disagreeing. Just tell me the rest and let's get it over with.'

'Two million,' Barry said. 'That's what it's going to cost you.'

Romanov looked horrified. 'Two million. You must be crazy.'

'No, just thinking of retiring. I'm not getting any younger, old son.' There was a heavy silence. He said, 'I have got it, Nikolai, believe me. No matter how much of a security clamp-down exists, your contacts in West Germany should be able to confirm what happened for you.'

'True.' Romanov nodded. 'I'm not able to

speak on the money though. I'll have to consult Moscow. I'll let you know.'

'By tomorrow morning,' Barry said. 'I don't want to hang about.'

Romanov said wearily. 'You're a bastard all the way through, Frank. I've always treated you fair and you do this to me. I should have known.'

Barry helped himself to another whisky. 'You learn something new every day.'

Romanov went into the living room and returned with the transcript of the message from London. 'Better read that.'

Barry started to work his way through and stopped smiling. 'Well, would you look at that now?' he whispered.

Romanov said, 'Have you seen the Paris papers this morning?'

'No, should I have done?'

Romanov tossed a newspaper across. 'Noon edition. Makes interesting reading.'

The story was there in full, together with photos of Savary and Brosnan. Barry read it through quickly. 'Brosnan dead? That doesn't seem possible.'

'It comes to us all.'

'Not Martin Brosnan. You didn't know him like I did. Tried to kill me once.'

'What for?'

'Oh, let's say he didn't approve of the way I carried on our particular war at that time.'

Romanov shrugged. 'Old history, none of which has any relevance now that he's dead.'

'But Devlin isn't,' Barry said.

Romanov frowned. 'You think he's a threat?'

'He could give the Devil points, that one.' Barry got up and walked to the rail. 'I wonder what he's up to right now, or what's more to the point, where is he?'

'Somewhere in the area of St Denise last night, waiting to receive Brosnan, must have been,' Romanov said.

'That's right and the Audin girl with him. So where are they now?'

'Back in Paris, perhaps.'

'Easy enough to find out. She must be in the phone book.'

* * *

Five minutes later, the phone rang in Anne-Marie's Paris apartment. Her daily maid, who was in the kitchen, dried her hands and went to answer it.

The voice at the other end spoke excellent French with a slight accent. 'Mademoiselle Audin?'

'No, monsieur, she isn't here. Who's speaking?'

'*Paris-Match*,' Barry lied smoothly. 'It's important I get hold of her. Do you know where she is?'

'But of course, monsieur. She phoned me here only an hour ago to say that she would be spending a few days on her farm.'

'Farm?' Barry laughed warmly. 'Sounds very unlike Anne-Marie.'

'Oh, it's just a small place, monsieur, near Vence in the hills above Nice. A village called St Martin. One old shepherd, a few sheep. Madermoiselle Audin uses it to get away from things. That's why she isn't on the telephone there.'

The maid was the kind of woman who obviously couldn't stop talking and Barry cut her off. 'Never mind,' he said. 'I'll wait till she gets back,' and he hung up.

'So what do you intend to do?' Romanov demanded.

'I think I'll take a plane down to Nice. After all, it only takes an hour. Scout this place of hers out. See if she's got Devlin there with her.'

'Why not let it go, Frank? As soon as I get your money confirmed from Moscow, you can be away. Why bother with this Devlin?'

'Old scores to settle there,' Barry said, 'and in any case, curiosity was always my besetting sin. You might say I have a compulsion to find out what the bastard's up to.'

'Have it your own way,' Romanov said wearily.

'I usually do, hadn't you noticed? One thing you can do is give me an address in Nice where I can pick up a little muscle if I need it. Nothing fancy, no nonsense about using their brains. Fist and boot men, that's what I want. Can you handle that?'

Romanov nodded. 'Yes, as it happens we have excellent connections in Nice. I can give you a suitable address.'

'Great, I knew I could rely on you. I'll be in touch as soon as I get back.' He grinned and slapped Romanov on the shoulder. 'Cheer up, old son. It might never happen.'

12

The small farm high on the hill above St Martin looked rather medieval, with a tower at one end, the roof covered in red pantiles, faded by the sun. Devlin looked down to the village, far below in the valley, the single ribbon of road that zig-zagged up the hill to the farm. The heat of the afternoon sun was warm on his back and he stretched lazily, turned back to the farm and went into the kitchen.

Anne-Marie stood at the wood stove, preparing a stew. She wore a tweed cap, open-necked shirt and overalls tucked into boots.

'How do you like it?' she demanded.

'A pleasant enough place. A man could be happy here or go stark, raving mad.' She laughed and he said, 'What about Martin?'

'Still fast asleep when I looked in.' She put

the pan on the stove. 'I'd like to have taken a picture, but I didn't want to risk waking him. He looked different.'

'How different?'

'I don't quite know how to put it. Very young.'

Devlin lit a cigarette and sat down, shaking his head. 'Sure and you're kidding yourself there, girl dear. There are no young men, not in Martin's generation or yours, for that matter. All the hopes, all the aspirations disappeared a long time ago, swallowed up by the swamp of Vietnam and the brickfields and back alleys of Ulster.'

She turned, wiping her hands on a cloth, and said gravely, 'Yes, I'm afraid you're probably right. The belief that life is a romantic affair is an essential ingredient missing in our generation. We learned, too young, that dishonesty is necessary for survival.'

'What's that, the thought for today?'

Brosnan stood in the doorway wearing a woollen shirt and jeans. He badly needed a shave and his hair, still almost shoulder length, was tousled.

Anne-Marie said, 'You look like a . . .'

She searched for words and he laughed. 'Like what? A thoroughly dangerous convict on the run?'

'No chance.' Devlin threw a newspaper across to him. 'Anne-Marie's been down to the village store. Noon edition just in from Nice. You're dead, old son, and that's official.'

Brosnan read the item through and showed no particular emotion. Anne-Marie said, 'Don't you feel anything? Anything at all?'

'Not really.' He ran his hands over his face. 'What I could do with is some fresh air and a sense of space. How about a look over this sheep farm of yours?'

She turned to Devlin. He nodded, 'Go on, get out of it, the both of you. I'll make myself a cup of tea and read a book or something.'

Brosnan and Anne-Marie went outside and he looked up towards the high hills, shielding his eyes from the sun. 'Those sheep up there?'

'That's right. Spanish mountain sheep.'

'A hell of a pull up those slopes to reach them.'

'Oh, old Louis, that's my shepherd, doesn't mind. He's been doing it all his life. I'm a little more up-to-date myself though.'

She opened the barn door and Brosnan saw a motorcycle on its stand. 'You mean you go up there on that?'

'That's what it's made for. It's Spanish as well. Montesa dirt bike. They'll do half a mile an hour if you want over rough ground in bottom gear. On the other hand, I usually do go rather faster than that.'

'Okay,' Brosnan said. 'Show me.'

'If you like.'

She pushed the bike off its stand, wheeled it outside and mounted, kick-starting expertly. The engine roared into life and he climbed on the pillion and put his hands round her waist.

'Now, let's see what you can do.'

She let in the clutch and they moved away.

The Montesa did everything she said it would, taking the slopes with a satisfying growl as she opened the throttle. When they ran out of track, she took to the hillside, climbing higher and higher until they went over a ridge and found sheep before them, scattered across the parched grass, grazing peacefully.

Finally, she braked to a halt beside a small whitewashed cottage with a roof of red pantiles in a slight depression surrounded by olive trees. To one side a wild and beautiful ravine dropped steeply.

'Old Louis uses this as a base when he's up here. Sometimes stays for weeks. He doesn't like it down there.' She nodded to the valley, far below, St Martin drowning in the late afternoon heat.

'I know what he means,' Brosnan said.

She tried the door and they went in. There was a living room and kitchen combined and a bedroom. The floors were stone flagged, the walls crudely plastered, but inside it was cool and dark as it was intended to be.

'He must be further up,' she said.

She lifted the wooden lid of a water cooler, took out a bottle of white wine and found two glasses. They went back outside and sat on the bench against the wall. From somewhere lower down there was the hollow jangle of a bell, remote, far away.

'That's the oldest ram, Hercules,' she said. 'Leader of the pack or should I say the flock?'

She filled his glass and her own and stood there, looking down at the valley. 'My favourite time of day. Everything seems to hang fire.'

She turned briefly to him and smiled and he realised, with a sense of discovery and as if it was the first time, that she was beautiful.

'People lived here once,' he said. 'In another world. Now they don't. Some of that lingers on. I suppose that's what your old Louis is trying to recapture.'

She sat down on the grass in front of him, ankles crossed. 'What happens now, Martin?'

'To us, you mean?'

She shook her head with a kind of impatience. 'No, to you.'

'Well, first there's Frank Barry to take care of. The object of the exercise, after all.'

She shook her head. 'Let him go, Martin. There's no profit in it. He's a walking dead man. Next week or next year.' She shrugged. 'Somewhere, someone's waiting for him. He must know that himself.'

'Very probably, but I'd prefer to be that someone myself.' Brosnan was quite calm, no evidence of emotion on his face. 'This is personal, but then you know that?'

'Norah?' She shook her head. 'You used to talk about her a lot, remember? From the sound of her, the last person to want you to pursue this thing.'

'Perhaps,' Brosnan said, 'but then Norah was always too good for this life. She never made that most important discovery of all.'

'And what would that be?'

'That it's not just a matter of the bastards like Frank Barry. Most people let you down, one way or the other, in the end. A fact of life.' There was an edge of bitterness in his voice when he said that.

She said, 'Like me, you mean, or Liam or Jean-Paul?' She put her glass down carefully, trying to control her anger. 'And what about Martin Brosnan, who hauled an old man out of Belle Isle with him when it would have been a damn sight easier to do it on his own?'

'I owed him,' Brosnan said. 'We shared a cell for four years. He sustained me with his wit and his humour and his wisdom.' He laughed harshly. 'That's ironic, isn't it? A gangster who's spent most of his life on the wrong side of the law and still he has real virtues.'

She got up and walked to the edge of the ravine and looked down into the valley again. When she turned, she was calmer. 'All right, let's move on from Frank Barry. After that, what happens?'

'I don't know,' he said. 'Ireland, I suppose. The only place left where I'm safe.'

'Back to that struggle of yours that was so important? My life for Ireland. Thompson guns by night and never wanting it to stop?'

'The only game we've got, you mean? When I picked up a rifle that night in Belfast, that first night, I was trying to stop people killing other people. Afterwards, I found myself on a course there was no turning back from. Remember what Yeats said? Too long a sacrifice can make a stone of the heart.' He shook his head. 'Too much blood, my love, too many dead. Nothing's worth that. No more causes for me.'

'So what will you do?'

'The Brosnans came from Kerry, did I ever tell you that? I bought a farm there a few years ago. Sheep mostly, just like this place.' He laughed. 'I like sheep. They don't take life too seriously.'

'So you'd like to go back there?'

'It's quite a place. Sea and mountains, green grass, soft rain, fuchsia growing in the hedges, glowing in the evening. *Deorini Dei* – the Tears of God, they call it.' He laughed softly. 'And the prettiest girls in all Ireland.'

He had stood to stretch himself and found her watching him, the shadow of pain in her eyes. He moved close and reached for her hand. 'You'd fit into the scene admirably.'

He pulled her to him and kissed her on the mouth. Her lips were soft and dry and he was trembling slightly, his stomach hollow with excitement. For a moment, she responded, then she took a deep shuddering breath and pushed him away.

'No, Martin, I'm not starting that again. You see, in spite of what you've said, I don't think you've changed. I think you'll always be the Movement's official undertaker. Now let's go.'

She turned and walked back to the motorcycle. Frank Barry alighted from the Paris plane at Nice airport at four-thirty. He picked up a Peugeot from one of the hire firms, checked on the location of St Martin and drove straight there. It only took him an hour. A drink at one of the village's two cafes and a talkative waiter gave him the location of Anne-Marie Audin's farm. By six o'clock he was crouched behind a wall in an olive grove on the other side of the valley, examining the farm through binoculars.

The only sign of life was the smoke from one of the chimneys rising in a straight line in the still air. He lit a cigarette and waited. About fifteen minutes later, the door opened and Liam Devlin strolled into the yard.

'Well now,' Barry said softly. 'Would you look at that?'

He became aware of a humming sound

somewhere in the distance, realised that it was an engine moving closer, swept the hillside above the farmhouse with his binoculars and found the motorcycle.

It looked like two men at first glance, Anne-Marie with the peak of her cap low over her eyes and he couldn't make out the face of the man behind. The motorcycle entered the yard and came to a halt. As Devlin moved towards them, Anne-Marie took off her cap, shaking her hair down and Brosnan paused to light a cigarette, giving Barry a clear look at his face.

Barry laughed, a feeling of intense pleasure coursing through him that he couldn't explain, even to himself. 'God save us, Martin,' he said softly, 'but you've done it again, you bastard.'

The three of them went into the house. Barry waited for a while, then got up and walked back down the track to where he had left the Peugeot.

'What's our next move?' Brosnan asked Devlin.

It was after dinner and they sat in the lamplight by the fire smoking. Through the half-open door Anne-Marie could be heard working in the kitchen.

'There is only one possible move,' Devlin said. 'Barry's KGB contact in Paris, this fella Romanov.'

'We can't exactly go knocking at the door of the Soviet Embassy.'

'No need. Ferguson supplied me with both his town and country address. He has an apartment on the Boulevard St Germain.'

'That's it, then,' Brosnan said. 'We start for Paris tomorrow.'

Anne-Marie walked in with tea and coffee on a tray in time to hear his words and Devlin's reply, 'Jesus, Martin, would you give us time to catch our breath?'

'I don't see any point in hanging about,' Brosnan told him.

'He can't wait to get to the funeral, you see,' Anne-Marie said and went back into the kitchen.

Devlin said, 'Since there's no help for it, I'd better get you tooled up.'

He went out. Brosnan poured the tea and drank it with conscious pleasure, a luxury denied him on Belle Isle. He was pouring a second cup when Devlin returned with a small suitcase which he placed on the table and opened.

'A parting gift from Jean-Paul Savary. I didn't bring any hardware through from London with me. Couldn't take a chance on the Customs.'

There were two Brownings, a short-barrelled Smith and Wesson revolver and a sinister looking Mauser with a bulbous silencer.

'Very interesting,' Brosnan said, and picked up the Mauser.

'That takes me back,' Devlin told him. 'Model 1932. Specially developed for German counter-intelligence operatives. Ten-round magazine.'

Brosnan reached in the case and took out a sleeveless jerkin whose nylon surface gleamed in the lamp light. 'Flak jacket?'

'What we call the up-market model for the man who has everything,' Devlin told him.

'Manufactured by the Wilkinson Sword Company. Nylon and titanium. Jean-Paul tells me they can stop a .44 magnum bullet at point-blank range.'

'Very impressive,' Anne-Marie said from the doorway. 'You're going to war again then?'

Brosnan said evenly, 'I think I'll get some sleep now. Let's make an early start in the morning.'

'All right,' Devlin said.

Brosnan brushed past Anne-Marie without speaking to her. After he had gone, she came to the table, shut the lid of the case angrily and sat down.

'I told you not to try and make him into something he isn't,' Devlin said.

She shook her head. 'He's changed, Liam. Different from what I expected.'

'Girl, dear, he was never what you thought he was in the first place. The dark hero who came headfirst out of the reeds in Vietnam to save you was a man, just as ill-formed and fallible as the rest of us. Those photos you took over the years showed only the surface of things. The danger in your profession.'

'I never truly understood him,' she said. 'I see that now.'

'A good feature for the centre page,' Devlin said. 'And the camera likes him. You always made him look good.'

'Him and his damn roses,' she said bitterly. 'Something else I never understood. Getting into the GOC's office at Army headquarters at Lisburn that time and leaving a rose instead of a bomb as if to say Brosnan was here. Games for children.'

'Oh, I don't know,' Devlin said. 'That's partly the poet in him, I suppose. The lover of what you French call the *beau geste*. But there's more to it than that. The Plains Indians in America, the Sioux and the Cheyenne had an interesting variation on the war theme. The bravest thing a warrior could do was get close enough in battle to touch the enemy with a stick. That was the real measure of a man's bravery, not whether he'd killed his enemy or not.'

'And you think that's what he was doing

with his roses? Saying, look how brave I am?'

'No,' Devlin said gravely. 'I think what he was really saying was, I could have killed you, but I didn't, so perhaps we should think again. Find another way.'

'I don't know, Liam.' She stood up wearily. 'Too complex for me and so is he. I'm going to bed.'

She kissed him on the forehead and went out.

Behind the golden façade of the Cote d'Azure, the underworld of Nice was as tough and as ruthless as that of Paris or Marseilles. Barry knew that. The address Romanov had given him turned out to be a back-street night club not far from the harbour, run by a man named Charles Chabert.

He was a small man, a surprisingly civilised-looking individual with a moustache and gold-rimmed glasses. His dark suit was of excellent cut and as sober as his general image. His cognac was excellent, too, and

Barry sipped a little and smiled his appreciation.

'Muscle,' he said. 'That's all I need. My contact in Paris assured me you were just the man to provide it.'

Chabert nodded. 'I have a certain reputation, Monsieur, that is true. How many men would you need?'

'Three.'

'To go up against?'

'Two.'

Chabert looked surprised. 'With you, that makes four. Is that necessary?'

'To take care of the two I have in mind it is.'

'I see. Formidable?'

'You could say that. I need them first thing tomorrow. A morning's work only. I'll pay you twenty thousand francs.'

'Would there be the possibility of a little shooting?'

'Definitely.'

Chabert nodded. 'I see. Then in that case, the price will be thirty thousand. Forty,' he added, 'to include my fee.'

'Done.' Barry smiled cheerfully and held out his hand. 'One thing, I'm in sole charge. You make that clear. No cowboys.'

'But naturally, monsieur. These are my own people. They do as I say.' He picked up the internal telephone and said, 'Send Jacaud, Leboef and Deville to my office.'

'They sound like a cabaret act,' Barry said.

'In a way, that's what they are. Excellent professional performers. Let me give you another cognac.'

A moment later, there was a knock at the door, it opened and three men filed in. They stood against the wall waiting. In spite of the good suits, Barry had only to look at the faces to know they were exactly what he was looking for.

'Satisfied, monsieur?' Chabert asked.

'Perfectly.'

'Good, then perhaps you would be kind enough to settle now. Cash in advance is the one policy I always strictly adhere to. Life, after all, is an uncertain matter and we are all vulnerable, even you, my friend, particularly when involved in an affair like this.'

Barry, who had come prepared, courtesy of Romanov, laughed and took a thick wad of notes from his inside pocket.

'You know, I like you, old son, I really do,' he said, and started to count out the agreed fee in thousand franc notes.

Devlin usually woke at dawn, the habit of years, but that following morning he overslept and discovered, when he opened his eyes, that it was eight-thirty. He got up quickly, had a shower and then dressed.

He hesitated, looking at the bullet-proof waistcoat, then decided to try it and put it on under his shirt. As it weighed sixteen pounds he knew he was wearing it, but it fitted snugly enough and was not particularly uncomfortable.

When he went into the kitchen, Brosnan was sitting at the table eating scrambled eggs. Anne-Marie turned from the stove. She looked tired, dark circles under her eyes as if she had slept badly.

'There you are. What would you like, eggs?'

Devlin shook his head. 'I haven't eaten breakfast in years. A cup of tea would be fine.' He sat down opposite Brosnan. 'And how are you this beautiful morning?'

'Couldn't be better,' Brosnan said. 'The first time I've done this in years.' He reached across and opened Devlin's shirt, disclosing the waistcoat. 'You've got a button undone. What are you wearing that for?'

'Oh, I thought I'd give it a try,' Devlin told him. 'You should try yours. It's fun.' He swallowed the tea Anne-Marie gave him and stood up. 'When are we leaving?'

'Whenever you like. How are we going, by road or air?'

'By road will take for ever. On the other hand, it might be safer. There's that face of yours to consider.'

'I'm dead, Liam,' Brosnan said. 'Nobody will look at me twice and that picture in the paper was five or six years old. Another thing, I had short hair then. A pair of sunglasses and I'm laughing.'

'All right,' Devlin said. 'Air it is. You get

ready. I'm just dropping down to the village to make a telephone call.'

'Ferguson?'

'He might just have something to say that's worth hearing.'

'If it's about Barry, I'll buy that.'

Devlin turned to Anne-Marie. 'I'll take the Citroen if I may.'

She handed him the keys. 'One thing, Liam, when you go it's without me.'

'I see.' He glanced at Brosnan who continued to eat stolidly. 'Whatever you think best, girl dear.' He held her hand for a brief moment, turned and went out.

Barry had driven up from Nice in the Peugeot followed by the three hoods in a small van with the name of a well-known Nice electrical contractor on the side panel. They drew into a lay-by just outside St Martin and Jacaud got out of the van, lifted the bonnet and pretended to be tinkering with the engine. Barry drove into the village. He was not sure of his next move. It certainly wasn't on just to drive up to the farm. On that narrow road, they would be seen coming all the way up from the village.

The situation was taken out of his hands, for as he pulled in beside the church, he saw Devlin at the wheel of the Citroen getting petrol at the filling station further along the street.

Barry got out of the Peugeot and dodged into the church, leaving the door slightly open, and watched.

Devlin pulled out of the filling station forecourt, turned across the street and parked under a tree. He got out and walked across to the cafe. The young woman was washing the half-dozen tables and chairs that stood outside.

'Morning, monsieur,' she said. 'You would like coffee?'

'Never touch the filthy stuff,' Devlin told her, 'But if you've got a cup of tea, that would be fine after I've used the telephone.'

'My father's using it at the moment, monsieur, phoning our weekly order to the wholesaler in Nice. He shouldn't be long. I could get you the tea while you wait.'

'And why not?' Devlin lit a cigarette, sat down and turned his face to the morning sun.

It was quiet in the church, winking candles and incense heavy on the cold air, and down by the altar the Virgin seemed to float out of darkness, a slight fixed smile on her face. No one waited by the confessional boxes. The place seemed empty, then Barry saw that there was a young boy down by the altar, kneeling in prayer. He stood up, crossed himself and walked to the door.

'Are you looking for the *curé*, monsieur? He's not here. He's gone to Vence.'

He was only nine or ten and Barry ruffled his hair and smiled. 'No, I'm watching a friend of mine. See, the man over there at the cafe?'

'I see, monsieur.'

'I tell you what,' Barry said. 'Let's play a trick on him.'

'A trick, monsieur?'

'That's right. You go over and tell him the priest wants to see him. Then, when he walks in, he'll get a big shock when he sees me.' He took out his wallet and produced a ten franc note.

The boy's eyes went round. 'For me, monsieur?'

Barry slipped it into his pocket. 'Off you go now, and mind you don't give the game away.'

Devlin's eyes closed as he gazed up at the sun and he was not aware of the boy's approach until he tugged at his sleeve.

'Monsieur?' the boy said timidly.

'What is it, son?'

'The priest, monsieur, in the church.' He waved vaguely. 'He asked me to get you.'

'The priest?' Devlin smiled good-humouredly. 'But I don't know him. There must be some mistake.'

'Oh, no, monsieur, he pointed you out to me. He said the gentleman at the table and you are the only one.'

Devlin looked around him. 'So I am, that's a fact. All right, let's see what he wants.'

He tried to take the boy's hand, but he turned and ran away. Devlin shrugged, walked across the street, passing the Peugeot, and went up the steps. He paused, the innate caution that was the product of years of living dangerously sending his hand into his pocket to feel for the butt of the Browning.

It was dark in the church after the bright morning sunshine. He stood just inside the door, waiting, and someone said in French in a hoarse whisper, 'Over here, Monsieur Devlin.'

He was aware of the cassock, the figure insubstantial in the gloom. 'What is it?' he demanded and moved forward.

'A message from Jacques Savary, monsieur. Please – in here.'

The priest moved into the confessional box, drawing the curtain, and Devlin went into the other side and sat down. The whole thing made perfect sense now, of course, for Savary and his son, after all, were the only people who knew where they were.

There was a movement on the other side of the grille and the voice said, 'Have you anything to confess, my son?'

'Well, I've sinned most grievously, Father, and that's a fact, but what about Savary?'

'He can roast in hell as far as I'm concerned, Liam, me old son, along with you!'

The Ceska in Barry's right hand coughed twice, ripping through the grille, slamming into Devlin, hurling him back against the side of the confessional box. There was a fractional moment when he fought for air and then total darkness.

Barry opened the curtain and looked down at him sprawled in the corner. 'All debts paid, Liam,' he said softly.

He pulled the cassock he had borrowed from the vestry over his head, flung it into a pew, closed the curtain on Devlin again and went out.

* * *

Unlike Devlin, Brosnan put the nylon and titanium waistcoat on over his shirt. It didn't look too bad at all. In fact it went quite well with his jeans. He pulled on the reefer coat and slipped one of the Brownings in his right-hand pocket. The Mauser went into his belt at the rear, snug against his back.

He smiled, remembering that it was Devlin who'd taught him that. He took the Smith and Wesson with the short barrel, hefted it in his hand and went into the bathroom. He found a roll of surgical tape in the cabinet over the washbasin, tore a couple of lengths off and taped the Smith and Wesson to the inside of his left leg, just above the ankle, covering it with his sock.

When he went into the kitchen the radio was playing, but there was no sign of Anne-Marie. He found her sitting on a bench outside in the morning sun, eyes closed. He strolled across and paused, uncertain what to say. Below him he could see the Citroen coming up the winding road.

'Liam's coming,' he said.

'Is he?'

He leaned on the wall. 'Do you still paint?'

'Yes,' she said. 'Only in watercolour now. I've given up oils.'

'Devlin once told me that any fool could paint in oils, but that it took a real painter to master watercolours.'

Behind him the Citroen moved into the courtyard and still she kept her eyes closed. 'Go away, Martin. Just go away.'

Brosnan turned to the Citroen and Jacaud leaned out of the window and pointed a revolver between his eyes. Frank Barry sat up in the rear seat, kicked the door open and got out, the Ceska in his hand.

The van drew into the yard and Leboef and Deville got out. 'Shall I see if he's carrying a gun, monsieur?' Jacaud asked.

'Oh, I think we can take that for granted.'

Jacaud discovered the Browning in Brosnan's right-hand pocket. 'Where's Liam?' Brosnan demanded.

'In hell, I shouldn't wonder. When last seen, he looked very dead indeed.'

Anne-Marie said, 'No, not that.'

Brosnan took a step forward, hands coming up. 'You bastard!' he said.

Jacaud slashed him across the kidneys with the barrel of his gun and Brosnan cried out and went down on one knee.

'The right place for you,' Barry said, and nodded to Jacaud. 'Frisk him again. He always was a tricky one. Favoured the back of his belt as I remember.'

Jacaud found the Mauser and passed it across. 'Nasty,' Barry said, and gave it back to him. 'A bit old-fashioned for me. Now let's have the girl.'

She tried to run and Leboef and Deville grabbed her between them and rammed her against the car. Brosnan fighting for breath, looked up. 'What do you want with her?'

'You can think about that in hell, Martin.'

Jacaud said, 'Do we kill her?'

For a second, Barry seemed to see Jenny Crowther stagger forward as his bullet struck her in the back. He said savagely, 'No, you bloody well don't. I'll take care of her myself.'

He took a black plastic case from his

pocket, opened it and produced a disposable syringe, ready filled. 'I don't mind you keeping Devlin company, Martin, but your girl-friend here. Now that seems an awful waste.'

Anne-Marie cried out as the needle went in. Within seconds, she was collapsing and Barry pushed her into the rear seat of the Citroen and tucked a travelling rug across her.

'She'll sleep like a baby, all the way to Paris.'

'Drugs,' Brosnan said through clenched teeth. 'Just your style.'

Barry frowned. 'Come off it, me old son. She'll sleep like a baby for ten hours and then wake without even a headache.'

He got into the Citroen and started the engine. Jacaud said, 'What do we do with him?'

'Officially he's dead already,' Barry said. 'So I suppose the answer is obvious.'

'Haven't you got the stomach to do it yourself, Frank?' Brosnan said. 'Look me in the eye while you pull the trigger, or maybe you'd prefer me to turn my back?'

Jacaud and Deville held him down as he struggled and Barry laughed. 'You used to despise me, Martin. I wasn't good enough for you and your bloody Cause. In the end, you're the one on his knees in the muck and that's how I want to remember you. Not even worth killing myself.'

He drove away. Jacaud and Deville hauled Brosnan to his feet and took him between them into the barn followed by Leboef. They sent him staggering forward with a vicious push that put him on his knees again.

Leboef moved across the barn to examine an old cart. 'What a dump,' he said.

Deville leaned against the wall by the door and Jacaud came forward, the Mauser in his hand. Brosnan got up, staggered to an old bench against the wall and slumped down.

'This is it then?' he said.

Jacaud shrugged. 'You should have stayed home, my friend.'

'So it would appear.'

Brosnan leaned over, groaning in pain and got his right hand to the butt of the Smith and Wesson he had taped so carefully to the inside of his left leg. He groaned again and sank to one knee. Jacaud moved in close, grabbed Brosnan by the hair, and yanked his head back, just as Brosnan tore his Smith and Wesson free and in the same motion fired at Jacaud's heart.

The force of the shot at such close range lifted Jacaud off his feet, slamming him into the ground. In the same instant, Brosnan shot Leboef in the back before he could turn, the bullet shattering his spine, driving him head-first into the cart.

At the door, Deville screamed, trying to draw his gun, already too late as the Smith and Wesson arced towards him. Brosnan's third bullet caught him in the centre of the forehead and Deville went backwards into the yard.

There was silence. Brosnan stood there for a moment, quite still, legs apart, perfectly balanced, the Smith and Wesson ready. He was like a different man, another human being altogether.

After a moment, he slipped the Smith and Wesson into his pocket and went and retrieved the Mauser and the Browning from Jacaud. Then he crossed to the Montesa, shoved it off its stand, kick-started it savagely and roared out across the yard and down the road towards St Martin.

13

Devlin surfaced to the sound of a querulous voice and a hand shaking him. 'Monsieur, are you all right?'

He opened his eyes and found an old priest bending over him. He felt as if he'd been kicked very hard several times in the body. He ran a hand over the general area of his heart and through a rent in his shirt found one of the bullets Barry had fired at him embedded in the waistcoat.

'Have you been drinking?' the priest demanded.

'Not at all, Father.' Devlin managed to smile. 'You can smell my breath. A touch of malaria, that's all.'

'Malaria?' the priest said, astonished as Devlin got up and righted the chair.

'Picked it up in the tropics years ago. Still get a touch now and then in the most unexpected places.'

He walked to the door and found that it hurt him to breath, so that when he went outside, he leaned against the wall at the top of the steps. Brosnan arrived on the motorcycle at that precise moment and braked to a halt beside the Citroen which was parked at the bottom of the steps.

Devlin said, 'How in the hell did that get there? I left it under the tree by the cafe.'

'Frank Barry took it to drive up to the farm. I thought it was you, Liam. He took us completely by surprise.'

'No more than he did me. Shot me twice in the heart in the church.' Devlin pulled the round out of the waistcoat and held it up. 'Jesus, Martin, but these things are a wonderful invention. All it did was knock me cold for a while. I'll see that bastard in hell yet.'

'Not if I see him first,' Brosnan said. 'He's taken Anne-Marie.'

'He's what?' Devlin was shocked. 'Then how come he left you in one piece?'

Brosnan explained. When he'd finished, Devlin said, 'So, he came down here, transferred her to his old car and cleared off. Come to think of it, there was another car here when I walked across to the church.'

'Can you remember what it was?'

'A Peugeot, I think. A saloon.'

'Right, let's get after him.'

Brosnan turned to go down the steps and Devlin lurched after him. 'Just a minute, Martin, where to?'

'Paris. When he gave her that shot in the arm he said it would keep her quiet all the way to Paris.'

'All right, so which way has he gone? Five miles north of here, you have a choice of three separate routes through the Alps to Lyons. On the other hand, maybe he's cut down towards the coast to take the route from Cannes to Avignon, or would you like me to make a few more suggestions?'

Brosnan kicked the side of the car in frustration. 'Why in the hell did he take her? What for?'

'The whim of the moment. Maybe he just

wanted you to know that he had her when you died. Like pulling the wings off flies. There is only one real certainty in this whole business. He's going to Paris and Paris means Romanov. Now, if we caught a plane from Nice, we'd be there before him. He has to drive all the way, can't do any other with Anne-Marie in the car.'

'By God, you're right,' Brosnan said. 'Let's get moving.'

'Not just yet.' Devlin tried to ease his sore ribs. 'One puzzle remains. How in the hell Frank Barry knew we were here. Just give me five minutes to phone Ferguson.'

It was Harry Fox who picked up the telephone. He listened for a moment, then turned to Ferguson. 'Devlin, sir.'

'Give it to me.' Ferguson snatched it from him. 'For God's sake, Devlin, where have you been?'

'Never mind that now. Can you explain to me how Frank Barry managed to trace Brosnan and me to the Audin girl's farm at St Martin?'

'Brosnan?' Ferguson said in astonishment. 'But I thought he was dead.'

'Well you shouldn't believe everything you read in the papers. But what about Barry? The bastard just tried to shoot me dead. Now he's gone haring off to Paris with Anne-Marie Audin.'

Ferguson said, 'Look, Devlin, it's a tricky one to explain. There was a leak here, I'm afraid. Someone passing on information to the KGB in London.'

'About our little affair?'

'I'm afraid so. I should imagine details were passed to Romanov in Paris and naturally, he would have alerted Barry.'

'Well thanks very much,' Devlin said. 'Nothing like efficiency. That's what built the Empire. You'll excuse me if I ring off now.'

'But Devlin,' Ferguson said hastily. 'What are you going to do?'

'Well, we don't exactly have a choice, do we? Go to Paris to see Colonel Nikolai Romanov.'

He left the cafe and got into the passenger seat of the Citroen. 'What did you find out?' Brosnan demanded.

'Nice Airport, quick as you like,' Devlin said. 'I'll tell you on the way.'

Barry took the scenic route through the High Alps. At Grenoble, he took the road for Lyons and stopped a few miles further on at a small roadside garage to fill his tank. Anne-Marie slept peacefully in the rear seat.

The old man on the pumps said, 'Madame looks as if she's enjoying herself.'

The travelling rug had slipped and Barry reached over and tucked it around her tenderly. 'Yes, we're on our way to Paris. The best way to pass the time on these long trips. Can I use your telephone?'

'But of course, monsieur. In the office.'

'Thanks,' Barry said. 'If you could check the oil, water and tyres, I'll be obliged.'

When he dialled Romanov's special number at the Embassy, it was Irana who answered. 'Barry here. Is he there?'

'Just a moment.'

Romanov said. 'How did things go?'

'Couldn't be better. You may be surprised to know that both gentlemen in question were still around.'

'Is that so?' Romanov said calmly. 'Presumably you took care of that?'

'Oh, yes. You might say I closed the books. Have you any news for me?'

'Yes, the business deal we discussed? I'm assured there will be no cash flow problem. You may proceed with the arrangements as soon as you like.'

'Good, then I'd like the transportation you promised arranged for tonight. Any problems?'

'None that I can see.'

'I'll see you at Croix, then, round about ten o'clock.'

As the old man came into the office, Barry put the phone down. 'What's the damage?'

'Two-fifty, monsieur.'

Barry paid him and slapped down an extra fifty franc note. 'That should cover the phone call.'

'Monsieur, please, it's too much,' the old man said.

'Nonsense,' Barry said. 'Things are going rather well for me at the moment. I'd like you to share my good fortune.'

He got behind the wheel and turned for a quick look at the girl. She still slept peacefully, all lines gone, no strain there at all. He smiled, patted her face and drove away.

Brosnan and Devlin arrived at Nice Airport to receive their first major setback. The departure schedule board indicated delays on all flights to Paris.

'I'll see what the problem is,' Devlin said.

He left Brosnan by the news-stand and approached the *Air France* ticket counter where a couple of charming and imperturbable young women were doing their best to placate a queue of angry passengers.

When it was Devlin's turn he said, 'What's the trouble at Paris?'

'The firemen are on strike at Charles de Gaulle. That means the guys at Orly and Le Bourget back them in the interests of union solidarity.'

Devlin said, 'And how long will the comedy continue?'

'I honestly don't know. Last time it was twenty-four hours, but they like to keep everyone guessing. You know how it is, monsieur?'

'Indeed I do.' Devlin turned and hurried back to Brosnan.

'Could be tomorrow.'

'To hell with that,' Brosnan said. 'Tomorrow could be too late. We'll just have to go by road and step on it, that's all.'

He took Devlin's arm and hurried him out of the entrance and across the concourse to the car park.

Croix was exactly what Barry had expected, a small airfield with a control tower, two hangars and three nissen huts, headquarters of an aero club according to the board on the gate.

The doors to one of the hangars were open and the Cessna 310 stood outside. There was a dark BMW saloon parked beside it and when Barry braked and switched off his engine he heard voices. Romanov and Irana Vronsky walked out, a small, dark man in white overalls following them.

Barry got out and went to meet them. 'Is this it?' he asked, nodding at the Cessna.

'That's right. The best Deforges could do at such short notice. He's Controller here.'

'Perhaps we could go to my office and discuss the destination?' Deforges said.

'Fine.' Barry opened the rear door of the Citroen, leaned inside, then stood up holding Anne-Marie in his arms. 'Have you got a couch or something handy in there. My friend here is still sleeping it off.'

Deforges glanced at Romanov as if for guidance, then shrugged. 'I suppose so.'

He led the way into the hangar and Barry followed, Romanov and Irana walking beside him. 'The Audin girl? This is crazy. What do you intend to do with her?'

'Take her with me.'

They had reached a glass-walled office and Deforges opened another door and showed him into a tiny room with a washbasin and a bed covered with army blankets.

'You can have this.'

He went out and Barry laid Anne-Marie on the bed. Irana leaned over her and put a hand on her forehead. 'How long will she be out?'

'Another hour.'

'But what are you playing at, Frank?' Romanov demanded.

'Well, it was either kill her or bring her along, and I've never been very good at knocking off women.'

'You're mad.'

'So they tell me.'

'Haven't you enough on your plate without the burden of this woman?'

'You let me worry about that.' Barry pushed him and Irana out and closed the door. 'Now, what about this plane?'

'It's outside on the tarmac,' Romanov replied.

'All right,' Barry said. 'The English Lake District, that's my target, particularly the coastal area.'

Deforges rummaged through his chart drawer and finally found what he was looking for. Barry ran his fingers down the Cumberland coast. 'Ravenglass. There should be an old RAF station a few miles south. Yes, there it is. Tanningley Field.'

'It's marked as no longer in use,' Deforges pointed out.

'That's right, but the runway is perfectly viable. I've seen it. How long should it take me in the Cessna?'

'Well, its cruising speed is a hundred and sixty, but it all depends on the weather. I'll call Orly and find out.'

He went into the other office and picked up the telephone. Barry lit a cigarette and said, 'I've been thinking, Nikolai, it would be very unfortunate if I arrived to find anyone waiting for me. That young fella who met me on Morecambe Pier last time, remember?'

Irana flushed angrily, opened her mouth to speak, but Romanov cut her off. 'Frank, why must you talk like this? We have a deal. I accept your terms. I want no further trouble or difficulty. All I want is that rocket pod.'

'Good,' Barry said, 'so there's nothing to worry about then.'

Deforges came back. 'There's a head wind and a low coming in from the Irish Sea that could bring heavy rain by morning. Even a chance of fog. In the circumstances, I'd allow four and a half hours flight time. Possibly five. You'll need light to land on such a field.'

'What time is dawn?'

'Just before five.'

'All right, I'll leave about midnight.'

'One problem,' Deforges said. 'You'll have to be officially routed both for leaving France and entering English air space.'

Barry nodded. 'So where do you think I should be going?'

Deforges looked at the map for a few moments. 'Ronaldsway Airport on the Isle of Man. Only fifty miles from your final destination on the English coast. At the last moment, tell the Ronaldsway Air Traffic Control people that you are diverting to Blackpool. Then I suggest you make an approach across the sea to Tanningley at under six hundred feet. At that height, you won't show up on any radar screens. Of course, someone may see you land, but at that time of the morning, there shouldn't be too many people around.'

'It doesn't matter anyway,' Barry said. 'I'll be out of it again before you know it. You get things moving then. I've got a telephone call to make.'

Deforges went out and Barry went into the other office, closed the door and picked up the phone. Irana and Romanov watched him through the glass wall.

'I don't trust him, Nikolai,' she said. 'He's made a fool of you once. He could do it again.'

'I don't really have much choice, my love. I must get my hands on that rocket pod . . .'

'So they can pat you on the head, promote you to General and transfer you to Moscow?' she said. 'To be perfectly frank, Nikolai, I'd rather stay in Paris.'

He frowned impatiently. 'I've warned you before about talking like that. One of these days you'll forget yourself and do it in the wrong company.'

'I only do it out of concern for you.'

'I know.' He kissed her on the cheek with genuine affection. 'No point in you hanging on here any longer, particularly as you have your own car with you. Go on back to the apartment.'

'What about you?'

'I'll see Barry off at midnight, then I'll join you.'

She squeezed his hand, picked up her fur coat and went out. Romanov lit a cigarette and watched Barry, who was now engaged in conversation with someone.

At March End, Henry Salter was just about to go up to bed when the phone rang. He answered it without hesitation, for in the funeral business one got used to the fact that people died at any time of the day or night.

'Henry Salter.'

'Is that you, me old son? Sinclair here.'

Salter's stomach turned hollow and he pulled a chair forward and sat down. 'What can I do for you, Mr Sinclair?' he asked, voice shaking.

'How are things with you since I left? Any problems?'

'A lot of police activity about twenty miles up the dale from here towards Wast Water.'

'Oh, yes. What happened?'

'Nobody seems to know.'

Barry laughed. 'That's really very good. When we parted, I said I'd be back and I will. You know the old airfield at Tanningley?'

'Yes.'

'I'll be landing there in a light plane around five in the morning. Meet me in the Land-Rover.'

'But it hasn't been used for years, that airfield,' Salter said.

'Five thousand pounds, in cash, for your very valuable assistance. I'll be away again within a couple of hours. How about it?'

Salter struggled against his natural greed and lost. 'I'll be there, Mr Sinclair.'

'See that you are,' Barry said and put down the phone.

* * *

Devlin and Brosnan reached Paris just after eleven and went straight to the address on the Boulevard St Germain. Romanov's apartment was at the top of a tower block, a luxury development of some distinction.

'What do we do if he isn't in?' Brosnan asked.

'How would I know, boy? Wait for him. Try picking the lock. We'll see.'

They walked along the thickly carpeted corridor and paused at the door numbered thirteen. 'Unlucky for some.' Devlin punched the bell.

There was a pause and then the door was flung open and Irana Vronsky said, 'What kept you, darling, I . . .'

The smile faded from her face. Brosnan moved fast, his hand on her jaw holding the mouth closed so that she couldn't scream, ramming her back into the apartment. Behind him Devlin closed the door.

Brosnan threw her on the couch and produced the silenced Mauser. 'This thing doesn't make a sound. Any trouble, I'll blow your head off. Now, where's Romanov?'

Irana took a deep breath to pull herself together. 'Go to hell!'

She wore a superb black silk dressing gown that gaped as she tried to get up, revealing black silk stockings and a hint of suspender. Brosnan shoved her down again.

Devlin said, 'Dressed that like, I think we can safely assume the lady is expecting the colonel at any moment. All we have to do is wait.' He sat down opposite her, helped himself to a Russian cigarette from a box on the table and sniffed it. 'Bolshevik fire-crackers. I had a friend once who smoked these things. Picked up a taste for them in the Winter War, but that was before your time. Would you by any chance know who I am?'

'You take a very good photo,' she said calmly.

'And my friend?'

'Mr Brosnan looks extremely healthy for a dead man.'

Which was a bad mistake and Devlin seized on it at once. 'So, you've either seen, or been in touch with, Frank Barry.'

She sat there, glaring at him, furiously angry with herself for being so stupid. 'What do you want?' she demanded.

'Well, a nice cup of tea would do for a start,' Liam Devlin told her.

Anne-Marie opened her eyes, stretched and lay there, staring up at the light bulb above her head. Her mind was blank and she wondered where on earth she was – and then she remembered the men at the farm, Martin on his knees. She sat up and found Barry sitting on the end of the bed watching her. Amazing how calm she was, no headache, no after-sleep drowsiness.

'Where are we?' she asked.

'A little aerodrome outside Paris.' There was a pot of coffee and a couple of cups on a tray beside him. He filled one and passed it across. 'Drink this.' She hesitated and he smiled and sipped some himself. 'Satisfied?'

She took the cup as the door opened and Romanov entered. 'Ready to go whenever you like, Frank. Deforges has got the engines turning over.' He glanced at Anne-Marie. 'Does she still go with you?'

Barry looked at her enquiringly. 'Well?'

'Do I have a choice?'

He laughed and turned to Romanov. 'She goes.'

Romanov shrugged and went out. Anne-Marie said, 'Is it permitted to ask the destination?'

'The English Lake District. You'll enjoy that. Lovely at this time of the year. Afterwards, if you're a good girl, Ireland. If you behave yourself, I'll let you go there.'

'Unexpected generosity, surely. Why take me along in the first place?'

'Oh, I've a lovely nature when you get to know me and in Ireland, you see, I'll be safe. Neither the British nor the French nor anyone else can extradite me. I'm a political offender, a most useful profession on occasion. The Irish Government won't like it, but you can scream the rooftops down once we're there and it still won't change the situation.'

She lay there, propped up on one arm, staring at him. 'Did you really kill Liam?'

'Yes,' he said. 'In the church at St Martin.'

'And Brosnan?' There was a silence between them. 'Why not me, too?'

He said, 'My friend who looked in a moment ago thinks I should.'

'Why don't you?'

'We all have our blind spots, my love, even a bastard like me. I don't kill women.' He hesitated, remembering Jenny Crowther. 'Not by intention, anyway.'

'Oh, I see,' she said. 'Not by intention? That really is a great comfort.'

He stood up, took the Ceska out, cocked it, then put the safety catch on and replaced it in his pocket. 'The choice is yours.'

Which was no choice at all as they both knew. 'Oh, I wouldn't miss it for anything.' She got to her feet. 'When do we leave?'

'Marvellous,' Barry said. 'I knew you'd see sense. Just think what a feature you could get out of it all. Now hold out your hands.' He produced a pair of handcuffs and snapped them into place, clamping her wrists together in front of her. 'The world's a deceitful old place and I like to be as certain as possible about things.'

'The only certainty at the moment is that you haven't killed me yet, Mr Barry,' Anne-Marie said.

'Oh ye of little faith.'

He opened the door and ushered her through.

There was fog heavy on the damp air and although Deforges had switched on the landing lights, it was not possible to see to the end of the runway. Romanov watched the Cessna turn and pause. As Barry boosted power, it rolled forward, the roaring of the engines filling the night. It started to lift off and was swallowed up by the fog instantly.

Deforges came across from the hangar, head turned to catch the muffled beat of the engines as Barry started to climb. 'Is he any good?'

'Oh, yes,' Romanov said. 'He has the Devil on his side, that one. Good night, Deforges,' and he turned and walked away to his car.

* * *

Barry climbed to six thousand feet, took a course from the Air Traffic Control at Orly that turned him towards the Channel coast. He switched to autopilot and turned, pushing his headphones down around his neck.

Anne-Marie sat amidships, strapped in, her wrists still handcuffed in front of her. 'Four and a half to five hours. You can be sensible and comfortable or just plain uncomfortable. The choice is yours.'

She held up her wrists without a word and he produced the key and unlocked them. 'Good girl,' he said. 'There's coffee and sandwiches and even a couple of half bottles of booze in the case at your feet. Feel free.'

He turned away, switched from autopilot and took control again.

It was half an hour past midnight when Romanov reached the apartment on the Boulevard St Germain. He was tired and cold and the prospect of Irana waiting filled him with a conscious pleasure. He got out his key, opened the door, and Irana called in Russian, 'Run, Nikolai!'

Romanov found himself staring into the barrel of a gun. And then Brosnan had him by the collar, kicked the door shut and pushed him into the living room.

Irana sat on the couch, Devlin standing behind her. Romanov stared at him in astonishment as Brosnan ran his hands over him expertly, finding the Walther PPK in Romanov's pocket and removing it.

Devlin said, 'You look surprised, Colonel Romanov, as well you might be, knowing who we are.'

Romanov tried to bluff it out. 'I don't know what you want and I certainly don't know who you are. If it's money, there's about four thousand francs in my wallet.'

'You can save it,' Devlin said. 'Your lady-friend here has already spilled the beans. She was surprised to see us because she thought we were both dead. That can only mean one thing. You've either spoken to, or heard from, Frank Barry. Where is he?'

Romanov took a Russian cigarette from

the box on the coffee table. 'You don't really expect me to answer that.'

'When last seen, he had a friend of ours with him, a lady named Anne-Marie Audin. We're very concerned about her, Colonel,' Devlin said. 'I think I may go as far as to say that my friend here is feeling rather upset about the whole business and when he gets angry, he becomes very unpredictable.'

Romanov glanced at Brosnan's hard, implacable face. 'I can't help that.'

Brosnan slid back the windows to the terrace. He moved close to Romanov and hit him under the breastbone, knuckles extended. The Russian went down on his knees.

Brosnan said, 'I don't give a damn who you are. I don't even care which side you're on. I'm only interested in saving that girl. You've got a minute – one minute to start talking. If you don't, I'm going to throw you off the balcony and by my reckoning, we must be fifteen storeys up.'

Irana cried out and tried to get to her feet. Brosnan pushed her down and said to Devlin, 'Keep her quiet.'

He shoved his foot into Romanov's rear, sending him sprawling towards the terrace. Irana looked up at Devlin and said desperately, 'Stop him! For God's sake, stop him! I'll tell you what you want to know.'

Romanov half-turned towards her on his hands and knees, shaking his head and Brosnan kicked his legs from under him, reached for his collar and started for the open window.

'No, please don't let him!' She grabbed at Devlin's coat.

'The whole truth,' he said. 'Everything.'

'I promise.'

He called to Brosnan. 'Okay, Martin, take him into the bathroom and let the poor fella clean himself up.'

Romanov stood at the washbasin examining his face in the mirror. His nose was bleeding and he sponged it carefully with a flannel.

'You play it rough, Mr Brosnan.'

'It worked, didn't it?'

'Oh, yes,' Romanov said. 'The old ploy. One guy's reasonable, the other is nasty. It never fails. I've used it myself many times.' He sighed. 'Only poor Irana didn't know that.'

'All Irana knows, if you want my opinion, is that she loves you.'

'Yes,' Romanov said soberly. 'So it would appear.'

The door opened and Devlin said, 'You can come out now.'

Irana got to her feet and ran into Romanov's arms. 'I'm sorry, Nikolai, but I wasn't prepared to see you killed.'

'That's all right.' He smoothed her hair with one hand. 'Actually, I'm rather flattered.'

Devlin turned to Brosnan. 'He left a small aerodrome outside Paris at midnight taking Anne-Marie with him. He's flying himself in a Cessna 310.'

'What's the destination?'

'The English Lake District. I'll explain it all later. Watch these two while I call Jean-Paul. Not Ferguson, right?.'

Brosnan smiled. 'Why bother the man? This isn't Ferguson's business any more.'

* * *

In Marseilles at the *Maison d'Or*, Jean-Paul Savary was counting the evening's takings from the casino with the assistance of the club manager and it was the manager who picked up the phone when it rang. He listened, then held it out to Jean-Paul.

'For you, boss. A Monsieur Devlin.'

Jean-Paul took it instantly. 'Savary here.'

'How's your father?'

'Sunning himself in Algeria. And you and Martin?'

'Things could be marginally worse, but I doubt it. You said anything at any time.'

'And meant it. What do you need?'

'We're in Paris. We need a light plane and the kind of pilot who doesn't ask questions to drop us at a disused airfield in the English Lake District.'

'When do you want to go?'

'Right now.'

'Give me your phone number. I'll call you back.'

'You can fix it?'

'My friend, the Union Corse can fix anything, except perhaps the Presidency.'

Jean-Paul put the phone down, took a small black book from a drawer in the desk and checked through it. He picked up the phone again and dialled a Paris number.

Leaning against the window, smoking a cigarette, Devlin said, 'I've been thinking about this whole business, Colonel, and it seems to me Barry's made a right old mug out of you.'

'Yes,' Romanov said evenly. 'I'm inclined to agree with you. So where is this conversation leading us?'

'I'd have thought it was obvious. You've promised him two million and you'll take delivery of this rocket pod in Ireland. Now from something the lady here let drop when she was being so informative, I understand the Germans have been rather reluctant to let their American allies have a look at this wonderful new weapon. Understandable, as feelings have not been exactly cordial there for some time.'

Romanov said carefully, 'So what are you suggesting?'

'I wouldn't want to spoil your evening, but if Frank Barry can get two million from you, I should have thought it likely that the CIA would give him five. Or do you think I'm being unreasonable?'

Romanov sat there, staring at him, and Irana hugged his arm. 'I warned you,' she said. 'I told you what he was like.'

'All supposition.'

The phone rang and Devlin picked it up. He listened for a few moments then said, 'God bless you, Jean-Paul.' He turned to Brosnan. 'Small aerodrome about half an hour's drive out of Paris near a place called Brie-Comte-Robert.'

'I know where that is,' Brosnan said.

Romanov said, 'You intend to take up the chase by plane?' He shrugged. 'Too late, my friend. Barry will have at least two hours' start on you.'

'We'll see,' Devlin told him.

Brosnan said, 'What are we going to do about these two?'

'A point.' Devlin stood looking down at

them, hands in pockets. 'I suppose you could try phoning this man Salter, tell him to warn Barry we're on our way in spite of what I said to you?' Romanov didn't reply, but the look in his eye said it all. 'I thought so. Have a look in the kitchen, Martin. Find some cord.' Brosnan went out and came back with a ball of twine and a clothes line. 'Fine.' Devlin turned to Irana, 'What time does the maid get in? Seven? Eight?'

She answered instinctively, 'Seven-thirty.'

'Good, she'll find you soon enough, you in one bedroom and him in the other. Too late to do us any harm.'

There was nothing Romanov could do except submit and within a few minutes he was tightly bound, hands behind his back, his ankles tied to his wrists. Brosnan gagged him and laid him on his side.

'Not too uncomfortable, I hope?'

Romanov's eyes flickered and Brosnan gave him an ironic salute, went out and closed and locked the door just as Devlin emerged from the other room.

'All right,' Devlin said. 'Let's move it,' and they went out quickly.

The fog was considerably worse and it was raining heavily by the time they reached Brie-Comte-Robert. They found the airfield with no difficulty, two miles on the other side of the town.

The gates in the perimeter wire stood open. The place was mainly in darkness and in the light from the Citroen's headlamps, Brosnan saw cracked concrete, grass growing high on either side of the runway. There were four hangars. They loomed out of the fog and a couple of lamps high on the wall had been turned on. In their light, the rain fell relentlessly.

A small door opened in one of the hangars and a man was silhouetted there. 'Mr Devlin?' he called in English, as Brosnan switched off the engine.

Devlin got out first. 'That's me.'

'Come on in.'

The hangar was dimly lit by only a couple

of bulbs. There were three planes. An old Dakota, a Beaver and a Navajo Chieftain.

'Barney Graham.' He held out his hand, a small, wiry-looking man with faded blue eyes. He wore a World War Two Irving flying jacket and sheepskin boots.

'You've heard from Savary?'

'Sure, you want to go to the Lake District. Come in the office.' They followed him and saw that several charts and maps had been laid out across the desk. 'A dirty night for dirty work.'

'You mean you're not prepared to do it?' Brosnan said.

Graham laughed. 'You don't say no to the *Union Corse*. They own this place. They're my bread and butter plus a considerable amount of jam. Now where exactly do you want to land?'

'An old RAF station from the war days, south of a place called Ravenglass. Tanningley Field.'

'That's bad flying country,' Graham said. 'Friend of mind hit the top of a mountain near there back in forty-three in a Lancaster bomber. Only the rear gunner survived and he had both legs broken.' He was going over the map as he spoke. 'There it is. No longer in use.'

'Apparently the runway is perfectly usable,' Devlin said. 'The man we're after is familiar with the place. He's flying there now. Left at midnight.'

'What in?'

'A Cessna 310.'

'There's a head wind tonight,' Graham said. 'I've checked the weather. That cuts him down to about a hundred and forty in one of those things. I'd say he'll get there about four-thirty. Maybe five, which would be about right. Dawn coming up, you see and on a field like that with no facilities, he can only make a visual approach so he needs light.' He folded the maps. 'Just like us.'

Devlin checked his watch and saw that it was two o'clock. 'So, he's got a two-hour start on us.'

Graham shook his head. 'My Navajo can better his speed by a hundred miles an hour and we won't be as bothered by that head wind. I reckon we can make it in three hours.'

'Arriving at five.' Brosnan turned to Devlin. 'Right up his backside, so let's get moving.'

'Just let me explain one thing before we leave,' Graham said. 'I'll need a destination to keep the air traffic people happy. I've already told Orly I'm making an emergency flight to Glasgow to pick up a supply of blood needed for an operation in Paris this afternoon.'

'Blood?' Brosnan said.

'Yes, a rare group. You know the sort of thing. A trick we use occasionally when we need to make a flight that's a little out of the ordinary. Jean-Paul's already arranged it by telephone with a contact in Glasgow since he spoke to you, so that gives me a legal reason for the flight.'

'And where do we come in?'

'The Lake District is directly *en route* and it isn't controlled air space. At the right moment, I go down fast, you jump out, and I take off again and keep my fingers crossed it isn't noticed on anyone's radar screen. A fair chance at that time in the morning.'

'And if it is?'

'I'll think of something,' Graham smiled. 'I took my wings in the RAF in nineteen thirty-nine, Mr Devlin. I've been at it a long time. Not much they can teach me. If I say I had instrument problems, they've got no proof otherwise. Anyway, let's get going.'

They got the hangar doors open and Devlin and Brosnan climbed into the Navajo. It was roomy enough inside with seating for ten people. Graham climbed in after them and pulled up the Airstair door.

'I've only got my wing lights to go by,' he said. 'With this fog the take-off's going to seem worse than it is. If you don't like heights, just close your eyes.'

The engines roared into life and Devlin and Brosnan strapped themselves in as he taxied outside, moved to the end of the runway and turned into the wind.

'You know what they say in the theatre, Martin?' Devlin said. 'It's bad luck to wish somebody good luck.'

'Thanks very much,' Brosnan told him. 'Just what I needed.'

And then they were ploughing into the fog, Graham easing back the column at precisely the correct moment for lift-off, refusing to sacrifice power for height, pulling the column back into his stomach when instinct told him it was right to do so.

At eight hundred feet they burst out of the fog; he put pressure on the right rudder and started to turn to starboard.

Anne-Marie had slept for some time and came awake to find the first grey light of dawn seeping across the sky. In the far distance to port, the Isle of Man was a shadow on the horizon. She could see from the altimeter that they were flying at two thousand feet. When she looked down, the sea was a desolate waste below.

She was aware of Barry's voice over the roaring of the twin engines as he spoke into his mike. 'Ronaldsway. This is Golphe Alpha Yankee Yankee Foxtrot. I am diverting to Blackpool.' There was a pause and then he said, 'No emergency, just a change of plan. Over and out.'

He switched to autopilot and turned to her, the handcuffs in one hand. 'Not that I think you'd be silly enough to start a fuss that would kill the both of us, but I'd feel happier if you put these back on.'

She didn't even struggle, there was little point, simply held out her wrists to receive the handcuffs.

'Good girl.' He grinned. 'Now just sit tight and enjoy yourself. This is the exciting bit.'

He took over the controls again and went down fast.

14

Henry Salter had the forethought to take a pair of twelve inch wire cutters with him when he drove out to Tanningley Field. They sliced easily enough through the rusting chain which was padlocked to the main gate, and he got back in the Land-Rover and drove inside.

He hadn't visited the place in years and there were signs of neglect everywhere. There was even grass growing through cracks in the old runway and the roofs of two of the hangars had fallen in.

The third looked in reasonable enough condition. It still bore the legend in faded white paint *Tanningley Aero Club*. With a bit of an effort, he managed to roll back the doors and venture inside. Even here, rain dripped through the holes in the roof.

It was cold and depressing and he shivered, turning up the collar of his coat. And then, in the distance, he heard the plane and ran outside.

The Cessna came in from the sea very low, banked to starboard and dropped straight in at the far end of the runway. Salter ran out waving his arms and the Cessna turned towards him and taxied inside the hangar, the roaring of the twin engines filling the place with their clamour. Barry switched off, opened the door and climbed out on the wing.

'Mr Sinclair,' Salter said weakly.

Barry reached inside the plane, pulled Anne-Marie out and helped her to the ground. Salter looked her over, noting the handcuffs with dismay.

'All right, let's get moving.' Barry ran Anne-Marie to the Land-Rover and pushed her into the rear, taking the driver's seat himself, switching on as Salter scrambled in to the passenger seat.

'But where are we going?'

'The Marsh. Your boat, the *Kathleen*, is still moored down there on the creek, I hope?'

'Of course she is.' Salter was bewildered. 'I don't understand.'

'You will,' Barry said and turned out of the main gates.

'Hang on,' Salter told him. 'I'd better close them or someone might notice and wonder what's been going on.'

Barry halted and Salter went back to the gates. He paused beside the Land-Rover as he came back, head turned, listening. Barry said impatiently, 'What is it?'

'I thought I heard another plane. I must have been mistaken.'

'Get in, man, for God's sake. I haven't got all day,' Barry said, exasperated, and he drove away quickly, without giving Salter time to get the door closed.

The sound Salter had heard was the Navajo making its first approach, but the weather had already deteriorated so much that the ceiling was down to eight hundred feet and Barney Graham turned out to sea again.

'It's too bloody dicey to go in blind. We'll be into the side of that mountain before you know what's happened.'

'You've got to get us down one way or another, it's absolutely essential,' Brosnan said.

'Maybe you'd like to jump out?' Graham swore softly. 'Okay, I'll try a sea approach.'

He turned out to sea, banked, went down low and burst out of the fog at five hundred feet, the mountain rushing to meet them.

It was Devlin who saw the runway and hangars a few hundred yards to starboard through driving rain. Graham went in fast and so low that when he banked at the last moment just before putting her down, the starboard wingtip was only six feet off the ground. The plane bounced heavily and ran towards the hangars.

'Out!' Graham shouted. 'Now!'

He was out of the cockpit and dropping the Airstair in seconds. Brosnan descended and Devlin went after him so fast that he stumbled and fell. The Airstair was hauled up behind them, and as they ran to get out of the way, the Navajo taxied towards the far end of the runway, paused briefly, then roared forward and took off.

Within a matter of moments it had climbed into the mist and was only a fast disappearing sound in the distance.

Devlin said, 'Let's hope this is it. No mistakes.'

Brosnan was already at the partly-open hangar door, pulling it back on its rollers, disclosing the Cessna. 'This is it all right. So where's Barry?'

'I should think this fella Salter will be able to tell us that, but just in case Barry intends to use this thing again, let's make sure he can't.'

Devlin produced a Browning from his pocket, took deliberate aim and fired at each wheel in turn. The Cessna lurched slightly as the tyres deflated.

'That's it,' Brosnan said. 'Now let's move it, Liam. According to that map, it's about five miles to Marsh End.'

But luck was with them, for as they were walking along the main road five minutes later, a farm truck with milk churns on the back passed them and stopped up ahead.

The man who leaned out of the window looked cheerful enough, in spite of the early hour. He badly needed a shave and his pyjama jacket showed under his old raincoat.

'In trouble?'

'We were last night,' Devlin said smoothly. 'Coming over the pass from the next valley when the car broke down.'

'Wast Water?'

'That's right. We must have walked five or six miles.'

'More like eight. Where are you making for?'

'You know Mr Salter's place?'

'Pass it every day. If that's where you're going, hop on the back and I'll drop you off.'

'Thanks,' Devlin said. 'We can phone the local garage from there.'

They climbed on board and squatted amongst the milk churns. Brosnan said, 'You're never at a loss, are you?'

Devlin grinned. 'All you have to do is live right.'

Barry drove along the track beside the creek and braked to a halt at the end of the jetty. The *Kathleen* waited, silent in the rain, and fog draped the marsh in a grey blanket. He helped Anne-Marie out and walked her along the jetty, a hand on her elbow.

Salter hurried behind. 'But what are you going to do, Mr Sinclair?'

Barry helped Anne-Marie over the rail. 'I'm going to retrieve something that belongs to me, Mr Salter, and for that, I need your boat. Afterwards, you collect your five thousand, take us back to Tanningley Field and I fly away into the grey morning like a departing spirit. I'm sure you'll be most relieved.'

Salter stayed on the jetty, staring at him stupidly. 'But we can't.'

'Why not?' Barry frowned. 'You told me when I was last here that you always keep the *Kathleen* ready for sea.'

'The ignition key,' Salter said. 'I can't start

the engines without that and it's up at the house.'

Barry swore. 'Then go and get it, you bloody idiot and be quick about it.'

Salter turned, hurried along the jetty and got into the Land-Rover. Barry pushed Anne-Marie along the deck and into the wheelhouse.

'How are you liking it so far?' His smile was fixed, the eyes were alive with excitement, and when he lit a cigarette his hands trembled.

'Careful,' Anne-Marie said. 'You're coming apart.'

'Who, me?' He laughed excitedly. 'Not till hell freezes over.'

He pulled down the inspection flap beneath the instrument panel. The Sterling and the Smith and Wesson were still in place. As he pushed it up again she said, 'So much for poor Mr Salter.'

'I know,' he said. 'But then I hate leaving loose ends. He shouldn't have joined, should he?'

He pulled her out of the way, lifted the lid

of the bench seat and rummaged around until he found the briefcase. He opened it, checked that the money was still there and closed it again.

'The war chest?' she said.

'Something like that.' He moved to the wheelhouse entrance and stood listening. 'Come on,' he said softly.

'Maybe he isn't coming back.'

'Don't be stupid.'

'Oh, I don't know. He looked frightened to death to me.'

He turned and glanced at her, the smile wiped from his face, then grabbed her arm, pulled her out of the wheelhouse and ran her along the deck and down the companionway to the saloon. He pushed her inside, locking the door on her, went back on deck, jumped over the rail and ran along the jetty.

The milk truck drove away into the fog and Devlin and Brosnan turned to the gold-painted sign beside the gate.

'Henry Salter, Undertaker, House of Rest

and Crematorium,' Devlin said. 'Very tasteful. Let's see if he's at home.'

The house was still, as if waiting for them, quiet in the morning rain as they moved towards the rear, keeping to the shelter of the rhododendron bushes. They paused, the courtyard before them, the barn door open. There was the sound of a vehicle approaching. The Land-Rover turned into the yard and rolled to a halt. Salter got out and went in the back door.

'I'd say that's our man,' Devlin whispered. 'He has a look of the corpse about him, wouldn't you agree?'

Salter wasn't happy – wasn't happy at all. The whole thing had a bad smell to it and Sinclair frightened him. On the other hand, he didn't really have much choice. He reached for the ignition key hanging on the key board above the refrigerator and the door burst open behind him. Before he knew what was happening, he was back across the table, Brosnan's hand on his throat, the muzzle of the Mauser rammed against his temple.

Salter had never been so terrified. 'Please, no!' he gabbled.

Devlin said, 'You are Henry Salter, I presume?'

'That's right,' Salter said, as Brosnan relaxed his grip.

'Where's Frank Barry?'

Salter said, 'Frank Barry? But I don't know anyone of that name.'

Brosnan's grip tightened. 'You picked him up at Tanningley Field no more than half an hour ago.'

'That was a man named Sinclair, Maurice Sinclair.'

'I see,' Devlin said. 'And he had the young woman with him?'

'That's right. When he took her off the plane she was in handcuffs.'

'And where are they now?'

'Down in the marsh on my boat, the *Kathleen*. He sent me up for the ignition key – look.'

He held up the key in his right hand and Brosnan said, 'I'll take that.'

Devlin said, 'He was here before?'

'That's right. A few days ago.'

'To get that rocket pod?'

Salter looked bewildered. 'I don't know what he was here for. I was paid to hire men for him. They were here for two days. They went. That's all I know.'

He was obviously telling the truth and Devlin nodded. 'How do we get to this boat of yours?'

'Turn left on to the main road. There's a sign post to the right saying Marsh End Creek. The *Kathleen*'s tied up at the jetty there. You can't miss her. She's the only boat there.'

Devlin reached up and ripped down the clothes-line that stretched across the sink. He threw it to Brosnan. 'All right, Martin, tie him up.'

He went outside, got into the Land-Rover's passenger seat and took out his Browning. He removed the clip, pushed the bullets out one by one with his thumb nail, and reloaded very carefully. As he finished, Brosnan came out of the kitchen door and got behind the wheel.

He turned to Devlin, his face pale. 'He's mine, Liam, remember that.'

Devlin said, 'The Japanese believe revenge is a purification, but personally, I doubt it.'

He leaned back, eyes closed, holding the Browning in his lap and Brosnan drove away.

Frank Barry, taking the short-cut through the garden saw the Landrover through the trees, still in the courtyard, and paused. What in the hell was Salter playing at? Perhaps the girl had been right after all. He started forward and saw Liam Devlin come out of the house and cross the yard.

Barry's instinct was to yell at the ghost, to frighten it away, but in fact it was he who was suddenly and strangely frightened. He cursed himself. He wasn't a superstitious idiot. And then he saw Martin Brosnan come out of the kitchen door, go round to the other side of the Land-Rover and disappear from view. A second ghost? Feeling himself trembling, he tried to take courage from the weight of the Ceska in his pocket. How many times do you have to kill a man?

By the time Barry reached the jetty, panting from his exertion, he was in control again. That Devlin and Brosnan were still alive was a fact. Any explanation of the situation was of secondary importance at the moment.

He ran along the jetty and paused, listening. Already the Land-Rover was close behind in the fog and without that damned ignition key, he couldn't move the boat, not under power anyway.

He cast off the lines at prow and stern, pushed as hard as he could against the rail and scrambled over as the gap suddenly widened between the *Kathleen* and the jetty. In a moment the gap was ten or twelve feet and then, suddenly, the boat started to drift broadside on back towards the jetty. When he looked over the rail, the reason was plain, for the tide was moving in through the marsh strongly.

Anne-Marie heard him thunder down the

companionway. The door to the saloon was flung open, he grabbed her and pulled her out and back up the companionway. She went cold, certain that he was about to kill her. Instead, he pushed her along the deck into the wheelhouse.

'What is it?' she demanded.

'The second coming,' he said savagely.

And then, the Land-Rover moved out of the fog, stopped at the end of the jetty and her heart nearly stopped beating.

Two things happened very quickly. Barry smashed the side window of the wheel-house with his elbow and Anne-Marie yelled at the top of her voice, 'Martin, look out!'

Barry shoved her down and loosed off a couple of shots through the broken window as Devlin and Brosnan ran, heads down, along the jetty. The gap between the *Kathleen* and the jetty was only about three feet now as Brosnan jumped for the stern and dived behind the deck housing. Devlin had chosen the prow and was down out of sight on the blind side of the wheelhouse.

'Now then, Frank,' he called, 'and how are you this fine morning?'

'Miracles is it now, Liam?' Barry called back.

'That's right. The Devil's sent us straight from Hell to fetch you!'

'He'll have to wait a while yet.' Barry got hold of Anne-Marie's hair in one hand. 'I'm going to stand up with your girl-friend, Martin,' he called. 'If I go, she goes. Remember that. Try and pick me off and my last act will be to squeeze this trigger.'

He pulled Anne-Marie up with him and stood holding her as close as if they were lovers, her head dragged back painfully, the muzzle of the Ceska under her chin.

'Two choices,' Barry said. 'She dies now, even if I have to die with her, or you come out here and lay down your guns.'

'No, Martin,' Anne-Marie called and Barry twisted his fingers in her hair.

'Don't muck me about. Yes or no.'

There was a pause, then Brosnan stood up

holding the Mauser. 'Throw it in the water!' Barry said.

Brosnan did so with an almost casual gesture, his eyes never leaving Barry's face. Devlin had moved out from the other side of the wheelhouse and stood only five or six feet away. He tossed his Browning into the creek without being told.

'Right,' Barry said. 'Come closer.' His voice cracked, the first real signs of stress beginning to show. 'I said closer.'

They stood together just outside the wheelhouse. 'Let the girl go, Frank,' Devlin said.

'Sure, why not?' Barry shoved her out of the wheelhouse into their arms. In the same moment he reached for the button on the instrument panel, the flap fell down and he tore the Sterling sub-machine gun from its brackets with his free hand.

'My ace-in-the-hole, Liam.' He grinned. 'I learned the importance of that one from you, remember?'

Devlin said, 'What happens now? Another execution?'

'Not yet,' Barry said. 'First, I'm going to

put you to work. A few hundred yards down that creek there's a pool in the reeds with a boat on the bottom. There's something in the cabin I very much want. You can go swimming for me, Martin.'

'The rocket pod?' Devlin said. 'Very ingenious.'

'You're remarkably well-informed,' Barry said. 'But enough conversation. Martin, you and the girl move along to the top of the companionway. Nice and slow. We'll have you two below in the saloon while we get this thing moving.' He swung the barrel at Devlin. 'You walk ahead of them right along to the stern.'

Devlin moved first. Brosnan pushed Anne-Marie in front of him and turned, backing away, protecting her with his body, his burning eyes never leaving Barry's face. Barry stayed where he was in the wheelhouse entrance, the Sterling ready.

Brosnan said, 'You should have stayed behind at the farm, Frank. You made a bad mistake using rubbish like those three hoods from Nice. They wouldn't have lasted one bad Saturday night in Belfast.'

'Yes, well this time I'll see to it myself,' Barry told him.

Brosnan turned, put a hand in Anne-Marie's back sending her tumbling down the steps, dived over the rail into the creek and went down deep into the brown stinking water, turning to pull himself under the hull, his feet kicking desperately in the thick ooze of the bottom.

The burst Barry fired from the Sterling chipped the rail, already too late, and he ran forward and fired again into the water. Of Brosnan there was no sign. Anne-Marie appeared, crouching in the companionway. Barry ran to the other rail and loosed off another burst into the water.

Devlin said, 'No good, Frank, you've lost him.'

'You shut your mouth,' Barry said.

Devlin took his time lighting a cigarette and Brosnan, clinging to the prow, heard him say, 'You always were a small man when it came down to it, weren't you, Frank?'

Barry moved towards him. 'Big enough to bury you.'

'You tried once and made one hell of a mess of it.' Devlin walked forward slowly. 'I don't think you can do any better now.'

Barry fired a single burst of four or five rounds that shredded Devlin's raincoat on the left side of his chest, spinning him round. He cried out and bounced off the side of the deckhouse.

Anne-Marie crawled towards him, pulling herself along on handcuffed hands and Brosnan slipped under the port rail and reached inside the wheelhouse for the Smith and Wesson.

Barry, aware of the movement, started to turn and Brosnan shot him in the right arm, the force of the blow spinning him round, the Sterling jumping into the air. It curved over the rail and disappeared under the surface of the water.

Barry stood there clutching his bloody arm. Brosnan said, 'The keys for the handcuffs, Frank. Let's have them.'

Barry felt in his pocket with bloodstained fingers, found the keys and dropped them on the deck where Anne-Marie retrieved them and set about unfastening herself.

'By God, but you're the tricky one, Martin, you always were, but I never thought to see you end up working for the opposition.'

'This isn't for them,' Brosnan said. 'This is for Norah. For what you did to her. She died screaming, Frank, strapped to a bed in a mental hospital and that's down to you.'

'Whoever told you that is a liar.' Barry looked genuinely horrified. 'It was the French who did that to Norah, those SDECE Service Five bastards. You know what the *barbouzes* are like. They tried electricity to break her. When that didn't work, they moved on to drugs and went too far.'

Liam Devlin, leaning against Anne-Marie, blood on his shoulder, said weakly, 'You're lying.'

'It's the God's truth.' Barry turned wildly to Brosnan. 'Kill Norah, is it? Martin, she was the only woman I ever loved. The only person I ever put before myself.'

'Liar!' Brosnan cried, and fired three times very fast, his first shot catching Barry in the shoulder, turning him, his next two in the back, driving him headfirst across the rail into the water.

Birds called wildly to each other, rising from the reeds in clouds. Brosnan slumped down on the deck housing.

'Liar,' he whispered and looked at Devlin. 'Wasn't he?'

But Devlin's eyes were closed in pain and there was no answer there, only the pity in Anne-Marie's face that he turned away from. He had to steel himself. The hired guns like Barry would always be replaced by other hired guns. Even the French torturers would be replaced by others. The blame went with the responsibility, whoever gave the orders. Ferguson? The Prime Minister?

He wished she wasn't a woman. It would be easier to kill a man.

The waistcoat had proved its worth again, taking the brunt of the burst Barry had fired at Devlin, but one round had caught him across the right shoulder and another had gone through his upper arm.

Brosnan finished bandaging it expertly, the boat's first-aid box open on the bunk beside him. When he was finished, he took out one of the emergency morphine ampoules.

'That should take care of the pain for a while.'

Devlin, his face grey, managed to smile. 'You'd have made a fine doctor, Martin.'

'Ranger training.'

Anne-Marie said, 'He needs a hospital now.'

'Yes, but not here, not in England. The surest way to a prison cell. Do you still have that launch in Nice like the old days?'

'Yes. Why do you ask?'

'So you could handle this?'

'Of course, no problem. This is a superb craft.'

'Good. I reckon you'll make Ireland in eight hours. Liam will tell you where to go in.'

'Liam?' She frowned. 'You mean you're not coming? But I don't understand?'

He ignored her, picked up Barry's brief-case which he had found in the wheelhouse and opened it, showing the money it contained to Devlin.

'At least thirty thousand quid there, Liam, probably more. Give me one name, one man in London who will do anything for that kind of money. No politics, just an honest crook.'

Devlin said wearily, 'Leave it, Martin. There's no profit in it now.'

'Ferguson lied to us about Norah, Liam.'

'All right,' Devlin said. 'So he lied. He thought the end justified the means. He wanted Frank Barry dead.'

'They all wanted Barry dead,' Brosnan said in a low voice. 'Ferguson, DI5, the Cabinet, the Prime Minister. Where does it stop? Somebody has to pay, Liam. I'm tired of being used for other people's purposes, dragged through the fire like some corn king for the sake of the rest of you.'

Devlin shook his head, 'No, Martin.'

Brosnan said deliberately, 'You owe me this one, Liam. You got me into it in the first place.'

'I helped you get free, damn you!' Devlin flared.

'Free?' Brosnan laughed harshly. 'Who's free?'

It was Anne-Marie who astonished them both by saying, 'Tell him, Liam. Give him what he asks and let's get out of here. Let him go to hell his own way.'

She turned and went up the companionway. Brosnan said, 'Well?'

Devlin reached for a cigarette and Brosnan lit it for him. 'I can't give you the name of a man, but there's a woman I knew some years back. Nothing to do with politics. Not even Irish. A German Jew originally. Lily Winter. She used to have a place on Great India Wharf in Wapping. I think she might be what you're looking for.'

Brosnan closed the briefcase and stood up. 'And Ferguson's telephone number.'

Devlin told him and Brosnan nodded. 'Thanks. Goodbye, Liam.' He turned and went up the companionway.

Anne-Marie was searching the wheelhouse and he took the ignition key from his pocket. 'Is this what you're looking for?'

She took it from him and switched on. The

engines rumbled into life. 'That's all right then,' Brosnan said.

'What do you want me to say? she demanded angrily. 'May you die in Ireland.'

It was the most ancient of Irish toasts. Brosnan said, 'An excellent sentiment, but hardly likely.'

He stepped over the rail and watched as the *Kathleen* pulled away from the jetty and turned downstream, disappearing into the fog. Only then did he turn and walk to the Land-Rover.

The selection of clothing in Salter's bedroom was so extensive that Brosnan could only assume that over the years the undertaker had made a practice of robbing the dead. He showered, washed the stink of the creek from him, and chose a grey tweed suit, woollen shirt and tie to go with it. He selected a raincoat and went downstairs to the living room where he'd left Salter tied to a chair.

He glanced at the clock. It was still only

seven a.m. and he said to Salter, 'What time does your staff come in?'

'After Sinclair phoned me, I told them to take the morning off.'

'So they'll be in around noon?'

'That's right.' Salter moistened dry lips.

'I'll do you a favour and leave them to find you tied up. That way it gives you a chance of claiming to be an unwilling party to whatever took place here when it comes out.'

Salter said, 'I'm very grateful. May I ask you something? Is Mr Sinclair dead?'

'Yes,' Brosnan said and he went out, closing the door.

A few moments later Salter heard the sound of the Land-Rover starting up. It moved away down the drive and faded into the distance. He eased his hands as much as he could and sat there, trying to work out what he was going to say to the police.

15

At one time, the Pool of London and the lower reaches of the Thames had been the centre for world shipping. Those days were long gone and as Brosnan walked down towards the docks through Wapping that Tuesday evening, he found only decay, rusting cranes pointing at the sky, empty warehouses, their windows boarded.

Somewhere a ship, easing down the river, sounded its fog horn; except for that sombre sound, he might have been the only living creature left in the world.

He turned on to Great India Wharf, walked on past docks empty of shipping and came to a warehouse at the end facing out across the river. The sign said *Winter & Co – Importers*. Brosnan opened the little judas gate in the main entrance and stepped in.

The place was crammed with old furniture of every description. It was dark, as it had been on his last visit, but this time music drifted down from the small glass office high above at the top of a flight of steep stairs.

'Mrs Winter?' he called.

The office door opened, the music flooding out. 'Is that you, Mr Brosnan?'

'Yes.'

She switched on another light to see him by and moved to the rail and looked down. She was at least seventy, her hair drawn back from a yellowing parchment face in an old-fashioned bun. She wore a tweed suit with a skirt that almost reached her ankles. Her right hand had a secure grip on the collar of one of the most superb dogs Brosnan had ever seen in his life – a black and tan Dobermann.

Her English was excellent, but with a German accent. 'You know, you interest me, Mr Brosnan. Karl didn't make a sound the first time you visited me and he hasn't now. I've never known him to do that before.'

'You know what they say?' Brosnan said. 'Children and dogs, they can always tell.'

He went up the stairs and gently caressed the dog's head as he followed her into the office. A cassette recorder on the desk was the source of the music. The song was *A Foggy Day in London Town* but Brosnan didn't recognise the singer.

'Al Bowlly,' she said. 'The best there ever was. He was killed in the London Blitz. I used to hear him sing at the Monseigneur restaurant in Piccadilly with Roy Fox and his band. That was back in nineteen thirty-two before I was foolish enough to return to Germany after my father died.'

Brosnan lit a cigarette and sat down on a chair on the other side of the desk, listening to that haunting voice singing a song from another world that for some reason touched something deep inside him.

'You like it?' she said.

'Oh, yes. I always loved cities by night or very early in the morning. Fog, wet streets, that total certainty that somewhere up ahead, just around the next corner, something marvellous and astonishing was waiting. That's when you're young, of course, and still believe.'

The song came to an end and she switched off the cassette player. 'I stopped believing in Dachau, Mr Brosnan.'

She pushed up her sleeve and showed him the number tattooed on her arm. Brosnan took off his jacket and unbuttoned the cuff of his shirt. She pulled his arm across the desk and examined his prison number incredulously. 'But you couldn't have been in the camps, you're too young. I don't understand.'

'Somewhere similar,' he said. 'We didn't have the ovens, but the usual way out was feet first.'

'Except for you?'

He pulled on his jacket. 'You might say I was an exception.'

She fitted a black gold-tipped cigarette into an ivory holder and looked at him searchingly as he gave her a light.

'You've brought the money?'

'Yes.' He put Barry's briefcase on the desk and opened it.

She looked at the packets of twenty pound notes inside and picked one up. 'How much is there?'

'Thirty-five thousand pounds.'

She sat staring down at the case, then closed it. 'That's a great deal of money. After Dachau, when I came back to England in nineteen forty-five, money was the only thing that mattered to me, Mr Brosnan. I'd stopped believing in people, you see.' She got up, went to a side table and poured coffee from an electric pot into two cups. 'I became, by chance really, a receiver of stolen goods, the most successful in London before I was finished. I dealt with all of them. All the princes of the underworld. The Kray brothers, the Richardson gang . . .'

'And Liam Devlin?'

'Liam, dear Liam.' She smiled. 'He was different. Him, I liked.'

'And the business he was involved in?'

'Didn't interest me in the slightest. When he needed passports, I got them for him. Arms dealers in Europe or the name of a reliable doctor. Things like that, but all that was a long time ago. Now, as you can see, I deal only in furniture.' She paused, then opened the brief-case again. 'It really is a great deal of money.'

'All yours if you can help me.'

'To do what, Mr Brosnan, that's the thing? What do you intend?'

'That's my business.'

She shook her head. 'You have an angry aura, Mr Brosnan and that is not good. Give me your hands.'

'My hands?' he said.

'Yes. I'm clairvoyant. Psychic. Surely you are aware of that? I'll show you.'

Her hands were cool and soft, making him remember, for no accountable reason, his maternal grandmother in Dublin when he was a child, clean linen sheets, rosemary and lavender. Then she tightened her grip and he was aware of a sudden tingle as from a minor electric shock. She had her eyes shut and opened them and reached out and touched his face and she was smiling.

'Yes,' she said. 'Now I see it all.'

Brosnan said, 'I don't understand?'

Her voice had changed and she was brisk

and businesslike. 'The woman you seek may be found at home tomorrow evening.'

'At home?' Brosnan's voice was hoarse. 'But that's Ten Downing Street. No way known to a man of getting there.'

'On the face of it, an impossibility. No one gets in without a personal invitation or official pass checked very thoroughly by the police on the doors and by officials inside. However, it is an interesting fact that all reception and official dinners are organised by outside caterers.'

'So?'

'Tomorrow evening at six-thirty the Prime Minister is giving a Christmas party for at least a hundred people. Mainly staff, past and present. Office workers, typists, the cleaners – they'll all be there. The function will take place in what's called the Pillared Room. I've already put arrangements in hand for you to join the staff the caterers are using as an extra waiter.'

Brosnan was stunned by the enormity of it. 'Can we get away with it? I mean, I don't even know my way about.'

She opened a drawer and took out a folded sheet of paper. 'There's a plan of the ground and first floors. It's quite simple.'

He opened it up to examine it. 'But where did you get this?'

'Information freely available in numerous magazines and newspaper articles over the years,' she said. 'You'll need an official pass with your photo. That kind of forgery presents no problem at all to the particular man I use. However, the question of your personal appearance is of prime importance. It will be necessary to alter it considerably before the photo is taken.'

'And how do I do that?'

'I have an old friend who specialises in such matters. I suggest you return here later on. Say at ten o'clock. Check out of that hotel room. Better if you stay here now.'

'All right.'

He got up and moved to the door. She said, 'Oh, I almost forgot. I have made enquiries in Dublin. Devlin is at present a patient in the Mountjoy Nursing Home. He is apparently doing well.'

'There was a young woman with him?'

'That's right. She moved yesterday to Devlin's cottage in Mayo.'

Brosnan nodded. 'Well, that's all right then.'

He went down the steel stairs and the Dobermann went to the rail silently and watched him go. Only when the outer door banged did he return to his mistress.

It was dark in the Prime Minister's study, the only light the single reading lamp on the desk. She was writing busily when Ferguson was shown in.

'Brigadier Ferguson, Prime Minister,' the secretary announced and left.

She didn't even bother looking up, simply kept on writing and Ferguson, forbidden by protocol from sitting without an invitation, was forced to stand before the desk like a schoolboy. Finally she stopped writing, sat back in her chair and looked up at him. The face was calm, but the eyes were cold.

'I've read your report on the Brosnan affair,

Brigadier. May I take it that nothing has been left out?'

'Nothing within my knowledge, ma'am, I give you my word,' Ferguson assured her.

'Right, then, to take the most important item first. You stated in your report your intention to seek for this rocket pod according to instructions given you by the man Brosnan. Have you had any success?'

'I'm happy to report that we recovered the item in question this very afternoon, Prime Minister. I was present myself.' A fact that he would long remember and he shuddered, remembering the bodies brought up by the divers, one-by-one.

'Which at least gives us some hope of restoring confidence between ourselves and the West German Government.' She opened the file and tapped it with a finger. 'In the copy of your original report found in the possession of the Baxter woman, there is no mention of the girl, Norah Cassidy. Details of that disgraceful business are only made plain in the report you have just submitted. Why, Brigadier? Were you perhaps ashamed?'

Ferguson could think of nothing to say.

She carried on, 'So, you lied about the Cassidy girl to Professor Devlin and through him, to Brosnan.'

'I thought it necessary, ma'am. I needed Brosnan's anger, you see and then, as so often happens with these things, it all got out of hand.'

'I don't believe that the end justifies the means, Brigadier. I believe in moral imperatives.' She was angry now. 'I don't hold the slightest brief for Martin Brosnan or anything he stands for. Or, if it comes to it, for Devlin, however devastatingly charming the rest of you seem to find him. A terrorist is a terrorist in my book, and that is exactly what these men were.'

'Yes, ma'am,' Ferguson said.

'Having said that, you lied to Brosnan; conned him, and for that he not only blames you, but me through you. Would you say that that is roughly the situation he outlined to you when he telephoned you the day before yesterday?'

'Yes, Prime Minister. To be explicit, his

actual words were, 'Somebody's got to pay. In the circumstances I'll deal with the lady herself direct." Then he put down the telephone.'

She nodded, very calm, not in the slightest bit afraid. 'Do you think he intends to assassinate me, Brigadier?'

'God knows, ma'am. He has a rather complex mind, this one.'

'I should say so.' She leafed through the file. 'Roses. What a conceit.' She closed it abruptly and sat up. 'I usually make my mind up about a man in ten seconds and I don't like to be proved wrong. In the circumstances, I'm going to put my personal safety in your hands, Brigadier. Now, how does that strike you?'

'As a very grave responsibility, Prime Minister.'

'Good, it's nice to be taken seriously. I haven't the slightest intention of changing my schedule, I'm far too busy. Another thing, I don't wish to see Brosnan's face next to mine on the front page of the *Daily Express* with melodramatic headlines such as mad IRA gunman stalks Prime Minister. Whatever you do must be handled discreetly.'

'As you say, ma'am.'

She passed a typed sheet across to him. 'There's my schedule for tomorrow. You will also find waiting below special passes for you and your aide, which will enable you to move in and out of Downing Street or the House of Commons at will.' She picked up her pen. 'Catch him, Brigadier, I should have thought it a simple enough task. Now you must go. I've work to do.'

She pressed a buzzer and by the time he reached the door, it was already being opened for him by the young secretary who had brought him up.

Ferguson told his driver to stop on the Embankment and said to Fox, 'Let's take a walk, Harry.'

They moved along the pavement, the driver trailing them. Finally Ferguson stopped and leaned on the wall, looking across the river.

'Bad, sir?' Fox enquired.

'She was not pleased, Harry. The last time I got a working over like that was by my housemaster at school. I was twelve at the time.' He took out his wallet, produced a card and gave it to Fox.

'What's this, sir?'

'Special pass, Harry, to get you into Downing Street or the Commons whenever you want. She's put me in charge of her personal security until this thing is sorted.'

'I see.' Fox put the card away carefully. 'I shouldn't think her personal detectives will be pleased about that.'

Ferguson produced the schedule she had given him and unfolded it. 'This is what she's doing tomorrow. Read it to me.'

He took a cheroot from a leather case and lit it carefully. Fox studied the sheet. 'Good God, sir, she starts at six-thirty in the morning and doesn't stop until one a.m. the following morning.'

'I know. Just give me the important features as they strike you.'

'Cabinet meeting in the morning for a

couple of hours. That's at Downing Street.' Fox frowned. 'I say, there's a possibility, sir.'

'What's that?'

'Memorial Service for Lord Mountbatten. You think he might chance his arm there?'

'I don't know,' Ferguson said. 'What else is there?'

'Back to Downing Street. House of Commons at three o'clock. Then back to Downing Street for a meeting with Ministers. Let's see, then she gives a radio interview and receives the West German Ambassador who's apparently retiring.'

'Anything else?'

'There's a staff Christmas party in the Pillared Room at six-thirty. She's due back at the Commons for dinner just before nine. After that, back home to work on papers.' He handed the sheet back to Ferguson. 'I wonder if they pay her overtime, sir?'

Ferguson said, 'So, the only soft spot seems to be the Mountbatten Memorial Service at St Paul's Cathedral. Who else will be there? Prince Charles, Princess Margaret.' He grimaced. 'The last place we want a bomb.'

Fox said, 'But Brosnan's never gone in for bombing, sir.'

'There's always a first time.'

'Do you really believe that, sir?'

'No.' Ferguson sighed. 'Not his style. He's the last of the Samurai, our lad, riding into the guns, sword in hand.'

They went back to the Bentley and got in. 'Still, the only soft spot is that service at St Paul's,' Fox said. 'Everything else is either at Downing Street or the Commons and he certainly hasn't a hope in hell of getting into Number Ten.'

'The Commons is a tricky one,' Ferguson said. 'Lot of people come and go. Constituents up to see their MP's and so on.'

Fox said, 'So what's our next move, sir?'

'Convene a meeting of all interested parties.' Ferguson glanced at his watch. 'We'll meet at my office at headquarters at eleven. No refusals accepted. Utmost priority. I want to see all heads of relevant departments at DI5. I also want Special Branch there. You know who to talk to?'

'Yes, sir,' Fox said. 'We'll get him, sir. Bound to.'

'I wish I could be so sanguine,' Charles Ferguson said and he leaned back and closed his eyes.

Brosnan sat in front of the dressing table, a towel around his shoulders, and watched as the old man ran a steel comb through the long hair which was now a pale straw colour.

'Good,' he said. 'I'm really very pleased with that. Now, of course, most of it must go.'

He picked up a pair of scissors and went to work, humming to himself. He was easily as old as Lily Winter and so similar in features that they might have been brother and sister.

Sitting on a stool watching, she lit a cigarette and passed it to Brosnan. 'Shlomo is so clever. He started in Yiddish cabaret in Amsterdam. Got out just ahead of the Germans.'

'I was at Elstree for years.' The old man

had exchanged the scissors for a cut-throat razor now. 'Margaret Lockwood, James Mason. I've worked with all the greats. Mr Noel Coward gave me a cigarette case once. It was engraved: *To Shlomo the Magician from the Master.*'

Brosnan's hair was now considerably more conventional in length and the old man quickly blow-dried it and parted it neatly. Amazing the difference it made, especially the bleached eyebrows.

'Fantastic,' Brosnan said.

'Not yet. Now you just look different. When I'm finished, I make you look like someone else. Stretch your upper lip and keep it stretched till I tell you to stop.'

Brosnan did as he was told. The old man carefully fitted a blond moustache into place. He reached for the scissors and trimmed it. 'I do this for famous people sometimes. You know, pop stars who want to go shopping at Harrods without being chased by the fans.'

'And me?' Brosnan said. 'Who do you think I don't want to be chased by?'

'I don't wish to know. I'm not interested.

You seem like a nice boy to me.' Shlomo shrugged. 'If Lily's satisfied, that's good enough. Open your mouth.' Brosnan did as he was told and the old man inserted cheek pads gently. He looked at the face over Brosnan's shoulder. 'I don't think we need nose rings, eh, Lily?'

She shook her head. 'Just the glasses.'

They were gold-framed, tinted blue and looked vaguely continental. The effect was quite astonishing. The man who stared back at Brosnan from the mirror was a total stranger.

'We'll not make you a foreigner,' Lily said. 'I mean, if we say you're Danish, you can be certain you'll run into a real Danish waiter, so plain George Jackson from Manchester will have to do.' She looked over his shoulder again and nodded. 'That really is very good. Now come and have your photo taken.'

Ferguson stood to one side of the steps at the main entrance of St Paul's Cathedral and watched the Royal party get into their cabs below. The Memorial Service for Mountbatten was over, had passed off without any kind of incident whatsoever. The Prime Minister, in a black suit, descended the steps, got into her car and was driven away.

Fox said, 'Well, that went off all right, thank God,' and they went down the steps as the Bentley drew up. 'The thing is, sir,' he added as they got in, 'as that really was the only time today when she was a soft target, what do we do now?'

'Stick to her like glue, Harry,' Ferguson told him. 'That's all we can do.' He rapped on the glass panel and his driver moved away at once, following the Prime Minister's car.

Below stairs at Number Ten Downing Street was a hive of activity as six-thirty approached. The first guests were already arriving, for many retired members of staff had been invited. The back entrance, a uniformed police sergeant on duty inside, stood open as half a dozen waiters ran back and forth, carrying crates of wine and other essentials for the function from a parked van.

Brosnan was one of them, and as he staggered in carrying two cartons of bottled beer, the police sergeant said, 'You can drop one of those off here any time you like.'

Brosnan grinned and kept on going to the kitchen where he was immediately ordered to help with the glasses. Some of the other waiters were already at work, he'd seen them go. It suddenly occurred to him that this might be it, that the sum total of all his efforts was going to be that he got as far as the kitchen. Then the Head Waiter came in and tapped him on the shoulder.

'You – what's your name?'

'Jackson, sir.'

'Right, put your gear on and get in there. You're needed.'

Brosnan took off his dark alpaca working jacket and hung it up, then he put on his white waiter's coat and took white gloves from the pocket. He pulled them on carefully and slipped a hand under his jacket, touching the Smith and Wesson flat against his back in his waistband under the shirt. Then he picked up a silver tray, took a deep breath and went along the corridor.

The Prime Minister, wearing a green evening dress, moved amongst the guests with her husband and daughter, thoroughly enjoying herself. From the other side of the room Brosnan watched as he worked his way through the crowd with glasses of white wine on his tray.

When it was empty, he went back to the serving table and the Head Waiter told him to collect empty glasses and take them to the kitchen. Brosnan did as he was told, journeying back and forth to the kitchen three times.

Now that he was here, the truth was he had no idea what came next. Then, as he returned from the kitchen for the third time, he noted the Prime Minister part from a group of people, a smile on her face, and go out through the open double doors and up the main staircase.

He remembered the plans he had studied

so carefully. Her private study, the White Drawing Room and the Blue Drawing Room were all up there.

They were opening champagne bottles at the serving table. He waited his turn with the other waiters and took one. Everything was busy confusion. He took a couple of glasses from the end of the table, placed them carefully on the tray with the champagne, then walked through the noisy crowd into the hall. It was, for the moment, empty. Without hesitation, he mounted the stairway to the first floor.

The Prime Minister was sitting at her desk, reading a memo and making notes, when there was a knock at the door. It opened and Brosnan entered. He closed the door carefully behind him and went forward.

She glanced up in surprise. 'What on earth have you got there?'

Brosnan's throat was dry, his heart pounded, he was acutely aware of the Smith and Wesson digging into his back. His voice was low and rather hoarse when he said, 'Champagne, ma'am.'

'I didn't order any champagne.'

'Well the Head Waiter told me to bring it up, ma'am, with two glasses. Very specific he was about that.'

'Two glasses.' She smiled suddenly. 'Oh, I see. Well, just leave it there on the table.'

She was writing again. There was sweat on Brosnan's forehead as he put the tray down on a small coffee table. He straightened and looked towards her and his right hand slid under his jacket, feeling for the butt of the Smith and Wesson. In three seconds it would be over.

For her, not for him.

Would it ever be over for him?

'You can go now,' she said, without looking up.

I don't exist for her, he thought, and yet I am her death. Oh Norah, will this or anything else avenge you?

He saw the roses in the crystal vase on the table to one side. White Christmas roses with long stems.

'Will that be all, ma'am?'

'Yes, thank you,' a touch of impatience in her voice.

She still didn't look up, even as, his heart beating rapidly, he slipped a rose from the vase and laid it on the silver tray beside the two glasses.

He opened the door, went out, and closed it again quietly.

The hall was deserted as he went down the stairs past the portraits of all those Prime Ministers who had gone before her. He moved straight into the crowd, picked up a tray and started to collect empty glasses. When his tray was full, he went back to the kitchen.

The passage was a frenzy of activity as the party drew to a close and the back door stood open, waiters carrying crates of empty bottles out to the van.

Brosnan went into the kitchen, took off his white waiter's coat and hung it up. Then he pulled on the dark alpaca working jacket, picked up a crate and moved out into the passage, past the sergeant standing at the open door. He joined the queue at the back of the van, passed up his crate, then walked round the other side and cut across a small courtyard with a little lawn in the centre.

Downing Street was crowded with departing guests, many of them on foot, moving out to look for taxis elsewhere. Brosnan simply joined the cheerful crowd, turned the corner into Whitehall and walked briskly away.

It was perhaps five minutes later that the Prime Minister finished her memo. She got up, went round the desk and started for the door, intending to go downstairs again. She glanced casually at the champagne and glasses on the tray as she went by and stopped abruptly. Then she turned, hurried back to her desk and flicked the intercom.

Ferguson said, 'He's gone, ma'am, not a sign of him.'

'There wouldn't be, would there? Not now.'

The rose lay on the desk between them. Ferguson said, almost plaintively, 'I don't understand. What on earth was he playing at?'

'But it's so simple, Brigadier, don't you see?' She picked up the rose. 'No one is safe, that's what your Mr Brosnan is saying to us. The kind of world we've created.'

Ferguson went cold as she laid the rose down very carefully. 'And now, Brigadier, I'd better get back to whatever guests I have left.'

He opened the door for her and she passed through.

Music was playing again as Brosnan stepped through the judas gate into the warehouse and the light was on in the office high above him. He went up the steel steps slowly and opened the door. Lily Winter was sitting at the desk, examining an antique necklace with an eyeglass. The Dobermann got up, moved across and pushed himself against Brosnan.

She took out the eyeglass and looked up at him for a long moment. 'So, you went to make war and made peace instead.'

'How did you know?'

'Fool.' She took a bottle of brandy from a drawer and a glass and filled it. 'Here. Do you think I would have helped you in the first place if I had not sensed it in you?'

'I stood as close to her as I am to you,' Brosnan said, and the glass shook in his hand. 'There were some winter roses in a vase. I put one on the tray and left.'

'A fine romantic gesture and what does it prove?'

'I've made a separate peace,' Brosnan said. 'A separate peace.' He lay down on the bunk against the wall and stared up at the ceiling. 'Suddenly I feel old – really old. You know what I mean?'

'I know,' she said.

Her voice seemed to come from a long distance. He closed his eyes and after a while, the glass slipped from his hand and he slept.

16

In a private room on the third floor of the Mountjoy Nursing Home in Dublin, Liam Devlin tried to possess himself in patience as the Staff Nurse removed the dressing from his shoulder and arm. The Matron, a formidable lady as stiff as her starched head-dress, stood behind the surgeon, watching as he inspected his handiwork.

'Very nice,' he said. 'Very nice indeed.' He nodded to the Staff Nurse. 'Fresh dressing, please.'

Devlin said plaintively, 'For God's sake, Patrick, when can I go home? A terrible place this. Not a drink in sight and they even try to stop you smoking.'

'A week, Liam,' said the surgeon, himself a distinguished professor of Trinity College.

'Another week and I'll think about it.' He turned to the Matron. 'Terrible injuries these car crashes cause. Terrible. He's a lucky man.'

'And tobacco and whiskey won't help,' she said. 'I'm sure you agree, professor?'

'Yes, of course. You're quite right.' She opened the door for him and he turned to Devlin and shrugged helplessly. 'I'll look in again tomorrow, Liam.'

When the door closed, Devlin said, 'God, she's a hard one and that's the truth.'

The Staff Nurse smiled as she finished replacing the dressing and bandages. 'Now you don't really expect me to comment on that, do you, Professor Devlin? I'll bring your tea in half an hour.'

She went out and he lay back against the pillow. There was a timid knock at the door and a young probationer looked in. She carried a long thin parcel wrapped in gold paper with a bow on it.

'And what in the blazes is that?' Devlin demanded.

'Interflora. It's just been delivered. Shall I open it for you?'

'That would seem to be a sound idea.'

He lay there watching as she stood at the table removing the wrapping. 'That's interesting.' She turned, holding a plastic cylinder containing a single rose. 'Somebody loves you, professor.'

Devlin lay there looking at it for a long moment. 'Is there a card?'

'Not that I can see.'

'No, there wouldn't be.'

'You know who it's from?'

'Oh, yes,' Devlin said softly. 'I know who it's from. Just leave it on the bed.'

She went out and he lay there looking at the rose and then he smiled. 'Now then, Martin,' he said softly. 'A small celebration would appear to be in order, surely.'

He reached over, wincing with pain, got the cupboard open at the side of his bed and took out a bottle of Bushmills and a pack of cigarettes.

It was one of the most beautiful evenings Anne-Marie Audin had ever known. She sat at an easel on the edge of the cliffs below Devlin's cottage, painting very fast, trying to catch the last of the evening light. Killala Bay was below her and across the water in the far distance, the mountains of Donegal were a purple shadow.

There was a step behind her. She didn't look round, some strange sixth sense telling her who it must be. Brosnan said, 'You get better all the time. That background wash is fantastic.'

She looked up and frowned. 'What happened to your hair?'

'It's a long story.' He lit a cigarette and crouched beside her.

'A change of heart?' she said.

'Something like that. I'd forgotten how peaceful it is here.'

She stopped painting and turned to look at him, her face sombre in the evening light. 'But for how long, Martin?'

He had no answer for her – no answer at all. The sea was calm, the sky the colour of brass. A storm petrel cried harshly as it dipped above their heads and fled across the water.